BRIDGERTON

AN OFFER FROM
A GENTLE MAN

AND

ROMANCING
MISTER BRIDGERTON

By Julia Quinn

THE BRIDGERTON PREQUELS

Because of Miss Bridgerton
The Girl with the Make-Believe Husband
The Other Miss Bridgerton
First Comes Scandal

THE BRIDGERTON SERIES

The Duke and I
The Viscount Who Loved Me
An Offer from a Gentleman
Romancing Mister Bridgerton
To Sir Phillip, With Love
When He Was Wicked
It's in His Kiss
On the Way to the Wedding
The Bridgertons: Happily Ever After

ANTHOLOGIES

The Further Observations of Lady Whistledown
Lady Whistledown Strikes Back

THE SMYTHE-SMITH QUARTET

Just Like Heaven
A Night Like This
The Sum of All Kisses
The Secrets of Sir Richard Kenworthy

THE BEVELSTOKE SERIES

The Secret Diaries of Miss Miranda Cheever
What Happens in London
Ten Things I Love About You

THE TWO DUKES OF WYNDHAM

The Lost Duke of Wyndham
Mr. Cavendish, I Presume

AGENTS OF THE CROWN

To Catch an Heiress
How to Marry a Marquis

THE LYNDON SISTERS

Everything and the Moon
Brighter Than the Sun

THE SPLENDID TRILOGY

Splendid
Dancing at Midnight
Minx

BRIDGERTON

AN OFFER FROM
A GENTLEMAN

ROMANCING
MISTER BRIDGERTON

JULIA QUINN

AVON
An Imprint of HarperCollins*Publishers*

"An Offer from a Gentleman: The 2nd Epilogue" and "Romancing Mister Bridgerton: The 2nd Epilogue" were originally published as ebooks.

"An Offer from a Gentleman: The 2nd Epilogue" copyright © 2009 by Julie Cotler Pottinger.

"Romancing Mister Bridgerton: The 2nd Epilogue" copyright © 2007 by Julie Cotler Pottinger.

AN OFFER FROM A GENTLEMAN. Copyright © 2001 by Julie Cotler Pottinger.

ROMANCING MISTER BRIDGERTON. Copyright © 2002 by Julie Cotler Pottinger.

HarperCollins books may be purchased for educational, business, or sales promotional use. For information, please email the Special Markets Department at SP-sales@harpercollins.com.

Originally published separately as *An Offer from a Gentleman* and *Romancing Mister Bridgerton* in the United States by Avon Books in 2001 and 2002.

Bridgerton Family Tree designed by Emily Cotler, Waxcreative Design

Library of Congress Cataloging-in-Publication Data has been applied for.

ISBN 978-0-06-338361-6

10 9 8 7 6 5 4 3 2 1

Table of Contents

An Offer from a Gentleman

1

Romancing Mister Bridgerton

385

Bridgerton FAMILY TREE

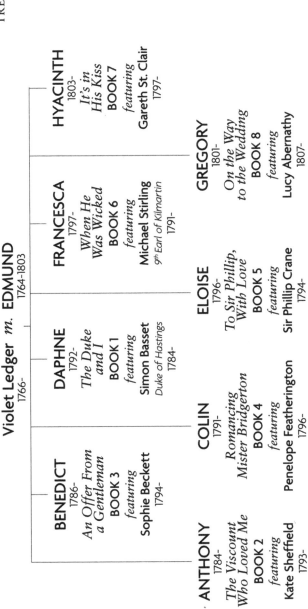

Violet Ledger *m.* EDMUND
1766-   1764-1803

BENEDICT
1786-
*An Offer From
a Gentleman*
BOOK 3
featuring
Sophie Beckett
1794-

ANTHONY
1784-
*The Viscount
Who Loved Me*
BOOK 2
featuring
Kate Sheffield
1793-

COLIN
1791-
*Romancing
Mister Bridgerton*
BOOK 4
featuring
Penelope Featherington
1796-

DAPHNE
1792-
*The Duke
and I*
BOOK 1
featuring
Simon Basset
Duke of Hastings
1784-

ELOISE
1796-
*To Sir Phillip,
With Love*
BOOK 5
featuring
Sir Phillip Crane
1794-

FRANCESCA
1797-
*When He
Was Wicked*
BOOK 6
featuring
Michael Stirling
9th Earl of Kilmartin
1791-

GREGORY
1801-
*On the Way
to the Wedding*
BOOK 8
featuring
Lucy Abernathy
1807-

HYACINTH
1803-
*It's in
His Kiss*
BOOK 7
featuring
Gareth St. Clair
1797-

FOR MORE INFORMATION
PLEASE VISIT JULIAQUINN.COM

BRIDGERTON

AN OFFER FROM A GENTLEMAN

For Cheyenne,
and the memory of a Frappucino summer.

And also for Paul,
even though he doesn't see anything wrong with watching
open heart surgery on TV while we're eating spaghetti.

Prologue

Everyone knew that Sophie Beckett was a bastard.

The servants all knew it. But they loved little Sophie, had loved her since she'd arrived at Penwood Park at the age of three, a small bundle wrapped in a too-big coat, left on the doorstep on a rainy July night. And because they loved her, they pretended that she was exactly what the sixth Earl of Penwood said she was—the orphaned daughter of an old friend. Never mind that Sophie's moss green eyes and dark blond hair matched the earl's precisely. Never mind that the shape of her face looked remarkably like that of the earl's recently deceased mother, or that her smile was an exact replica of the earl's sister's. No one wanted to hurt Sophie's feelings—or risk their livelihoods—by pointing that out.

The earl, one Richard Gunningworth, never discussed Sophie or her origins, but he must have known she was his bastard. No one knew what had been in the letter the housekeeper had fished from Sophie's pocket when she'd been discovered that rainy midnight; the earl had burned the missive mere seconds after reading it. He'd watched the paper shrivel and curl in the flames, then ordered a room made up for Sophie near the nursery. She'd remained there ever since. He called her Sophia, and she called him "my lord," and they saw each other a few times a year, whenever the earl returned home from London, which wasn't very often.

But perhaps most importantly, Sophie knew she was a bastard. She wasn't entirely certain how she knew it, just that she did, and probably had her entire life. She had few memories of her life before her arrival at Penwood Park, but she could remember a long coach journey across England, and she could remember her grandmother, coughing and wheezing and looking terribly thin, telling her she was going to live with her father. And most of all, she could remember standing on the doorstep in the rain, knowing that her grandmother was hiding in the bushes, waiting to see if Sophie was taken inside.

The earl had touched his fingers to the little girl's chin, tipped her face up to the light, and in that moment they both knew the truth.

Everyone knew Sophie was a bastard, and no one talked about it, and they were all quite happy with this arrangement.

Until the earl decided to marry.

Sophie had been quite pleased when she'd heard the news. The housekeeper had said that the butler had said that the earl's secretary had said that the earl planned to spend more time at Penwood Park now that he would be a family man. And while Sophie didn't exactly miss the earl when he was gone—it was hard to miss someone who didn't pay her much attention even when he was there— she rather thought she *might* miss him if she got to know him better, and if she got to know him better, maybe he wouldn't go away so often. Plus, the upstairs maid had said that the housekeeper had said that the neighbors' butler had said that the earl's intended wife already had two daughters, and they were near in age to Sophie.

After seven years alone in the nursery, Sophie was delighted. Unlike the other children in the district, she was never invited to local parties and events. No one actually came out and called her a bastard—to do so was tantamount to calling the earl, who had made one declaration that Sophie was his ward and then never revisited the subject, a liar. But at the same time, the earl never made any great attempt to force Sophie's acceptance. And so at the age of ten,

Sophie's best friends were maids and footmen, and her parents might as well have been the housekeeper and butler.

But now she was getting sisters for real.

Oh, she knew she could not call them her sisters. She knew that she would be introduced as Sophia Maria Beckett, the earl's ward, but they would *feel* like sisters. And that was what really mattered.

And so, one February afternoon, Sophie found herself waiting in the great hall along with the assembled servants, watching out the window for the earl's carriage to pull up the drive, carrying in it the new countess and her two daughters. And, of course, the earl.

"Do you think she'll like me?" Sophie whispered to Mrs. Gibbons, the housekeeper. "The earl's wife, I mean."

"Of course she'll like you, dearling," Mrs. Gibbons whispered back. But her eyes hadn't been as certain as her tone. The new countess might not take kindly to the presence of her husband's by-blow.

"And I'll take lessons with her daughters?"

"No point in having you take your lessons separately."

Sophie nodded thoughtfully, then started to squirm when she saw the carriage rolling up the drive. "They're here!" she whispered.

Mrs. Gibbons reached out to pat her on the head, but Sophie had already dashed off to the window, practically pressing her face up to the glass.

The earl stepped down first, then reached in and helped down two young girls. They were dressed in matching black coats. One wore a pink ribbon in her hair; the other yellow. Then, as the two girls stepped aside, the earl reached up to help one last person from the carriage.

Sophie's breath caught in her throat as she waited for the new countess to emerge. Her little fingers crossed and a single, "Please," whispered over her lips.

Please let her love me.

Maybe if the countess loved her, then the earl would love her as well, and maybe, even if he didn't actually call her daughter, he'd treat her as one, and they'd be a family truly.

As Sophie watched through the window, the new countess stepped down from the carriage, her every movement so graceful and pure that Sophie was reminded of the delicate lark that occasionally came to splash in the birdbath in the garden. Even the countess's hat was adorned by a long feather, its turquoise plume glittering in the hard winter sun.

"She's beautiful," Sophie whispered. She darted a quick look back at Mrs. Gibbons to gauge her reaction, but the housekeeper was standing at strict attention, eyes straight ahead, waiting for the earl to bring his new family inside for introductions.

Sophie gulped, not exactly certain where she was meant to stand. Everyone else seemed to have a designated place. The servants were lined up according to rank, from the butler right down to the lowliest scullery maid. Even the dogs were sitting dutifully in the corner, their leads held tight by the Keeper of the Hounds.

But Sophie was rootless. If she were truly the daughter of the house, she'd be standing with her governess, awaiting the new countess. If she were truly the earl's ward, she'd be in much the same place. But Miss Timmons had caught a head cold and refused to leave the nursery and come downstairs. None of the servants believed for a second that the governess was truly ill. She'd been fine the night before, but no one blamed her for the deception. Sophie was, after all, the earl's bastard, and no one wanted to be the one to offer potential insult to the new countess by introducing her to her husband's by-blow.

And the countess would have to be blind, stupid, or both not to realize in an instant that Sophie was something more than the earl's ward.

Suddenly overcome with shyness, Sophie shrank into a corner as two footmen threw open the front doors with a flourish. The two girls entered first, then stepped to the side as the earl led the countess in. The earl introduced the countess and her daughters to the butler, and the butler introduced them to the servants.

And Sophie waited.

The butler presented the footmen, the chef, the housekeeper, the grooms.

And Sophie waited.

He presented the kitchen maids, the upstairs maids, the scullery maids.

And Sophie waited.

And then finally the butler—Rumsey was his name—presented the lowliest of the lowest of maids, a scullery girl named Dulcie who had been hired a mere week earlier. The earl nodded and murmured his thanks, and Sophie was still waiting, completely unsure of what to do.

So she cleared her throat and stepped forward, a nervous smile on her face. She didn't spend much time with the earl, but she was trotted out before him whenever he visited Penwood Park, and he always gave her a few minutes of his time, asking about her lessons before shooing her back up to the nursery.

Surely he'd still want to know how her studies were progressing, even now that he'd married. Surely he'd want to know that she'd mastered the science of multiplying fractions, and that Miss Timmons had recently declared her French accent, "perfection."

But he was busy saying something to the countess's daughters, and he didn't hear her. Sophie cleared her throat again, this time more loudly, and said, "My lord?" in a voice that came out a bit more squeaky than she'd intended.

The earl turned around. "Ah, Sophia," he murmured, "I didn't realize you were in the hall."

Sophie beamed. He hadn't been ignoring her, after all.

"And who might this be?" the countess asked, stepping forward to get a better look.

"My ward," the earl replied. "Miss Sophia Beckett."

The countess speared Sophie with an assessing look, then her eyes narrowed.

And narrowed.

And narrowed some more.

"I see," she said.

And everyone in the room knew instantly that she *did* see.

"Rosamund," the countess said, turning to her two girls, "Posy, come with me."

The girls moved immediately to their mother's side. Sophie hazarded a smile in their direction. The smaller one smiled back, but the older one, whose hair was the color of spun gold, took her cue from her mother, pointed her nose in the air, and looked firmly away.

Sophie gulped and smiled again at the friendly girl, but this time the little girl chewed on her lower lip in indecision, then cast her eyes toward the floor.

The countess turned her back on Sophie and said to the earl, "I assume you have had rooms prepared for Rosamund and Posy."

He nodded. "Near the nursery. Right next to Sophie."

There was a long silence, and then the countess must have decided that certain battles should not be conducted before the servants, because all she said was, "I would like to go upstairs now."

And she left, taking the earl and her daughters along with her.

Sophie watched the new family walk up the stairs, and then, as they disappeared onto the landing, she turned to Mrs. Gibbons and asked, "Do you think I should go up to help? I could show the girls the nursery."

Mrs. Gibbons shook her head. "They looked tired," she lied. "I'm sure they'll be needing a nap."

Sophie frowned. She'd been told that Rosamund was eleven and Posy was ten. Surely that was a bit old for taking naps.

Mrs. Gibbons patted her on the back. "Why don't you come with me? I could use a bit of company, and Cook told me that she just made a fresh batch of shortbread. I think it's still warm."

Sophie nodded and followed her out of the hall. She'd have plenty of time that evening to get to know the two girls. She'd show them the nursery, and then they'd become friends, and before long they'd be as sisters.

Sophie smiled. It would be glorious to have sisters.

As it happened, Sophie did not encounter Rosamund and Posy—or the earl and countess, for that matter—until the next day. When Sophie entered the nursery to take her supper, she noticed that the table had been set for two, not four, and Miss Timmons (who had miraculously recovered from her ailment) said that the new countess had told her that Rosamund and Posy were too tired from their travels to eat that evening.

But the girls had to have their lessons, and so the next morning they arrived in the nursery, trailing the countess by one step each. Sophie had been working at her lessons for an hour already, and she looked up from her arithmetic with great interest. She didn't smile at the girls this time. Somehow it seemed best not to.

"Miss Timmons," the countess said.

Miss Timmons bobbed a curtsy, murmuring, "My lady."

"The earl tells me you will teach my daughters."

"I will do my best, my lady."

The countess motioned to the older girl, the one with golden hair and cornflower eyes. She looked, Sophie thought, as pretty as the porcelain doll the earl had sent up from London for her seventh birthday.

"This," the countess said, "is Rosamund. She is eleven. And this"—she then motioned to the other girl, who had not taken her eyes off of her shoes—"is Posy. She is ten."

Sophie looked at Posy with great interest. Unlike her mother and sister, her hair and eyes were quite dark, and her cheeks were a bit pudgy.

"Sophie is also ten," Miss Timmons replied.

The countess's lips thinned. "I would like you to show the girls around the house and garden."

Miss Timmons nodded. "Very well. Sophie, put your slate down. We can return to arithmetic—"

"Just *my* girls," the countess interrupted, her voice somehow hot and cold at the same time. "I will speak with Sophie alone."

Sophie gulped and tried to bring her eyes to the countess's, but she only made it as far as her chin. As Miss Timmons ushered Rosamund and Posy out of the room she stood up, awaiting further direction from her father's new wife.

"I know who you are," the countess said the moment the door clicked shut.

"M-my lady?"

"You're his bastard, and don't try to deny it."

Sophie said nothing. It was the truth, of course, but no one had ever said it aloud. At least not to her face.

The countess grabbed her chin and squeezed and pulled until Sophie was forced to look her in the eye. "You listen to me," she said in a menacing voice. "You might live here at Penwood Park, and you might share lessons with my daughters, but you are nothing but a bastard, and that is all you will ever be. Don't you ever, *ever* make the mistake of thinking you are as good as the rest of us."

Sophie let out a little moan. The countess's fingernails were biting into the underside of her chin.

"My husband," the countess continued, "feels some sort of misguided duty to you. It's admirable of him to see to his mistakes, but it is an insult to me to have you in my home—fed, clothed, and educated as if you were his real daughter."

But she *was* his real daughter. And it had been her home much longer than the countess's.

Abruptly, the countess let go of her chin. "I don't want to see you," she hissed. "You are never to speak to me, and you shall endeavor never to be in my company. Furthermore, you are not to speak to Rosamund and Posy except during lessons. They are the daughters of the house now, and should not have to associate with the likes of *you*. Do you have any questions?"

Sophie shook her head.

"Good."

And with that, she swept out of the room, leaving Sophie with wobbly legs and a quivering lip.

And an awful lot of tears.

In time, Sophie learned a bit more about her precarious position in the house. The servants always knew everything, and it all reached Sophie's ears eventually.

The countess, whose given name was Araminta, had insisted that very first day that Sophie be removed from the house. The earl had refused. Araminta didn't have to love Sophie, he'd said coolly. She didn't even have to like her. But she had to put up with her. He had owned up to his responsibility to the girl for seven years, and he wasn't going to stop now.

Rosamund and Posy took their cues from Araminta and treated Sophie with hostility and disdain, although Posy's heart clearly wasn't into torture and cruelty in the way Rosamund's was. Rosamund liked nothing better than to pinch and twist the skin on the back of Sophie's hand when Miss Timmons wasn't looking. Sophie never said anything; she rather doubted that Miss Timmons would have the courage to reprimand Rosamund (who would surely run to Araminta with a false tale), and if anyone noticed that Sophie's hands were perpetually black-and-blue, no one ever said so.

Posy showed her the occasional kindness, although more often than not she just sighed, and said, "My mummy says I'm not to be nice to you."

As for the earl, he never intervened.

Sophie's life continued in this vein for four years, until the earl surprised everyone by clutching his hand to his chest while taking tea in the rose garden, letting out one ragged gasp, and falling face-first to the stone cobbles.

He never regained consciousness.

Everyone was quite shocked. The earl was only forty years old. Who could have known that his heart would give out at such a young age? No one was more stunned than Araminta, who had been trying quite desperately since her wedding night to conceive the all-important heir.

"I might be with child!" she hastened to tell the earl's solicitors. "You can't give the title over to some distant cousin. I could very well be with child."

But she wasn't with child, and when the earl's will was read one month later (the solicitors had wanted to be sure to give the count-ess enough time to know for sure if she was pregnant) Araminta was forced to sit next to the new earl, a rather dissolute young man who was more often drunk than not.

Most of the earl's wishes were standard fare. He left bequests to loyal servants. He settled funds on Rosamund, Posy, and even Sophie, ensuring that all three girls would have respectable dowries.

And then the solicitor reached Araminta's name.

To my wife, Araminta Gunningworth, Countess of Penwood, I leave a yearly income of two thousand pounds—

"That's all?" Araminta cried out.

—unless she agrees to shelter and care for my ward, Miss Sophia Maria Beckett, until the latter reaches the age of twenty, in which case her yearly income shall be trebled to six thousand pounds.

"I don't want her," Araminta whispered.

"You don't have to take her," the solicitor reminded her. "You can—"

"Live on a measly two thousand a year?" she snapped. "I don't think so."

The solicitor, who lived on considerably less than two thousand a year, said nothing.

The new earl, who'd been drinking steadily throughout the meeting, just shrugged.

Araminta stood.

"What is your decision?" the solicitor asked.

"I'll take her," she said in a low voice.

"Shall I find the girl and tell her?"

Araminta shook her head. "I'll tell her myself."

But when Araminta found Sophie, she left out a few important facts . . .

Part One

Chapter 1

This year's most sought-after invitation must surely be that of the Bridgerton masquerade ball, to be held Monday next. Indeed, one cannot take two steps without being forced to listen to some society mama speculating on who will attend, and perhaps more importantly, who will wear what.

Neither of the aforementioned topics, however, are nearly as interesting as that of the two unmarried Bridgerton brothers, Benedict and Colin. (Before anyone points out that there is a third unmarried Bridgerton brother, let This Author assure you that she is fully aware of the existence of Gregory Bridgerton. He is, however, fourteen years of age, and therefore not pertinent to this particular column, which concerns, as This Author's columns often do, that most sacred of sports: husband-hunting.)

Although the Misters Bridgerton are just that—merely Misters—they are still considered two of the prime catches of the season. It is a well-known fact that both are possessed of respectable fortunes, and it does not require perfect sight to know that they also possess, as do all eight of the Bridgerton offspring, the Bridgerton good looks.

*Will some fortunate young lady use the mystery of a masquer-
ade night to snare one of the eligible bachelors?*
This Author isn't even going to attempt to speculate.
LADY WHISTLEDOWN'S SOCIETY PAPERS,
31 MAY 1815

"Sophie! Sophieeeeeeeeeeeeeeee!"

As screeches went, it was enough to shatter glass. Or at least an eardrum.

"Coming, Rosamund! I'm coming!" Sophie hitched up the hem of her coarse woolen skirts and hurried up the stairs, slipping on the fourth step and only just barely managing to grab the bannister before landing on her bottom. She should have remembered that the stairs would be slick; she'd helped the downstairs maid wax them just that morning.

Skidding to a halt in the doorway to Rosamund's bedroom and still catching her breath, Sophie said, "Yes?"

"My tea is cold."

What Sophie wanted to say was, "It was warm when I brought it an hour ago, you lazy fiend."

What she did say was, "I'll get you another pot."

Rosamund sniffed. "See that you do."

Sophie stretched her lips into what the nearly blind might call a smile and picked up the tea service. "Shall I leave the biscuits?" she asked.

Rosamund gave her pretty head a shake. "I want fresh ones."

Shoulders slightly stooped from the weight of the overloaded tea service, Sophie exited the room, careful not to start grumbling until she'd safely reached the hall. Rosamund was forever ordering tea, then not bothering to drink it until an hour passed. By then, of course, it was cold, so she had to order a fresh pot.

Which meant Sophie was forever running up and down the stairs, up and down, up and down. Sometimes it seemed that was all she did with her life.

Up and down, up and down.

And of course the mending, the pressing, the hairdressing, the shoe polishing, the darning, the bedmaking . . .

"Sophie!"

Sophie turned around to see Posy heading toward her.

"Sophie, I've been meaning to ask you, do you think this color is becoming on me?"

Sophie assessed Posy's mermaid costume. The cut wasn't quite right for Posy, who had never lost all of her baby fat, but the color did indeed bring out the best in her complexion. "It is a lovely shade of green," Sophie replied quite honestly. "It makes your cheeks very rosy."

"Oh, good. I'm so glad you like it. You do have such a knack for picking out my clothing." Posy smiled as she reached out and plucked a sugared biscuit from the tray. "Mother has been an absolute bear all week about the masquerade ball, and I know I shall never hear the end of it if I do not look my best. Or"—Posy's face twisted into a grimace—"if she *thinks* I do not look my best. She is determined that one of us snare one of the remaining Bridgerton brothers, you know."

"I know."

"And to make matters worse, that Whistledown woman has been writing about them again. It only"—Posy finished chewing and paused while she swallowed—"whets her appetite."

"Was the column very good this morning?" Sophie asked, shifting the tray to rest on her hip. "I haven't had a chance to read it yet."

"Oh, the usual stuff," Posy said with a wave of her hand. "Really, it can be quite humdrum, you know."

Sophie tried to smile and failed. She'd like nothing more than to live a day of Posy's humdrum life. Well, perhaps she wouldn't want

Araminta for a mother, but she wouldn't mind a life of parties, routs, and musicales.

"Let's see," Posy mused. "There was a review of Lady Worth's recent ball, a bit about Viscount Guelph, who seems rather smitten with some girl from Scotland, and then a longish piece on the upcoming Bridgerton masquerade."

Sophie sighed. She'd been reading about the upcoming masquerade for weeks, and even though she was nothing but a lady's maid (and occasionally a housemaid as well, whenever Araminta decided she wasn't working hard enough) she couldn't help but wish that she could attend the ball.

"I for one will be thrilled if that Guelph viscount gets himself engaged," Posy remarked, reaching for another biscuit. "It will mean one fewer bachelor for Mother to go on and on about as a potential husband. It's not as if I have any hope of attracting his attention anyway." She took a bite of the biscuit; it crunched loudly in her mouth. "I do hope Lady Whistledown is right about him."

"She probably is," Sophie answered. She had been reading *Lady Whistledown's Society Papers* since it had debuted in 1813, and the gossip columnist was almost always correct when it came to matters of the Marriage Mart.

Not, of course, that Sophie had ever had the chance to see the Marriage Mart for herself. But if one read *Whistledown* often enough, one could almost feel a part of London Society without actually attending any balls.

In fact, reading *Whistledown* was really Sophie's one true enjoyable pastime. She'd already read all of the novels in the library, and as neither Araminta, Rosamund, nor Posy was particularly enamored of reading, Sophie couldn't look forward to a new book entering the house.

But *Whistledown* was great fun. No one actually knew the columnist's true identity. When the single-sheet newspaper had debuted two years earlier, speculation had been rampant. Even now, whenever Lady Whistledown reported a particularly juicy bit of gossip, people starting talking and guessing anew, wondering who on earth was able to report with such speed and accuracy.

And for Sophie, *Whistledown* was a tantalizing glimpse into the world that might have been hers, had her parents actually made their union legal. She would have been an earl's daughter, not an earl's bastard; her name Gunningworth instead of Beckett.

Just once, she'd like to be the one stepping into the coach and attending the ball.

Instead, she was the one dressing others for their nights on the town, cinching Posy's corset or dressing Rosamund's hair or polishing a pair of Araminta's shoes.

But she could not—or at least should not—complain. She might have to serve as maid to Araminta and her daughters, but at least she had a home. Which was more than most girls in her position had.

When her father had died, he'd left her nothing. Well, nothing but a roof over her head. His will had ensured that she could not be turned out until she was twenty. There was no way that Araminta would forfeit four thousand pounds a year by giving Sophie the boot.

But that four thousand pounds was Araminta's, not Sophie's, and Sophie hadn't ever seen a penny of it. Gone were the fine clothes she'd used to wear, replaced by the coarse wool of the servants. And she ate what the rest of the maids ate—whatever Araminta, Rosamund, and Posy chose to leave behind.

Sophie's twentieth birthday, however, had come and gone almost a year earlier, and here she was, still living at Penwood House, still waiting on Araminta hand and foot. For some unknown reason— probably because she didn't want to train (or pay) a new maid— Araminta had allowed Sophie to remain in her household.

And Sophie had stayed. If Araminta was the devil she knew, then the rest of the world was the devil she didn't. And Sophie had no idea which would be worse.

"Isn't that tray getting heavy?"

Sophie blinked her way out of her reverie and focused on Posy, who was reaching for the last biscuit on the tray. Drat. She'd been hoping to snitch it for herself. "Yes," she murmured. "Yes, it is quite. I should really be getting to the kitchen with it."

Posy smiled. "I won't keep you any longer, but when you're done with that, could you press my pink gown? I'm going to wear it tonight. Oh, and I suppose the matching shoes should be readied as well. I got a bit of dirt on them last time I wore them, and you know how Mother is about shoes. Never mind that you can't even see them under my skirt. She'll notice the tiniest speck of dirt the instant I lift my hem to climb a step."

Sophie nodded, mentally adding Posy's requests to her daily list of chores.

"I'll see you later, then!" Biting down on that last biscuit, Posy turned and disappeared into her bedchamber.

And Sophie trudged down to the kitchen.

A few days later, Sophie was on her knees, pins clamped between her teeth as she made last-minute alterations on Araminta's masquerade costume. The Queen Elizabeth gown had, of course, been delivered from the dressmaker as a perfect fit, but Araminta insisted that it was now a quarter inch too large in the waist.

"How is that?" Sophie asked, speaking through her teeth so the pins wouldn't fall.

"Too tight."

Sophie adjusted a few pins. "What about that?"

"Too loose."

Sophie pulled out a pin and stuck it back in precisely the same spot. "There. How does that feel?"

Araminta twisted this way and that, then finally declared, "It'll do."

Sophie smiled to herself as she stood to help Araminta out of the gown.

"I'll need it done in an hour if we're to get to the ball on time," Araminta said.

"Of course," Sophie murmured. She'd found it easiest just to say "of course" on a regular basis in conversations with Araminta.

"This ball is very important," Araminta said sharply. "Rosamund must make an advantageous match this year. The new earl—" She shuddered with distaste; she still considered the new earl an interloper, never mind that he was the old earl's closest living male relative. "Well, he has told me that this is the last year we may use Penwood House in London. The nerve of the man. I am the dowager countess, after all, and Rosamund and Posy are the earl's daughters."

Stepdaughters, Sophie silently corrected.

"We have every right to use Penwood House for the season. What he plans to do with the house, I'll never know."

"Perhaps he wishes to attend the season and look for a wife," Sophie suggested. "He'll be wanting an heir, I'm sure."

Araminta scowled. "If Rosamund doesn't marry into money, I don't know what we'll do. It is so difficult to find a proper house to rent. And so expensive as well."

Sophie forbore to point out that at least Araminta didn't have to pay for a lady's maid. In fact, until Sophie had turned twenty, she'd received four thousand pounds per year, just for *having* a lady's maid.

Araminta snapped her fingers. "Don't forget that Rosamund will need her hair powdered."

Rosamund was attending dressed as Marie Antoinette. Sophie had asked if she was planning to put a ring of faux blood around her neck. Rosamund had not been amused.

Araminta pulled on her dressing gown, cinching the sash with swift, tight movements. "And Posy—" Her nose wrinkled. "Well, Posy will need your help in some manner or other, I'm sure."

"I'm always glad to help Posy," Sophie replied.

Araminta narrowed her eyes as she tried to figure out if Sophie was being insolent. "Just see that you do," she finally said, her syllables clipped. She stalked off to the washroom.

Sophie saluted as the door closed behind her.

"Ah, there you are, Sophie," Rosamund said as she bustled into the room. "I need your help immediately."

"I'm afraid it'll have to wait until—"

"I said immediately!" Rosamund snapped.

Sophie squared her shoulders and gave Rosamund a steely look. "Your mother wants me to alter her gown."

"Just pull the pins out and tell her you pulled it in. She'll never notice the difference."

Sophie had been considering the very same thing, and she groaned. If she did as Rosamund asked, Rosamund would tattle on her the very next day, and then Araminta would rant and rage for a week. Now she would definitely have to do the alteration.

"What do you need, Rosamund?"

"There is a tear at the hem of my costume. I have no idea how it happened."

"Perhaps when you tried it on—"

"Don't be impertinent!"

Sophie clamped her mouth shut. It was far more difficult to take orders from Rosamund than from Araminta, probably because they'd once been equals, sharing the same schoolroom and governess.

"It must be repaired immediately," Rosamund said with an affected sniff.

Sophie sighed. "Just bring it in. I'll do it right after I finish with your mother's. I promise you'll have it in plenty of time."

"I won't be late for this ball," Rosamund warned. "If I am, I shall have *your* head on a platter."

"You won't be late," Sophie promised.

Rosamund made a rather huffy sound, then hurried out the door to retrieve her costume.

"Ooof!"

Sophie looked up to see Rosamund crashing into Posy, who was barreling through the door.

"Watch where you're going, Posy!" Rosamund snapped.

"You could watch where you're going, too," Posy pointed out.

"I *was* watching. It's impossible to get out of *your* way, you big oaf."

Posy's cheeks stained red, and she stepped aside.

"Did you need something, Posy?" Sophie asked, as soon as Rosamund had disappeared.

Posy nodded. "Could you set aside a little extra time to dress my hair tonight? I found some green ribbons that look a little like seaweed."

Sophie let out a long breath. The dark green ribbons weren't likely to show up very well against Posy's dark hair, but she didn't have the heart to point that out. "I'll try, Posy, but I have to mend Rosamund's dress and alter your mother's."

"Oh." Posy looked crestfallen. It nearly broke Sophie's heart. Posy was the only person who was even halfway nice to her in Araminta's household, save for the servants. "Don't worry," she assured her. "I'll make sure your hair is lovely no matter how much time we have."

"Oh, thank you, Sophie! I—"

"Haven't you gotten started on my gown yet?" Araminta thundered as she returned from the washroom.

Sophie gulped. "I was talking with Rosamund and Posy. Rosamund tore her gown and—"

"Just get to work!"

"I will. Immediately." Sophie plopped down on the settee and turned the gown inside out so that she could take in the waist.

"Faster than immediately," she muttered. "Faster than a humming-bird's wings. Faster than——"

"What are you chattering about?" Araminta demanded.

"Nothing."

"Well, cease your prattle immediately. I find the sound of your voice particularly grating."

Sophie ground her teeth together.

"Mama," Posy said, "Sophie is going to dress my hair tonight like——"

"Of course she's going to dress your hair. Quit your dilly-dallying this minute and go put compresses on your eyes so they don't look so puffy."

Posy's face fell. "My eyes are puffy?"

Sophie shook her head on the off chance that Posy decided to look down at her.

"Your eyes are always puffy," Araminta replied. "Don't you think so, Rosamund?"

Posy and Sophie both turned toward the door. Rosamund had just entered, carrying her Marie Antoinette gown. "Always," she agreed. "But a compress will help, I'm sure."

"You look stunning tonight," Araminta told Rosamund. "And you haven't even started getting ready. That gold in your gown is an exquisite match to your hair."

Sophie shot a sympathetic look at the dark-haired Posy, who never received such compliments from her mother.

"You shall snare one of those Bridgerton brothers," Araminta continued. "I'm sure of it."

Rosamund looked down demurely. It was an expression she'd perfected, and Sophie had to admit it looked lovely on her. But then again, most everything looked lovely on Rosamund. Her golden hair and blue eyes were all the rage that year, and thanks to the generous dowry settled upon her by the late earl, it was widely assumed that she would make a brilliant match before the season was through.

Sophie glanced back over at Posy, who was staring at her mother with a sad, wistful expression. "You look lovely, too, Posy," Sophie said impulsively.

Posy's eyes lit up. "Do you think so?"

"Absolutely. And your gown is terribly original. I'm sure there won't be any other mermaids."

"How would you know, Sophie?" Rosamund asked with a laugh. "It's not as if you've ever been out in society."

"I'm sure you'll have a lovely time, Posy," Sophie said pointedly, ignoring Rosamund's jibe. "I'm terribly jealous. I do wish I could go."

Sophie's little sigh and wish was met with absolute silence . . . followed by the raucous laughter of both Araminta and Rosamund. Even Posy giggled a bit.

"Oh, that's rich," Araminta said, barely able to catch her breath. "Little Sophie at the Bridgerton ball. They don't allow bastards out in society, you know."

"I didn't say I expected to go," Sophie said defensively, "just that I wish I *could*."

"Well, you shouldn't even bother doing that," Rosamund chimed in. "If you wish for things you can't possibly hope for, you're only going to be disappointed."

But Sophie didn't hear what she had to say, because in that moment, the oddest thing happened. As she was turning her head toward Rosamund, she caught sight of the housekeeper standing in the doorway. It was Mrs. Gibbons, who had come up from Penwood Park in the country when the town housekeeper had passed away. And when Sophie's eyes met hers, she winked.

Winked!

Sophie didn't think she'd ever seen Mrs. Gibbons wink.

"Sophie! Sophie! Are you listening to me?"

Sophie turned a distracted eye toward Araminta. "I'm sorry," she murmured. "You were saying?"

"I was saying," Araminta said in a nasty voice, "that you had better get to work on my gown this instant. If we are late for the ball, *you* will answer for it tomorrow."

"Yes, of course," Sophie said quickly. She jabbed her needle into the fabric and started sewing but her mind was still on Mrs. Gibbons.

A wink?

Why on earth would she wink?

Three hours later, Sophie was standing on the front steps of Penwood House, watching first Araminta, then Rosamund, then Posy each take the footman's hand and climb up into the carriage. Sophie waved at Posy, who waved back, then watched the carriage roll down the street and disappear around the corner. It was barely six blocks to Bridgerton House, where the masquerade was to be held, but Araminta would have insisted upon the carriage if they'd lived right next door.

It was important to make a grand entrance, after all.

With a sigh, Sophie turned around and made her way back up the steps. At least Araminta had, in the excitement of the moment, forgotten to leave her with a list of tasks to complete while she was gone. A free evening was a luxury indeed. Perhaps she'd reread a novel. Or maybe she could find today's edition of *Whistledown*. She'd thought she'd seen Rosamund take it into her room earlier that afternoon.

But as Sophie stepped through the front door of Penwood House, Mrs. Gibbons materialized as if from nowhere and grabbed her arm. "There's no time to lose!" the housekeeper said.

Sophie looked at her as if she'd lost her mind. "I beg your pardon?"

Mrs. Gibbons tugged at her elbow. "Come with me."

Sophie allowed herself to be led up the three flights of stairs to her room, a tiny little chamber tucked under the eaves. Mrs. Gibbons was acting in a most peculiar manner, but Sophie humored her and followed along. The housekeeper had always treated her with exceptional kindness, even when it was clear that Araminta disapproved.

"You'll need to get undressed," Mrs. Gibbons said as she grasped the doorknob.

"*What?*"

"We really must rush."

"Mrs. Gibbons, you . . ." Sophie's mouth fell open, and her words trailed off as she took in the scene in her bedroom. A steaming tub of water lay right in the center, and all three housemaids were bustling about. One was pouring a pitcher of water into the tub, another was fiddling with the lock on a rather mysterious-looking trunk, and the third was holding a towel and saying, "Hurry! Hurry!"

Sophie cast bewildered eyes at the lot of them. "What is going on?"

Mrs. Gibbons turned to her and beamed. "You, Miss Sophia Maria Beckett, are going to the masquerade!"

One hour later, Sophie was transformed. The trunk had held dresses belonging to the late earl's mother. They were all fifty years out of date, but that was no matter. The ball was a masquerade; no one expected the gowns to be of the latest styles.

At the very bottom of the trunk they'd found an exquisite creation of shimmering silver, with a tight, pearl-encrusted bodice and the flared skirts that had been so popular during the previous century. Sophie felt like a princess just touching it. It was a bit musty from its years in the trunk, and one of the maids quickly took it outside to dab a bit of rosewater on the fabric and air it out.

She'd been bathed and perfumed, her hair had been dressed, and one of the housemaids had even applied a touch of rouge to her lips. "Don't tell Miss Rosamund," the maid had whispered. "I nicked it from her collection."

"Ooooh, look," Mrs. Gibbons said. "I found matching gloves."

Sophie looked up to see the housekeeper holding up a pair of long, elbow-length gloves. "Look," she said, taking one from Mrs. Gibbons and examining it. "The Penwood crest. And it's monogrammed. Right at the hem."

Mrs. Gibbons turned over the one in her hand. "SLG. Sarah Louisa Gunningworth. Your grandmother."

Sophie looked at her in surprise. Mrs. Gibbons had never referred to the earl as her father. No one at Penwood Park had ever verbally acknowledged Sophie's blood ties to the Gunningworth family.

"Well, she *is* your grandmother," Mrs. Gibbons declared. "We've all danced around the issue long enough. It's a crime the way Rosamund and Posy are treated like daughters of the house, and you, the earl's true blood, must sweep and serve like a maid!"

The three housemaids nodded in agreement.

"Just once," Mrs. Gibbons said, "for just one night, *you* will be the belle of the ball." With a smile on her face, she slowly turned Sophie around until she was facing the mirror.

Sophie's breath caught. "Is that me?"

Mrs. Gibbons nodded, her eyes suspiciously bright. "You look lovely, dearling," she whispered.

Sophie's hand moved slowly up to her hair.

"Don't muss it!" one of the maids yelped.

"I won't," Sophie promised, her smile wobbling a bit as she fought back a tear. A touch of shimmery powder had been sprinkled onto her hair, so that she sparkled like a fairy princess. Her dark blond curls had been swept atop her head in a loose topknot, with one thick lock allowed to slide down the length of her neck. And her eyes, normally moss green, shone like emeralds.

Although Sophie suspected that might have had more to do with her unshed tears than anything else.

"Here is your mask," Mrs. Gibbons said briskly. It was a demi-mask, the sort that tied at the back so that Sophie would not have to use one of her hands to hold it up. "Now all we need are shoes."

Sophie glanced ruefully at her serviceable and ugly work shoes that sat in the corner. "I have nothing suitable for such finery, I'm afraid."

The housemaid who had rouged Sophie's lips held up a pair of white slippers. "From Rosamund's closet," she said.

Sophie slid her right foot into one of the slippers and just as quickly slid it back out. "It's much too big," she said, glancing up at Mrs. Gibbons. "I'll never be able to walk in them."

Mrs. Gibbons turned to the maid. "Fetch a pair from Posy's closet."

"Hers are even bigger," Sophie said. "I know. I've cleaned enough scuff marks from them."

Mrs. Gibbons let out a long sigh. "There's nothing for it, then. We shall have to raid Araminta's collection."

Sophie shuddered. The thought of walking anywhere in Araminta's shoes was somewhat creepy. But it was either that or go without, and she didn't think that bare feet would be acceptable at a fancy London masquerade.

A few minutes later the maid returned with a pair of white satin slippers, stitched in silver and adorned with exquisite faux-diamond rosettes.

Sophie was still apprehensive about wearing Araminta's shoes, but she slipped one of her feet in, anyway. It fit perfectly.

"And they match, too," one of the maids said, pointing to the silver stitching. "As if they were made for the dress."

"We don't have time for admiring shoes," Mrs. Gibbons suddenly said. "Now listen to these instructions very carefully. The coachman has returned from taking the countess and her girls, and he will take you to Bridgerton House. But he has to be waiting outside when they wish to depart, which means you must leave by midnight and not a second later. Do you understand?"

Sophie nodded and looked at the clock on the wall. It was a bit after nine, which meant she'd have more than two hours at the masquerade. "Thank you," she whispered. "Oh, thank you so much."

Mrs. Gibbons dabbed her eyes with a handkerchief. "You just have a good time, dearling. That's all the thanks I need."

Sophie looked again at the clock. Two hours.

Two hours that she'd have to make last a lifetime.

Chapter 2

The Bridgertons are truly a unique family. Surely there cannot be anyone in London who does not know that they all look remarkably alike, or that they are famously named in alphabetical order: Anthony, Benedict, Colin, Daphne, Eloise, Francesca, Gregory, and Hyacinth.

It does make one wonder what the late viscount and (still very-much alive) dowager viscountess would have named their next child had their offspring numbered nine. Imogen? Inigo?

Perhaps it is best they stopped at eight.

LADY WHISTLEDOWN'S SOCIETY PAPERS,
2 JUNE 1815

Benedict Bridgerton was the second of eight children, but sometimes it felt more like a hundred.

This ball his mother had insisted upon hosting was supposed to be a masquerade, and Benedict had dutifully donned a black demimask, but everyone knew who he was. Or rather, they all *almost* knew.

"A Bridgerton!" they would exclaim, clapping their hands together with glee.

"You must be a Bridgerton!"

"A Bridgerton! I can spot a Bridgerton anywhere."

Benedict was a Bridgerton, and while there was no family to which he'd rather belong, he sometimes wished he were considered a little less a Bridgerton and a little more himself.

Just then, a woman of somewhat indeterminate age dressed as a shepherdess sauntered over. "A Bridgerton!" she trilled. "I'd recognize that chestnut hair anywhere. Which are you? No, don't say. Let me guess. You're not the viscount, because I just saw him. You must be Number Two or Number Three."

Benedict eyed her coolly.

"Which one? Number Two or Number Three?"

"Two," he bit off.

She clapped her hands together. "That's what I thought! Oh, I must find Portia. I told her you were Number Two—"

Benedict, he nearly growled.

"—but she said, no, he's the younger one, but I—"

Benedict suddenly had to get away. It was either that or kill the twittering ninnyhammer, and with so many witnesses, he didn't think he could get away with it. "If you'll excuse me," he said smoothly. "I see someone with whom I must speak."

It was a lie, but he didn't much care. With a curt nod toward the overage shepherdess, he made a beeline toward the ballroom's side door, eager to escape the throng and sneak into his brother's study, where he might find some blessed peace and quiet and perhaps a glass of fine brandy.

"Benedict!"

Damn. He'd nearly made a clean escape. He looked up to see his mother hurrying toward him. She was dressed in some sort of Elizabethan costume. He supposed she was meant to be a character in one of Shakespeare's plays, but for the life of him, he had no idea which.

"What can I do for you, Mother?" he asked. "And don't say 'Dance with Hermione Smythe-Smith.' Last time I did that I nearly lost three toes in the process."

"I wasn't going to ask anything of the sort," Violet replied. "I was going to ask you to dance with Prudence Featherington."

"Have mercy, Mother," he moaned. "She's even worse."

"I'm not asking you to marry the chit," she said. "Just dance with her."

Benedict fought a groan. Prudence Featherington, while essentially a nice person, had a brain the size of a pea and a laugh so grating he'd seen grown men flee with their hands over their ears. "I'll tell you what," he wheedled. "I'll dance with Penelope Featherington if you keep Prudence at bay."

"That'll do," his mother said with a satisfied nod, leaving Benedict with the sinking sensation that she'd wanted him to dance with Penelope all along.

"She's over there by the lemonade table," Violet said, "dressed as a leprechaun, poor thing. The color is good for her, but someone really must take her mother in hand next time they venture out to the dressmaker. A more unfortunate costume, I can't imagine."

"You obviously haven't seen the mermaid," Benedict murmured.

She swatted him lightly on the arm. "No poking fun at the guests."

"But they make it so easy."

She shot him a look of warning before saying, "I'm off to find your sister."

"Which one?"

"One of the ones who isn't married," Violet said pertly. "Viscount Guelph might be interested in that Scottish girl, but they aren't betrothed yet."

Benedict silently wished Guelph luck. The poor bloke was going to need it.

"And thank you for dancing with Penelope," Violet said pointedly.

He gave her a rather ironic half smile. They both knew that her words were meant as a reminder, not as thanks.

His arms crossed in a somewhat forbidding stance, he watched his mother depart before drawing a long breath and turning to make his way to the lemonade table. He adored his mother to distraction, but she did tend to err on the side of meddlesome when it came to the social lives of her children. And if there was one thing that bothered her even more than Benedict's unmarried state, it was the sight of a young girl's glum face when no one asked her to dance. As a result, Benedict spent a lot of time on the ballroom floor, sometimes with girls she wanted him to marry, but more often with the overlooked wallflowers.

Of the two, he rather thought he preferred the wallflowers. The popular girls tended to be shallow and, to be frank, just a little bit dull.

His mother had always had a particular soft spot for Penelope Featherington, who was on her . . . Benedict frowned. On her *third* season? It must be her third. And with no marriage prospects in sight. Ah, well. He might as well do his duty. Penelope was a nice enough girl, with a decent wit and personality. Someday she'd find herself a husband. It wouldn't be *him*, of course, and in all honesty it probably wouldn't be anyone he even knew, but surely she'd find *some*one.

With a sigh, Benedict started to make his way toward the lemonade table. He could practically taste that brandy, smooth and mellow in his mouth, but he supposed that a glass of lemonade would tide him over for a few minutes.

"Miss Featherington!" he called out, trying not to shudder when three Miss Featheringtons turned around. With what he knew could not possibly be anything but the weakest of smiles, he added, "Er, Penelope, that is."

From about ten feet away, Penelope beamed at him, and Benedict was reminded that he actually *liked* Penelope Featherington. Truly, she wouldn't be considered so antidotal if she weren't always lumped together with her unfortunate sisters, who could easily make a grown man wish himself aboard a ship to Australia.

He'd nearly closed the gap between them when he heard a low rumble of whispers rippling across the ballroom behind him. He knew he ought to keep going and get this duty-dance over with, but God help him, his curiosity got the best of him and he turned around.

And found himself facing what had to be the most breathtaking woman he'd ever seen.

He couldn't even tell if she was beautiful. Her hair was a rather ordinary dark blond, and with her mask tied securely around her head he couldn't even see half of her face.

But there was something about her that held him mesmerized. It was her smile, the shape of her eyes, the way she held herself and looked about the ballroom as if she'd never seen a more glorious sight than the silly members of the *ton* all dressed up in ridiculous costumes.

Her beauty came from within.

She shimmered. She glowed.

She was utterly radiant, and Benedict suddenly realized that it was because she looked so damned *happy*. Happy to be where she was, happy to be *who* she was.

Happy in a way Benedict could barely remember. His was a good life, it was true, maybe even a great life. He had seven wonderful siblings, a loving mother, and scores of friends. But this woman—

This woman knew joy.

And Benedict had to know *her*.

Penelope forgotten, he pushed his way through the crowd until he was but a few steps from her side. Three other gentlemen had beaten him to his destination and were presently showering her with flattery and praise. Benedict watched her with interest; she did not react as any woman of his acquaintance might.

She did not act coy. Nor did she act as if she expected their compliments as her due. Nor was she shy, or tittering, or arch, or ironic, or any of those things one might expect from a woman.

She just smiled. Beamed, actually. Benedict supposed that compliments were meant to bring a measure of happiness to the receiver, but never had he seen a woman react with such pure, unadulterated joy.

He stepped forward. He wanted that joy for himself.

"Excuse me, gentlemen, but the lady has already promised this dance to me," he lied.

Her mask's eye-holes were cut a bit large, and he could see that her eyes widened considerably, then crinkled with amusement. He held out his hand to her, silently daring her to call his bluff.

But she just smiled at him, a wide, radiant grin that pierced his skin and traveled straight to his soul. She put her hand in his, and it was only then that Benedict realized he'd been holding his breath.

"Have you permission to dance the waltz?" he murmured once they reached the dance floor.

She shook her head. "I do not dance."

"You jest."

"I'm afraid I do not. The truth is—" She leaned forward and with a glimmer of a smile said, "I don't know how."

He looked at her with surprise. She moved with an inborn grace, and furthermore, what gently bred lady could reach her age without learning how to dance? "There is only one thing to do, then," he murmured. "I shall teach you."

Her eyes widened, then her lips parted, and a surprised laugh burst forth.

"What," he asked, trying to sound serious, "is so funny?"

She grinned at him—the sort of grin one expects from an old school chum, not a debutante at a ball. Still smiling, she said, "Even I know that one does not conduct dancing lessons at a ball."

"What does that mean, I wonder," he murmured, *"even you?"*

She said nothing.

"I shall have to take the upper hand, then," he said, "and force you to do my bidding."

"Force me?"

But she was smiling as she said it, so he knew she took no offense, and he said, "It would be ungentlemanly of me to allow this sorrowful state of affairs to continue."

"Sorrowful, you say?"

He shrugged. "A beautiful lady who cannot dance. It seems a crime against nature."

"If I allow you to teach me . . ."

"*When* you allow me to teach you."

"*If* I allow you to teach me, where shall you conduct the lesson?"

Benedict lifted his chin and scanned the room. It wasn't difficult to see over the heads of most of the partygoers; at an inch above six feet, he was one of the tallest men in the room. "We shall have to retire to the terrace," he said finally.

"The terrace?" she echoed. "Won't it be terribly crowded? It's a warm night, after all."

He leaned forward. "Not the *private* terrace."

"The private terrace, you say?" she asked, amusement in her voice. "And how, pray tell, would you know of a private terrace?"

Benedict stared at her in shock. Could she possibly not know who he was? It wasn't that he held such a high opinion of himself that he expected all of London to be aware of his identity. It was just that he was a Bridgerton, and if a person met one Bridgerton, that generally meant he could recognize another. And as there was no one in London who had not crossed paths with one Bridgerton or another, Benedict was generally recognized everywhere. Even, he thought ruefully, when that recognition was simply as "Number Two."

"You did not answer my question," his mystery lady reminded him.

"About the private terrace?" Benedict raised her hand to his lips and kissed the fine silk of her glove. "Let us just say that I have my ways."

She appeared undecided, and so he tugged at her fingers, pulling her closer—only by an inch, but somehow it seemed she was only a kiss away. "Come," he said. "Dance with me."

She took a step forward, and he knew his life had been changed forever.

Sophie hadn't seen him when she'd first walked into the room, but she'd felt magic in the air, and when he'd appeared before her, like some charming prince from a children's tale, she somehow knew that *he* was the reason she'd stolen into the ball.

He was tall, and what she could see of his face was very handsome, with lips that hinted of irony and smiles, and skin that was just barely touched by the beginnings of a beard. His hair was a dark, rich brown, and the flickering candlelight lent it a faint reddish cast.

People seemed to know who he was, as well. Sophie noticed that when he moved, the other partygoers stepped out of his path. And when he'd lied so brazenly and claimed her for a dance, the other men had deferred and stepped away.

He was handsome and he was strong, and for this one night, he was hers.

When the clock struck midnight, she'd be back to her life of drudgery, of mending and washing, and attending to Araminta's every wish. Was she so wrong to want this one heady night of magic and love?

She felt like a princess—a reckless princess—and so when he asked her to dance, she put her hand in his. And even though she knew that this entire evening was a lie, that she was a nobleman's bastard and a countess's maid, that her dress was borrowed and her shoes practically stolen—none of that seemed to matter as their fingers twined.

For a few hours, at least, Sophie could pretend that this gentleman could be *her* gentleman, and that from this moment on, her life would be changed forever.

It was nothing but a dream, but it had been so terribly long since she'd let herself dream.

Banishing all caution, she allowed him to lead her out of the ballroom. He walked quickly, even as he wove through the pulsing crowd, and she found herself laughing as she tripped along after him.

"Why is it," he said, halting for a moment when they reached the hall outside the ballroom, "that you always seem to be laughing at me?"

She laughed again; she couldn't help it. "I'm happy," she said with a helpless shrug. "I'm just so happy to be here."

"And why is that? A ball such as this must be routine for one such as yourself."

Sophie grinned. If he thought she was a member of the *ton*, an alumna of dozens of balls and parties, then she must be playing her role to perfection.

He touched the corner of her mouth. "You keep smiling," he murmured.

"I like to smile."

His hand found her waist, and he pulled her toward him. The distance between their bodies remained respectable, but the increasing nearness robbed her of breath.

"I like to watch you smile," he said. His words were low and seductive, but there was something oddly hoarse about his voice, and Sophie could almost let herself believe that he really meant it, that she wasn't merely that evening's conquest.

But before she could respond, an accusing voice from down the hall suddenly called out, "There you are!"

Sophie's stomach lurched well into her throat. She'd been found out. She'd be thrown into the street, and tomorrow probably into jail for stealing Araminta's shoes, and—

And the man who'd called out had reached her side and was saying to her mysterious gentleman, "Mother has been looking all over for you. You weaseled out of your dance with Penelope, and *I* had to take your place."

"So sorry," her gentleman murmured.

That didn't seem to be enough of an apology for the newcomer, because he scowled mightily as he said, "If you flee the party and leave me to that pack of she-devil debutantes, I swear I shall exact revenge to my dying day."

"A chance I'm willing to take," her gentleman said.

"Well, I covered up for you with Penelope," the other man grumbled. "You're just lucky that I happened to be standing by. The poor girl's heart looked broken when you turned away."

Sophie's gentleman had the grace to blush. "Some things are unavoidable, I'm afraid."

Sophie looked from one man to the other. Even under their demimasks, it was more than obvious that they were brothers, and she realized in a blinding flash that they must be the Bridgerton brothers, and this must be their house, and—

Oh, good Lord, had she made a total and utter fool of herself by asking him how he knew of a private terrace?

But which brother was he? Benedict. He had to be Benedict. Sophie sent a silent thank-you to Lady Whistledown, who'd once written a column completely devoted to the task of telling the Bridgerton siblings apart. Benedict, she recalled, had been singled out as the tallest.

The man who made her heart flip in triple time stood a good inch above his brother—

—who Sophie suddenly realized was looking at her quite intently.

"I see why you departed," Colin said (for he must be Colin; he certainly wasn't Gregory, who was only fourteen, and Anthony was married, so he wouldn't care if Benedict fled the party and left him to fend off the debutantes by himself). He looked at Benedict with a sly expression. "Might I request an introduction?"

Benedict raised a brow. "You can try your best, but I doubt you'll meet with success. I haven't learned her name yet myself."

"You haven't asked," Sophie could not help pointing out.

"And would you tell me if I did?"

"I'd tell you *some*thing," she returned.

"But not the truth."

She shook her head. "This isn't a night for truth."

"My favorite kind of night," Colin said in a jaunty voice.

"Don't you have somewhere to *be*?" Benedict asked.

Colin shook his head. "I'm sure Mother would prefer that I *be* in the ballroom, but it's not exactly a requirement."

"*I* require it," Benedict returned.

Sophie felt a giggle bubbling in her throat.

"Very well," Colin sighed. "I shall take myself off."

"Excellent," Benedict said.

"All alone, to face the ravenous wolves . . ."

"Wolves?" Sophie queried.

"Eligible young ladies," Colin clarified. "A pack of ravenous wolves, the lot of them. Present company excluded, of course."

Sophie thought it best not to point out that she was not an "eligible young lady" at all.

"My mother——" Colin began.

Benedict groaned.

"——would like nothing better than to see my dear elder brother married off." He paused and pondered his words. "Except, perhaps, to see *me* married off."

"If only to get you out of the house," Benedict said dryly.

This time Sophie *did* giggle.

"But then again, he's considerably more ancient," Colin continued, "so perhaps we should send him to the gallows—er, altar first."

"Do you have a *point*?" Benedict growled.

"None whatsoever," Colin admitted. "But then again, I rarely do."

Benedict turned to Sophie. "He speaks the truth."

"So then," Colin said to Sophie with a grand flourish of his arm, "will you take pity on my poor, long-suffering mother and chase my dear brother up the aisle?"

"Well, he hasn't asked," Sophie said, trying to join the humor of the moment.

"How much have you had to drink?" Benedict grumbled.

"Me?" Sophie queried.

"*Him.*"

"Nothing at all," Colin said jovially, "but I'm thinking quite seriously of remedying that. In fact, it might be the only thing that will make this eve bearable."

"If the procurement of drink removes you from my presence," Benedict said, "then it will certainly be the only thing that will make *my* night bearable as well."

Colin grinned, gave a jaunty salute, and was gone.

"It's nice to see two siblings who love each other so well," Sophie murmured.

Benedict, who had been staring somewhat menacingly at the doorway through which his brother had just disappeared, snapped his attention back to her. "You call *that* love?"

Sophie thought of Rosamund and Posy, who were forever sniping at each other, and not in jest. "I do," she said firmly. "It's obvious you would lay your life down for him. And vice versa."

"I suppose you're right." Benedict let out a beleaguered sigh, then ruined the effect by smiling. "Much as it pains me to admit it." He leaned against the wall, crossing his arms and looking terribly sophisticated and urbane. "So tell me," he said, "have you any siblings?"

Sophie pondered that question for a moment, then gave a decisive, "No."

One of his brows rose into a curiously arrogant arch. He cocked his head very slightly to the side as he said, "I find myself rather curious as to why it took you so long to determine the answer to that question. One would think the answer would be an easy one to reach."

Sophie looked away for a moment, not wanting him to see the pain that she knew must show in her eyes. She had always wanted a family. In fact, there was nothing in life she had ever wanted more. Her father had never recognized her as his daughter, even in private, and her mother had died at her birth. Araminta treated her like the plague, and Rosamund and Posy had certainly never been sisters to her. Posy had occasionally been a friend, but even she spent most of the day asking Sophie to mend her dress, or style her hair, or polish her shoes . . .

And in all truth, even though Posy asked rather than ordered, as her sister and mother did, Sophie didn't exactly have the option of saying no.

"I am an only child," Sophie finally said.

"And that is all you're going to say on the subject," Benedict murmured.

"And that is all I'm going to say on the subject," she agreed.

"Very well." He smiled, a lazy masculine sort of smile. "What, then, am I permitted to ask you?"

"Nothing, really."

"Nothing at all?"

"I suppose I might be induced to tell you that my favorite color is green, but beyond that I shall leave you with no clues to my identity."

"Why so many secrets?"

"If I answered that," Sophie said with an enigmatic smile, truly warming to her role as a mysterious stranger, "then that would be the end of my secrets, wouldn't it?"

He leaned forward ever so slightly. "You could always develop new secrets."

Sophie backed up a step. His gaze had grown hot, and she had heard enough talk in the servants' quarters to know what that meant. Thrilling as that was, she was not quite as daring as she pretended to be. "This entire night," she said, "is secret enough."

"Then ask me a question," he said. "I have no secrets."

Her eyes widened. "None? Truly? Doesn't everyone have secrets?"

"Not I. My life is hopelessly banal."

"*That* I find difficult to believe."

"It's true," he said with a shrug. "I've never seduced an innocent, or even a married lady, I have no gambling debts, and my parents were completely faithful to one another."

Meaning he wasn't a bastard. Somehow the thought brought an ache to Sophie's throat. Not, of course, because he was legitimate, but rather because she knew he would never pursue her—at least not in an honorable fashion—if he knew that she wasn't.

"You haven't asked me a question," he reminded her.

Sophie blinked in surprise. She hadn't thought he'd been serious. "A-all right," she half stammered, caught off guard. "What, then, is your favorite color?"

He grinned. "You're going to waste your question on that?"

"I only get one question?"

"More than fair, considering you're granting me none." Benedict leaned forward, his dark eyes glinting. "And the answer is blue."

"Why?"

"Why?" he echoed.

"Yes, why? Is it because of the ocean? Or the sky? Or perhaps just because you like it?"

Benedict eyed her curiously. It seemed such an odd question—*why* his favorite color was blue. Everyone else would have taken blue for an answer and left it at that. But this woman—whose name he still didn't even know—went deeper, beyond the whats and into the whys.

"Are you a painter?" he queried.

She shook her head. "Just curious."

"Why is your favorite color green?"

She sighed, and her eyes grew nostalgic. "The grass, I suppose, and maybe the leaves. But mostly the grass. The way it feels when one runs barefoot in the summer. The smell of it after the gardeners have gone through with their scythes and trimmed it even."

"What does the feel and smell of grass have to do with the color?"

"Nothing, I suppose. And maybe everything. I used to live in the country, you see . . ." She caught herself. She hadn't meant to tell him even that much, but there didn't seem to be harm in his knowing such an innocent fact.

"And you were happier there?" he asked quietly.

She nodded, a faint rush of awareness shivering across her skin. Lady Whistledown must never have had a conversation with Benedict Bridgerton beyond the superficial, because she'd never written that he was quite the most perceptive man in London. When he looked into her eyes, Sophie had the oddest sense that he could see straight into her soul.

"You must enjoy walking in the park, then," he said.

"Yes," Sophie lied. She never had time to go to the park. Araminta didn't even give her a day off like the other servants received.

"We shall have to take a stroll together," Benedict said.

Sophie avoided a reply by reminding him, "You never did tell me why your favorite color is blue."

His head cocked slightly to the side, and his eyes narrowed just enough so that Sophie knew that he had noticed her evasion. But he simply said, "I don't know. Perhaps, like you, I'm reminded of something I miss. There is a lake at Aubrey Hall—that is where I grew up, in Kent—but the water always seemed more gray than blue."

"It probably reflects the sky," Sophie commented.

"Which is, more often than not, more gray than blue," Benedict said with a laugh. "Perhaps that is what I miss—blue skies and sunshine."

"If it weren't raining," Sophie said with a smile, "this wouldn't be England."

"I went to Italy once," Benedict said. "The sun shone constantly."

"It sounds like heaven."

"You'd think," he said. "But I found myself missing the rain."

"I can't believe it," she said with a laugh. "I feel like I spend half my life staring out the window and grumbling at the rain."

"If it were gone, you'd miss it."

Sophie grew pensive. Were there things in her life she'd miss if they were gone? She wouldn't miss Araminta, that was for certain, and she wouldn't miss Rosamund. She'd probably miss Posy, and she'd definitely miss the way the sun shone through the window in her attic room in the mornings. She'd miss the way the servants laughed and joked and occasionally included her in their fun, even though they all knew she was the late earl's bastard.

But she wasn't going to miss these things—she wouldn't even have the opportunity to miss them—because she wasn't going anywhere. After this evening—this one amazing, wonderful, magical evening—it would be back to life as usual.

She supposed that if she were stronger, braver, she'd have left Penwood House years ago. But would that have really made much difference? She might not like living with Araminta, but she wasn't likely to improve her lot in life by leaving. She might have liked to have been a governess, and she was certainly well qualified for the position, but jobs were scarce for those without references, and Araminta certainly wasn't going to give her one.

"You're very quiet," Benedict said softly.

"I was just thinking."

"About?"

"About what I'd miss—and what I wouldn't miss—should my life drastically change."

His eyes grew intense. "And do you expect it to drastically change?"

She shook her head and tried to keep the sadness out of her voice when she answered, "No."

His voice grew so quiet it was almost a whisper. "Do you want it to change?"

"Yes," she sighed, before she could stop herself. "Oh, *yes.*"

He took her hands and brought them to his lips, gently kissing each one in turn. "Then we shall begin right now," he vowed. "And tomorrow you shall be transformed."

"Tonight I am transformed," she whispered. "Tomorrow I shall disappear."

Benedict drew her close and dropped the softest, most fleeting of kisses onto her brow. "Then we must pack a lifetime into this very night."

Chapter 3

This Author waits with bated breath to see what costumes the ton will choose for the Bridgerton masquerade. It is rumored that Eloise Bridgerton plans to dress as Joan of Arc, and Penelope Featherington, out for her third season and recently returned from a visit with Irish cousins, will don the costume of a leprechaun. Miss Posy Reiling, stepdaughter to the late Earl of Penwood, plans a costume of mermaid, which This Author personally cannot wait to behold, but her elder sister, Miss Rosamund Reiling, has been very close-lipped about her own attire.

As for the men, if previous masquerade balls are any indication, the portly will dress as Henry VIII, the more fit as Alexander the Great or perhaps the devil, and the bored (the eligible Bridgerton brothers sure to be among these ranks) as themselves—basic black evening kit, with only a demi-mask as a nod to the occasion.

LADY WHISTLEDOWN'S SOCIETY PAPERS,
5 JUNE 1815

"Dance with me," Sophie said impulsively.

His smile was amused, but his fingers twined tightly with hers as he murmured, "I thought you didn't know how."

"You said you would teach me."

He stared at her for a long moment, his eyes boring into hers, then he tugged on her hand and said, "Come with me."

Pulling her along behind him, they slipped down a hallway, climbed a flight of stairs, and then rounded a corner, emerging in front of a pair of French doors. Benedict jiggled the wrought-iron handles and swung the doors open, revealing a small private terrace, adorned with potted plants and two chaise lounges.

"Where are we?" Sophie asked, looking around.

"Right above the ballroom terrace." He shut the doors behind them. "Can't you hear the music?"

Mostly, what Sophie could hear was the low rumble of endless conversation, but if she strained her ears, she could hear the faint lilt of the orchestra. "Handel," she said with a delighted smile. "My governess had a music box with this very tune."

"You loved your governess very much," he said quietly.

Her eyes had been closed as she hummed along with the music, but when she heard his words, she opened them in a startled fashion. "How did you know?"

"The same way I knew you were happier in the country." Benedict reached out and touched her cheek, one gloved finger trailing slowly along her skin until it reached the line of her jaw. "I can see it in your face."

She held silent for a few moments, then pulled away, saying, "Yes, well, I spent more time with her than with anyone else in the household."

"It sounds a lonely upbringing," he said quietly.

"Sometimes it was." She walked over to the edge of the balcony and rested her hands on the balustrade as she stared out into the inky night. "Sometimes it wasn't." Then she turned around quite suddenly, her smile bright, and Benedict knew that she would not reveal anything more about her childhood.

"Your upbringing must have been the complete opposite of lonely," she said, "with so many brothers and sisters about."

"You know who I am," he stated.

She nodded. "I didn't at first."

He walked over to the balustrade and leaned one hip against it, crossing his arms. "What gave me away?"

"It was your brother, actually. You looked so alike—"

"Even with our masks?"

"Even with your masks," she said with an indulgent smile. "Lady Whistledown writes about you quite often, and she never passes up an opportunity to comment upon how alike you look."

"And do you know which brother I am?"

"Benedict," she replied. "If indeed Lady Whistledown is correct when she says that you are tallest among your brothers."

"You're quite the detective."

She looked slightly embarrassed. "I merely read a gossip sheet. It makes me no different from the rest of the people here."

Benedict watched her for a moment, wondering if she realized that she'd revealed another clue to the puzzle of her identity. If she'd recognized him only from *Whistledown*, then she'd not been out in society for long, or perhaps not at all. Either way, she was not one of the many young ladies to whom his mother had introduced him.

"What else do you know about me from *Whistledown*?" he asked, his smile slow and lazy.

"Are you fishing for compliments?" she asked, returning the half smile with the vaguest tilt of her lips. "For you must know that the Bridgertons are almost always spared her rapier quill. Lady Whistledown is nearly always complimentary when writing about your family."

"It's led to quite a bit of speculation about her identity," he admitted. "Some think she must be a Bridgerton."

"Is she?"

He shrugged. "Not that I'm aware of. And you didn't answer my question."

"Which question was that?"

"What you know of me from *Whistledown*."

She looked surprised. "Are you truly interested?"

"If I cannot know anything about *you*, at least I might know what you know about *me*."

She smiled, and touched the tip of her index finger to her lower lip in an endearingly absentminded gesture. "Well, let's see. Last month you won some silly horse race in Hyde Park."

"It wasn't the least bit silly," he said with a grin, "and I'm a hundred quid richer for it."

She shot him an arch look. "Horse races are almost always silly."

"Spoken just like a woman," he muttered.

"Well—"

"Don't point out the obvious," he interrupted.

That made her smile.

"What else do you know?" he asked.

"From *Whistledown*?" She tapped her finger against her cheek. "You once lopped the head off your sister's doll."

"And I'm still trying to figure out how she knew about that," Benedict muttered.

"Maybe Lady Whistledown is a Bridgerton, after all."

"Impossible. Not," he added rather forcefully, "that we're not smart enough to pull it off. Rather, the rest of the family would be too smart not to figure it out."

She laughed out loud at that, and Benedict studied her, wondering if she was aware that she'd given away yet another tiny clue to her identity. Lady Whistledown had written of the doll's unfortunate encounter with a guillotine two years earlier, in one of her very earliest columns. Many people now had the gossip sheet delivered all the way out in the country, but in the beginning, *Whistledown* had been strictly for Londoners.

Which meant that his mystery lady had been in London two years ago. And yet she hadn't known who he was until she'd met Colin.

She'd been in London, but she'd not been out in society. It wasn't enough to figure out who she was, but it was a start.

"What else do you know?" he asked, eager to see if she'd inadvertently reveal anything else.

She chuckled, clearly enjoying herself. "Your name has not been seriously linked with any young lady, and your mother despairs of ever seeing you married."

"The pressure has lessened a bit now that my brother's gone and got himself a wife."

"The viscount?"

Benedict nodded.

"Lady Whistledown wrote about that as well."

"In great detail. Although—" He leaned toward her and lowered his voice. "She didn't get all the facts."

"Really?" she asked with great interest. "What did she leave out?"

He tsked-tsked and shook his head at her. "I'm not about to reveal the secrets of my brother's courtship if you won't reveal even your name."

She snorted at that. "*Courtship* might be too strong a word. Why, Lady Whistledown wrote—"

"Lady Whistledown," he interrupted with a vaguely mocking half smile, "is not privy to all that goes on in London."

"She certainly seems privy to *most*."

"Do you think?" he mused. "I tend to disagree. For example, I suspect that if Lady Whistledown were here on the terrace, she would not know your identity."

Her eyes widened under her mask. Benedict took some satisfaction in that.

He crossed his arms. "Is that true?"

She nodded. "But I am so well disguised that no one would recognize me right now."

He raised a brow. "What if you removed your mask? Would she recognize you then?"

She pushed herself away from the railing and took a few steps toward the center of the terrace. "I'm not going to answer that."

He followed her. "I didn't think you would. But I wanted to ask, nonetheless."

Sophie turned around, then caught her breath as she realized he was mere inches away. She'd heard him following her, but she hadn't thought he was quite that close. She parted her lips to speak, but to her great surprise, she hadn't a thing to say. All she could seem to do was stare up at him, at those dark, dark eyes peering at her from behind his mask.

Speech was impossible. Even breathing was difficult.

"You still haven't danced with me," he said.

She didn't move, just stood there as his large hand came to rest at the small of her back. Her skin tingled where he touched her, and the air grew thick and hot.

This was desire, Sophie realized. This was what she'd heard the maids whispering about. This was what no gently bred lady was even supposed to *know* about.

But she was no gently bred lady, she thought defiantly. She was a bastard, a nobleman's by-blow. She was not a member of the *ton* and never would be. Did she really have to abide by their rules?

She'd always sworn that she would never become a man's mistress, that she'd never bring a child into this world to suffer her fate as a bastard. But she wasn't planning anything quite so brazen. This was one dance, one evening, perhaps one kiss.

It was enough to ruin a reputation, but what sort of reputation did she have to begin with? She was outside society, beyond the pale. And she wanted one night of fantasy.

She looked up.

"You're not going to run, then," he murmured, his dark eyes flaring with something hot and exciting.

She shook her head, realizing that once again, he'd known what she was thinking. It should have scared her that he so effortlessly read her thoughts, but in the dark seduction of the night, with the wind tugging at the loose strands of her hair, and the music floating up from below, it was somehow thrilling instead. "Where do I put my hand?" she asked. "I want to dance."

"Right here on my shoulder," he instructed. "No, just a touch lower. There you are."

"You must think me the veriest ninny," she said, "not knowing how to dance."

"I think you're very brave, actually, for admitting it." His free hand found hers and slowly lifted it into the air. "Most women of my acquaintance would have feigned an injury or disinterest."

She looked up into his eyes even though she knew it would leave her breathless. "I haven't the acting skills to feign disinterest," she admitted.

The hand at the small of her back tightened.

"Listen to the music," he instructed, his voice oddly hoarse. "Do you feel it rising and falling?"

She shook her head.

"Listen harder," he whispered, his lips drawing closer to her ear. "*One*, two, three; *one*, two, three."

Sophie closed her eyes and somehow filtered out the endless chatter of the guests below them until all she heard was the soft swell of the music. Her breathing slowed, and she found herself swaying in time with the orchestra, her head rocking back and forth with Benedict's softly uttered numerical instructions.

"*One*, two, three; *one* two three."

"I feel it," she whispered.

He smiled. She wasn't sure how she knew that; her eyes were still closed. But she felt the smile, heard it in the tenor of his breath.

"Good," he said. "Now watch my feet and allow me to lead you."

Sophie opened her eyes and looked down.

"*One*, two, three; *one*, two, three."

Hesitantly, she stepped along with him—right onto his foot.

"Oh! I'm sorry!" she blurted out.

"My sisters have done far worse," he assured her. "Don't give up."

She tried again, and suddenly her feet knew what to do. "Oh!" she breathed in surprise. "This is wonderful!"

"Look up," he ordered gently.

"But I'll stumble."

"You won't," he promised. "I won't let you. Look into my eyes."

Sophie did as he asked, and the moment her eyes touched his, something inside her seemed to lock into place, and she could not look away. He twirled her in circles and spirals around the terrace, slowly at first, then picking up speed, until she was breathless and giddy.

And all the while, her eyes remained locked on his.

"What do you feel?" he asked.

"Everything!" she said, laughing.

"What do you hear?"

"The music." Her eyes widened with excitement. "I hear the music as I've never heard it before."

His hands tightened, and the space between them diminished by several inches. "What do you see?" he asked.

Sophie stumbled, but she never took her eyes off his. "My soul," she whispered. "I see my very soul."

He stopped dancing. "What did you say?" he whispered.

She held silent. The moment seemed too charged, too meaningful, and she was afraid she'd spoil it.

No, that wasn't true. She was afraid she'd make it even better, and that would make it hurt all the more when she returned to reality at midnight.

How on earth was she going to go back to polishing Araminta's shoes after this?

"I know what you said," Benedict said hoarsely. "I heard you, and—"

"Don't say anything," Sophie cut in. She didn't want him to tell her that he felt the same way, didn't want to hear anything that would leave her pining for this man forever.

But it was probably already too late for that.

He stared at her for an agonizingly long moment, then murmured, "I won't speak. I won't say a word." And then, before she even had a second to breathe, his lips were on hers, exquisitely gentle and achingly tender.

With deliberate slowness, he brushed his lips back and forth across hers, the bare hint of friction sending shivers and tingles spiraling through her body.

He touched her lips and she felt it in her toes. It was a singularly odd—and singularly wonderful—sensation.

Then his hand at the small of her back—the one that had guided her so effortlessly in their waltz—started to pull her toward him. The pressure was slow but inexorable, and Sophie grew hot as their bodies grew closer, then positively burned when she suddenly felt the length of him pressing against her.

He seemed very large, and very powerful, and in his arms she felt like she must be the most beautiful woman in the world.

Suddenly anything seemed possible, maybe even a life free of servitude and stigma.

His mouth grew more insistent, and his tongue darted out to tickle the corner of her mouth. His hand, which had still been holding hers in a waltz-pose, slid down the length of her arm and then up her back until it rested at the nape of her neck, his fingers tugging her hair loose from its coiffure.

"Your hair is like silk," he whispered, and Sophie actually giggled, because he was wearing gloves.

He pulled away. "What," he asked with an amused expression, "are you laughing about?"

"How can you know what my hair feels like? You're wearing gloves."

He smiled, a crooked, boyish sort of a smile that sent her stomach into flips and melted her heart. "I don't know how I know," he said, "but I do." His grin grew even more lopsided, and then he added, "But just to be sure, perhaps I'd better test with my bare skin."

He held out his hand before her. "Will you do the honors?"

Sophie stared at his hand for a few seconds before she realized what he meant. With a shaky, nervous breath, she took a step back and brought both of her hands to his. Slowly she pinched the end of each of the glove's fingertips and gave it a little tug, loosening the fine fabric until she could slide the entire glove from his hand.

Glove still dangling from her fingers, she looked up. He had the oddest expression in his eyes. Hunger . . . and something else. Something almost spiritual.

"I want to touch you," he whispered, and then his bare hand cupped her cheek, the pads of his fingers lightly stroking her skin, whispering upward until they touched the hair near her ear. He tugged gently until he pulled one lock loose. Freed from the coiffure, her hair sprang into a light curl, and Sophie could not take her eyes off it, wrapped golden around his index finger.

"I was wrong," he murmured. "It's softer than silk."

Sophie was suddenly gripped by a fierce urge touch him in the same way, and she held out her hand. "It's my turn," she said softly.

His eyes flared, and then he went to work on her glove, loosening it at the fingers the same way she had done. But then, rather than pulling it off, he brought his lips to the edge of the long glove, all the way above her elbow, and kissed the sensitive skin on the inside of her arm. "Also softer than silk," he murmured.

Sophie used her free hand to grip his shoulder, no longer confident of her ability to stand.

He tugged at the glove, allowing it to slide off her arm with agonizing slowness, his lips following its progress until they reached the inside of her elbow. Barely breaking the kiss, he looked up and said, "You don't mind if I stay here for a bit."

Helplessly, Sophie shook her head.

His tongue darted out and traced the bend of her arm.

"Oh, my," she moaned.

"I thought you might like that," he said, his words hot against her skin.

She nodded. Or rather, she meant to nod. She wasn't sure if she actually did.

His lips continued their trail, sliding sensuously down her forearm until they reached the inside of her wrist. They remained there for a moment before finally coming to rest in the absolute center of her palm.

"Who are you?" he asked, lifting his head but not letting go of her hand.

She shook her head.

"I have to know."

"I can't say." And then, when she saw that he would not take no for an answer, she lied and added, "Yet."

He took one of her fingers and rubbed it gently against his lips. "I want to see you tomorrow," he said softly. "I want to call on you and see where you live."

She said nothing, just held herself steady, trying not to cry.

"I want to meet your parents and pet your damned dog," he continued, somewhat unsteadily. "Do you understand what I mean?"

Music and conversation still drifted up from below, but the only sound on the terrace was the harsh rasp of their breath.

"I want—" His voice dropped to a whisper, and his eyes looked vaguely surprised, as if he couldn't quite believe the truth of his own words. "I want your future. I want every little piece of you."

"Don't say anything more," she begged him. "*Please*. Not another word."

"Then tell me your name. Tell me how to find you tomorrow."

"I—" But then she heard a strange sound, exotic and ringing. "What is that?"

"A gong," he replied. "To signal the unmasking."

Panic rose within her. "What?"

"It must be midnight."

"Midnight?" she gasped.

He nodded. "Time to remove your mask."

One of Sophie's hands flew up to her temple, pressing the mask harshly against her skin, as if she could somehow glue it onto her face through sheer force of will.

"Are you all right?" Benedict asked.

"I have to go," she blurted out, and then, with no further warning, she hitched up her skirts and ran from the terrace.

"Wait!" she heard him call out, felt the rush of air as his arm swiped forward in a futile attempt to grab her dress.

But Sophie was fast, and perhaps more importantly, she was in a state of utter panic, and she tore down the stairs as if the fires of hell were nipping at her heels.

She plunged into the ballroom, knowing that Benedict would prove a determined pursuer, and she'd have the best chance of losing him in a large crowd. All she had to do was make it across the room, and then she could exit via the side door and scoot around the outside of the house to her waiting carriage.

The revelers were still removing their masks, and the party was loud with raucous laughter. Sophie pushed and jostled, anything to beat her way to the other side of the room. She threw one desperate glance over her shoulder. Benedict had entered the ballroom, his face intense as he scanned the crowd. He didn't seem to have seen her yet, but she knew that he would; her silver gown would make her an easy target.

Sophie kept shoving people out of her way. At least half of them didn't seem to notice; probably too drunk. "Excuse me," she muttered, elbowing Julius Caesar in the ribs. "Beg pardon," came out more like a grunt; that was when Cleopatra stepped on her toe.

"Excuse me, I—" And then the breath was quite literally sucked out of her, because she found herself face-to-face with Araminta.

Or rather, face to mask. Sophie was still disguised. But if anyone could recognize her, it would be Araminta. And—

"Watch where you're going," Araminta said haughtily. Then, while Sophie stood openmouthed, she swished her Queen Elizabeth skirts and swept away.

Araminta hadn't recognized her! If Sophie hadn't been so frantic about getting out of Bridgerton House before Benedict caught up with her, she would have laughed with delight.

Sophie glanced desperately behind her. Benedict had spotted her and was pushing his way through the crowd with considerably more efficiency than she had done. With an audible gulp and renewed energy, she pushed forth, almost knocking two Grecian goddesses to the ground before finally reaching the far door.

She looked behind her just long enough to see that Benedict had been waylaid by some elderly lady with a cane, then ran out of the building and around front, where the Penwood carriage was waiting, just as Mrs. Gibbons had said it would.

"Go, go, go!" Sophie shouted frantically to the driver.

And she was gone.

Chapter 4

*More than one masquerade attendee has reported to This Author
that Benedict Bridgerton was seen in the company of an unknown
lady dressed in a silver gown.*

*Try as she might, This Author has been completely unable to
discern the mystery lady's identity. And if This Author cannot
uncover the truth, you may be assured that her identity is a well-
kept secret indeed.*

LADY WHISTLEDOWN'S SOCIETY PAPERS,
7 JUNE 1815

She was gone.

Benedict stood on the pavement in front of Bridgerton House,
surveying the street. All of Grosvenor Square was a mad crush of
carriages. She could be in any one of them, just sitting there on the
cobbles, trying to escape the traffic. Or she could be in one of the
three carriages that had just escaped the tangle and rolled around
the corner.

Either way, she was gone.

He was half-ready to strangle Lady Danbury, who'd jammed her
cane onto his toe and insisted upon giving him her opinion on most
of the partygoers' costumes. By the time he'd managed to free him-

self, his mystery lady had disappeared through the ballroom's side door.

And he knew that she had no intention of letting him see her again.

Benedict let out a low and rather viciously uttered curse. With all the ladies his mother had trotted out before him—and there had been many—he'd never once felt the same soul-searing connection that had burned between him and the lady in silver. From the moment he'd seen her—no, from the moment *before* he'd seen her, when he'd only just felt her presence, the air had been alive, crackling with tension and excitement. And he'd been alive, too—alive in a way he hadn't felt for years, as if everything were suddenly new and sparkling and full of passion and dreams.

And yet . . .

Benedict cursed again, this time with a touch of regret.

And yet he didn't even know the color of her eyes.

They definitely hadn't been brown. Of that much he was positive. But in the dim light of the candled night, he'd been unable to discern whether they were blue or green. Or hazel or gray. And for some reason he found this the most upsetting. It ate at him, leaving a burning, hungry sensation in the pit of his stomach.

They said eyes were the windows to the soul. If he'd truly found the woman of his dreams, the one with whom he could finally imagine a family and a future, then by God he ought to know the color of her eyes.

It wasn't going to be easy to find her. It was never easy to find someone who didn't want to be found, and she'd made it more than clear that her identity was a secret.

His clues were paltry at best. A few dropped comments concerning Lady Whistledown's column and . . .

Benedict looked down at the single glove still clutched in his right hand. He'd quite forgotten that he'd been holding it as he'd dashed through the ballroom. He brought it to his face and inhaled its scent, but much to his surprise, it didn't smell of rosewater and soap, as had his mystery lady. Rather, its scent was a bit musty, as if it had been packed away in an attic trunk for many years.

Odd, that. Why would she be wearing an ancient glove?

He turned it over in his hand, as if the motion would somehow bring her back, and that was when he noticed a tiny bit of stitching at the hem.

SLG. Someone's initials.

Were they hers?

And a family crest. One he did not recognize.

But his mother would. His mother always knew that sort of thing. And chances were, if she knew the crest, she'd know who the initials SLG belonged to.

Benedict felt his first glimmer of hope. He would find her.

He would find her, and he would make her his. It was as simple as that.

It took a mere half hour to return Sophie to her regular, drab state. Gone were the dress, the glittering earbobs, and the fancy coiffure. The jeweled slippers were tucked neatly back in Araminta's closet, and the rouge the maid had used for her lips was resting in its place on Rosamund's dressing table. She'd even taken five minutes to massage the skin on her face, to remove the indentations left by the mask.

Sophie looked as she always looked before bed—plain, simple, and unassuming, her hair pulled into a loose braid, her feet tucked into warm stockings to keep out the chill night air.

She was back to looking what she was in truth—nothing more than a housemaid. Gone were all traces of the fairy princess she'd been for one short evening.

And saddest of all, gone was her fairy prince.

Benedict Bridgerton had been everything she'd read in *Whistledown*. Handsome, strong, debonair. He was the stuff of a young girl's dreams, but not, she thought glumly, of *her* dreams. A man like that didn't marry an earl's by-blow. And he certainly didn't marry a housemaid.

But for one night he'd been hers, and she supposed that would have to be enough.

She picked up a little stuffed dog she'd had since she'd been a small girl. She'd kept it all these years as a reminder of happier times. It usually sat on her dresser, but for some reason she wanted it closer right now. She crawled into bed, the little dog tucked under her arm, and curled up under the covers.

Then she squeezed her eyes shut, biting her lip as silent tears trickled onto her pillow.

It was a long, long night.

"Do you recognize this?"

Benedict Bridgerton was sitting next to his mother in her very feminine rose-and-cream drawing room, holding out his only link to the woman in silver. Violet Bridgerton took the glove and examined the crest. She needed only a second before she announced, "Penwood."

"As in 'Earl of'?"

Violet nodded. "And the G would be for Gunningworth. The title recently passed out of their family, if I recall correctly. The earl died without issue . . . oh, it must have been six or seven years ago. The title went to a distant cousin. And," she added with a disapproving nod of her head, "you forgot to dance with Penelope Featherington last night. You're lucky your brother was there to dance in your stead."

Benedict fought a groan and tried to ignore her scolding. "Who, then, is SLG?"

Violet's blue eyes narrowed. "Why are you interested?"

"I don't suppose," Benedict said on a groan, "that you will simply answer my question without posing one of your own."

She let out a ladylike snort. "You know me far better than that."

Benedict just managed to stop himself from rolling his eyes.

"Who," Violet asked, "does the glove belong to, Benedict?" And then, when he didn't answer quickly enough for her taste, she added, "You might as well tell me everything. You know I will figure it out on my own soon enough, and it will be far less embarrassing for you if I don't have to ask any questions."

Benedict sighed. He was going to have to tell her everything. Or at least, almost everything. There was little he enjoyed less than sharing such details with his mother—she tended to grab hold of any hope that he might actually marry and cling on to it with the tenacity of a barnacle. But he had little choice. Not if he wanted to find *her*.

"I met someone last night at the masquerade," he finally said.

Violet clapped her hands together with delight. "Really?"

"She's the reason I forgot to dance with Penelope."

Violet looked nearly ready to die of rapture. "Who? One of Penwood's daughters?" She frowned. "No, that's impossible. He had no daughters. But he did have two stepdaughters." She frowned again. "Although I must say, having met those two girls . . . well . . ."

"Well, what?"

Violet's brow wrinkled as she fumbled for polite words. "Well, I simply wouldn't have guessed you'd be interested in either of them, that's all. But if you *are*," she added, her face brightening considerably, "then I shall surely invite the dowager countess over for tea. It's the very least I can do."

Benedict started to say something, then stopped when he saw that his mother was frowning yet again. "What now?" he asked.

"Oh, nothing," Violet said. "Just that . . . well . . ."

"Spit it out, Mother."

She smiled weakly. "Just that I don't particularly *like* the dowager countess. I've always found her rather cold and ambitious."

"Some would say you're ambitious as well, Mother," Benedict pointed out.

Violet pulled a face. "Of course I have great ambition that my children marry well and happily, but I am not the sort who'd marry her daughter off to a seventy-year-old man just because he was a duke!"

"Did the dowager countess do that?" Benedict couldn't recall any seventy-year-old dukes making recent trips to the altar.

"No," Violet admitted, "but she would. Whereas I——"

Benedict bit back a smile as his mother pointed to herself with great flourish.

"I would allow my children to marry paupers if it would bring them happiness."

Benedict raised a brow.

"They would be well-principled and hardworking paupers, of course," Violet explained. "No gamblers need apply."

Benedict didn't want to laugh at his mother, so instead he coughed discreetly into his handkerchief.

"But you should not concern yourself with me," Violet said, giving her son a sideways look before punching him lightly in the arm.

"Of course I must," he said quickly.

She smiled serenely. "I shall put aside my feelings for the dowager countess if you care for one of her daughters . . ." She looked up hopefully. "Do you care for one of her daughters?"

"I have no idea," Benedict admitted. "I never got her name. Just her glove."

Violet gave him a stern look. "I'm not even going to ask how you obtained her glove."

"It was all very innocent, I assure you."

Violet's expression was dubious in the extreme. "I have far too many sons to believe *that*," she muttered.

"The initials?" Benedict reminded her.

Violet examined the glove again. "It's rather old," she said.

Benedict nodded. "I thought so as well. It smelled a bit musty, as if it had been packed away for some time."

"And the stitches show wear," she commented. "I don't know what the L is for, but the S could very well be for Sarah. The late earl's mother, who has also passed on. Which would make sense, given the age of the glove."

Benedict stared down at the glove in his mother's hands for a moment before saying, "As I'm fairly certain I did not converse with a ghost last night, who do you think the glove might belong to?"

"I have no idea. Someone in the Gunningworth family, I imagine."

"Do you know where they live?"

"At Penwood House, actually," Violet replied. "The new earl hasn't given them the boot yet. Don't know why. Perhaps he's afraid they'll want to live with him once he takes up residence. I don't think he's even in town for the season. Never met him myself."

"Do you happen to know—"

"Where Penwood House is?" Violet cut in. "Of course I do. It's not far, only a few blocks away." She gave him directions, and Benedict, in his haste to be on his way, was already on his feet and halfway out the door before she finished.

"Oh, Benedict!" Violet called out, her smile very amused.

He turned around. "Yes?"

"The countess's daughters are named Rosamund and Posy. Just in case you're interested."

Rosamund and Posy. Neither seemed fitting, but what did he know? Perhaps he didn't seem a proper Benedict to people he met. He turned on his heel and tried to exit once again, but his mother stopped him with yet another, "Oh, Benedict!"

He turned around. "Yes, Mother?" he asked, sounding purposefully beleaguered.

"You will tell me what happens, won't you?"

"Of course, Mother."

"You're lying to me," she said with a smile, "but I forgive you. It's so nice to see you in love."

"I'm not—"

"Whatever you say, dear," she said with a wave.

Benedict decided there was little point in replying, so with nothing more than a roll of his eyes, he left the room and hurried out of the house.

"Sophieeeeeeeeeeeeeeeee!"

Sophie's chin snapped up. Araminta sounded even more irate than usual, if that were possible. Araminta was *always* upset with her.

"Sophie! Drat it, where is that infernal girl?"

"The infernal girl is right here," Sophie muttered, setting down the silver spoon she'd been polishing. As lady's maid to Araminta, Rosamund, and Posy, she shouldn't have had to add the polishing to her list of chores, but Araminta positively reveled in working her to the bone.

"Right here," she called out, rising to her feet and walking out into the hall. The Lord only knew what Araminta was upset about this time. She looked this way and that. "My lady?"

Araminta came storming around the corner. "What," she snapped, holding something up in her right hand, "is the meaning of *this*?"

Sophie's eyes fell to Araminta's hand, and she only just managed to stifle a gasp. Araminta was holding the shoes that Sophie had borrowed the night before. "I—I don't know what you mean," she stammered.

"These shoes are *brand-new*. Brand-new!"

Sophie stood quietly until she realized that Araminta required a reply. "Um, what is the problem?"

"Look at this!" Araminta screeched, jabbing her finger toward one of the heels. "It's scuffed. Scuffed! How could something like this happen?"

"I'm sure I don't know, my lady," Sophie said. "Perhaps—"

"There is no perhaps about it," Araminta huffed. "Someone has been wearing my shoes."

"I assure you no one has been wearing your shoes," Sophie replied, amazed that she was able to keep her voice even. "We all know how particular you are about your footwear."

Araminta narrowed her eyes suspiciously. "Are you being sarcastic?"

Sophie rather thought that if Araminta had to ask, then she was playing her sarcasm very well indeed, but she lied, and said, "No! Of course not. I merely meant that you take very good care of your shoes. They last longer that way."

Araminta said nothing, so Sophie added, "Which means you don't have to buy as many pairs."

Which was, of course, utter ridiculousness, as Araminta already owned more pairs of shoes than any one person could hope to wear in a lifetime.

"This is your fault," Araminta growled.

According to Araminta, everything was always Sophie's fault, but this time she was actually correct, so Sophie just gulped and said, "What would you like me to do about it, my lady?"

"I want to know who wore my shoes."

"Perhaps they were scuffed in your closet," Sophie suggested. "Maybe you accidentally kicked them last time you walked by."

"I never *accidentally* do anything," Araminta snapped.

Sophie silently agreed. Araminta was deliberate in all things. "I can ask the maids," Sophie said. "Perhaps one of them knows something."

"The maids are a pack of idiots," Araminta replied. "What they know could fit on my littlest fingernail."

Sophie waited for Araminta to say, "Present company excluded," but of course she did not. Finally, Sophie said, "I can try to polish the shoe. I'm sure we can do something about the scuff mark."

"The heels are covered in satin," Araminta sneered. "If you can find a way to polish that, then we should have you admitted to the Royal College of Fabric Scientists."

Sophie badly wanted to ask if there even *existed* a Royal College of Fabric Scientists, but Araminta didn't have much of a sense of humor even when she wasn't in a complete snit. To poke fun now would be a clear invitation for disaster. "I could try to rub it out," Sophie suggested. "Or brush it."

"You do that," Araminta said. "In fact, while you're at it . . ."

Oh, *blast*. All bad things began with Araminta saying, "While you're at it."

". . . you might as well polish all of my shoes."

"All of them?" Sophie gulped. Araminta's collection must have numbered at least eighty pair.

"All of them. And while you're at it . . ."

Not *again*.

"Lady Penwood?"

Araminta blessedly stopped in mid-command to turn and see what the butler wanted.

"A gentleman is here to see you, my lady," he said, handing her a crisp, white card.

Araminta took it from him and read the name. Her eyes widened, and she let out a little, "Oh!" before turning back to the butler, and barking out, "Tea! And biscuits! The best silver. At once."

The butler hurried out, leaving Sophie staring at Araminta with unfeigned curiosity. "May I be of any help?" Sophie asked.

Araminta blinked twice, staring at Sophie as if she'd forgotten her presence. "No," she snapped. "I'm far too busy to bother with you. Go upstairs at once." She paused, then added, "What are you doing down here, anyway?"

Sophie motioned toward the dining room she'd recently exited. "You asked me to polish—"

"I asked you to see to my shoes," Araminta fairly yelled.

"All—all right," Sophie said slowly. Araminta was acting very odd, even for Araminta. "I'll just put away—"

"Now!"

Sophie hurried to the stairs.

"Wait!"

Sophie turned around. "Yes?" she asked hesitantly.

Araminta's lips tightened into an unattractive frown. "Make sure that Rosamund's and Posy's hair is properly dressed."

"Of course."

"Then you may instruct Rosamund to lock you in my closet."

Sophie stared at her. She actually wanted Sophie to give the order to have herself locked in the closet?

"Do you understand me?"

Sophie couldn't quite bring herself to nod. Some things were simply too demeaning.

Araminta marched over until their faces were quite close. "You didn't answer," she hissed. "Do you understand me?"

Sophie nodded, but just barely. Every day, it seemed, brought more evidence of the depth of Araminta's hatred for her. "Why do you keep me here?" she whispered before she had time to think better of it.

"Because I find you useful," was Araminta's low reply.

Sophie watched as Araminta stalked from the room, then hurried up the stairs. Rosamund's and Posy's hair looked quite acceptable, so she sighed, turned to Posy, and said, "Lock me in the closet, if you will."

Posy blinked in surprise. "I beg your pardon?"

"I was instructed to ask Rosamund, but I can't quite bring myself to do so."

Posy peered in the closet with great interest. "May I ask why?"

"I'm meant to polish your mother's shoes."

Posy swallowed uncomfortably. "I'm sorry."

"So am I," Sophie said with a sigh. "So am I."

Chapter 5

And in other news from the masquerade ball, Miss Posy Reiling's costume as a mermaid was somewhat unfortunate, but not, This Author thinks, as dreadful as that of Mrs. Featherington and her two eldest daughters, who went as a bowl of fruit—Philippa as an orange, Prudence as an apple, and Mrs. Featherington as a bunch of grapes.

Sadly, none of the three looked the least bit appetizing.

LADY WHISTLEDOWN'S SOCIETY PAPERS,
7 JUNE 1815

What had his life come to, Benedict wondered, that he was obsessed with a glove? He'd patted his coat pocket about a dozen times since he'd taken a seat in Lady Penwood's sitting room, silently reassuring himself that it was still there. Uncharacteristically anxious, he wasn't certain what he planned to say to the dowager countess once she arrived, but he was usually fairly glib of tongue; surely he'd figure out something as he went along.

His foot tapping, he glanced over at the mantel clock. He'd given his card to the butler about fifteen minutes earlier, which meant that Lady Penwood ought to be down soon. It seemed an unwritten rule that all ladies of the *ton* must keep their callers waiting for at least fifteen minutes, twenty if they were feeling particularly peevish.

A bloody stupid rule, Benedict thought irritably. Why the rest of the world didn't value punctuality as he did, he would never know, but—

"Mr. Bridgerton!"

He looked up. A rather attractive, extremely fashionable blond woman in her forties glided into the room. She looked vaguely familiar, but that was to be expected. They'd surely attended many of the same society functions, even if they had not been introduced.

"You must be Lady Penwood," he murmured, rising to his feet and offering her a polite bow.

"Indeed," she replied with a gracious incline of her head. "I am so delighted that you have chosen to honor us with a call. I have, of course, informed my daughters of your presence. They shall be down shortly."

Benedict smiled. That was exactly what he'd hoped she'd do. He would have been shocked if she'd behaved otherwise. No mother of marriageable daughters ever ignored a Bridgerton brother. "I look forward to meeting them," he said.

Her brow furrowed slightly. "Then you have not yet met them?"

Blast. Now she'd be wondering why he was there. "I have heard such lovely things about them," he improvised, trying not to groan. If Lady Whistledown caught hold of this—and Lady Whistledown seemed to catch hold of everything—it would soon be all over town that he was looking for a wife, *and* that he'd zeroed in on the countess's daughters. Why else would he call upon two women to whom he had not even been introduced?

Lady Penwood beamed. "My Rosamund is considered one of the loveliest girls of the season."

"And your Posy?" Benedict asked, somewhat perversely.

The corners of her mouth tightened. "Posy is, er, delightful."

He smiled benignly. "I cannot wait to meet Posy."

Lady Penwood blinked, then covered up her surprise with a slightly hard smile. "I'm sure Posy will be delighted to meet you."

A maid entered with an ornate silver tea service, then set it down on a table at Lady Penwood's nod. Before the maid could depart, however, the countess said (somewhat sharply, in Benedict's opinion), "Where are the Penwood spoons?"

The maid bobbed a rather panicked curtsy, then replied, "Sophie was polishing the silver in the dining room, my lady, but she had to go upstairs when you—"

"Silence!" Lady Penwood cut in, even though she'd been the one to ask about the spoons in the first place. "I'm sure Mr. Bridgerton is not so high in the instep that he needs monogrammed spoons for his tea."

"Of course not," Benedict murmured, thinking that Lady Penwood must be a bit too high in the instep herself if she even thought to bring it up.

"Go! Go!" the countess ordered the maid, waving her briskly away. "Begone."

The maid hurried out, and the countess turned back to him, explaining, "Our better silver is engraved with the Penwood crest."

Benedict leaned forward. "Really?" he asked with obvious interest. This would be an excellent way to verify that the crest on the glove was indeed that of the Penwoods. "We don't have anything like that at Bridgerton House," he said, hoping he wasn't lying. In all truth, he'd never even noticed the pattern of the silver. "I should love to see it."

"Really?" Lady Penwood asked, her eyes lighting up. "I knew you were a man of taste and refinement."

Benedict smiled, mostly so he wouldn't groan.

"I shall have to send someone to the dining room to fetch a piece. Assuming, of course, that infernal girl managed to do her job." The corners of her lips turned down in a most unattractive manner, and Benedict noticed that her frown lines were deep indeed.

"Is there a problem?" he asked politely.

She shook her head and waved her hand dismissively. "Merely

that it is so difficult to find good help. I'm sure your mother says the same thing all the time."

His mother never said any such thing, but that was probably because all of the Bridgerton servants were treated very well and thus were utterly devoted to the family. But Benedict nodded all the same.

"One of these days I'm going to have to give Sophie the boot," the countess said with a sniff. "She cannot do anything right."

Benedict felt a vague pang of pity for the poor, unseen Sophie. But the last thing he wanted to do was get into a discussion on servants with Lady Penwood, and so he changed the subject by motioning to the teapot, and saying, "I imagine it's well steeped by now."

"Of course, of course." Lady Penwood looked up and smiled. "How do you take yours?"

"Milk, no sugar."

As she prepared his cup, Benedict heard the clatter of feet coming down the stairs, and his heart began to race with excitement. Any minute now the countess's daughters would slip through the door, and surely one of them would be the woman he'd met the night before. It was true that he had not seen most of her face, but he knew her approximate size and height. And he was fairly certain that her hair was a long, light brown.

Surely he'd recognize her when he saw her. How could he not?

But when the two young ladies entered the room, he knew instantly that neither was the woman who'd haunted his every thought. One of them was far too blond, and besides, she held herself with a prissy, rather affected manner. There was no joy in her aspect, no mischief in her smile. The other looked friendly enough, but she was too chubby, and her hair was too dark.

Benedict did his best not to look disappointed. He smiled during the introductions and gallantly kissed each of their hands, murmuring some nonsense about how delighted he was to meet them. He made a point of fawning over the chubby one, if only because her mother so obviously preferred the other.

Mothers like that, he decided, didn't deserve to be mothers.

"And do you have any other children?" Benedict asked Lady Penwood, once the introductions were through.

She gave him an odd look. "Of course not. Else I would have brought them out to meet you."

"I thought you might have children still in the schoolroom," he demurred. "Perhaps from your union with the earl."

She shook her head. "Lord Penwood and I were not blessed with children. Such a pity it was that the title left the Gunningworth family."

Benedict could not help but notice that the countess looked more irritated than saddened by her lack of Penwood progeny. "Did your husband have any brothers or sisters?" he asked. Maybe his mystery lady was a Gunningworth cousin.

The countess shot him a suspicious look, which, Benedict had to admit, was well deserved, considering that his questions were not at all the usual fare for an afternoon call. "Obviously," she replied, "my late husband did not have any brothers, as the title passed out of the family."

Benedict knew he should keep his mouth shut, but something about the woman was so bloody irritating he had to say, "He could have had a brother who predeceased him."

"Well, he did not."

Rosamund and Posy were watching the exchange with great interest, their heads bobbing back and forth like balls at a tennis match.

"And any sisters?" Benedict inquired. "The only reason I ask is that I come from such a large family." He motioned to Rosamund and Posy. "I cannot imagine having only one sibling. I thought perhaps that your daughters might have cousins to keep them company."

It was, he thought, rather paltry as far as explanations went, but it would have to do.

"He did have one sister," the countess replied with a disdainful sniff. "But she lived and died a spinster. She was a woman of great faith," she explained, "and chose to devote her life to charitable works."

So much for *that* theory.

"I very much enjoyed your masquerade ball last night," Rosamund suddenly said.

Benedict looked at her in surprise. The two girls had been so silent he'd forgotten they could even speak. "It was really my mother's ball," he answered. "I had no part in the planning. But I shall convey your compliments."

"Please do," Rosamund said. "Did you enjoy the ball, Mr. Bridgerton?"

Benedict stared at her for a moment before answering. She had a hard look in her eyes, as if she was searching for a specific piece of information. "I did indeed," he finally said.

"I noticed you spent a great deal of time with one lady in particular," Rosamund persisted.

Lady Penwood twisted her head sharply to look at him, but she did not say anything.

"Did you?" Benedict murmured.

"She was wearing silver," Rosamund said. "Who was she?"

"A mystery woman," he said with an enigmatic smile. No need for them to know that she was a mystery to him as well.

"Surely you can share her name with us," Lady Penwood said.

Benedict just smiled and stood. He wasn't going to get any more information here. "I'm afraid I must be going, ladies," he said affably, offering them a smooth bow.

"You never did see the spoons," Lady Penwood reminded him.

"I'll have to save them for another time," Benedict said. It was unlikely that his mother would have incorrectly identified the Penwood crest, and besides, if he spent much more time in the company of the hard and brittle Countess of Penwood, he might retch.

"It has been lovely," he lied.

"Indeed," Lady Penwood said, rising to walk him to the door. "Brief, but lovely."

Benedict didn't bother to smile again.

"What," Araminta said as she heard the front door close behind Benedict Bridgerton, "do you suppose that was about?"

"Well," Posy said, "he might—"

"I didn't ask you," Araminta bit off.

"Well, then, who *did* you ask?" Posy returned with uncharacteristic gumption.

"Perhaps he saw me from afar," Rosamund said, "and—"

"He didn't see you from afar," Araminta snapped as she strode across the room.

Rosamund lurched backward in surprise. Her mother rarely spoke to her in such impatient tones.

Araminta continued, "You yourself said he was besotted with some woman in a silver dress."

"I didn't say 'besotted' precisely . . ."

"Don't argue with me over such trivialities. Besotted or not, he didn't come here looking for either of *you*," Araminta said with a fair amount of derision. "I don't know what he was up to. He . . ."

Her words trailed off as she reached the window. Pulling the sheer curtain back, she saw Mr. Bridgerton standing on the pavement, pulling something from his pocket. "What is he doing?" she whispered.

"I think he's holding a glove," Posy said helpfully.

"It's not a—" Araminta said automatically, too used to contradicting everything Posy had to say. "Why, it *is* a glove."

"I should think I know a glove when I see one," Posy muttered.

"What is he looking at?" Rosamund asked, nudging her sister out of the way.

"There's something on the glove," Posy said. "Perhaps it's a piece of embroidery. We've some gloves with the Penwood crest embroidered on the hem. Maybe that glove has the same."

Araminta went white.

"Are you feeling all right, Mother?" Posy asked. "You look rather pale."

"He came here looking for her," Araminta whispered.

"Who?" Rosamund asked.

"The woman in silver."

"Well, he isn't going to find her here," Posy replied, "as I was a mermaid and Rosamund was Marie Antoinette. And you, of course, were Queen Elizabeth."

"The shoes," Araminta gasped. "The shoes."

"What shoes?" Rosamund asked irritably.

"They were scuffed. Someone wore my shoes." Araminta's face, already impossibly pale, blanched even more. "It was *her*. How did she do it? It had to be her."

"Who?" Rosamund demanded.

"Mother, are you certain you're all right?" Posy asked again. "You're not at all yourself."

But Araminta had already run out of the room.

"Stupid, stupid shoe," Sophie grumbled, scrubbing at the heel of one of Araminta's older pieces of footwear. "She hasn't even worn this one for years."

She finished polishing the toe and put it back in its place in the neatly ordered row of shoes. But before she could reach for another pair, the door to the closet burst open, slamming against the wall with such force that Sophie nearly screamed with surprise.

"Oh, goodness, you gave me a fright," she said to Araminta. "I didn't hear you coming, and—"

"Pack your things," Araminta said in a low, cruel voice. "I want you out of this house by sunrise."

The rag Sophie had been using to polish the shoes fell from her hand. "What?" she gasped. "Why?"

"Do I really need a reason? We both know I ceased receiving any funds for your care nearly a year ago. It's enough that I don't want you here any longer."

"But where will I go?"

Araminta's eyes narrowed to nasty slits. "That's not my concern, now, is it?"

"But—"

"You're twenty years of age. Certainly old enough to make your way in the world. There will be no more coddling from me."

"You never coddled me," Sophie said in a low voice.

"Don't you dare talk back to me."

"Why not?" Sophie returned, her voice growing shrill. "What have I to lose? You're booting me out of the house, anyway."

"You might treat me with a little respect," Araminta hissed, planting her foot on Sophie's skirt so that she was pinned in her kneeling position, "considering that I have clothed and sheltered you this past year out of the goodness of my heart."

"You do nothing out of the goodness of your heart." Sophie tugged at her skirt, but it was firmly trapped under Araminta's heel. "Why did you really keep me here?"

Araminta cackled. "You're cheaper than a regular maid, and I do enjoy ordering you about."

Sophie hated being Araminta's virtual slave, but at least Penwood House was home. Mrs. Gibbons was her friend, and Posy was usually sympathetic, and the rest of the world was . . . well . . . rather scary. Where would she go? What would she do? How would she support herself?

"Why now?" Sophie asked.

Araminta shrugged. "You're no longer useful to me."

Sophie looked at the long row of shoes she'd just polished. "I'm not?"

Araminta ground the pointy heel of her shoe into Sophie's skirt, tearing the fabric. "You went to the ball last night, didn't you?"

Sophie felt the blood drain from her face, and she knew that Araminta saw the truth in her eyes. "N-no," she lied. "How would I—"

"I don't know how you did it, but I know you were there." Araminta kicked a pair of shoes in Sophie's direction. "Put these on."

Sophie just stared at the shoes in dismay. They were white satin, stitched in silver. They were the shoes she'd worn the night before.

"Put them on!" Araminta screamed. "I know that Rosamund's and Posy's feet are too large. You're the only one who could have worn my shoes last night."

"And from that you think I went to the ball?" Sophie asked, her voice breathy with panic.

"Put on the shoes, Sophie."

Sophie did as she was told. They were, of course, a perfect fit.

"You have overstepped your bounds," Araminta said in a low voice. "I warned you years ago not to forget your place in this world. You are a bastard, a by-blow, the product of—"

"I *know* what a bastard is," Sophie snapped.

Araminta raised one haughty brow, silently mocking Sophie's outburst. "You are unfit to mingle with polite society," she continued, "and yet you *dared* to pretend you are as good as the rest of us by attending the masquerade."

"Yes, I dared," Sophie cried out, well past caring that Araminta had somehow discovered her secret. "I dared, and I'd dare again. My blood is just as blue as yours, and my heart far kinder, and—"

One minute Sophie was on her feet, screaming at Araminta, and the next she was on the floor, clutching her cheek, made red by Araminta's palm.

"Don't you ever compare yourself to me," Araminta warned.

Sophie remained on the floor. How could her father have done this to her, leaving her in the care of a woman who so obviously detested her? Had he cared so little? Or had he simply been blind?

"You will be gone by morning," Araminta said in a low voice. "I don't ever want to see your face again."

Sophie started to make her way to the door.

"But not," Araminta said, planting the heel of her hand against Sophie's shoulder, "until you finish the job I have assigned you."

"It will take me until morning just to finish," Sophie protested.

"That is your problem, not mine." And with that, Araminta slammed the door shut, turning the lock with a very loud click.

Sophie stared down at the flickering candle she'd brought in to help illuminate the long, dark closet. There was no way the wick would last until morning.

And there was no way—absolutely no way in hell—that she was going to polish the rest of Araminta's shoes.

Sophie sat down on the floor, arms crossed and legs crossed, and stared at the candle flame until her eyes crossed, too. When the sun rose tomorrow, her life would be forever altered. Penwood House might not have been terribly welcoming, but at least it was safe.

She had almost no money. She hadn't received so much as a farthing from Araminta in the past seven years. Luckily, she still had a bit of the pin money she'd received when her father had been alive and she'd been treated as his ward, not his wife's slave. There had been many opportunities to spend it, but Sophie had always known that this day might come, and it had seemed prudent to hold on to what little funds she possessed.

But her paltry few pounds wasn't going to get her very far. She needed a ticket out of London, and that cost money. Probably well over half what she had saved. She supposed she could stay in town for a bit, but the London slums were dirty and dangerous, and Sophie knew that her budget would not place her in any of the better neighborhoods. Besides, if she were going to be on her own, she might as well return to the countryside she loved.

Not to mention that Benedict Bridgerton was here. London was a large city, and Sophie had no doubt that she could successfully avoid him for years, but she was desperately afraid that she wouldn't *want* to avoid him, that she'd find herself gazing at his house, hoping for the merest of glimpses as he came through the front door.

And if he saw her . . . Well, Sophie didn't know what would happen. He might be furious at her deception. He might want to make her his mistress. He might not recognize her at all.

The only thing she was certain he would not do was to throw himself at her feet, declare his undying devotion, and demand her hand in marriage.

Sons of viscounts did not marry baseborn nobodies. Not even in romantic novels.

No, she'd have to leave London. Keep herself far from temptation. But she'd need more money, enough to keep her going until she found employment. Enough to—

Sophie's eyes fell on something sparkly—a pair of shoes tucked away in the corner. Except she'd cleaned those shoes just an hour earlier, and she knew that those sparklies weren't the shoes but a pair of jeweled shoe clips, easily detachable and small enough to fit in her pocket.

Did she dare?

She thought about all the money that Araminta had received for her upkeep, money Araminta had never seen fit to share.

She thought about all those years she'd toiled as a lady's maid, without drawing a single wage.

She thought about her conscience, then quickly squelched it. In times like these, she didn't have room for a conscience.

She took the shoe clips.

And then, several hours later when Posy came (against her mother's wishes) and let her out, she packed up all of her belongings and left.

Much to her surprise, she didn't look back.

Part Two

Chapter 6

It has now been three years since any of the Bridgerton siblings have wed, and Lady Bridgerton has been heard to declare on several occasions that she is nearing her wit's end. Benedict has not taken a bride (and it is the opinion of This Author that as he has attained the age of thirty, he is far past due), and neither has Colin, although he may be forgiven his tardiness, since he is, after all, merely six-and-twenty.

The dowager viscountess also has two girls about which she must worry. Eloise is nearly one-and-twenty and although she has received several proposals, she has shown no inclination to marry. Francesca is nearly twenty (the girls quite coincidentally share a birthday), and she, too, seems more interested in the season than she does in marriage.

This Author feels that Lady Bridgerton does not need to worry. It is inconceivable that any of the Bridgertons might not eventually make an acceptable match, and besides, her two married children have already given her a total of five grandchildren, and surely that is her heart's desire.

LADY WHISTLEDOWN'S SOCIETY PAPERS,
30 APRIL 1817

Alcohol and cheroots. Card games and lots of hired women. It was just the sort of party Benedict Bridgerton would have enjoyed immensely when he was fresh out of university.

Now he was just bored.

He wasn't even certain why he'd agreed to attend. More boredom, he supposed. The London season of 1817 had thus far been a repeat of the previous year, and he hadn't found 1816 terribly scintillating to begin with. To do the whole thing over again was beyond banal.

He didn't even really know his host, one Phillip Cavender. It was one of those friend of a friend of a friend situations, and now Benedict was fervently wishing he'd remained in London. He'd just gotten over a blistering head cold, and he should have used that as an excuse to cry off, but his friend—whom he hadn't even seen in the past four hours—had prodded and cajoled, and finally Benedict had given in.

Now he heartily regretted it.

He walked down the main hall of Cavender's parents' home. Through the doorway to his left he could see a high-stakes card game in process. One of the players was sweating profusely. "Stupid idiot," Benedict muttered. The poor bloke was probably just a breath away from losing his ancestral home.

The door to his right was closed, but he could hear the sound of feminine giggling, followed by masculine laughter, followed by some rather unattractive grunting and squealing.

This was madness. He didn't want to be here. He hated card games where the stakes were higher than the participants could afford, and he'd never had any interest in copulating in such a public manner. He had no idea what had happened to the friend who had brought him here, and he didn't much like any of the other guests.

"I'm leaving," he declared, even though there was no one in the hall to hear him. He had a small piece of property not so very far away, just an hour's ride, really. It wasn't much more than a cottage, but it was his, and right now it sounded like heaven.

But good manners dictated that he find his host and inform him of his departure, even if Mr. Cavender was so sotted that he wouldn't remember the conversation the next day.

After about ten minutes of fruitless searching, however, Benedict was beginning to wish that his mother had not been so adamant in her quest to instill good manners in all of her children. It would have been a great deal easier just to leave and be done with it. "Three more minutes," he grumbled. "If I don't find the bloody idiot in three more minutes, I'm leaving."

Just then, a pair of young men stumbled by, tripping over their own feet as they exploded in raucous laughter. Alcoholic fumes filled the air, and Benedict took a discreet step back, lest one of them was suddenly compelled to cast up the contents of his stomach.

Benedict had always been fond of his boots.

"Bridgerton!" one of them called out.

Benedict gave them a curt nod in greeting. They were both about five years younger than he was, and he didn't know them well.

"Tha's not a Bridgerton," the other fellow slurred. "Tha's a—why, it *is* a Bridgerton. Got the hair and the nose." His eyes narrowed. "But which Bridgerton?"

Benedict ignored his question. "Have you seen our host?"

"We have a host?"

"Course we have a host," the first man replied. "Cavender. Damned fine fellow, you know, t'let us use his house—"

"Hiss parents' house," the other one corrected. "Hasn't inherited yet, poor bloke."

"Just so! His parents' house. Still jolly of him."

"Have either of you *seen* him?" growled Benedict.

"Just outside," replied the one who previously hadn't recalled that they had a host. "In the front."

"Thank you," Benedict said shortly, then strode past them to the front door of the house. He'd head down the front steps, pay his respects to Cavender, then make his way to the stables to collect his phaeton. He'd barely even have to break his stride.

It was, thought Sophie Beckett, high time she found a new job.

It had been almost two years since she'd left London, two years since she'd finally stopped being Araminta's virtual slave, two years since she'd been completely on her own.

After she'd left Penwood House, she'd pawned Araminta's shoe clips, but the diamonds Araminta had liked to boast about had turned out not to be diamonds at all, but rather simple paste, and they hadn't brought much money. She'd tried to find a job as a governess, but none of the agencies she'd queried was willing to take her on. She was obviously well educated, but she'd had no references, and besides, most women did not like to hire someone quite so young and pretty.

Sophie had eventually purchased a ticket on a coach to Wiltshire, since that was as far as she could go while still reserving the bulk of her pin money for emergencies. Luckily, she'd found employment quickly, as an upstairs maid for Mr. and Mrs. John Cavender. They were an ordinary sort of couple, expecting good work from their servants but not demanding the impossible. After toiling for Araminta for so many years, Sophie found the Cavenders a positive vacation.

But then their son had returned from his tour of Europe, and everything had changed. Phillip was constantly cornering her in the hall, and when his innuendo and suggestions were rebuffed, he'd grown more aggressive. Sophie had just started to think that maybe she ought to find employment elsewhere when Mr. and Mrs. Cavender had left for a week to visit Mrs. Cavender's sister in Brighton, and Phillip had decided to throw a party for two dozen of his closest friends.

It had been difficult to avoid Phillip's advances before, but at least Sophie had felt reasonably protected. Phillip would never dare attack her while his mother was in residence.

But with Mr. and Mrs. Cavender gone, Phillip seemed to think that he could do and take anything he wanted, and his friends were no better.

Sophie knew she should have left the grounds immediately, but Mrs. Cavender had treated her well, and she didn't think it was polite to leave without giving two weeks' notice. After two hours of being chased around the house, however, she decided that good manners were not worth her virtue, and so she'd told the (thankfully sympathetic) housekeeper that she could not stay, packed her meager belongings in one small bag, stolen down the side stairs, and let herself out. It was a two-mile hike into the village, but even in the dead of night, the road to town seemed infinitely safer than remaining at the Cavender home, and besides, she knew of a small inn where she could get a hot meal and a room for a reasonable price.

She'd just come 'round the house and had stepped onto the front drive, however, when she heard a raucous shout.

She looked up. Oh, *blast*. Phillip Cavender, looking even drunker and meaner than usual.

Sophie broke into a run, praying that alcohol had impaired Phillip's coordination because she knew she could not match him for speed.

But her flight must have only served to excite him, because she heard him yell out with glee, then felt his footsteps rumbling on the ground, growing closer and closer until she felt his hand close round the back collar of her coat, jerking her to a halt.

Phillip laughed triumphantly, and Sophie had never been so terrified in her entire life.

"Look what I have here," he cackled. "Little Miss Sophie. I shall have to introduce you to my friends."

Sophie's mouth went dry, and she wasn't sure whether her heart started to beat double time or stopped altogether. "Let me go, Mr. Cavender," she said in her sternest voice. She knew that he liked her helpless and pleading, and she refused to cater to his wishes.

"I don't think so," he said, turning her around so that she was forced to watch his lips stretch into a slippery smile. He turned his head to the side and called out, "Heasley! Fletcher! Look what I have here!"

Sophie watched with horror as two more men emerged from the shadows. From the looks of them, they were just as drunk, or maybe even more so, than Phillip.

"You always host the best parties," one of them said in an oily voice.

Phillip puffed out with pride.

"Let me go!" Sophie said again.

Phillip grinned. "What do you think, boys? Should I do as the lady asks?"

"Hell, no!" came the reply from the younger of the two men.

" 'Lady,' " said the other—the same one who had told Phillip that he hosted the best parties, "might be a bit of a misnomer, don't you think?"

"Quite right!" Phillip replied. "This one's a housemaid, and as we all know, that breed is born to serve." He gave Sophie a shove, pushing her toward one of his friends. "Here. Have a look at the goods."

Sophie cried out as she was propelled forward, and she clutched tightly to her small bag. She was about to be raped; that much was clear. But her panicked mind wanted to hold on to some last shred of dignity, and she refused to allow these men to spill her every last belonging onto the cold ground.

The man who caught her fondled her roughly, then shoved her toward the third one. He'd just snaked his hand around her waist, when she heard someone yell out, "Cavender!"

Sophie shut her eyes in agony. *A fourth man. Dear God, weren't three enough?*

"Bridgerton!" Phillip called out. "Come join us!"

Sophie's eyes snapped open. Bridgerton?

A tall, powerfully built man emerged from the shadows, moving forward with easy, confident grace.

"What have we here?"

Dear God, she'd recognize that voice anywhere. She heard it often enough in her dreams.

It was Benedict Bridgerton. Her Prince Charming.

The night air was chilly, but Benedict found it refreshing after being forced to breathe the alcohol and tobacco fumes inside. The moon was nearly full, glowing round and fat, and a gentle breeze ruffled the leaves on the trees. All in all, it was an excellent night to leave a boring party and ride home.

But first things first. He had to find his host, go through the motions of thanking him for his hospitality, and inform him of his departure. As he reached the bottom step, he called out, "Cavender!"

"Over here!" came the reply, and Benedict turned his head to the right. Cavender was standing under a stately old elm with two other gentlemen. They appeared to be having a bit of fun with a housemaid, pushing her back and forth between them.

Benedict groaned. He was too far away to determine whether the housemaid was enjoying their attentions, and if she was not, then he was going to have to save her, which was not how he'd planned to spend his evening. He'd never been particularly enamored of playing the hero, but he had far too many younger sisters—four, to be precise—to ignore any female in distress.

"Ho there!" he called out as he ambled over, keeping his posture purposefully casual. It was always better to move slowly and assess the situation than it was to charge in blindly.

"Bridgerton!" Cavender called out. "Come join us!"

Benedict drew close just as one of the men snaked an arm around the young woman's waist and pinned her to him, her back to his front. His other hand was on her bottom, squeezing and kneading.

Benedict brought his gaze to the maid's eyes. They were huge and filled with terror, and she was looking at him as if he'd just dropped fully formed from the sky.

"What have we here?" he asked.

"Just a bit of sport," Cavender chortled. "My parents were kind enough to hire this prime morsel as the upstairs maid."

"She doesn't appear to be enjoying your attentions," Benedict said quietly.

"She likes it just fine," Cavender replied with a grin. "Fine enough for me, anyway."

"But not," Benedict said, stepping forward, "for me."

"You can have your turn with her," Cavender said, ever jovial. "Just as soon as we're through."

"You misunderstand."

There was a hard edge to Benedict's voice, and the three men all froze, looking over at him with wary curiosity.

"Release the girl," he said.

Still stunned by the sudden change of atmosphere, and with reflexes most likely dulled by alcohol, the man holding the girl did nothing.

"I don't want to fight you," Benedict said, crossing his arms, "but I will. And I can assure you that the three-to-one odds don't frighten me."

"Now, see here," Cavender said angrily. "You can't come here and order me about on my own property."

"It's your parents' property," Benedict pointed out, reminding them all that Cavender was still rather wet behind the ears.

"It's my home," Cavender shot back, "and she's my maid. And she'll do what I want."

"I wasn't aware that slavery was legal in this country," Benedict murmured.

"She has to do what I say!"

"Does she?"

"I'll fire her if she doesn't."

"Very well," Benedict said with a tiny quirk of a smile. "Ask her then. Ask the girl if she wants to tup with all three of you. Because that is what you had in mind, isn't it?"

Cavender sputtered as he fought for words.

"Ask her," Benedict said again, grinning now, mostly because he knew his smile would infuriate the younger man. "And if she says no, you can fire her right here on the spot."

"I'm not going to ask her," Cavender whined.

"Well, then, you can't really expect her to do it, can you?" Benedict looked at the girl. She was a fetching thing, with a short bob of light brown curls and eyes that loomed almost too large in her face. "Fine," he said, sparing a brief glance back at Cavender. "I'll ask her."

The girl's lips parted slightly, and Benedict had the oddest sensation that they had met before. But that was impossible, unless she'd worked for some other aristocratic family. And even then, he would have only seen her in passing. His taste in women had never run to housemaids, and in all truth, he tended not to notice them.

"Miss . . ." He frowned. "I say, what's your name?"

"Sophie Beckett," she gasped, sounding as if there were a very large frog caught in her throat.

"Miss Beckett," he continued, "would you be so kind as to answer the following question?"

"No!" she burst out.

"You're not going to answer?" he asked, his eyes amused.

"No, I do *not* want to tup with these three men!" The words practically exploded from her mouth.

"Well, that seems to settle that," Benedict said. He glanced up at the man still holding her. "I suggest you release her so that Cavender here may relieve her of employment."

"And where will she go?" Cavender sneered. "I can assure you she won't work in this district again."

Sophie turned to Benedict, wondering much the same thing.

Benedict gave a careless shrug. "I'll find her a position in my mother's household." He looked over at her and raised a brow. "I assume that's acceptable?"

Sophie's mouth dropped open in horrified surprise. He wanted to take her to his *home*?

"That's not quite the reaction I expected," Benedict said dryly. "It will certainly be more pleasant than your employment here. At the very least, I can assure you you won't be raped. What do you say?"

Sophie glanced frantically at the three men who had intended to rape her. She really didn't have a choice. Benedict Bridgerton was her only means off the Cavender property. She knew she couldn't possibly work for his mother; to be in such close proximity to Benedict and still have to be a servant would be more than she could bear. But she could find a way to avoid that later. For now she just needed to get away from Phillip.

She turned to Benedict and nodded, still afraid to use her voice. She felt as if she were choking inside, although she wasn't certain whether that was from fear or relief.

"Good," he said. "Shall we be off?"

She gave a rather pointed look at the arm that was still holding her hostage.

"Oh, for the love of God," Benedict snarled. "Will you let go of her or will I have to shoot your damned hand off?"

Benedict wasn't even holding a gun, but the tone of his voice was such that the man let go instantly.

"Good," Benedict said, holding his arm out toward the maid. She stepped forward, and with trembling fingers placed her hand on his elbow.

"You can't just take her!" Phillip yelled.

Benedict gave him a supercilious look. "I just did."

"You'll be sorry you did this," Phillip said.

"I doubt it. Now get out of my sight."

Phillip made a huffy sound, then turned his friends and said, "Let's get out of here." Then he turned to Benedict and added, "Don't think you shall ever receive another invitation to one of my parties."

"My heart is breaking," Benedict drawled.

Phillip let out one more outraged snort, and then he and his two friends stalked back to the house.

Sophie watched them walk away, then slowly dragged her gaze back to Benedict. When she'd been trapped by Phillip and his leering friends, she'd known what they wanted to do to her, and she'd almost wanted to die. And then, all of a sudden, there was Benedict Bridgerton, standing before her like a hero from her dreams, and she'd thought maybe she *had* died, because why else would he be here with her unless she was in heaven?

She'd been so completely and utterly stunned, she'd almost forgotten that Phillip's friend still held her pinned against him and was grabbing her behind in a most humiliating manner. For one brief second the world had melted away, and the only thing she could see, the only thing she *knew*, was Benedict Bridgerton.

It had been a moment of perfection.

But then the world had come crashing back, and all she could think was—what on earth was he doing here? It was a disgusting party, full of drunkards and whores. When she'd met him two years ago, he hadn't seemed the sort who would frequent such events. But she'd only known him for a few short hours. Perhaps she'd misjudged him. She closed her eyes in agony. For the past two years, the memory of Benedict Bridgerton had been the brightest light in her drab and dreary life. If she'd misjudged him, if he was little better than Phillip and his friends, then she'd be left with nothing.

Not even a memory of love.

But he *had* saved her. That was irrefutable. Maybe it didn't really matter why he'd come to Phillip's party, only that he had, and he had saved her.

"Are you all right?" he suddenly asked.

Sophie nodded, looking him squarely in the eye, waiting for him to recognize her.

"Are you certain?"

She nodded again, still waiting. It had to happen soon.

"Good. They were handling you roughly."

"I'll be all right." Sophie chewed on her lower lip. She had no idea how he would react once he realized who she was. Would he be delighted? Furious? The suspense was killing her.

"How much time will it take for you to pack your things?"

Sophie blinked rather dumbly, then realized she was still holding her satchel. "It's all right here," she said. "I was trying to leave when they caught me."

"Smart girl," he murmured approvingly.

Sophie just stared at him, unable to believe he hadn't recognized her.

"Let's be off, then," he said. "It makes me ill just to be on Cavender's property."

Sophie said nothing, but her chin jutted slightly forward, and her head tilted to the side as she watched his face.

"Are you certain you're all right?" he asked.

And then Sophie started to think.

Two years ago, when she'd met him, half of her face had been covered by a mask.

Her hair had been lightly powdered, making it seem blonder than it actually was. Furthermore, she'd since cut it and sold the locks to a wigmaker. Her previous long waves were now short curls.

Without Mrs. Gibbons to feed her, she'd lost nearly a stone.

And when one got right down to it, they'd only been in each other's company a mere hour and a half.

She stared at him, right into his eyes. And that was when she knew.

He wasn't going to recognize her.

He had no idea who she was.

Sophie didn't know whether to laugh or to cry.

Chapter 7

It was clear to all of the guests at the Mottram ball Thursday last that Miss Rosamund Reiling has set her cap for Mr. Phillip Cavender.

It is the opinion of This Author that the two are well matched indeed.

LADY WHISTLEDOWN'S SOCIETY PAPERS,
30 APRIL 1817

Ten minutes later, Sophie was sitting next to Benedict Bridgerton in his phaeton.

"Is there something in your eye?" he asked politely.

That caught her attention. "I-I beg your pardon?"

"You keep blinking," he explained. "I thought perhaps you had something in your eye."

Sophie swallowed hard, trying to suppress a round of nervous laughter. What was she supposed to say to him? The truth? That she was blinking because she kept expecting to wake up from what could only be a dream? Or maybe a nightmare?

"Are you certain you're all right?" he asked.

She nodded.

"Just the aftereffects of shock, I imagine," he said.

She nodded again, letting him think that was all that affected her.

How could he not have recognized her? She'd been dreaming of this moment for years. Her Prince Charming had finally come to rescue her, and he didn't even know who she was.

"What was your name again?" he asked. "I'm terribly sorry. It always takes me twice to remember a name."

"Miss Sophia Beckett." There seemed little reason to lie; she hadn't told him her name at the masquerade.

"I'm pleased to meet you, Miss Beckett," he said, keeping his eyes on the dark road. "I'm Mr. Benedict Bridgerton."

Sophie acknowledged his greeting with a nod even though he wasn't looking at her. She held silent for a moment, mostly because she simply didn't know what to say in such an unbelievable situation. It was, she realized, the introduction that had never taken place two years earlier. Finally, she just said, "That was a very brave thing you did."

He shrugged.

"There were three of them and only one of you. Most men would not have intervened."

This time he did look at her. "I hate bullies," was all he said.

She nodded again. "They would have raped me."

"I know," he replied. And then he added, "I have four sisters."

She almost said "I know," but caught herself just in time. How was a housemaid from Wiltshire supposed to know that? So instead she said, "I expect that is why you were so sensitive to my plight."

"I would like to think another man would come to their aid, should they ever find themselves in a similar situation."

"I pray you never have to find out."

He nodded grimly. "As do I."

They rode on, silence cloaking the night. Sophie remembered the masquerade ball, when they hadn't lacked for conversation, even for a moment. It was different now, she realized. She was a housemaid, not a glorious woman of the *ton*. They had nothing in common.

But still, she kept waiting for him to recognize her, to yank the

carriage to a halt, clasp her to his chest, and tell her he'd been looking for her for two years. But that wasn't going to happen, she soon
realized. He couldn't recognize the lady in the housemaid, and in all
truth, why should he?

People saw what they expected to see. And Benedict Bridgerton
surely didn't expect to see a fine lady of the *ton* in the guise of a
humble housemaid.

Not a day had gone by that she hadn't thought of him, hadn't
remembered his lips on hers, or the heady magic of that costumed
night. He had become the centerpiece of her fantasies, dreams in
which she was a different person, with different parents. In her
dreams, she'd met him at a ball, maybe her own ball, hosted by her
devoted mother and father. He courted her sweetly, with fragrant
flowers and stolen kisses. And then, on a mellow spring day, while
the birds were singing and a gentle breeze ruffled the air, he got
down on one knee and asked her to marry him, professing his everlasting love and adoration.

It was a fine daydream, surpassed only by the one in which they
lived happily ever after, with three or four splendid children, born
safely within the sacrament of marriage.

But even with all her fantasies, she never imagined she'd actually
see him again, much less be rescued by him from a trio of licentious
attackers.

She wondered if he ever thought of the mysterious woman in
silver with whom he'd shared one passionate kiss. She liked to think
that he did, but she doubted that it had meant as much to him as
it had to her. He was a man, after all, and had most likely kissed
dozens of women.

And for him, that one night had been much like any other. Sophie
still read *Whistledown* whenever she could get her hands on it. She
knew that he attended scores of balls. Why should one masquerade
stand out in his memory?

Sophie sighed and looked down at her hands, still clutching the drawstring to her small bag. She wished she owned gloves, but her only pair had worn out earlier that year, and she hadn't been able to afford another. Her hands looked rough and chapped, and her fingers were growing cold.

"Is that everything you own?" Benedict asked, motioning to the bag.

She nodded. "I haven't much, I'm afraid. Just a change of clothing and a few personal mementos."

He was silent for a moment, then said, "You have quite a refined accent for a housemaid."

He was not the first to make that observation, so Sophie gave him her stock answer. "My mother was a housekeeper to a very kind and generous family. They allowed me to share some of their daughters' lessons."

"Why do you not work there?" With an expert twist of his wrists, he guided his team to the left side of the fork in the road. "I assume you do not speak of the Cavenders."

"No," she replied, trying to devise a proper answer. No one had ever bothered to probe deeper than her offered explanation. No one had ever been interested enough to care. "My mother passed on," she finally replied, "and I did not deal well with the new housekeeper."

He seemed to accept that, and they rode on for a few minutes. The night was almost silent, save for the wind and the rhythmic clip-clop of the horses' hooves. Finally, Sophie, unable to contain her curiosity, asked, "Where are we going?"

"I have a cottage not far away," he replied. "We'll stay there a night or two, then I'll take you to my mother's home. I'm certain she'll find a position for you in her household."

Sophie's heart began to pound. "This cottage of yours . . ."

"You will be properly chaperoned," he said with a faint smile. "The caretakers will be in attendance, and I assure you that Mr. and Mrs. Crabtree are not likely to let anything untoward occur in their house."

"I thought it was *your* house."

His smile grew deeper. "I have been trying to get them to think of it as such for years, but I have never been successful."

Sophie felt her lips tug up at the corners. "They sound like people I would like very much."

"I expect you would."

And then there was more silence. Sophie kept her eyes scrupulously straight ahead. She had the most absurd fear that if their eyes met, he would recognize her. But that was mere fancy. He'd already looked her squarely in the eye, more than once even, and he still thought her nothing but a housemaid.

After a few minutes, however, she felt the oddest tingling in her cheek, and as she turned to face him she saw that he kept glancing at her with an odd expression.

"Have we met?" he blurted out.

"No," she said, her voice a touch more choked than she would have preferred. "I don't believe so."

"I'm sure you're right," he muttered, "but still, you do seem rather familiar."

"All housemaids look the same," she said with a wry smile.

"I used to think so," he mumbled.

She turned her face forward, her jaw dropping. Why had she said that? Didn't she *want* him to recognize her? Hadn't she spent the last half hour hoping and wishing and dreaming and—

And that was the problem. She was dreaming. In her dreams he loved her. In her dreams he asked her to marry him. In reality, he might ask her to become his mistress, and that was something she'd sworn she would never do. In reality, he might feel honor bound to return her to Araminta, who would probably turn her straightaways over to the magistrate for stealing her shoe clips (and Sophie didn't for one moment think that Araminta hadn't noticed their disappearance).

No, it was best if he did not recognize her. It would only complicate her life, and considering that she had no source of income, and in fact very little beyond the clothes on her back, her life did not need complications at this point.

And yet she felt unaccountably disappointed that he had not instantly known who she was.

"Is that a raindrop?" Sophie asked, eager to keep the conversation on more benign topics.

Benedict looked up. The moon was now obscured by clouds. "It didn't look like rain when we left," he murmured. A fat raindrop landed on his thigh. "But I do believe you're correct."

She glanced at the sky. "The wind has picked up quite a bit. I hope it doesn't storm."

"It's sure to storm," he said wryly, "as we are in an open carriage. If I had taken my coach, there wouldn't be a cloud in the sky."

"How close are we to your cottage?"

"About half an hour away, I should think." He frowned. "Provided we are not slowed by the rain."

"Well, I do not mind a bit of rain," she said gamely. "There are far worse things than getting wet."

They both knew exactly what she was talking about.

"I don't think I remembered to thank you," she said, her words quiet.

Benedict turned his head sharply. By all that was holy, there was something damned familiar about her voice. But when his eyes searched her face, all he saw was a simple housemaid. A very attractive housemaid, to be sure, but a housemaid nonetheless. No one with whom he would ever have crossed paths.

"It was nothing," he finally said.

"To you, perhaps. To me it was everything."

Uncomfortable with such appreciation, he just nodded and gave one of those grunts men tended to emit when they didn't know what to say.

"It was a very brave thing you did," she said.

He grunted again.

And then the heavens opened up in earnest.

It took about one minute for Benedict's clothes to be soaked through. "I'll get there as quickly as I can," he yelled, trying to make himself heard over the wind.

"Don't worry about me!" Sophie called back, but when he looked over at her, he saw that she was huddling into herself, her arms wrapped tightly over her chest as she tried to conserve the heat of her body.

"Let me give you my coat."

She shook her head and actually laughed. "It'll probably make me even wetter, soaked as it is."

He nudged the horses into a faster pace, but the road was growing muddy, and the wind was whipping the rain every which way, reducing the already mediocre visibility.

Bloody hell. This was just what he needed. He'd had a head cold all last week, and he probably wasn't completely recovered. A ride in the freezing rain would most likely set him back, and he'd spend the next month with a runny nose, watery eyes . . . all those infuriating, unattractive symptoms.

Of course . . .

Benedict couldn't quite contain a smile. Of course, if he were ill again, his mother couldn't try to cajole him into attending every single party in town, all in the hopes that he would find some suitable young lady and settle down into a quiet and happy marriage.

To his credit, he always kept his eyes open, was always on the lookout for a prospective bride. He certainly wasn't opposed to marriage on principle. His brother Anthony and his sister Daphne had made splendidly happy matches. But Anthony's and Daphne's marriages were splendidly happy because they'd been smart enough to wed the right people, and Benedict was quite certain he had not yet met the right person.

No, he thought, his mind wandering back a few years, that wasn't entirely true. He'd once met someone . . .

The lady in silver.

When he'd held her in his arms and twirled her around the balcony in her very first waltz, he'd felt something different inside, a fluttering, tingling sensation. It should have scared the hell out of him.

But it hadn't. It had left him breathless, excited . . . and determined to have her.

But then she'd disappeared. It was as if the world were actually flat, and she'd fallen right off the edge. He'd learned nothing in that irritating interview with Lady Penwood, and when he'd queried his friends and family, no one knew anything about a young woman wearing a silver dress.

She hadn't arrived with anyone and she hadn't left with anyone. For all intents and purposes, she hadn't even existed.

He'd watched for her at every ball, party, and musicale he attended. Hell, he attended twice as many functions as usual, just in the hopes that he'd catch a glimpse of her.

But he'd always come home disappointed.

He'd thought he would stop looking for her. He was a practical man, and he'd assumed that eventually he would simply give up. And in some ways, he had. After a few months he found himself back in the habit of turning down more invitations than he accepted. A few months after that, he realized that he was once again able to meet women and not automatically compare them to her.

But he couldn't stop himself from watching for her. He might not feel the same urgency, but whenever he attended a ball or took a seat at a musicale, he found his eyes sweeping across the crowd, his ears straining for the lilt of her laughter.

She was out there somewhere. He'd long since resigned himself to the fact that he wasn't likely to find her, and he hadn't searched actively for over a year, but . . .

He smiled wistfully. He just couldn't stop from looking. It had become, in a very strange way, a part of who he was. His name was Benedict Bridgerton, he had seven brothers and sisters, was rather skilled with both a sword and a sketching crayon, and he always kept his eyes open for the one woman who had touched his soul.

He kept hoping . . . and wishing . . . and watching. And even though he told himself it was probably time to marry, he just couldn't muster the enthusiasm to do so.

Because what if he put his ring on some woman's finger, and the next day he saw *her*?

It would be enough to break his heart.

No, it would be more than that. It would be enough to shatter his soul.

Benedict breathed a sigh of relief as he saw the village of Rosemeade approaching. Rosemeade meant that his cottage was a mere five minutes away, and lud, but he couldn't wait to get inside and throw himself into a steaming tub of water.

He glanced over at Miss Beckett. She, too, was shivering, but, he thought with a touch of admiration, she hadn't let out even a peep of complaint. Benedict tried to think of another woman of his acquaintance who would have stood up to the elements with such fortitude and came up empty-handed. Even his sister Daphne, who was as good a sport as any, would have been howling about the cold by now.

"We're almost there," he assured her.

"I'm all—Oh! Are you all right?"

Benedict was gripped by wave of coughs, the deep, hacking kind that rumble down in one's chest. His lungs felt as if they were on fire, and his throat like someone had taken a razor blade to it.

"I'm fine," he gasped, jerking slightly on the reins to make up for the lack of direction he'd given the horses while he was coughing.

"You don't sound fine."

"Had a head cold last week," he said with a wince. Damn, but his lungs felt sore.

"That didn't sound like your head," she said, giving him what she obviously hoped was a teasing smile. But it didn't look like a teasing smile. In truth, she looked terribly concerned.

"Must've moved," he muttered.

"I don't want you getting sick on my account."

He tried to grin, but his cheekbones ached too much. "I would've been caught in the rain whether I'd taken you along or not."

"Still—"

Whatever she'd intended to say was lost under another stream of deep, chesty coughs.

"Sorry," he mumbled.

"Let me drive," she said, reaching for the reins.

He turned to her in disbelief. "This is a phaeton, not a single-horse wagon."

Sophie fought the urge to throttle him. His nose was running, his eyes were red, he couldn't stop coughing, and still he found the energy to act like an arrogant peacock. "I assure you," she said slowly, "that I know how to drive a team of horses."

"And where did you acquire that skill?"

"The same family that allowed me to share in their daughters' lessons," Sophie lied. "I learned to drive a team when the girls learned."

"The lady of the house must have taken quite a liking to you," he said.

"She did quite," Sophie replied, trying not to laugh. Araminta had been the lady of the house, and she'd fought tooth and nail every time her father had insisted that she be allowed to receive the same instruction as Rosamund and Posy. They'd all three learned how to drive teams the year before the earl had died.

"I'll drive, thank you," Benedict said sharply. Then he ruined the entire effect by launching into yet another coughing fit.

Sophie reached for the reins. "For the love of—"

"Here," he said, thrusting them toward her, as he wiped his eyes. "Take them. But I'll be watching you."

"I would expect no less," she said peevishly. The rain didn't exactly make for ideal driving conditions, and it had been years since she'd held reins in her hands, but she thought she acquitted herself rather nicely. There were some things one didn't forget, she supposed.

It felt rather nice, actually, to do something she hadn't done since her previous life, when she'd been, officially at least, an earl's ward. She'd had fine clothes then, and good food, and interesting lessons, and . . .

She sighed. It hadn't been perfect, but it had been better than anything that had come after.

"What's wrong?" Benedict asked.

"Nothing. Why should you think something is wrong?"

"You sighed."

"You heard me over the wind?" she asked incredulously.

"I've been paying close attention. I'm sick enough"—cough cough—"without you landing us in a ditch."

Sophie decided not even to credit him with a reply.

"Turn right up ahead," he directed. "It'll take us directly to my cottage."

She did as he asked. "Does your cottage have a name?"

"My Cottage."

"I might have known," she muttered.

He smirked. Quite a feat, in her opinion, since he looked sick as a dog. "I'm not kidding," he said.

Sure enough, in another minute they pulled up in front of an elegant country house, complete with a small, unobtrusive sign in front reading, MY COTTAGE.

"The previous owner coined the name," Benedict said as he directed her toward the stables, "but it seemed to fit me as well."

Sophie looked over at the house, which, while fairly small, was no humble dwelling. "You call this a cottage?"

"No, the previous owner did," he replied. "You should have seen his other house."

A moment later they were out of the rain, and Benedict had hopped down and was unhitching the horses. He was wearing gloves, but they were completely sodden and slipping on the bridle, and so he peeled them off and flung them away. Sophie watched him as he went about his work. His fingers were wrinkled like prunes and trembling from the cold. "Let me help," she said, stepping forward.

"I can do it."

"Of course you can," she said placatingly, "but you can do it faster with my help."

He turned, presumably to refuse her again, then doubled over as he was wracked by coughs. Sophie quickly rushed in and led him to a nearby bench. "Sit down, please," she implored him. "I'll finish up the job."

She thought he'd disagree, but this time he gave in. "I'm sorry," he said hoarsely. "I—"

"There's nothing to feel sorry about," she said, making quick work of the job. Or as quick as she could; her fingers were still numb, and bits of her skin had turned white from having been wet for so long.

"Not very . . ." He coughed again, this one lower and deeper than before. ". . . gentlemanly of me."

"Oh, I think I can forgive you this time, considering the way you saved me earlier this evening." Sophie tried to give him a jaunty smile, but for some reason it wobbled, and without warning she found herself inexplicably near tears. She turned quickly away, not wanting him to see her face.

But he must have seen something, or maybe just sensed that something was wrong, because he called out, "Are you all right?"

"I'm fine!" she replied, but her voice came out strained and choked, and before she knew it, he was next to her, and she was in his arms.

"It's all right," he said soothingly. "You're safe now."

The tears burst forth. She cried for what could have been her fate that evening, and she cried for what had been her fate for the past nine years. She cried for the memory of when he'd held her in his arms at the masquerade, and she cried because she was in his arms right now.

She cried because he was so damned *nice*, and even though he was clearly ill, even though she was, in his eyes, nothing but a housemaid, he still wanted to care for her and protect her.

She cried because she hadn't let herself cry in longer than she could remember, and she cried because she felt so alone.

And she cried because she'd been dreaming of him for so very long, and he hadn't recognized her. It was probably best that he did not, but her heart still ached from it.

Eventually her tears subsided, and he stepped back, touching her chin as he said, "Do you feel better now?"

She nodded, surprised that it was true.

"Good. You had a scare, and—" He jerked away from her, doubling over as he coughed.

"We really need to get you inside," Sophie said, brushing away the last streaks of her tears. "Inside the house, that is."

He nodded. "I'll race you to the door."

Her eyes widened in shock. She couldn't believe that he had the spirit to make a joke of this, when he was obviously feeling so poorly. But she wrapped the drawstring of her bag around her hands, hitched up her skirts, and ran for the front door to the cottage. By the time she reached the steps, she was laughing from the exertion, giggling at the ridiculousness of running wildly to get out of the rain when she was already soaked to the bone.

Benedict had, not surprisingly, beaten her to the small portico. He might have been ill, but his legs were significantly longer and stronger. When she skidded to a halt at his side, he was banging on the front door.

"Don't you have a key?" Sophie yelled. The wind was still howling, making it difficult to be heard.

He shook his head. "I wasn't planning on stopping here."

"Do you think the caretakers will even hear you?"

"I bloody well hope so," he muttered.

Sophie wiped away the rivulets of water running over her eyes and peeked in a nearby window. "It's very dark," she told him. "Do you think they might not be home?"

"I don't know where else they'd be."

"Shouldn't there at least be a maid or a footman?"

Benedict shook his head. "I'm so rarely here it seemed foolish to hire a full staff. The maids only come in for the day."

Sophie grimaced. "I'd suggest we look for an open window, but that's rather unlikely in the rain."

"Not necessary," Benedict said grimly. "I know where the spare key is hidden."

Sophie looked at him in surprise. "Why do you sound so glum about it?"

He coughed several times before answering, "Because it means I have to go back out into the bloody storm."

Sophie knew he was truly reaching the end of his patience. He'd already sworn twice in front of her, and he didn't seem the sort to curse in front of a woman, even a mere housemaid.

"Wait here," he ordered, and then before she could reply, he'd left the shelter of the portico and dashed away.

A few minutes later she heard a key turning in the lock, and the front door swung open to reveal Benedict, holding a candle and dripping all over the floor. "I don't know where Mr. and Mrs. Crabtree are," he said, his voice raspy from all his coughing, "but they're definitely not here."

Sophie gulped. "We're alone?"

He nodded. "Completely."

She edged toward the stairs. "I'd better find the servants' quarters."

"Oh, no you won't," he growled, grabbing hold of her arm.

"I won't?"

He shook his head. "You, dear girl, aren't going anywhere."

Chapter 8

It seems one cannot take two steps at a London ball these days without stumbling across a society matron lamenting the difficulties of finding good help. Indeed, This Author thought that Mrs. Featherington and Lady Penwood were going to come to blows at last week's Smythe-Smith musicale. It seems that Lady Penwood stole Mrs. Featherington's lady's maid right out from under her nose one month ago, promising higher wages and free cast-off clothing. (It should be noted that Mrs. Featherington also gave the poor girl cast-off clothing, but anyone who has ever observed the attire of the Featherington girls would understand why the lady's maid would not view this as a benefit.)

The plot thickened, however, when the lady's maid in question fled back to Mrs. Featherington, begging to be rehired. It seemed that Lady Penwood's idea of a lady's maid included duties more accurately ascribed to the scullery maid, upstairs maid, and cook.

Someone ought to tell the woman that one girl cannot do the work of three.

LADY WHISTLEDOWN'S SOCIETY PAPERS, 2 MAY 1817

"We're going to build a fire," Benedict said, "and get warm before either of us goes off to bed. I didn't save you from Cavender just so you could die of influenza."

Sophie watched him cough anew, the spasms wracking his body and forcing him to bend over at the waist. "Begging your pardon, Mr. Bridgerton," she could not help commenting, "but of the two of us, I should think you're more in danger of contracting influenza."

"Just so," he gasped, "and I assure you I have no desire to be so afflicted, either. So——" He bent over again as he was once again engulfed by coughs.

"Mr. Bridgerton?" Sophie asked, concern in her voice.

He swallowed convulsively and barely managed to say, "Just help me get a fire blazing before I cough myself into oblivion."

Sophie's brow knit with worry. His coughing fits were coming closer and closer together, and each time they were deeper, more rumbly, as if they were coming from the very pit of his chest.

She made easy work of the fire; she'd certainly had enough experience setting them as a housemaid, and soon they were both holding their hands as close to the flames as they dared.

"I don't suppose your change of clothing remained dry," Benedict said, nodding toward Sophie's sodden satchel.

"I doubt it," she said ruefully. "But it's no matter. If I stand here long enough, I'll dry out."

"Don't be silly," he scoffed, turning around so that the fire might heat his back. "I'm sure I can find you a change of clothing."

"You have women's clothing here?" she asked doubtfully.

"You're not so fussy that you can't wear breeches and a shirt for one evening, are you?"

Until that very moment, Sophie had probably been *exactly* that fussy, but put that way, it did seem a little silly. "I suppose not," she said. Dry clothing certainly sounded appealing.

"Good," he said briskly. "Why don't you light the furnaces in two bedrooms, and I'll find us both some clothing?"

"I can stay in the servants' quarters," Sophie said quickly.

"Not necessary," he said, striding out of the room and motioning for her to follow. "I've extra rooms, and you are not a servant here."

"But I *am* a servant," she pointed out, hurrying after him.

"Do whatever you please then." He started to march up the stairs, but had to stop halfway up to cough. "You can find a tiny little room in the servants' quarters with a hard little pallet, or you can avail yourself of a guest bedroom, all of which I assure you come equipped with feather mattresses and goosedown coverlets."

Sophie knew that she should remember her place in the world and march right up the next flight of stairs to the attic, but by God above, a feather mattress and down coverlet sounded like heaven on earth. She hadn't slept in such comfort in years. "I'll just find a small guest bedroom," she acceded. "The, er, smallest you have."

Half of Benedict's mouth quirked up in a dry, I-told-you-so sort of smile. "Pick whichever room you like. But not that one," he said, pointing to the second door on the left. "That's mine."

"I'll get the furnace started in there immediately," she said. He needed the warmth more than she did, and besides, she found herself inordinately curious to see what the inside of his bedroom looked like. One could tell a lot about a person by the décor of his bedchamber. Provided, of course, she thought with a grimace, that one possessed enough funds to decorate in the manner one preferred. Sophie sincerely doubted that anyone could have told anything about her from her little attic turret at the Cavenders'—except for the fact that she had not a penny to her name.

Sophie left her satchel in the hall and scurried into Benedict's bedchamber. It was a lovely room, warm and masculine and very comfortable. Despite the fact that Benedict had said he was rarely in residence, there were all sorts of personal items on the desk and tables—miniatures of what had to be his brothers and sisters, leather-bound books, and even a small glass bowl filled with . . .

Rocks?

"How odd," Sophie murmured, moving forward even though she knew she was being dreadfully invasive and nosy.

"Each one is meaningful in some way," came a deep voice from behind her. "I've collected them since—" He stopped to cough. "Since I was a child."

Sophie's face flushed red at having been caught so shamelessly snooping, but her curiosity was still piqued, so she held one up. It was of a pinkish hue, with a ragged gray vein running straight through the middle. "What about this one?"

"I picked that one up on a hike," Benedict said softly. "It happened to be the day my father died."

"Oh!" Sophie dropped the rock back on the pile as if burned. "I'm so sorry."

"It was long ago."

"I'm still sorry."

He smiled sadly. "As am I." Then he coughed, so hard that he had to lean against the wall.

"You need to get warm," Sophie said quickly. "Let me get to work on that fire."

Benedict tossed a bundle of clothing onto the bed. "For you," he said simply.

"Thank you," she said, keeping her attention focused on the small furnace. It was dangerous to remain in the same room as him. She didn't think he was likely to make an untoward advance; he was far too much of a gentleman to foist himself on a woman he barely knew. No, the danger lay squarely within herself. Frankly, she was terrified that if she spent too much time in his company she might fall head over heels in love.

And what would that get her?

Nothing but a broken heart.

Sophie huddled in front of the small iron furnace for several minutes, stoking the flame until she was confident that it would not flicker out. "There," she announced once she was satisfied. She stood up, arching her back slightly as she stretched and turned around. "That should take care of—Oh my!"

Benedict Bridgerton looked positively green.

"Are you all right?" she asked, hurrying to his side.

"Don' feel too well," he slurred, leaning heavily against the bed-post. He sounded vaguely intoxicated, but Sophie had been in his company for at least two hours, and she knew that he had not been drinking.

"You need to get into bed," she said, stumbling under his weight when he decided to lean against her instead of the bedpost.

He grinned. "You coming?"

She lurched back. "Now I know you're feverish."

He lifted his hand to touch his forehead, but he smacked his nose instead. "Ow!" he yelped.

Sophie winced in sympathy.

His hand crept up to his forehead. "Hmmm, maybe I am a bit hot."

It was horribly familiar of her, but a man's health was at stake, so Sophie reached out and touched her hand to his brow. It wasn't burning, but it certainly wasn't cool. "You need to get out of those wet clothes," she said. "Immediately."

Benedict looked down, blinking as if the sight of his sodden clothing was a surprise. "Yes," he murmured thoughtfully. "Yes, I believe I do." His fingers went to the buttons on his shirt, but they were clammy and numb and kept slipping and sliding. Finally, he just shrugged at her and said helplessly, "I can't do it."

"Oh, dear. Here, I'll . . ." Sophie reached out to undo his but-tons, jerked her hands back nervously, then finally gritted her teeth and reached out again. She made quick work of the buttons, doing her best to keep her gaze averted as each undone button revealed another two inches of his skin. "Almost done," she muttered. "Just a moment now."

He didn't say anything in reply, so she looked up. His eyes were closed, and his entire body was swaying slightly. If he weren't stand-ing up, she'd have sworn that he was asleep.

"Mr. Bridgerton?" she asked softly. "Mr. Bridgerton!"

Benedict's head jerked up violently. "What? What?"

"You fell asleep."

He blinked confusedly. "Is there a reason that's bad?"

"You can't fall asleep in your clothing."

He looked down. "How'd my shirt get undone?"

Sophie ignored the question, instead nudging him until his behind was leaning against the mattress. "Sit," she ordered.

She must have sounded suitably bossy, because he did.

"Have you something dry we can change you into?" she asked.

He shrugged the shirt off, letting it land on the floor in a messy heap. "Never sleep with clothes."

Sophie felt her stomach lurch. "Well, tonight I think you should, and—*What* are you doing?"

He looked over at her as if she'd asked the most inane question in the world. "Taking my breeches off."

"Couldn't you at least wait until I'd turned my back?"

He stared at her blankly.

She stared back.

He stared some more. Finally, he said, "Well?"

"Well what?"

"Aren't you going to turn your back?"

"Oh!" she yelped, spinning around as if someone had lit a fire under her feet.

Benedict shook his head wearily as he sat on the edge of the bed and pulled off his stockings. God save him from prudish misses. She was a housemaid, for God's sake. Even if she was a virgin—and given her behavior, he rather suspected she was—she'd surely seen a male form before. Housemaids were always slipping in and out of rooms without knocking, carrying towels and sheets and what have you. It was inconceivable she'd never accidentally barged in on a naked man.

He stripped off his breeches—not an easy task considering they were still more than a little damp and he had quite literally to peel them from his skin. When he was well and truly naked, he quirked a brow in the direction of Sophie's back. She was standing rigidly, her hands fisted tightly at her sides.

With surprise, he realized the sight of her made him smile.

He was starting to feel a bit sluggish, and it took him two tries before he was able to lift his leg high enough to climb into bed. With considerable effort he leaned forward and grabbed the edge of his coverlet, dragging it over his body. Then, completely worn-out, he sagged back against the pillows and groaned.

"Are you all right?" Sophie called.

He made an effort to say, "Fine," but it came out more like, "Fmmph."

He heard her moving about, and when he summoned up the energy to lift one eyelid halfway open, he saw that she'd moved to the side of the bed. She looked concerned.

For some reason that seemed rather sweet. It had been quite a long time since any woman who wasn't related to him had been concerned for his welfare.

"I'm fine," he mumbled, trying to give her a reassuring smile. But his voice sounded like it was coming through a long, narrow tunnel. He reached up and tugged at his ear. His mouth felt like he was talking properly; the problem must be with his ears.

"Mr. Bridgerton? Mr. Bridgerton?"

He pried an eyelid open again. "Go da bed," he grunted. "Get dry."

"Are you certain?"

He nodded. It was getting too difficult to speak.

"Very well. But I'm going to leave your door open. If you need me in the night, just call out."

He nodded again. Or at least he tried to. Then he slept.

It took Sophie barely a quarter of an hour to get ready for bed. A surfeit of nervous energy kept her going as she changed into dry clothing and readied the furnace in her room, but once her head hit her pillow, she felt herself succumbing to an exhaustion so total it seemed to come from her very bones.

It had been a long day, she thought groggily. A really long day, between attending to her morning chores, dashing around the house to escape Cavender and his friends . . . Her eyelids drifted shut. It had been an extraordinarily long day, and . . .

Sophie sat up suddenly, her heart pounding. The fire in the furnace had burned low, so she must have fallen asleep. She'd been dead tired, though, so something must have woken her. Was it Mr. Bridgerton? Had he called out? He'd not looked well when she'd left him, but neither had he seemed at death's door.

Sophie hopped out of bed, grabbed a candle, then dashed toward the door of her room, grabbing hold of the waistband of the too-big breeches Benedict had lent her when they started to slip down her hips. When she reached the hall she heard the sound that must have woken her up.

It was a deep groan, followed by a thrashing noise, followed by what could only be called a whimper.

Sophie dashed into Benedict's room, stopping briefly at the furnace to light her candle. He was lying in his bed, almost preternaturally still. Sophie edged toward him, her eyes focusing on his chest. She knew he couldn't possibly be dead, but she'd feel an awful lot better once she saw his chest rise and fall.

"Mr. Bridgerton?" she whispered. "Mr. Bridgerton?"

No response.

She crept closer, leaning over the edge of the bed. "Mr. Bridgerton?"

His hand shot out and grabbed her shoulder, pulling her off-balance until she fell onto the bed.

"Mr. Bridgerton!" Sophie squealed. "Let go!"

But he'd started to thrash and moan, and there was enough heat coming off his body that Sophie knew he was in the grips of a fever.

She somehow managed to wrench herself free, and she went tumbling off the bed while he continued to toss and turn, mumbling streams of words that made no sense.

Sophie waited for a quiet moment, then darted her hand out to touch his forehead. It was on fire.

She chewed on her lower lip as she tried to decide what to do. She had no experience nursing the feverish, but it seemed to her that the logical thing would be to cool him off. On the other hand, sickrooms always seemed to be kept closed, stuffy, and warm, so maybe . . .

Benedict started to thrash again, and then, out of nowhere, he murmured, "Kiss me."

Sophie lost hold of her breeches; they fell to the floor. She let out a little yelp of surprise as she quickly bent to retrieve them. Clutching the waistband securely with her right hand, she reached out to pat his hand with her left, then thought the better of it. "You're just dreaming, Mr. Bridgerton," she told him.

"Kiss me," he repeated. But he did not open his eyes.

Sophie leaned in closer. Even by the light of one solitary candle she could see his eyeballs moving quickly under his lids. It was bizarre, she thought, to see another person dream.

"God damn it!" he suddenly yelled. "Kiss me!"

Sophie lurched back in surprise, setting her candle hastily on the bedside table. "Mr. Bridgerton, I—" she began, fully intending to explain why she could not even begin to think about kissing him, but then she thought—*Why not?*

Her heart fluttering wildly, she leaned down and brushed the barest, lightest, most gentle of kisses on his lips.

"I love you," she whispered. "I've always loved you."

To Sophie's everlasting relief, he didn't move. It wasn't the sort of moment she wanted him to remember in the morning. But then, just when she was convinced that he'd settled back into a deep sleep, his head began to toss from side to side, leaving deep indentations in his feather pillow.

"Where'd you go?" he grunted hoarsely. "Where'd you go?"

"I'm right here," Sophie replied.

He opened his eyes, and for the barest of seconds appeared completely lucid, as he said, "Not *you*." Then his eyes rolled back and his head started tossing from side to side again.

"Well, I'm all you've got," Sophie muttered. "Don't go anywhere," she said with a nervous laugh. "I'll be right back."

And then, her heart pounding with fear and nerves, she ran out of the room.

If there was one thing Sophie had learned in her days as a housemaid, it was that most households were run in essentially the same way. It was for that reason that she had no trouble at all finding spare linens to replace Benedict's sweat-soaked sheets. She also scavenged a pitcher full of cool water and a few small towels for dampening his brow.

Upon her return to his bedroom, she found him lying still again, but his breathing was shallow and rapid. Sophie reached out and touched his brow again. She couldn't be certain, but it seemed to her that it was growing warmer.

Oh, dear. This was not good, and she was singularly unqualified to care for a feverish patient. Araminta, Rosamund, and Posy had never had a sick day in their lives, and the Cavenders had all been uncommonly healthy as well. The closest she'd ever come to nursing had been helping Mrs. Cavender's mother, who'd been unable to walk. But she'd never taken care of someone with a fever.

She dunked a cloth in the pitcher of water, then wrung it out until it was no longer dripping from the corners. "This ought to make you feel a little better," she whispered, placing it gingerly on his brow. Then she added, in a rather unconfident voice, "At least I hope it will."

He didn't flinch when she touched him with the cloth. Sophie took that as an excellent sign, and she prepared another cool towel. She had no idea where to put it, though. His chest somehow didn't seem right, and she certainly wasn't going to allow the bedsheet to drift any lower than his waist unless the poor man was at death's door (and even then, she wasn't certain what she could possibly do down there that would resurrect him). So she finally just dabbed with it behind his ears, and a little on the sides of his neck.

"Does that feel better?" she asked, not expecting any sort of an answer but feeling nonetheless that she ought to continue with her one-sided conversation. "I really don't know very much about caring for the ill, but it just *seems* to me like you'd want something cool on your brow. I know if *I* were sick, that's how I'd feel."

He shifted restlessly, mumbling something utterly incoherent.

"Really?" Sophie replied, trying to smile but failing miserably. "I'm glad you feel that way."

He mumbled something else.

"No," she said, dabbing the cool cloth on his ear, "I'd have to agree with what you said the first time."

He went still again.

"I'd be happy to reconsider," she said worriedly. "Please don't take offense."

He didn't move.

Sophie sighed. One could only converse so long with an unconscious man before one started to feel extremely silly. She lifted up the cloth she'd placed on his forehead and touched his skin. It felt kind of clammy now. Clammy and still warm, which was a combination she wouldn't have thought possible.

She decided to leave the cloth off for now, and she laid it over the top of the pitcher. There seemed little she could do for him at that very moment, so Sophie stretched her legs and walked slowly around his room, shamelessly examining everything that wasn't nailed down, and quite a bit that was.

The collection of miniatures was her first stop. There were nine on the writing desk; Sophie surmised that they were of Benedict's parents and seven brothers and sisters. She started to put the sib-

lings in order according to their ages, but then it occurred to her
that the miniatures most likely hadn't been painted all at the same
time, so she could be looking at a likeness of his older brother at
fifteen and younger brother at twenty.

She was struck by how alike they all were, with the same deep
chestnut hair, wide mouths, and elegant bone structure. She looked
closely to try to compare eye color but found it impossible in the
dim candlelight, and besides, eye color often wasn't easily discerned
on a miniature, anyway.

Next to the miniatures was the bowl with Benedict's rock collection. Sophie picked a few of them up in turn, rolling them lightly
over her palm. "Why are these so special to you, I wonder?" she
whispered, placing them carefully back in the bowl. They just
looked like rocks to her, but she supposed that they might appear
more interesting and unique to Benedict if they represented special
memories for him.

She found a small wooden box that she absolutely could not open;
it must have been one of those trick boxes she'd heard about that
came from the Orient. And most intriguing, leaning against the
side of the desk was a large sketchbook, filled with pencil drawings,
mostly of landscapes but with a few portraits as well. Had Benedict
drawn them? Sophie squinted at the bottom of each drawing. The
small squiggles certainly looked like two Bs.

Sophie sucked in her breath, an unbidden smile lighting her face.
She'd never dreamed that Benedict was an artist. There had never
even been a peep about it in *Whistledown*, and it seemed like the sort
of thing the gossip columnist would have figured out over the years.

Sophie drew the sketchbook closer to her candle and flipped
through the pages. She wanted to sit with the book and spend ten
minutes perusing each sketch, but it seemed too intrusive to examine his drawings in such detail. She was probably just trying to justify her nosiness, but somehow it didn't seem as bad just to give
them a glance.

The landscapes were varied. Some were of My Cottage (or should she call it His Cottage?) and some were of a larger house, which Sophie supposed was the country home of the Bridgerton family. Most of the landscapes featured no architecture at all, just a babbling brook, or a windswept tree, or a rain-dappled meadow. And the amazing thing about his drawings was that they seemed to capture the whole and true moment. Sophie could swear that she could hear that brook babbling or the wind ruffling the leaves on that tree.

The portraits were fewer in number, but Sophie found them infinitely more interesting. There were several of what had to be his littlest sister, and a few of what she thought must be his mother. One of Sophie's favorites was of what appeared to be some kind of outdoor game. At least five Bridgerton siblings were holding long mallets, and one of the girls was depicted at the forefront, her face screwed up in determination as she tried to aim a ball through a wicket.

Something about the picture almost made Sophie laugh out loud. She could feel the merriment of the day, and it made her long desperately for a family of her own.

She glanced back at Benedict, still sleeping quietly in his bed. Did he realize how lucky he was to have been born into such a large and loving clan?

With a sigh, Sophie flipped through a few more pages until she reached the end of the book. The very last sketch was different from the rest, if only because it appeared to be of a night scene, and the woman in it was holding her skirts above her ankles as she ran across—

Good God! Sophie gasped, thunderstruck. It was her!

She brought the sketch closer to her face. He'd gotten the details of her dress—that wonderful, magical silver concoction that had been hers for only a single evening—perfectly. He'd even remembered her long, elbow-length gloves and the exact manner in which her hair had been styled. Her face was a little less recognizable, but one would have to make allowances for that given that he'd never actually seen it in its entirety.

Well, not until now.

Benedict suddenly groaned, and when Sophie glanced over she saw that he was shifting restlessly in the bed. She closed up the sketchbook and put it back into its place before hurriedly making her way to his side.

"Mr. Bridgerton?" she whispered. She wanted desperately to call him Benedict. That was how she thought of him; that was what she'd called him in her dreams these long two years. But that would be inexcusably familiar and certainly not in keeping with her position as a servant.

"Mr. Bridgerton?" she whispered again. "Are you all right?"

His eyelids fluttered open.

"Do you need anything?"

He blinked several times, and Sophie couldn't be sure whether he'd heard her or not. He looked so unfocused, she couldn't even be sure whether he'd truly seen her.

"Mr. Bridgerton?"

He squinted. "Sophie," he said hoarsely, his throat sounding terribly dry and scratchy. "The housemaid."

She nodded. "I'm here. What do you need?"

"Water," he rasped.

"Right away." Sophie had been dunking the cloths into the water in the pitcher, but she decided that now was no time to be fussy, so she grabbed hold of the glass she'd brought up from the kitchen and filled it. "Here you are," she said, handing it to him.

His fingers were shaky, so she did not let go of the glass as he brought it to his lips. He took a couple of sips, then sagged back against his pillows.

"Thank you," he whispered.

Sophie reached out and touched his brow. It was still quite warm, but he seemed lucid once again, and she decided to take that as a sign that the fever had broken. "I think you'll be better in the morning."

He laughed. Not hard, and not with anything approaching vigor, but he actually laughed. "Not likely," he croaked.

"Well, not recovered," she allowed, "but I think you'll feel better than you do right now."

"It would certainly be hard to feel worse."

Sophie smiled at him. "Do you think you can scoot to one side of your bed so I can change your sheets?"

He nodded and did as she asked, closing his weary eyes as she changed the bed around him. "That's a neat trick," he said when she was done.

"Mrs. Cavender's mother often came to visit," Sophie explained. "She was bedridden, so I had to learn how to change the sheets without her leaving the bed. It's not terribly difficult."

He nodded. "I'm going back to sleep now."

Sophie gave his shoulder a reassuring pat. She just couldn't help herself. "You'll feel better in the morning," she whispered. "I promise."

Chapter 9

*It has oft been said that physicians make the worst patients, but
it is the opinion of This Author that any man makes a terrible
patient. One might say it takes patience to be a patient, and
heaven knows, the males of our species lack an abundance of patience.*

LADY WHISTLEDOWN'S SOCIETY PAPERS,
2 MAY 1817

The first thing Sophie did the following morning was scream.

She'd fallen asleep in the straight-backed chair next to Benedict's
bed, her limbs sprawled most inelegantly and her head cocked to
the side in a rather uncomfortable position. Her sleep had been light
at first, her ears perked to listen for any sign of distress from the
sickbed. But after an hour or so of complete, blessed silence, exhaustion claimed her, and she fell into a deeper slumber, the kind from
which one ought to awaken in peace, with a restful, easy smile on
one's face.

Which may have been why, when she opened her eyes and saw
two strange people staring at her, she had such a fright that it took
a full five minutes for her heart to stop racing.

"Who are you?" The words tumbled out of Sophie's mouth before she realized exactly who they must be: Mr. and Mrs. Crabtree, the caretakers of My Cottage.

"Who are *you*?" the man demanded, not a little bit belligerently.

"Sophie Beckett," she said with a gulp. "I . . ." She pointed desperately at Benedict. "He . . ."

"Spit it out, girl!"

"Don't torture her," came a croak from the bed.

Three heads swiveled in Benedict's direction. "You're awake!" Sophie exclaimed.

"Wish to God I weren't," he muttered. "My throat feels like it's on fire."

"Would you like me to fetch you some more water?" Sophie asked solicitously.

He shook his head. "Tea. Please."

She shot to her feet. "I'll go get it."

"*I'll* get it," Mrs. Crabtree said firmly.

"Would you like help?" Sophie asked timidly. Something about this pair made her feel like she were ten years old. They were both short and squat, but they positively exuded authority.

Mrs. Crabtree shook her head. "A fine housekeeper I am if I can't prepare a pot of tea."

Sophie gulped. She couldn't tell whether Mrs. Crabtree was miffed or joking. "I never meant to imply—"

Mrs. Crabtree waved off her apology. "Shall I bring you a cup?"

"You shouldn't fetch anything for me," Sophie said. "I'm a ser—"

"Bring her a cup," Benedict ordered.

"But—"

He jabbed his finger at her, grunting, "Be quiet," before turning to Mrs. Crabtree and bestowing upon her a smile that could have melted an ice cap. "Would you be so kind as to include a cup for Miss Beckett on the tray?"

"Of course, Mr. Bridgerton," she replied, "but may I say—"

"You can say anything you please once you return with the tea," he promised.

She gave him a stern look. "I have a lot to say."

"Of that I have no doubt."

Benedict, Sophie, and Mr. Crabtree waited in silence while Mrs. Crabtree left the room, and then, when she was safely out of earshot, Mr. Crabtree positively chortled, and said, "You're in for it now, Mr. Bridgerton!"

Benedict smiled weakly.

Mr. Crabtree turned to Sophie and explained, "When Mrs. Crabtree has a lot to say, she has a *lot* to say."

"Oh," Sophie replied. She would have liked to have said something slightly more articulate, but "oh" was truly the best she could come up with on such short notice.

"And when she has a lot to say," Mr. Crabtree continued, his smile growing wide and sly, "she likes to say it with great vigor."

"Fortunately," Benedict said in a dry voice, "we'll have our tea to keep us occupied."

Sophie's stomach grumbled loudly.

"And," Benedict continued, shooting her an amused glance, "a fair bit of breakfast, too, if I know Mrs. Crabtree."

Mr. Crabtree nodded. "Already prepared, Mr. Bridgerton. We saw your horses in the stables when we returned from our daughter's house this morning, and Mrs. Crabtree got to work on breakfast straightaway. She knows how you love your eggs."

Benedict turned to Sophie and gave her a conspiratorial sort of smile. "I do love eggs."

Her stomach grumbled again.

"We didn't know there'd be two of you, though," Mr. Crabtree said.

Benedict chuckled, then winced at the pain. "I can't imagine that Mrs. Crabtree didn't make enough to feed a small army."

"Well, she didn't have time to prepare a proper breakfast with beef pie and fish," Mr. Crabtree said, "but I believe she has bacon and ham and eggs and toast."

Sophie's stomach positively growled. She clapped a hand to her belly, just barely resisting the urge to hiss, "Be quiet!"

"You should have told us you were coming," Mr. Crabtree added, shaking a finger at Benedict. "We never would have gone visiting if we'd known to expect you."

"It was a spur-of-the-moment decision," Benedict said, stretching his neck from side to side. "Went to a bad party and decided to leave."

Mr. Crabtree jerked his head toward Sophie. "Where'd she come from?"

"She was at the party."

"I wasn't *at* the party," Sophie corrected. "I just happened to be there."

Mr. Crabtree squinted at her suspiciously. "What's the difference?"

"I wasn't attending the party. I was a servant at the house."

"You're a servant?"

Sophie nodded. "That's what I've been trying to tell you."

"You don't look like a servant." Mr. Crabtree turned to Benedict. "Does she look like a servant to you?"

Benedict shrugged helplessly. "I don't know *what* she looks like."

Sophie scowled at him. It might not have been an insult, but it certainly wasn't a compliment.

"If she's somebody else's servant," Mr. Crabtree persisted, "then what's she doing here?"

"May I save my explanations until Mrs. Crabtree returns?" Benedict asked. "Since I'm certain she'll repeat all of your questions?"

Mr. Crabtree looked at him for a moment, blinked, nodded, then turned back to Sophie. "Why're you dressed like that?"

Sophie looked down and realized with horror that she'd completely forgotten she was wearing men's clothes. Men's clothes so big that she could barely keep the breeches from falling to her feet. "My clothes were wet," she explained, "from the rain."

Mr. Crabtree nodded sympathetically. "Quite a storm last night. That's why we stayed over at our daughter's. We'd planned to come home, you know."

Benedict and Sophie just nodded.

"She doesn't live terribly far away," Mr. Crabtree continued. "Just on the other side of the village." He glanced over at Benedict, who nodded immediately.

"Has a new baby," he added. "A girl."

"Congratulations," Benedict said, and Sophie could see from his face that he was not merely being polite. He truly meant it.

A loud clomping sound came from the stairway; surely Mrs. Crabtree returning with breakfast. "I ought to help," Sophie said, jumping up and dashing for the door.

"Once a servant, always a servant," Mr. Crabtree said sagely.

Benedict wasn't sure, but he thought he saw Sophie wince.

A minute later, Mrs. Crabtree entered, bearing a splendid silver tea service.

"Where's Sophie?" Benedict asked.

"I sent her down to get the rest," Mrs. Crabtree replied. "She should be up in no time. Nice girl," she added in a matter-of-fact tone, "but she needs a belt for those breeches you lent her."

Benedict felt something squeeze suspiciously in his chest at the thought of Sophie-the-housemaid, with her breeches 'round her ankles. He gulped uncomfortably when he realized the tight sensation might very well be desire.

Then he groaned and grabbed at his throat, because uncomfortable gulps were even more uncomfortable after a night of harsh coughing.

"You need one of my tonics," Mrs. Crabtree said.

Benedict shook his head frantically. He'd had one of her tonics before; it had had him retching for three hours.

"I won't take no for an answer," she warned.

"She never does," Mr. Crabtree added.

"The tea will work wonders," Benedict said quickly, "I'm sure."

But Mrs. Crabtree's attention had already been diverted. "Where is that girl?" she muttered, walking back to the door and looking out. "Sophie! Sophie!"

"If you can keep her from bringing me a tonic," Benedict whispered urgently to Mr. Crabtree, "it's a fiver in your pocket."

Mr. Crabtree beamed. "Consider it done!"

"There she is," Mrs. Crabtree declared. "Oh, heaven above."

"What is it, dearie?" Mr. Crabtree asked, ambling toward the door.

"The poor thing can't carry a tray and keep her breeches up at the same time," she replied, clucking sympathetically.

"Aren't you going to help her?" Benedict asked from the bed.

"Oh yes, of course." She hurried out.

"I'll be right back," Mr. Crabtree said over his shoulder. "Don't want to miss this."

"Someone get the bloody girl a belt!" Benedict yelled grumpily. It didn't seem quite fair that everyone got to go out to the hall and watch the sideshow while he was stuck in bed.

And he definitely was stuck there. Just the thought of getting up made him dizzy.

He must have been sicker than he'd realized the night before. He no longer felt the urge to cough every few seconds, but his body felt worn-out, exhausted. His muscles ached, and his throat was damned sore. Even his teeth didn't feel quite right.

He had vague recollections of Sophie taking care of him. She'd put cool compresses on his forehead, watched over him, even sung him a lullaby. But he'd never quite seen her face. Most of the time he hadn't had the energy to open his eyes, and even when he had, the room had been dark, always leaving her in shadows, reminding him of—

Benedict sucked in his breath, his heart thumping crazily in his chest as, in a sudden flash of clarity, he remembered his dream.

He'd dreamed of *her.*

It was not a new dream, although it had been months since he'd been visited by it. It was not a fantasy for the innocent, either. Benedict was no saint, and when he dreamed of the woman from the masquerade, she was not wearing her silver dress.

She was not, he thought with a wicked smile, wearing anything.

But what perplexed him was why this dream would return now, after so many months of dormancy. Was there something about Sophie that had triggered it? He'd thought—he'd hoped—that the disappearance of the dream had meant he was over her.

Obviously not.

Sophie certainly didn't look like the woman he'd danced with two years earlier. Her hair was all wrong, and she was far too thin. He distinctly remembered the lush, curvy feel of the masked woman in his arms; in comparison, Sophie could only be called scrawny. He supposed their voices were a bit similar, but he had to admit to himself that as time passed, his memories of that night grew less vivid, and he could no longer recall his mystery woman's voice with perfect clarity. Besides, Sophie's accent, while exceptionally refined for a housemaid, was not as upper-crust as *hers* had been.

Benedict let out a frustrated snort. How he hated calling her *her.* That seemed the cruelest of her secrets. She'd kept from him even her name. Part of him wished she'd just lied and given him a false name. At least then he'd have something to think of her by in his mind.

Something to whisper in the night, when he was staring out the window, wondering where in hell she was.

Benedict was saved from further reflection by the sounds of stumbling and bumbling in the hallway. Mr. Crabtree was the first to return, staggering under the weight of the breakfast tray.

"What happened to the rest?" Benedict asked suspiciously, eyeing the door.

"Mrs. Crabtree went off to find Sophie some proper clothing," Mr. Crabtree replied, setting the tray down on Benedict's desk. "Ham or bacon?"

"Both. I'm famished. And what the devil does she mean by 'proper clothing'?"

"A dress, Mr. Bridgerton. That's what women wear."

Benedict seriously considered lobbing a candle stump at him. "I meant," he said with what he considered saintly patience, "where is she going to *find* a dress?"

Mr. Crabtree walked over with a plate of food on a footed tray that would fit over Benedict's lap. "Mrs. Crabtree has several extras. She's always happy to share."

Benedict choked on the bite of egg he'd shoveled into his mouth. "Mrs. Crabtree and Sophie are hardly the same size."

"Neither are you," Mr. Crabtree pointed out, "and she wore your clothes just fine."

"I thought you said the breeches fell off in the hall."

"Well, we don't have to worry about that with the dress, do we? I hardly think her shoulders are going to slip through the neck hole."

Benedict decided it was safer for his sanity to mind his own business, and he turned his full attention to his breakfast. He was on his third plate when Mrs. Crabtree bustled in.

"Here we are!" she announced.

Sophie slunk in, practically drowning in Mrs. Crabtree's voluminous dress. Except, of course, at her ankles. Mrs. Crabtree was a good five inches shorter than Sophie.

Mrs. Crabtree beamed. "Doesn't she look smashing?"

"Oh, yes," Benedict replied, lips twitching.

Sophie glared at him.

"You'll have plenty of room for breakfast," he said gamely.

"It's only until I get her clothing cleaned up," Mrs. Crabtree explained. "But at least it's decent." She waddled over to Benedict. "How is your breakfast, Mr. Bridgerton?"

"Delicious," he replied. "I haven't eaten so well in months."

Mrs. Crabtree leaned forward and whispered, "I like your Sophie. May we keep her?"

Benedict choked. On what, he didn't know, but he choked nonetheless. "I beg your pardon?"

"Mr. Crabtree and I aren't as young as we used to be. We could use another set of hands around here."

"I, ah, well . . ." He cleared his throat. "I'll think about it."

"Excellent." Mrs. Crabtree crossed back to the other side of the room and grabbed Sophie's arm. "You come with me. Your stomach has been growling all morning. When was the last time you ate?"

"Er, sometime yesterday, I should think."

"When yesterday?" Mrs. Crabtree persisted.

Benedict hid a smile under his napkin. Sophie looked utterly overwhelmed. Mrs. Crabtree tended to do that to a person.

"Er, well, actually—"

Mrs. Crabtree planted her hands on her hips. Benedict grinned. Sophie was in for it now.

"Are you going to tell me that you didn't eat yesterday?" Mrs. Crabtree boomed.

Sophie shot a desperate look at Benedict. He replied with a don't-look-to-*me*-for-help shrug. Besides, he rather enjoyed watching Mrs. Crabtree fuss over her. He'd be willing to bet that the poor girl hadn't been fussed over in years.

"I was very busy yesterday," Sophie hedged.

Benedict frowned. She'd probably been busy running from Phillip Cavender and the pack of idiots he called friends.

Mrs. Crabtree shoved Sophie into the seat behind the desk. "Eat," she ordered.

Benedict watched as Sophie tucked into the food. It was obvious that she was trying to put on her best manners, but eventually hunger must have gotten the best of her, because after a minute she was practically shoveling the food into her mouth.

It was only when Benedict noticed that his jaw was clamped together like a vise that he realized he was absolutely furious. At whom, he wasn't precisely certain. But he did *not* like seeing Sophie so hungry.

They had an odd little bond, he and the housemaid. He'd saved her and she'd saved him. Oh, he doubted his fever from the night before would have killed him; if it had been truly serious, he'd still be battling it now. But she had cared for him and made him comfortable and probably hastened his road to recovery.

"Will you make certain she eats at least another plateful?" Mrs. Crabtree asked Benedict. "I'm going to make up a room for her."

"In the servants' quarters," Sophie said quickly.

"Don't be a silly. Until we hire you on, you're not a servant here."

"But—"

"Nothing more about it," Mrs. Crabtree interrupted.

"Would you like my help, dearie?" Mr. Crabtree asked.

Mrs. Crabtree nodded, and in a moment the couple was gone.

Sophie paused in her quest to consume as much food as humanly possible to stare at the door through which they'd just disappeared. She supposed they considered her one of their own, because if she'd been anything but a servant, they'd never have left her alone with Benedict. Reputations could be ruined on far less.

"You didn't eat at all yesterday, did you?" Benedict asked quietly.

Sophie shook her head.

"Next time I see Cavender," he growled, "I'm going to beat him to a bloody pulp."

If she were a better person, she would have been horrified, but Sophie couldn't quite prevent a smile at the thought of Benedict further defending her honor. Or of seeing Phillip Cavender with his nose relocated to his forehead.

"Fill up your plate again," Benedict said. "If only for my sake. I assure you that Mrs. Crabtree counted how many eggs and strips of bacon were on the platter when she left, and she'll have my head if the numbers haven't gone down by the time she returns."

"She's a very nice lady," Sophie said, reaching for the eggs. The first plate of food had barely touched upon her hunger; she needed no further urging to eat.

"The best."

Sophie expertly balanced a slice of ham between a serving fork and spoon and moved it to her plate. "How are you feeling this morning, Mr. Bridgerton?"

"Very well, thank you. Or if not well, then at least a damn sight better than I did last night."

"I was very worried about you," she said, spearing a corner of the ham with her fork and then cutting a piece off with her knife.

"It was very kind of you to care for me."

She chewed, swallowed, then said, "It was nothing, really. Anyone would have done it."

"Perhaps," he said, "but not with such grace and good humor."

Sophie's fork froze in midair. "Thank you," she said softly. "That is a lovely compliment."

"I didn't . . . er . . ." He cleared his throat.

Sophie eyed him curiously, waiting for him to finish whatever it was he wanted to say.

"Never mind," he mumbled.

Disappointed, she put a piece of ham in her mouth.

"I didn't do anything for which I ought to apologize, did I?" he suddenly blurted out.

Sophie spat the ham out into her napkin.

"I'll take that as a yes," he muttered.

"No!" she said quickly. "Not at all. You merely startled me."

His eyes narrowed. "You wouldn't lie to me about this, would you?"

Sophie shook her head as she remembered the single, perfect kiss she'd given him. He hadn't done anything that required an apology, but that didn't mean that *she* hadn't.

"You're blushing," he accused.

"No, I'm not."

"Yes," he said, "you are."

"If I'm blushing," she replied pertly, "it's because I'm wondering why *you* would think you had any reason to apologize."

"You have a rather smart mouth for a servant," he said.

"I'm sorry," Sophie said quickly. She had to remember her place. But that was hard to do with this man, the one member of the *ton* who had treated her—if only for a few hours—as an equal.

"I meant it as a compliment," he said. "Do not stifle yourself on my account."

She said nothing.

"I find you rather . . ." He paused, obviously searching for the correct word. "Refreshing."

"Oh." She set her fork down. "Thank you."

"Have you plans for the rest of the day?" he asked.

She looked down at her huge garments and grimaced. "I thought I'd wait for my clothes to be readied, and then I suppose I'll see if any of the nearby houses are in need of housemaids."

Benedict scowled at her. "I told you I would find you a position with my mother."

"And I do appreciate that," she said quickly. "But I would prefer to stay in the country."

He shrugged the shrug of one who has never been thrown one of life's great stumbles. "You can work at Aubrey Hall, then. In Kent."

Sophie chewed on her lower lip. She couldn't exactly come out and say she didn't want to work for his mother because then she'd have to see *him*.

She couldn't think of a torture that would be more exquisitely painful.

"You shouldn't think of me as your responsibility," she finally said.

He gave her a rather superior glance. "I told you I would find you a new position."

"But—"

"What could there possibly be to discuss?"

"Nothing," she grumbled. "Nothing at all." Clearly, it was no use arguing with him just then.

"Good." He leaned back contentedly against his pillows. "I'm glad you see it my way."

Sophie stood. "I should be going."

"To do what?"

She felt rather stupid as she said, "I don't know."

He grinned. "Have fun with it, then."

Her hand tightened around the handle of the serving spoon.

"Don't do it," he warned.

"Do what?"

"Throw the spoon."

"I wouldn't dream of it," she said tightly.

He laughed aloud. "Oh, yes you would. You're dreaming of it right now. You just wouldn't *do* it."

Sophie's hand was gripping the spoon so hard it shook.

Benedict was chuckling so hard his bed shook.

Sophie stood, still holding the spoon.

Benedict smiled. "Are you planning to take that with you?"

Remember your place, Sophie was screaming at herself. *Remember your place.*

"Whatever could you be thinking," Benedict mused, "to look so adorably ferocious? No, don't tell me," he added. "I'm sure it involves my untimely and painful demise."

Slowly and carefully, Sophie turned her back to him and put the spoon down on the table. She didn't want to risk any sudden movements. One false move and she knew she'd be hurling it at his head.

Benedict raised his brows approvingly. "That was very mature of you."

Sophie turned around slowly. "Are you this charming with everyone or only me?"

"Oh, only you." He grinned. "I shall have to make sure you take me up on my offer to find you employment with my mother. You do bring out the best in me, Miss Sophie Beckett."

"This is the best?" she asked with obvious disbelief.

"I'm afraid so."

Sophie just shook her head as she walked to the door. Conversations with Benedict Bridgerton could be exhausting.

"Oh, Sophie!" he called out.

She turned around.

He smiled slyly. "I knew you wouldn't throw the spoon."

What happened next was surely not Sophie's fault. She was, she was convinced, temporarily and fleetingly possessed by a demon. Because she absolutely did not recognize the hand that shot out to the small table next to her and picked up a stump of a candle. True, the hand appeared to be connected quite firmly to her arm, but it didn't look the least bit familiar as it drew back and hurled the stump across the room.

Straight at Benedict Bridgerton's head.

Sophie didn't even wait to see if her aim had been true. But as she stalked out the door, she heard Benedict explode with laughter. Then she heard him shout out, "Well done, Miss Beckett!"

And she realized that for the first time in years, her smile was one of pure, unadulterated joy.

Chapter 10

Although he responded in the affirmative (or so says Lady Covington) Benedict Bridgerton did not make an appearance at the annual Covington Ball. Complaints were heard from young women (and their mamas) across the ballroom.

According to Lady Bridgerton (his mother, not his sister-in-law), Mr. Bridgerton left for the country last week and has not been heard from since. Those who might fear for Mr. Bridgerton's health and well-being should not fret; Lady Bridgerton sounded more annoyed than worried. Last year no less than four couples met their future spouses at the Covington Ball; the previous year, three.

Much to Lady Bridgerton's dismay, if any matches are made at this year's Covington Ball, her son Benedict will not be among the grooms.

LADY WHISTLEDOWN'S SOCIETY PAPERS, 5 MAY 1817

There were advantages, Benedict soon discovered, to a long, drawn-out recovery.

The most obvious was the quantity and variety of most excellent food brought forth from Mrs. Crabtree's kitchen. He'd always been fed well at My Cottage, but Mrs. Crabtree truly rose to the occasion when she had someone tucked away in the sickroom.

And even better, Mr. Crabtree had managed to intercept all of Mrs. Crabtree's tonics and replace them with Benedict's best brandy. Benedict dutifully drank every drop, but the last time he looked out the window, it appeared that three of his rosebushes had died, presumably where Mr. Crabtree had dumped the tonic.

It was a sad sacrifice, but one Benedict was more than willing to make after his last experience with Mrs. Crabtree's tonics.

Another perk of staying abed was the simple fact that, for the first time in years, he could enjoy some quiet time. He read, sketched, and even closed his eyes and just daydreamed—all without feeling guilty for neglecting some other task or chore.

Benedict soon decided that he'd be perfectly happy leading the life of the indolent.

But the best part of his recovery, by far, was Sophie. She popped into his room several times a day, sometimes to fluff his pillows, sometimes to bring him food, sometimes just to read to him. Benedict had a feeling that her industriousness was due to her desire to feel useful, and to thank him with deeds for saving her from Phillip Cavender.

But he didn't much care why she came to visit; he just liked it that she did.

She'd been quiet and reserved at first, obviously trying to adhere to the standard that servants should be neither seen nor heard. But Benedict had had none of that, and he'd purposefully engaged her in conversation, just so she couldn't leave. Or he'd goad and needle her, simply to get a rise out of her, because he liked her far better when she was spitting fire than when she was meek and submissive.

But mostly he just enjoyed being in the same room with her. It didn't seem to matter if they were talking or if she was just sitting in a chair, leafing through a book while he stared out the window. Something about her presence brought him peace.

A sharp knock at the door broke him out of his thoughts, and he looked up eagerly, calling out, "Enter!"

Sophie poked her head in, her shoulder-length curls shaking slightly as they brushed against the edge of the door. "Mrs. Crabtree thought you might like tea."

"Tea? Or tea and biscuits?"

Sophie grinned, pushing the door open with her hip as she balanced the tray. "Oh, the latter, to be sure."

"Excellent. And will you join me?"

She hesitated, as she always did, but then she nodded, as she also always did. She'd long since learned that there was no arguing with Benedict when he had his mind set on something.

Benedict rather liked it that way.

"The color is back in your cheeks," she commented as she set the tray down on a nearby table. "And you don't look nearly so tired. I should think you'll be up and out of bed soon."

"Oh, soon, I'm sure," he said evasively.

"You're looking healthier every day."

He smiled gamely. "Do you think so?"

She lifted the teapot and paused before she poured. "Yes," she said with an ironic smile. "I wouldn't have said so otherwise."

Benedict watched her hands as she prepared his tea. She moved with an innate sense of grace, and she poured the tea as if she'd been to the manner born. Clearly the art of afternoon tea had been another one of those lessons she'd learned from her mother's generous employers. Or maybe she'd just watched other ladies closely while they'd prepared tea. Benedict had noticed that she was a very observant woman.

They'd enacted this ritual often enough that she didn't have to ask how he liked his tea. She handed him his cup—milk, no sugar—and then placed a selection of biscuits and scones on a plate.

"Fix yourself a cup," Benedict said, biting into a biscuit, "and come sit by me."

She hesitated again. He knew she'd hesitate, even though she'd already agreed to join him. But he was a patient man, and his patience was rewarded with a soft sigh as she reached out and plucked another cup off the tray.

After she'd fixed her own cup—two lumps of sugar, just the barest splash of milk—she sat in the velvet-covered, straight-backed chair by his bed, regarding him over the rim of her teacup as she took a sip.

"No biscuits for you?" Benedict asked.

She shook her head. "I had a few straight out of the oven."

"Lucky you. They're always best when they're warm." He polished off another biscuit, brushed a few crumbs off of his sleeve, and reached for another. "And how have you spent your day?"

"Since I last saw you two hours earlier?"

Benedict shot her a look that said he recognized her sarcasm but chose not to respond to it.

"I helped Mrs. Crabtree in the kitchen," Sophie said. "She's making a beef stew for supper and needed some potatoes peeled. Then I borrowed a book from your library and read in the garden."

"Really? What did you read?"

"A novel."

"Was it good?"

She shrugged. "Silly, but romantic. I enjoyed it."

"And do you long for romance?"

Her blush was instantaneous. "That's a rather personal question, don't you think?"

Benedict shrugged and started to say something utterly flip, like "It was worth a try," but as he watched her face, her cheeks turning delightfully pink, her eyes cast down to her lap, the strangest thing happened.

He realized he wanted her.

He really, really wanted her.

He wasn't certain why this so surprised him. Of course he *wanted* her. He was as red-blooded as any man, and one couldn't spend a protracted amount of time around a woman as gamine and adorable as Sophie without wanting her. Hell, he wanted half the women he met, in a purely low-intensity, non-urgent sort of way.

But in that moment, with this woman, it became urgent.

Benedict changed positions. Then he bunched the coverlet up over his lap. Then he changed positions again.

"Is your bed uncomfortable?" Sophie asked. "Do you need me to fluff your pillows?"

Benedict's first urge was to reply in the affirmative, grab her as she leaned across him, and then have his wicked way with her, since they would, rather conveniently, be in bed.

But he had a sneaking suspicion that that particular plan would not go over well with Sophie, so instead he said, "I'm fine," then winced when he realized his voice sounded oddly squeaky.

She smiled as she eyed the biscuits on his plate, saying, "Maybe just one more."

Benedict moved his arm out of the way to allow her easy access to his plate, which was, he realized somewhat belatedly, resting on his lap. The sight of her hand reaching toward his groin—even if she was aiming for a plate of biscuits—did funny things to him, to his groin, to be precise.

Benedict had a sudden vision of things . . . *shifting* down there, and he hastily grabbed the plate, lest it become unbalanced.

"Do you mind if I take the last—"

"Fine!" he croaked.

She plucked a ginger biscuit off the plate and frowned. "You look better," she said, giving the biscuit a little sniff, "but you don't sound better. Is your throat bothering you?"

Benedict took a quick sip of his tea. "Not at all. I must've swallowed a piece of dust."

"Oh. Drink some more tea, then. That shouldn't bother you for long." She set her teacup down. "Would you like me to read to you?"

"Yes!" Benedict said quickly, bunching up his coverlet around his waist. She might try to take away the strategically placed plate, and then where would he be?

"Are you certain you're all right?" she asked, looking far more suspicious than concerned.

He smiled tightly. "Just fine."

"Very well," she said, standing up. "What would you like me to read?"

"Oh, anything," he said with a blithe wave of his hand.

"Poetry?"

"Splendid." He would have said, "Splendid," had she offered to read a dissertation on botany in the arctic tundra.

Sophie wandered over to a recessed bookshelf and idly perused its contents. "Byron?" she asked. "Blake?"

"Blake," he said quite firmly. A hour's worth of Byron's romantic drivel would probably send him quite over the edge.

She slid a slim volume of poetry off the shelf and returned to her chair, swishing her rather unattractive skirts before she sat down.

Benedict frowned. He'd never really noticed before how ugly her dress was. Not as bad as the one Mrs. Crabtree had lent her, but certainly not anything designed to bring out the best in a woman.

He ought to buy her a new dress. She would never accept it, of course, but maybe if her current garments were accidentally *burned . . .*

"Mr. Bridgerton?"

But how could he manage to burn her dress? She'd have to not be wearing it, and that posed a certain challenge in and of itself . . .

"Are you even listening to me?" Sophie demanded.

"Hmmm?"

"You're *not* listening to me."

"Sorry," he admitted. "My apologies. My mind got away from me. Please continue."

She began anew, and in his attempt to show how much attention he was paying her, he focused his eyes on her lips, which proved to be a *big* mistake.

Because suddenly those lips were all he could see, and he couldn't stop thinking about kissing her, and he knew—absolutely knew—that if one of them didn't leave the room in the next thirty seconds, he was going to do something for which he'd owe her a thousand apologies.

Not that he didn't plan to seduce her. Just that he'd rather do it with a bit more finesse.

"Oh, dear," he blurted out.

Sophie gave him an odd look. He didn't blame her. He sounded like a complete idiot. He didn't think he'd uttered the phrase, "Oh, dear," in years. If ever.

Hell, he sounded like his mother.

"Is something wrong?" Sophie asked.

"I just remembered something," he said, rather stupidly, in his opinion.

She raised her brows in question.

"Something that I'd forgotten," Benedict said.

"The things one remembers," she said, looking exceedingly amused, "are most often things one had forgotten."

He scowled at her. "I'll need a bit of privacy."

She stood instantly. "Of course," she murmured.

Benedict fought off a groan. Damn. She looked hurt. He hadn't meant to injure her feelings. He just needed to get her out of the room so that he didn't yank her into the bed. "It's a personal matter," he told her, trying to make her feel better but suspecting that all he was doing was making himself look like a fool.

"Ohhhhh," she said knowingly. "Would you like me to bring you the chamber pot?"

"I can walk to the chamber pot," he retorted, forgetting that he didn't need to use the chamber pot.

She nodded and stood, setting the book of poetry onto a nearby table. "I'll leave you to your business. Just ring the bellpull when you need me."

"I'm not going to summon you like a servant," he growled.

"But I *am* a—"

"Not for me you're not," he said. The words emerged a little more harshly than was necessary, but he'd always detested men who preyed on helpless female servants. The thought that he might be turning into one of those repellent creatures was enough to make him gag.

"Very well," she said, her words meek like a servant. Then she nodded like a servant—he was fairly certain she did it just to annoy him—and left.

The minute she was gone, Benedict leapt out of the bed and ran to the window. Good. No one was in sight. He shrugged off his dressing gown, replaced it with a pair of breeches and a shirt and jacket, and looked out the window again. Good. Still no one.

"Boots, boots," he muttered, glancing around the room. Where the hell were his boots? Not his good boots—the pair for mucking around in the mud . . . ah, there they were. He grabbed the boots and yanked them on.

Back to the window. Still no one. Excellent. Benedict threw one leg over the sill, then another, then grabbed hold of the long, sturdy branch that jutted out from a nearby elm tree. From there it was an easy shimmy, wiggle, and balancing act down to the ground.

And from there it was straight to the lake. To the very cold lake.

To take a very cold swim.

"If he needed the chamber pot," Sophie muttered to herself, "he could have just said so. It's not as if I haven't fetched chamber pots before."

She stamped down the stairs to the main floor, not entirely certain why she was going downstairs (she had nothing specific to do there) but heading in that direction simply because she couldn't think of anything better to do.

She didn't understand why he had so much trouble treating her like what she was—a servant. He kept insisting that she didn't work for him and didn't have to do anything to earn her keep at My Cottage, and then in the same breath assured her that he would find her a position in his mother's household.

If he would just treat her like a servant, she'd have no trouble remembering that she was an illegitimate nobody and he was a member of one of the *ton*'s wealthiest and most influential families. Every time he treated her like a real person (and it was her experience that most aristocrats did not treat servants like anything remotely approaching a real person) it brought her back to the night of the masquerade, when she'd been, for one perfect evening, a lady of glamour and grace—the sort of woman who had a right to dream about a future with Benedict Bridgerton.

He acted as if he actually liked her and enjoyed her company. And maybe he did. But that was the cruelest twist of all, because he was making her love him, making a small part of her think she had the right to dream about him.

And then, inevitably, she had to remind herself of the truth of the situation, and it hurt so damned much.

"Oh, there you are, Miss Sophie!"

Sophie lifted up her eyes, which had been absently following the cracks in the parquet floor, to see Mrs. Crabtree descending the stairs behind her.

"Good day, Mrs. Crabtree," Sophie said. "How is that beef stew coming along?"

"Fine, fine," Mrs. Crabtree said absently. "We were a bit short on carrots, but I think it will be tasty nonetheless. Have you seen Mr. Bridgerton?"

Sophie blinked in surprise at the question. "In his room. Just a minute ago."

"Well, he's not there now."

"I think he had to use the chamber pot."

Mrs. Crabtree didn't even blush; it was the sort of conversation servants often had about their employers. "Well, if he did use it, he didn't *use* it, if you know what I mean," she said. "The room smelled as fresh as a spring day."

Sophie frowned. "And he wasn't there?"

"Neither hide nor hair."

"I can't imagine where he might have gone."

Mrs. Crabtree planted her hands on her ample hips. "I'll search the downstairs and you search the up. One of us is bound to find him."

"I'm not sure that's such a good idea, Mrs. Crabtree. If he's left his room, he probably had a good reason. Most likely, he doesn't want to be found."

"But he's ill," Mrs. Crabtree protested.

Sophie considered that, then pictured his face in her mind. His skin had held a healthy glow and he hadn't looked the least bit tired. "I'm not so certain about that, Mrs. Crabtree," she finally said. "I think he's malingering on purpose."

"Don't be silly," Mrs. Crabtree scoffed. "Mr. Bridgerton would never do something like that."

Sophie shrugged. "I wouldn't have thought so, but truly, he doesn't look the least bit ill any longer."

"It's my tonics," Mrs. Crabtree said with a confident nod. "I told you they'd speed up his recovery."

Sophie had seen Mr. Crabtree dump the tonics in the rosebushes; she'd also seen the aftermath. It hadn't been a pretty sight. How she managed to smile and nod, she'd never know.

"Well, I for one would like to know where he went," Mrs. Crabtree continued. "He shouldn't be out of bed, and he knows it."

"I'm sure he'll return soon," Sophie said placatingly. "In the meantime, do you need any help in the kitchen?"

Mrs. Crabtree shook her head. "No, no. All that stew needs to do now is cook. And besides, Mr. Bridgerton has been scolding me for allowing you to work."

"But—"

"No arguments, if you please," Mrs. Crabtree cut in. "He's right, of course. You're a guest here, and you shouldn't have to lift a finger."

"I'm not a guest," Sophie protested.

"Well, then, what are you?"

That gave Sophie pause. "I have no idea," she finally said, "but I'm definitely not a guest. A guest would be . . . A guest would be . . ." She struggled to make sense of her thoughts and feelings. "I suppose a guest would be someone who is of the same social rank, or at least close to it. A guest would be someone who has never had to wait upon another person, or scrub floors, or empty chamber pots. A guest would be—"

"Anyone the master of the house chooses to invite as a guest," Mrs. Crabtree retorted. "That's the beauty of being the master of the house. You can do anything you please. And you should stop belittling yourself. If Mr. Bridgerton chooses to regard you as a houseguest, then you should accept his judgment and enjoy yourself. When was the last time you were able to live in comfort without having to work your fingers to the bone in return?"

"He can't truly regard me as a houseguest," Sophie said quietly. "If he did, he would have installed a chaperone for the protection of my reputation."

"As if *I* would allow anything untoward in my house," Mrs. Crabtree bristled.

"Of course you wouldn't," Sophie assured her. "But where reputations are at stake, appearance is just as important as fact. And in the eyes of society, a housekeeper does not qualify as a chaperone, no matter how strict and pure her morals may be."

"If that's true," Mrs. Crabtree protested, "then you need a chaperone, Miss Sophie."

"Don't be silly. I don't need a chaperone because I'm not of his class. No one cares if a housemaid lives and works in the household of a single man. No one thinks any less of her, and certainly no one who would consider her for marriage would consider her ruined." Sophie shrugged. "It's the way of the world. And obviously it's the way Mr. Bridgerton thinks, whether he'll admit it or not, because he has never once said a word about it being improper for me to be here."

"Well, I don't like it," Mrs. Crabtree announced. "I don't like it one bit."

Sophie just smiled, because it was so sweet of the housekeeper to care. "I think I'm going to take myself off for a walk," she said, "as long as you're certain you don't need any help in the kitchen. And," she added with a sly grin, "as long as I'm in this strange, hazy position. I might not be a guest, but it is the first time in years I'm not a servant, and I'm going to enjoy my free time while it lasts."

Mrs. Crabtree gave her a hearty pat on the shoulder. "You do that, Miss Sophie. And pick a flower for me while you're out there."

Sophie grinned and headed out the front door. It was a lovely day, unseasonably warm and sunny, and the air held the gentle fragrance of the first blooms of spring. She couldn't recall the last time she'd taken a walk for the simple pleasure of enjoying the fresh air.

Benedict had told her about a nearby pond, and she thought she might amble that way, maybe even dip her toes in the water if she was feeling particularly daring.

She smiled up at the sun. The air might be warm, but the water was surely still freezing, so early in May. Still, it would feel good. Anything felt good that represented leisure time and peaceful, solitary moments.

She paused for a moment, frowning thoughtfully at the horizon. Benedict had mentioned that the lake was south of My Cottage, hadn't he? A southward route would take her right through a rather densely wooded patch, but a bit of a hike certainly wouldn't kill her.

Sophie picked her way through the forest, stepping over tree roots, and pushing aside low-lying branches, letting them snap back behind her with reckless abandon. The sun barely squeaked through the canopy of leaves above her, and down at ground level, it felt more like dusk than midday.

Up ahead, she could see a clearing, which she assumed must be the pond. As she drew closer, she saw the glint of sunlight on water, and she breathed a little sigh of satisfaction, happy to know that she'd gone in the correct direction.

But as she drew even closer, she heard the sound of someone splashing about, and she realized with equal parts terror and curiosity that she was not alone.

She was only ten or so feet from the edge of the pond, easily visible to anyone in the water, so she quickly flattened herself behind the trunk of a large oak. If she had a sensible bone in her body, she'd turn right around and run back to the house, but she just couldn't quite keep herself from peeking around the tree and looking to see who might be mad enough to splash about in a lake so early in the season.

With slow, silent movements, she crept out from behind the tree, trying to keep as much of herself concealed as possible.

And she saw a man.

A *naked* man.

A naked . . .

Benedict?

Chapter 11

The housemaid wars rage on in London. Lady Penwood called Mrs. Featherington a conniving, ill-bred thief in front of no less than three society matrons, including the very popular dowager Viscountess Bridgerton!

Mrs. Featherington responded by calling Lady Penwood's home no better than a workhouse, citing the ill treatment of her lady's maid (whose name, This Author has learned, is not Estelle as was originally claimed, and furthermore, she is not remotely French. The girl's name is Bess, and she hails from Liverpool).

Lady Penwood stalked away from the altercation in quite a huff, followed by her daughter, Miss Rosamund Reiling. Lady Penwood's other daughter, Posy (who was wearing an unfortunate green gown) remained behind with a somewhat apologetic look in her eyes until her mother returned, grabbed her by the sleeve, and dragged her off.

This Author certainly does not make up the guest lists at society parties, but it is difficult to imagine that the Penwoods will be invited to Mrs. Featherington's next soirée.

LADY WHISTLEDOWN'S SOCIETY PAPERS, 7 MAY 1817

It was wrong of her to stay.

So wrong.

So very, very wrong.

And yet she did not move an inch.

She found a large, bald-pated rock, mostly obscured by a short, squat bush, and sat down, never once taking her eyes off of him.

He was *naked*. She still couldn't quite believe it.

He was, of course, partially submerged, with the edge of the water rippling against his rib cage.

The *lower*—she thought giddily—edge of his rib cage.

Or perhaps if she were to be honest with herself, she'd have to rephrase her previous thought to: He was, *unfortunately*, partially submerged.

Sophie was as innocent as the next . . . as, well, the next innocent, but dash it all, she was curious, and she was more than halfway in love with this man. Was it so very wicked to wish for a huge gust of wind, powerful enough to create a small tidal wave that would whip the water away from his body and deposit it somewhere else? Anywhere else?

Very well, it was wicked. *She* was wicked, and she didn't care.

She'd spent her life taking the safe road, the prudent path. Only one night in her short life had she completely thrown caution to the wind. And that night had been the most thrilling, the most magical, the most stupendously wonderful night of her life.

And so she decided to remain right where she was, stay the course, and see what she saw. It wasn't as if she had anything to lose. She had no job, no prospects save for Benedict's promise to find her a position in his mother's household (and she had a feeling that would be a very bad idea, anyway).

And so she sat back, tried not to move a muscle, and kept her eyes wide, wide open.

Benedict had never been a superstitious man, and he'd certainly never thought himself the sort with a sixth sense, but once or twice in his life, he'd experienced a strange surge of awareness, a sort of mystical tingling feeling that warned him that something important was afoot.

The first time had been the day his father had died. He'd never told anyone about this, not even his older brother Anthony, who'd been utterly devastated by their father's death, but that afternoon, as he and Anthony had raced across the fields of Kent in some silly horse race, he'd felt an odd, numb feeling in his arms and legs, followed by the strangest pounding in his head. It hadn't hurt, precisely, but it had sucked the air from his lungs and left him with the most intense sensation of terror he could ever imagine.

He'd lost the race, of course; it was difficult to grip reins when one's fingers refused to work properly. And when he'd returned home, he'd discovered that his terror had not been unwarranted. His father was already dead, having collapsed after being stung by a bee. Benedict still had difficulty believing that a man as strong and vital as his father could be felled by a bee, but there had been no other explanation.

The second time it had happened, however, the feeling had been completely different. It had been the night of his mother's masquerade, right before he'd seen the woman in the silver dress. Like the time before, the sensation had started in his arms and legs, but instead of feeling numb, this time he felt an odd tingling, as if he'd just suddenly come alive after years of sleepwalking.

Then he'd turned and seen her, and he'd known she was the reason he was there that night; the reason he lived in England; hell, the very reason he'd been born.

Of course, she had gone and proven him wrong by disappearing into thin air, but at the time he'd believed all that, and if she'd let him, he would have proven it to her as well.

Now, as he stood in the pond, the water lapping at his midriff, just above his navel, he was struck once again by that odd sense of somehow being more alive than he'd been just seconds earlier. It was a good feeling, an exciting, breathless rush of emotion.

It was like before. When he'd met *her*.

Something was about to happen, or maybe someone was near.

His life was about to change.

And he was, he realized with wry twist of his lips, naked as the day he was born. It didn't exactly put a man at an advantage, at least not unless he was in between a pair of silk sheets with an attractive young woman at his side.

Or underneath.

He took a step into slightly deeper waters, the soft sludge of the pondbottom squishing between his toes. Now the water reached a couple of inches higher. He was bloody well freezing, but at least he was mostly covered up.

He scanned the shore, looking up into trees and down in the bushes. There had to be someone there. Nothing else could account for the strange, tingling feeling that had now spread throughout his body.

And if his body could tingle while submerged in a lake so cold, he was terrified to see his own privates (the poor things felt like they'd shrunk to nothing, which was *not* what a man liked to imagine), then it must be a very strong tingle indeed.

"Who is out there?" he called out.

No answer. He hadn't really expected one, but it had been worth a try.

He squinted as he searched the shore again, turning a full three hundred and sixty degrees as he watched for any sign of movement. He saw nothing but the gentle ruffling of the leaves in the wind, but as he finished his sweep of the area, he somehow *knew*.

"Sophie!"

He heard a gasp, followed by a huge flurry of activity.

"Sophie Beckett," he yelled, "if you run from me right now, I swear I will follow you, and I will not take the time to don my clothing."

The noises coming from the shore slowed.

"I *will* catch up with you," he continued, "because I'm stronger and faster. And I might very well feel compelled to tackle you to the ground, just to be certain you do not escape."

The sounds of her movement ceased.

"Good," he grunted. "Show yourself."

She didn't.

"Sophie," he warned.

There was a beat of silence, followed by the sound of slow, hesitant footsteps, and then he saw her, standing on the shore in one of those awful dresses he'd like to see sunk to the bottom of the Thames.

"What are you doing here?" he demanded.

"I went for a walk. What are *you* doing here?" she countered. "You're supposed to be ill. That"—she waved her arm toward him and, by extension, the pond—"can't possibly be good for you."

He ignored her question and comment. "Were you following me?"

"Of course not," she replied, and he rather believed her. He didn't think she possessed the acting talents to fake that level of righteousness.

"I would never follow you to a swimming hole," she continued. "It would be indecent."

And then her face went completely red, because they both knew she hadn't a leg to stand on with that argument. If she had truly been concerned about decency, she'd have left the pond the second she'd seen him, accidentally or not.

He lifted one hand from the water and pointed toward her, twisting his wrist as he motioned for her to turn around. "Give me your back while you wait for me," he ordered. "It will only take me a moment to pull on my clothing."

"I'll go home right now," she offered. "You'll enjoy greater privacy, and—"

"You'll stay," he said firmly.

"But—"

He crossed his arms. "Do I look like a man in the mood to be argued with?"

She stared at him mutinously.

"If you run," he warned, "I *will* catch you."

Sophie eyed the distance between them, then tried to judge the distance back to My Cottage. If he stopped to pull on his clothing she might have a chance of escaping, but if he *didn't* . . .

"Sophie," he said, "I can practically see the steam coming out of your ears. Stop taxing your brain with useless mathematical computations and do as I asked."

One of her feet twitched. Whether it was itching to run home or merely turn around, she'd never know.

"Now," he ordered.

With a loud sigh and grumble, Sophie crossed her arms and turned around to stare at a knothole in the tree trunk in front of her as if her very life depended on it. The infernal man wasn't being particularly quiet as he went about his business, and she couldn't seem to keep herself from listening to and trying to identify every sound that rustled and splashed behind her. Now he was emerging from the water, now he was reaching for his breeches, now he was . . .

It was no use. She had a dreadfully wicked imagination, and there was no getting around it.

He should have just let her return to the house. Instead she was forced to wait, utterly mortified, while he dressed. Her skin felt like it was on fire, and she was certain her cheeks must be eight different shades of red. A gentleman would have let her weasel out of her embarrassment and hole up in her room back at the house for at least three days in hopes that he'd just forget about the entire affair.

But Benedict Bridgerton was obviously determined not to be a gentleman this afternoon, because when she moved one of her feet—just to flex her toes, which were falling asleep in her shoes, honest!—barely half a second passed before he growled, "Don't even think about it."

"I wasn't!" she protested. "My foot was falling asleep. And hurry up! It can't possibly take so long to get dressed."

"Oh?" he drawled.

"You're doing this just to torture me," she grumbled.

"You may feel free to face me at any time," he said, his voice laced with quiet amusement. "I assure you that I asked you to turn your back for the sake of *your* sensibilities, not mine."

"I'm just fine where I am," she replied.

After what seemed like an hour but what was probably only three minutes, she heard him say, "You may turn around now."

Sophie was almost afraid to do so. He had just the sort of perverse sense of humor that would compel him to order her around before he'd donned his clothing.

But she decided to trust him—not, she was forced to admit, that she had much choice in the matter—and so she turned around. Much to her relief and, if she was to be honest with herself, a fair bit of disappointment, he was quite decently dressed, save for a smattering of damp spots where the water from his skin had seeped through the fabric of his clothing.

"Why didn't you just let me run home?" she asked.

"I wanted you here," he said simply.

"But why?" she persisted.

He shrugged. "I don't know. Punishment, perhaps, for spying on me."

"I wasn't—" Sophie's denial was automatic, but she cut herself off halfway through, because of course she'd been spying on him.

"Smart girl," he murmured.

She scowled at him. She would have liked to have said something utterly droll and witty, but she had a feeling that anything emerging from her mouth just then would have been quite the opposite, so she held her tongue. Better to be a silent fool than a talkative one.

"It's very bad form to spy on one's host," he said, planting his hands on his hips and somehow managing to look both authoritative and relaxed at the same time.

"It was an accident," she grumbled.

"Oh, I believe you there," he said. "But even if you didn't intend to spy on me, the fact remains that when the opportunity arose, you took it."

"Do you blame me?"

He grinned. "Not at all. I would have done precisely the same thing."

Her mouth fell open.

"Oh, don't pretend to be offended," he said.

"I'm not pretending."

He leaned a bit closer. "To tell the truth, I'm quite flattered."

"It was academic curiosity," she ground out. "I assure you."

His smile grew sly. "So you're telling me that you would have spied upon any naked man you'd come across?"

"Of course not!"

"As I said," he drawled, leaning back against a tree, "I'm flattered."

"Well, now that we have that settled," Sophie said with a sniff, "I'm going back to Your Cottage."

She made it only two steps before his hand shot out and grabbed a small measure of the fabric of her dress. "I don't think so," he said.

Sophie turned back around with a weary sigh. "You have already embarrassed me beyond repair. What more could you possibly wish to do to me?"

Slowly, he reeled her in. "That's a very interesting question," he murmured.

Sophie tried to plant her heels into the ground, but she was no match for the inexorable tug of his hand. She stumbled slightly, then found herself mere inches away from him. The air suddenly felt hot, very hot, and Sophie had the bizarre sense that she no longer quite knew how to work her hands and feet. Her skin tingled, her heart raced, and the bloody man was just staring at her, not moving a muscle, not pulling her the final few inches against him.

Just staring at her.

"Benedict?" she whispered, forgetting that she still called him Mr. Bridgerton.

He smiled. It was a small, knowing sort of smile, one that sent chills right down her spine to another area altogether. "I like when you say my name," he said.

"I didn't mean to," she admitted.

He touched a finger to her lips. "Shhh," he admonished. "Don't tell me that. Don't you know that's not what a man wishes to hear?"

"I don't have much experience with men," she said.

"Now that's what a man wishes to hear."

"Really?" she asked dubiously. She knew men wanted innocence in their wives, but Benedict wasn't about to marry a girl like her.

He touched her cheek with one fingertip. "It's what I want to hear from *you*."

A soft rush of air crossed Sophie's lips as she gasped. He was going to kiss her.

He was going to kiss her. It was the most wonderful and awful thing that could possibly happen.

But oh, how she wanted this.

She knew she was going to regret this tomorrow. She let out a smothered, choking sort of laugh. Who was she kidding? She'd regret it in ten minutes. But she had spent the last two years remembering what it felt like to be in his arms, and she wasn't sure she'd make it through the rest of her days without at least one more memory to keep her going.

His finger floated across her cheek to her temple, and then from there traced her eyebrow, ruffling the soft hairs as it moved to the bridge of her nose. "So pretty," he said softly, "like a storybook fairy. Sometimes I think you couldn't possibly be real."

Her only reply was a quickening of breath.

"I think I'm going to kiss you," he whispered.

"You think?"

"I think I *have* to kiss you," he said, looking as if he couldn't quite believe his own words. "It's rather like breathing. One doesn't have much choice in the matter."

Benedict's kiss was achingly tender. His lips brushed across hers in a feather-light caress, back and forth with just the barest hint of friction. It was utterly breathtaking, but there was something more, something that made her dizzy and weak. Sophie clutched at his shoulders, wondering why she felt so off-balance and strange, and then it suddenly came to her—

It was just like before.

The way his lips brushed hers so soft and sweet, the way he began with gentle titillation, rather than forcing entry—it was just what he'd done at the masquerade. After two years of dreams, Sophie was finally reliving the single most exquisite moment of her life.

"You're crying," Benedict said, touching her cheek.

Sophie blinked, then reached up to wipe away the tears she hadn't even known were falling.

"Do you want me to stop?" he whispered.

She shook her head. No, she didn't want him to stop. She wanted him to kiss her just as he had at the masquerade, the gentle caress giving way to a more passionate joining. And then she wanted him to kiss her some more, because this time the clock wasn't going to strike midnight, and she wouldn't have to flee.

And she wanted him to know that she was the woman from the masquerade. And she desperately prayed that he would never recognize her. And she was just so bloody confused, and . . .

And he kissed her.

Really kissed her, with fierce lips and probing tongue, and all the passion and desire a woman could ever want. He made her feel beautiful, precious, priceless. He treated her like a woman, not some serving wench, and until that very moment, she hadn't realized just how much she missed being treated like a person. Gentry and aristocrats didn't see their servants, they tried not to hear them, and when they were forced to converse, they kept it as short and perfunctory as possible.

But when Benedict kissed her, she felt real.

And when he kissed her, he did so with his entire body. His lips, which had begun the intimacy with such gentle reverence, were now fierce and demanding on hers. His hands, so large and strong they seemed to cover half her back, held her to him with a strength that left her breathless. And his body—dear God, it ought to be illegal the way it was pressed against hers, the heat of it seeping through her clothing, searing her very soul.

He made her shiver. He made her melt.

He made her want to give herself to him, something she'd sworn she would never do outside the sacrament of marriage.

"Oh, Sophie," he murmured, his voice husky against her lips. "I've never felt—"

Sophie stiffened, because she was fairly certain he'd intended to say he'd never felt that way before, and she had no idea how she felt about that. On the one hand, it was thrilling to be the one woman who could bring him to his knees, make him dizzy with desire and need.

On the other hand, he'd kissed her before. Hadn't he felt the same exquisite torture then, too?

Dear God, was she jealous of herself?

He pulled back a half inch. "What's wrong?"

She gave her head a little shake. "Nothing."

Benedict touched his fingers to the tip of her chin and tilted her face up. "Don't lie to me, Sophie. What's wrong?"

"I'm—I'm only nervous," she stammered. "That's all."

His eyes narrowed with concerned suspicion. "Are you certain?"

"Absolutely certain." She tugged herself from his grasp and took a few steps away from him, her arms hugging over her chest. "I don't do this sort of thing, you know."

Benedict watched her walk away, studying the bleak line of her back. "I know," he said softly. "You're not the sort of girl who would."

She gave a little laugh at that, and even though he could not see her face, he could well imagine its expression. "How do you know that?" she asked.

"It's obvious in everything you do."

She didn't turn around. She didn't say anything.

And then, before he had any idea what he was saying, the most bizarre question tumbled from his mouth. "Who are you, Sophie?" he asked. "Who are you, really?"

She still didn't turn around, and when she spoke, her voice was barely above a whisper. "What do you mean?"

"Something isn't quite right about you," he said. "You speak too well to be a maid."

Her hand was nervously fidgeting with the folds of her skirt as she said, "Is it a crime to wish to speak well? One can't get very far in this country with a lowborn accent."

"One could make the argument," he said with deliberate softness, "that you haven't gotten very far."

Her arms straightened into sticks. Straight rigid sticks with little tight fists at the end. And then, while he waited for her to say something, she started walking away.

"Wait!" he called out, and he caught up with her in under three strides, grabbing hold of her wrist. He tugged at her until she was forced to turn around. "Don't go," he said.

"It is not my habit to remain in the company of people who insult me."

Benedict nearly flinched, and he knew he would be forever haunted by the stricken look in her eyes. "I wasn't insulting you," he said, "and you know it. I was speaking the truth. You're not meant to be a housemaid, Sophie. It's clear to me, and it ought to be clear to you."

She laughed—a hard, brittle sound he'd never thought to hear from her. "And what do you suggest I do, Mr. Bridgerton?" she asked. "Find work as a governess?"

Benedict thought that was a fine idea, and he started to tell her so, but she interrupted him, saying, "And who do you think will hire me?"

"Well . . ."

"No one," she snapped. "No one will hire me. I have no references, and I look far too young."

"And pretty," he said grimly. He'd never given much thought to the hiring of governesses, but he knew that the duty usually fell to the mother of the house. And common sense told him that no mother wanted to bring such a pretty young thing into her household. Just look what Sophie had had to endure at the hands of Phillip Cavender.

"You could be a lady's maid," he suggested. "At least then you wouldn't be cleaning chamber pots."

"You'd be surprised," she muttered.

"A companion to an elderly lady?"

She sighed. It was a sad, weary sound, and it nearly broke his heart. "You're very kind to try to help me," she said, "but I have already explored all of those avenues. Besides, I am not your responsibility."

"You could be."

She looked at him in surprise.

In that moment, Benedict knew that he had to have her. There was a connection between them, a strange, inexplicable bond that he'd felt only one other time in his life, with the mystery lady from the masquerade. And while she was gone, vanished into thin air, Sophie was very real. He was tired of mirages. He wanted someone he could see, someone he could touch.

And she needed him. She might not realize it yet, but she needed him. Benedict took her hand and tugged, catching her off-balance and wrapping her to him when she fell against his body.

"Mr. Bridgerton!" she yelped.

"Benedict," he corrected, his lips at her ear.

"Let me—"

"Say my name," he persisted. He could be very stubborn when it suited his interests, and he wasn't going to let her go until he heard his name cross her lips.

And maybe not even then.

"Benedict," she finally relented. "I—"

"Hush." He silenced her with his mouth, nibbling at the corner of her lips. When she went soft and compliant in his arms, he drew back, just far enough so that he could focus on her eyes. They looked impossibly green in the late-afternoon light, deep enough to drown in.

"I want you to come back to London with me," he whispered, the words tumbling forth before he had a chance to consider them. "Come back and live with me."

She looked at him in surprise.

"Be mine," he said, his voice thick and urgent. "Be mine right now. Be mine forever. I'll give you anything you want. All I want in return is you."

Chapter 12

Speculation continues to abound concerning the disappearance of Benedict Bridgerton. According to Eloise Bridgerton, who as his sister ought to know, he was due back in town several days ago.

But as Eloise must be the first to admit, a man of Mr. Bridgerton's age and stature need hardly report his whereabouts to his younger sister.

LADY WHISTLEDOWN'S SOCIETY PAPERS, 9 MAY 1817

"You want me to be your mistress," she said flatly.

He gave her a confused look, although she couldn't be sure whether that was because her statement was so obvious or because he objected to her choice of words. "I want you to be with me," he persisted.

The moment was so staggeringly painful and yet she found herself almost smiling. "How is that different from being your mistress?"

"Sophie—"

"How is it different?" she repeated, her voice growing strident.

"I don't know, Sophie." He sounded impatient. "Does it matter?"

"It does to me."

"Fine," he said in a short voice. "Fine. Be my mistress, and have *this.*"

Sophie had just enough time to gasp before his lips descended on hers with a ferocity that turned her knees to water. It was like no kiss they'd ever shared, harsh with need, and laced with an odd, strange anger.

His mouth devoured hers in a primitive dance of passion. His hands seemed to be everywhere, on her breasts, around her waist, even under her skirt. He touched and squeezed, caressed and stroked.

And all the while, he had her pressed up so tightly against him she was certain she'd melt into his skin.

"I want you," he said roughly, his lips finding the hollow at the base of her throat. "I want you right now. I want you here."

"Benedict—"

"I want you in my bed," he growled. "I want you tomorrow. And I want you the next day."

She was wicked, and she was weak, and she gave in to the moment, arching her neck to allow him greater access. His lips felt so good against her skin, sending shivers and tingles to the very center of her being. He made her long for him, long for all the things she couldn't have, and curse the things she could.

And then somehow she was on the ground, and he was there with her, half-on and half-off of her body. He seemed so large, so powerful, and in that moment, so perfectly *hers*. A very small part of Sophie's mind was still functioning, and she knew that she had to say no, had to put a stop to the madness, but God help her, she couldn't. Not yet.

She'd spent so long dreaming about him, trying desperately to remember the scent of his skin, the sound of his voice. There had been many nights when the fantasy of him had been all that had kept her company.

She had been living on dreams, and she wasn't a woman for whom many had come true. She didn't want to lose this one just yet.

"Benedict," she murmured, touching the crisp silkiness of his hair and pretending—pretending that he hadn't just asked her to be his mistress, that she was someone else—anyone else.

Anyone but the bastard daughter of a dead earl, with no means of support besides waiting on others.

Her murmurings seemed to embolden him, and his hand, which had been tickling her knee for so long, started to inch upward, squeezing the soft skin of her thigh. Years of hard work had made her lean, not fashionably curvy, but he didn't seem to mind. In fact, she could feel his heart begin to beat even more rapidly, hear his breath coming in hoarser gasps.

"Sophie, Sophie, Sophie," he groaned, his lips moving frantically along her face until they found her mouth again. "I need you." He pressed his hips hotly against hers. "Do you feel how I need you?"

"I need you, too," she whispered. And she did. There was a fire burning within her that had been simmering quietly for years. The sight of him had ignited it anew, and his touch was like kerosene, sending her into a conflagration.

His fingers wrestled with the large, poorly made buttons on the back of her dress. "I'm going to burn this," he grunted, his other hand relentlessly stroking the tender skin at the back of her knee. "I'll dress you in silks, in satins." He moved to her ear, nipping at her lobe, then licking the tender skin where her ear met her cheek. "I'll dress you in nothing at all."

Sophie stiffened in his arms. He'd managed to say the one thing that could remind her why she was here, why he was kissing her. It wasn't love, or any of those tender emotions she'd dreamed about, but lust. And he wanted to make her a kept woman.

Just as her mother had been.

Oh, God, it was so tempting. So impossibly tempting. He was offering her a life of ease and luxury, a life with *him*.

At the price of her soul.

No, that wasn't entirely true, or entirely a problem. She might be able to live as a man's mistress. The benefits—and how could she consider life with Benedict anything but a benefit—might outweigh the drawbacks. But while she might be willing to make such decisions with her own life and reputation, she would not do so for a child. And how could there not be a child? All mistresses eventually had children.

With a tortured cry, she gave him a shove and wrenched herself away, rolling to the side until she found herself on her hands and knees, stopping to catch her breath before hauling herself to her feet.

"I can't do this, Benedict," she said, barely able to look at him.

"I don't see why not," he muttered.

"I can't be your mistress."

He rose to his feet. "And why is that?"

Something about him pricked at her. Maybe it was the arrogance of his tone, maybe it was the insolence in his posture. "Because I don't want to," she snapped.

His eyes narrowed, not with suspicion, but with anger. "You wanted to just a few seconds ago."

"You're not being fair," she said in a low voice. "I wasn't thinking."

His chin jutted out belligerently. "You're not supposed to be thinking. That's the point of it."

She blushed as she redid her buttons. He'd done a very good job of making her not think. She'd almost thrown away a lifetime of vows and morals, all at one wicked kiss. "Well, I won't be your mistress," she said again. Maybe if she said it enough, she'd feel more confident that he wouldn't be able to break down her defenses.

"And what are you going to do instead?" he hissed. "Work as a housemaid?"

"If I have to."

"You'd rather wait on people—polish their silver, scrub out their damned chamber pots—than come and live with me."

She said only one word, but it was low and true. "Yes."

His eyes flashed furiously. "I don't believe you. No one would make that choice."

"I did."

"You're a fool."

She said nothing.

"Do you understand what you're giving up?" he persisted, his arm waving wildly as he spoke. She'd hurt him, she realized. She'd hurt him and insulted his pride, and he was lashing out like a wounded bear.

Sophie nodded, even though he wasn't looking at her face.

"I could give you whatever you wanted," he bit off. "Clothes, jewels—Hell, forget about the clothes and jewels, I could give you a bloody roof over your head, which is more than you have now."

"That is true," she said quietly.

He leaned forward, his eyes burning hot into hers. "I could give you everything."

Somehow she managed to stand up straight, and somehow she managed not to cry. And somehow she even managed to keep her voice even as she said, "If you think that's everything, then you probably wouldn't understand why I must refuse."

She took a step back, intending to head to His Cottage and pack her meager bag, but he obviously wasn't through with her yet, because he stopped her with a strident, "Where are you going?"

"Back to the cottage," she said. "To pack my bag."

"And where do you think you're going to go with that bag?"

Her mouth fell open. Surely he didn't expect her to *stay*.

"Do you have a job?" he demanded. "A place to go?"

"No," she replied, "but—"

He planted his hands on his hips and glared at her. "And you think I'm going to just let you leave here, with no money or prospects?"

Sophie was so surprised she started to blink uncontrollably. "W-well," she stammered, "I didn't think—"

"No, you *didn't* think," he snapped.

She just stared at him, eyes wide and lips parted, unable to believe what she was hearing.

"You bloody fool," he swore. "Do you have any idea how dangerous it is in the world for a woman alone?"

"Er, yes," she managed. "Actually, I do."

If he heard her, he gave no indication, just went on about "men who take advantage" and "helpless women" and "fates worse than death." Sophie wasn't positive, but she thought she even heard the phrase, "roast beef and pudding." About halfway through his tirade, she lost all ability to focus on his words. She just kept watching his mouth and hearing the tone of his voice, all the while trying to comprehend the fact that he seemed remarkably concerned for her welfare, considering that she'd just summarily rejected him.

"Are you even listening to a word I'm saying?" Benedict demanded.

Sophie didn't nod or shake her head, instead doing an odd combination of both.

Benedict swore under his breath. "That's it," he announced. "You're coming back to London with me."

That seemed to wake her up. "I just said I'm not!"

"You don't have to be my damned mistress," he bit off. "But I'm not leaving you to fend for yourself."

"I was fending for myself quite adequately before I met you."

"Adequately?" he sputtered. "At the Cavenders'? You call that adequate?"

"You're not being fair!"

"And you're not being intelligent."

Benedict thought that his argument was most reasonable, if a little overbearing, but Sophie obviously did not agree, because, much to his surprise, he found himself lying faceup on the ground, having been felled by a remarkably quick right hook.

"Don't you ever call me stupid," she hissed.

Benedict blinked, trying to get his eyesight back to the point where he only saw one of her. "I wasn't—"

"Yes, you were," she replied in a low, angry voice. Then she turned on her heel, and in the split second before she stalked away, he realized he had only one way to stop her. He certainly wasn't going to make it to his feet with anything resembling speed in his current befuddled state, so he reached out and grabbed one of her ankles with both of his hands, sending her sprawling onto the ground right next to him.

It wasn't a particularly gentlemanly maneuver, but beggars really couldn't be choosers, and besides, she had thrown the first punch.

"You're not going anywhere," he growled.

Sophie slowly lifted her head, spitting out dirt as she glared at him. "I cannot believe," she said scathingly, "that you just did that."

Benedict let go of her foot and hauled himself to a crouching position. "Believe it."

"You—"

He held up a hand. "Don't say anything now. I beg you."

Her eyes bugged out. "You're begging me?"

"I hear your voice," he informed her, "therefore you must be speaking."

"But—"

"And as for begging you," he said, effectively cutting her off again, "I assure you it was merely a figure of speech."

She opened her mouth to say something, then obviously thought the better of it, clamping her lips shut with the petulant look of a three-year-old. Benedict let out a short breath, then offered her his hand. She was, after all, still sitting in the dirt and not looking especially happy about it.

She stared at his hand with remarkable revulsion, then moved her gaze to his face and glared at him with such ferocity that Benedict wondered if he had recently sprouted horns. Still not saying a word, she ignored his offer of help and hefted herself to her feet.

"As you like," he murmured.

"A poor choice of words," she snapped, then started marching away.

As Benedict was on his feet this time, he felt no need to incapacitate her. Instead, he dogged her every step, remaining a mere (and annoying, he was sure) two paces behind her. Finally, after about a minute, she turned around and said, "Please leave me alone."

"I'm afraid I can't," he said.

"Can't or won't?"

He thought about that for a moment. "Can't."

She scowled at him and kept walking.

"I find it as difficult to believe as you do," Benedict called out, keeping pace with her.

She stopped and turned around. "That is impossible."

"I can't help it," he said with a shrug. "I find myself completely unwilling to let you go."

" 'Unwilling' is a far cry from 'can't.' "

"I didn't save you from Cavender just to let you squander your life away."

"That isn't your choice to make."

She had a point there, but he wasn't inclined to give it to her. "Perhaps," he allowed, "but I'm going to make it, anyway. You're coming with me to London. We will discuss it no further."

"You're trying to punish me," she said, "because I refused you."

"No," he said slowly, considering her words even as he answered. "No, I'm not. I'd like to punish you, and in my current state of mind I'd even go so far as to say you deserve to be punished, but that's not why I'm doing it."

"Then why are you?"

"It's for your own good."

"That's the most condescending, patronizing—"

"I'm sure you're right," he allowed, "but nonetheless, in this particular case, at this particular moment, I know what's best for you, and you clearly don't, so—*don't* hit me again," he warned.

Sophie looked down at her fist, which she hadn't even realized was pulled back and ready to fly. He was turning her into a monster. There was no other explanation. She didn't think she'd ever hit anyone in her life, and here she was ready to do it for the second time that day.

Eyes never leaving her hand, she slowly unclenched her fist, stretching her fingers out like a starfish and holding them there for the count of three. "How," she said in a very low voice, "do you intend to stop me from going my way?"

"Does it really matter?" he asked, shrugging nonchalantly. "I'm sure I'll think of something."

Her mouth fell open. "Are you saying you'd tie me up and—"

"*I* didn't say anything of the sort," he cut in with a wicked grin. "But the idea certainly has its charms."

"You are despicable," she spat.

"And you sound like the heroine of a very poorly written novel," he replied. "What did you say you were reading this morning?"

Sophie felt the muscles working frenetically in her cheek, felt her jaw clenching to the point where she was certain her teeth would shatter. How Benedict managed to be the most wonderful and the most awful man in the world at the very same time, she would never understand. Right now, though, the awful side seemed to be winning, and she was quite certain—logic aside—that if she remained in his company one more second, her head would explode.

"I'm leaving!" she said, with, in her opinion, great drama and resolve.

But he just answered her with a sly half smile, and said, "I'm following."

And the bloody man remained two strides behind her the entire way home.

———————

Benedict didn't often go out of his way to annoy people (with the notable exception of his siblings), but Sophie Beckett clearly brought out the devil in him. He stood in the doorway to her room as she packed, casually lounging against the doorframe. His arms were crossed in a manner that he somehow knew would vex her, and his right leg was slightly bent, the toe of his boot stubbed up against the floor.

"Don't forget your dress," he said helpfully.

She glared at him.

"The ugly one," he added, as if clarification were necessary.

"They're both ugly," she spat out.

Ah, a reaction. "I know."

She went back to shoving her belongings into her satchel.

He waved an arm expansively. "Feel free to take a souvenir."

She straightened, her hands planted angrily on her hips. "Does that include the silver tea service? Because I could live for several years on what that would fetch."

"You may certainly take the tea service," he replied genially, "as you will not be out of my company."

"I will not be your mistress," she hissed. "I told you, I won't do it. I *can't* do it."

Something about her use of the word "can't" struck him as significant. He mulled that over for a few moments while she gathered up the last of her belongings and cinched shut the drawstring to her satchel.

"That's it," he murmured.

She ignored him, instead marching toward the door and giving him a pointed look.

He knew she wanted him to get out of the way so she could depart. He didn't move a muscle, save for one finger that thoughtfully stroked the side of his jaw. "You're illegitimate," he said.

The blood drained from her face.

"You are," he said, more to himself than to her. Strangely, he felt rather relieved by the revelation. It explained her rejection of him, made it into something that had nothing to do with him and everything to do with her.

It took the sting out.

"I don't care if you're illegitimate," he said, trying not to smile. It was a serious moment, but by God, he wanted to break out in a grin because now she'd come to London with him and be his mistress. There were no more obstacles, and—

"You don't understand anything," she said, shaking her head. "It's not about whether I'm good enough to be your mistress."

"I would care for any children we might have," he said solemnly, pushing himself away from the doorframe.

Her stance grew even more rigid, if that were possible. "And what about your wife?"

"I don't have a wife."

"Ever?"

He froze. A vision of the masquerade lady danced through his mind. He'd pictured her many ways. Sometimes she wore her silver ballgown, sometimes nothing at all.

Sometimes she wore a wedding dress.

Sophie's eyes narrowed as she watched his face, then she snorted derisively as she stalked past him.

He followed. "That's not a fair question, Sophie," he said, dogging her heels.

She moved down the hall, not even pausing when she reached the stairs. "I think it's more than fair."

He raced down the stairs until he was below her, halting her progress. "I have to marry someday."

Sophie stopped. She had to; he was blocking her path. "Yes, you do," she said. "But I don't have to be anyone's mistress."

"Who was your father, Sophie?"

"I don't know," she lied.

"Who was your mother?"

"She died at my birth."

"I thought you said she was a housekeeper."

"Clearly I misrepresented the truth," she said, past the point of caring that she'd been caught in a lie.

"Where did you grow up?"

"It's of no interest," she said, trying to squirm her way past him.

One of his hands wrapped itself around her upper arm, holding her firmly in place. "I find it very interesting."

"Let me go!"

Her cry pierced the silence of the hall, loud enough so that the Crabtrees would certainly come running to save her. Except that Mrs. Crabtree had gone to the village, and Mr. Crabtree was outside, out of earshot. There was no one to help her, and she was at his mercy.

"I can't let you go," he whispered. "You're not cut out for a life of servitude. It will kill you."

"If it were going to kill me," she returned, "it would have done so years ago."

"But you don't have to do this any longer," he persisted.

"Don't you dare try to make this about me," she said, nearly shaking with emotion. "You're not doing this out of concern for my welfare. You just don't like being thwarted."

"That is true," he admitted, "but I also won't see you cast adrift."

"I have been adrift all my life," she whispered, and she felt the traitorous sting of tears prick her eyes. God above, she didn't want to cry in front of this man. Not now, not when she felt so off-balance and weak.

He touched her chin. "Let me be your anchor."

Sophie closed her eyes. His touch was painfully sweet, and a not very small part of her was aching to accept his offer, to leave the life she'd been forced to live and cast her lot with him, this marvelous, wonderful, infuriating man who had haunted her dreams for years.

But the pain of her childhood was still too fresh. And the stigma of her illegitimacy felt like a brand on her soul.

She would not do this to another child.

"I can't," she whispered. "I wish——"

"What do you wish?" he asked urgently.

She shook her head. She'd been about to tell him that she wished that she could, but she knew that such words would be unwise. He would only latch on to them, and press his cause anew.

And that would make it all the harder to say no.

"You leave me no choice, then," he stated grimly.

Her eyes met his.

"Either you come with me to London, and——" He held up a silencing hand when she tried to protest. "And I will find you a position in my mother's household," he added pointedly.

"Or?" she asked, her voice sullen.

"Or I will have to inform the magistrate that you have stolen from me."

Her mouth abruptly tasted like acid. "You wouldn't," she whispered.

"I certainly don't want to."

"But you would."

He nodded. "I would."

"They'd hang me," she said. "Or send me to Australia."

"Not if I requested otherwise."

"And what would you request?"

His brown eyes looked strangely flat, and she suddenly realized that he wasn't enjoying the conversation any more than she was.

"I would request," he said, "that you be released into my custody."

"That would be very convenient for you."

His fingers, which had been touching her chin all the while, slid down to her shoulder. "I'm only trying to save you from yourself."

Sophie walked to a nearby window and looked out, surprised that he hadn't tried to stop her. "You're making me hate you, you know," she said.

"I can live with that."

She gave him a curt nod. "I will wait for you in the library, then. I would like to leave today."

Benedict watched her walk away, stood utterly still as the door to the library closed behind her. He knew she would not flee. She was not the sort to go back on her word.

He couldn't let this one go. *She* had left—the great and mysterious "she," he thought with a bitter smile—the one woman who had touched his heart.

The same woman who had not even given him her name.

But now there was Sophie, and she *did* things to him. Things he hadn't felt since *her*. He was sick of pining for a woman who practically didn't exist. Sophie was here, and Sophie would be his.

And, he thought with grim determination, Sophie was *not* going to leave him.

"I can live with you hating me," he said to the closed door. "I just can't live without *you*."

Chapter 13

It was previously reported in this column that This Author predicted a possible match between Miss Rosamund Reiling and Mr. Phillip Cavender. This Author can now say that this is not likely to occur. Lady Penwood (Miss Reiling's mother) has been heard to say that she will not settle for a mere mister, even though Miss Reiling's father, while certainly wellborn, was not a member of the aristocracy.

Not to mention, of course, that Mr. Cavender has begun to show a decided interest in Miss Cressida Cowper.

LADY WHISTLEDOWN'S SOCIETY PAPERS, 9 MAY 1817

Sophie started feeling ill the minute the carriage departed My Cottage. By the time they stopped for the night at an inn in Oxfordshire, she was downright queasy. And when they reached the outskirts of London . . . Well, she was quite convinced she would throw up.

Somehow she managed to keep the contents of her stomach where they belonged, but as their carriage wended farther into the tangled streets of London, she was filled with an intense sense of apprehension.

No, not apprehension. Doom.

It was May, which meant that the season was in full swing. Which meant that Araminta was in residence.

Which meant that Sophie's arrival was a bad, bad idea.

"Very bad," she muttered.

Benedict looked up. "Did you say something?"

She crossed her arms mutinously. "Just that you're a very bad man."

He chuckled. She'd known he would chuckle, and it still irritated her.

He pulled the curtain away from the window and looked out. "We're nearly there," he said.

He'd said that he was taking her directly to his mother's residence. Sophie remembered the grand house in Grosvenor Square as if she'd been there the night before. The ballroom was huge, with hundreds of sconces on the walls, each adorned by a perfect beeswax candle. The smaller rooms had been decorated in the Adam style, with exquisitely scalloped ceilings and pale, pastel walls.

It had been Sophie's dream house, quite literally. In all her dreams of Benedict and their fictional future together, she'd always seen herself in that house. It was silly, she knew, since he was a second son and thus not in line to inherit the property, but still, it was the most beautiful home she'd ever beheld, and dreams weren't meant to be about reality, anyway. If Sophie had wanted to dream her way right into Kensington Palace, that was her prerogative.

Of course, she thought with a wry smile, she wasn't likely ever to see the interior of Kensington Palace.

"What are you smiling about?" Benedict demanded.

She didn't bother to glance up as she replied, "I'm plotting your demise."

He grinned—not that she was looking at him, but it was one of those smiles she could hear in the way he breathed.

She hated that she was that sensitive to his every nuance. Especially since she had a sneaking suspicion that he was the same way about her.

"At least it sounds entertaining," he said.

"What does?" she asked, finally moving her eyes from the lower hem of the curtain, which she'd been staring at for what seemed like hours.

"My demise," he said, his smile crooked and amused. "If you're going to kill me, you might as well enjoy yourself while you're at it, because Lord knows, I won't."

Her jaw dropped a good inch. "You're mad," she said.

"Probably." He shrugged rather casually before settling back in his seat and propping his feet up on the bench across from him. "I've all but kidnapped you, after all. I should think that would qualify as the maddest thing I've ever done."

"You could let me go now," she said, even though she knew he never would.

"Here in London? Where you could be attacked by footpads at any moment? That would be most irresponsible of me, don't you think?"

"It hardly compares to abducting me against my will!"

"I didn't abduct you," he said, idly examining his fingernails. "I blackmailed you. There's a world of difference."

Sophie was saved from having to reply by the jolt of the carriage as it ground to a halt.

Benedict flipped back the curtains one last time, then let them fall into place. "Ah. Here we are."

Sophie waited while he disembarked, then moved to the doorway. She briefly considered ignoring his outstretched hand and jumping down herself, but the carriage was quite high off the ground, and she really didn't wish to make a fool of herself by tripping and landing in the gutter.

It would be nice to insult him, but not at the cost of a sprained ankle.

With a sigh, she took his hand.

"Very smart of you," Benedict murmured.

Sophie looked at him sharply. How did he know what she'd been thinking?

"I almost always know what you're thinking," he said.

She tripped.

"Whoa!" he called out, catching her expertly before she landed in the gutter.

He held her just a moment longer than was necessary before depositing her on the pavement. Sophie would have said something, except that her teeth were ground together far too tightly for words.

"Doesn't the irony just kill you?" Benedict asked, smiling wickedly.

She pried open her jaw. "No, but it may very well kill *you*."

He laughed, the blasted man. "Come along," he said. "I'll introduce you to my mother. I'm sure she'll find some position or another for you."

"She may not have any openings," Sophie pointed out.

He shrugged. "She loves me. She'll make an opening."

Sophie held her ground, refusing to take a single step alongside him until she'd made her point. "I'm not going to be your mistress."

His expression was remarkably bland as he murmured, "Yes, you've said as much."

"No, I mean, your plan isn't going to work."

He was all innocence. "I have a plan?"

"Oh, please," she scoffed. "You're going to try to wear me down in hopes that eventually I'll give in."

"I would never dream of it."

"I'm sure you dream of quite a bit more," she muttered.

He must have heard her, because he chuckled. Sophie crossed her arms mutinously, not caring that she looked most undignified in such a position, standing right there on the pavement in full view of the world. No one would pay her half a mind, anyway, dressed as she was in the coarse woolens of a servant. She supposed she ought to adopt a brighter outlook and approach her new position with a more optimistic attitude, but drat it all, she *wanted* to be sullen just then.

Frankly, she thought she'd earned it. If anyone had a right to be sullen and disgruntled, it was she.

"We *could* stand here on the pavement all day," Benedict said, his voice lightly laced with sarcasm.

She started to shoot him an angry glare, but that was when she noticed where they were standing. They weren't in Grosvenor Square. Sophie wasn't even certain where they were. Mayfair, to be sure, but the house before them definitely wasn't the house at which she'd attended the masquerade.

"Er, is this Bridgerton House?" she asked.

He quirked a brow. "How did you know my home is called Bridgerton House?"

"You've mentioned it." Which was, thankfully, true. He'd talked about both Bridgerton House, and the Bridgertons' country residence, Aubrey Hall, several times during their conversations.

"Oh." He seemed to accept that. "Well, no, actually, it's not. My mother moved out of Bridgerton House nearly two years ago. She hosted one last ball—it was a masquerade, actually—and then turned the residence over to my brother and his wife. She'd always said she would leave just as soon as he married and started a family of his own. I believe his first child was born a mere month after she left."

"Was it a boy or a girl?" she asked, even though she knew the answer. Lady Whistledown always reported such things.

"A boy. Edmund. They had another son, Miles, earlier this year."

"How nice for them," Sophie murmured, even though it felt like her heart were strangling. She wasn't likely to have children of her own, and that was one of the saddest realizations she'd ever reached. Children required a husband, and marriage seemed a pipe dream. She hadn't been raised to be a servant, and thus she had very little in common with most of the men she met in her daily life. Not that the other servants weren't good and honorable people, but it was difficult to imagine sharing her life with someone who, for example, couldn't read.

Sophie didn't need to marry someone of particularly high birth, but even the middle class was out of her reach. No self-respecting man in trade would marry a housemaid.

Benedict motioned for her to follow him, and she did, until they reached the front steps.

Sophie shook her head. "I'll use the side entrance."

His lips thinned. "You'll use the front entrance."

"I'll use the side entrance," she said firmly. "No woman of breeding will hire a maid who enters through the front."

"You're with me," he ground out. "You'll use the front entrance."

A bubble of mirth escaped her lips. "Benedict, just yesterday you wanted me to become your mistress. Would you dare bring your mistress to meet your mother through the front door?"

She'd confounded him with that. Sophie grinned as she watched his face twist with frustration.

She felt better than she had in days.

"Would you," she continued, mostly just to torture him further, "bring your mistress to meet her at all?"

"You're not my mistress," he bit off.

"Indeed."

His chin jutted out, and his eyes bored into hers with barely leashed fury. "You're a bloody little housemaid," he said, his voice low, "because you've insisted upon being a housemaid. And as a housemaid, you are, if somewhat low on the social scale, still utterly respectable. Certainly respectable enough for my mother."

Sophie's smile faltered. She might have pushed him too far.

"Good," Benedict grunted, once it was clear that she was not going to argue the point any further. "Come with me."

Sophie followed him up the steps. This might actually work to her advantage. Benedict's mother surely would not hire a maid who had the effrontery to use the front door. And since she had steadfastly refused to be Benedict's mistress, he would have to accept defeat and allow her to return to the country.

Benedict pushed open the front door, holding it until Sophie entered before him. The butler arrived within seconds.

"Wickham," Benedict said, "kindly inform my mother that I am here."

"I will indeed, Mr. Bridgerton," Wickham replied. "And might I take the liberty of informing you that she has been rather curious as to your whereabouts this past week?"

"I would be shocked if she hadn't been," Benedict replied.

Wickham nodded toward Sophie with an expression that hovered somewhere between curiosity and disdain. "Might I inform her of your guest's arrival?"

"Please do."

"Might I inform her of your guest's identity?"

Sophie looked over at Benedict with great interest, wondering what he'd say.

"Her name is Miss Beckett," Benedict replied. "She is here to seek employment."

One of Wickham's brows rose. Sophie was surprised. She didn't think that butlers were supposed to show any expression whatsoever.

"As a maid?" Wickham inquired.

"As whatever," Benedict said, his tone beginning to show the first traces of impatience.

"Very good, Mr. Bridgerton," Wickham said, and then he disappeared up the staircase.

"I don't think he thought it was very good at all," Sophie whispered to Benedict, careful to hide her smile.

"Wickham is not in charge here."

Sophie let out a little whatever-you-say sort of sigh. "I imagine Wickham would disagree."

He looked at her with disbelief. "He's the butler."

"And I'm a housemaid. I know all about butlers. More, I daresay, than you do."

His eyes narrowed. "You act less like a housemaid than any woman of my acquaintance."

She shrugged and pretended to inspect a still life painting on the wall. "You bring out the worst in me, Mr. Bridgerton."

"Benedict," he hissed. "You've called me by my given name before. Use it now."

"Your mother is about to descend the stairs," she reminded him, "and you are insisting that she hire me as a housemaid. Do many of your servants call you by your given name?"

He glared at her, and she knew he knew she was right. "You can't have it both ways, Mr. Bridgerton," she said, allowing herself a tiny smile.

"I only wanted it *one* way," he growled.

"Benedict!"

Sophie looked up to see an elegant, petite woman descending the stairs. Her coloring was fairer than Benedict's, but her features marked her clearly as his mother.

"Mother," he said, striding to meet her at the bottom of the stairs. "It is good to see you."

"It would be better to see you," she said pertly, "had I known where you were this past week. The last I'd heard you'd gone off to the Cavender party, and then everyone returned without you."

"I left the party early," he replied, "then went off to My Cottage."

His mother sighed. "I suppose I can't expect you to notify me of your every movement now that you're thirty years of age."

Benedict gave her an indulgent smile.

She turned to Sophie. "This must be your Miss Beckett."

"Indeed," Benedict replied. "She saved my life while I was at My Cottage."

Sophie started. "I didn't—"

"She did," Benedict cut in smoothly. "I took ill from driving in the rain, and she nursed me to health."

"You would have recuperated without me," she insisted.

"But not," Benedict said, directing his words at his mother, "with such speed or in such comfort."

"Weren't the Crabtrees at home?" Violet asked.

"Not when we arrived," Benedict replied.

Violet looked at Sophie with such obvious curiosity that Benedict was finally forced to explain, "Miss Beckett had been employed by the Cavenders, but certain circumstances made it impossible for her to stay."

"I . . . see," Violet said unconvincingly.

"Your son saved me from a most unpleasant fate," Sophie said quietly. "I owe him a great deal of thanks."

Benedict looked to her in surprise. Given the level of her hostility toward him, he hadn't expected her to volunteer complimentary information. But he supposed he should have done; Sophie was highly principled, not the sort to let anger interfere with honesty.

It was one of the things he liked best about her.

"I see," Violet said again, this time with considerably more feeling.

"I was hoping you might find her a position in your household," Benedict said.

"But not if it's too much trouble," Sophie hastened to add.

"No," Violet said slowly, her eyes settling on Sophie's face with a curious expression. "No, it wouldn't be any trouble at all, but . . ."

Both Benedict and Sophie leaned forward, awaiting the rest of the sentence.

"Have we met?" Violet suddenly asked.

"I don't think so," Sophie said, stammering slightly. How could

Lady Bridgerton think she knew her? She was positive their paths had not crossed at the masquerade. "I can't imagine how we could have done."

"I'm certain you're right," Lady Bridgerton said with a wave of her hand. "There is something vaguely familiar about you. But I'm sure it's just that I've met someone with similar features. It happens all the time."

"Especially to me," Benedict said with a crooked smile.

Lady Bridgerton looked to her son with obvious affection. "It's not my fault all my children ended up looking remarkably alike."

"If the blame can't be placed with you," Benedict asked, "then where may we place it?"

"Entirely upon your father," Lady Bridgerton replied jauntily. She turned to Sophie. "They all look just like my late husband."

Sophie knew she should remain silent, but the moment was so lovely and comfortable that she said, "I think your son resembles you."

"Do you think?" Lady Bridgerton asked, clasping her hands together with delight. "How lovely. And here I've always just considered myself a vessel for the Bridgerton family."

"Mother!" Benedict said.

She sighed. "Am I speaking too plainly? I do that more and more in my old age."

"You are hardly elderly, Mother."

She smiled. "Benedict, why don't you go visit with your sisters while I take your Miss Bennett—"

"Beckett," he interrupted.

"Yes, of course, Beckett," she murmured. "I shall take her upstairs and get her settled in."

"You need only take me to the housekeeper," Sophie said. It was most odd for a lady of the house to concern herself with the hiring of a housemaid. Granted, the entire situation was unusual, what with Benedict asking that she be hired on, but it was very strange that Lady Bridgerton would take a personal interest in her.

"Mrs. Watkins is busy, I'm sure," Lady Bridgerton said. "Besides, I believe we have need for another lady's maid upstairs. Have you any experience in that area?"

Sophie nodded.

"Excellent. I thought you might. You speak very well."

"My mother was a housekeeper," Sophie said automatically. "She worked for a very generous family and—" She broke off in horror, belatedly remembering that she'd told Benedict the truth—that her mother had died at her birth. She shot him a nervous look, and he answered it with a vaguely mocking tilt of his chin, silently telling her that he wasn't going to expose her lie.

"The family she worked for was very generous," Sophie continued, a relieved rush of air passing across her lips, "and they allowed me to share many lessons with the daughters of the house."

"I see," Lady Bridgerton said. "That explains a great deal. I find it difficult to believe you've been toiling as a housemaid. You are clearly educated enough to pursue loftier positions."

"She reads quite well," Benedict said.

Sophie looked to him in surprise.

He ignored her, instead saying to his mother, "She read to me a great deal during my recuperation."

"Do you write, as well?" Lady Bridgerton asked.

Sophie nodded. "My penmanship is quite neat."

"Excellent. It is always handy to have an extra pair of hands at my disposal when we are addressing invitations. And we do have a ball coming up later in the summer. I have two girls out this year," she explained to Sophie. "I'm hopeful that one of them will choose a husband before the season is through."

"I don't think Eloise wants to marry," Benedict said.

"Quiet your mouth," Lady Bridgerton said.

"Such a statement is sacrilege around here," Benedict said to Sophie.

"Don't listen to him," Lady Bridgerton said, walking toward the stairs. "Here, come with me, Miss Beckett. What did you say your given name was?"

"Sophia. Sophie."

"Come with me, Sophie. I'll introduce you to the girls. And," she added, her nose crinkling with distaste, "we'll find you something new to wear. I cannot have one of our maids dressed so shabbily. A person would think we didn't pay you a fair wage."

It had never been Sophie's experience that members of the *ton* were concerned about paying their servants fairly, and she was touched by Lady Bridgerton's generosity.

"You," Lady Bridgerton said to Benedict. "Wait for me downstairs. We have much to discuss, you and I."

"I'm quaking in my boots," he deadpanned.

"Between him and his brother, I don't know which one of them will kill me first," Lady Bridgerton muttered.

"Which brother?" Sophie asked.

"Either. Both. All three. Scoundrels, the lot of them."

But they were scoundrels she clearly loved. Sophie could hear it in the way she spoke, see it in her eyes when they lit with joy upon seeing her son.

And it made Sophie lonely and wistful and jealous. How different her life might have been had her mother lived through childbirth. They might have been unrespectable, Mrs. Beckett a mistress and Sophie a bastard, but Sophie liked to think that her mother would have loved her.

Which was more than she received from any other adult, her father included.

"Come along, Sophie," Lady Bridgerton said briskly.

Sophie followed her up the stairs, wondering why, if she were merely about to begin a new job, she felt as if she were entering a new family.

It felt . . . nice.

And it had been a long, long while since her life had felt nice.

Chapter 14

Rosamund Reiling swears that she saw Benedict Bridgerton back in London. This Author is inclined to believe the veracity of the account; Miss Reiling can spot an unmarried bachelor at fifty paces.

Unfortunately for Miss Reiling, she can't seem to land one.
LADY WHISTLEDOWN'S SOCIETY PAPERS,
12 MAY 1817

Benedict had barely taken two steps toward the sitting room when his sister Eloise came dashing down the hall. Like all the Bridgertons, she had thick, chestnut hair and a wide smile. Unlike Benedict, however, her eyes were a clear, crisp gray, a shade quite unlike that possessed by any of her brothers and sisters.

"Benedict!" she called out, throwing her arms rather exuberantly around him. "Where have you been? Mother has been grumbling all week, wondering where you'd gone off to."

"Funny, when I spoke to Mother, not two minutes ago, her grumbles were about *you*, wondering when you were finally planning to marry."

Eloise pulled a face. "When I meet someone worth marrying, that's when. I do wish someone new would move to town. I feel as though I meet the same hundred or so people over and over again."

"You *do* meet the same hundred or so people over and over again."

"Exactly my point," she said. "There are no secrets left in London. I already know everything about everyone."

"Really?" Benedict asked, with no small measure of sarcasm.

"Mock me all you want," she said, jabbing her finger toward him in a manner he was *sure* his mother would deem unladylike, "but I am not exaggerating."

"Not even a little bit?" he grinned.

She scowled at him. "Where *were* you this past week?"

He walked into the sitting room and plopped down on a sofa. He probably should have waited for her to sit, but she was just his sister, after all, and he'd never felt the need to stand on ceremony when they were alone. "Went to the Cavender party," he said, propping his feet up on a low table. "It was abominable."

"Mother will kill you if she catches you with your feet up," Eloise said, sitting down in a chair that was kitty-corner to him. "And why was the party so dreadful?"

"The company." He looked at his feet and decided to leave them where they were. "A more boring bunch of lazy louts, I've never met."

"As long as you don't mince words."

Benedict raised a brow at her sarcasm. "You are hereby forbidden from marrying anyone who was in attendance."

"An order I shall probably have no difficulty obeying." She tapped her hands against the arms of her chair. Benedict had to smile; Eloise had always been a bundle of nervous energy.

"But," she said, looking up with narrowed eyes, "that doesn't explain where you were all *week*."

"Has anyone ever told you that you are exceedingly nosy?"

"Oh, all the time. Where were you?"

"And persistent, too."

"It's the only way to be. Where were you?"

"Have I mentioned I'm considering investing in a company that manufactures human-sized muzzles?"

She threw a pillow at him. "Where *were* you?"

"As it happens," he said, gently tossing the pillow back in her direction, "the answer isn't the least bit interesting. I was at My Cottage, recuperating from a nasty cold."

"I thought you'd already recuperated."

He regarded her with an expression that was an unlikely cross between amazement and distaste. "How do you *know* that?"

"I know everything. You should know that by now." She grinned. "Colds can be so nasty. Did you have a setback?"

He nodded. "After driving in the rain."

"Well, that wasn't very smart of you."

"Is there any reason," he asked, glancing about the room as if he were directing his question at someone other than Eloise, "why I am allowing myself to be insulted by my ninnyhammer of a younger sister?"

"Probably because I do it so well." She kicked at his foot, trying to knock it off the table. "Mother will be here at any second, I'm sure."

"No, she won't," he returned. "She's busy."

"Doing what?"

He waved his hand toward the ceiling. "Orienting the new maid."

She sat up straight. "We have a new maid? Nobody told me about it."

"Heavens," he drawled, "something has happened and Eloise doesn't know about it."

She leaned back in her chair, then kicked his foot again. "House-maid? Lady's maid? Scullery?"

"Why do you care?"

"It's always good to know what's what."

"Lady's maid, I believe."

Eloise took all of one half second to digest that. "And how do you know?"

Benedict figured he might as well tell her the truth. The Lord knew, she'd know the whole story by sundown, even if he didn't. "Because I brought her here."

"The maid?"

"No, Mother. Of course the maid."

"Since when do you trouble yourself with the hiring of servants?"

"Since this particular young lady nearly saved my life by nursing me while I was ill."

Eloise's mouth fell open. "You were *that* ill?"

Might as well let her believe he'd been at death's door. A little pity and concern might work to his advantage next time he needed to wheedle her into something. "I have felt better," he said mildly. "Where are you going?"

She'd already risen to her feet. "To go find Mother and meet the new maid. She's probably going to wait on Francesca and me, now that Marie is gone."

"You lost your maid?"

Eloise scowled. "She left us for that odious Lady Penwood."

Benedict had to grin at her description. He remembered his one meeting with Lady Penwood quite well; he, too, had found her odious.

"Lady Penwood is notorious for mistreating her servants. She's gone through three lady's maids this year. Stole Mrs. Featherington's right out from under her nose, but the poor girl only lasted a fortnight."

Benedict listened patiently to his sister's tirade, amazed that he was even interested. And yet for some strange reason, he was.

"Marie will come crawling back in a week, asking us to take her back on, you mark my words," Eloise said.

"I always mark your words," he replied, "I just don't always care."

"You," Eloise returned, pointing her finger at him, "are going to regret that you said that."

He shook his head, smiling faintly. "Doubtful."

"Hmmph. I'm going upstairs."

"Do enjoy yourself."

She poked her tongue out at him—surely not appropriate behavior for a woman of twenty-one—and left the room. Benedict managed to enjoy just three minutes of solitude before footsteps once again sounded in the hall, tapping rhythmically in his direction. When he looked up, he saw his mother in the doorway.

He stood immediately. Certain manners could be ignored for one's sister, but never for one's mother.

"I saw your feet on the table," Violet said before he could even open his mouth.

"I was merely polishing the surface with my boots."

She raised her brows, then made her way to the chair so recently vacated by Eloise and sat down. "All right, Benedict," she said in an extremely no-nonsense voice. "Who is she?"

"Miss Beckett, you mean?"

Violet gave him one businesslike nod.

"I have no idea, save that she worked for the Cavenders and was apparently mistreated by their son."

Violet blanched. "Did he . . . Oh dear. Was she . . ."

"I don't think so," Benedict said grimly. "In fact, I'm certain she wasn't. But not for lack of trying on his part."

"The poor thing. How lucky for her that you were there to save her."

Benedict found he didn't like to relive that night on the Cavenders' lawn. Even though the escapade had ended quite favorably, he could not seem to stop himself from racing through the gamut of "what-ifs." What if he hadn't come along in time? What if Cavender and his friends had been a little less drunk and a little more obstinate? Sophie could have been raped. Sophie *would* have been raped.

And now that he knew Sophie, had grown to care about her, the very notion chilled him to the bone.

"Well," Violet said, "she is not who she says she is. Of that I'm certain."

Benedict sat up straight. "Why do you say that?"

"She is far too educated to be a housemaid. Her mother's employers may have allowed her to share in some of their daughters' lessons, but all of them? I doubt it. Benedict, the girl speaks French!"

"She does?"

"Well, I can't be positive," Violet admitted, "but I caught her looking at a book on Francesca's desk that was written in French."

"Looking is not the same as reading, Mother."

She shot him a peevish look. "I'm telling you, I was looking at the way her eyes were moving. She was reading it."

"If you say so, you must be correct."

Violet's eyes narrowed. "Are you being sarcastic?"

"Normally," Benedict said with a smile, "I would say yes, but in this case, I was speaking quite seriously."

"Perhaps she is the cast-off daughter of an aristocratic family," Violet mused.

"Cast-off?"

"For getting herself with child," she explained.

Benedict was not used to his mother speaking quite so frankly. "Er, no," he said, thinking about Sophie's steadfast refusal to become his mistress. "I don't think so."

But then he thought—why not? Maybe she refused to bring an illegitimate child into this world because she had already *had* an illegitimate child and didn't want to repeat the mistake.

Benedict's mouth suddenly tasted quite sour. If Sophie had had a child, then Sophie had had a lover.

"Or maybe," Violet continued, warming to the endeavor, "she's the illegitimate child of a nobleman."

That was considerably more plausible—and more palatable. "One would think he'd have settled enough funds on her so that she didn't have to work as a housemaid."

"A great many men completely ignore their by-blows," Violet said, her face wrinkling with distaste. "It's nothing short of scandalous."

"More scandalous than their having the by-blows in the first place?"

Violet's expression turned quite peevish.

"Besides," Benedict said, leaning back against the sofa and propping one ankle on the other knee, "if she were the bastard of a nobleman, and he'd cared for her enough to make sure she had schooling as a child, then why is she completely penniless now?"

"Hmmm, that's a good point." Violet tapped her index finger against her cheek, pursed her lips, then continued tapping. "But have no fear," she finally said, "I shall discover her identity within a month."

"I'd recommend asking Eloise for help," Benedict said dryly.

Violet nodded thoughtfully. "Good idea. That girl could get Napoleon to spill his secrets."

Benedict stood. "I must be going. I'm weary from the road and would like to get home."

"You can always avail yourself here."

He gave her a half smile. His mother liked nothing better than to have her children close at hand. "I need to get back to my own lodgings," he said, leaning down and dropping a kiss on her cheek. "Thank you for finding a position for Sophie."

"Miss Beckett, you mean?" Violet asked, her lips curving slyly.

"Sophie, Miss Beckett," Benedict said, feigning indifference. "Whatever you wish to call her."

When he left, he did not see his mother smiling broadly at his back.

Sophie knew that she should not allow herself to grow too comfortable at Bridgerton House—she would, after all, be leaving just as soon as she could make the arrangements—but as she looked around her room, surely the nicest any servant had ever been assigned, and she thought about Lady Bridgerton's friendly manner and easy smile . . .

She just couldn't help wishing that she could stay forever.

But that was impossible. She knew that as well as she knew that her name was Sophia Maria Beckett, not Sophia Maria Gunningworth.

First and foremost, there was always the danger that she'd come into contact with Araminta, especially now that Lady Bridgerton had elevated her from housemaid to lady's maid. A lady's maid might, for example, find herself acting as a chaperone or escort on outings outside the house. Outings to places where Araminta and the girls might choose to frequent.

And Sophie had no doubt that Araminta would find a way to make her life a living hell. Araminta hated her in a way that defied reason, went beyond emotion. If she saw Sophie in London, she would not be content simply to ignore her. Sophie had no doubt that Araminta would lie, cheat, and steal just to make Sophie's life more difficult.

She hated Sophie that much.

But if Sophie were to be honest with herself, the true reason she could not remain in London was not Araminta. It was Benedict.

How could she avoid him when she lived in his mother's household? She was furious with him right now—beyond furious, in all truth—but she knew, deep down, that anger could only be short-lived. How could she resist him, day in and day out, when the mere sight of him made her weak with longing? Someday soon he'd smile at her, one of those sideways, crooked sorts of smiles, and she'd find herself clutching on to the furniture, just to keep herself from melting into a pathetic pool on the floor.

She'd fallen in love with the wrong man. She could never have him on her terms, and she refused to go to him on his.

It was hopeless.

Sophie was saved from any further depressing thoughts by a brisk knock on her door. When she called out, "Yes?" the door opened, and Lady Bridgerton entered the room.

Sophie immediately jumped to her feet and bobbed a curtsy. "Was there anything you needed, my lady?" she asked.

"No, not at all," Lady Bridgerton replied. "I was merely checking to see if you were getting settled in. Is there anything I can get for you?"

Sophie blinked. Lady Bridgerton was asking *her* if *she* needed anything? Rather the reverse of the usual ladyservant relationship. "Er, no thank you," Sophie said. "I would be happy to get something for you, though."

Lady Bridgerton waved her offer way. "No need. You shouldn't feel you have to do anything for us today. I'd prefer that you get yourself settled in first so that you do not feel distracted when you begin."

Sophie cast her eyes toward her small bag. "I don't have much to unpack. Truly, I should be happy to begin work immediately."

"Nonsense. It's already nearly the end of the day, and we are not planning to go out this evening, anyway. The girls and I have made do with only one lady's maid for the past week; we shall certainly survive for one more night."

"But—"

Lady Bridgerton smiled. "No arguments, if you please. One last day free is the least I can do after you saved my son."

"I did very little," Sophie said. "He would have been fine without me."

"Nonetheless, you aided him when he needed help, and for that I am in your debt."

"It was my pleasure," Sophie replied. "It was the very least I owed him after what he did for me."

Then, to her great surprise, Lady Bridgerton walked forward and sat down in the chair behind Sophie's writing desk.

Writing desk! Sophie was still trying to fathom that. What maid had ever been blessed with a writing desk?

"So tell me, Sophie," Lady Bridgerton said with a winning smile—one that instantly reminded her of Benedict's easy grin. "Where are you from?"

"East Anglia, originally," Sophie replied, seeing no reason to lie. The Bridgertons were from Kent; it was unlikely that Lady Bridgerton would be familiar with Norfolk, where Sophie had grown up. "Not so very far from Sandringham, if you know where that is."

"I do indeed," Lady Bridgerton said. "I haven't been, but I've heard that it is a lovely building."

Sophie nodded. "It is, quite. Of course, I've never been inside. But the exterior is beautiful."

"Where did your mother work?"

"Blackheath Hall," Sophie replied, this lie slipping easily off her tongue. She'd been asked that question often enough; she'd long since settled upon a name for her fictional home. "Are you familiar with it?"

Lady Bridgerton's brow furrowed. "No, I don't believe so."

"A bit north of Swaffham."

Lady Bridgerton shook her head. "No, I do not know it."

Sophie gave her a gentle smile. "Not many people do."

"Do you have any brothers or sisters?"

Sophie was unused to an employer wanting to know so much about her personal background; usually all they cared about were her employment record and references. "No," she said. "There was only me."

"Ah, well, at least you had the company of the girls with whom you shared lessons. That must have been nice for you."

"It was good fun," Sophie lied. In all truth, studying with Rosamund and Posy had been sheer torture. She'd much preferred lessons when she'd been alone with her governess, before they'd come to live at Penwood Park.

"I must say, it was very generous of your mother's employers—I'm sorry," Lady Bridgerton interrupted herself, her brow furrowing, "what did you say their name was?"

"Grenville."

Her forehead wrinkled again. "I'm not familiar with them."

"They don't often come to London."

"Ah, well, that explains it," Lady Bridgerton said. "But as I was saying, it was very generous of them to allow you to share in their daughters' lessons. What did you study?"

Sophie froze, not sure whether she was being interrogated or if Lady Bridgerton were truly interested. No one had ever cared to delve so deeply into the faux background she had created for herself. "Er, the usual subjects," she hedged. "Arithmetic and literature. History, a bit of mythology. French."

"French?" Lady Bridgerton asked, looking quite surprised. "How interesting. French tutors can be very dear."

"The governess spoke French," Sophie explained. "So it didn't cost any extra."

"How *is* your French?"

Sophie wasn't about to tell her the truth and say that it was perfect. Or almost perfect. She'd gotten out of practice these past few years and lost a bit of her fluency. "It's tolerable," she said. "Good enough to pass for a French maid, if that's what you desire."

"Oh, no," Lady Bridgerton said, laughing merrily. "Heavens, no. I know it is all the rage to have French maids, but I would never ask you to go about your chores trying to remember to speak with a French accent."

"That's very thoughtful of you," Sophie said, trying not to let her suspicion show on her face. She was sure that Lady Bridgerton was a nice lady; she'd *have* to be a nice lady to have raised such a nice family. But this was almost *too* nice.

"Well, it's—oh, good day, Eloise. What brings you up here?"

Sophie looked to the doorway and saw what could only be a

Bridgerton daughter standing there. Her thick, chestnut hair was coiled elegantly at the back of her neck, and her mouth was wide and expressive, just like Benedict's.

"Benedict told me we have a new maid," Eloise said.

Lady Bridgerton motioned to Sophie. "This is Sophie Beckett. We were just chatting. I think we shall deal famously."

Eloise gave her mother an odd look—or at least Sophie thought it was an odd look. She supposed that it was possible that Eloise always looked at her mother with a slightly suspicious, slightly confused, sideways glance. But somehow Sophie didn't think so.

"My brother tells me you saved his life," Eloise said, turning from her mother to Sophie.

"He exaggerates," Sophie said, a faint smile touching her lips.

Eloise regarded her with an oddly shrewd glance, and Sophie had the distinct impression that Eloise was analyzing her smile, trying to decide whether or not she was poking fun at Benedict, and if so, whether it was in jest or unkindness.

The moment seemed suspended in time, and then Eloise's lips curved in a surprisingly sly manner. "I think my mother is correct," she said. "We shall deal famously."

Sophie rather thought she had just passed some sort of crucial test.

"Have you met Francesca and Hyacinth?" Eloise asked.

Sophie shook her head, just as Lady Bridgerton said, "They are not at home. Francesca is visiting Daphne, and Hyacinth is off at the Featheringtons. She and Felicity seem to be over their row and are once again inseparable."

Eloise chuckled. "Poor Penelope. I think she was enjoying the relative peace and quiet with Hyacinth gone. I know *I* was enjoying the respite from Felicity."

Lady Bridgerton turned to Sophie and explained, "My daughter Hyacinth can more often than not be found at the home of her best friend, Felicity Featherington. And when she is not, then Felicity can be found here."

Sophie smiled and nodded, wondering once again why they were sharing such tidbits with her. They were treating her like family, something even her own family had never done.

It was very odd.

Odd and wonderful.

Odd and wonderful and horrible.

Because it could never last.

But maybe she could stay just a little while. Not long. A few weeks—maybe even a month. Just long enough to get her affairs and thoughts in order. Just long enough to relax and pretend she was more than just a servant.

She knew she could never be a part of the Bridgerton family, but maybe she could be a friend.

And it had been so long since she had been anyone's friend.

"Is something wrong, Sophie?" Lady Bridgerton asked. "You have a tear in your eye."

Sophie shook her head. "Just a speck of dust," she mumbled, pretending to busy herself with the unpacking of her small bag of possessions. She knew that no one believed her, but she didn't much care.

And even though she had no idea where she intended to go from this moment on, she had the oddest feeling that her life had just begun.

Chapter 15

This Author is quite certain that the male half of the population will be uninterested in the following portion of the column, so you are all given leave to skip to the next section. However, for the ladies, let This Author be the first to inform you that the Bridgerton family was recently sucked into the battle of the maids that has been raging all season between Lady Penwood and Mrs. Featherington. It seems that the maid attending to the daughters Bridgerton has defected to the Penwoods, replacing the maid who fled back to the Featherington household after Lady Penwood forced her to polish three hundred pairs of shoes.

And in other Bridgerton news, Benedict Bridgerton is most definitely back in London. It seems he took ill while in the country and extended his stay. One wishes that there were a more interesting explanation (especially when one is, like This Author, dependent upon interesting stories to earn one's living), but sadly, that is all there is to it.

LADY WHISTLEDOWN'S SOCIETY PAPERS,
14 MAY 1817

By the following morning, Sophie had met five of Benedict's seven siblings. Eloise, Francesca, and Hyacinth all still lived with their mother, Anthony had stopped by with his young son for breakfast, and Daphne—who was now the Duchess of Hastings—had been summoned to help Lady Bridgerton plan the end-of-the-season ball. The only Bridgertons Sophie hadn't met were Gregory, who was off at Eton, and Colin, who was off, in Anthony's words, God-knows-where.

Although, if one wanted to put a fine point on it, Sophie already had met Colin—two years earlier at the masquerade. She was rather relieved that he was out of town. She doubted that he would recognize her; Benedict, after all, had not. But somehow the thought of meeting him again was quite stressful and unsettling.

Not that that should matter, she thought ruefully. Everything seemed quite stressful and unsettling these days.

Much to Sophie's extreme *lack* of surprise, Benedict showed up at his mother's home the following morning for breakfast. Sophie should have been able to avoid him completely, except that he was loitering in the hall as she tried to make her way down to the kitchen, where she planned to take her morning meal with the rest of the servants.

"And how was your first night at Number Five, Bruton Street?" he inquired, his smile lazy and masculine.

"Splendid," Sophie replied, stepping aside so that she might make a clean half circle around him.

But as she stepped to her left, he stepped to his right, effectively blocking her path. "I'm so glad you're enjoying yourself," he said smoothly.

Sophie stepped back to her right. "I *was*," she said pointedly.

Benedict was far too debonair to step back to his left, but he somehow managed to turn and lean against a table in just the right way to once again block her movement. "Have you been given a tour of the house?" he asked.

"By the housekeeper."

"And of the grounds?"

"There are no grounds."

He smiled, his brown eyes warm and melting. "There's a garden."

"About the size of a pound note," she retorted.

"Nonetheless . . ."

"Nonetheless," Sophie cut in, "I have to eat breakfast."

He stepped gallantly aside. "Until next time," he murmured.

And Sophie had the sinking feeling that next time would come quickly indeed.

Thirty minutes later, Sophie edged slowly out of the kitchen, half-expecting Benedict to jump out at her from around a corner. Well, maybe not half-expecting. Judging from the way she couldn't quite breathe, she was probably whole-expecting.

But he wasn't there.

She inched forward. Surely he would come bounding down the stairs at any moment, ambushing her with his very presence.

Still no Benedict.

Sophie opened her mouth, then bit her tongue when she realized she'd been about to call out his name.

"Stupid girl," she muttered.

"Who's stupid?" Benedict asked. "Surely not *you*."

Sophie nearly jumped a foot. "Where did you come from?" she demanded, once she'd almost caught her breath.

He pointed to an open doorway. "Right there," he answered, his voice all innocence.

"So now you're jumping out at me from *closets*?"

"Of course not." He looked affronted. "That was a staircase."

Sophie peered around him. It was the side staircase. The *servants'* staircase. Certainly not anyplace a family member would just *happen* to be walking. "Do you often creep down the side staircase?" she asked, crossing her arms.

He leaned forward, just close enough to make her slightly uncomfortable, and, although she would never admit it to anyone, barely even herself, slightly excited. "Only when I want to sneak up on someone."

She attempted to brush past him. "I have to get to work."

"Now?"

She gritted her teeth. "Yes, now."

"But Hyacinth is eating breakfast. You can hardly dress her hair while she's eating."

"I also attend to Francesca and Eloise."

He shrugged, smiling innocently. "They're eating breakfast, too. Truly, you have nothing to do."

"Which shows how little you know about working for a living," she shot back. "I have ironing, mending, polishing—"

"They make you polish the silver?"

"Shoes!" she fairly yelled. "I have to polish shoes."

"Oh." He leaned back, one shoulder resting against the wall as he crossed his arms. "It sounds dull."

"It *is* dull," she ground out, trying to ignore the tears that suddenly pricked her eyes. *She* knew her life was dull, but it was painful to hear someone else point it out.

One corner of his mouth lifted into a lazy, seductive smile. "Your life doesn't *have* to be dull, you know."

She tried to step past him. "I prefer it dull."

He waved his arm grandly to the side, motioning for her to pass. "If that is how you wish it."

"I do." But the words didn't come out nearly as firmly as she'd intended. "I *do*," she repeated. Oh, very well, no use lying to herself. She didn't. Not entirely. But that was the way it had to be.

"Are you trying to convince yourself, or me?" he asked softly.

"I won't even dignify that with an answer," she replied. But she didn't meet his eyes as she said it.

"You'd best get yourself upstairs, then," he said, raising one brow when she didn't move. "I'm sure you have a great many shoes to polish."

Sophie ran up the stairs—the servants' stairs—and didn't look back.

He next found her in the garden—that tiny patch of green she'd so recently (and accurately) mocked as the size of a pound note. The Bridgerton sisters had gone off to visit the Featherington sisters, and Lady Bridgerton was taking a nap. Sophie had all of their gowns pressed and ready for that evening's social event, hair ribbons were selected and matched to each dress, and enough shoes had been polished to last a week.

With all her work done, Sophie decided to take a short break and read in the garden. Lady Bridgerton had told her that she might borrow freely from her small library of books, so Sophie selected a recently published novel and settled herself into a wrought-iron chair on the small patio. She'd only read a chapter before she heard footsteps approaching from the house. Somehow she managed not to look up until a shadow fell across her. Predictably, it was Benedict.

"Do you *live* here?" Sophie asked dryly.

"No," he said, plopping down into the chair next to her, "although my mother is constantly telling me to make myself right at home."

She could think of no witty rejoinder, so she merely "hmmphed" and stuck her nose back in her book.

He plunked his feet on the small table in front. "And what are we reading today?"

"That question," she said, snapping the book shut but leaving her finger in to mark her place, "implies that I am actually reading, which I assure you I am unable to do while you are sitting here."

"My presence is that compelling, eh?"

"It's that *disturbing*."

"Better than dull," he pointed out.

"I like my life dull."

"If you like your life dull, then that can only mean that you do not understand the nature of excitement."

The condescension in his tone was appalling. Sophie gripped her book so hard her knuckles turned white. "I have had enough excite-ment in my life," she said through gritted teeth. "I assure you."

"I would be pleased to participate in this conversation to a greater degree," he drawled, "except that you have not seen fit to share with me *any* of the details of your life."

"It was not an oversight on my part."

He clucked disapprovingly. "So hostile."

Her eyes bugged out. "You abducted me—"

"Coerced," he reminded her.

"Do you *want* me to hit you?"

"I wouldn't mind it," he said mildly. "And besides, now that you're here, was it really so very terrible that I browbeat you into coming? You like my family, don't you?"

"Yes, but—"

"And they treat you fairly, right?"

"Yes, but—"

"Then what," he asked, his tone most supercilious, "is the problem?"

Sophie almost lost her temper. She almost jumped to her feet and grabbed his shoulders and shook and shook and shook, but at the last moment she realized that that was exactly what he wanted her to do. And so instead she merely sniffed and said, "If you cannot recognize the problem, there is no way that I could explain it to you."

He laughed, damn the man. "My goodness," he said, "that was an expert sidestep."

She picked up her book and opened it. "I'm reading."

"Trying, at least," he murmured.

She flipped a page, even though she hadn't read the last two para-graphs. She was really just trying to make a show of ignoring him, and besides, she could always go back and read them later, after he left.

"Your book is upside down," he pointed out.

Sophie gasped and looked down. "It is not!"

He smiled slyly. "But you still had to look to be sure, didn't you?"

She stood up and announced, "I'm going inside."

He stood immediately. "And leave the splendid spring air?"

"And leave *you*," she retorted, even though his gesture of respect was not lost on her. Gentlemen did not ordinarily stand for mere servants.

"Pity," he murmured. "I was having such fun."

Sophie wondered how much injury he'd sustain if she threw the book at him. Probably not enough to make up for the loss to her dignity.

It amazed her how easily he could infuriate her. She loved him desperately—she'd long since given up lying to herself about that—and yet he could make her entire body shake with anger with one little quip.

"Good-*bye*, Mr. Bridgerton."

He waved her off. "I'll see you later, I'm sure."

Sophie paused, not sure she liked his dismissive demeanor.

"I thought you were leaving," he said, looking faintly amused.

"I am," she insisted.

He cocked his head to the side but didn't say anything. He didn't have to. The vaguely mocking expression in his eyes did the job quite well.

She turned and walked toward the door leading inside, but when she was about halfway to her destination, she heard him call out, "Your new dress is quite fetching."

She stopped and sighed. She might have gone from faux-guardian of an earl to a mere lady's maid, but good manners were good manners, and there was no way she could ignore a compliment. Turning around, she said, "Thank you. It was a gift from your mother. I believe it used to belong to Francesca."

He leaned against the fence, his posture deceptively lazy. "That's a custom, isn't it, to share frocks with one's maid?"

Sophie nodded. "When one is through with them, of course. No one would give a new frock away."

"I see."

Sophie eyed him suspiciously, wondering why on earth he cared about the status of her new dress.

"Didn't you want to go inside?" he inquired.

"What are you up to?" she asked.

"Why would you think I'm up to anything?"

Her lips pursed before she said, "You wouldn't be you if you weren't up to something."

He smiled at that. "I do believe that was a compliment."

"It wasn't necessarily intended as such."

"But nonetheless," he said mildly, "that's how I choose to take it."

She wasn't sure how best to respond, so she said nothing. She also didn't move toward the door. She wasn't sure why, since she'd been quite vocal about her desire to be alone. But what she said and what she felt weren't always one and the same. In her heart she longed for this man, dreamed of a life that could never be.

She shouldn't be so angry with him. He shouldn't have forced her against her wishes to come to London, that was true, but she couldn't fault him for offering her a position as his mistress. He had done what any man in his position would have done. Sophie had no illusions about her place in London society. She was a maid. A servant. And the only thing that separated her from other maids and servants was that she'd had a taste of luxury as a child. She'd been reared gently, if without love, and the experience had shaped her ideals and values. Now she was forever stuck between two worlds, with no clear place in either.

"You look very serious," he said quietly.

Sophie heard him, but she couldn't quite break herself from her thoughts.

Benedict stepped forward. He reached out to touch her chin, then checked himself. There was something untouchable about her just then, something unreachable. "I can't bear it when you look so sad," he said, surprised by his own words. He hadn't intended to say anything; it had just slipped out.

She looked up at that. "I'm not sad."

He gave his head the tiniest shake. "There's a sorrow deep in your eyes. It's rarely gone."

Her hand flew to her face, as if she could actually touch that sorrow, as if it were solid, something that could be massaged away.

Benedict took her hand and raised it to his lips. "I wish you would share your secrets with me."

"I have no—"

"Don't lie," he cut in, his tone harsher than he'd intended. "You have more secrets than any woman I've—" He broke off, a sudden image of the woman from the masquerade flashing through his mind. "More than almost any woman I've known," he finished.

Her eyes met his for the briefest of seconds, and then she looked away. "There is nothing wrong with secrets. If I choose—"

"Your secrets are eating you alive," he said sharply. He didn't want to stand there and listen to her excuses, and his frustration gnawed at his patience. "You have the opportunity to change your life, to reach out and grasp happiness, and yet you won't do it."

"I can't," she said, and the pain in her voice nearly unmanned him.

"Nonsense," he said. "You can do anything you choose. You just don't want to."

"Don't make this harder than it already is," she whispered.

When she said that, something snapped inside of him. He felt it palpably, a strange popping sensation that released a rush of blood, feeding the frustrated anger that had been simmering inside of him for days. "You think it's not hard?" he asked. "You think it's not *hard?*"

"I didn't say that!"

He grabbed her hand and pulled her body against his, so she could see for herself just how hard he was. "I burn for you," he said, his lips touching her ear. "Every night, I lie in bed, thinking of you, wondering why the hell you're here with my mother, of all people, and not with me."

"I didn't want—"

"You don't know what you want," he cut in. It was a cruel statement, condescending in the extreme, but he was beyond caring. She'd wounded him in a way he hadn't even known was possible, with a power he'd never dreamed she possessed. She'd chosen a life of drudgery over a life with him, and now he was doomed to see her almost every day, to see her and taste her and smell her just enough to keep his desire sharp and strong.

It was his own fault, of course. He could have let her stay in the country, could have saved himself this wrenching torture. But he'd surprised even himself by insisting that she come to London. It was odd, and he was almost afraid to analyze what it meant, but he needed to know that she was safe and protected more than he needed her for himself.

She said his name, but her voice was laced with longing, and he knew that she was not indifferent to him. She might not fully understand what it meant to want a man, but she wanted him all the same.

He captured her mouth with his, swearing to himself as he did so that if she said no, if she made any sort of indication that she didn't want this, he'd stop. It'd be the hardest thing he'd ever done, but he would do it.

But she didn't say no, and she didn't push against him or struggle or squirm. Instead, she positively melted into him, her hands twining in his hair as her lips parted beneath his. He didn't know why she'd suddenly decided to let him kiss her—no, to kiss *him*—but he wasn't about to lift his lips from hers to wonder why.

He seized the moment, tasting her, drinking her, *breathing* her. He was no longer quite so confident that he would be able to convince her to become his mistress, and it was suddenly imperative that this kiss be more than just a kiss. It might have to last him a lifetime.

He kissed her with renewed vigor, pushing away the niggling voice in his head, telling him that he'd been here, done this before. Two years earlier he'd danced with a woman, kissed her, and she'd told him that he'd have to pack a lifetime into a single kiss.

He'd been overconfident then; he hadn't believed her. And he'd lost her, maybe lost everything. He certainly hadn't met anyone since with whom he could even imagine building a life.

Until Sophie.

Unlike the lady in silver, she wasn't someone he could hope to marry, but also unlike the lady in silver, she was *here*.

And he wasn't going to let her get away.

She was here, with him, and she felt like heaven. The soft scent of her hair, the slight taste of salt on her skin—she was, he thought, born to rest in the shelter of his arms. And he was born to hold her.

"Come home with me," he whispered in her ear.

She said nothing, but he felt her stiffen.

"Come home with me," he repeated.

"I can't," she said, the breath of each word whispering across his skin.

"You *can*."

She shook her head, but she didn't pull away, so he took advantage of the moment and brought his lips to hers one more time. His tongue darted in, exploring the warm recesses of her mouth, tasting the very essence of her. His hand found the swell of her breast and he squeezed gently, his breath catching as he felt her pucker beneath him. But it wasn't enough. He wanted to feel her skin, not the fabric of her dress.

But this was not the place. They were in his mother's garden, for God's sake. Anyone could come across them, and to be frank, if he hadn't pulled her into the alcove right by the door, anyone could have seen them. It was the sort of thing that could cause Sophie to lose her job.

Maybe he should be pulling her out into the open, where all the world would see, because then she'd be on her own again, and she'd have no choice but to be his mistress.

Which was, he reminded himself, what he wanted.

But it occurred to him—and frankly, he was rather surprised he had the presence of mind at such a moment for *anything* to occur to him—that part of the reason he cared so much for her was her remarkably solid and unflinching sense of herself. She knew who she was, and unfortunately for him, that person didn't stray from the bounds of respectable society.

If he ruined her so publicly, in front of people she admired and respected, he'd break her spirit. And that would be an unforgivable crime.

Slowly, he pulled away. He still wanted her, and he still wanted her to be his mistress, but he wasn't going to force the issue by compromising her in his mother's household. When she came to him—and she *would*, he vowed—it would be of her own free will.

In the meantime, he would woo her, wear her down. In the meantime, he'd—

"You stopped," she whispered, looking surprised.

"This isn't the place," he replied.

For a moment her face showed no change of expression. Then, almost as if someone were pulling a shade over her face, horror dawned. It started in her eyes, which grew impossibly round and somehow even more green than usual, then it reached her mouth, her lips parting as a gasp of air rushed in.

"I didn't think," she whispered, more to herself than to him.

"I know." He smiled. "I know. I hate it when you think. It always ends badly for me."

"We can't do this again."

"We certainly can't do it *here*."

"No, I mean—"

"You're spoiling it."

"But—"

"Humor me," he said, "and let me believe the afternoon ended without your telling me this will never happen again."

"But—"

He pressed a finger to her lips. "You're not humoring me."

"But—"

"Don't I deserve this one little fantasy?"

At last, he broke through. She smiled.

"Good," he said. "That's more like it."

Her lips quivered, then, amazingly, her smile grew.

"Excellent," he murmured. "Now then, I'm going to leave. And you have only one task while I go. You will stay right here, and you will keep smiling. Because it breaks my heart to see any other expression on your face."

"You won't be able to see me," she pointed out.

He touched her chin. "I'll know."

And then, before her expression could change from that enchanting combination of shock and adoration, he left.

Chapter 16

*The Featheringtons hosted a small dinner party yesterday eve,
and, although This Author was not privileged enough to attend,
it has been said that the evening was deemed quite a success.
Three Bridgertons attended, but sadly for the Featherington
girls, none of the Bridgertons were of the male variety. The
always amiable Nigel Berbrooke was there, paying great attention to Miss Philippa Featherington.*

    *This Author is told that both Benedict and Colin Bridgerton
were invited, but had to send their regrets.*

LADY WHISTLEDOWN'S SOCIETY PAPERS,
19 MAY 1817

As the days melted into a week, Sophie discovered that working for
the Bridgertons could keep a girl very busy indeed. Her job was to
be maid to all three unmarried girls, and her days were filled with
hairdressing, mending, pressing gowns, polishing shoes . . . She
hadn't left the house even once—unless one counted time out in the
back garden.

    But where such a life under Araminta had been dreary and demean-
ing, the Bridgerton household was filled with laughter and smiles.
The girls bickered and teased, but never with the malice Sophie
had seen Rosamund show to Posy. And when tea was informal—

upstairs, with only Lady Bridgerton and the girls in attendance—
Sophie was always invited to partake. She usually brought her
basket of mending and darned or sewed buttons while the Bridgertons chattered away, but it was so lovely to be able to sit and sip a
fine cup of tea, with fresh milk and warm scones. And after a few
days, Sophie even began to feel comfortable enough to occasionally
add to the conversation.

It had become Sophie's favorite time of day.

"Where," Eloise asked, one afternoon about a week after what
Sophie was now referring to as *the big kiss*, "do you suppose Benedict is?"

"Ow!"

Four Bridgerton faces turned to Sophie. "Are you all right?" Lady
Bridgerton asked, her teacup suspended halfway between her saucer
and her mouth.

Sophie grimaced. "I pricked my finger."

Lady Bridgerton's lips curved into a small, secret smile.

"Mother has told you," fourteen-year-old Hyacinth said, "at least
a *thousand* times—"

"A thousand times?" Francesca asked with arched brows.

"A hundred times," Hyacinth amended, shooting an annoyed
look at her older sister, "that you do not have to bring your mending
to tea."

Sophie suppressed a smile of her own. "I should feel very lazy if
I did not."

"Well, I'm not going to bring my embroidery," Hyacinth announced, not that anyone had asked her to.

"Feeling lazy?" Francesca queried.

"Not in the least," Hyacinth returned.

Francesca turned to Sophie. "You're making Hyacinth feel lazy."

"I do not!" Hyacinth protested.

Lady Bridgerton sipped at her tea. "You *have* been working on the same piece of embroidery for quite some time, Hyacinth. Since February, if my memory serves."

"Her memory always serves," Francesca said to Sophie.

Hyacinth glared at Francesca, who smiled into her teacup.

Sophie coughed to cover a smile of her own. Francesca, who at twenty was merely one year younger than Eloise, had a sly, subversive sense of humor. Someday Hyacinth would be her match, but not yet.

"Nobody answered my question," Eloise announced, letting her teacup clatter into its saucer. "Where is Benedict? I haven't seen him in an age."

"It's been a week," Lady Bridgerton said.

"Ow!"

"Do you need a thimble?" Hyacinth asked Sophie.

"I'm not usually this clumsy," Sophie muttered.

Lady Bridgerton lifted her cup to her lips and held it there for what seemed like a rather long time.

Sophie gritted her teeth together and returned to her mending with a vengeance. Much to her surprise, Benedict had not made even the barest of appearances since *the big kiss* last week. She'd found herself peering out windows, peeking around corners, always expecting to catch a glimpse of him.

And yet he was never there.

Sophie couldn't decide whether she was crushed or relieved. Or both.

She sighed. Definitely both.

"Did you say something, Sophie?" Eloise asked.

Sophie shook her head and murmured, "No," refusing to look up from her poor, abused index finger. Grimacing slightly, she pinched her skin, watching blood slowly bead up on her fingertip.

"Where *is* he?" Eloise persisted.

"Benedict is thirty years of age," Lady Bridgerton said in a mild voice. "He doesn't need to inform us of his every activity."

Eloise snorted loudly. "That's a fine about-face from last week, Mother."

"Whatever do you mean?"

"'Where is Benedict?'" Eloise mocked, doing a more-than-fair imitation of her mother. "'How dare he go off without a word? It's as if he's dropped off the face of the earth.'"

"That was different," Lady Bridgerton said.

"How so?" This, from Francesca, who was wearing her usual sly smile.

"He'd said he was going to that awful Cavender boy's party, and then never came back, whereas *this* time . . ." Lady Bridgerton stopped, pursing her lips. "*Why* am I explaining myself to you?"

"I can't imagine," Sophie murmured.

Eloise, who was sitting closest to Sophie, choked on her tea.

Francesca whacked Eloise on the back as she leaned forward to inquire, "Did you say something, Sophie?"

Sophie shook her head as she stabbed her needle into the dress she was mending, completely missing the hem.

Eloise gave her a dubious sideways glance.

Lady Bridgerton cleared her throat. "Well, I think—" She stopped, cocking her head to the side. "I say, is that someone in the hall?"

Sophie stifled a groan and looked over toward the doorway, expecting the butler to enter. Wickham always gave her a disapproving frown before imparting whatever news he was carrying. He didn't approve of the maid taking tea with the ladies of the house, and while he never vocalized his thoughts on the issue in front of the Bridgertons, he rarely took pains to keep his opinions from showing on his face.

But instead of Wickham, Benedict walked through the doorway.

"Benedict!" Eloise called out, rising to her feet. "We were just talking about you."

He looked at Sophie. "Were you?"

"*I* wasn't," Sophie muttered.

"Did you say something, Sophie?" Hyacinth asked.

"Ow!"

"I'm going to have to take that mending away from you," Lady Bridgerton said with an amused smile. "You'll have lost a pint of blood before the day is through."

Sophie lurched to her feet. "I'll get a thimble."

"You don't have a *thimble*?" Hyacinth asked. "I would never *dream* of doing mending without a thimble."

"Have you *ever* dreamed of mending?" Francesca smirked.

Hyacinth kicked her, nearly upsetting the tea service in the process.

"Hyacinth!" Lady Bridgerton scolded.

Sophie stared at the door, trying desperately to keep her eyes focused on anything but Benedict. She'd spent all week hoping for a glimpse, but now that he was here, all she wanted was to escape. If she looked at his face, her eyes inevitably strayed to his lips. And if she looked at his lips, her thoughts immediately went to their kiss. And if she thought about the kiss . . .

"I need that thimble," she blurted out, jumping to her feet. There were some things one just shouldn't think about in public.

"So you said," Benedict murmured, one of his eyebrows quirking up into a perfect—and perfectly arrogant—arch.

"It's downstairs," she muttered. "In my room."

"But your room is upstairs," Hyacinth said.

Sophie could have killed her. "That's what I said," she ground out.

"No," Hyacinth said in a matter-of-fact tone, "you didn't."

"Yes," Lady Bridgerton said, "she did. I heard her."

Sophie twisted her head sharply to look at Lady Bridgerton and knew in an instant that the older woman had lied. "I have to get that thimble," she said, for what seemed like the thirtieth time. She hurried toward the doorway, gulping as she grew close to Benedict.

"Wouldn't want you to hurt yourself," he said, stepping aside to allow her through the doorway. But as she brushed past him, he leaned forward, whispering, "Coward."

Sophie's cheeks burned, and she was halfway down the stairs before she realized that she'd meant to go back to her room. Dash it all, she didn't want to march back up the stairs and have to walk past Benedict again. He was probably still standing in the doorway, and his lips would tilt upward as she passed—one of those faintly mocking, faintly seductive smiles that never failed to leave her breathless.

This was a disaster. There was no way she was going to be able to stay here. How could she remain with Lady Bridgerton, when every glimpse of Benedict turned her knees to water? She just wasn't strong enough. He was going to wear her down, make her forget all of her principles, all of her vows. She was going to have to leave. There was no other option.

And that was really too bad, because she *liked* working for the Bridgerton sisters. They treated her like a human being, not like some barely paid workhorse. They asked her questions and seemed to care about her answers.

Sophie knew she wasn't one of them, would never be one of them, but they made it so easy to pretend. And in all truth, all that Sophie had ever really wanted out of life was a family.

With the Bridgertons, she could almost pretend that she had one.

"Lost your way?"

Sophie looked up to see Benedict at the top of the stairs, leaning lazily against the wall. She looked down and realized that she was still standing on the stairs. "I'm going out," she said.

"To buy a thimble?"

"Yes," she said defiantly.

"Don't you need money?"

She could lie, and say that she had money in her pocket, or she could tell the truth, and show herself for the pathetic fool she was.

Or she could just run down the stairs and out of the house. It was the cowardly thing to do, but . . .

"I have to go," she muttered, and dashed away so quickly that she completely forgot she ought to be using the servants' entrance. She skidded across the foyer and pushed open the heavy door, stumbling her way down the front steps. When her feet hit the pavement, she turned north, not for any particular reason, just because she had to go somewhere, and then she heard a voice.

An awful, horrible, terrible voice.

Dear God, it was Araminta.

Sophie's heart stopped, and she quickly pressed herself back against the wall. Araminta was facing the street, and unless she turned around, she'd never notice Sophie.

At least it was easy to remain silent when one couldn't even breathe.

What was she doing here? Penwood House was at least eight blocks away, closer to—

Then Sophie remembered. She'd read it in *Whistledown* last year, one of the few copies she'd been able to get her hands on while she was working for the Cavenders. The new Earl of Penwood had finally decided to take up residence in London. Araminta, Rosamund, and Posy had been forced to find new accommodations.

Next door to the Bridgertons? Sophie couldn't have imagined a worse nightmare if she tried.

"Where is that insufferable girl?" she heard Araminta say.

Sophie immediately felt sorry for the girl in question. As Araminta's former "insufferable girl," she knew that the position came with few benefits.

"Posy!" Araminta yelled, then marched into a waiting carriage.

Sophie chewed on her lip, her heart sinking. In that moment, she knew exactly what must have happened when she left. Araminta would have hired a new maid, and she was probably just beastly to the poor girl, but she wouldn't have been able to degrade and demean her in quite the same fashion she'd done with Sophie. You had to know a person, really hate them, to be so cruel. Any old servant wouldn't do.

And since Araminta had to put someone down—she didn't know how to feel good about herself without making someone else feel bad—she'd obviously chosen Posy as her whipping boy—or girl, as the case might be.

Posy came dashing out the door, her face pinched and drawn. She looked unhappy, and perhaps a bit heavier than she had been two years earlier. Araminta wouldn't like that, Sophie thought glumly. She'd never been able to accept that Posy wasn't petite and blond and beautiful like Rosamund and herself. If Sophie had been Araminta's nemesis, then Posy had always been her disappointment.

Sophie watched as Posy stopped at the top of the steps, then reached down to fiddle with the laces of her short boots. Rosamund poked her head out of the carriage, yelling, "Posy!" in what Sophie thought was a rather unattractively shrill voice.

Sophie ducked back, turning her head away. She was right in Rosamund's line of sight.

"I'm coming!" Posy called out.

"Hurry up!" Rosamund snapped.

Posy finished tying her laces, then hurried forward, but her foot slipped on the final step, and a moment later she was sprawled on the pavement. Sophie lurched forward, instinctively moving to help Posy, but she jammed herself back against the wall. Posy was unhurt, and there was nothing in life Sophie wanted less than for Araminta to know that she was in London, practically right next door.

Posy picked herself off the pavement, stopping to stretch her neck, first to the right, then to the left, then . . .

Then she saw her. Sophie was sure of it. Posy's eyes widened, and her mouth fell open slightly. Then her lips came together, pursed to make the "S" to begin "Sophie?"

Sophie shook her head frantically.

"Posy!" came Araminta's irate cry.

Sophie shook her head again, her eyes begging, pleading with Posy not to give her away.

"I'm coming, Mother!" Posy called. She gave Sophie a single short nod, then climbed up into the carriage, which thankfully rolled off in the opposite direction.

Sophie sagged against the building. She didn't move for a full minute.

And then she didn't move for another five.

Benedict didn't mean to take anything away from his mother and sisters, but once Sophie ran out of the upstairs sitting room, he lost his interest in tea and scones.

"I was just wondering where you'd been," Eloise was saying.

"Hmmm?" He craned his head slightly to the right, wondering how much of the streetscape he could see through the window from this angle.

"I said," Eloise practically hollered, "I was just wondering—"

"Eloise, lower your voice," Lady Bridgerton interjected.

"But he's not listening."

"If he's not listening," Lady Bridgerton said, "then shouting isn't going to get his attention."

"Throwing a scone might work," Hyacinth suggested.

"Hyacinth, don't you da—"

But Hyacinth had already lobbed the scone. Benedict ducked out of the way, barely a second before it would have bounced off the side of his head. He looked first to the wall, which now bore a slight smudge where the scone had hit, then to the floor, where it had landed, remarkably in one piece.

"I believe that is my cue to leave," he said smoothly, shooting a cheeky smile at his youngest sister. Her airborne scone had given him just the excuse he needed to duck out of the room and see if he couldn't trail Sophie to wherever it was she thought she was going.

"But you just got here," his mother pointed out.

Benedict immediately regarded her with suspicion. Unlike her usual moans of "But you just got here," she didn't sound the least bit upset at his leaving.

Which meant she was up to something.

"I could stay," he said, just to test her.

"Oh, no," she said, lifting her teacup to her lips even though he was fairly certain it was empty. "Don't let us keep you if you're busy."

Benedict fought to school his features into an impassive expression, or at least to hide his shock. The last time he'd informed his mother that he was "busy," she'd answered with, "Too busy for your mother?"

His first urge was to declare, "I'll stay," and park himself in a chair, but he had just enough presence of mind to realize that staying to thwart his mother was rather ridiculous when what he really wanted to do was leave. "I'll go, then," he said slowly, backing toward the door.

"Go," she said, shooing him away. "Enjoy yourself."

Benedict decided to leave the room before she managed to befuddle him any further. He reached down and scooped up the scone, gently tossing it to Hyacinth, who caught it with a grin. He then nodded at his mother and sisters and headed out into the hall, reaching the stairs just as he heard his mother say, "I thought he'd never leave."

Very odd, indeed.

With long, easy strides, he made his way down the steps and out the front door. He doubted that Sophie would still be near the house, but if she'd gone shopping, there was really only one direction in which she would have headed. He turned right, intending to stroll until he reached the small row of shops, but he'd only gone three steps before he saw Sophie, pressed up against the brick exterior of his mother's house, looking as if she could barely remember how to breathe.

"Sophie?" Benedict rushed toward her. "What happened? Are you all right?"

She started when she saw him, then nodded.

He didn't believe her, of course, but there seemed little point in saying so. "You're shaking," he said, looking at her hands. "Tell me what happened. Did someone bother you?"

"No," she said, her voice uncharacteristically quavery. "I just . . . I, ah . . ." Her gaze fell on the stairs next to them. "I tripped on my way down the stairs and it scared me." She smiled weakly. "I'm sure you know what I mean. When you feel as if your insides have flipped upside down."

Benedict nodded, because of course he knew what she meant. But that didn't mean that he believed her. "Come with me," he said.

She looked up, and something in the green depths of her eyes broke his heart. "Where?" she whispered.

"Anywhere but here."

"I—"

"I live just five houses down," he said.

"You do?" Her eyes widened, then she murmured, "No one told me."

"I promise that your virtue will be safe," he interrupted. And then he added, because he couldn't quite help himself: "Unless *you* want it otherwise."

He had a feeling she would have protested if she weren't so dazed, but she allowed him to lead her down the street. "We'll just sit in my front room," he said, "until you feel better."

She nodded, and he led her up the steps and into his home, a modest town house just a bit south of his mother's.

Once they were comfortably ensconced, and Benedict had shut

the door so that they wouldn't be bothered by any of his servants, he turned to her, prepared to say, "Now, why don't you tell me what really happened," but at the very last minute something compelled him to hold his tongue. He could ask, but he knew she wouldn't answer. She'd be put on the defensive, and that wasn't likely to help his cause any.

So instead, he schooled his face into a neutral mask and asked, "How are you enjoying your work for my family?"

"They are very nice," she replied.

"Nice?" he echoed, sure that his disbelief showed clearly on his face. "Maddening, perhaps. Maybe even exhausting, but nice?"

"I think they are very nice," Sophie said firmly.

Benedict started to smile, because he loved his family dearly, and he loved that Sophie was growing to love them, but then he realized that he was cutting off his nose to spite his face, because the more attached Sophie became to his family, the less likely she was to potentially shame herself in their eyes by agreeing to be his mistress.

Damn. He'd made a serious miscalculation last week. But he'd been so focused on getting her to come to London, and a position in his mother's household had seemed the only way to convince her to do it.

That, combined with a fair bit of coercion.

Damn. Damn. Damn. Why hadn't he coerced her into something that would segue a little more easily into his arms?

"You should thank your lucky stars that you have them," Sophie said, her voice more forceful than it had been all afternoon. "I'd give anything for—"

But she didn't finish her sentence.

"You'd give anything for what?" Benedict asked, surprised by how much he wanted to hear her answer.

She gazed soulfully out the window as she replied, "To have a family like yours."

"You have no one," he said, his words a statement, not a question.

"I've never had anyone."

"Not even your—" And then he remembered that she'd slipped and told him that her mother had died at her birth. "Sometimes," he said, keeping his voice purposefully light and gentle, "it's not so easy being a Bridgerton."

Her head slowly turned around. "I can't imagine anything nicer."

"There isn't anything nicer," he replied, "but that doesn't mean it's always easy."

"What do you mean?"

And Benedict found himself giving voice to feelings he'd never shared with any other living soul, not even—no, especially not his family. "To most of the world," he said, "I'm merely a Bridgerton. I'm not Benedict or Ben or even a gentleman of means and hopefully a bit of intelligence. I'm merely"—he smiled ruefully—"a Bridgerton. Specifically, Number Two."

Her lips trembled, then they smiled. "You're much more than that," she said.

"I'd like to think so, but most of the world doesn't see it that way."

"Most of the world are fools."

He laughed at that. There was nothing more fetching than Sophie with a scowl. "You will not find disagreement here," he said.

But then, just when he thought the conversation was over, she surprised him by saying, "You're nothing like the rest of your family."

"How so?" he asked, not quite meeting her gaze. He didn't want her to see just how important her reply was to him.

"Well, your brother Anthony . . ." Her face scrunched in thought. "His whole life has been altered by the fact that he's the eldest. He quite obviously feels a responsibility to your family that you do not."

"Now wait just one—"

"Don't interrupt," she said, placing a calming hand on his chest. "I didn't say that you didn't love your family, or that you wouldn't give your life for any one of them. But it's different with your brother. He feels responsible, and I truly believe he would consider himself a failure if any of his siblings were unhappy."

"How many times have you met Anthony?" he muttered.

"Just once." The corners of her mouth tightened, as if she were suppressing a smile. "But that was all I needed. As for your younger brother, Colin . . . well, I haven't met him, but I've heard plenty—"

"From whom?"

"Everyone," she said. "Not to mention that he is forever being mentioned in *Whistledown*, which I must confess I've read for years."

"Then you knew about me before you met me," he said.

She nodded. "But I didn't *know* you. You're much more than Lady Whistledown realizes."

"Tell me," he said, placing his hand over hers. "What do you see?"

Sophie brought her eyes to his, gazed into those chocolatey depths, and saw something there she'd never dreamed existed. A tiny spark of vulnerability, of need.

He needed to know what she thought of him, that he was important to her. This man, so self-assured and so confident, needed her approval.

Maybe he needed *her.*

She curled her hand until their palms touched, then used her other index finger to trace circles and swirls on the fine kid of his glove. "You are . . ." she began, taking her time because she knew that every word weighed heavier in such a powerful moment. "You are not quite the man you present to the rest of the world. You'd like to be thought of as debonair and ironic and full of quick wit, and you *are* all those things, but underneath, you're so much more.

"You care," she said, aware that her voice had grown raspy with emotion. "You care about your family, and you even care about me, although God knows I don't always deserve it."

"Always," he interrupted, raising her hand to his lips and kissing her palm with a fervency that sucked her breath away. "Always."

"And . . . and . . ." It was hard to continue when his eyes were on hers with such single-minded emotion.

"And what?" he whispered.

"Much of who you are comes from your family," she said, the words tumbling forth in a rush. "That much is true. You can't grow up with such love and loyalty and not become a better person because of it. But deep within you, in your heart, in your very soul, is the man you were born to be. *You*, not someone's son, not someone's brother. Just you."

Benedict watched her intently. He opened his mouth to speak, but he discovered that he had no words. There *were* no words for a moment like this.

"Deep inside," she murmured, "you've the soul of an artist."

"No," he said, shaking his head.

"Yes," she insisted. "I've seen your sketches. You're brilliant. I don't think I knew how much until I met your family. You captured them all perfectly, from the sly look in Francesca's smile to the mischief in the very way Hyacinth holds her shoulders."

"I've never shown anyone else my sketches," he admitted.

Her head snapped up. "You can't be serious."

He shook his head. "I haven't."

"But they're brilliant. *You're* brilliant. I'm sure your mother would love to see them."

"I don't know why," he said, feeling sheepish, "but I never wanted to share them."

"You shared them with me," she said softly.

"Somehow," he said, touching his fingers to her chin, "it felt right."

And then his heart skipped a beat, because all of a sudden *everything* felt right.

He loved her. He didn't know how it had happened, only that it was true.

It wasn't just that she was convenient. There had been lots of convenient women. Sophie was different. She made him laugh. She made him want to make *her* laugh. And when he was with her—Well, when he was with her he wanted her like hell, but during those few moments when his body managed to keep itself in check . . .

He was content.

It was strange, to find a woman who could make him happy just with her mere presence. He didn't even have to see her, or hear her voice, or even smell her scent. He just had to know that she was there.

If that wasn't love, he didn't know what was.

He stared down at her, trying to prolong the moment, to hold on to these few moments of complete perfection. Something softened in her eyes, and the color seemed to melt right then and there, from a shiny, glowing emerald to a soft and lilting moss. Her lips parted and softened, and he knew that he had to kiss her. Not that he wanted to, that he had to.

He needed her next to him, below him, on top of him.

He needed her in him, around him, a part of him.

He needed her the way he needed air.

And, he thought in that last rational moment before his lips found hers, he needed her right now.

Chapter 17

Sophie had been kissed before—she had been kissed by Benedict before—but nothing, not a single moment of a single kiss, prepared her for this.

It wasn't a kiss. It was heaven.

He kissed her with an intensity she could barely comprehend, his lips teasing hers, stroking, nibbling, caressing. He stoked a fire within her, a desire to be loved, a need to love in return. And God help her, when he kissed her, all she wanted to do was kiss him back.

She heard him murmuring her name, but it barely registered over the roaring in her ears. This was desire. This was need. How foolish of her ever to think that she could deny this. How self-important to think that she could be stronger than passion.

"Sophie, Sophie," he said, over and over, his lips on her cheek, her neck, her ear. He said her name so many times it seemed to soak into her skin.

She felt his hands on the buttons of her dress, could feel the fabric loosening as each slipped through its buttonhole. This was everything she'd always sworn she would never do, and yet when her bodice tumbled to her waist, leaving her shamelessly exposed, she groaned his name and arched her back, offering herself to him like some sort of forbidden fruit.

Benedict stopped breathing when he saw her. He'd pictured this moment in his mind so many times—every night as he lay in bed, and in every dream when he actually slept. But this—reality—was far sweeter than a dream, and far more erotic.

His hand, which had been stroking the warm skin on her back, slowly slid over her rib cage. "You're so beautiful," he whispered, knowing that the words were hopelessly inadequate. As if mere words could describe what he felt. And then, when his trembling fingers finished their journey and cupped her breast, he let out a shuddering groan. Words were impossible now. His need for her was so intense, so primitive. It robbed him of his ability to speak. Hell, he could barely think.

He wasn't certain how this woman had come to mean so much to him. It seemed that one day she was a stranger, and the next she was as indispensable as air. And yet it hadn't happened in a blinding flash. It had been a slow, sneaky process, quietly coloring his emotions until he realized that without her, his life lacked all meaning.

He touched her chin, lifting her face until he could peer into her eyes. They seemed to glow from within, glistening with unshed tears. Her lips were trembling, too, and he knew that she was as affected by the moment as he.

He leaned forward . . . slowly, slowly. He wanted to give her the chance to say no. It would kill him if she did, but it would be far worse to listen to her regrets in the proverbial morning.

But she didn't say no, and when he was but a few inches away, her eyes closed and her head tilted slightly to the side, silently inviting him to kiss her.

It was remarkable, but every time he kissed her, her lips seemed to grow sweeter, her scent more beguiling. And his need grew, too. His blood was racing with desire, and it was taking his every last shred of restraint not to push her back onto the sofa and tear her clothes from her body.

That would come later, he thought with a secret smile. But this—surely her first time—would be slow and tender and everything a young girl dreamed.

Well, maybe not. His smile turned into an outright grin. Half the things he was going to do to her, she wouldn't have even *thought* to dream about.

"What are you smiling about?" she asked.

He drew back a few inches, cupping her face with both hands. "How did you know I was smiling?"

"I could feel it on my lips."

He brought a finger to those lips, tracing the outline, then running the edge of his fingernail along the plump skin. "You make me smile," he whispered. "When you don't make me want to scream, you make me smile."

Her lips trembled, and her breath was hot and moist against his finger. He took her hand and brought it to his mouth, rubbing one finger against his lips in much the same way he had done with hers. But as he watched her eyes widen, he dipped her finger into his mouth, softly sucking at the fingertip, tickling her skin with his teeth and tongue.

She gasped, and the sound was sweet and erotic at the same time.

There were a thousand things that Benedict wanted to ask her— How did she feel? What did she feel? But he was so damned afraid that she'd change her mind if he gave her the opportunity to put any of her thoughts into words. And so instead of questions, he gave her kisses, returning his lips to hers in a searing, barely controlled dance of desire.

He murmured her name like a benediction as he lowered her onto the sofa, her bare back rubbing up against the upholstery. "I want you," he groaned. "You have no idea. No idea."

Her only response was a soft mewling sound that came from deep in her throat. For some reason that was like oil on the fire within him, and his fingers clutched at her even tighter, pressing into her skin, as his lips traveled down the swanlike column of her throat.

He moved lower, lower, burning a hot trail on her skin, pausing only briefly when he reached the gentle swell of her breast. She was completely beneath him now, her eyes glazed with desire, and it was so much better than any of his dreams.

And oh, how he'd dreamed of her.

With a low, possessive growl, Benedict took her nipple into his mouth. She let out a soft squeal, and he was unable to suppress his own low rumble of satisfaction. "Shhh," he crooned, "just let me—"

"But—"

He pressed one of his fingers against her lips, probably a little too roughly, but it was getting harder and harder to control his movements. "Don't think," he murmured. "Just lie back and let me pleasure you."

She looked dubious, but when he moved his mouth to her other breast and renewed his sensual onslaught, her eyes grew dazed, her lips parted, and her head lolled back against the cushions.

"Do you like this?" he whispered, tracing the peak of her breast with his tongue.

Sophie couldn't quite manage to open her eyes, but she nodded.

"Do you like this?" Now his tongue moved to the underside of her breast, and he nibbled the sensitive skin over her rib cage.

Her breath shallow and fast, she nodded again.

"What about this?" He pushed her dress further down, nibbling a trail along her skin until he reached her navel.

This time Sophie couldn't even manage a nod. Dear God, she was practically naked before him, and all she could do was moan and sigh and beg for more.

"I need you," she panted.

His words were murmured into the soft skin of her abdomen. "I know."

Sophie squirmed beneath him, unnerved by this primitive need to move. Something very strange was growing within her, something hot and tingling. It was as if she were growing, getting ready to burst through her skin. It was as if, after twenty-two years of life, she were finally coming alive.

She wanted desperately to feel his skin, and she grabbed at the fine linen of his shirt, bunching it in her hands until it came loose of his breeches. She touched him, skimming her hands along his lower back, surprised and delighted when his muscles quivered beneath her fingers.

"Ah, Sophie," he grunted, shuddering as her hands slipped under his shirt to caress his skin.

His reaction emboldened her, and she stroked him more, moving up until she reached his shoulders, broad and firmly muscled.

He groaned again, then cursed under his breath as he lifted himself off of her. "Damn thing is in the way," he muttered, tearing the shirt off and flinging it across the room. Sophie had just an instant to stare at his bare chest before he was atop her again, and this time they were skin against skin.

It was the most glorious feeling she could ever imagine.

He was so warm, and even though his muscles were hard and powerful, his skin was seductively soft. He even smelled good, a warm masculine mixture of sandalwood and soap.

Sophie touched her fingers to his hair as he moved to nuzzle her neck. It was thick and springy, and it tickled her chin as he tickled her neck. "Oh, Benedict," she sighed. "This is so perfect. I can't imagine anything better."

He looked up, his dark eyes as wicked as his smile. "I can."

She felt her lips part and knew she must look terribly foolish, just lying there staring at him like an idiot.

"Just you wait," he said. "Just you wait."

"But— Oh!" She let out a squeal as he flipped off her shoes. One of his hands wrapped around her ankle, then teased its way up her leg.

"Did you imagine this?" he asked, tracing the crease at the back of her knee.

She shook her head frantically, trying not to squirm.

"Really?" he murmured. "Then I'm sure you didn't imagine *this*." He reached up and unsnapped her garters.

"Oh, Benedict, you mustn't—"

"Oh, no, I *must*." He slid her stockings down her legs with agonizing slowness. "I really must."

Sophie watched with openmouthed delight as he tossed them over his head. Her stockings weren't of the highest quality, but they were nonetheless fairly light, and they floated through the air like dandelion tufts until they landed, one on a lamp and the other on the floor.

Then, while she was still laughing and looking at the stocking, hanging drunkenly from the lampshade, he sneaked up on her, sliding his hands back up her legs until they reached all the way to her thighs.

"I daresay no one has ever touched you here," he said wickedly.

Sophie shook her head.

"And I daresay you never imagined it."

She shook her head again.

"If you didn't imagine this . . ." He squeezed her thighs, causing her to squeal and arch off the sofa. ". . . then I'm sure you won't have imagined *this*." He trailed his fingers ever upward as he spoke, the rounded curves of his nails lightly grazing her skin until he reached the soft thatch of her womanhood.

"Oh, no," she said, more out of reflex than anything else. "You can't—"

"Oh, but I can. I assure you."

"But— Ooooooh." It was suddenly as if her brain had flown right out the window, because it was near impossible to think of anything while his fingers were tickling her. Well, almost anything. She seemed able to think about how utterly naughty this was and how very much she didn't want him to stop.

"What are you doing to me?" she gasped, her every muscle tightening as he moved his fingers in a particularly wicked manner.

"Everything," he returned, capturing her lips with his. "Anything you want."

"I want— Oh!"

"Like that, do you?" His words were murmured against her cheek.

"I don't know what I want," she breathed.

"I do." He moved to her ear, nibbling softly on her lobe. "I know exactly what you want. Trust me."

And it was as easy as that. She gave herself over to him completely—not that she hadn't been nearly to that point already. But when he said, "Trust me," and she realized that she did, something changed slightly inside. She was ready for this. It was still wrong, but she was ready, and she wanted it, and for once in her life she was going to do something wild and crazy and completely out of character.

Just because she wanted to.

As if he'd read her thoughts, he pulled away a few inches and cupped one cheek with his large hand. "If you want me to stop," he said, his voice achingly hoarse, "you need to tell me now. Not in ten minutes, not even in one. It has to be now."

Touched that he would even take the time to ask, she reached up and cupped his cheek in the same way he held hers. But when she opened her mouth to speak, the only word she could manage was, "Please."

His eyes flared with need, and then, as if something snapped within him, he changed in an instant. Gone was the gentle, languorous lover. In his place was a man gripped by desire. His hands were everywhere, on her legs, around her waist, touching her face. And before Sophie knew it, her dress was gone, on the floor next to one of her stockings. She was completely nude, and it felt very odd but somehow also very right as long as he was touching her.

The sofa was narrow, but that didn't seem to matter as Benedict yanked off his boots and breeches. He perched alongside her as his boots went flying, unable to stop touching her, even as he divested himself of his clothing. It took longer to get naked, but on the other hand, he had the oddest notion that he might perish on the spot if he moved from her side.

He'd thought he'd wanted a woman before. He'd thought he'd needed one. But this—this went beyond both. This was spiritual. This was in his soul.

His clothes finally gone, he lay back on top of her, pausing for one shuddering moment to savor the feel of her beneath him, skin to skin, head to toe. He was hard as a rock, harder than he could ever remember, but he fought against his impulses, and tried to move slowly.

This was her first time. It had to be perfect.

Or if not perfect, then damn good.

He snaked a hand between them and touched her. She was ready—more than ready for him. He slipped one finger inside of her, grinning with satisfaction as her entire body jerked and tensed around him.

"That's very—" Her voice was raspy, her breathing labored. "Very—"

"Strange?" he finished for her.

She nodded.

He smiled. Slowly, like a cat. "You'll get used to it," he promised. "I plan to get you very used to it."

Sophie's head lolled back. This was madness. Fever. Something was building inside of her, deep in her gut, coiling, pulsing, making her rigid. It was something that needed release, something that grabbed at her, and yet even with all this pressure, it felt so spectacularly wonderful, as if she'd been born for this very moment.

"Oh, Benedict," she sighed. "Oh, my love."

He froze—just for a fraction of a second, but it was long enough for her to know that he'd heard her. But he didn't say a word, just kissed her neck and squeezed her leg as he positioned himself between her thighs and nudged at her entrance.

Her lips parted with shock.

"Don't worry," he said in an amused voice, reading her mind as always. "It will work."

"But—"

"Trust me," he said, the words murmured against her lips.

Slowly, she felt him entering her. She was being stretched, invaded, and yet she wouldn't say it felt bad, exactly. It was . . . It was . . .

He touched her cheek. "You look serious."

"I'm trying to decide how this feels," she admitted.

"If you have the presence of mind to do that, then I'm certainly not doing a good enough job."

Startled, she looked up. He was smiling at her, that crooked grin that never failed to reduce her to mush.

"Stop thinking so hard," he whispered.

"But it's difficult not to— Oh!" And then her eyes rolled back as she arched beneath him.

Benedict buried his head in her neck so she wouldn't see his amused expression. It seemed the best way for him to keep her from overanalyzing a moment that should have been pure sensation and emotion was for him to keep moving.

And he did. Inexorably forward, sliding in and out until he reached the fragile barrier of her maidenhead.

He winced. He'd never been with a virgin before. He'd heard it hurt, that there was nothing a man could do to eliminate the pain for the woman, but surely if he was gentle, it would go easier for her.

He looked down. Her face was flushed, and her breath was rapid. Her eyes were glazed, dazed, clearly rapt with passion.

It fueled his own fire. God, he wanted her so badly his bones ached.

"This might hurt," he lied. It *would* hurt. But he was stuck between wanting to give her the truth so that she would be prepared and giving her the softer version so that she would not be nervous.

"I don't care," she gasped. "Please. I need you."

Benedict leaned down for one final, searing kiss as his hips surged forward. He felt her stiffen slightly around him as he broke through her maidenhead, and he bit—he actually *bit* his hand to keep himself from coming at that very second.

It was like he was a green lad of sixteen, not an experienced man of thirty.

She did this to him. Only her. It was a humbling thought.

Gritting his teeth against his baser urges, Benedict began to move within her, slowly stroking when what he really wanted to do was let go completely.

"Sophie, Sophie," he grunted, repeating her name, trying to remind himself that this time was about *her*. He was here to please *her* needs, not his own.

It would be perfect. It had to be perfect. He needed her to love this. He needed her to love *him*.

She was quickening beneath him, and every wiggle, every squirm whipped up his own frenzy of desire. He was trying to be extra gentle for her, but she was making it so damn hard to hold back. Her hands were everywhere—on his hips, on his back, squeezing his shoulders.

"Sophie," he moaned again. He couldn't hold off much longer. He wasn't strong enough. He wasn't noble enough. He wasn't—

"Ohhhhhhhhhhhhh!"

She convulsed beneath him, her body arching off the sofa as she screamed. Her fingers bit into his back, nails raking his skin, but he didn't care. All he knew was that she'd found her release, and it was good, and for the love of God, he could finally—

"Ahhhhhhhhhhhhh!"

He exploded. There was simply no other word for it.

He couldn't stop moving, couldn't stop shaking, and then, in an instant, he collapsed, dimly aware that he was probably crushing her, but unable to move a single muscle.

He should say something, tell her something about how wonderful it had been. But his tongue felt thick and his lips felt heavy, and on top of all that, he could barely open his eyes. Pretty words would have to wait. He was only a man, and he had to catch his breath.

"Benedict?" she whispered.

He flopped his hand slightly against her. It was the only thing he could manage to indicate that he'd heard.

"Is it always like this?"

He shook his head, hoping that she'd feel the motion and know what it meant.

She sighed and seemed to sink deeper into the cushions. "I didn't think so."

Benedict kissed the side of her head, which was all that he could reach. No, it wasn't always like this. He'd dreamed of her so many times, but this . . . This . . .

This was more than dreams.

Sophie wouldn't have thought it possible, but she must've dozed off, even with the thrilling weight of Benedict pressing her down against the sofa, making it slightly difficult to breathe. He must've fallen asleep, too, and she woke when he woke, aroused by the sudden rush of cool air when he lifted himself off of her body.

He placed a blanket on top of her before she even had a chance to be embarrassed by her nakedness. She smiled even as she blushed, for there was little that could be done to ease her embarrassment. Not that she regretted her actions. But a woman didn't lose her virginity on a sofa and not feel a little bit embarrassed. It simply wasn't possible.

Still, the blanket had been a thoughtful gesture. Not a surprising one, though. Benedict was a thoughtful man.

He obviously didn't share her modesty, though, because he made no attempt to cover himself as he crossed the room and gathered his carelessly flung garments. Sophie stared shamelessly as he pulled on his breeches. He stood straight and proud, and the smile he gave her when he caught her watching was warm and direct.

God, how she loved this man.

"How do you feel?" he asked.

"Fine," she answered. "Good." She smiled shyly. "Splendid."

He picked up his shirt and stuck one arm into it. "I'll send someone over to collect your belongings."

Sophie blinked. "What do you mean?"

"Don't worry, I'll make sure he's discreet. I know it might be embarrassing for you now that you know my family."

Sophie clutched the blanket to her, wishing that her dress wasn't out of reach. Because she suddenly felt ashamed. She'd done the one thing she'd always sworn she would never do, and now Benedict assumed she would be his mistress. And why shouldn't he? It was a fairly natural assumption.

"Please don't send anyone over," she said, her voice small.

He glanced at her in surprise. "You'd rather go yourself?"

"I'd rather my things stayed where they were," she said softly. It was so much easier saying that than telling him directly that she would not become his mistress.

Once, she could forgive. Once, she could even cherish. But a lifetime with a man who was not her husband—that she knew she could not do.

Sophie looked down at her belly, praying that there would be no child to be brought into the world illegitimately.

"What are you telling me?" he said, his eyes intent upon her face.

Damn. He wasn't going to allow her to take the easy way out. "I'm saying," she said, gulping against the boulder-sized lump that had suddenly developed in her throat, "that I cannot be your mistress."

"What do you call this?" he asked in a tight voice, waving his arm at her.

"I call it a lapse in judgment," she said, not meeting his eyes.

"Oh, so I'm a lapse?" he said, his tone unnaturally pleasant. "How nice. I don't believe I've ever been someone's lapse before."

"You know that's not the way I meant it."

"Do I?" He grabbed one of his boots and perched on the arm of a chair so that he could yank it on. "Frankly, my dear, I have no idea what you mean anymore."

"I shouldn't have done this—"

He whipped his head around to face her, his hot, flashing eyes at odds with his bland smile. "Now I'm a *shouldn't*? Excellent. Even better than a lapse. Shouldn't sounds much naughtier, don't you think? A lapse is merely a mistake."

"There is no need to be so ugly about this."

He cocked his head to the side as if he were truly considering her words. "Is that what I'm being? I rather thought I was acting in a most friendly and understanding manner. Look, no yelling, no histrionics . . ."

"I'd prefer yelling and histrionics to *this*."

He scooped up her dress and threw it at her, none too gently. "Well, we don't always get what we prefer, do we, Miss Beckett? I can certainly attest to that."

She grabbed her dress and stuffed it under the covers with her, hoping that she'd eventually find a way to don it without moving the blanket.

"It'll be a neat trick if you figure out how to do it," he said, giving her a condescending glance.

She glared at him. "I'm not asking you to apologize."

"Well, that's a relief. I doubt I could find the words."

"Please don't be so sarcastic."

His smile was mocking in the extreme. "You're hardly in a position to ask me anything."

"Benedict . . ."

He loomed over her, leering rudely. "Except, of course, to rejoin you, which I'd gladly do."

She said nothing.

"Do you understand," he said, his eyes softening slightly, "what it feels like to be pushed away? How many times do you expect you can reject me before I stop trying?"

"It's not that I want to—"

"Oh, stop with that old excuse. It's grown tired. If you wanted to be with me, you would be with me. When you say no, it's because you want to say no."

"You don't understand," she said in a low voice. "You've always been in a position where you could do what you wanted. Some of us don't have that luxury."

"Silly me. I thought I was offering you that very luxury."

"The luxury to be your mistress," she said bitterly.

He crossed his arms, his lips twisting as he said, "You won't have to do anything you haven't already done."

"I got carried away," Sophie said slowly, trying to ignore his insult. It was no more than she deserved. She had slept with him. Why shouldn't he think she would be his mistress? "I made a mistake," she continued. "But that doesn't mean I should do it again."

"I can offer you a better life," he said in a low voice.

She shook her head. "I won't be your mistress. I won't be any man's mistress."

Benedict's lips parted with shock as he digested her words. "Sophie," he said incredulously, "you know I cannot *marry* you."

"Of course I know that," she snapped. "I'm a servant, not an idiot."

Benedict tried for a moment to put himself in her shoes. He knew she wanted respectability, but she had to know that he could not give it to her. "It would be hard for you as well," he said softly, "even if I were to marry you. You would not be accepted. The *ton* can be cruel."

Sophie let out a loud, hollow laugh. "I know," she said, her smile utterly humorless. "Believe me, I know."

"Then why—"

"Grant me a favor," she interrupted, turning her face so that she was no longer looking at him. "Find someone to marry. Find someone acceptable, who will make you happy. And then leave me alone."

Her words struck a chord, and Benedict was suddenly reminded of the lady from the masquerade. She had been of his world, his class. She would have been acceptable. And he realized, as he stood there, staring down at Sophie, who was huddled on the sofa, trying not to look at him, that she was the one he'd always pictured in his mind, whenever he thought to the future. Whenever he imagined himself with a wife and children.

He'd spent the last two years with one eye on every door, always waiting for his lady in silver to enter the room. He felt silly sometimes, even stupid, but he'd never been able to erase her from his thoughts.

Or purge the dream—the one in which he pledged his troth to her, and they lived happily ever after.

It was a silly fantasy for a man of his reputation, sickly sweet and sentimental, but he hadn't been able to help himself. That's what came from growing up in a large and loving family—one tended to want the same for oneself.

But the woman from the masquerade had become barely more than a mirage. Hell, he didn't even know her name. And Sophie was *here.*

He couldn't marry her, but that didn't mean they couldn't be together. It would mean compromise, mostly on her part, he admitted. But they could do it. And they'd certainly be happier than if they remained apart.

"Sophie," he began, "I know the situation is not ideal—"

"Don't," she interrupted, her voice low, barely audible.

"If you'd only listen—"

"*Please.* Don't."

"But you're not—"

"Stop!" she said, her voice rising perilously in volume.

She was holding her shoulders so tightly they were practically at her ears, but Benedict forged on, anyway. He loved her. He needed her. He had to make her see reason. "Sophie, I know you'll agree if—"

"I won't have an illegitimate child!" she finally yelled, struggling to keep the blanket around her as she rose to her feet. "I won't do it! I love you, but not that much. I don't love anyone that much."

His eyes fell to her midsection. "It may very well be too late for that, Sophie."

"I know," she said quietly, "and it's already eating me up inside."

"Regrets have a way of doing that."

She looked away. "I don't regret what we did. I wish I could. I know I should. But I can't."

Benedict just stared at her. He wanted to understand her, but he just couldn't grasp how she could be so adamant about not wanting to be his mistress and have his children and at the same time *not* regret their lovemaking.

How could she say she loved him? It made the pain that much more intense.

"If we don't have a child," she said quietly, "then I shall consider myself very lucky. And I won't tempt the fates again."

"No, you'll merely tempt *me*," he said, hearing the sneer in his voice and hating it.

She ignored him, drawing the blanket closer around her as she stared sightlessly at a painting on the wall. "I'll have a memory I will forever cherish. And that, I suppose, is why I can't regret what we did."

"It won't keep you warm at night."

"No," she agreed sadly, "but it will keep my dreams full."

"You're a coward," he accused. "A coward for not chasing after those dreams."

She turned around. "No," she said, her voice remarkably even considering the way he was glaring at her. "What I am is a bastard. And before you say you don't care, let me assure you that I do. And so does everyone else. Not a day has gone by that I am not in some way reminded of the baseness of my birth."

"Sophie . . ."

"If I have a child," she said, her voice starting to crack, "do you know how much I would love it? More than life, more than breath, more than anything. How could I hurt my own child the way I've been hurt? How could I subject her to the same kind of pain?"

"Would you reject your child?"

"Of course not!"

"Then she wouldn't feel the same sort of pain," Benedict said with a shrug. "Because I wouldn't reject her either."

"You don't understand," she said, the words ending on a whimper.

He pretended he hadn't heard her. "Am I correct in assuming that *you* were rejected by your parents?"

Her smile was tight and ironic. "Not precisely. Ignored would be a better description."

"Sophie," he said, rushing toward her and gathering her in his arms, "you don't have to repeat the mistakes of your parents."

"I know," she said sadly, not struggling in his embrace, but not returning it either. "And that's why I cannot be your mistress. I won't relive my mother's life."

"You wouldn't—"

"They say that a smart person learns from her mistakes," she interrupted, her voice forcefully ending his protest. "But a truly smart person learns from other people's mistakes." She pulled away, then turned to face him. "I'd like to think I'm a truly smart person. Please don't take that away from me."

There was a desperate, almost palpable, pain in her eyes. It hit him in the chest, and he staggered back a step.

"I'd like to get dressed," she said, turning away. "I think you should leave."

He stared at her back for several seconds before saying, "I could make you change your mind. I could kiss you, and you would—"

"You wouldn't," she said, not moving a muscle. "It isn't in you."

"It *is*."

"You would kiss me, and then you would hate yourself. And it would only take a second."

He left without another word, letting the click of the door signal his departure.

Inside the room, Sophie's quivering hands dropped the blanket, and she crumpled onto the sofa, forever staining its delicate fabric with her tears.

Chapter 18

Pickings have been slim this past fortnight for marriage-minded misses and their mamas. The crop of bachelors is low to begin with this season, as two of 1816's most eligible, the Duke of Ashbourne and the Earl of Macclesfield, got themselves leg-shackled last year.

To make matters worse, the two unmarried Bridgerton brothers (discounting Gregory, who is only sixteen and hardly in a position to aid any poor, young misses on the marriage mart) have made themselves very scarce. Colin, This Author is told, is out of town, possibly in Wales or Scotland (although no one seems to know why he would go to Wales or Scotland in the middle of the season). Benedict's story is more puzzling. He is apparently in London, but he eschews all polite social gatherings in favor of less genteel milieus.

Although if truth be told, This Author should not give the impression that the aforementioned Mr. Bridgerton has been spending his every waking hour in debauched abandon. If accounts are correct, he has spent most of the past fortnight in his lodgings on Bruton Street.

As there have been no rumors that he is ill, This Author can

only assume that he has finally come to the conclusion that the
London season is utterly dull and not worth his time.
Smart man, indeed.

LADY WHISTLEDOWN'S SOCIETY PAPERS, 9 JUNE 1817

Sophie didn't see Benedict for a full fortnight. She didn't know whether to be pleased, surprised, or disappointed. She didn't know whether she *was* pleased, surprised, or disappointed.

She didn't know anything these days. Half the time she felt like she didn't even know herself.

She was certain that she had made the right decision in yet again refusing Benedict's offer. She knew it in her head, and even though she ached for the man she loved, she knew it in her heart. She had suffered too much pain from her bastardy ever to risk imposing the same on a child, especially one of her own.

No, that was not true. She had risked it once. And she couldn't quite make herself regret it. The memory was too precious. But that didn't mean she should do it again.

But if she was so certain that she'd done the right thing, why did it hurt so much? It was as if her heart were perpetually breaking. Every day, it tore some more, and every day, Sophie told herself that it could not get worse, that surely her heart was finished breaking, that it was finally well and fully broken, and yet every night she cried herself to sleep, aching for Benedict.

And every day she felt even worse.

Her tension was intensified by the fact that she was terrified to step outside the house. Posy would surely be looking for her, and Sophie thought it best if Posy didn't find her.

Not that she thought Posy was likely to reveal her presence here in London to Araminta; Sophie knew Posy well enough to trust that Posy would never deliberately break a promise. And Posy's nod when Sophie had been frantically shaking her head could definitely be considered a promise.

But as true of heart as Posy was when it came to keeping promises, the same could not, unfortunately, be said of her lips. And Sophie could easily imagine a scenario—many scenarios as a matter of fact—in which Posy would accidentally blurt out that she'd seen Sophie. Which meant that Sophie's one big advantage was that Posy didn't know where Sophie was staying. For all she knew, Sophie had just been out for a stroll. Or maybe Sophie had come to spy on Araminta.

In all truth, that seemed an awful lot more plausible than the truth, which was that Sophie just happened to have been blackmailed into taking a job as a lady's maid just down the street.

And so, Sophie's emotions kept darting back and forth from melancholy to nervous, brokenhearted to downright fearful.

She'd managed to keep most of this to herself, but she knew she had grown distracted and quiet, and she also knew that Lady Bridgerton and her daughters had noticed it. They looked at her with concerned expressions, spoke with an extra gentleness. And they kept wondering why she did not come to tea.

"Sophie! There you are!"

Sophie had been hurrying to her room, where a small pile of mending awaited, but Lady Bridgerton had caught her in the hall.

She stopped and tried to manage a smile of greeting as she bobbed a curtsy. "Good afternoon, Lady Bridgerton."

"Good afternoon, Sophie. I have been looking all over for you."

Sophie stared at her blankly. She seemed to do a lot of that lately. It was difficult to focus on anything. "You have?" she asked.

"Yes. I was wondering why you haven't been to tea all week. You know that you are always invited when we are taking it informally."

Sophie felt her cheeks grow warm. She'd been avoiding tea because it was just so hard to be in the same room with all those Bridgertons at once and not to think of Benedict. They all looked so alike, and whenever they were together they were such a family.

It forced Sophie to remember everything that she didn't have, reminded her of what she'd never have: a family of her own.

Someone to love. Someone who'd love her. All within the bounds of respectability and marriage.

She supposed there were women who could throw over respectability for passion and love. A very large part of her wished she were one of those women. But she was not. Love could not conquer all. At least not for her.

"I've been very busy," she finally said to Lady Bridgerton.

Lady Bridgerton just smiled at her—a small, vaguely inquisitive smile, imposing a silence that forced Sophie to say more.

"With the mending," she added.

"How terrible for you. I wasn't aware that we'd poked holes in quite so many stockings."

"Oh, you haven't!" Sophie replied, biting her tongue the minute she said it. There went her excuse. "I have some mending of my own," she improvised, gulping as she realized how bad that sounded. Lady Bridgerton well knew that Sophie had no clothes other than the ones she had given her, which were all, needless to say, in perfect condition. And besides, it was very bad form for Sophie to be doing her own mending during the day, when she was meant to be waiting on the girls. Lady Bridgerton was an understanding employer; she probably wouldn't have minded, but it went against Sophie's own code of ethics. She'd been given a job—a good one, even if it did involve getting her heart broken on a day to day basis—and she took pride in her work.

"I see," Lady Bridgerton said, that enigmatic smile still in place on her face. "You may, of course, bring your own mending to tea."

"Oh, but I could not dream of it."

"But I am telling you that you *can.*"

And Sophie could tell by the tone of her voice that what she was really saying was that she *must.*

"Of course," Sophie murmured, and followed her into the upstairs sitting room.

The girls were all there, in their usual places, bickering and smiling and tossing jokes (although thankfully no scones). The eldest Bridgerton daughter, Daphne—now the Duchess of Hastings—was there as well, with her youngest daughter, Caroline, in her arms.

"Sophie!" Hyacinth said with a beam. "I thought you must have been ill."

"But you just saw me this morning," Sophie reminded her, "when I dressed your hair."

"Yes, but you didn't seem quite yourself."

Sophie had no suitable reply, since she really *hadn't* been quite herself. She couldn't very well contradict the truth. So she just sat in a chair and nodded when Francesca inquired if she wanted some tea.

"Penelope Featherington said she would drop by today," Eloise said to her mother just as Sophie was taking her first sip. Sophie had never met Penelope, but she was frequently written about in *Whistledown*, and she knew that she and Eloise were fast friends.

"Has anyone noticed that Benedict hasn't visited in some time?" Hyacinth asked.

Sophie jabbed her finger but thankfully managed to keep from yelping with pain.

"He hasn't been by to see Simon and me, either," Daphne said.

"Well, he told me he would help me with my arithmetic," Hyacinth grumbled, "and he has most certainly reneged on his word."

"I'm sure it has merely slipped his mind," Lady Bridgerton said diplomatically. "Perhaps if you sent him a note."

"Or simply banged on his door," Francesca said, giving her eyes a slight roll. "It's not as if he lives very far away."

"I am an unmarried female," Hyacinth said with a huff. "I cannot visit bachelor lodgings."

Sophie coughed.

"You're fourteen," Francesca said disdainfully.

"Nevertheless!"

"You should ask Simon for help, anyway," Daphne said. "He's much better with numbers than Benedict."

"You know, she's right," Hyacinth said, looking at her mother after shooting one last glare at Francesca. "Pity for Benedict. He's completely without use to me now."

They all giggled, because they knew she was joking. Except for Sophie, who didn't think she knew how to giggle anymore.

"But in all seriousness," Hyacinth continued, "what *is* he good at? Simon's better at numbers, and Anthony knows more of history. Colin's funnier, of course, and—"

"Art," Sophie interrupted in a sharp voice, a little irritated that Benedict's own family didn't see his individuality and strengths.

Hyacinth looked at her in surprise. "I beg your pardon?"

"He's good at art," Sophie repeated. "Quite a bit better than any of you, I imagine."

That got everyone's attention, because while Sophie had let them see her naturally dry wit, she was generally soft-spoken, and she certainly had never said a sharp word to any of them.

"I didn't even know he drew," Daphne said with quiet interest. "Or does he paint?"

Sophie glanced at her. Of the Bridgerton women, she knew Daphne the least, but it would have been impossible to miss the look of sharp intelligence in her eyes. Daphne was curious about her brother's hidden talent, she wanted to know why she didn't know about it, and most of all, she wanted to know why Sophie *did*.

In less than a second Sophie was able to see all of that in the young duchess's eyes. And in less than a second she decided that she'd made a mistake. If Benedict hadn't told his family about his art, then it wasn't her place to do so.

"He draws," she finally said, in a voice that she hoped was curt enough to prevent further questions.

It was. No one said a word, although five pairs of eyes remained focused quite intently on her face.

"He sketches," Sophie muttered.

She looked from face to face. Eloise's eyes were blinking rapidly. Lady Bridgerton wasn't blinking at all. "He's quite good," Sophie muttered, mentally kicking herself even as she said it. There was something about silence among the Bridgertons that compelled her to fill the void.

Finally, after the longest moment of silence ever to fill the space of a second, Lady Bridgerton cleared her throat and said, "I should like to see one of his sketches." She dabbed a napkin to her lips even though she hadn't taken a sip of her tea. "Provided, of course, that he cares to share it with me."

Sophie stood up. "I think I should go."

Lady Bridgerton speared her with her eyes. "Please," she said, in a voice that was velvet over steel, "stay."

Sophie sat back down.

Eloise jumped to her feet. "I think I hear Penelope."

"You do not," Hyacinth said.

"Why would I lie?"

"I certainly don't know, but—"

The butler appeared in the doorway. "Miss Penelope Featherington," he intoned.

"*See,*" Eloise shot at Hyacinth.

"Is this a bad time?" Penelope asked.

"No," Daphne replied with a small, vaguely amused smile, "just an odd one."

"Oh. Well, I could come back later, I suppose."

"Of course not," Lady Bridgerton said. "Please sit down and have some tea."

Sophie watched as the young woman took a seat on the sofa next to Francesca. Penelope was no sophisticated beauty, but she was rather fetching in her own, uncomplicated way. Her hair was a brownish red, and her cheeks were lightly dusted with freckles. Her complexion was a touch sallow, although Sophie had a suspicion that that had more to do with her unattractive yellow frock than anything else.

Come to think of it, she rather thought that she'd read something in Lady Whistledown's column about Penelope's awful clothes. Pity the poor girl couldn't talk her mother into letting her wear blue.

But as Sophie surreptitiously studied Penelope, she became aware that Penelope was not-so-surreptitiously studying her.

"Have we met?" Penelope suddenly asked.

Sophie was suddenly gripped by an awful, premonition-like feeling. Or maybe it was déjà vu. "I don't think so," she said quickly.

Penelope's gaze didn't waver from her face. "Are you certain?"

"I—I don't see how we could have done."

Penelope let out a little breath and shook her head, as if clearing cobwebs from her mind. "I'm sure you're correct. But there is something terribly familiar about you."

"Sophie is our new lady's maid," Hyacinth said, as if that would explain anything. "She usually joins us for tea when we're only family."

Sophie watched Penelope as she murmured something in response, and then suddenly it hit her. She *had* seen Penelope before! It had been at the masquerade, probably no more than ten seconds before she'd met Benedict.

She'd just made her entrance, and the young men who had quickly surrounded her had still been making their way to her side. Penelope had been standing right there, dressed in some rather strange green costume with a funny hat. For some reason she hadn't been wearing a mask. Sophie had stared at her for a moment, trying to figure out what her costume was meant to be, when a young gentleman had bumped into Penelope, nearly knocking her to the floor.

Sophie had reached out and helped her up, and had just managed to say something like, "There you are," when several more gentlemen had rushed in, separating the two women.

Then Benedict had arrived, and Sophie had had eyes for no one but him. Penelope—and the abominable way she had been treated by the young gentlemen at the masquerade—had been forgotten until this very moment.

And clearly the event had remained buried at the back of Penelope's mind as well.

"I'm sure I must be mistaken," Penelope said as she accepted a cup of tea from Francesca. "It's not your looks, precisely, but rather the way you hold yourself, if that makes any sense."

Sophie decided that a smooth intervention was necessary and so she pasted on her best conversational smile, and said, "I shall take that as a compliment, since I am sure that the ladies of your acquaintance are gracious and kind indeed."

The minute she shut her mouth, however, she realized that that had been overkill. Francesca was looking at her as if she'd sprouted horns, and the corners of Lady Bridgerton's mouth were twitching as she said, "Why, Sophie, I vow that is the longest sentence you have uttered in a fortnight."

Sophie lifted her teacup to her face and mumbled, "I haven't been feeling well."

"Oh!" Hyacinth suddenly blurted out. "I hope you are not feeling too sickly, because I was hoping you could help me this evening."

"Of course," Sophie said, eager for an excuse to turn away from Penelope, who was still studying her as if she were a human puzzle. "What is it you need?"

"I have promised to entertain my cousins this eve."

"Oh, that's right," Lady Bridgerton said, setting her saucer down on the table. "I'd nearly forgotten."

Hyacinth nodded. "Could you help? There are four of them, and I'm sure to be overrun."

"Of course," Sophie said. "How old are they?"

Hyacinth shrugged.

"Between the ages of six and ten," Lady Bridgerton said with a dissaproving expression. "You should know that, Hyacinth."

Sophie said to Hyacinth, "Fetch me when they arrive. I love children and would be happy to help."

"Excellent," Hyacinth said, clasping her hands together. "They are so young and active. They would have worn me out."

"Hyacinth," Francesca said, "you're hardly old and decrepit."

"When was the last time you spent two hours with four children under the age of ten?"

"Stop," Sophie said, laughing for the first time in two weeks. "I'll help. No one will be worn-out. And you should come, too, Francesca. We'll have a lovely time, I'm sure."

"Are you—" Penelope started to say something, then cut herself off. "Never mind."

But when Sophie looked over at her, she was still staring at her face with a most perplexed expression. Penelope opened her mouth, closed it, then opened it again, saying, "I *know* I know you."

"I'm sure she's right," Eloise said with a jaunty grin. "Penelope never forgets a face."

Sophie blanched.

"Are you quite all right?" Lady Bridgerton asked, leaning forward. "You don't look well."

"I think something didn't agree with me," Sophie hastily lied, clutching her stomach for effect. "Perhaps the milk was off."

"Oh, dear," Daphne said with a concerned frown as she looked down at her baby. "I gave some to Caroline."

"It tasted fine to me," Hyacinth said.

"It might have been something from this morning," Sophie said, not wanting Daphne to worry. "But all the same, I think I had better lie down." She stood and took a step toward the door. "If that is agreeable to you, Lady Bridgerton."

"Of course," she replied. "I hope you feel better soon."

"I'm sure I will," Sophie said, quite truthfully. She'd feel better just as soon as she left Penelope Featherington's line of vision.

"I'll come get you when my cousins arrive," Hyacinth called out.

"If you're feeling better," Lady Bridgerton added.

Sophie nodded and hurried out of the room, but as she left, she caught sight of Penelope Featherington watching her with a most intent expression, leaving Sophie filled with a horrible sense of dread.

Benedict had been in a bad mood for two weeks. And, he thought as he trudged down the pavement toward his mother's house, his bad mood was about to get worse. He'd been avoiding coming here because he didn't want to see Sophie; he didn't want to see his mother, who was sure to sense his bad mood and question him about it; he didn't want to see Eloise, who was sure to sense his mother's interest and try to interrogate him; he didn't want to see—

Hell, he didn't want to see anyone. And considering the way he'd been snapping off the heads of his servants (verbally, to be sure, although occasionally quite literally in his dreams) the rest of the world would do well if they didn't care to see him, either.

But, as luck would have it, right as he placed his foot on the first step, he heard someone call out his name, and when he turned around, both of his adult brothers were walking toward him along the pavement.

Benedict groaned. No one knew him better than Anthony and Colin, and they weren't likely to let a little thing like a broken heart go unnoticed or unmentioned.

"Haven't seen you in an age," Anthony said. "Where have you been?"

"Here and there," Benedict said evasively. "Mostly at home." He turned to Colin. "Where have *you* been?"

"Wales."

"Wales? Why?"

Colin shrugged. "I felt like it. Never been there before."

"Most people require a slightly more compelling reason to take off in the middle of the season," Benedict said.

"Not I."

Benedict stared at him. Anthony stared at him.

"Oh, very well," Colin said with a scowl. "I needed to get away. Mother has started in on me with this bloody marriage thing."

"'Bloody marriage thing'?" Anthony asked with an amused smile. "I assure you, the deflowering of one's wife is not quite so gory."

Benedict kept his expression scrupulously impassive. He'd found a small spot of blood on his sofa after he'd made love to Sophie. He'd thrown a pillow over it, hoping that by the time any of the servants noticed, they'd have forgotten that he'd had a woman over. He liked to think that none of the staff had been listening at doors or gossiping, but Sophie herself had once told him that servants generally knew everything that went on in a household, and he tended to think that she was right.

But if he had indeed blushed—and his cheeks did feel a touch warm—neither of his brothers saw it, because they didn't say anything, and if there was anything in life as certain as, say, the sun rising in the east, it was that a Bridgerton never passed up the opportunity to tease and torment another Bridgerton.

"She's been talking about Penelope Featherington nonstop," Colin said with a scowl. "I tell you, I've known the girl since we were both in short pants. Er, since I was in short pants, at least. She was in . . ." He scowled some more, because both his brothers were laughing at him. "She was in whatever it is that young girls wear."

"Frocks?" Anthony supplied helpfully.

"Petticoats?" was Benedict's suggestion.

"The point is," Colin said forcefully, "that I have known her forever, and I can assure you I am not likely to fall in love with her."

Anthony turned to Benedict and said, "They'll be married within a year. Mark my words."

Colin crossed his arms. "Anthony!"

"Maybe two," Benedict said. "He's young yet."

"Unlike *you*," Colin retorted. "Why am I besieged by Mother, I wonder? Good God, you're thirty-one—"

"Thirty," Benedict snapped.

"Regardless, one would think you'd be getting the brunt of it."

Benedict frowned. His mother had been uncharacteristically reserved these past few weeks when it came to her opinions on Benedict and marriage and why the two ought to meet and soon. Of course, Benedict had been avoiding his mother's house like the plague, but even before that, she'd not mentioned a word.

It was most odd.

"At any rate," Colin was still grumbling, "I am not going to marry soon, and I am certainly not going to marry Penelope Featherington!"

"Oh!"

It was a feminine "oh," and without looking up, Benedict somehow knew that he was about to experience one of life's most awkward moments. Heart filled with dread, he lifted his head and turned toward the front door. There, framed perfectly in the open doorway, was Penelope Featherington, her lips parted with shock, her eyes filled with heartbreak.

And in that moment, Benedict realized what he'd probably been too stupid (and stupidly male) to notice: Penelope Featherington was in love with his brother.

Colin cleared his throat. "Penelope," he squeaked, his voice sounding as if he'd regressed ten years and gone straight back to puberty, "uh . . . good to see you." He looked to his brothers to leap in and save him, but neither chose to intervene.

Benedict winced. It was one of those moments that simply could not be saved.

"I didn't know you were there," Colin said lamely.

"Obviously not," Penelope said, but her words lacked an edge.

Colin swallowed painfully. "Were you visiting Eloise?"

She nodded. "I was invited."

"I'm sure you were!" he said quickly. "Of course you were. You're a great friend of the family."

Silence. Horrible, awkward silence.

"As if you would come uninvited," Colin mumbled.

Penelope said nothing. She tried to smile, but she obviously couldn't quite manage it. Finally, just when Benedict thought she would brush by them all and flee down the street, she looked straight at Colin and said, "I never asked you to marry me."

Colin's cheeks turned a deeper red than Benedict would have thought humanly possible. Colin opened his mouth, but no sound came out.

It was the first—and quite possibly would be the only—moment of Benedict's recollection for which his younger brother was at a complete loss for words.

"And I never—" Penelope added, swallowing convulsively when the words came out a bit tortured and broken. "I never said to anyone that I wanted you to ask me."

"Penelope," Colin finally managed, "I'm so sorry."

"You have nothing to apologize for," she said.

"No," Colin insisted, "I do. I hurt your feelings, and—"

"You didn't know I was there."

"But nevertheless—"

"You are not going to marry me," she said hollowly. "There is nothing wrong with that. I am not going to marry your brother Benedict."

Benedict had been trying not to look, but he snapped to attention at that.

"It doesn't hurt his feelings when I announce that I am not going to marry him." She turned to Benedict, her brown eyes focusing on his. "Does it, Mr. Bridgerton?"

"Of course not," Benedict answered quickly.

"It's settled, then," she said tightly. "No feelings were hurt. Now then, if you will excuse me, gentlemen, I should like to go home."

Benedict, Anthony, and Colin parted as if drops in the Red Sea as she made her way down the steps.

"Don't you have a maid?" Colin asked.

She shook her head. "I live just around the corner."

"I know, but—"

"I'll escort you," Anthony said smoothly.

"That's really not necessary, my lord."

"Humor me," he said.

She nodded, and the two of them took off down the street.

Benedict and Colin watched their retreating forms in silence for a full thirty seconds before Benedict turned to his brother and said, "That was very well done of you."

"I didn't know she was there!"

"Obviously," Benedict drawled.

"Don't. I feel terrible enough already."

"As well you should."

"Oh, and you have never inadvertently hurt a woman's feelings before?" Colin's voice was defensive, just defensive enough so that Benedict knew he felt like an utter heel inside.

Benedict was saved from having to reply by the arrival of his mother, standing at the top of the steps, framed in the doorway much the same way Penelope had been just a few minutes earlier.

"Has your brother arrived yet?" Violet asked.

Benedict jerked his head toward the corner. "He is escorting Miss Featherington home."

"Oh. Well, that's very thoughtful of him. I—Where are you going, Colin?"

Colin paused briefly but didn't even turn his head as he grunted, "I need a drink."

"It's a bit early for——" She stopped mid-sentence when Benedict laid his hand on her arm.

"Let him go," he said.

She opened her mouth as if to protest, then changed her mind and merely nodded. "I'd hoped to gather the family for an announcement," she said with a sigh, "but I suppose that can wait. In the meantime, why don't you join me for tea?"

Benedict glanced at the clock in the hall. "Isn't it a bit late for tea?"

"Skip the tea then," she said with a shrug. "I was merely looking for an excuse to speak with you."

Benedict managed a weak smile. He wasn't in the mood to converse with his mother. To be frank, he wasn't in the mood to converse with any person, a fact to which anyone with whom he'd recently crossed paths would surely attest.

"It's nothing serious," Violet said. "Heavens, you look as if you're ready to go to the gallows."

It probably would have been rude to point out that that was exactly how he felt, so instead he just leaned down and kissed her on the cheek.

"Well, that's a nice surprise," she said, beaming up at him. "Now come with me," she added, motioning toward the downstairs sitting room. "I have someone I want to tell you about."

"Mother!"

"Just hear me out. She's a lovely girl . . ."

The gallows indeed.

Chapter 19

Miss Posy Reiling (younger step-daughter to the late Earl of Pen-wood) isn't a frequent subject of this column (nor, This Author is sad to say, a frequent subject of attention at social functions) but one could not help but notice that she was acting very strangely at her mother's musicale on Tuesday eve. She insisted upon sitting by the window, and she spent most of the performance staring at the streetscape, as if looking for something . . . or perhaps someone?

LADY WHISTLEDOWN'S SOCIETY PAPERS,
11 JUNE 1817

Forty-five minutes later, Benedict was slouching in his chair, his eyes glazed. Every now and then he had to stop and make sure his mouth wasn't hanging open.

His mother's conversation was *that* boring.

The young lady she had wanted to discuss with him had actually turned out to be seven young ladies, each of which she *assured* him was better than the last.

Benedict thought he might go mad. Right there in his mother's sitting room he was going to go stark, raving mad. He'd suddenly pop out of his chair, fall to the floor in a frenzy, his arms and legs waving, mouth frothing—

"Benedict, are you even *listening* to me?"

He looked up and blinked. Damn. Now he would have to focus on his mother's list of possible brides. The prospect of losing his sanity had been infinitely more appealing.

"I was trying to tell you about Mary Edgeware," Violet said, looking more amused than frustrated.

Benedict was instantly suspicious. When it came to her children dragging their feet to the altar, his mother was never amused. "Mary who?"

"Edge—Oh, never mind. I can see that I cannot compete with whatever is plaguing you just now."

"Mother," Benedict said abruptly.

She cocked her head slightly to the side, her eyes intrigued and perhaps a bit surprised. "Yes?"

"When you met Father—"

"It happened in an instant," she said softly, somehow knowing what he'd meant to ask.

"So you knew that he was the one?"

She smiled, and her eyes took on a faraway, misty look. "Oh, I wouldn't have admitted it," she said. "At least not right away. I fancied myself a practical sort. I'd always scoffed at the notion of love at first sight." She paused for a moment, and Benedict knew she was no longer in the room with him, but at some long-ago ball, meeting his father for the first time. Finally, just when he thought she'd completely forgotten the conversation, she looked back up and said, "But I knew."

"From the first moment you saw him?"

"Well, from the first time we spoke, at least." She took his offered handkerchief and dabbed at her eyes, smiling sheepishly, as if embarrassed by her tears.

Benedict felt a lump forming in his throat, and he looked away, not wanting her to see the moisture forming in his own eyes. Would anyone cry for him more than a decade after he died? It was a humbling thing to be in the presence of true love, and Benedict suddenly felt so damned jealous—of his own *parents*.

They'd found love and had the good sense to recognize and cherish it. Few people were so fortunate.

"There was something about his voice that was so soothing, so warm," Violet continued. "When he spoke, you felt like you were the only person in the room."

"I remember," Benedict said with a warm, nostalgic smile. "It was quite a feat, to be able to do that with eight children."

His mother swallowed convulsively, then said, her voice once again brisk, "Yes, well, he never knew Hyacinth, so I suppose it was only seven."

"Still . . ."

She nodded. "Still."

Benedict reached out and patted her on the hand. He didn't know why; he hadn't planned to. But somehow it seemed the right thing to do.

"Yes, well," she said, giving his hand a little squeeze before returning hers to her lap. "Was there any particular reason you asked about your father?"

"No," he lied. "At least not . . . Well . . ."

She waited patiently, with that mildly expectant expression that made it impossible to keep one's feelings to oneself.

"What happens," he asked, as surprised by the words tumbling forth as she undoubtedly was, "when one falls in love with someone unsuitable?"

"Someone unsuitable," she repeated.

Benedict nodded painfully, immediately regretting his words. He should never have said anything to his mother, and yet . . .

He sighed. His mother had always been a remarkably good listener. And truly, for all her annoying matchmaking ways, she was more qualified to give advice on matters of the heart than anyone he knew.

When she spoke, she appeared to be choosing her words carefully. "What do you mean by unsuitable?"

"Someone . . ." He stopped, paused. "Someone someone like me probably shouldn't marry."

"Someone perhaps who is not of our social class?"

He glanced at a painting on the wall. "Someone like that."

"I see. Well . . ." Violet's brow scrunched a bit, then she said, "I suppose it would depend on how far out of our social class this person is."

"Far."

"A little bit far or quite a lot far?"

Benedict was convinced that no man of his age and reputation had ever had such a conversation with his mother, but he nonetheless answered, "Quite a lot."

"I see. Well, I would have to say . . ." She chewed on her lower lip for a moment before continuing. "I would have to say," she said, slightly more forcefully (although not, if one was judging in absolute terms, forceful at all).

"I would have to say," she said for a third time, "that I love you very much and will support you in all things." She cleared her throat. "If indeed we are talking about *you*."

It seemed useless to deny it, so Benedict just nodded.

"But," Violet added, "I would caution you to consider what you are doing. Love is, of course, the most important element in any union, but outside influences can put a strain on a marriage. And if you marry someone of, say"—she cleared her throat—"the servant class, then you will find yourself the subject of a great deal of gossip and no small amount of ostracism. And that will be difficult for one such as you to bear."

"One such as me?" he asked, bristling at her choice of words.

"You must know I mean no insult. But you and your brothers do lead charmed lives. You're handsome, intelligent, personable. Everyone likes you. I cannot tell you how happy that makes me." She smiled, but it was a wistful, slightly sad smile. "It is not easy to be a wallflower."

And suddenly Benedict understood why his mother was always forcing him to dance with the girls like Penelope Featherington. The ones who stood at the fringes of the ballroom, the ones who always pretended they didn't actually *want* to dance.

She had been a wallflower herself.

It was difficult to imagine. His mother was hugely popular now, with an easy smile and piles of friends. And if Benedict had heard the story correctly, his father had been considered the catch of the season.

"Only you will be able to make this decision," Violet continued, bringing Benedict's thoughts back to the here and now, "and I'm afraid it won't be an easy one."

He stared out the window, his silence his agreement.

"But," she added, "should you decide to join your life with someone not of our class, I will of course support you in every possible manner."

Benedict looked up sharply. There were few women of the *ton* who would say the same to their sons.

"You are my son," she said simply. "I would give my life for you."

He opened his mouth to speak but was surprised to find that he couldn't make a sound.

"I certainly wouldn't banish you for marrying someone unsuitable."

"Thank you," he said. It was all he could manage to say.

Violet sighed, loudly enough to regain his full attention. She looked tired, wistful. "I wish your father were here," she said.

"You don't say that very often," he said quietly.

"I always wish your father were here." She closed her eyes for a brief moment. "Always."

And then somehow it became clear. As he watched his mother's face, finally realizing—no, finally *understanding*—the depth of his parents' love for one another, it all became clear.

Love. He loved Sophie. That was all that should have mattered.

He'd thought he'd loved the woman from the masquerade. He'd thought he'd wanted to marry her. But he understood now that that had been nothing but a dream, a fleeting fantasy of a woman he barely knew.

But Sophie was . . .

Sophie was Sophie. And that was everything he needed.

Sophie wasn't a great believer in destiny or fate, but after one hour with Nicholas, Elizabeth, John, and Alice Wentworth, young cousins to the Bridgerton clan, she was beginning to think that maybe there was a reason she had never managed to obtain a position as a governess.

She was exhausted.

No, no, she thought, with more than a touch of desperation. Exhaustion didn't really provide an adequate description for the current state of her existence. Exhaustion didn't quite capture the slight edge of insanity the foursome had brought to her mind.

"No, no, no, that's *my* doll," Elizabeth said to Alice.

"It's mine," Alice returned.

"It is not!"

"Is too!"

"I'll settle this," ten-year-old Nicholas said, swaggering over with his hands on his hips.

Sophie groaned. She had a feeling that it was not a terribly good idea to allow the dispute to be settled by a ten-year-old boy who happened to think he was a pirate.

"Neither of you will want the doll," he said, with a devious gleam in his eye, "if I simply *lop* off its—"

Sophie leapt to intervene. "You will not lop off its head, Nicholas Wentworth."

"But then they'll stop—"

"No," Sophie said forcefully.

He looked at her, obviously assessing her commitment to that particular course of action, then grumbled and walked away.

"I think we need a new game," Hyacinth whispered to Sophie.

"I *know* we need a new game," Sophie muttered.

"Let go of my soldier!" John screeched. "Let go let go let go!"

"I'm never having children," Hyacinth announced. "In fact, I may never get married."

Sophie forbore to point out that when Hyacinth married and had children, she would certainly have a flotilla of nurses and nannies to aid her with their keeping and care.

Hyacinth winced as John pulled Alice's hair, then swallowed uncomfortably as Alice slugged John in the stomach. "The situation is growing desperate," she whispered to Sophie.

"Blind man's bluff!" Sophie suddenly exclaimed. "What do you think, everyone? How about a game of blind man's bluff?"

Alice and John nodded enthusiastically, and Elizabeth gave a reluctant, "All right," after carefully considering the issue.

"What do you say, Nicholas?" Sophie asked, addressing the last remaining holdout.

"It could be fun," he said slowly, terrifying Sophie with the devilish gleam in his eye.

"Excellent," she said, trying to keep the wariness out of her voice.

"But *you* must be the blind man," he added.

Sophie opened her mouth to protest, but at that moment, the other three children started jumping up and down and squealing with delight. Then her fate was sealed when Hyacinth turned to her with a sly smile and said, "Oh, you must."

Sophie knew that protest was useless, so she let out a long-suffering sigh—exaggerated, just to delight the children—and turned around so that Hyacinth could fasten a scarf over her eyes.

"Can you see?" Nicholas demanded.

"No," Sophie lied.

He turned to Hyacinth with a grimace. "She can see."

How could he tell?

"Add a second scarf," he said. "This one is too sheer."

"The indignity," Sophie muttered, but nonetheless, she leaned down slightly so that Hyacinth could tie another scarf over her eyes.

"She's blind now!" John hooted.

Sophie gave them all a sickly-sweet smile.

"All right now," Nicholas said, clearly in charge. "You wait ten seconds so that we can take our places."

Sophie nodded, then tried not to wince as she heard the sounds of a mad scramble around the room. "Try not to break anything!" she yelled, as if that would make any difference to an overexcited six-year-old.

"Are you ready?" she asked.

No response. That meant yes.

"Blind Man!" she called out.

"Bluff!" came five voices in unison.

Sophie frowned in concentration. One of the girls was definitely behind the sofa. She took a few baby steps to the right.

"Blind Man!"

"Bluff!" Followed, of course, by a few titters and chuckles.

"Blind M— OW!"

More hoots and squeals of laughter. Sophie grunted as she rubbed her bruised shin.

"Blind Man!" she called, with considerably less enthusiasm.

"Bluff!"

"Bluff!"

"BLUFF!"

"BLUFF!"

"BLUFF!"

"You are all mine, Alice," she muttered under her breath, deciding to go for the smallest and presumably weakest of the bunch. "All mine."

Benedict had nearly made a clean escape. After his mother had left the sitting room, he'd downed a much-needed glass of brandy and headed out toward the door, only to be caught by Eloise, who informed him that he absolutely *couldn't* leave yet, that Mother was trying *very* hard to assemble all of her children in one place because Daphne had an *important* announcement to make.

"With child again?" Benedict asked.

"Act surprised. You weren't supposed to know."

"I'm not going to act anything. I'm leaving."

She made a desperate leap forward and somehow managed to grab his sleeve. "You can't."

Benedict let out a long breath and tried to pry her fingers off of his arm, but she had his shirt in a death grip. "I am going to pick up one foot," he said in slow, tedious tones, "and step forward. Then I will pick up the next foot—"

"You promised Hyacinth you would help her with her arithmetic," Eloise blurted out. "She hasn't seen hide nor hair of you in two weeks."

"It's not as if she has a school to flunk out of," Benedict muttered.

"Benedict, that is a terrible thing to say!" Eloise exclaimed.

"I know," he groaned, hoping to stave off a lecture.

"Just because we of the female gender are not allowed to study at places like Eton and Cambridge doesn't mean our educations are any less precious," Eloise ranted, completely ignoring her brother's weak "I know."

"Furthermore—" she carried on.

Benedict sagged against the wall.

"—I am of the opinion that the reason we are *not* allowed access is that if we *were*, we would trounce you men in all subjects!"

"I'm sure you're right," he sighed.

"Don't patronize me."

"Believe me, Eloise, the last thing I would dream of doing is patronizing you."

She eyed him suspiciously before crossing her arms and saying, "Well, don't disappoint Hyacinth."

"I won't," he said wearily.

"I believe she's in the nursery."

Benedict gave her a distracted nod, turning toward the stairs.

But as he trudged on up, he didn't see Eloise turn toward his mother, who was peeking out of the music room, and give her a big wink and a smile.

The nursery was located on the second floor. Benedict didn't often come up that high; most of his siblings' bedrooms were on the first floor. Only Gregory and Hyacinth still lived adjacent to the nursery, and with Gregory off at Eton most of the year and Hyacinth usually terrorizing someone in some other section of the house, Benedict simply didn't have much reason to visit.

It didn't escape him that aside from the nursery, the second floor was home to bedrooms for the higher servants. Including the lady's maids.

Sophie.

She was probably off in some corner somewhere with her mending—certainly not in the nursery, which was the domain of nurses and nannies. A lady's maid would have no reason to—

"Heeheeheehahaha!"

Benedict raised his brows. That was most definitely the sound of childish laughter, not something likely to come out of fourteen-year-old Hyacinth's mouth.

Oh, right. His Wentworth cousins were visiting. His mother had mentioned something about that. Well, that would be a bonus. He hadn't seen them in a few months, and they were nice enough children, if a little high-spirited.

As he approached the nursery door, the laughter increased, with a few squeals thrown in for good measure. The sounds brought a smile to Benedict's face, and he turned when he reached the open doorway, and then—

He saw her.

Her.

Not Sophie.

Her.

And yet it *was* Sophie.

She was blindfolded, smiling as she groped her hands toward the giggling children. He could see only the bottom half of her face, and that's when he knew.

There was only one other woman in the world for whom he'd seen only the bottom half of her face.

The smile was the same. The gamine little point at the end of her chin was the same. It was *all* the same.

She was the woman in silver, the woman from the masquerade ball.

It suddenly made sense. Only twice in his life had he felt this inexplicable, almost mystical attraction to a woman. He'd thought it remarkable, to have found two, when in his heart he'd always believed there was only one perfect woman out there for him.

His heart had been right. There *was* only one.

He'd searched for her for months. He'd pined for her even longer. And here she'd been right under his nose.

And she hadn't told him.

Did she understand what she'd put him through? How many hours he'd lain awake, feeling that he was betraying the lady in silver—the woman he'd dreamed of marrying—all because he was falling in love with a housemaid?

Dear God, it bordered on the absurd. He'd finally decided to let the lady in silver go. He was going to ask Sophie to marry him, social consequences be damned.

And they were one and the same.

A strange roaring filled his head, as if two enormous seashells had been clapped to his ears, whistling, whirring, humming; and the air suddenly smelled a bit acrid and everything looked a little bit red, and—

Benedict could not take his eyes off of her.

"Is something wrong?" Sophie asked. All the children had gone silent, staring at Benedict with open mouths and large, large eyes.

"Hyacinth," he bit off, "will you please evacuate the room?"

"But—"

"Now!" he roared.

"Nicholas, Elizabeth, John, Alice, come along now," Hyacinth said quickly, her voice cracking. "There are biscuits in the kitchen, and I know that . . ."

But Benedict didn't hear the rest. Hyacinth had managed to clear the room out in record time and her voice was disappearing down the hall as she ushered the children away.

"Benedict?" Sophie was saying, fumbling with the knot at the back of her head. "Benedict?"

He shut the door. The click was so loud she jumped. "What's wrong?" she whispered.

He said nothing, just watched her as she tore at the scarf. He liked it that she was helpless. He didn't feel terribly kind and charitable at the moment.

"Do you have something you need to tell me?" he asked. His voice was controlled, but his hands were shaking.

She went still, so still that he would have sworn that he could see the heat rise from her body. Then she cleared her throat—an uncomfortable, awkward sort of sound—and went back to work on the knot. Her movements tightened her dress around her breasts, but Benedict felt not one speck of desire.

It was, he thought ironically, the first time he *hadn't* felt desire for this woman, in either of her incarnations.

"Can you help me with this?" she asked. But her voice was hesitant.

Benedict didn't move.

"Benedict?"

"It's interesting to see you with a scarf tied around your head, Sophie," he said softly.

Her hands dropped slowly to her sides.

"It's almost like a demi-mask, wouldn't you say?"

Her lips parted, and the soft rush of air that crossed them was the room's only noise.

He walked toward her, slowly, inexorably, his footsteps just loud enough so that she had to know he was stalking her. "I haven't been to a masquerade in many years," he said.

She knew. He could see it in her face, the way she held her mouth, tight at the corners, and yet still slightly open. She knew that he knew.

He hoped she was terrified.

He took another two steps toward her, then abruptly turned to the right, his arm brushing past her sleeve. "Were you ever going to tell me that we'd met before?"

Her mouth moved, but she didn't speak.

"Were you?" he asked, his voice low and controlled.

"No," she said, her voice wavering.

"Really?"

She didn't make a sound.

"Any particular reason?"

"It—it didn't seem pertinent."

He whirled around. "It didn't seem *pertinent*?" he snapped. "I fell in love with you two years ago, and it didn't seem pertinent?"

"Can I please remove the scarf?" she whispered.

"You can remain blind."

"Benedict, I—"

"Like *I* was blind this past month," he continued angrily. "Why don't you see how you like it?"

"You didn't fall in love with me two years ago," she said, yanking at the too-tight scarf.

"How would you know? *You* disappeared."

"I *had* to disappear," she cried out. "I didn't have a choice."

"We always have choices," he said condescendingly. "We call it free will."

"That's easy for you to say," she snapped, tugging frantically at the blindfold. "You, who have everything! I had to—Oh!" With one wrenching movement, she somehow managed to yank down the scarves until they hung loosely around her neck.

Sophie blinked against the sudden onslaught of light. Then she caught sight of Benedict's face and stumbled back a step.

His eyes were on fire, burning with a rage, and yes, a hurt that she could barely comprehend. "It's good to see you, Sophie," he said in a dangerously low voice. "If indeed that is your real name."

She nodded.

"It occurs to me," he said, a little too casually, "if you were at the masquerade, then you are not exactly of the servant class, are you?"

"I didn't have an invitation," she said hastily. "I was a fraud. A pretender. I had no right to be there."

"You lied to me. Through everything, all this, you lied to me."

"I had to," she whispered.

"Oh, please. What could possibly be so terrible that you must conceal your identity from *me*?"

Sophie gulped. Here in the Bridgerton nursery, with him looming over her, she couldn't quite remember why she'd decided not to tell him that she was the lady at the masquerade.

Maybe she'd feared that he would want her to become his mistress.

Which had happened anyway.

Or maybe she hadn't said anything because by the time she'd realized that this wasn't going to be a chance meeting, that he wasn't about to let Sophie-the-housemaid out of his life, it was too late. She'd gone too long without telling him, and she feared his rage.

Which was exactly what had happened.

Proving her point. Of course, that was cold consolation as she stood across from him, watching his eyes go hot with anger and cold with disdain—all at the same time.

Maybe the truth—as unflattering as it might be—was that her pride had been stung. She'd been disappointed that he hadn't recognized her himself. If the night of the masquerade had been as magical for him as it had been for her, shouldn't he have known instantly who she was?

Two years she'd spent dreaming about him. Two years she'd seen his face every night in her mind. And yet when he'd seen hers, he'd seen a stranger.

Or maybe, just maybe, it hadn't been any of those things. Maybe it was simpler than that. Maybe she'd just wanted to protect her heart. She didn't know why, but she'd felt a little safer, a little less exposed as an anonymous housemaid. If Benedict had known who she was—or at least known that she'd been the woman at the masquerade—then he would have pursued her. Relentlessly.

Oh, he had certainly pursued her when he'd thought she'd been a maid. But it would have been different if he'd known the truth. Sophie was sure of it. He wouldn't have perceived the class differences as being quite so great, and Sophie would have lost an important barrier between them. Her social status, or lack thereof, had been a protective wall around her heart. She *couldn't* get too close because, quite honestly, she couldn't get too close. A man such as Benedict—son of and brother to viscounts—would never marry a servant.

But an earl's by-blow—now that was a much trickier situation. Unlike a servant, an aristocratic bastard could dream.

But like those of a servant, the dreams weren't likely to come true. Making the dreaming all that much more painful. And she'd known—every time it had been on the tip of her tongue to blurt out her secret she had known—that telling him the truth would lead straight to a broken heart.

It almost made Sophie want to laugh. Her heart couldn't possibly feel worse than it did now.

"I searched for you," he said, his low, intense voice cutting into her thoughts.

Her eyes widened, grew wet. "You did?" she whispered.

"For six bloody months," he cursed. "It was as if you fell right off the face of the earth."

"I had nowhere to go," she said, not sure why she was telling him that.

"You had *me*."

The words hung in the air, heavy and dark. Finally, Sophie, propelled by some perverse sense of belated honesty, said, "I didn't know you searched for me. But—but—" She choked on the word, closing her eyes tightly against the pain of the moment.

"But what?"

She swallowed convulsively, and when she did open her eyes, she did not look at his face. "Even if I'd known you were looking," she said, hugging her arms to her body, "I wouldn't have let you find me."

"Was I that repulsive to you?"

"No!" she cried out, her eyes flying to his face. There was hurt there. He hid it well, but she knew him well. There was hurt in his eyes.

"No," she said, trying to make her voice calm and even. "It wasn't that. It could never be that."

"Then what?"

"We're from different worlds, Benedict. Even then I knew that there could be no future for us. And it would have been torture. To tease myself with a dream that couldn't come true? I couldn't do that."

"Who are you?" he asked suddenly.

She just stared at him, frozen into inaction.

"Tell me," he bit off. "Tell me who you are. Because you're no damned lady's maid, that's for certain."

"I'm exactly who I said I was," she said, then, at his murderous glare, hastily added, "Almost."

He advanced on her. "Who *are* you?"

She backed up another step. "Sophia Beckett."

"Who are you?"

"I've been a servant since I was fourteen."

"And who were you before that?"

Her voice dropped to a whisper. "A bastard."

"Whose bastard?"

"Does it matter?"

His stance grew more belligerent. "It matters to me."

Sophie felt herself deflate. She hadn't expected him to ignore the duties of his birth and actually *marry* someone like her, but she'd hoped he wouldn't care quite that much.

"Who were your parents?" Benedict persisted.

"No one you know."

"Who were your parents?" he roared.

"The Earl of Penwood," she cried out.

He stood utterly still, not a muscle moving. He didn't even blink.

"I am a nobleman's bastard," she said harshly, years of anger and resentment pouring forth. "My father was the Earl of Penwood and my mother was a maid. Yes," she spat out when she saw his face grow pale, "my mother was a lady's maid. Just as I am a lady's maid."

A heavy pause filled the air, and then Sophie said in a low voice, "I won't be like my mother."

"And yet, if she'd behaved otherwise," he said, "you wouldn't be here to tell me about it."

"That's not the point."

Benedict's hands, which had been fisted at his sides, began to twitch. "You lied to me," he said in a low voice.

"There was no need to tell you the truth."

"Who the hell are you to decide?" he exploded. "Poor little Benedict, he can't handle the truth. He can't make up his own mind. He—"

He broke off, disgusted by the whiny edge to his voice. She was turning him into someone he didn't know, someone he didn't like.

He had to get out of there. He had to—

"Benedict?" She was looking at him oddly. Her eyes were concerned.

"I have to go," he muttered. "I can't see you right now."

"Why?" she asked, and he could see from her face that she instantly regretted the question.

"I am so angry right now," he said, each word a slow, staccato beat in the sentence, "that I don't know myself. I—" He looked down at his hands. They were shaking. He wanted to hurt her, he realized. No, he didn't want to hurt her. He would never want to hurt her. And yet . . .

And yet . . .

It was the first time in his life he'd felt so out of control. It scared him.

"I have to go," he said again, and he brushed roughly past her as he strode out the door.

Chapter 20

While we are on the topic, Miss Reiling's mother, the Countess of Penwood, has also been acting very strange of late. According to servants' gossip (which we all know is always the most reliable sort), the countess threw quite the tantrum last night, hurling no fewer than seventeen shoes at her servants.

One footman sports a bruised eye, but other than that, all remain in good health.

LADY WHISTLEDOWN'S SOCIETY PAPERS,
11 JUNE 1817

Within an hour, Sophie had her bag packed. She didn't know what else to do. She was gripped—painfully gripped—by nervous energy, and she could not sit still. Her feet kept moving and her hands were shaking, and every few minutes, she found herself taking a big spontaneous gulp of air, as if the extra breath could somehow calm her inside.

She could not imagine that she would be allowed to remain here in Lady Bridgerton's household after such a horrible falling-out with Benedict. Lady Bridgerton was fond of Sophie, it was true, but Benedict was her son. Blood really was thicker than just about anything else, especially when it was Bridgerton blood.

It was sad, really, she thought as she sat down on her bed, her hands still torturing a hopelessly mangled handkerchief. For all her inner turmoil over Benedict, she'd *liked* living in the Bridgerton household. Sophie had never before had the honor of living amongst a group of people who truly understood the meaning of the word family.

She would miss them.

She would miss Benedict.

And she would mourn the life she could not have.

Unable to sit still, she jumped back to her feet and walked to the window. "Damn you, Papa," she said, looking up at the skies. "There. I've called you Papa. You never let me do that. You never wanted to *be* that." She gasped convulsively, using the back of her hand to wipe at her nose. "I've called you Papa. How does it feel?"

But there was no sudden clap of thunder, no gray cloud appearing out of nowhere to cover up the sun. Her father would never know how angry she was with him for leaving her penniless, leaving her with Araminta. Most likely, he wouldn't have cared.

She felt rather weary, and she leaned against the window frame, rubbing her eyes with her hand. "You gave me a taste of another life," she whispered, "and then left me in the wind. It would have been so much easier if I'd been raised a servant.

"I wouldn't have wanted so much. It would have been easier."

She turned back around, her eyes falling upon her single, meager bag. She hadn't wanted to take any of the dresses that Lady Bridgerton and her daughters had given her, but she'd had little choice in the matter, as her old dresses had already been relegated to the rag bin. So she'd chosen only two, the same number with which she'd arrived—the one she happened to be wearing when Benedict had discovered her identity, and a spare, which she'd tucked in the bag. The rest had been left hanging, neatly pressed, in the wardrobe.

Sophie sighed, closing her eyes for a moment. It was time to go. Where, she didn't know, but she couldn't stay here.

She leaned down and picked up the bag. She had a little money saved. Not much, but if she worked and was frugal, she'd have enough funds for passage to America within a year. She'd heard that things were easier there for those of less-than-respectable birth, that the boundaries of class weren't quite as strict as they were here in England.

She poked her head out into the hall, which was blessedly vacant. She knew she was a coward, but she didn't want to have to say goodbye to the Bridgerton daughters. She might do something *really* stupid, like cry, and then she'd feel even worse. Never in her life had she had the chance to spend time with women of her own age who treated her with respect and affection. She'd once hoped that Rosamund and Posy would be her sisters, but that had never come to pass. Posy might have tried, but Araminta wouldn't allow it, and Posy, for all her sweetness, had never been strong enough to stand up to her mother.

But she did have to bid farewell to Lady Bridgerton. There was no getting around that. Lady Bridgerton had been kind to her far beyond any expectations, and Sophie would not thank her by sneaking out and disappearing like some criminal. If she was lucky, Lady Bridgerton would not yet have heard of her altercation with Benedict. Sophie could give her notice, bid her farewell, and be off.

It was late afternoon, well past tea time, so Sophie decided to take a chance and see if Lady Bridgerton was in the small office she kept off of her bedchamber. It was a warm and cozy little room, with a writing desk and several bookshelves—a place where Lady Bridgerton penned her correspondence and settled the household accounts.

The door was ajar, so Sophie knocked softly, allowing the door to swing open a few inches as her knuckles connected with the wood.

"Enter!" came Lady Bridgerton's bidding.

Sophie pushed the door open and poked her head in. "Am I interrupting?" she asked quietly.

Lady Bridgerton set down her quill. "Yes, but it's a welcome interruption. I've never enjoyed balancing the household accounts."

"I would—" Sophie bit her tongue. She had been about to say that she would have been happy to take over the task; she'd always been good with numbers.

"You were saying?" Lady Bridgerton asked, her eyes warm.

Sophie gave her head a little shake. "Nothing."

The room lapsed into silence until Lady Bridgerton gave Sophie a slightly amused smile, and asked, "Was there a specific reason you knocked on my door?"

Sophie took a deep breath that was meant to settle her nerves (but didn't) and said, "Yes."

Lady Bridgerton looked at her expectantly but didn't say anything.

"I'm afraid I must resign my position here," Sophie said.

Lady Bridgerton actually rose out of her seat. "But why? Aren't you happy? Have any of the girls been mistreating you?"

"No, no," Sophie hastened to assure her. "That could not be further from the truth. Your daughters are so lovely—in heart as well as in appearance. I've never— That is to say, no one has ever—"

"What is it, Sophie?"

Sophie clutched at the doorframe, desperately trying to find her balance. Her legs felt unsteady, her heart felt unsteady. Any moment now she was going to burst into tears, and why? Because the man she loved would never marry her? Because he hated her for lying to him? Because he'd broken her heart twice—once by asking her to be his mistress, and once by making her love his family and then forcing her to leave?

He might not have demanded that she go, but it couldn't have been more obvious that she could not stay.

"It's Benedict, isn't it?"

Sophie's head snapped up.

Lady Bridgerton smiled sadly. "It's obvious that there is some feeling between you," she said gently, answering the question that Sophie knew must show in her eyes.

"Why didn't you fire me?" Sophie whispered. She didn't think that Lady Bridgerton knew that Sophie and Benedict had been intimate, but no one of Lady Bridgerton's position would want her son pining for a housemaid.

"I don't know," Lady Bridgerton replied, looking more conflicted than Sophie could ever have imagined. "I probably should have done." She shrugged, her eyes strangely helpless. "But I like you."

The tears Sophie had been working so hard to keep in check began to roll down her face, but beyond that, she somehow managed to keep her composure. She didn't shake, and she didn't make a sound. She just stood there, utterly still, as the tears came forth.

When Lady Bridgerton spoke again, her words held a very careful and measured quality, as if she were choosing them with great care, searching for a specific reply. "You are," she said, her eyes never leaving Sophie's face, "the sort of woman I would like for my son. Our acquaintance has not been a long one, but I know your character and I know your heart. And I wish—"

A small, choked sob burst forth from Sophie's mouth, but she swallowed it down as quickly as she could.

"I wish that you were of a different background," Lady Bridgerton continued, acknowledging Sophie's cry with a sympathetic tilt of her head and a sad, slow blink of her eyes. "Not that I hold such a thing against you, or think the less of you, but it makes things very difficult."

"Impossible," Sophie whispered.

Lady Bridgerton didn't say anything, and Sophie knew that in her heart she agreed—if not completely, then ninety-eight percent—with her assessment.

"Is it possible," Lady Bridgerton asked, her words even more measured and careful than before, "that your background is not quite what it seems?"

Sophie said nothing.

"There are things about you that don't add up, Sophie."

Sophie knew that she expected her to ask what, but she had a fair idea what Lady Bridgerton meant.

"Your accent is impeccable," Lady Bridgerton said. "I know you told me that you had lessons with the children your mother worked for, but that doesn't seem like enough of an explanation to me. Those lessons wouldn't have started until you were a bit older, six at the very earliest, and your speech patterns would have already been rather set by that point."

Sophie felt her eyes widen. She'd never seen that particular hole in her story, and she was rather surprised that no one else had until now. But then again, Lady Bridgerton was a good deal smarter than most of the people to whom she had told her fabricated history.

"And you know Latin," Lady Bridgerton said. "Don't try to deny it. I heard you muttering under your breath the other day when Hyacinth vexed you."

Sophie kept her gaze fixed firmly on the window just to Lady Bridgerton's left. She couldn't quite bring herself to meet her eyes.

"Thank you for not denying it," Lady Bridgerton said. And then she waited for Sophie to say something, waited so long that finally Sophie had to fill the interminable silence.

"I'm not a suitable match for your son," was all she said.

"I see."

"I really have to go." She had to get the words out quickly, before she changed her mind.

Lady Bridgerton nodded. "If that is your wish, there is nothing I can do to stop you. Where is it you plan to go?"

"I have relatives in the north," Sophie lied.

Lady Bridgerton clearly didn't believe her, but she answered, "You will, of course, use one of our carriages."

"No, I couldn't possibly."

"You can't think I would permit you to do otherwise. I consider you to be my responsibility—at least for the next few days—and it is far too dangerous for you to leave unescorted. It's not safe for women alone in this world."

Sophie couldn't quite suppress a rueful smile. Lady Bridgerton's tone might be different, but her words were almost exactly those uttered by Benedict a few weeks earlier. And look where that had gotten her. She would never say that she and Lady Bridgerton were close friends, but she knew her well enough to know that she would not be budged on this issue.

"Very well," Sophie acceded. "Thank you." She could have the carriage drop her off somewhere, preferably not too far from a port where she could eventually book passage to America, and then decide where to go from there.

Lady Bridgerton offered her a small, sad smile. "I assume you already have your bags packed?"

Sophie nodded. It didn't seem necessary to point out that she only had one bag, singular.

"Have you made all of your good-byes?"

Sophie shook her head. "I'd rather not," she admitted.

Lady Bridgerton stood and nodded. "Sometimes that is best," she agreed. "Why don't you await me in the front hall? I will see to having a coach brought 'round."

Sophie turned and started to walk out, but when she reached the doorway, she stopped and turned around. "Lady Bridgerton, I—"

The older lady's eyes lit up, as if she were expecting some good news. Or if not good, then at least something different. "Yes?"

Sophie swallowed. "I just wanted to thank you."

The light in Lady Bridgerton's eyes dimmed a little. "Whatever for?"

"For having me here, for accepting me, and allowing me to pretend I was a part of your family."

"Don't be sil—"

"You didn't have to let me take tea with you and the girls," Sophie interrupted. If she didn't get this all out now, she'd lose her courage.

"Most women wouldn't have done. It was lovely . . . and new . . . and . . ." She gulped. "I will miss you all."

"You don't have to go," Lady Bridgerton said softly.

Sophie tried to smile, but it came out all wobbly, and it tasted like tears. "Yes," she said, almost choking on the word. "I do."

Lady Bridgerton stared at her for a very long moment, her pale blue eyes filled with compassion and then maybe a touch of realization. "I see," she said quietly.

And Sophie feared that she did see.

"I'll meet you downstairs," Lady Bridgerton said.

Sophie nodded as she stood aside to let the dowager viscountess pass. Lady Bridgerton paused in the hallway, looking down at Sophie's well-worn bag. "Is that all you have?" she asked.

"Everything in the world."

Lady Bridgerton swallowed uncomfortably, and her cheeks took on the slightest hue of pink, almost as if she were actually embarrassed by her riches—and Sophie's lack thereof.

"But that . . ." Sophie said, motioning to the bag, "that's not what's important. What you have . . ." She stopped and swallowed, doing battle with the lump in her throat. "I don't mean what you own . . ."

"I know what you mean, Sophie." Lady Bridgerton dabbed at her eyes with her fingers. "Thank you."

Sophie's shoulders rose and fell in a tiny shrug. "It's the truth."

"Let me give you some money before you go, Sophie, Lady Bridgerton blurted out.

Sophie shook her head. "I couldn't. I've already taken two of the dresses you gave me. I didn't want to, but—"

"It's all right," Lady Bridgerton assured her. "What else could you do? The ones you came with are gone." She cleared her throat. "But please, let me give you some money." She saw Sophie open her mouth to protest and said, "*Please*. It would make me feel better."

Lady Bridgerton had a way of looking at a person that truly made one want to do as she asked, and besides that, Sophie really did need the money. Lady Bridgerton was a generous lady; she might even give Sophie enough to book third-class passage across the ocean. Sophie found herself saying, "Thank you," before her conscience had a chance to grapple with the offer.

Lady Bridgerton gave her a brief nod and disappeared down the hall.

Sophie took a long, shaky breath, then picked up her bag and walked slowly down the stairs. She waited in the foyer for a moment, then decided she might as well wait outside. It was a fine spring day, and Sophie thought that a bit of sun on her nose might be just the thing to make her feel better. Well, at least a little bit better. Besides, she'd be less likely to run into one of the Bridgerton daughters, and much as she was going to miss them, she just didn't want to have to say good-bye.

Still clutching her bag in one hand, she pushed open the front door and descended the steps.

It shouldn't take too long for the coach to be brought around. Five minutes, maybe ten, maybe—

"Sophie Beckett!"

Sophie's stomach dropped right down to her ankles. Araminta. How could she have forgotten?

Frozen into inaction, she looked around and up the stairs, trying to figure out which way to flee. If she ran back into the Bridgerton house, Araminta would know where to find her, and if she took off on foot—

"Constable!" Araminta shrieked. "I want a constable!"

Sophie dropped her bag and took off running.

"Someone stop her!" Araminta screamed. "Stop thief! Stop thief!"

Sophie kept running, even though she knew it would make her

look guilty. She ran with every last fiber in her muscles, with every gulp of air she could force into her lungs. She ran and she ran and she ran . . .

Until someone tackled her, thumping into her back and knocking her to the ground.

"I got her!" the man yelled. "I got her for you!"

Sophie blinked and gasped at the pain. Her head had hit the pavement with a stunning blow, and the man who had caught her was practically sitting on her abdomen.

"There you are!" Araminta crowed as she hurried over. "Sophie Beckett. The nerve!"

Sophie glared at her. Words didn't exist to express the loathing in her heart. Not to mention that she was in too much pain to speak.

"I've been looking for you," Araminta said, smiling evilly. "Posy told me she'd seen you."

Sophie closed her eyes for longer than the usual blink. *Oh, Posy.* She doubted that she'd meant to give her away, but Posy's tongue had a way of getting ahead of her mind.

Araminta planted her foot very close to Sophie's hand—the one that was being held immobile by her captor's fingers around her wrist—then smiled as she moved her foot *onto* Sophie's hand. "You shouldn't have stolen from me," Araminta said, her blue eyes glinting.

Sophie just grunted. It was all she could manage.

"You see," Araminta continued gleefully, "now I can have you thrown in jail. I suppose I could have done so before, but now I have the truth on my side."

Just then, a man ran up, skidding to a halt before Araminta. "The authorities are on the way, milady. We'll have this thief taken away in no time."

Sophie caught her lower lip between her teeth, torn between praying that the authorities would be delayed until Lady Bridgerton came outside, and praying that they'd come right away, so that the Bridgertons would never see her shame.

And in the end, she got her wish. The latter one, that was. Not two minutes later the authorities arrived, threw her into a wagon, and carted her off to jail.

And all Sophie could think of as she rode away was that the Bridgertons would never know what had happened to her, and maybe that was for the best.

Chapter 21

La, but such excitement yesterday on the front steps of Lady Bridgerton's residence on Bruton Street!

First, Penelope Featherington was seen in the company of not one, not two, but THREE Bridgerton brothers, surely a heretofore impossible feat for the poor girl, who is rather infamous for her wallflower ways. Sadly (but perhaps predictably) for Miss Featherington, when she finally departed, it was on the arm of the viscount, the only married man in the bunch.

If Miss Featherington were to somehow manage to drag a Bridgerton brother to the altar, it would surely mean the end of the world as we know it, and This Author, who freely admits she would not know heads from tails in such a world, would be forced to resign her post on the spot.

If Miss Featherington's gathering weren't enough gossip, not three hours later, a woman was accosted right in front of the town house by the Countess of Penwood, who lives three doors down. It seems the woman, who This Author suspects was working in the Bridgerton household, used to work for Lady Penwood. Lady Penwood alleges that the unidentified woman stole from her two years ago and immediately had the poor thing carted off to jail.

This Author is not certain what the punishment is these days

*for theft, but one has to suspect that if one has the audacity to
steal from a countess, the punishment is quite strict. The poor
girl in question is likely to be hanged, or at the very least, find
herself transported.*

*The previous housemaid wars (reported last month in This
Column) seem rather trivial now.*

LADY WHISTLEDOWN'S SOCIETY PAPERS,
13 JUNE 1817

Benedict's first inclination the following morning was to pour himself a good, stiff drink. Or maybe three. It might have been scandalously early in the day for spirits, but alcoholic oblivion sounded rather appealing after the emotional skewering he'd received the previous evening at the hands of Sophie Beckett.

But then he remembered that he'd made a date that morning for a fencing match with his brother Colin. Suddenly, skewering his brother sounded rather appealing, no matter that he'd had nothing to do with Benedict's wretched mood.

That, Benedict thought with a grim smile as he pulled on his gear, was what brothers were for.

"I've only an hour," Colin said as he attached the safety tip to his foil. "I have an appointment this afternoon."

"No matter," Benedict replied, lunging forward a few times to loosen up the muscles in his leg. He hadn't fenced in some time; the sword felt good in his hand. He drew back and touched the tip to the floor, letting the blade bend slightly. "It won't take more than an hour to best you."

Colin rolled his eyes before he drew down his mask.

Benedict walked to the center of the room. "Are you ready?"

"Not quite," Colin replied, following him.

Benedict lunged again.

"I said I wasn't ready!" Colin hollered as he jumped out of the way.

"You're too slow," Benedict snapped.

Colin cursed under his breath, then added a louder, "Bloody hell," for good measure. "What's gotten into you?"

"Nothing," Benedict nearly snarled. "Why would you say so?"

Colin took a step backward until they were a suitable distance apart to start the match. "Oh, I don't know," he intoned, sarcasm evident. "I suppose it could be because you nearly took my head off."

"I've a tip on my blade."

"And you were slashing like you were using a sabre," Colin shot back.

Benedict gave a hard smile. "It's more fun that way."

"Not for my neck." Colin passed his sword from hand to hand as he flexed and stretched his fingers. He paused and frowned. "You sure you have a foil there?"

Benedict scowled. "For the love of God, Colin, I would never use a real weapon."

"Just making sure," Colin muttered, touching his neck lightly. "Are you ready?"

Benedict nodded and bent his knees.

"Regular rules," Colin said, assuming a fencer's crouch. "*No* slashing."

Benedict gave him a curt nod.

"*En garde!*"

Both men raised their right arms, twisting their wrists until their palms were up, foils gripped in their fingers.

"Is that new?" Colin suddenly asked, eyeing the handle of Benedict's foil with interest.

Benedict cursed at the loss of his concentration. "Yes, it's new," he bit off. "I prefer an Italian grip."

Colin stepped back, completely losing his fencing posture as he looked at his own foil, with a less elaborate French grip. "Might I borrow it some time? I wouldn't mind seeing if—"

"Yes!" Benedict snapped, barely resisting the urge to advance and lunge that very second. "Will you get back *en garde*?"

Colin gave him a lopsided smile, and Benedict just *knew* that he had asked about his grip simply to annoy him. "As you wish," Colin murmured, assuming position again.

They held still for one moment, and then Colin said, "Fence!"

Benedict advanced immediately, lunging and attacking, but Colin had always been particularly fleet of foot, and he retreated carefully, meeting Benedict's attack with an expert parry.

"You're in a bloody bad mood today," Colin said, lunging forward and just nearly catching Benedict on the shoulder.

Benedict stepped out of his way, lifting his blade to block the attack. "Yes, well, I had a bad"—he advanced again, his foil stretched straight forward—*"day."*

Colin sidestepped his attack neatly. "Nice riposte," he said, touching his forehead with the handle of his foil in a mock salute.

"Shut up and fence," Benedict snapped.

Colin chuckled and advanced, swishing his blade this way and that, keeping Benedict on the retreat. "It must be a woman," he said.

Benedict blocked Colin's attack and quickly began his own advance. "None of your damned business."

"It's a woman," Colin said, smirking.

Benedict lunged forward, the tip of his foil catching Colin on the collarbone. "Point," he grunted.

Colin gave a curt nod. "Touch for you." They walked back to the center of the room. "Are you ready?" he asked.

Benedict nodded.

"En garde. Fence!"

This time Colin was the first to take the attack. "If you need some advice about women . . ." he said, driving Benedict back to the corner.

Benedict raised his foil, blocking Colin's attack with enough force to send his younger brother stumbling backward. "If I need advice about women," he returned, "the last person I'd go to would be *you.*"

"You wound me," Colin said, regaining his balance.

"No," Benedict drawled. "That's what the safety tip is for."

"I certainly have a better record with women than *you*."

"Oh really?" Benedict said sarcastically. He stuck his nose in the air, and in a fair imitation of Colin said, " 'I am certainly *not* going to marry Penelope Featherington!' "

Colin winced.

"You," Benedict said, "shouldn't be giving advice to anyone."

"I didn't know she was there."

Benedict lunged forward, just barely missing Colin's shoulder. "That's no excuse. You were in public, in broad daylight. Even if she hadn't been there, someone would have heard and the bloody thing would have ended up in *Whistledown*."

Colin met his lunge with a parry, then riposted with blinding speed, catching Benedict neatly in the belly. "My touch," he grunted.

Benedict gave him a nod, acknowledging the point.

"I was foolish," Colin said as they walked back to the center of the room. "You, on the other hand, are stupid."

"What the hell does that mean?"

Colin sighed as he pushed up his mask. "Why don't you just do us all a favor and marry the girl?"

Benedict just stared at him, his hand going limp around the handle of his sword. Was there any possibility that Colin didn't know who they were talking about?

He removed his mask and looked into his brother's dark green eyes and nearly groaned. Colin knew. He didn't know how Colin knew, but he definitely knew. He supposed he shouldn't have been surprised. Colin always knew everything. In fact, the only person who ever seemed to know more gossip than Colin was Eloise, and it never took her more than a few hours to impart all of her dubious wisdom to Colin.

"How did you know?" Benedict finally asked.

One corner of Colin's mouth tilted up into a crooked smile. "About Sophie? It's rather obvious."

"Colin, she's—"

"A maid? Who cares? What is going to happen to you if you marry her?" Colin asked with a devil-may-care shrug of his shoulders. "People you couldn't care less about will ostracize you? Hell, I wouldn't mind being ostracized by some of the people with whom I'm forced to socialize."

Benedict shrugged dismissively. "I'd already decided I didn't care about all that," he said.

"Then what in bloody hell is the problem?" Colin demanded.

"It's complicated."

"Nothing is ever as complicated as it is in one's mind."

Benedict mulled that over, planting the tip of his foil against the floor and allowing the flexible blade to wiggle back and forth. "Do you remember Mother's masquerade?" he asked.

Colin blinked at the unexpected question. "A few years ago? Right before she moved out of Bridgerton House?"

Benedict nodded. "That's the one. Do you remember meeting a woman dressed in silver? You came upon us in the hall."

"Of course. You were rather taken with—" Colin's eyes suddenly bugged out. "That wasn't *Sophie*?"

"Remarkable, isn't it?" Benedict murmured, his every inflection screaming understatement.

"But . . . How . . ."

"I don't know how she got there, but she's not a maid."

"She's not?"

"Well, she is a maid," Benedict clarified, "but she's also the bastard daughter of the Earl of Penwood."

"Not the current—"

"No, the one who died several years back."

"And you knew all this?"

"No," Benedict said, the word short and staccato on his tongue, "I did not."

"Oh." Colin caught his lower lip between his teeth as he digested the meaning of his brother's short sentence. "I see." He stared at Benedict. "What are you going to do?"

Benedict's sword, whose blade had been wiggling back and forth as he pressed the tip against the floor, suddenly sprang straight and skittered out of his hand. He watched it dispassionately as it slid across the floor, and didn't look back up as he said, "That's a very good question."

He was still furious with Sophie for her deception, but neither was he without blame. He shouldn't have demanded that Sophie be his mistress. It had certainly been his right to ask, but it had also been her right to refuse. And once she had done so, he should have let her be.

Benedict hadn't been brought up a bastard, and if her experience had been sufficiently wretched so that she refused to risk bearing a bastard herself—well, then, he should have respected that.

If he respected *her*, then he had to respect her beliefs.

He shouldn't have been so flip with her, insisting that anything was possible, that she was free to make any choice her heart desired. His mother was right; he *did* live a charmed life. He had wealth, family, happiness . . . and nothing was truly out of his reach. The only awful thing that had ever happened in his life was the sudden and untimely death of his father, and even then, he'd had his family to help him through. It was difficult for him to imagine certain pains and hurts because he'd never experienced them.

And unlike Sophie, he'd never been alone.

What now? He had already decided that he was prepared to brave social ostracism and marry her. The unrecognized bastard daughter of an earl was a slightly more acceptable match than a servant, but only slightly. London society might accept her if he forced them to, but they wouldn't go out of their way to be kind. He and Sophie would most likely have to live quietly in the country, eschewing the London society that would almost certainly shun them.

But it took his heart less than a second to know that a quiet life with Sophie was by far preferable to a public life without her.

Did it matter that she was the woman from the masquerade? She'd lied to him about her identity, but he knew her soul. When they kissed, when they laughed, when they simply sat and talked— she had never feigned a moment.

The woman who could make his heart sing with a simple smile, the woman who could fill him with contentment just through the simple act of sitting by him while he sketched—that was the real Sophie.

And he loved her.

"You look as if you've reached a decision," Colin said quietly.

Benedict eyed his brother thoughtfully. When had he grown so perceptive? Come to think of it, when had he grown up? Benedict had always thought of Colin as a youthful rascal, charming and deb- onair, but not one who had ever had to assume any sort of respon- sibility.

But when he regarded his brother now, he saw someone else. His shoulders were a little broader, his posture a little more steady and subdued. And his eyes looked wiser. That was the biggest change. If eyes truly were windows to the soul, then Colin's soul had gone and grown up on him when Benedict hadn't been paying attention.

"I owe her a few apologies," Benedict said.

"I'm sure she'll forgive you."

"She owes me several as well. More than several."

Benedict could tell that his brother wanted to ask, "What for?" but to his credit, all Colin said was, "Are you willing to forgive her?"

Benedict nodded.

Colin reached out and plucked Benedict's foil from his hands. "I'll put this away for you."

Benedict stared at his brother's fingers for a rather stupidly long moment before snapping to attention. "I have to go," he blurted out.

Colin barely suppressed a grin. "I surmised as much."

Benedict stared at his brother and then, for no other reason than an overwhelming urge, he reached out and pulled him into a quick hug. "I don't say this often," he said, his voice starting to sound gruff in his ears, "but I love you."

"I love you, too, big brother." Colin's smile, always a little bit lopsided, grew. "Now get the hell out of here."

Benedict tossed his mask at his brother and strode out of the room.

"What do you mean, she's gone?"

"Just that, I'm afraid," Lady Bridgerton said, her eyes sad and sympathetic. "She's gone."

The pressure behind Benedict's temples began to build; it was a wonder his head didn't explode. "And you just let her *go*?"

"It would hardly have been legal for me to force her to stay."

Benedict nearly groaned. It had hardly been legal for him to force her to come to London, but he'd done it, anyway.

"Where did she go?" he demanded.

His mother seemed to deflate in her chair. "I don't know. I had insisted that she take one of our coaches, partly because I feared for her safety but also because I wanted to know where she went."

Benedict slammed his hands on the desk. "Well, then, what happened?"

"As I was *trying* to say, I attempted to get her to take one of our coaches, but it was obvious she didn't want to, and she disappeared before I could have the carriage brought 'round."

Benedict cursed under his breath. Sophie was probably still in London, but London was huge and hugely populated. It would be damn near impossible to find someone who didn't want to be found.

"I had assumed," Violet said delicately, "that the two of you had a falling-out."

Benedict raked his hand through his hair, then caught sight of his white sleeve. "Oh, Jesus," he muttered. He'd run over here in his fencing clothes. He looked up at his mother with a roll of his eyes. "No lectures on blasphemy just now, Mother. Please."

Her lips twitched. "I wouldn't dream of it."

"Where am I going to find her?"

The levity left Violet's eyes. "I don't know, Benedict. I wish I did. I quite liked Sophie."

"She's Penwood's daughter," he said.

Violet frowned. "I suspected something like that. Illegitimate, I assume?"

Benedict nodded.

His mother opened her mouth to say something, but he never did find out what, because at that moment, the door to her office came flying open, slamming against the wall with an amazing crash. Francesca, who had obviously been running across the house, smashed into her mother's desk, followed by Hyacinth, who smashed into Francesca.

"What is wrong?" Violet asked, rising to her feet.

"It's Sophie," Francesca panted.

"I know," Violet said. "She's gone. We—"

"No!" Hyacinth cut in, slapping a piece of paper down on the desk. "Look."

Benedict tried to grab the paper, which he immediately recognized as an issue of *Whistledown*, but his mother got there first. "What is it?" he asked, his stomach sinking as he watched her face pale.

She handed him the paper. He scanned it quickly, passing by bits about the Duke of Ashbourne, the Earl of Macclesfield, and Penelope Featherington before he reached the section about what had to be Sophie.

"Jail?" he said, the word mere breath on his lips.

"We must see her released," his mother said, throwing her shoulders back like a general girding for battle.

But Benedict was already out the door.

"Wait!" Violet yelled, dashing after him. "I'm coming, too."

Benedict stopped short just before he reached the stairs. "You are not coming," he ordered. "I will not have you exposed to—"

"Oh, please," Violet returned. "I'm hardly a wilting flower. And I can vouch for Sophie's honesty and integrity."

"I'm coming, too," Hyacinth said, skidding to a halt alongside Francesca, who had also followed them out into the upstairs hall.

"No!" came the simultaneous reply from her mother and brother.

"But—"

"I said *no*," Violet said again, her voice sharp.

Francesca let out a sullen snort. "I suppose it would be fruitless for me to insist upon—"

"Don't even finish that sentence," Benedict warned.

"As if you would let me even try."

Benedict ignored her and turned to his mother. "If you want to go, we leave immediately."

She nodded. "Have the carriage brought 'round, and I'll be waiting out front."

Ten minutes later, they were on their way.

Chapter 22

Such a scurry on Bruton Street. The dowager Viscountess Bridgerton and her son, Benedict Bridgerton, were seen dashing out of her house Friday morning. Mr. Bridgerton practically threw his mother into a carriage, and they took off at breakneck speed. Francesca and Hyacinth Bridgerton were seen standing in the doorway, and This Author has it on the best authority that Francesca was heard to utter a very unladylike word.

But the Bridgerton household was not the only one to see such excitement. The Penwoods also experienced a great deal of activity, culminating in a public row right on the front steps between the countess and her daughter, Miss Posy Reiling.

As This Author has never liked Lady Penwood, she can only say, "Huzzah for Posy!"

LADY WHISTLEDOWN'S SOCIETY PAPERS,
16 JUNE 1817

It was cold. Really cold. And there was an awful scurrying noise that definitely belonged to a small, four-legged creature. Or even worse, a large, four-legged creature. Or to be more precise, a large version of a small, four-legged creature.

Rats.

"Oh, God," Sophie moaned. She didn't often take the Lord's name in vain, but now seemed as good a time as any to start. Maybe He would hear, and maybe He would smite the rats. Yes, that would do very nicely. A big jolt of lightning. Huge. Of biblical proportions. It could hit the earth, spread little electrical tentacles around the globe, and sizzle all the rats dead.

It was a lovely dream. Right up there with the ones in which she found herself living happily ever after as Mrs. Benedict Bridgerton.

Sophie took a quick gasp as a sudden stab of pain pierced her heart. Of the two dreams, she feared that the genocide of the rats might be the more likely to come true.

She was on her own now. Well and truly on her own. She didn't know why this was so upsetting. In all truth, she'd always been on her own. Not since her grandmother had deposited her on the front steps of Penwood Park had she had a champion, someone who put her interests above—or even at the same level—as their own.

Her stomach growled, reminding her that she could add hunger to her growing list of miseries.

And thirst. They hadn't even brought her so much as a sip of water. She was starting to have very strange fantasies about tea.

Sophie let out a long, slow breath, trying to remember to breathe through her mouth when it came time to inhale. The stench was overwhelming. She'd been given a crude chamber pot to use for her bodily functions, but so far she'd been holding it in, trying to relieve herself with as little frequency as possible. The chamber pot had been emptied before it had been tossed into her cell, but it hadn't been cleaned, and in fact when Sophie had picked it up it had been wet, causing her to drop it immediately as her entire body shuddered with revulsion.

She had, of course, emptied many chamber pots in her time, but the people she'd worked for had generally managed to hit their mark, so to speak. Not to mention that Sophie had always been able to wash her hands afterward.

Now, in addition to the cold and the hunger, she didn't feel clean in her own skin.

It was a horrible sensation.

"You have a visitor."

Sophie jumped to her feet at the warden's gruff, unfriendly voice. Could Benedict have found out where she was? Would he even wish to come to her aid? Did he—

"Well, well, well."

Araminta. Sophie's heart sank.

"Sophie Beckett," she clucked, approaching the cell and then holding a handkerchief to her nose, as if Sophie were the sole cause of the stench. "I would never have guessed that you would have the audacity to show your face in London."

Sophie clamped her mouth together in a mutinous line. She knew that Araminta wanted to get a rise out of her, and she refused to give her the satisfaction.

"Things aren't going well for you, I'm afraid," Araminta continued, shaking her head in a parody of sympathy. She leaned forward and whispered, "The magistrate doesn't take very kindly to thieves."

Sophie crossed her arms and stared stubbornly at the wall. If she so much as looked at Araminta, she probably wouldn't be able to restrain herself from lunging at her, and the metal bars of her cell were likely to do serious damage to her face.

"The shoe clips were bad enough," Araminta said, tapping her chin with her forefinger, "but he grew so very angry when I informed him of the theft of my wedding ring."

"I didn't—" Sophie caught herself before she yelled any more. That was exactly what Araminta wanted.

"Didn't you?" she returned, smiling slyly. She waggled her fingers in the air. "I don't appear to be wearing it, and it's your word against mine."

Sophie's lips parted, but not a sound emerged. Araminta was

right. And no judge would take her word over the Countess of Penwood's.

Araminta smiled slightly, her expression vaguely feline. "The man in front—I think he said he was the warden—said you're not likely to be hanged, so you needn't worry on that score. Transportation is a much more likely outcome."

Sophie almost laughed. Just the day before she'd been considering emigrating to America. Now it seemed she'd be leaving for certain—except her destination would be Australia. And she'd be in chains.

"I'll plead for clemency on your behalf," Araminta said. "I don't want you killed, only . . . gone."

"A model of Christian charity," Sophie muttered. "I'm sure the justice will be touched."

Araminta brushed her fingers against her temple, idly pushing back her hair. "Won't he, though?" She looked directly at Sophie and smiled. It was a hard and hollow expression, and suddenly Sophie had to know—

"Why do you hate me?" she whispered.

Araminta did nothing but stare at her for a moment, and then she whispered, "Because he loved you."

Sophie was stunned into silence.

Araminta's eyes grew impossibly brittle. "I will never forgive him for that."

Sophie shook her head in disbelief. "He never loved me."

"He clothed you, he fed you." Araminta's mouth tightened. "He forced me to live with you."

"That wasn't love," Sophie said. "That was guilt. If he loved me he wouldn't have left me with *you*. He wasn't stupid; he had to have known how much you hated me. If he loved me he wouldn't have forgotten me in his will. If he loved me—" She broke off, choking on her own voice.

Araminta crossed her arms.

"If he loved me," Sophie continued, "he might have taken the time to talk to me. He might have asked me how my day went, or what I was studying, or did I enjoy my breakfast." She swallowed convulsively, turning away. It was too hard to look at Araminta just then. "He never loved me," she said quietly. "He didn't know how to love."

No words passed between the two women for many moments, and then Araminta said, "He was punishing me."

Slowly, Sophie turned back around.

"For not giving him an heir." Araminta's hands began to shake. "He hated me for that."

Sophie didn't know what to say. She didn't know if there was anything to say.

After a long moment, Araminta said, "At first I hated you because you were an insult to me. No woman should have to shelter her husband's bastard."

Sophie said nothing.

"But then . . . But then . . ."

To Sophie's great surprise, Araminta sagged against the wall, as if the memories were sucking away her very strength.

"But then it changed," Araminta finally said. "How could he have had you with some whore, and I could not give him a child?"

There seemed little point in Sophie's defending her mother.

"I didn't just hate *you*, you know," Araminta whispered. "I hated seeing you."

Somehow, that didn't surprise Sophie.

"I hated hearing your voice. I hated the fact that your eyes were his. I hated knowing that you were in my house."

"It was my house, too," Sophie said quietly.

"Yes," Araminta replied. "I know. I hated that, too."

Sophie turned quite sharply, looking Araminta in the eye. "Why are you here?" she asked. "Haven't you done enough? You've already ensured my transportation to Australia."

Araminta shrugged. "I can't seem to stay away. There's something so lovely about seeing you in jail. I shall have to bathe for three hours straight to rid myself of the stench, but it's worth it."

"Then excuse me if I go sit in the corner and pretend to read a book," Sophie spat out. "There is nothing lovely about seeing *you*." She marched over to the wobbly three-legged stool that was her cell's only piece of furniture and sat down, trying not to look as miserable as she felt. Araminta had bested her, it was true, but her spirit had not been broken, and she refused to let Araminta think otherwise.

She sat, arms crossed, her back to the cell opening, listening for signs that Araminta was leaving.

But Araminta stayed.

Finally, after about ten minutes of this nonsense, Sophie jumped to her feet and yelled, "Would you *go?*"

Araminta cocked her head slightly to the side. "I'm thinking."

Sophie would have asked, "About what?" but she was rather afraid of the answer.

"I wonder what it is like in Australia," Araminta mused. "I've never been, of course; no civilized person of my acquaintance would even consider it. But I hear it is dreadfully warm. And you with your fair skin. That lovely complexion of yours isn't likely to survive the hot sun. In fact—"

But whatever Araminta had been about to say was cut off (*thankfully*—because Sophie feared she might be moved to attempt murder if she had to listen to another word) by a commotion erupting around the corner.

"What the devil . . . ?" Araminta said, taking a few steps back and craning her neck for a better view.

And then Sophie heard a very familiar voice.

"Benedict?" she whispered.

"What did you say?" Araminta demanded.

But Sophie had already jumped to her feet and had her face pressed up against the bars of her cell.

"I said," Benedict boomed, *"let us pass!"*

"Benedict!" Sophie yelled. She forgot that she didn't particularly want the Bridgertons to see her in such demeaning surroundings. She forgot that she had no future with him. All she could think was that he had come for her, and he was *here*.

If Sophie could have fit her head through the bars, she would have.

A rather sickening smack, obviously that of flesh against bone, echoed through the air, followed by a duller thud, most probably that of body against floor.

Running steps, and then . . .

"Benedict!"

"Sophie! My God, are you well?" His hands reached through the bars, cupping her cheeks. His lips found hers; the kiss was not one of passion but of terror and relief.

"Mr. Bridgerton?" Araminta squeaked.

Sophie somehow managed to pull her eyes off of Benedict and onto Araminta's shocked face. In the flurry of excitement, she'd quite forgotten that Araminta was still unaware of her ties to the Bridgerton family.

It was one of life's most perfect moments. Maybe it meant she was a shallow person. Maybe it meant that she didn't have her priorities in the proper order. But Sophie just *loved* that Araminta, for whom position and power were everything, had just witnessed Sophie being kissed by one of London's most eligible bachelors.

Of course, Sophie was also rather glad to see Benedict.

Benedict pulled away, his reluctant hands trailing lightly across Sophie's face as he drew back out of her cell. As he crossed his arms, he gave Araminta a glare that Sophie was convinced would scorch earth.

"What are your charges against her?" Benedict demanded.

Sophie's feelings for Araminta could best be categorized as "extreme dislike," but even so, she never would have described the older woman as stupid. She was now, however, prepared to reassess that judgment because Araminta, instead of quaking and cowering as any sane person might do under such fire, instead planted her hands on her hips and belted out, "Theft!"

At that very moment, Lady Bridgerton came scurrying around the corner. "I can't believe Sophie would do any such thing," she said, rushing to her son's side. Her eyes narrowed as she regarded Araminta. "And," she added rather peevishly, "I never liked you, Lady Penwood."

Araminta drew back and planted an affronted hand on her chest. "This is not about me," she huffed. "It is about that girl"—(said with a scathing glance toward Sophie)—"who had the audacity to steal my wedding band!"

"I never stole your wedding band, and you know it!" Sophie protested. "The last thing I would want of yours—"

"You stole my shoe clips!"

Sophie's mouth shut into a belligerent line.

"Ha! See!" Araminta looked about, trying to gauge how many people had seen. "A clear admission of guilt."

"She is your stepdaughter," Benedict ground out. "She should never have been in a position where she felt she had to—"

Araminta's face twisted and grew red. "Don't you *ever*," she warned, "call her my stepdaughter. She is nothing to me. Nothing!"

"I beg your pardon," Lady Bridgerton said in a remarkably polite voice, "but if she truly meant nothing to you, you'd hardly be here in this filthy jail, attempting to have her hanged for theft."

Araminta was saved from having to reply by the arrival of the magistrate, who was followed by an extremely grumpy-looking warden, who also happened to be sporting a rather stunning black eye.

As the warden had spanked her on the bottom while shoving her into her cell, Sophie really couldn't help but smile.

"What is going on here?" the magistrate demanded.

"This woman," Benedict said, his loud, deep voice effectively blotting out all other attempts at an answer, "has accused my fiancée of theft."

Fiancée?

Sophie just managed to snap her mouth closed, but even so, she had to clutch tightly on to the bars of her cell, because her legs had turned to instant water.

"Fiancée?" Araminta gasped.

The magistrate straightened. "And precisely who are you, sir?" he asked, clearly aware that Benedict was someone important, even if he wasn't positive who.

Benedict crossed his arms as he said his name.

The magistrate paled. "Er, any relation to the viscount?"

"He's my brother."

"And she's"—he gulped as he pointed to Sophie—"your fiancée?"

Sophie waited for some sort of supernatural sign to stir the air, branding Benedict as a liar, but to her surprise, nothing happened. Lady Bridgerton was even nodding.

"You can't marry her," Araminta insisted.

Benedict turned to his mother. "Is there any reason I need to consult Lady Penwood about this?"

"None that I can think of," Lady Bridgerton replied.

"She is nothing but a whore," Araminta hissed. "Her mother was a whore, and blood runs—urp!"

Benedict had her by the throat before anyone was even aware that he had moved. "Don't," he warned, "make me hit you."

The magistrate tapped Benedict on the shoulder. "You really ought to let her go."

"Might I muzzle her?"

The magistrate looked torn, but eventually he shook his head.

With obvious reluctance, Benedict released Araminta.

"If you marry her," Araminta said, rubbing her throat, "I shall make sure everyone knows *exactly* what she is—the bastard daughter of a whore."

The magistrate turned to Araminta with a stern expression. "I don't think we need that sort of language."

"I can assure you I am not in the habit of speaking in such a manner," she replied, sniffing disdainfully, "but the occasion warrants strong speech."

Sophie actually bit her knuckle as she stared at Benedict, who was flexing and unflexing his fingers in a most menacing manner. Clearly *he* felt the occasion warranted strong fists.

The magistrate cleared his throat. "You accuse her of a very serious crime." He gulped. "And she's going to be married to a Bridgerton."

"I am the Countess of Penwood," she shrilled. "Countess!"

The magistrate looked back and forth between the occupants of the room. As a countess, Araminta outranked everyone, but at the same time, she was only one Penwood against two Bridgertons, one of whom was very large, visibly angry, and had already planted his fist in the warden's eye.

"She stole from me!"

"No, you stole from her!" Benedict roared.

The room fell into instant silence.

"You stole her very childhood," Benedict said, his body shaking with rage. There were huge gaps in his knowledge of Sophie's life, but somehow he knew that this woman had caused much of the pain that lurked behind her green eyes. And he'd have been willing to bet that her dear, departed papa was responsible for the rest.

Benedict turned to the magistrate and said, "My fiancée is the bastard daughter of the late Earl of Penwood. And that is why the dowager countess has falsely accused her of theft. It is revenge and hate, pure and simple."

The magistrate looked from Benedict to Araminta and then finally to Sophie. "Is this true?" he asked her. "Have you been falsely accused?"

"She took the shoe clips!" Araminta shrieked. "I swear on my husband's grave, she took the shoe clips!"

"Oh, for the love of God, Mother, *I* took the shoe clips."

Sophie's mouth fell open. "Posy?"

Benedict looked at the newcomer, a short, slightly pudgy young woman who was obviously the countess's daughter, then glanced back to Sophie, who had gone white as a sheet.

"Get out of here," Araminta hissed. "You have no place in these proceedings."

"Obviously she does," the magistrate said, turning to Araminta, "if she took the shoe clips. Do you want to have her charged?"

"She's my daughter!"

"Put me in the cell with Sophie!" Posy said dramatically, clasping one of her hands to her breast with great effect. "If she is transported for theft, then I must be as well."

For the first time in several days, Benedict found himself smiling.

The warden took out his keys. "Sir?" he said hesitantly, nudging the magistrate.

"Put those away," the magistrate snapped. "We're not incarcerating the countess's daughter."

"Do not put those away," Lady Bridgerton cut in. "I want my future daughter-in-law released immediately."

The warden looked helplessly at the magistrate.

"Oh, very well," the magistrate said, jabbing his finger in Sophie's direction. "Let that one free. But no one is going anywhere until I have this sorted out."

Araminta bristled in protest, but Sophie was duly released. She started to run to Benedict, but the magistrate held out a restraining arm. "Not so fast," he warned. "We'll be having no lovey-dovey reunions until I figure out who is to be arrested."

"No one is to be arrested," Benedict growled.

"She is going to Australia!" Araminta cried out, pointing toward Sophie.

"Put me in the cell!" Posy sighed, placing the back of her hand against her brow. "I did it!"

"Posy, will you be quiet?" Sophie whispered. "Trust me, you do not want to be in that cell. It's dreadful. And there are rats."

Posy started inching away from the cell.

"You will never see another invitation again in this town," Lady Bridgerton said to Araminta.

"I am a countess!" Araminta hissed.

"And I am more popular," Lady Bridgerton returned, the snide words so out of character that both Benedict's and Sophie's mouths dropped open.

"Enough!" the magistrate said. He turned to Posy, pointing to Araminta as he said, "Is she your mother?"

Posy nodded.

"And you said you stole the shoe clips?"

Posy nodded again. "And no one stole her wedding ring. It's in her jewelry box at home."

No one gasped, because no one was terribly surprised.

But Araminta said, nonetheless, "It is not!"

"Your other jewelry box," Posy clarified. "The one you keep in the third drawer from the left."

Araminta paled.

The magistrate said, "You don't seem to have a very good case against Miss Beckett, Lady Penwood."

Araminta began to shake with rage, her outstretched arm quivering as she pointed one long finger at Sophie. "She stole from me," she said in a deadly low voice before turning furious eyes on Posy. "My daughter is lying. I do not know why, and I certainly do not know what she hopes to gain, but she is lying."

Something very uncomfortable began to churn in Sophie's stomach. Posy was going to be in horrible trouble when she went home. There was no telling what Araminta would do in retaliation for such public humiliation. She couldn't let Posy take the blame for her. She had to—

"Posy didn't—" The words burst forth from her mouth before she had a chance to think, but she didn't manage to finish her sentence because Posy elbowed her in the belly.

Hard.

"Did you say something?" the magistrate inquired.

Sophie shook her head, completely unable to speak. Posy had knocked her breath clear to Scotland.

The magistrate let out a weary sigh and raked his hand through his thinning blond hair. He looked at Posy, then at Sophie, then Araminta, then Benedict. Lady Bridgerton cleared her throat, forcing him to look at her, too.

"Clearly," the magistrate said, looking very much as if he'd rather be anywhere other than where he was, "this is about a great deal more than a stolen shoe clip."

"Shoe *clips*," Araminta sniffed. "There were two of them."

"Regardless," the magistrate ground out, "you all obviously detest one another, and I would like to know why before I go ahead and charge anyone."

For a second, no one spoke. Then everyone spoke.

"Silence!" the magistrate roared. "You," he said, pointing at Sophie, "start."

"Uhhhh . . ." Now that Sophie actually had the floor, she felt terribly self-conscious.

The magistrate cleared his throat. Loudly.

"What he said was correct," Sophie said quickly, pointing to Benedict. "I am the daughter of the Earl of Penwood, although I was never acknowledged as such."

Araminta opened her mouth to say something, but the magistrate sent her such a withering glare that she kept quiet.

"I lived at Penwood Park for seven years before she married the earl," she continued, motioning to Araminta. "The earl said that he was my guardian, but everyone knew the truth." She paused, remembering her father's face, and thinking that she ought not be so surprised that she couldn't picture him with a smile. "I look a great deal like him," she said.

"I knew your father," Lady Bridgerton said softly. "And your aunt. It explains why I've always thought you looked so familiar."

Sophie flashed her a small, grateful smile. Something in Lady Bridgerton's tone was very reassuring, and it made her feel a little warmer inside, a little more secure.

"Please continue," the magistrate said.

Sophie gave him a nod, then added, "When the earl married the countess, she didn't want me living there, but the earl insisted. I rarely saw him, and I don't think he thought very much of me, but he did see me as his responsibility, and he wouldn't allow her to boot me out. But when he died . . ."

Sophie stopped and swallowed, trying to get past the lump in her throat. She'd never actually told her story to anyone before; the words seemed strange and foreign coming from her mouth. "When he died," she continued, "his will specified that Lady Penwood's portion would be trebled if she kept me in her household until I turned twenty. So she did. But my position changed dramatically. I became a servant. Well, not really a servant." Sophie smiled wryly. "A servant is paid. So I was really more like a slave."

Sophie looked over at Araminta. She was standing with her arms crossed and her nose tipped in the air. Her lips were pursed tightly, and it suddenly struck Sophie how very many times before she had seen that exact same expression on Araminta's face. More times than she could dare to count. Enough times to have broken her soul.

Yet here she was, dirty and penniless to be sure, but with her mind and spirit still strong.

"Sophie?" Benedict asked, gazing at her with a concerned expression. "Is everything all right?"

She nodded slowly, because she was just coming to realize that everything *was* all right. The man she loved had (in a rather roundabout way) just asked her to marry him, Araminta was finally about to receive the drubbing she deserved—at the hands of the Bridgertons, no less, who would leave her in shreds by the time they were through, and Posy . . . now that might have been the loveliest of all. Posy, who had always wanted to be a sister to her, who had never quite had the courage to be herself, had stood up to her mother and quite possibly saved the day. Sophie was one hundred percent certain that if Benedict had not come and declared her his fiancée, Posy's testimony would have been the only thing to save her from transportation—or maybe even execution. And Sophie knew better than anyone that Posy would pay dearly for her courage. Araminta was probably already plotting how to make her life a living hell.

Yes, everything *was* all right, and Sophie suddenly found herself standing a little straighter as she said, "Allow me to finish my story. After the earl died, Lady Penwood kept me on as her unpaid lady's maid. Although in truth I was made to do the work of three maids."

"You know, Lady Whistledown said that very thing just last month!" Posy said excitedly. "I told Mother that she—"

"Posy, shut *up*!" Araminta snapped.

"When I turned twenty," Sophie continued, "she didn't turn me out. To this day I don't know why."

"I think we've heard enough," Araminta said.

"I don't think we've heard nearly enough," Benedict snapped.

Sophie looked to the magistrate for guidance. At his nod she continued. "I can only deduce that she rather enjoyed having someone to order about. Or maybe she just liked having a maid she didn't have to pay. There was nothing left from his will."

"That's not true," Posy blurted out.

Sophie turned to her in shock.

"He did leave you money," Posy insisted.

Sophie felt her jaw go slack. "That's not possible. I had nothing. My father saw to my welfare up to age twenty, but after that—"

"After that," Posy said rather forcefully, "you had a dowry."

"A dowry?" Sophie whispered.

"That's not true!" Araminta shrilled.

"It *is* true," Posy insisted. "You ought not leave incriminating evidence about, Mother. I read a copy of the earl's will last year." She turned to the rest of the room and said, "It was in the same box where she put her wedding band."

"You stole my dowry?" Sophie said, her voice barely more than breath. All these years she'd thought her father had left her with nothing. She'd known that he'd never loved her, that he saw her as little more than his responsibility, but it had stung that he'd left dowries for Rosamund and Posy—who were not even his blood daughters—and not for her.

She'd never really thought that he'd ignored her on purpose; in all truth, she'd mostly felt . . . forgotten.

Which had felt worse than a deliberate snub would have done.

"He left me a dowry," she said dazedly. Then to Benedict, "I have a dowry."

"I don't care if you have a dowry," Benedict replied. "I don't need it."

"I care," Sophie said. "I thought he'd forgotten me. All these years I'd thought he'd written up his will and simply forgotten about me. I know he couldn't really leave money to his bastard daughter, but he'd told all the world I was his ward. There was no reason he couldn't provide for his ward." For some reason she looked to Lady

Bridgerton. "He could have provided for a ward. People do that all the time."

The magistrate cleared his throat and turned on Araminta, "And what has happened to her dowry?"

Araminta said nothing.

Lady Bridgerton cleared her throat. "I don't think it's terribly legal," she said, "to embezzle a young woman's dowry." She smiled—a slow, satisfied sort of smile. "Eh, Araminta?"

Chapter 23

Lady Penwood appears to have left town. So does Lady Bridgerton. Interesting . . .

LADY WHISTLEDOWN'S SOCIETY PAPERS,
18 JUNE 1817

Benedict decided he had never loved his mother more than he did at that very minute. He was trying not to grin, but it was exceedingly difficult with Lady Penwood gasping like a fish on land.

The magistrate's eyes bugged out. "You're not suggesting I arrest the *countess*?"

"No, of course not," Violet demurred. "She'd likely go free. The aristocracy rarely pays for its crimes. But," she added, tilting her head slightly to the side as she gave Lady Penwood a very pointed glance, "if you *were* to arrest her, it would be terribly embarrassing while she defended the charges."

"What are you trying to say?" Lady Penwood asked through decidedly clenched teeth.

Violet turned to the magistrate. "Might I have a few moments alone with Lady Penwood?"

"Of course, my lady." He gave her a gruff nod, then barked, "Everyone! Out!"

"No, no," Violet said with a sweet smile as she pressed something that looked suspiciously like a pound note into his palm. "My family may stay."

The magistrate blushed slightly, then grabbed the warden's arm and yanked him out of the room.

"There now," Violet murmured. "Where were we?"

Benedict beamed with pride as he watched his mother march right up to Lady Penwood and stare her down. He stole a glance at Sophie. Her mouth was hanging open.

"My son is going to marry Sophie," Violet said, "and you are going to tell anyone who will listen that she was the ward of your late husband."

"I will never lie for her," Lady Penwood shot back.

Violet shrugged. "Fine. Then you can expect my solicitors to begin looking for Sophie's dowry immediately. After all, Benedict will be entitled to it once he marries her."

Benedict slipped his arm around Sophie's waist and gave her a light squeeze.

"If someone asks me," Lady Penwood ground out, "I will confirm whatever story you bandy about. But do not expect me to go out of my way to help her."

Violet pretended to mull that over, then said, "Excellent. I do believe that will do nicely." She turned to her son. "Benedict?"

He gave her a sharp nod.

His mother turned back to Lady Penwood. "Sophie's father was named Charles Beckett and he was a distant cousin of the earl's, no?"

Lady Penwood looked as if she'd swallowed a bad clam, but she nodded nonetheless.

Violet pointedly turned her back on the countess, and said, "I'm sure some members of the *ton* will consider her a bit shabby, since obviously nobody will be familiar with her family, but at least she will be respectable. After all"—she turned back around and flashed a wide smile at Araminta—"there is that connection with the Penwoods."

Araminta let out a strange, growling sound. It was all Benedict could do not to laugh.

"Oh, magistrate!" Violet called out, and when he bustled back into the room, she smiled gamely at him and said, "I believe my work here is done."

He let out a sigh of relief, saying, "Then I don't have to arrest anyone?"

"It seems not."

He practically sagged against the wall.

"Well, I am leaving!" Lady Penwood announced, as if anyone might possibly miss her. She turned to her daughter with furious eyes. "Come along, Posy."

Benedict watched as the blood quite literally drained from Posy's face. But before he could intervene, Sophie jumped forward, blurting out, "Lady Bridgerton!" just as Araminta roared, *"Now!"*

"Yes, dear?"

Sophie grabbed Violet's arm and pulled her close enough to whisper something in her ear.

"Quite right," Violet said. She turned to Posy. "Miss Gunningworth?"

"Actually, it's Miss Reiling," Posy corrected. "The earl never adopted me."

"Of course. Miss Reiling. How old are you?"

"One-and-twenty, my lady."

"Well, that's certainly old enough to make your own decisions. Would you like to come to my home for a visit?"

"Oh, *yes!*"

"Posy, you may *not* go live with the Bridgertons!" Araminta ordered.

Violet ignored her completely as she said to Posy, "I believe I will quit London early this season. Would you care to join us for an extended stay in Kent?"

Posy nodded quickly. "I would be much obliged."

"That settles it, then."

"That does not settle it," Araminta snapped. "She is my daughter, and—"

"Benedict," Lady Bridgerton said in a rather bored voice, "what was the name of my solicitor?"

"Go!" Araminta spat at Posy. "And don't ever darken my door again."

For the first time that afternoon, Posy began to look a little scared. It didn't help when her mother stalked right up to her and hissed straight in her face, "If you go with them now, you are dead to me. Do you understand? *Dead!*"

Posy threw a panicked look at Violet, who immediately stepped forward and linked their arms together.

"It's all right, Posy," Violet said softly. "You may stay with us as long as you wish."

Sophie stepped forward and slid her arm through Posy's free one. "Now we will be sisters truly," she said, leaning forward and giving her a kiss on the cheek.

"Oh, Sophie," Posy cried out, a well of tears bursting forth. "I'm so sorry! I never stood up for you. I should have said something. I should have done something, but—"

Sophie shook her head. "You were young. I was young. And I know better than anyone how difficult it is to defy *her*." She threw a scathing glare at Araminta.

"Don't you speak to me that way," Araminta seethed, raising her hand as if to strike.

"Ah ah ah!" Violet cut in. "The solicitors, Lady Penwood. Don't forget the solicitors."

Araminta dropped her hand, but she looked as if she might spontaneously burst into flame at any moment.

"Benedict?" Violet called out. "How quickly could we be at the solicitors' office?"

Grinning inside, he gave his chin a thoughtful stroke. "They're not too terribly far away. Twenty minutes? Thirty if the roads are full."

Araminta shook with rage as she directed her words at Violet. "Take her then. She's never been anything to me but a disappointment. And you can expect to be stuck with her until your dying day, as no one is likely to offer for her. I have to bribe men just to ask her to dance."

And then the strangest thing occurred. Sophie began to shake. Her skin turned red, her teeth clenched, and the most amazing roar burst forth from her mouth. And before anyone could even think to intervene, she had planted her fist squarely into Araminta's left eye and sent the older woman sprawling.

Benedict had thought that nothing could have surprised him more than his mother's heretofore undetected Machiavellian streak.

He was wrong.

"That," Sophie hissed, "is *not* for stealing my dowry. It's not for all the times you tried to boot me out of my house before my father died. And it's not even for turning me into your personal slave."

"Er, Sophie," Benedict said mildly, "what, then, is it for?"

Sophie's eyes never wavered off of Araminta's face as she said, "*That* was for not loving your daughters equally."

Posy began to bawl.

"There's a special place in hell for mothers like you," Sophie said, her voice dangerously low.

"You know," the magistrate squeaked, "we really do need to clear this cell out for the next occupant."

"He's right," Violet said quickly, stepping in front of Sophie before she decided to start kicking Araminta. She turned to Posy. "Have you any belongings you wish to retrieve?"

Posy shook her head.

Violet's eyes turned sad as she gave Posy's hand a little squeeze. "We shall make new memories for you, my dear."

Araminta rose to her feet, gave Posy one last horrific glare, then stalked away.

"Well," Violet declared, planting her hands on her hips. "I thought she would never leave."

Benedict disengaged his arm from Sophie's waist with a murmur of, "Don't move a muscle," then walked quickly to his mother's side.

"Have I told you lately," he whispered in her ear, "how much I love you?"

"No," she said with a jaunty smile, "but I know, anyway."

"Have I mentioned that you're the best of mothers?"

"No, but I know that, too."

"Good." He leaned down and dropped a kiss on her cheek. "Thank you. It's a privilege to be your son."

His mother, who had held her own throughout the day, and indeed proven herself the most hardheaded and quick-witted of them all, burst into tears.

"What did you say to her?" Sophie demanded.

"It's all right," Violet said, sniffling mightily. "It's . . ." She threw her arms around Benedict. "I love you, too!"

Posy turned to Sophie and said, "This is a nice family."

Sophie turned to Posy and said, "I know."

One hour later Sophie was in Benedict's sitting room, perched on the very same sofa on which she had lost her innocence just a few weeks earlier. Lady Bridgerton had questioned the wisdom (and propriety) of Sophie's going to Benedict's home by herself, but he had given her such a look that she had quickly backed down, saying only, "Just have her home by seven."

Which gave them one hour together.

"I'm sorry," Sophie blurted out, the instant her bottom touched the sofa. For some reason they hadn't said anything during the carriage ride home. They'd held hands, and Benedict had brought her fingers to his lips, but they hadn't said anything.

Sophie had been relieved. She hadn't been ready for words. It had been easy at the jail, with all the commotion and so many people, but now that they were alone . . .

She didn't know what to say.

Except, she supposed, "I'm sorry."

"No, I'm sorry," Benedict replied, sitting beside her and taking her hands in his.

"No, I'm—" She suddenly smiled. "This is very silly."

"I love you," he said.

Her lips parted.

"I want to marry you," he said.

She stopped breathing.

"And I don't care about your parents or my mother's bargain with Lady Penwood to make you respectable." He stared down at her, his dark eyes meltingly in love. "I would have married you no matter what."

Sophie blinked. The tears in her eyes were growing fat and hot, and she had a sneaking suspicion that she was about to make a fool of herself by blubbering all over him. She managed to say his name, then found herself completely lost from there.

Benedict squeezed her hands. "We couldn't have lived in London, I know, but we don't need to live in London. When I thought about what it was in life I really needed—not what I wanted, but what I needed—the only thing that kept coming up was you."

"I—"

"No, let me finish," he said, his voice suspiciously hoarse. "I shouldn't have asked you to be my mistress. It wasn't right of me."

"Benedict," she said softly, "what else would you have done? You thought me a servant. In a perfect world we could have married, but this isn't a perfect world. Men like you don't marry—"

"Fine. I wasn't wrong to ask, then." He tried to smile. It came out lopsided. "I would have been a fool not to ask. I wanted you so badly, and I think I already loved you, and—"

"Benedict, you don't have to—"

"Explain? Yes, I do. I should never have pressed the issue once you refused my offer. It was unfair of me to ask, especially when we both knew that I would eventually be expected to marry. I would die before sharing you. How could I ask you to do the same?"

She reached out and brushed something off of his cheek. Jesus, was he crying? He couldn't remember the last time he'd cried. When his father had died, perhaps? Even then, his tears had fallen in private.

"There are so many reasons I love you," he said, each word emerging with careful precision. He knew that he had won her. She wasn't going to run away; she *would* be his wife. But he still wanted this to be perfect. A man only got one shot at declaring himself to his true love; he didn't want to muck it up completely.

"But one of the things I love best," he continued, "is the fact that you know yourself. You know who you are, and what you value. You have principles, Sophie, and you stick by them." He took her hand and brought it to his lips. "That is so rare."

Her eyes were filling with tears, and all he wanted to do was hold her, but he knew he had to finish. So many words had been welling up inside of him, and they all had to be said.

"And," he said, his voice dropping in volume, "you took the time to see *me*. To know me. Benedict. Not Mr. Bridgerton, not 'Number Two.' Benedict."

She touched his cheek. "You're the finest person I know. I adore your family, but I love *you*."

He crushed her to him. He couldn't help it. He had to feel her in his arms, to reassure himself that she was there and that she would always be there. With him, by his side, until death did they part. It was strange, but he was driven by the oddest compulsion to hold her . . . just hold her.

He wanted her, of course. He always wanted her. But more than that, he wanted to hold her. To smell her, to feel her.

He was, he realized, comforted by her presence. They didn't need to talk. They didn't even need to touch (although he wasn't about to let go just then). Simply put, he was a happier man—and quite possibly a better man—when she was near.

He buried his face in her hair, inhaling her scent, smelling . . .

Smelling . . .

He drew back. "Would you care for a bath?"

Her face turned an instant scarlet. "Oh, no," she moaned, the words muffled into the hand she'd clapped over her mouth. "It was so filthy in jail, and I was forced to sleep on the ground, and—"

"Don't tell me any more," he said.

"But—"

"Please." If he heard more he might have to kill someone. As long as there had been no permanent damage, he didn't want to know the details.

"I think," he said, the first hint of a smile tugging at the left corner of his mouth, "that you should take a bath."

"Right." She nodded as she rose to her feet. "I'll go straight to your mother's—"

"Here."

"Here?"

The smile spread to the right corner of his mouth. "Here."

"But we told your mother—"

"That you'd be home by nine."

"I think she said seven."

"Did she? Funny, I heard nine."

"Benedict . . ."

He took her hand and pulled her toward the door. "Seven sounds an *awful* lot like nine."

"Benedict . . ."

"Actually, it sounds even more like eleven."

"Benedict!"

He deposited her right by the door. "Stay here."

"I beg your pardon?"

"Don't move a muscle," he said, touching his fingertip to her nose.

Sophie watched helplessly as he slipped out into the hall, only to return two minutes later. "Where did you go?" she asked.

"To order a bath."

"But—"

His eyes grew very, very wicked. "For two."

She gulped.

He leaned forward. "They happened to have water heating already."

"They did?"

He nodded. "It'll only take a few minutes to fill the tub."

She glanced toward the front door. "It's nearly seven."

"But I'm allowed to keep you until twelve."

"Benedict!"

He pulled her close. "You want to stay."

"I never said that."

"You don't have to. If you really disagreed with me, you'd have something more to say than, 'Benedict'!"

She had to smile; he did *that* good an imitation of her voice.

His mouth curved into a devilish grin. "Am I wrong?"

She looked away, but she knew her lips were twitching.

"I thought not," he murmured. He motioned with his head toward the stairs. "Come with me."

She went.

To Sophie's great surprise, Benedict vacated the room while she undressed for her bath. She held her breath as she pulled her dress over her head. He was right; she did smell rank.

The maid who had drawn the bath had scented it with oil and a sudsy soap that left bubbles floating on the surface. Once Sophie had shed all of her clothing, she dipped her toe into the steaming water. The rest of her soon followed.

Heaven. It was hard to believe it had only been two days since she'd had a bath. One night in jail made it feel more like a year.

Sophie tried to clear her mind and enjoy the hedonism of the moment, but it was difficult to enjoy with the anticipation growing within her veins. She knew when she'd decided to stay that Benedict planned on joining her. She could have refused; for all his wheedling and cajoling, he would have taken her back home to his mother's.

But she had decided to stay. Somewhere between the sitting-room doorway and the base of the stairs she'd realized she *wanted* to stay. It had been such a long road to this moment, and she wasn't quite ready to relinquish him, even if it would only be until the following morning, when he was sure to come by his mother's for breakfast.

He would be here soon. And when he was . . .

She shivered. Even in the steaming hot tub, she shivered. And then, as she was sinking deeper into the water, allowing it to rise above her shoulders and neck, even right up to her nose, she heard the click of the door opening.

Benedict. He was wearing a dark green dressing gown, tied with a sash at his waist. His feet were bare, as were his legs from the knees down.

"I hope you don't mind if I have this destroyed," he said, glancing down at her dress.

She smiled at him and shook her head. It wasn't what she'd been expecting him to say, and she knew that he'd done it to set her at ease.

"I'll send someone to fetch you another," he said.

"Thank you." She shifted slightly in the water to make room for him, but he surprised her by walking to her end of the tub.

"Lean forward," he murmured.

She did, and sighed with pleasure as he began to wash her back.

"I've dreamed of doing this for years."

"Years?" she asked, amused.

"Mmm-hmm. I had *many* dreams about you after the masquerade."

Sophie was glad she was leaning forward, her forehead resting on her bent knees, because she blushed.

"Dunk your head so I can wash your hair," he ordered.

She slid under the water, then quickly came back up.

Benedict rubbed the bar of soap in his hands and then began to work the lather through her hair. "It was longer before," he commented.

"I had to cut it," she said. "I sold it to a wigmaker."

She wasn't sure, but she thought she might have heard him growl.

"It used to be much shorter," she added.

"Ready to rinse."

She dunked back in the tub, swishing her head this way and that under the water before coming back up for air.

Benedict cupped his hands and filled them with water. "You've still got some in the back," he said, letting the water pour over her hair.

Sophie let him repeat that process a few times, then finally asked, "Aren't you coming in?" It was dreadfully brazen of her, and she knew she must be blushing like a raspberry, but she simply had to know.

He shook his head. "I'd planned to, but this is too much fun."

"Washing me?" she asked doubtfully.

One corner of his mouth quirked into the faintest of half smiles. "I'm rather looking forward to drying you off as well." He reached down and picked up a large white towel. "Up you go."

Sophie chewed on her lower lip in indecision. She had, of course, already been as close to him as two people could be, but she wasn't so sophisticated that she could rise naked from the tub without a large degree of embarrassment.

Benedict smiled faintly as he stood and unfolded the towel. Holding it wide, he averted his gaze and said, "I'll have you all wrapped up before I can see a thing."

Sophie took a deep breath and stood, somehow feeling that that one action might mark the beginning of the rest of her life.

Benedict gently wrapped the towel around her, his hands bringing the corners to her face when he was done. He dabbed at her cheeks, where light droplets of water were still clinging to her skin, then leaned down and kissed her nose. "I'm glad you're here," he murmured.

"I'm glad, too."

He touched her chin. His eyes never left hers, and she almost felt as if he'd touched those as well. And then, with the softest, most tender caress imaginable, he kissed her. Sophie didn't just feel loved; she felt revered.

"I should wait until Monday," he said, "but I don't want to."

"I don't want you to wait," she whispered.

He kissed her again, this time with a bit more urgency. "You're so beautiful," he murmured. "Everything I ever dreamed of."

His lips found her cheek, her chin, her neck, and every kiss, every nibble robbed her of balance and breath. She was sure her legs would give out, sure her strength would fail her under his tender onslaught, and just when she was convinced she'd crumple to the floor, he scooped her into his arms and carried her to the bed.

"In my heart," he vowed, settling her against the quilts and pillows, "you are my wife."

Sophie's breath caught.

"After our wedding it will be legal," he said, stretching out alongside her, "blessed by God and country, but right now—" His voice grew hoarse as he propped himself up on one elbow so that he could gaze into her eyes. "Right now it is *true*."

Sophie reached up and touched his face. "I love you," she whispered. "I have always loved you. I think I loved you before I even knew you."

He leaned down to kiss her anew, but she stopped him with a breathy, "No, wait."

He paused, mere inches from her lips.

"At the masquerade," she said, her voice uncharacteristically shaky, "even before I saw you, I *felt* you. Anticipation. Magic. There was something in the air. And when I turned, and you were there, it was as if you'd been waiting for me, and I knew that you were the reason I'd stolen into the ball."

Something wet hit her cheek. A single tear, fallen from his eye.

"You are the reason I exist," she said softly, "the very reason I was born."

He opened his mouth, and for a moment she was certain he would say something, but the only sound that emerged was a rough, halting noise, and she realized that he was overcome, that he could not speak.

She was undone.

Benedict kissed her again, trying to show in deeds what he could not say in words. He hadn't thought he could love her any more than he did just five seconds earlier, but when she'd said . . . when she'd told him . . .

His heart had grown, and he'd thought it might burst.

He loved her. Suddenly the world was a very simple place. He loved her, and that was all that mattered.

His robe and her towel melted away, and when they were skin to skin he worshipped her with his hands and lips. He wanted her to realize the extent of his need for her, and he wanted her to know the same desire.

"Oh, Sophie," he groaned, her name the only word he could manage to say. "Sophie, Sophie, Sophie."

She smiled up at him, and he was struck by the most remarkable desire to laugh. He was happy, he realized. So damned happy.

And it felt good.

He positioned himself over her, ready to enter her, ready to make her his. This was different from the last time, when they'd both been swept away by emotion. This time they had been deliberate. They had chosen more than passion; they had chosen each other.

"You're mine," he said, his eyes never leaving hers as he slid inside. "You're mine."

And much later, when they were exhausted and spent, lying in each other's arms, he brought his lips to her ear and whispered, "And I'm yours."

Several hours later, Sophie yawned and blinked herself awake, wondering why she felt so lovely and warm, and—

"Benedict!" she gasped. "What time is it?"

He didn't respond, so she clutched at his shoulder and shook hard. "Benedict! Benedict!"

He grunted as he rolled over. "I'm sleeping."

"What time is it?"

He buried his face in the pillow. "Haven't the foggiest."

"I'm supposed to be at your mother's by seven."

"Eleven," he mumbled.

"Seven!"

He opened one eye. It looked like it took a great deal of effort. "You knew you weren't going to make it back by seven when you decided to take a bath."

"I know, but I didn't think I'd be much past nine."

Benedict blinked a few times as he looked around the room. "I don't think you're going to make it—"

But she'd already caught sight of the mantel clock and was presently choking frantically.

"Are you all right?" he inquired.

"It's three in the morning!"

He smiled. "You might as well spend the night, then."

"Benedict!"

"You wouldn't want to put out any of the servants, would you? They're all quite asleep, I'm sure."

"But I—"

"Have mercy, woman," he finally declared. "I'm marrying you next week."

That got her attention. "Next week?" she squeaked.

He tried to assume a serious mien. "It's best to take care of these things quickly."

"Why?"

"Why?" he echoed.

"Yes, why?"

"Er, ah, stemming gossip and all that."

Her lips parted and her eyes grew round. "Do you think Lady Whistledown will write about me?"

"God, I hope not," he muttered.

Her face fell.

"Well, I suppose she *might*. Why on earth would you want her to?"

"I've been reading her column for years. I always dreamed of seeing my name there."

He shook his head. "You have very strange dreams."

"Benedict!"

"Very well, yes, I imagine Lady Whistledown will report our marriage, if not before the ceremony, then certainly very quickly after the fact. She's diabolical that way."

"I wish I knew who she was."

"You and half of London."

"Me and *all* of London, I should think." She sighed, then said, not very convincingly, "I really should go. Your mother is surely worried about me."

He shrugged. "She knows where you are."

"But she'll think less of me."

"I doubt it. She'll give you a bit of latitude, I'm sure, considering we're to be married in three days."

"Three days?" she yelped. "I thought you said next week."

"Three days *is* next week."

Sophie frowned. "Oh. You're right. Monday, then?"

He nodded, looking very satisfied.

"Imagine that," she said. "I'll be in *Whistledown*."

He propped himself up on one elbow, eyeing her suspiciously. "Are you looking forward to marrying me," he asked in an amused voice, "or is it merely the *Whistledown* mention that has you so excited?"

She gave him a playful swat on the shoulder.

"Actually," he said thoughtfully, "you've already been in *Whistledown*."

"I have? When?"

"After the masquerade. Lady Whistledown remarked that I'd been rather taken with a mystery woman in silver. Try as she might, she couldn't deduce your identity." He grinned. "It very well may be the only secret in London she *hasn't* uncovered."

Sophie's face went instantly serious and she scooted a foot or so away from him on the bed. "Oh, Benedict. I have to . . . I want to . . . That is to say . . ." She stopped, looking away for a few seconds before turning back. "I'm sorry."

He considered yanking her back into his arms, but she looked so damned earnest he had no choice but to take her seriously. "What for?"

"For not telling you who I was. It was wrong of me." She bit her lip. "Well, not *wrong* precisely."

He drew back slightly. "If it wasn't wrong, then what was it?"

"I don't know. I can't explain exactly why I did what I did, but it just . . ." She chewed on her lips some more. He started to think that she might do herself permanent harm.

She sighed. "I didn't tell you right away because it didn't seem to make any sense to do so. I was so sure we'd part ways just as soon as we left the Cavenders. But then you grew ill, and I had to care for you, and you didn't recognize me, and . . ."

He lifted a finger to her lips. "It doesn't matter."

Her brows rose. "It seemed to matter a great deal the other night."

He didn't know why, but he just didn't want to get into a serious discussion at that moment. "A lot has changed since then."

"Don't you want to know why I didn't tell you who I was?"

He touched her cheeks. "I know who you are."

She chewed on her lip.

"And do you want to hear the funniest part?" he continued. "Do you know one of the reasons I was so hesitant to give my heart completely to you? I'd been saving a piece of it for the lady from the masquerade, always hoping that one day I'd find her."

"Oh, Benedict," she sighed, thrilled by his words, and at the same time miserable that she had hurt him so.

"Deciding to marry you meant I had to abandon my dream of marrying *her*," he said quietly. "Ironic, isn't it?"

"I'm sorry I hurt you by not revealing my identity," she said, not quite looking at his face, "but I'm not sure that I'm sorry I did it. Does that make any sense?"

He didn't say anything.

"I think I would do the same thing again."

He still didn't say anything. Sophie started to feel very uneasy inside.

"It just seemed like the right thing to do at the time," she persisted. "Telling you that I'd been at the masquerade would have served no purpose."

"I would have known the truth," he said softly.

"Yes, and what would you have done with that truth?" She sat up, pulling the covers until they were tucked under her arms. "You would have wanted your mystery woman to be your mistress, just as you wanted the housemaid to be your mistress."

He said nothing, just stared at her face.

"I guess what I'm saying," Sophie said quickly, "is that if I'd known at the beginning what I know now, I would have said something. But I didn't know, and I thought I'd just be positioning myself for heartbreak, and—" She choked on her final words, frantically searching his face for some kind of clue to his feelings. "*Please* say something."

"I love you," he said.

It was all she needed.

Epilogue

Sunday's bash at Bridgerton House is sure to be the event of the season. The entire family will gather, along with a hundred or so of their closest friends, to celebrate the dowager vis countess's birthday.

It is considered crass to mention a lady's age, and so This Author will not reveal which birthday Lady Bridgerton is celebrating.

But have no fear . . . This Author knows!

LADY WHISTLEDOWN'S SOCIETY PAPERS,
9 APRIL 1824

"Stop! Stop!"

Sophie shrieked with laughter as she ran down the stone steps that led to the garden behind Bridgerton House. After three children and seven years of marriage, Benedict could still make her smile, still make her laugh . . . and he still chased her around the house any chance he could get.

"Where are the children?" she gasped, once he'd caught her at the base of the steps.

"Francesca is watching them."

"And your mother?"

He grinned. "I daresay Francesca is watching her, too."

"Anyone could stumble upon us out here," she said, looking this way and that.

His smile turned wicked. "Maybe," he said, catching hold of her green-velvet skirt and reeling her in, "we should adjourn to the *private* terrace."

The words were oh-so-familiar, and it was only a second before she was transported back nine years to the masquerade ball. "The private terrace, you say?" she asked, amusement dancing in her eyes. "And how, pray tell, would you know of a *private* terrace?"

His lips brushed against hers. "I have my ways," he murmured.

"And I," she returned, smiling slyly, "have my secrets."

He drew back. "Oh? And will you share?"

"We five," she said with a nod, "are about to be six."

He looked at her face, then looked at her belly. "Are you sure?"

"As sure as I was last time."

He took her hand and raised it to lips. "This one will be a girl."

"That's what you said last time."

"I know, but—"

"And the time before."

"All the more reason for the odds to favor me *this* time."

She shook her head. "I'm glad you're not a gambler."

He smiled at that. "Let's not tell anyone yet."

"I think a few people already suspect," Sophie admitted.

"I want to see how long it takes that Whistledown woman to figure it out," Benedict said.

"Are you serious?"

"The blasted woman knew about Charles, and she knew about Alexander, and she knew about William."

Sophie smiled as she let him pull her into the shadows. "Do you realize that I have been mentioned in Whistledown *two hundred* and thirty-two times?"

That stopped him cold. "You've been counting?"

"Two hundred and thirty-three if you include the time after the masquerade."

"I can't believe you've been counting."

She gave him a nonchalant shrug. "It's exciting to be mentioned."

Benedict thought it was a bloody nuisance to be mentioned, but he wasn't about to spoil her delight, so instead he just said, "At least she always writes nice things about you. If she didn't, I might have to hunt her down and run her out of the country."

Sophie couldn't help but smile. "Oh, *please*. I hardly think you could discover her identity when no one else in the *ton* has managed it."

He raised one arrogant brow. "That doesn't sound like wifely devotion and confidence to me."

She pretended to examine her glove. "You needn't expend the energy. She's obviously very good at what she does."

"Well, she won't know about Violet," Benedict vowed. "At least not until it's obvious to the world."

"Violet?" Sophie asked softly.

"It's time my mother had a grandchild named after her, don't you think?"

Sophie leaned against him, letting her cheek rest against the crisp linen of his shirt. "I think Violet is a lovely name," she murmured, nestling deeper into the shelter of his arms. "I just hope it's a girl. Because if it's a boy, he's never going to forgive us . . ."

Later that night, in a town house in the very best part of London, a woman picked up her quill and wrote:

Lady Whistledown's Society Papers
12 April 1824

Ah, Gentle Reader, This Author has learned that the Bridgerton grandchildren will soon number eleven . . .

But when she tried to write more, all she could do was close her eyes and sigh. She'd been doing this for so very long now. Could it have possibly been eleven years already?

Maybe it was time to move on. She was tired of writing about everyone else. It was time to live her own life.

And so Lady Whistledown set down her quill and walked to her window, pushing aside her sage green curtains and looking out into the inky night.

"Time for something new," she whispered. "Time to finally be me."

Dear Reader,

Have you ever wondered what happened to your favorite characters after you closed the final page? Wanted just a little bit more of a favorite novel? I have, and if the questions from my readers are any indication, I'm not the only one. So after countless requests from Bridgerton fans, I decided to try something a little different, and I wrote a "2nd Epilogue" for each of the novels. These are the stories that come after *the stories.*

At first, the Bridgerton 2nd Epilogues were available exclusively online; later they were published (along with a novella about Violet Bridgerton) in a collection called The Bridgertons: Happily Ever After. *Now, for the first time, each 2nd Epilogue is being included with the novel it follows. I hope you enjoy Benedict and Sophie as they continue their journey.*

Warmly,
Julia Quinn

An Offer from a Gentleman: The 2nd Epilogue

At five and twenty, Miss Posy Reiling was considered *nearly* a spinster. There were those who might have considered her past the cutoff from young miss to hopeless ape leader; three and twenty was often cited as the unkind chronological border. But Posy was, as Lady Bridgerton (her unofficial guardian) often remarked, a unique case.

In debutante years, Lady Bridgerton insisted, Posy was only twenty, *maybe* twenty-one.

Eloise Bridgerton, the eldest unmarried daughter of the house, put it a little more bluntly: Posy's first few years out in society had been worthless and should not be counted against her.

Eloise's youngest sister, Hyacinth, never one to be verbally outdone, simply stated that Posy's years between the ages of seventeen and twenty-two had been "utter rot."

It was at this point that Lady Bridgerton had sighed, poured herself a stiff drink, and sunk into a chair. Eloise, whose mouth was as sharp as Hyacinth's (though thankfully tempered by some discretion), had remarked that they had best get Hyacinth married off quickly or their mother was going to become an alcoholic. Lady Bridgerton had not appreciated the comment, although she privately thought it might be true.

Hyacinth was like that.

But this is a story about Posy. And as Hyacinth has a tendency to take over anything in which she is involved . . . please do forget about her for the remainder of the tale.

The truth was, Posy's first few years on the Marriage Mart *had* been utter rot. It was true that she'd made her debut at a proper age of seventeen. And, indeed, she was the stepdaughter of the late Earl of Penwood, who had so prudently made arrangements for her dowry before his untimely death several years prior.

She was perfectly pleasant to look at, if perhaps a little plump, she had all of her teeth, and it had been remarked upon more than once that she had uncommonly kind eyes.

Anyone assessing her on paper would not understand why she'd gone so long without even a single proposal.

But anyone assessing her on paper might not have known about Posy's mother, Araminta Gunningworth, the dowager Countess of Penwood.

Araminta was splendidly beautiful, even more so than Posy's elder sister, Rosamund, who had been blessed with fair hair, a rose-bud mouth, and eyes of cerulean blue.

Araminta was ambitious, too, and enormously proud of her ascension from the gentry to the aristocracy. She'd gone from Miss Wincheslea to Mrs. Reiling to Lady Penwood, although to hear her speak of it, her mouth had been dripping silver spoons since the day of her birth.

But Araminta had failed in one regard; she had not been able to provide the earl with an heir. Which meant that despite the *Lady* before her name, she did not wield a terribly large amount of power. Nor did she have access to the type of fortune she felt was her due.

And so she pinned her hopes on Rosamund. Rosamund, she was sure, would make a splendid match. Rosamund was achingly beautiful. Rosamund could sing and play the pianoforte, and if she wasn't talented with a needle, then she knew exactly how to poke Posy, who was. And since Posy did not enjoy repeated needle-sized skin punctures, it was Rosamund's embroidery that always looked exquisite.

Posy's, on the other hand, generally went unfinished.

And since money was not as plentiful as Araminta would have her peers believe, she lavished what they had on Rosamund's wardrobe, and Rosamund's lessons, and Rosamund's *everything*.

She wasn't about to let Posy look embarrassingly shabby, but really, there was no point in spending more than she had to on her. You couldn't turn a sow's ear into a silk purse, and you certainly couldn't turn a Posy into a Rosamund.

But.

(And this is a rather large but.)

Things didn't turn out so well for Araminta. It's a terribly long story, and one probably deserving of a book of its own, but suffice it to say that Araminta cheated another young girl of her inheritance, one Sophia Beckett, who happened to be the earl's illegitimate daughter. She would have got away with it completely, because who cares about a bastard, except that Sophie had had the temerity to fall in love with Benedict Bridgerton, second son in the aforementioned (and extremely well-connected) Bridgerton family.

This would not have been enough to seal Araminta's fate, except that Benedict decided he loved Sophie back. Quite madly. And while he might have overlooked embezzlement, he certainly could not do the same for having Sophie hauled off to jail (on mostly fraudulent charges).

Things were looking grim for dear Sophie, even with intervention on the part of Benedict and his mother, the also aforementioned Lady Bridgerton. But then who should show up to save the day but Posy?

Posy, who had been ignored for most of her life.

Posy, who had spent years feeling guilty for not standing up to her mother.

Posy, who was still a little bit plump and never would be as beautiful as her sister, but who would always have the *kindest* eyes.

Araminta had disowned her on the spot, but before Posy had even a moment to wonder if this constituted good or bad fortune, Lady Bridgerton had invited her to live in her home, for as long as she wished.

Posy might have spent twenty-two years being poked and pricked by her sister, but she was no fool. She accepted gladly, and did not even bother to return home to collect her belongings.

As for Araminta, well, she'd quickly ascertained that it was in her best interest not to make any public comment about the soon-to-be Sophia Bridgerton unless it was to declare her an absolute joy and delight.

Which she didn't do. But she didn't go around calling her a bastard, either, which was all anyone could have expected.

All of this explains (in an admittedly roundabout way) why Lady Bridgerton was Posy's unofficial guardian, and why she considered her a unique case. To her mind, Posy had not truly debuted until she came to live with her. Penwood dowry or no, who on earth would have looked twice at a girl in ill-fitting clothes, always stuck off in the corner, trying her best not to be noticed by her own mother?

And if she was still unmarried at twenty-five, why, that was certainly equal to a mere twenty for anyone else. Or so Lady Bridgerton said.

And no one really wanted to contradict her.

As for *Posy*, she often said that her life had not really begun until she went to jail.

This tended to require some explaining, but most of Posy's statements did.

Posy didn't mind. The Bridgertons actually *liked* her explanations. They liked *her*.

Even better, she rather liked herself.

Which was more important than she'd ever realized.

Sophie Bridgerton considered her life to be almost perfect. She adored her husband, loved her cozy home, and was quite certain that her two little boys were the most handsome, brilliant creatures ever to be born anywhere, anytime, any . . . well, any *any* one could come up with.

It was true that they *had* to live in the country because even with the sizable influence of the Bridgerton family, Sophie was, on account of her birth, not likely to be accepted by some of the more particular London hostesses.

(Sophie called them particular. Benedict called them something else entirely.)

But that didn't matter. Not really. She and Benedict preferred life in the country, so it was no great loss. And even though it would always be whispered that Sophie's birth was not what it should be, the official story was that she was a distant—and completely legitimate—relative of the late Earl of Penwood. And even though no one *really* believed Araminta when she'd confirmed the story, confirmed it she had.

Sophie knew that by the time her children were grown, the rumors would be old enough so that no doors would be closed to them, should they wish to take their spots in London society.

All was well. All was perfect.

Almost. Really, all she needed to do was find a husband for Posy. Not just any husband, of course. Posy deserved the best.

"She is not for everyone," Sophie had admitted to Benedict the previous day, "but that does not mean she is not a brilliant catch."

"Of course not," he murmured. He was trying to read the newspaper. It was three days old, but to his mind it was all still news to him.

She looked at him sharply.

"I mean, of course," he said quickly. And then, when she did not immediately carry on, he amended, "I mean whichever one means that she will make someone a splendid wife."

Sophie let out a sigh. "The problem is that most people don't seem to realize how lovely she is."

Benedict gave a dutiful nod. He understood his role in this particular tableau. It was the sort of conversation that wasn't really a conversation. Sophie was thinking aloud, and he was there to provide the occasional verbal prompt or gesture.

"Or at least that's what your mother reports," Sophie continued.

"Mmm-hmm."

"She doesn't get asked to dance nearly as often as she ought."

"Men are beasts," Benedict agreed, flipping to the next page.

"It's true," Sophie said with some emotion. "Present company excluded, of course."

"Oh, of course."

"Most of the time," she added, a little waspishly.

He gave her a wave. "Think nothing of it."

"Are you listening to me?" she asked, her eyes narrowing.

"Every word," he assured her, actually lowering the paper enough to see her above the top edge. He hadn't actually *seen* her eyes narrow, but he knew her well enough to hear it in her voice.

"We need to find a husband for Posy."

He considered that. "Perhaps she doesn't want one."

"Of course she wants one!"

"I have been told," Benedict opined, "that every woman wants a husband, but in my experience, this is not precisely true."

Sophie just stared at him, which he did not find surprising. It was a fairly lengthy statement, coming from a man with a newspaper.

"Consider Eloise," he said. He shook his head, which was his usual inclination while thinking of his sister. "How many men has she refused now?"

"At least three," Sophie said, "but that's not the point."

"What *is* the point, then?"

"*Posy.*"

"Right," he said slowly.

Sophie leaned forward, her eyes taking on an odd mix of bewilderment and determination. "I don't know why the gentlemen don't see how wonderful she is."

"She's an acquired taste," Benedict said, momentarily forgetting that he wasn't supposed to offer a real opinion.

"*What?*"

"*You* said she's not for everyone."

"But you're not supposed to—" She slumped a bit in her seat. "Never mind."

"What were you going to say?"

"Nothing."

"*Sophie*," he prodded.

"Just that you weren't supposed to agree with me," she muttered. "But even I can recognize how ridiculous that is."

It was a splendid thing, Benedict had long since realized, to have a sensible wife.

Sophie didn't speak for some time, and Benedict would have resumed his perusal of the newspaper, except that it was too interesting watching her face. She'd chew on her lip, then let out a weary sigh, then straighten a bit, as if she'd got a good thought, then frown.

Really, he could have watched her all afternoon.

"Can *you* think of anyone?" she suddenly asked.

"For Posy?"

She gave him a look. A whom-else-might-I-be-speaking-of look.

He let out a breath. He should have anticipated the question, but he'd begun to think of the painting he was working on his studio. It was a portrait of Sophie, the fourth he'd done in their three years of marriage. He was beginning to think that he'd not got her mouth quite right. It wasn't the lips so much as the corners of her mouth.

A good portraitist needed to understand the muscles of the human body, even those on the face, and—

"Benedict!"

"What about Mr. Folsom?" he said quickly.

"The solicitor?"

He nodded.

"He looks shifty."

She was right, he realized, now that he thought on it. "Sir Reginald?"

Sophie gave him another look, visibly disappointed with his selection. "He's *fat*."

"So is—"

"She is *not*," Sophie cut in. "She is pleasantly plump."

"I was going to say that so is Mr. Folsom," Benedict said, feeling the need to defend himself, "but that you had chosen to comment upon his shiftiness."

"Oh."

He allowed himself the smallest of smiles.

"Shiftiness is far worse than excess weight," she mumbled.

"I could not agree more," Benedict said. "What about Mr. Woodson?"

"Who?"

"The new vicar. The one you said—"

"—has a brilliant smile!" Sophie finished excitedly. "Oh, Benedict, that's perfect! Oh, I love you love you love you!" At that, she practically leapt across the low table between them and into his arms.

"Well, I love you, too," he said, and he congratulated himself on having had the foresight to shut the door to the drawing room earlier.

The newspaper flew over his shoulder, and all was right with the world.

———

The season drew to a close a few weeks later, and so Posy decided to accept Sophie's invitation for an extended visit. London was hot and sticky and rather smelly in the summer, and a sojourn in the country seemed just the thing. Besides, she had not seen either of her godsons in several months, and she had been *aghast* when Sophie had written to say that Alexander had already begun to lose some of his baby fat.

Oh, he was just the most squeezable, adorable thing. She had to go see him before he grew too thin. She simply had to.

And it would be nice to see Sophie, too. She'd written that she was still feeling a bit weak, and Posy did like to be a help.

A few days into the visit, she and Sophie were taking tea, and talk turned, as it occasionally did, to Araminta and Rosamund, whom Posy occasionally bumped into in London. After over a year of silence, her mother finally had begun to acknowledge her, but even so, conversation was brief and stilted. Which, Posy had decided, was for the best. Her mother might have had nothing to say to her, but she didn't have anything to say to her mother, either.

As far as epiphanies went, it had been rather liberating.

"I saw her outside the milliner," Posy said, fixing her tea just the way she liked it, with extra milk and no sugar. "She'd just come down the steps, and I couldn't avoid her, and then I realized I didn't want to avoid her. Not that I wished to speak with her, of course." She took a sip. "Rather, I didn't wish to expend the energy needed to hide."

Sophie nodded approvingly.

"And then we spoke, and said nothing, really, although she did manage to get in one of her clever little insults."

"I hate that."

"I know. She's *so* good at it."

"It's a talent," Sophie remarked. "Not a good one, but a talent nonetheless."

"Well," Posy continued, "I must say, I was rather mature about the entire encounter. I let her say what she wished, and then I bid her good-bye. And then I had the most amazing realization."

"What is that?"

Posy gave a smile. "I like myself."

"Well, of course you do," Sophie said, blinking with confusion.

"No, no, you don't understand," Posy said. It was strange, because Sophie ought to have understood perfectly. She was the only person in the world who knew what it meant to live as Araminta's unfavored child. But there was something so sunny about Sophie. There always had been. Even when Araminta treated her as a virtual slave, Sophie had never seemed beaten. There had always been a singular spirit to her, a sparkle. It wasn't defiance; Sophie was the least defiant person Posy knew, except perhaps for herself.

Not defiance . . . resilience. Yes, that was it exactly.

At any rate, Sophie ought to have understood what Posy had meant, but she didn't, so Posy said, "I didn't always like myself. And why should I have done? My own mother didn't like me."

"Oh, Posy," Sophie said, her eyes brimming with tears, "you mustn't—"

"No, no," Posy said good-naturedly. "Don't think anything of it. It doesn't bother me."

Sophie just looked at her.

"Well, not anymore," Posy amended. She eyed the plate of biscuits sitting on the table between them. She really oughtn't to eat one. She'd had three, and she *wanted* three more, so maybe that meant that if she had one, she was really abstaining from two . . .

She twiddled her fingers against her leg. Probably she shouldn't have one. Probably she should leave them for Sophie, who had just had a baby and needed to regain her strength. Although Sophie did look perfectly recovered, and little Alexander was already four months old . . .

"Posy?"

She looked up.

"Is something amiss?"

Posy gave a little shrug. "I can't decide whether I wish to eat a biscuit."

Sophie blinked. "A biscuit? Really?"

"There are at least two reasons why I should not, and probably more than that." She paused, frowning.

"You looked quite serious," Sophie remarked. "Almost as if you were conjugating Latin."

"Oh, no, I should look far more at peace if I were conjugating Latin," Posy declared. "That would be quite simple, as I know nothing about it. Biscuits, on the other hand, I ponder endlessly." She sighed and looked down at her middle. "Much to my dismay."

"Don't be silly, Posy," Sophie scolded. "You are the loveliest woman of my acquaintance."

Posy smiled and took the biscuit. The marvelous thing about Sophie was that she wasn't lying. Sophie really did think her the loveliest woman of her acquaintance. But then again, Sophie had always been that sort of person. She saw kindness where others saw . . . Well, where others didn't even bother to look, to be frank.

Posy took a bite and chewed, deciding that it was absolutely worth it. Butter, sugar, and flour. What could be better?

"I received a letter from Lady Bridgerton today," Sophie remarked.

Posy looked up in interest. Technically, Lady Bridgerton could mean Sophie's sister-in-law, the wife of the current viscount. But they both knew she referred to Benedict's mother. To them, she would always be Lady Bridgerton. The other one was Kate. Which was just as well, as that was Kate's preference within the family.

"She said that Mr. Fibberly called." When Posy did not comment, Sophie added, "He was looking for you."

"Well, of course he was," Posy said, deciding to have that fourth biscuit after all. "Hyacinth is too young and Eloise terrifies him."

"Eloise terrifies me," Sophie admitted. "Or at least she used to. Hyacinth I'm quite sure will terrify me to the grave."

"You just need to know how to manage her," Posy said with a wave. It was true, Hyacinth Bridgerton *was* terrifying, but the two of them had always got on quite well. It was probably due to Hyacinth's firm (some might say unyielding) sense of justice. When she'd found out that Posy's mother had never loved her as well as Rosamund . . .

Well, Posy had never told tales, and she wasn't going to begin now, but let it be said that Araminta had never again eaten fish.

Or chicken.

Posy had got this from the servants, and they always had the most accurate gossip.

"But you were about to tell me about Mr. Fibberly," Sophie said, still sipping at her tea.

Posy shrugged, even though she hadn't been about to do any such thing. "He's so dull."

"Handsome?"

Posy shrugged again. "I can't tell."

"One generally need only look at the face."

"I can't get past his dullness. I don't think he laughs."

"It can't be that bad."

"Oh, it can, I assure you." She reached out and took another biscuit before she realized she hadn't meant to. Oh well, it was already in her hand now, she couldn't very well put it back. She waved it in the air as she spoke, trying to make her point. "He sometimes makes this dreadful noise like, 'Ehrm ehrm ehrm,' and I think he thinks he's laughing, but he's clearly not."

Sophie giggled even though she looked as if she thought she shouldn't.

"And he doesn't even look at my bosom!"

"Posy!"

"It's my *only* good feature."

"It is not!" Sophie glanced about the drawing room, even though there was precisely no one about. "I can't believe you said that."

Posy let out a frustrated exhale. "I can't say *bosom* in London and now I can't do so in Wiltshire, either?"

"Not when I'm expecting the new vicar," Sophie said.

A chunk of Posy's biscuit fell off and fell into her lap. "What?"

"I didn't tell you?"

Posy eyed her suspiciously. Most people thought Sophie was a poor liar, but that was only because she had such an angelic look about her. And she rarely lied. So everyone assumed that if she did, she'd be dreadful at it.

Posy, however, knew better. "No," she said, brushing off her skirts, "you did not tell me."

"How very unlike me," Sophie murmured. She picked up a biscuit and took a bite.

Posy stared at her. "Do you know what I'm not doing now?"

Sophie shook her head.

"I am not rolling my eyes, because I am trying to act in a fashion that befits my age and maturity."

"You do look very grave."

Posy stared her down a bit more. "He is unmarried, I assume."

"Er, yes."

Posy lifted her left brow, the arch expression possibly the only useful gift she'd received from her mother. "How old is this vicar?"

"I do not know," Sophie admitted, "but he has all of his hair."

"And it has come to this," Posy murmured.

"I thought of you when I met him," Sophie said, "because he smiles."

Because he *smiled*? Posy was beginning to think that Sophie was a bit cracked. "I beg your pardon?"

"He smiles so often. And so well." At that *Sophie* smiled. "I couldn't help but think of you."

Posy did roll her eyes this time, then followed it with an immediate "I have decided to forsake maturity."

"By all means."

"I shall meet your vicar," Posy said, "but you should know I have decided to aspire to eccentricity."

"I wish you the best with that," Sophie said, not without sarcasm.

"You don't think I can?"

"You're the least eccentric person I know."

It was true, of course, but if Posy had to spend her life as an old maid, she wanted to be the eccentric one with the large hat, not the desperate one with the pinched mouth.

"What is his name?" she asked.

But before Sophie could answer, they heard the front door opening, and then it was the butler giving her her answer as he announced, "Mr. Woodson is here to see you, Mrs. Bridgerton."

Posy stashed her half-eaten biscuit under a serviette and folded her hands prettily in her lap. She was a little miffed with Sophie for inviting a bachelor for tea without warning her, but still, there seemed little reason not to make a good impression. She looked expectantly at the doorway, waiting patiently as Mr. Woodson's footsteps drew near.

And then . . .

And then . . .

Honestly, it wouldn't do to try to recount it, because she remembered almost nothing of what followed.

She saw him, and it was as if, after twenty-five years of life, her heart finally began to beat.

Hugh Woodson had never been the most admired boy at school. He had never been the most handsome, or the most athletic. He had never been the cleverest, or the snobbiest, or the most foolish. What he had been, and what he had been all of his life, was the most well liked.

People liked him. They always had. He supposed it was because he liked most everybody in return. His mother swore he'd emerged from the womb smiling. She said so with great frequency, although Hugh suspected she did so only to give her father the lead-in for: "Oh, Georgette, you know it was just gas."

Which never failed to set the both of them into fits of giggles.

It was a testament to Hugh's love for them both, and his general ease with himself, that he usually laughed as well.

Nonetheless, for all his likeability, he'd never seemed to attract the females. They adored him, of course, and confided their most desperate secrets, but they always did so in a way that led Hugh to believe he was viewed as a jolly, dependable sort of creature.

The worst part of it was that every woman of his acquaintance was absolutely positive that she knew the *perfect* woman for him, or if not, then she was quite sure that a perfect woman did indeed exist.

That no woman ever thought *herself* the perfect woman had not gone unnoticed. Well, by Hugh, at least. Everyone else was oblivious.

But he carried on, because there could be no point in doing otherwise. And as he had always suspected that women were the cleverer sex, he still held out hope that the perfect woman was indeed out there.

After all, no fewer than four dozen women had said so. They couldn't *all* be wrong.

But Hugh was nearing thirty, and Miss Perfection had not yet seen fit to reveal herself. Hugh was beginning to think that he should take matters into his own hands, except that he hadn't the slightest idea how to do such a thing, especially as he'd just taken a living in a rather quiet corner of Wiltshire, and there didn't seem to be a single appropriately-aged unmarried female in his parish.

Remarkable but true.

Maybe he should wander over to Gloucestershire Sunday next. There was a vacancy there, and he'd been asked to pitch in and deliver a sermon or two until they found a new vicar. There had to be at least one unattached female. The whole of the Cotswolds couldn't be bereft.

But this wasn't the time to dwell on such things. He was just arriving for tea with Mrs. Bridgerton, an invitation for which he was enormously grateful. He was still familiarizing himself with the area and its inhabitants, but it had taken but one church service to know that Mrs. Bridgerton was universally liked and admired. She seemed quite clever and kind as well.

He hoped she liked to gossip. He really needed someone to fill him in on the neighborhood lore. One really couldn't tend to one's flock without knowing its history.

He'd also heard that her cook laid a very fine tea. The biscuits had been mentioned in particular.

"Mr. Woodson to see you, Mrs. Bridgerton."

Hugh stepped into the drawing room as the butler stated his name. He was rather glad he'd forgotten to eat lunch, because the house smelled heavenly and—

And then he quite forgot everything.

Why he'd come.

Who he was.

The color of the sky, even, and the smell of the grass.

Indeed, as he stood there in the arched doorway of the Bridgertons' drawing room, he knew one thing, and one thing only.

The woman on the sofa, the one with the extraordinary eyes who was not Mrs. Bridgerton, was Miss Perfection.

Sophie Bridgerton knew a thing or two about love at first sight. She had, once upon a time, been hit by its proverbial lightning bolt, struck dumb with breathless passion, heady bliss, and an odd tingling sensation across her entire body.

Or at least, that was how she remembered it.

She also remembered that while Cupid's arrow had, in her case, proven remarkably accurate, it had taken quite a while for her and Benedict to reach their happily ever after. So even though she wanted to bounce in her seat with glee as she watched Posy and Mr. Woodson stare at each other like a pair of lovesick puppies, another part of her—the extremely practical, born-on-the-wrong-side-of-the-blanket, I-am-well-aware-that-the-world-is-not-made-up-of-rainbows-and-angels part of her—was trying to hold back her excitement.

But the thing about Sophie was, no matter how awful her childhood had been (and parts of it had been quite dreadfully awful), no matter what cruelties and indignities she'd faced in her life (and there, too, she'd not been fortunate), she was, at heart, an incurable romantic.

Which brought her to Posy.

It was true that Posy visited several times each year, and it was also true that one of those visits almost always coincided with the end of the season, but Sophie *might* have added a little extra entreaty to her recently tendered invitation. She might have exaggerated a bit when describing how quickly the children were growing, and there was a chance that she had actually lied when she said that she was feeling poorly.

But in this case, the ends absolutely justified the means. Oh, Posy had told her that she would be perfectly content to remain unmarried, but Sophie did not believe her for a second. Or to be more precise, Sophie believed that Posy believed that she would be perfectly content. But one had only to look at Posy snuggling little William and Alexander to know that she was a born mother, and that the world would be a much poorer place if Posy did not have a passel of children to call her own.

It was true that Sophie had, one time or twelve, made a point of introducing Posy to whichever unattached gentleman was to be found at the moment in Wiltshire, but *this time* . . .

This time Sophie knew.

This time it was love.

"Mr. Woodson," she said, trying not to grin like a madwoman, "may I introduce you to my dear sister, Miss Posy Reiling?"

Mr. Woodson looked as if he thought he was saying something, but the truth was, he was staring at Posy as if he'd just met Aphrodite.

"Posy," Sophie continued, "this is Mr. Woodson, our new vicar. He is only recently arrived, what was it, three weeks ago?"

He had been in residence for nearly two months. Sophie knew this perfectly well, but she was eager to see if he'd been listening well enough to correct her.

He just nodded, never taking his eyes off Posy.

"Please, Mr. Woodson," Sophie murmured, "do sit down."

He managed to understand her meaning, and he lowered himself into a chair.

"Tea, Mr. Woodson?" Sophie inquired.

He nodded.

"Posy, will you pour?"

Posy nodded.

Sophie waited, and then when it became apparent that Posy wasn't going to do much of anything besides smile at Mr. Woodson, she said, "*Posy.*"

Posy turned to look at her, but her head moved so slowly and with such reluctance, it was as if a giant magnet had turned its force onto her.

"Will you pour Mr. Woodson's tea?" Sophie murmured, trying to restrict her smile to her eyes.

"Oh. Of course." Posy turned back to the vicar, that silly smile returning to her face. "Would you like some tea?"

Normally Sophie might have mentioned that she had already

asked Mr. Woodson if he wanted tea, but there was nothing normal about this encounter, so she decided to simply sit back and observe.

"I would love some," Mr. Woodson said to Posy. "Above all else."

Really, Sophie thought, it was as if she weren't even there.

"How do you take it?" Posy asked.

"However you wish."

Oh now, this was too much. No man fell so blindingly into love that he no longer held a preference for his tea. This was England, for heaven's sake. More to the point, this was *tea*.

"We have both milk and sugar," Sophie said, unable to help herself. She'd intended to sit and watch, but really, even the most hopeless romantic couldn't have remained silent.

Mr. Woodson didn't hear her.

"Either of them would be appropriate in your cup," she added.

"You have the most extraordinary eyes," he said, and his voice was full of wonder, as if he couldn't quite believe that he was right there in this room, with Posy.

"Your smile," Posy said in return. "It's . . . lovely."

He leaned forward. "Do you like roses, Miss Reiling?"

Posy nodded.

"I must bring you some."

Sophie gave up trying to appear serene and finally let herself grin. It wasn't as if either of them was looking at her, anyway. "We have roses," she said.

No response.

"In the back garden."

Again, nothing.

"Where the two of you might go for a stroll."

It was as if someone had just stuck a pin in both of them.

"Oh, shall we?"

"I would be delighted."

"Please, allow me to—"

"Take my arm."

"I would—"

"You must—"

By the time Posy and Mr. Woodson were at the door, Sophie could hardly tell who was saying what. And not a drop of tea had entered Mr. Woodson's cup.

Sophie waited for a full minute, and then burst out laughing, clapping her hand over her mouth to stifle the sound, although she wasn't sure why she needed to. It was a laugh of pure delight. Pride, too, at having orchestrated the whole thing.

"What are you laughing about?" It was Benedict, wandering into the room, his fingers stained with paint. "Ah, biscuits. Excellent. I'm famished. Forgot to eat this morning." He took the last one and frowned. "You might have left more for me."

"It's Posy," Sophie said, grinning. "And Mr. Woodson. I predict a very short engagement."

Benedict's eyes widened. He turned to the door, then to the window. "Where are they?"

"In the back. We can't see them from here."

He chewed thoughtfully. "But we could from my studio."

For about two seconds neither moved. But only two seconds.

They ran for the door, pushing and shoving their way down the hall to Benedict's studio, which jutted out of the back of the house, giving it light from three directions. Sophie got there first, although not by entirely fair means, and let out a shocked gasp.

"What is it?" Benedict said from the doorway.

"They're kissing!"

He strode forward. "They are not."

"Oh, they are."

He drew up beside her, and his mouth fell open. "Well, I'll be damned."

And Sophie, who never cursed, responded, "I know. I *know*."

"And they only just met? Really?"

"You kissed me the first night we met," she pointed out.

"That was different."

Sophie managed to pull her attention from the kissing couple on the lawn for just long enough to demand, "How?"

He thought about that for a moment, then answered, "It was a masquerade."

"Oh, so it's all right to kiss someone if you don't know who they are?"

"Not fair, Sophie," he said, clucking as he shook his head. "I asked you, and you wouldn't tell me."

That was true enough to put an end to that particular branch of the conversation, and they stood there for another moment, shamelessly watching Posy and the vicar. They'd stopped kissing and were now talking—from the looks of it, a mile a minute. Posy would speak, and then Mr. Woodson would nod vigorously and interrupt her, and then she would interrupt him, and then he looked like he was giggling, of all things, and then Posy began to speak with such animation that her arms waved all about her head.

"What on earth could they be saying?" Sophie wondered.

"Probably everything they should have said before he kissed her." Benedict frowned, crossing his arms. "How long have they been at this, anyway?"

"You've been watching just as long as I have."

"No, I meant, when did he arrive? Did they even speak before . . ." He waved his hand toward the window, gesturing to the couple, who looked about ready to kiss again.

"Yes, of course, but . . ." Sophie paused, thinking. Both Posy and Mr. Woodson had been rather tongue-tied at their meeting. In fact, she couldn't recall a single substantive word that was spoken. "Well, not very much, I'm afraid."

Benedict nodded slowly. "Do you think I should go out there?"

Sophie looked at him, then at the window, and then back. "Are you mad?"

He shrugged. "She is my sister now, and it *is* my house . . ."

"Don't you dare!"

"So I'm not supposed to protect her honor?"

"It's her first kiss!"

He quirked a brow. "And here we are, spying on it."

"It's my right," Sophie said indignantly. "I arranged the whole thing."

"Oh you did, did you? I seem to recall that *I* was the one to suggest Mr. Woodson."

"But you didn't *do* anything about it."

"That's your job, darling."

Sophie considered a retort, because his tone was rather annoying, but he did have a point. She did rather enjoy trying to find a match for Posy, and she was *definitely* enjoying her obvious success.

"You know," Benedict said thoughtfully, "we might have a daughter someday."

Sophie turned to him. He wasn't normally one for such non sequiturs. "I beg your pardon?"

He gestured to the lovebirds on the lawn. "Just that this could be excellent practice for me. I'm quite certain I wish to be an overbearingly protective father. I could storm out and tear him apart from limb to limb."

Sophie winced. Poor Mr. Woodson wouldn't stand a chance.

"Challenge him to a duel?"

She shook her head.

"Very well, but if he lowers her to the ground, I am interceding."

"He won't— Oh dear heavens!" Sophie leaned forward, her face nearly to the glass. "Oh my God."

And she didn't even cover her mouth in horror at having blasphemed.

Benedict sighed, then flexed his fingers. "I really don't want to injure my hands. I'm halfway through your portrait, and it's going so well."

Sophie had one hand on his arm, holding him back even though he wasn't really moving anywhere. "No," she said, "don't—" She gasped. "Oh, my. Maybe we should do something."

"They're not on the ground yet."

"Benedict!"

"Normally I'd say to call the priest," he remarked, "except that seems to be what got us into this mess in the first place."

Sophie swallowed. "Perhaps you can procure a special license for them? As a wedding gift?"

He grinned. "Consider it done."

It was a splendid wedding. And that kiss at the end . . .

No one was surprised when Posy produced a baby nine months later, and then at yearly intervals after that. She took great care in the naming of her brood, and Mr. Woodson, who was as beloved a vicar as he'd been in every other stage of his life, adored her too much to argue with any of her choices.

First there was Sophia, for obvious reasons, and then Benedict. The next would have been Violet, except that Sophie begged her not to. She'd always wanted the name for her daughter, and it would be far too confusing with the families living so close. So Posy went with Georgette, after Hugh's mother, whom she thought had just the *nicest* smile.

After that was John, after Hugh's father. For quite some time it appeared that he would remain the baby of the family. After giving birth every June for four years in a row, Posy stopped getting pregnant. She wasn't doing anything differently, she confided in Sophie; she and Hugh were still very much in love. It just seemed that her body had decided it was through with childbearing.

Which was just as well. With two girls and two boys, all in the single digits, she had her hands full.

But then, when John was five, Posy rose from bed one morning and threw up on the floor. It could only mean one thing, and the following autumn, she delivered a girl.

Sophie was present at the birth, as she always was. "What shall you name her?" she asked.

Posy looked down at the perfect little creature in her arms. It was sleeping quite soundly, and even though she knew that newborns did not smile, the baby really did look as if it were rather pleased about something.

Maybe about being born. Maybe this one was going to attack life with a smile. Good humor would be her weapon of choice.

What a splendid human being she would be.

"Araminta," Posy said suddenly.

Sophie nearly fell over from the shock of it. *"What?"*

"I want to name her Araminta. I'm quite certain." Posy stroked the baby's cheek, then touched her gently under the chin.

Sophie could not seem to stop shaking her head. "But your mother . . . I can't believe you would—"

"I'm not naming her *for* my mother," Posy cut in gently. "I'm naming her *because* of my mother. It's different."

Sophie looked dubious, but she leaned over to get a closer peek at the baby. "She's really quite sweet," she murmured.

Posy smiled, never once taking her eyes off the baby's face. "I know."

"I suppose I could grow accustomed to it," Sophie said, her head bobbing from side to side in acquiescence. She wiggled her finger between the baby's hand and body, giving the palm a little tickle until the tiny fingers wrapped instinctively around her own. "Good evening, Araminta," she said. "Very nice to meet you."

"Minty," Posy said.

Sophie looked up. "What?"

"I'm calling her Minty. Araminta will do well in the family Bible, but I do believe she's a Minty."

Sophie pressed her lips together in an effort not to smile. "Your mother would hate that."

"Yes," Posy murmured, "she would, wouldn't she?"

"Minty," Sophie said, testing the sound on her tongue. "I like it. No, I think I love it. It suits her."

Posy kissed the top of Minty's head. "What kind of girl will you be?" she whispered. "Sweet and docile?"

Sophie chuckled at that. She had been present at twelve birthings—four of her own, five of Posy's, and three of Benedict's sister Eloise. Never had she heard a baby enter this world with as loud a cry as little Minty. "This one," she said firmly, "is going to lead you a merry chase."

And she did. But that, dear reader, is another story . . .

BRIDGERTON

— ···—

ROMANCING
MISTER BRIDGERTON

*For the women on avonloop, colleagues and friends
all—thanks for giving me someone to talk to
all day long. Your support and friendship have
meant more to me than I could ever say.*

*And for Paul, even though the closest thing
you'd ever find to a romance in his field is a
lecture called "The Kiss of Death."*

Acknowledgments

With utmost thanks to Lisa Kleypas and Stephanie Laurens for the gracious use of their characters.

Prologue

On the sixth of April, in the year 1812—precisely two days before her sixteenth birthday—Penelope Featherington fell in love.

It was, in a word, thrilling. The world shook. Her heart leaped. The moment was breathtaking. And, she was able to tell herself with some satisfaction, the man in question—one Colin Bridgerton—felt precisely the same way.

Oh, not the love part. He certainly didn't fall in love with her in 1812 (and not in 1813, 1814, 1815, or—oh, blast, not in all the years 1816–1822, either, and certainly not in 1823, when he was out of the country the whole time, anyway). But his earth shook, his heart leaped, and Penelope knew without a shadow of a doubt that his breath was taken away as well. For a good ten seconds.

Falling off a horse tended to do that to a man.

It happened thus:

She'd been out for a walk in Hyde Park with her mother and two older sisters when she felt a thunderous rumbling under her feet (see above: the bit about the earth shaking). Her mother wasn't paying much attention to her (her mother rarely did), so Penelope slipped away for a moment to see what was about. The rest of the Featheringtons were in rapt conversation with Viscountess Bridgerton and her daughter Daphne, who had just begun her second season in London, so they were pretending to ignore the rumbling. The

Bridgertons were an important family indeed, and conversations with them were not to be ignored.

As Penelope skirted around the edge of a particularly fat-trunked tree, she saw two riders coming her way, galloping along hell-for-leather or whatever expression people liked to use for fools on horseback who care not for their safety and well-being. Penelope felt her heart quicken (it would have been difficult to maintain a sedate pulse as a witness to such excitement, and besides, this allowed her to say that her heart leaped when she fell in love).

Then, in one of those inexplicable quirks of fate, the wind picked up quite suddenly and lifted her bonnet (which, much to her mother's chagrin, she had not tied properly since the ribbon chafed under her chin) straight into the air and, splat! right onto the face of one of the riders.

Penelope gasped (taking her breath away!), and then the man fell off his horse, landing most inelegantly in a nearby mud puddle.

She rushed forward, quite without thinking, squealing something that was meant to inquire after his welfare, but that she suspected came out as nothing more than a strangled shriek. He would, of course, be furious with her, since she'd effectively knocked him off his horse and covered him with mud—two things guaranteed to put any gentleman in the foulest of moods. But when he finally rose to his feet, brushing off whatever mud could be dislodged from his clothing, he didn't lash out at her. He didn't give her a stinging setdown, he didn't yell, he didn't even glare.

He laughed.

He laughed.

Penelope hadn't much experience with the laughter of men, and what little she *had* known had not been kind. But this man's eyes—a rather intense shade of green—were filled with mirth as he wiped a rather embarrassingly placed spot of mud off his cheek and said, "Well, that wasn't very well done of me, was it?"

And in that moment, Penelope fell in love.

When she found her voice (which, she was pained to note, was a good three seconds after a person of any intelligence would have replied), she said, "Oh, no, it is I who should apologize! My bonnet came right off my head, and . . ."

She stopped talking when she realized he hadn't actually apologized, so there was little point in contradicting him.

"It was no trouble," he said, giving her a somewhat amused smile. "I—Oh, good day, Daphne! Didn't know you were in the park."

Penelope whirled around to find herself facing Daphne Bridgerton, standing next to her mother, who promptly hissed, "What have you done, Penelope Featherington?" and Penelope couldn't even answer with her stock, *Nothing*, because in truth, the accident was completely her fault, and she'd just made a fool of herself in front of what was obviously—judging from the expression on her mother's face—a very eligible bachelor indeed.

Not that her mother would have thought that *she* had a chance with him. But Mrs. Featherington held high matrimonial hopes for her older girls. Besides, Penelope wasn't even "out" in society yet.

But if Mrs. Featherington intended to scold her any further, she was unable to do so, because that would have required that she remove her attention from the all-important Bridgertons, whose ranks, Penelope was quickly figuring out, included the man presently covered in mud.

"I hope your son isn't injured," Mrs. Featherington said to Lady Bridgerton.

"Right as rain," Colin interjected, making an expert sidestep before Lady Bridgerton could maul him with motherly concern.

Introductions were made, but the rest of the conversation was unimportant, mostly because Colin quickly and accurately sized up Mrs. Featherington as a matchmaking mama. Penelope was not at all surprised when he beat a hasty retreat.

But the damage had already been done. Penelope had discovered a reason to dream.

Later that night, as she replayed the encounter for about the thousandth time in her mind, it occurred to her that it would have been nice if she could have said that she'd fallen in love with him as he kissed her hand before a dance, his green eyes twinkling devilishly while his fingers held hers just a little more tightly than was proper. Or maybe it could have happened as he rode boldly across a windswept moor, the (aforementioned) wind no deterrent as he (or rather, his horse) galloped ever closer, his (Colin's, not the horse's) only intention to reach her side.

But no, she had to go and fall in love with Colin Bridgerton when he fell off a horse and landed on his bottom in a mud puddle. It was highly irregular, and *highly* unromantic, but there was a certain poetic justice in that, since nothing was ever going to come of it.

Why waste romance on a love that would never be returned? Better to save the windswept-moor introductions for people who might actually have a future together.

And if there was one thing Penelope knew, even then, at the age of sixteen years minus two days, it was that her future did not feature Colin Bridgerton in the role of husband.

She simply wasn't the sort of girl who attracted a man like him, and she feared that she never would be.

On the tenth of April, in the year 1813—precisely two days after her seventeenth birthday—Penelope Featherington made her debut into London society. She hadn't wanted to do it. She begged her mother to let her wait a year. She was at least two stone heavier than she ought to be, and her face still had an awful tendency to develop spots whenever she was nervous, which meant that she *always* had spots, since nothing in the world could make her as nervous as a London ball.

She tried to remind herself that beauty was only skin deep, but that didn't offer any helpful excuses when she was berating herself for never knowing what to *say* to people. There was nothing more depressing than an ugly girl with no personality. And in that first year on the marriage mart, that was exactly what Penelope was. An ugly girl with no—oh, very well, she had to give herself *some* credit—with very little personality.

Deep inside, she knew who she was, and that person was smart and kind and often even funny, but somehow her personality always got lost somewhere between her heart and her mouth, and she found herself saying the wrong thing or, more often, nothing at all.

To make matters even less attractive, Penelope's mother refused to allow Penelope to choose her own clothing, and when she wasn't in the requisite white that most young ladies wore (and which of course didn't flatter her complexion one bit), she was forced to wear yellow and red and orange, all of which made her look perfectly wretched. The one time Penelope had suggested green, Mrs. Featherington had planted her hands on her more-than-ample hips and declared that green was too melancholy.

Yellow, Mrs. Featherington declared, was a *happy* color and a *happy* girl would snare a husband.

Penelope decided then and there that it was best not to try to understand the workings of her mother's mind.

So Penelope found herself outfitted in yellow and orange and the occasional red, even though such colors made her look decidedly *un*-happy, and in fact were positively ghastly with her brown eyes and red-tinged hair. There was nothing she could do about it, though, so she decided to grin and bear it, and if she couldn't manage a grin, at least she wouldn't cry in public.

Which, she took some pride in noting, she never did.

And if that weren't enough, 1813 was the year that the mysterious (and fictitious) Lady Whistledown began publishing her thrice-weekly *Society Papers*. The single-sheet newspaper became an instant sensation. No one knew who Lady Whistledown really was, but everyone seemed to have a theory. For weeks—no, months, really—London could speak of nothing else. The paper had been delivered for free for two weeks—just long enough to addict the *ton*—and then suddenly there was no delivery, just paperboys charging the outrageous price of five pennies a paper.

But by then, no one could live without the almost-daily dose of gossip, and everyone paid their pennies.

Somewhere some woman (or maybe, some people speculated, some man) was growing very rich indeed.

What set *Lady Whistledown's Society Papers* apart from any previous society newssheets was that the author actually listed her subjects' names in full. There was no hiding behind abbreviations such as Lord P—— or Lady B——. If Lady Whistledown wanted to write about someone, she used his full name.

And when Lady Whistledown wanted to write about Penelope Featherington, she did. Penelope's first appearance in *Lady Whistledown's Society Papers* went as follows:

> *Miss Penelope Featherington's unfortunate gown left the unfortunate girl looking like nothing more than an overripe citrus fruit.*

A rather stinging blow, to be sure, but nothing less than the truth. Her second appearance in the column was no better.

> *Not a word was heard from Miss Penelope Featherington, and no wonder! The poor girl appeared to have drowned amidst the ruffles of her dress.*

Not, Penelope was afraid, anything that would enhance her popularity.

But the season wasn't a complete disaster. There were a few people with whom she seemed able to speak. Lady Bridgerton, of all people, took a liking to her, and Penelope found that she could often tell things to the lovely viscountess that she would never dream of saying to her own mother. It was through Lady Bridgerton that she met Eloise Bridgerton, the younger sister of her beloved Colin. Eloise was also just turned seventeen, but her mother had wisely allowed her to delay her debut by a year, even though Eloise possessed the Bridgerton good looks and charm in abundance.

And while Penelope spent her afternoons in the green-and-cream drawing room at Bridgerton House (or, more often, up in Eloise's bedchamber where the two girls laughed and giggled and discussed everything under the sun with great earnestness), she found herself coming into occasional contact with Colin, who at two-and-twenty had not yet moved out of the family home and into bachelor lodgings.

If Penelope had thought she loved him before, that was nothing compared to what she felt after actually getting to know him. Colin Bridgerton was witty, he was dashing, he had a devil-may-care jokester quality to him that made women swoon, but most of all . . .

Colin Bridgerton was nice.

Nice. Such a silly little word. It should have been banal, but somehow it fit him to perfection. He always had something nice to say to Penelope, and when she finally worked up the courage to say something back (other than the very basic greetings and farewells), he actually listened. Which made it all the easier the next time around.

By the end of the season, Penelope judged that Colin Bridgerton was the only man with whom she'd managed an entire conversation.

This was love. Oh, this was love love love love love love. A silly repetition of words, perhaps, but that was precisely what Penelope doodled on a ridiculously expensive sheet of writing paper, along with the words, "Mrs. Colin Bridgerton" and "Penelope Bridgerton" and "Colin Colin Colin." (The paper went into the fire the moment Penelope heard footsteps in the hall.)

How wonderful it was to feel love—even the one-sided sort—for a nice person. It made one feel so positively sensible.

Of course, it didn't hurt that Colin possessed, as did all the Bridgerton men, fabulous good looks. There was that famous

Bridgerton chestnut hair, the wide and smiling Bridgerton mouth, the broad shoulders, the six-foot height, and in Colin's case, the most devastating green eyes ever to grace a human face.

They were the sort of eyes that haunted a girl's dreams.

And Penelope dreamed and dreamed and dreamed.

April of 1814 found Penelope back in London for a second season, and even though she attracted the same number of suitors as the year before (zero), the season wasn't, in all honesty, quite so bad. It helped that she'd lost nearly two stone and could now call herself "pleasantly rounded" rather than "a hideous pudge." She was still nowhere near the slender ideal of womanhood that ruled the day, but at least she'd changed enough to warrant the purchase of a completely new wardrobe.

Unfortunately, her mother once again insisted on yellow, orange, and the occasional splash of red. And this time, Lady Whistledown wrote:

> *Miss Penelope Featherington (the least inane of the Feather-ington sisters) wore a gown of lemon yellow that left a sour taste in one's mouth.*

Which at least seemed to imply that Penelope was the most intelligent member of her family, although the compliment was backhanded, indeed.

But Penelope wasn't the only one singled out by the acerbic gossip columnist. Dark-haired Kate Sheffield was likened to a singed daffodil in her yellow dress, and Kate went on to marry Anthony Bridgerton, Colin's older brother and a viscount to boot!

So Penelope held out hope.

Well, not really. She knew Colin wasn't going to marry her, but at least he danced with her at every ball, and he made her laugh, and every now and then she made him laugh, and she knew that that would have to be enough.

And so Penelope's life continued. She had her third season, then her fourth. Her two older sisters, Prudence and Philippa, finally found husbands of their own and moved away. Mrs. Featherington held out hope that Penelope might still make a match, since it had taken both Prudence and Philippa five seasons to snare husbands, but Penelope knew that she was destined to remain a spinster. It wouldn't be fair to marry someone when she was still so desperately in love with Colin. And maybe, in the far reaches of her mind—in the farthest-back corner, tucked away behind the French verb conjugations she'd never mastered and the arithmetic she never used—she still held out a tiny shred of hope.

Until *that* day.

Even now, seven years later, she still referred to it as *that* day.

She'd gone to the Bridgerton household, as she frequently did, to take tea with Eloise and her mother and sisters. It was right before Eloise's brother Benedict had married Sophie, only he didn't know who she really was, and—well, that didn't signify, except that it may have been the one truly great secret in the last decade that Lady Whistledown had never managed to unearth.

Anyway, she was walking through the front hall, listening to her feet tap along the marble tile as she saw herself out. She was adjusting her pelisse and preparing to walk the short distance to her own home (just around the corner, really) when she heard voices. Male voices. Male Bridgerton voices.

It was the three elder Bridgerton brothers: Anthony, Benedict, and Colin. They were having one of those conversations that men have, the kind in which they grumble a lot and poke fun at each other. Penelope had always liked to watch the Bridgertons interact in this manner; they were such a *family*.

Penelope could see them through the open front door, but she couldn't hear what they were saying until she'd reached the threshold. And in a testament to the bad timing that had plagued her throughout her life, the first voice she heard was Colin's, and the words were not kind.

". . . *and I am certainly not going to marry Penelope Featherington!*"

"Oh!" The word slipped over her lips before she could even think, the squeal of it piercing the air like an off-key whistle.

The three Bridgerton men turned to face her with identical horrified faces, and Penelope knew that she had just entered into what would certainly be the most awful five minutes of her life.

She said nothing for what seemed like an eternity, and then, finally, with a dignity she never dreamed she possessed, she looked straight at Colin and said, "I never asked you to marry me."

His cheeks went from pink to red. He opened his mouth, but not a sound came out. It was, Penelope thought with wry satisfaction, probably the only time in his life he'd ever been at a loss for words.

"And I never—" She swallowed convulsively. "I never said to anyone that I wanted you to ask me."

"Penelope," Colin finally managed, "I'm so sorry."

"You have nothing to apologize for," she said.

"No," he insisted, "I do. I hurt your feelings, and—"

"You didn't know I was there."

"But nevertheless—"

"You are not going to marry me," she said, her voice sounding very strange and hollow to her ears. "There is nothing wrong with that. I am not going to marry your brother Benedict."

Benedict had clearly been trying not to look, but he snapped to attention at that.

Penelope fisted her hands at her sides. "It doesn't hurt his feelings when I announce that I am not going to marry him." She turned to Benedict, forcing her eyes directly on his. "Does it, Mr. Bridgerton?"

"Of course not," Benedict answered quickly.

"It's settled, then," she said tightly, amazed that, for once, *exactly* the right words were coming out of her mouth. "No feelings were hurt. Now, then, if you will excuse me, gentlemen, I should like to go home."

The three gentlemen immediately stood back to let her pass, and she would have made a clean escape, except that Colin suddenly blurted out, "Don't you have a maid?"

She shook her head. "I live just around the corner."

"I know, but——"

"I'll escort you," Anthony said smoothly.

"That's really not necessary, my lord."

"Humor me," he said, in a tone that told her quite clearly she hadn't any choice in the matter.

She nodded, and the two of them took off down the street. After they had passed about three houses, Anthony said in a strangely respectful voice, "He didn't know you were there."

Penelope felt her lips tighten at the corners—not out of anger, just out of a weary sense of resignation. "I know," she replied. "He's not the sort to be cruel. I expect your mother has been hounding him to get married."

Anthony nodded. Lady Bridgerton's intentions to see each and every one of her eight offspring happily married were legendary.

"She likes me," Penelope said. "Your mother, that is. She can't see beyond that, I'm afraid. But the truth is, it doesn't matter so much if she likes Colin's bride."

"Well, I wouldn't say *that*," Anthony mused, sounding not so much like a highly feared and respected viscount and rather more like a well-behaved son. "I shouldn't like to be married to someone my mother didn't like." He shook his head in a gesture of great awe and respect. "She's a force of nature."

"Your mother or your wife?"

He considered that for about half a second. "Both."

They walked for a few moments, and then Penelope blurted out, "Colin should go away."

Anthony eyed her curiously. "I beg your pardon?"

"He should go away. Travel. He's not ready to marry, and your mother won't be able to restrain herself from pressuring him. She means well. . . ." Penelope bit her lip in horror. She hoped the viscount didn't think she was actually criticizing Lady Bridgerton. As far as she was concerned, there was no greater lady in England.

"My mother always means well," Anthony said with an indulgent smile. "But maybe you're right. Perhaps he should get away. Colin does enjoy travel. Although he did just return from Wales."

"Did he?" Penelope murmured politely, as if she didn't know perfectly well that he'd been in Wales.

"Here we are," he said as he nodded his reply. "This is your house, is it not?"

"Yes. Thank you for accompanying me home."

"It was my pleasure, I assure you."

Penelope watched as he left, then she went inside and cried.

The very next day, the following account appeared in *Lady Whistledown's Society Papers*:

> *La, but such excitement yesterday on the front steps of Lady Bridgerton's residence on Bruton Street!*
>
> *First, Penelope Featherington was seen in the company of not one, not two, but THREE Bridgerton brothers, surely a heretofore impossible feat for the poor girl, who is rather infamous for her wallflower ways. Sadly (but perhaps predictably) for Miss Featherington, when she finally departed, it was on the arm of the viscount, the only married man in the bunch.*
>
> *If Miss Featherington were to somehow manage to drag a Bridgerton brother to the altar, it would surely mean the end of the world as we know it, and This Author, who freely admits she would not know heads from tails in such a world, would be forced to resign her post on the spot.*

It seemed even Lady Whistledown understood the futility of Penelope's feelings for Colin.

The years drifted by, and somehow, without realizing it, Penelope ceased to be a debutante and found herself sitting with the chaperones, watching her younger sister Felicity—surely the only Featherington sister blessed with both natural beauty and charm—enjoying her own London seasons.

Colin developed a taste for travel and began to spend more and more time outside of London; it seemed that every few months he was off to some new destination. When he was in town, he always saved a dance and a smile for Penelope, and somehow she managed to pretend that nothing had ever happened, that he'd never declared his distaste for her on a public street, that her dreams had never been shattered.

And when he was in town, which wasn't often, they seemed to settle into an easy, if not terribly deep, friendship. Which was all an almost twenty-eight-year-old spinster could hope for, right?

Unrequited love was never easy, but at least Penelope Featherington was used to it.

Chapter 1

Matchmaking mamas are united in their glee—Colin Bridgerton has returned from Greece!

For those gentle (and ignorant) readers who are new to town this year, Mr. Bridgerton is third in the legendary string of eight Bridgerton siblings (hence the name Colin, beginning with C; he follows Anthony and Benedict, and precedes Daphne, Eloise, Francesca, Gregory, and Hyacinth).

Although Mr. Bridgerton holds no noble title and is unlikely ever to do so (he is seventh in line for the title of Viscount Bridgerton, behind the two sons of the current viscount, his elder brother Benedict, and his three sons) he is still considered one of the prime catches of the season, due to his fortune, his face, his form, and most of all, his charm. It is difficult, however, to predict whether Mr. Bridgerton will succumb to matrimonial bliss this season; he is certainly of an age to marry (three-and-thirty), but he has never shown a decided interest in any lady of proper parentage, and to make matters even more complicated, he has an appalling tendency to leave London at the drop of a hat, bound for some exotic destination.

LADY WHISTLEDOWN'S SOCIETY PAPERS,
2 April 1824

"Look at this!" Portia Featherington squealed. "Colin Bridgerton is back!"

Penelope looked up from her needlework. Her mother was clutching the latest edition of *Lady Whistledown's Society Papers* the way Penelope might clutch, say, a rope while hanging off a building. "I know," she murmured.

Portia frowned. She hated when someone—anyone—was aware of gossip before she was. "How did you get to *Whistledown* before I did? I told Briarly to set it aside for me and not to let anyone touch—"

"I didn't see it in *Whistledown*," Penelope interrupted, before her mother went off to castigate the poor, beleaguered butler. "Felicity told me. Yesterday afternoon. Hyacinth Bridgerton told her."

"Your sister spends a great deal of time over at the Bridgerton household."

"As do I," Penelope pointed out, wondering where this was leading.

Portia tapped her finger against the side of her chin, as she always did when she was plotting or scheming. "Colin Bridgerton is of an age to be looking for a wife."

Penelope managed to blink just before her eyes bugged right out of her head. "Colin Bridgerton is not going to marry Felicity!"

Portia gave a little shrug. "Stranger things have happened."

"Not that I've ever seen," Penelope muttered.

"Anthony Bridgerton married that Kate Sheffield girl, and she was even less popular than *you*."

That wasn't exactly true; Penelope rather thought they'd been on equally low rungs of the social ladder. But there seemed little point in telling this to her mother, who probably thought she'd complimented her third daughter by saying she'd not been the least popular girl that season.

Penelope felt her lips tightening. Her mother's "compliments" had a habit of landing rather like wasps.

"Do not think I mean to criticize," Portia said, suddenly all concern. "In truth, I am glad for your spinsterhood. I am alone in this world save for my daughters, and it's comforting to know that one of you shall be able to care for me in my older years."

Penelope had a vision of the future—the future as described by her mother—and she had a sudden urge to run out and marry the chimney sweep. She'd long since resigned herself to a life of eternal spinsterhood, but somehow she'd always pictured herself off in her own neat little terrace house. Or maybe a snug cottage by the sea.

But lately Portia had been peppering her conversations with references to her old age and how lucky she was that Penelope could care for her. Never mind that both Prudence and Philippa had married well-heeled men and possessed ample funds to see to their mother's every comfort. Or that Portia was moderately wealthy in her own right; when her family had settled money on her as a dowry, one-fourth had been set aside for her own personal account.

No, when Portia talked about being "cared for," she wasn't referring to money. What Portia wanted was a slave.

Penelope sighed. She was being overly harsh with her mother, if only in her own mind. She did that too often. Her mother loved her. She knew her mother loved her. And she loved her mother back.

It was just that sometimes she didn't much *like* her mother.

She hoped that didn't make her a bad person. But truly, her mother could try the patience of even the kindest, gentlest of daughters, and as Penelope was the first to admit, she could be a wee bit sarcastic at times.

"Why don't you think Colin would marry Felicity?" Portia asked.

Penelope looked up, startled. She'd thought they were done with that subject. She should have known better. Her mother was nothing if not tenacious. "Well," she said slowly, "to begin with, she's twelve years younger than he is."

"Pfft," Portia said, waving her hand dismissively. "That's nothing, and you know it."

Penelope frowned, then yelped as she accidentally stabbed her finger with her needle.

"Besides," Portia continued blithely, "he's"—she looked back down at *Whistledown* and scanned it for his exact age—"three-and-thirty! How is he meant to avoid a twelve-year difference between him and his wife? Surely you don't expect him to marry someone *your* age."

Penelope sucked on her abused finger even though she knew it was hopelessly uncouth to do so. But she needed to put something in her mouth to keep her from saying something horrible *and* horribly spiteful.

Everything her mother said was true. Many *ton* weddings— maybe even most of them—saw men marrying girls a dozen or more years their junior. But somehow the age gap between Colin and Felicity seemed even larger, perhaps because . . .

Penelope was unable to keep the disgust off her face. "She's like a sister to him. A little sister."

"Really, Penelope. I hardly think—"

"It's almost incestuous," Penelope muttered.

"What did you say?"

Penelope snatched up her needlework again. "Nothing."

"I'm sure you said something."

Penelope shook her head. "I did clear my throat. Perhaps you heard—"

"I heard you saying something. I'm sure of it!"

Penelope groaned. Her life loomed long and tedious ahead of her. "Mother," she said, with the patience of, if not a saint, at least a very devout nun, "Felicity is practically engaged to Mr. Albansdale."

Portia actually began rubbing her hands together. "She won't be engaged to him if she can catch Colin Bridgerton."

"Felicity would *die* before chasing after Colin."

"Of course not. She's a smart girl. Anyone can see that Colin Bridgerton is a better catch."

"But Felicity loves Mr. Albansdale!"

Portia deflated into her perfectly upholstered chair. "There is that."

"And," Penelope added with great feeling, "Mr. Albansdale is in possession of a perfectly respectable fortune."

Portia tapped her index finger against her cheek. "True. Not," she said sharply, "as respectable as a Bridgerton portion, but it's nothing to sneeze at, I suppose."

Penelope knew it was time to let it go, but she couldn't stop her mouth from opening one last time. "In all truth, Mother, he's a wonderful match for Felicity. We should be delighted for her."

"I know, I know," Portia grumbled. "It's just that I so wanted one of my daughters to marry a Bridgerton. What a coup! I would be the talk of London for weeks. Years, maybe."

Penelope stabbed her needle into the cushion beside her. It was a rather foolish way to vent her anger, but the alternative was to jump to her feet and yell, *What about me?* Portia seemed to think that once Felicity was wed, her hopes for a Bridgerton union were forever dashed. But Penelope was still unmarried—didn't that count for anything?

Was it so much to wish that her mother thought of her with the same pride she felt for her other three daughters? Penelope knew that Colin wasn't going to choose her as his bride, but shouldn't a mother be at least a little bit blind to her children's faults? It was obvious to Penelope that neither Prudence, Philippa, nor even Felicity had ever had a chance with a Bridgerton. Why did her mother seem to think their charms so exceeded Penelope's?

Very well, Penelope had to admit that Felicity enjoyed a popularity that exceeded that of her three older sisters combined. But Prudence and Philippa had never been Incomparables. They'd hovered on the perimeters of ballrooms just as much as Penelope had.

Except, of course, that they were married now. Penelope wouldn't have wanted to cleave herself unto either of their husbands, but at least they were wives.

Thankfully, however, Portia's mind had already moved on to greener pastures. "I must pay a call upon Violet," she was saying. "She'll be so relieved that Colin is back."

"I'm sure Lady Bridgerton will be delighted to see you," Penelope said.

"That poor woman," Portia said, her sigh dramatic. "She worries about him, you know—"

"I know."

"Truly, I think it is more than a mother should be expected to bear. He goes gallivanting about, the good Lord only knows where, to countries that are positively *heathen*—"

"I believe they practice Christianity in Greece," Penelope murmured, her eyes back down on her needlework.

"Don't be impertinent, Penelope Anne Featherington, and they're *Catholics*!" Portia shuddered on the word.

"They're not Catholics at all," Penelope replied, giving up on the needlework and setting it aside. "They're Greek Orthodox."

"Well, they're not Church of England," Portia said with a sniff.

"Seeing as how they're Greek, I don't think they're terribly worried about that."

Portia's eyes narrowed disapprovingly. "And how do you know about this Greek religion, anyway? No, don't tell me," she said with a dramatic flourish. "You read it somewhere."

Penelope just blinked as she tried to think of a suitable reply.

"I wish you wouldn't read so much," Portia sighed. "I probably could have married you off years ago if you had concentrated more on the social graces and less on . . . less on . . ."

Penelope had to ask. "Less on what?"

"I don't know. Whatever it is you do that has you staring into space and daydreaming so often."

"I'm just thinking," Penelope said quietly. "Sometimes I just like to stop and think."

"Stop what?" Portia wanted to know.

Penelope couldn't help but smile. Portia's query seemed to sum up all that was different between mother and daughter. "It's nothing, Mother," Penelope said. "Really."

Portia looked as if she wanted to say more, then thought the better of it. Or maybe she was just hungry. She did pluck a biscuit off the tea tray and pop it into her mouth.

Penelope started to reach out to take the last biscuit for herself, then decided to let her mother have it. She might as well keep her mother's mouth full. The last thing she wanted was to find herself in another conversation about Colin Bridgerton.

"Colin's back!"

Penelope looked up from her book—*A Brief History of Greece*—to see Eloise Bridgerton bursting into her room. As usual, Eloise had not been announced. The Featherington butler was so used to seeing her there that he treated her like a member of the family.

"Is he?" Penelope asked, managing to feign (in her opinion) rather realistic indifference. Of course, she did set *A Brief History of Greece* down behind *Mathilda*, the novel by S. R. Fielding that had been all the rage a year earlier. Everyone had a copy of *Mathilda* on their bedstand. And it was thick enough to hide *A Brief History of Greece*.

Eloise sat down in Penelope's desk chair. "Indeed, and he's very tanned. All that time in the sun, I suppose."

"He went to Greece, didn't he?"

Eloise shook her head. "He said the war there has worsened, and it was too dangerous. So he went to Cyprus instead."

"My, my," Penelope said with a smile. "Lady Whistledown got something wrong."

Eloise smiled that cheeky Bridgerton smile, and once again Penelope realized how lucky she was to have her as her closest friend. She and Eloise had been inseparable since the age of seventeen. They'd had their London seasons together, reached adulthood together, and, much to their mothers' dismay, had become spinsters together.

Eloise claimed that she hadn't met the right person.

Penelope, of course, hadn't been asked.

"Did he enjoy Cyprus?" Penelope inquired.

Eloise sighed. "He said it was brilliant. How I should love to travel. It seems everyone has been somewhere but me."

"And me," Penelope reminded her.

"And you," Eloise agreed. "Thank goodness for you."

"Eloise!" Penelope exclaimed, throwing a pillow at her. But she thanked goodness for Eloise, too. Every day. Many women went through their entire lives without a close female friend, and here she had someone to whom she could tell anything. Well, almost anything. Penelope had never told her of her feelings for Colin, although she rather thought Eloise suspected the truth. Eloise was far too tactful to mention it, though, which only validated Penelope's certainty that Colin would never love her. If Eloise had thought, for even one moment, that Penelope actually had a chance at snaring Colin as a husband, she would have been plotting her matchmaking strategies with a ruthlessness that would have impressed any army general.

When it came right down to it, Eloise was a rather managing sort of person.

". . . and then he said that the water was so choppy that he actually cast up his accounts over the side of the boat, and—" Eloise scowled. "You're not listening to me."

"No," Penelope admitted. "Well, yes, actually, parts of it. I cannot believe Colin actually told you he vomited."

"Well, I *am* his sister."

"He'd be furious with you if he knew you'd told me."

Eloise waved off her protest. "He won't mind. You're like another sister to him."

Penelope smiled, but she sighed at the same time.

"Mother asked him—of course—whether he was planning to remain in town for the season," Eloise continued, "and—of course—he was terribly evasive, but then I decided to interrogate him myself—"

"Terribly smart of you," Penelope murmured.

Eloise threw the pillow back at her. "And I finally got him to admit to me that yes, he thinks he will stay for at least a few months. But he made me promise not to tell Mother."

"Now, that's not"—Penelope cleared her throat—"terribly intelligent of him. If your mother thinks his time here is limited, she will redouble her efforts to see him married. I should think that was what he wanted most to avoid."

"It does seem his usual aim in life," Eloise concurred.

"If he lulled her into thinking that there was no rush, perhaps she might not badger him quite so much."

"An interesting idea," Eloise said, "but probably more true in theory than in practice. My mother is so determined to see him wed that it matters not if she increases her efforts. Her regular efforts are enough to drive him mad as it is."

"Can one go doubly mad?" Penelope mused.

Eloise cocked her head. "I don't know," she said. "I don't think I should want to find out."

They both fell silent for a moment (a rare occurrence, indeed) and then Eloise quite suddenly jumped to her feet and said, "I must go."

Penelope smiled. People who didn't know Eloise very well thought she had a habit of changing the subject frequently (and abruptly), but Penelope knew that the truth was something else altogether. When Eloise had her mind set on something, she was completely unable to let it go. Which meant that if Eloise suddenly wanted to leave, it probably had to do with something they'd been talking about earlier in the afternoon, and—

"Colin is expected for tea," Eloise explained.

Penelope smiled. She loved being right.

"You should come," Eloise said.

Penelope shook her head. "He'll want it to be just family."

"You're probably right," Eloise said, nodding slightly. "Very well, then, I must be off. Terribly sorry to cut my visit so short, but I wanted to be sure that you knew Colin was home."

"*Whistledown,*" Penelope reminded her.

"Right. Where does that woman get her information?" Eloise said, shaking her head in wonder. "I vow sometimes she knows so much about my family I wonder if I ought to be frightened."

"She can't go on forever," Penelope commented, getting up to see her friend out. "Someone will eventually figure out who she is, don't you think?"

"I don't know." Eloise put her hand on the doorknob, twisted, and pulled. "I used to think so. But it's been ten years. More, actually. If she were going to be caught, I think it would have happened already."

Penelope followed Eloise down the stairs. "Eventually she'll make a mistake. She has to. She's only human."

Eloise laughed. "And here I thought she was a minor god."

Penelope found herself grinning.

Eloise stopped and whirled around so suddenly that Penelope crashed right into her, nearly sending both of them tumbling down the last few steps on the staircase. "Do you know what?" Eloise demanded.

"I couldn't begin to speculate."

Eloise didn't even bother to pull a face. "I'd wager that she *has* made a mistake," she said.

"I beg your pardon?"

"You said it yourself. She—or it could be he, I suppose—has been writing the column for over a decade. No one could do that for so long without making a mistake. Do you know what I think?"

Penelope just spread her hands in an impatient gesture.

"I think the problem is that the rest of us are too stupid to notice her mistakes."

Penelope stared at her for a moment, then burst out laughing. "Oh, Eloise," she said, wiping tears from her eyes. "I do love you."

Eloise grinned. "And it's a good thing you do, spinster that I am. We shall have to set up a household together when we are thirty and truly crones."

Penelope caught hold of the idea like a lifeboat. "Do you think we could?" she exclaimed. And then, in a hushed voice, after looking furtively up and down the hall, "Mother has begun to speak of her old age with alarming frequency."

"What's so alarming about that?"

"I'm in all of her visions, waiting on her hand and foot."

"Oh, dear."

"A milder expletive than had crossed my mind."

"Penelope!" But Eloise was grinning.

"I love my mother," Penelope said.

"I know you do," Eloise said, in a rather placating sort of voice.

"No, I really do."

The left corner of Eloise's mouth began to twitch. "I know you really do. Really."

"It's just that—"

Eloise put up a hand. "You don't need to say any more. I understand perfectly. I—Oh! Good day, Mrs. Featherington!"

"Eloise," Portia said, bustling down the hall. "I didn't realize you were here."

"I'm sneaky as always," Eloise said. "Cheeky, even."

Portia gave her an indulgent smile. "I heard your brother is back in town."

"Yes, we are all overjoyed."

"I'm sure you must be, especially your mother."

"Indeed. She is beside herself. I believe she is drawing up a list right now."

Portia's entire aspect perked up, as it did at the mention of anything that might be construed as gossip. "A list? What sort of list?"

"Oh, you know, the same list she has made for all of her adult children. Prospective spouses and all that."

"It makes me wonder," Penelope said in a dry voice, "what constitutes 'all that.'"

"Sometimes she includes one or two people who are hopelessly unsuitable so as to highlight the qualities of the *real* possibilities."

Portia laughed. "Perhaps she'll put you on Colin's list, Penelope!"

Penelope didn't laugh. Neither did Eloise. Portia didn't seem to notice.

"Well, I'd best be off," Eloise said, clearing her throat to cover a moment that was awkward to two of the three people in the hall. "Colin is expected for tea. Mother wants the entire family in attendance."

"Will you all fit?" Penelope asked. Lady Bridgerton's home was large, but the Bridgerton children, spouses, and grandchildren numbered twenty-one. It was a large brood, indeed.

"We're going to Bridgerton House," Eloise explained. Her mother had moved out of the Bridgertons' official London residence after her eldest son had married. Anthony, who had been viscount since the age of eighteen, had told Violet that she needn't go, but she had insisted that he and his wife needed their privacy. As a result, Anthony and Kate lived with their three children in Bridgerton House, while Violet lived with her unmarried children (with the exception of Colin, who kept his own lodgings) just a few blocks away at 5 Bruton Street. After a year or so of unsuccessful attempts to name Lady Bridgerton's new home, the family had taken to calling it simply Number Five.

"Do enjoy yourself," Portia said. "I must go and find Felicity. We are late for an appointment at the modiste."

Eloise watched Portia disappear up the stairs, then said to Penelope, "Your sister seems to spend a great deal of time at the modiste."

Penelope shrugged. "Felicity is going mad with all the fittings, but she's Mother's only hope for a truly grand match. I'm afraid she's convinced that Felicity will catch a duke if she's wearing the right gown."

"Isn't she practically engaged to Mr. Albansdale?"

"I imagine he'll make a formal offer next week. But until then, Mother is keeping her options open." She rolled her eyes. "You'd best warn your brother to keep his distance."

"Gregory?" Eloise asked in disbelief. "He's not even out of university."

"Colin."

"*Colin?*" Eloise exploded with laughter. "Oh, that's rich."

"That's what I told her, but you know how she is once she gets an idea in her head."

Eloise chuckled. "Rather like me, I imagine."

"Tenacious to the end."

"Tenacity can be a very good thing," Eloise reminded her, "at the proper time."

"Right," Penelope returned with a sarcastic smile, "and at the improper time, it's an absolute nightmare."

Eloise laughed. "Cheer up, friend. At least she let you rid yourself of all those yellow frocks."

Penelope looked down at her morning dress, which was, if she did say so herself, a rather flattering shade of blue. "She stopped choosing my clothing once she finally realized I was officially on the shelf. A girl with no marriage prospects isn't worth the time and energy it takes her to offer fashion advice. She hasn't accompanied me to the modiste in over a year! Bliss!"

Eloise smiled at her friend, whose complexion turned the loveliest peaches and cream whenever she wore cooler hues. "It was apparent to all, the moment you were allowed to choose your own clothing. Even Lady Whistledown commented upon it!"

"I hid that column from Mother," Penelope admitted. "I didn't want her feelings to be hurt."

Eloise blinked a few times before saying, "That was very kind of you, Penelope."

"I have my moments of charity and grace."

"One would think," Eloise said with a snort, "that a vital component of charity and grace is the ability not to draw attention to one's possession of them."

Penelope pursed her lips as she pushed Eloise toward the door. "Don't you need to go home?"

"I'm leaving! I'm leaving!"

And she left.

It was, Colin Bridgerton decided as he took a sip of some truly excellent brandy, rather nice to be back in England.

It was quite strange, actually, how he loved returning home just as much as he did the departure. In another few months—six at the most—he'd be itching to leave again, but for now, England in April was positively brilliant.

"It's good, isn't it?"

Colin looked up. His brother Anthony was leaning against the front of his massive mahogany desk, motioning to him with his own glass of brandy.

Colin nodded. "Hadn't realized how much I missed it until I returned. Ouzo has its charms, but this"—he lifted his glass—"is heaven."

Anthony smiled wryly. "And how long do you plan to remain this time?"

Colin wandered over to the window and pretended to look out. His eldest brother made little attempt to disguise his impatience with Colin's wanderlust. In truth, Colin really couldn't blame him. Occasionally, it was difficult to get letters home; he supposed that his family often had to wait a month or even two for word of his welfare. But while he knew that he would not relish being in their shoes—never knowing if a loved one was dead or alive, constantly waiting for the knock of the messenger at the front door—that just wasn't enough to keep his feet firmly planted in England.

Every now and then, he simply had to get *away*. There was no other way to describe it.

Away from the *ton*, who thought him a charming rogue and nothing else, away from England, which encouraged younger sons to enter the military or the clergy, neither of which suited his temperament. Even away from his family, who loved him unconditionally but had no clue that what he really wanted, deep down inside, was something to do.

His brother Anthony held the viscountcy, and with that came myriad responsibilities. He ran estates, managed the family's finances, and saw to the welfare of countless tenants and servants. Benedict, his elder by four years, had gained renown as an artist. He'd started with pencil and paper, but at the urging of his wife had moved on to oils. One of his landscapes now hung in the National Gallery.

Anthony would be forever remembered in family trees as the seventh Viscount Bridgerton. Benedict would live through his paintings, long after he left this earth.

But Colin had nothing. He managed the small property given to him by his family and he attended parties. He would never dream of claiming he didn't have fun, but sometimes he wanted something a little more than fun.

He wanted a purpose.

He wanted a legacy.

He wanted, if not to know then at least to hope, that when he was gone, he'd be memorialized in some manner other than in *Lady Whistledown's Society Papers*.

He sighed. No wonder he spent so much time traveling.

"Colin?" his brother prompted.

Colin turned to him and blinked. He was fairly certain Anthony had asked him a question, but somewhere in the meanderings of his mind, he'd forgotten what.

"Oh. Right." Colin cleared his throat. "I'll be here for the rest of the season, at least."

Anthony said nothing, but it was difficult to miss the satisfied expression on his face.

"If nothing else," Colin added, affixing his legendary crooked grin on his face, "someone has to spoil your children. I don't think Charlotte has nearly enough dolls."

"Only fifty," Anthony agreed in a deadpan voice. "The poor girl is horribly neglected."

"Her birthday is at the end of this month, is it not? I shall have to neglect her some more, I think."

"Speaking of birthdays," Anthony said, settling into the large chair behind his desk, "Mother's is a week from Sunday."

"Why do you think I hurried to return?"

Anthony raised a brow, and Colin had the distinct impression that he was trying to decide if Colin had truly rushed home for their mother's birthday, or if he was simply taking advantage of some very good timing.

"We're holding a party for her," Anthony said.

"She's letting you?" It was Colin's experience that women of a certain age did not enjoy birthday celebrations. And although his mother was still exceedingly lovely, she was definitely of a certain age.

"We were forced to resort to blackmail," Anthony admitted. "She agreed to the party or we revealed her true age."

Colin shouldn't have taken a sip of his brandy; he choked on it and just barely managed to avert spraying it all over his brother. "I should have liked to have seen *that*."

Anthony offered a rather satisfied smile. "It was a brilliant maneuver on my part."

Colin finished the rest of his drink. "What, do you think, are the chances she won't use the party as an opportunity to find me a wife?"

"Very small."

"I thought so."

Anthony leaned back in his chair. "You *are* thirty-three now, Colin . . ."

Colin stared at him in disbelief. "God above, don't *you* start on me."

"I wouldn't dream of it. I was merely going to suggest that you keep your eyes open this season. You needn't actively look for a wife, but there's no harm in remaining at least amenable to the possibility."

Colin eyed the doorway, intending to pass through it very shortly. "I assure you I am not averse to the idea of marriage."

"I didn't think you were," Anthony demurred.

"I see little reason to rush, however."

"There's never a reason to rush," Anthony returned. "Well, rarely, anyway. Just humor Mother, will you?"

Colin hadn't realized he was still holding his empty glass until it slipped through his fingers and landed on the carpet with a loud thunk. "Good God," he whispered, "is she ill?"

"No!" Anthony said, his surprise making his voice loud and forceful. "She'll outlive us all, I'm sure of it."

"Then what is this about?"

Anthony sighed. "I just want to see you happy."

"I am happy," Colin insisted.

"Are you?"

"Hell, I'm the happiest man in London. Just read Lady Whistledown. She'll tell you so."

Anthony glanced down at the paper on his desk.

"Well, maybe not this column, but anything from last year. I've been called charming more times than Lady Danbury has been called opinionated, and we both know what a feat *that* is."

"Charming doesn't necessarily equal happy," Anthony said softly.

"I don't have time for this," Colin muttered. The door had never looked so good.

"If you were truly happy," Anthony persisted, "you wouldn't keep leaving."

Colin paused with his hand on the doorknob. "Anthony, I *like* to travel."

"Constantly?"

"I must, or I wouldn't do it."

"That's an evasive sentence if ever I've heard one."

"And this"—Colin flashed his brother a wicked smile—"is an evasive maneuver."

"Colin!"

But he'd already left the room.

Chapter 2

It has always been fashionable among the ton *to complain of ennui, but surely this year's crop of partygoers has raised boredom to an art form. One cannot take two steps at a society function these days without hearing the phrase "dreadfully dull," or "hopelessly banal." Indeed, This Author has even been informed that Cressida Twombley recently remarked that she was convinced that she might perish of eternal boredom if forced to attend one more off-key musicale.*

(This Author must concur with Lady Twombley on that note; while this year's selection of debutantes are an amiable bunch, there is not a decent musician among them.)

If there is to be an antidote for the disease of tedium, surely it will be Sunday's fête at Bridgerton House. The entire family will gather, along with a hundred or so of their closest friends, to celebrate the dowager viscountess's birthday.

It is considered crass to mention a lady's age, and so This Author will not reveal which birthday Lady Bridgerton is celebrating.

But have no fear! This Author knows!

LADY WHISTLEDOWN'S SOCIETY PAPERS,
9 April 1824

Spinsterhood was a word that tended to invoke either panic or pity, but Penelope was coming to realize that there were decided advantages to the unmarried state.

First of all, no one really expected the spinsters to dance at balls, which meant that Penelope was no longer forced to hover at the edge of the dance floor, looking this way and that, pretending that she didn't really want to dance. Now she could sit off to the side with the other spinsters and chaperones. She still wanted to dance, of course—she rather liked dancing, and she was actually quite good at it, not that anyone ever noticed—but it was much easier to feign disinterest the farther one got from the waltzing couples.

Second, the number of hours spent in dull conversation had been drastically reduced. Mrs. Featherington had officially given up hope that Penelope might ever snag a husband, and so she'd stopped thrusting her in the path of every third-tier eligible bachelor. Portia had never really thought Penelope had a prayer of attracting the attention of a first- or second-tier bachelor, which was probably true, but most of the third-tier bachelors were classified as such for a reason, and sadly, that reason was often personality, or lack thereof. Which, when combined with Penelope's shyness with strangers, didn't tend to promote sparkling conversation.

And finally, she could eat again. It was maddening, considering the amount of food generally on display at *ton* parties, but women on the hunt for husbands weren't supposed to exhibit anything more robust than a bird's appetite. This, Penelope thought gleefully (as she bit into what had to be the most heavenly éclair outside of France), had to be the best spinster perk of all.

"Good heavens," she moaned. If sin could take a solid form, surely it would be a pastry. Preferably one with chocolate.

"That good, eh?"

Penelope choked on the éclair, then coughed, sending a fine spray of pastry cream through the air. "Colin," she gasped, fervently praying the largest of the globs had missed his ear.

"Penelope." He smiled warmly. "It's good to see you."

"And you."

He rocked on his heels—once, twice, thrice—then said, "You look well."

"And you," she said, too preoccupied with trying to figure out where to set down her éclair to offer much variety to her conversation.

"That's a nice dress," he said, motioning to her green silk gown.

She smiled ruefully, explaining, "It's not yellow."

"So it's not." He grinned, and the ice was broken. It was strange, because one would think her tongue would be tied the tightest around the man she loved, but there was something about Colin that set everyone at ease.

Maybe, Penelope had thought on more than one occasion, part of the reason she loved him was that he made her feel comfortable with herself.

"Eloise tells me you had a splendid time in Cyprus," she said.

He grinned. "Couldn't resist the birthplace of Aphrodite, after all."

Penelope found herself smiling as well. His good humor was infectious, even if the last thing she wanted to do was take part in a discussion of the goddess of love. "Was it as sunny as everyone says?" she asked. "No, forget I asked. I can see from your face that it was."

"I did acquire a bit of a tan," he said with a nod. "My mother nearly fainted when she saw me."

"From delight, I'm sure," Penelope said emphatically. "She misses you terribly when you're gone."

He leaned in. "Come, now, Penelope, surely you're not going to start in on me? Between my mother, Anthony, Eloise, and Daphne, I'm liable to perish of guilt."

"Not Benedict?" she couldn't help quipping.

He shot her a slightly smirky look. "He's out of town."

"Ah, well, that explains his silence."

His narrowed eyes matched his crossed arms to perfection. "You've always been cheeky, did you know that?"

"I hide it well," she said modestly.

"It's easy to see," he said in a dry voice, "why you are such good friends with my sister."

"I'm assuming you intended that as a compliment?"

"I'm fairly certain I'd be endangering my health if I'd intended it any other way."

Penelope was standing there hoping she'd think of a witty rejoinder when she heard a strange, wet, splattish sound. She looked down to discover that a large yellowish blob of pastry cream had slid from her half-eaten éclair and landed on the pristine wooden floor. She looked back up to find Colin's oh-so-green eyes dancing with laughter, even as his mouth fought for a serious expression.

"Well, now, that's embarrassing," Penelope said, deciding that the only way to avoid dying of mortification was to state the painfully obvious.

"I suggest," Colin said, raising one brow into a perfectly debonair arch, "that we flee the scene."

Penelope looked down at the empty carcass of the éclair still in her hand. Colin answered her with a nod toward a nearby potted plant.

"No!" she said, her eyes growing wide.

He leaned in closer. "I dare you."

Her eyes darted from the éclair to the plant and back to Colin's face. "I couldn't," she said.

"As far as naughty things go, this one is fairly mild," he pointed out.

It was a dare, and Penelope was usually immune to such childish ploys, but Colin's half-smile was difficult to resist. "Very well," she said, squaring her shoulders and dropping the pastry onto the soil. She took a step back, examined her handiwork, looked around to see if anyone besides Colin was watching her, then leaned down and rotated the pot so that a leafy branch covered the evidence.

"I didn't think you'd do it," Colin said.

"As you said, it's not terribly naughty."

"No, but it is my mother's favorite potted palm."

"Colin!" Penelope whirled around, fully intending to sink her hand right back into the plant to retrieve the éclair. "How could you let me—Wait a second." She straightened, her eyes narrowed. "This isn't a palm."

He was all innocence. "It's not?"

"It's a miniature orange tree."

He blinked. "Is it, now?"

She scowled at him. Or at least she hoped it was a scowl. It was difficult to scowl at Colin Bridgerton. Even his mother had once remarked that it was nearly impossible to reprimand him.

He would just smile and look contrite and say something funny, and you just couldn't stay angry with him. You simply couldn't do it.

"You were trying to make me feel guilty," Penelope said.

"Anyone could confuse a palm with an orange tree."

She fought the urge to roll her eyes. "Except for the oranges."

He chewed on his lower lip, his eyes thoughtful. "Yes, hmmm, one would think they'd be a bit of a giveaway."

"You're a terrible liar, did you know that?"

He straightened, tugging slightly at his waistcoat as he lifted his chin. "Actually, I'm an excellent liar. But what I'm really good at is appearing appropriately sheepish and adorable after I'm caught."

What, Penelope wondered, was she meant to say to *that*? Because surely there was no one more adorably sheepish (sheepishly adorable?) than Colin Bridgerton with his hands clasped behind his back, his eyes flitting along the ceiling, and his lips puckered into an innocent whistle.

"When you were a child," Penelope asked, abruptly changing the subject, "were you ever punished?"

Colin immediately straightened to attention. "I beg your pardon?"

"Were you ever punished as a child?" she repeated. "Are you ever punished now?"

Colin just stared at her, wondering if she had any idea what she was asking. Probably not. "Errr . . ." he said, mostly because he hadn't anything else to say.

She let out a vaguely patronizing sigh. "I thought not."

If he were a less indulgent man, and if this were anyone but Penelope Featherington, whom he knew did not possess a malicious bone in her body, he might take offense. But he was an uncommonly easygoing fellow, and this *was* Penelope Featherington, who had been a faithful friend to his sister for God knows how many years, so instead of adopting a hard, cynical stare (which, admittedly, was an expression at which he'd never excelled), he merely smiled and murmured, "Your point being?"

"Do not think I mean to criticize your parents," she said with an expression that was innocent and sly at the same time. "I would never dream of implying that you were spoiled in any way."

He nodded graciously.

"It's just that"—she leaned in, as if imparting a grave secret—"I rather think you could get away with murder if you so chose."

He coughed—not to clear his throat and not because he wasn't feeling well, but rather because he was so damned startled. Penelope was such a funny character. No, that wasn't quite right. She was . . . *surprising.* Yes, that seemed to sum her up. Very few people really knew her; she had certainly never developed a reputation as a sterling conversationalist. He was fairly certain she'd made it through three-hour parties without ever venturing beyond words of a single syllable.

But when Penelope was in the company of someone with whom she felt comfortable—and Colin realized that he was probably privileged to count himself among that number—she had a dry wit, a sly smile, and evidence of a very intelligent mind, indeed.

He wasn't surprised that she'd never attracted any serious suitors for her hand; she wasn't a beauty by any stretch, although upon close examination she was more attractive than he'd remembered her to be. Her brown hair had a touch of red to it, highlighted nicely by the flickering candles. And her skin was quite lovely—that perfect peaches-and-cream complexion that ladies were always slathering their faces with arsenic to achieve.

But Penelope's attractiveness wasn't the sort that men usually noticed. And her normally shy and occasionally even stuttering demeanor didn't exactly showcase her personality.

Still, it was too bad about her lack of popularity. She would have made someone a perfectly good wife.

"So you're saying," he mused, steering his mind back to the matter at hand, "that I should consider a life of crime?"

"Nothing of the sort," she replied, a demure smile on her face. "Just that I rather suspect you could talk your way out of anything." And then, unexpectedly, her mien grew serious, and she quietly said, "I envy that."

Colin surprised himself by holding out his hand and saying, "Penelope Featherington, I think you should dance with me."

And then Penelope surprised *him* by laughing and saying, "That's very sweet of you to ask, but you don't have to dance with me any longer."

His pride felt oddly pricked. "What the devil do you mean by that?"

She shrugged. "It's official now. I'm a spinster. There's no longer a reason to dance with me just so that I don't feel left out."

"That's not why I danced with you," he protested, but he knew that it was exactly the reason. And half the time he'd only remembered to ask because his mother had poked him—*hard*—in the back and reminded him.

She gave him a faintly pitying look, which galled him, because he'd never thought to be pitied by Penelope Featherington.

"If you think," he said, feeling his spine grow stiff, "that I'm going to allow you to wiggle out of a dance with me *now*, you're quite delusional."

"You don't have to dance with me just to prove you don't mind doing it," she said.

"I *want* to dance with you," he fairly growled.

"Very well," she said, after what seemed to be a ridiculously long pause. "It would surely be churlish for me to refuse."

"It was probably churlish of you to doubt my intentions," he said as he took her arm, "but I'm willing to forgive you if you can forgive yourself."

She stumbled, which made him smile.

"I do believe I'll manage," she choked out.

"Excellent." He offered her a bland smile. "I'd hate to think of you living with the guilt."

The music was just beginning, so Penelope took his hand and curtsied as they began the minuet. It was difficult to talk during the dance, which gave Penelope a few moments to catch her breath and gather her thoughts.

Perhaps she'd been a bit too harsh with Colin. She shouldn't have scolded him for asking her to dance, when the truth was, those dances were among her most cherished memories. Did it really matter if he'd only done it out of pity? It would have been worse if he'd never asked her at all.

She grimaced. Worse still, did this mean she had to apologize?

"Was something wrong with that éclair?" Colin inquired the next time they stepped toward each other.

A full ten seconds passed before they were close enough again for her to say, "I beg your pardon?"

"You look as if you've swallowed something vile," he said, loudly this time, for he'd clearly lost patience with waiting for the dance to allow them to speak.

Several people looked over, then stepped discreetly away, as if Penelope might actually be sick right there on the ballroom floor.

"Do you need to shout it to the entire world?" Penelope hissed.

"You know," he said thoughtfully, bending into an elegant bow as the music drew to a close, "that was the loudest whisper I've ever heard."

He was insufferable, but Penelope wasn't going to say so, because it would only make her sound like a character in a very bad romantic novel. She'd read one just the other day in which the heroine used the word (or one of its synonyms) on every other page.

"Thank you for the dance," she said, once they'd reached the perimeter of the room. She almost added, *You can now tell your mother that you've fulfilled your obligations*, but immediately regretted her impulse. Colin hadn't done anything to deserve such sarcasm. It wasn't his fault that men only danced with her when forced to by their mothers. He'd always at least smiled and laughed while doing his duty, which was more than she could say for the rest of the male population.

He nodded politely and murmured his own thanks. They were just about to part ways when they heard a loud female voice bark out, "Mr. Bridgerton!"

They both froze. It was a voice they both knew. It was a voice everyone knew.

"Save me," Colin groaned.

Penelope looked over her shoulder to see the infamous Lady Danbury pushing her way through the crowd, wincing when her ever-present cane landed on the foot of some hapless young lady. "Maybe she means a different Mr. Bridgerton?" Penelope suggested. "There are quite a few of you, after all, and it's possible—"

"I'll give you ten pounds if you don't leave my side," Colin blurted out.

Penelope choked on air. "Don't be silly, I—"

"Twenty."

"Done!" she said with a smile, not because she particularly needed the money but rather because it was strangely enjoyable to be extorting it from Colin. "Lady Danbury!" she called out, hurrying to the elderly lady's side. "How nice to see you."

"Nobody ever thinks it's nice to see me," Lady Danbury said sharply, "except maybe my nephew, and half the time I'm not even sure about him. But I thank you for lying all the same."

Colin said nothing, but she still turned in his direction and swatted his leg with her cane. "Good choice dancing with this one," she said. "I've always liked her. More brains than the rest of her family put together."

Penelope opened her mouth to defend at least her younger sister, when Lady Danbury barked out, "Ha!" after barely a second's pause, adding, "I noticed neither of you contradicted me."

"It is always a delight to see you, Lady Danbury," Colin said, giving her just the sort of smile he might have directed at an opera singer.

"Glib, this one is," Lady Danbury said to Penelope. "You'll have to watch out for him."

"It is rarely necessary that I do so," Penelope said, "as he is most often out of the country."

"See!" Lady Danbury crowed again. "I told you she was bright."

"You'll notice," Colin said smoothly, "that I did not contradict you."

The old lady smiled approvingly. "So you didn't. You're getting smart in your old age, Mr. Bridgerton."

"It has occasionally been remarked that I possessed a small modicum of intelligence in my youth, as well."

"Hmmph. The important word in that sentence being *small*, of course."

Colin looked at Penelope through narrowed eyes. She appeared to be choking on laughter.

"We women must look out for one another," Lady Danbury said to no one in particular, "since it is clear that no one else will do so."

Colin decided it was definitely time to go. "I think I see my mother."

"Escape is impossible," Lady Danbury crowed. "Don't bother to attempt it, and besides, I know for a fact you don't see your mother. She's attending to some brainless twit who tore the hem off her dress." She turned to Penelope, who was now exerting such effort to control her laughter that her eyes were glistening with unshed tears. "How much did he pay you not to leave him alone with me?"

Penelope quite simply exploded. "I beg your pardon," she gasped, clasping a hand over her horrified mouth.

"Oh, no, go right ahead," Colin said expansively. "You've been such a help already."

"You don't have to give me the twenty pounds," she said.

"I wasn't planning to."

"Only twenty pounds?" Lady Danbury asked. "Hmmph. I would have thought I'd be worth at least twenty-five."

Colin shrugged. "I'm a third son. Perpetually short of funds, I'm afraid."

"Ha! You're as plump in the pocket as at least three earls," Lady Danbury said. "Well, maybe not earls," she added, after a bit of thought. "But a few viscounts, and most barons, to be sure."

Colin smiled blandly. "Isn't it considered impolite to talk about money in mixed company?"

Lady Danbury let out a noise that was either a wheeze or a giggle—Colin wasn't sure which—then said, "It's always impolite to talk about money, mixed company or no, but when one is my age, one can do almost anything one pleases."

"I do wonder," Penelope mused, "what one *can't* do at your age."

Lady Danbury turned to her. "I beg your pardon?"

"You said that one could do *almost* anything one pleases."

Lady Danbury stared at her in disbelief, then cracked a smile. Colin realized he was smiling as well.

"I like her," Lady D said to him, pointing at Penelope as if she were some sort of statue for sale. "Did I tell you I like her?"

"I believe you did," he murmured.

Lady Danbury turned to Penelope and said, her face a mask of utter seriousness, "I do believe I couldn't get away with murder, but that might be all."

All at once, both Penelope and Colin burst out laughing.

"Eh?" Lady Danbury said. "What's so funny?"

"Nothing," Penelope gasped. As for Colin, he couldn't even manage that much.

"It's not nothing," Lady D persisted. "And I shall remain here and pester you all night until you tell me what it is. Trust me when I tell you that that is *not* your desired course of action."

Penelope wiped a tear from her eye. "I just got through telling him," she said, motioning with her head toward Colin, "that he probably could get away with murder."

"Did you, now?" Lady Danbury mused, tapping her cane lightly against the floor the way someone else might scratch her chin while pondering a deep question. "Do you know, but I think you might be right. A more charming man I don't think London has ever seen."

Colin raised a brow. "Now, why don't I think you meant that as a compliment, Lady Danbury?"

"Of course it's a compliment, you dunderhead."

Colin turned to Penelope. "As opposed to *that*, which was clearly a compliment."

Lady Danbury beamed. "I declare," she said (or in all truth, de-clared), "this is the most fun I've had all season."

"Happy to oblige," Colin said with an easy smile.

"It's been an especially dull year, don't you think?" Lady Danbury asked Penelope.

Penelope nodded. "Last year was a bit tedious as well."

"But not as bad as this year," Lady D persisted.

"Don't ask me," Colin said affably. "I've been out of the country."

"Hmmph. I suppose you're going to say that your absence is the reason we've all been so bored."

"I would never dream of it," Colin said with a disarming smile. "But clearly, if the thought has crossed your mind, it must have some merit."

"Hmmph. Whatever the case, I'm bored."

Colin looked over at Penelope, who appeared to be holding herself very, very still—presumably to stave off laughter.

"Haywood!" Lady Danbury suddenly called out, waving over a middle-aged gentleman. "Wouldn't you agree with me?"

A vaguely panicked expression drifted across Lord Haywood's face, and then, when it became clear that he could not escape, he said, "I try to make a policy of *always* agreeing with you."

Lady Danbury turned to Penelope and said, "Is it my imagination, or are men getting more sensible?"

Penelope's only answer was a noncommittal shrug. Colin decided she was a wise girl, indeed.

Haywood cleared his throat, his blue eyes blinking fast and furious in his rather fleshy face. "Er, what, precisely, am I agreeing to?"

"That the season is boring," Penelope supplied helpfully.

"Ah, Miss Featherington," Haywood said in a blustery sort of voice. "Didn't see you there."

Colin stole just enough of a glance at Penelope to see her lips straighten into a small, frustrated smile. "Right here next to you," she muttered.

"So you are," Haywood said jovially, "and yes, the season is dreadfully boring."

"Did someone say the season is dull?"

Colin glanced to his right. Another man and two ladies had just joined the group and were avidly expressing their agreement.

"Tedious," one of them murmured. "Appallingly tedious."

"I have never attended a more banal round of parties," one of the ladies announced with an affected sigh.

"I shall have to inform my mother," Colin said tightly. He was among the most easygoing of men, but really, there were some insults he could not let pass.

"Oh, not this gathering," the woman hastened to add. "This ball is truly the only shining light in an otherwise dark and dismal string of gatherings. Why, I was just saying to—"

"Stop now," Lady Danbury ordered, "before you choke on your foot."

The lady quickly silenced herself.

"It's odd," Penelope murmured.

"Oh, Miss Featherington," said the lady who'd previously been going on about dark and dismal gatherings. "Didn't see you there."

"What's odd?" Colin asked, before anyone else could tell Penelope how unremarkable they found her.

She gave him a small, grateful smile before explaining herself. "It's odd how the *ton* seems to entertain themselves by pointing out how unentertained they are."

"I beg your pardon?" Haywood said, looking confused.

Penelope shrugged. "I think the lot of you are having a jolly good time talking about how bored you are, that's all."

Her comment was met with silence. Lord Haywood continued to look confused, and one of the two ladies must have had a speck of dust in her eye, because she couldn't seem to do anything but blink.

Colin couldn't help but smile. He hadn't thought Penelope's statement was such a terribly complicated concept.

"The only interesting thing to do is read *Whistledown*," said the nonblinking lady, as if Penelope had never even spoken.

The gentleman next to her murmured his assent.

And then Lady Danbury began to smile.

Colin grew alarmed. The old lady had a look in her eye. A frightening look.

"I have an idea," she said.

Someone gasped. Someone else groaned.

"A brilliant idea."

"Not that any of your ideas are anything but," Colin murmured in his most affable voice.

Lady Danbury shushed him with a wave of her hand. "How many great mysteries are there in life, really?"

No one answered, so Colin guessed, "Forty-two?"

She didn't even bother to scowl at him. "I am telling you all here and now. . . ."

Everyone leaned in. Even Colin. It was impossible not to indulge the drama of the moment.

"You are all my witnesses. . . ."

Colin thought he heard Penelope mutter, "Get *on* with it."

"One thousand pounds," Lady Danbury said.

The crowd surrounding her grew.

"One thousand pounds," she repeated, her voice growing in volume. Really, she would have been a natural on the stage. "One thousand pounds . . ."

It seemed the entire ballroom had hushed into reverent silence.

". . . to the person who unmasks Lady Whistledown!"

Chapter 3

This Author would be remiss if it was not mentioned that the most talked-about moment at last night's birthday ball at Bridgerton House was not the rousing toast to Lady Bridgerton (age not to be revealed) but rather Lady Danbury's impertinent offer of one thousand pounds to whomever unmasks . . .

Me.

Do your worst, ladies and gentlemen of the ton. *You haven't a prayer of solving this mystery.*

LADY WHISTLEDOWN'S SOCIETY PAPERS,
12 April 1824

Precisely three minutes were required for news of Lady Danbury's outrageous dare to spread throughout the ballroom. Penelope knew this to be true because she happened to be facing a large (and, according to Kate Bridgerton, extremely precise) grandfather clock when Lady Danbury made her announcement. At the words, "One thousand pounds to the person who unmasks Lady Whistledown," the clock read forty-four minutes past ten. The long hand had advanced no farther than forty-seven when Nigel Berbrooke stumbled into the rapidly growing circle of people surrounding Lady Danbury and proclaimed her latest scheme "scrumbly good fun!"

And if Nigel had heard about it, that meant everyone had, because Penelope's brother-in-law was not known for his intelligence, his attention span, or his listening ability.

Nor, Penelope thought wryly, for his vocabulary. Scrumbly, indeed.

"And who do you think Lady Whistledown is?" Lady Danbury asked Nigel.

"No earthly idea," he admitted. "Ain't me, that's all I know!"

"I think we all know that," Lady D replied.

"Who do you think it is?" Penelope asked Colin.

He offered her a one-shouldered shrug. "I've been out of town too often to speculate."

"Don't be silly," Penelope said. "Your cumulative time in London certainly adds up to enough parties and routs to form a few theories."

But he just shook his head. "I really couldn't say."

Penelope stared at him for a moment longer than was necessary, or, in all honesty, socially acceptable. There was something odd in Colin's eyes. Something fleeting and elusive. The *ton* often thought him nothing more than a devil-may-care charmer, but he was far more intelligent than he let on, and she'd have bet her life that he had a few suspicions.

But for some reason, he wasn't willing to share them with her.

"Who do you think it is?" Colin asked, avoiding her question with one of his own. "You've been out in society just about as long as Lady Whistledown. Surely you must have thought about it."

Penelope looked about the ballroom, her eyes resting on this person and that, before finally returning to the small crowd around her. "I think it could very well be Lady Danbury," she replied. "Wouldn't that be a clever joke on everyone?"

Colin looked over at the elderly lady, who was having a grand old time talking up her latest scheme. She was thumping her cane on the ground, chattering animatedly, and smiling like a cat with cream, fish, and an entire roast turkey. "It makes sense," he said thoughtfully, "in a rather perverse sort of way."

Penelope felt the corners of her mouth twist. "She's nothing if not perverse."

She watched Colin watching Lady D for another few seconds, then quietly said, "But you don't think it's her."

Colin slowly turned his head to face her, raising one brow in silent question.

"I can tell by the expression on your face," Penelope explained.

He grinned, that loose easy grin he so often used in public. "And here I thought I was inscrutable."

"Afraid not," she replied. "Not to me, anyway."

Colin sighed. "I fear it will never be my destiny to be a dark, brooding hero."

"You may well find yourself *some*one's hero," Penelope allowed. "There's time for you yet. But dark and brooding?" She smiled. "Not very likely."

"Too bad for me," he said jauntily, giving her another one of his well-known smiles—this one the lopsided, boyish one. "The dark, brooding types get all the women."

Penelope coughed discreetly, a bit surprised he'd be speaking of such things with her, not to mention the fact that Colin Bridgerton had never had trouble attracting women. He was grinning at her, awaiting a response, and she was trying to decide whether the correct reaction was polite maidenly outrage or a laugh and an I'm-such-a-good-sport sort of chuckle, when Eloise quite literally skidded to a halt in front of them.

"Did you hear the news?" Eloise asked breathlessly.

"Were you *running*?" Penelope returned. Truly a remarkable feat in such a crowded ballroom.

"Lady Danbury has offered one thousand pounds to whomever unmasks Lady Whistledown!"

"We know," Colin said in that vaguely superior tone exclusive to older brothers.

Eloise let out a disappointed sigh. "You do?"

Colin motioned to Lady Danbury, who was still a scant few yards away. "We were right here when it happened."

Eloise looked annoyed in the extreme, and Penelope knew exactly what she was thinking (and would most probably relate to her the following afternoon). It was one thing to miss an important moment. It was another entirely to discover that one's brother had seen the entire thing.

"Well, people are already talking about it," Eloise said. "Gushing, really. I haven't been witness to such excitement in years."

Colin turned to Penelope and murmured, "This is why I so often choose to leave the country."

Penelope tried not to smile.

"I know you're talking about me and I don't care," Eloise continued, barely pausing to take a breath. "I tell you, the *ton* has gone mad. Everyone—and I mean everyone—is speculating on her identity, although the shrewdest ones won't say a word. Don't want others to win on their hunch, don't you know."

"I think," Colin announced, "that I am not so in need of a thousand pounds that I care to worry about this."

"It's a lot of money," Penelope said thoughtfully.

He turned to her in disbelief. "Don't tell me you're going to join in this ridiculous game."

She cocked her head to the side, lifting her chin in what she hoped was an enigmatic—or if not enigmatic, at the very least slightly mysterious—manner. "I am not so well heeled that I can ignore the offer of one thousand pounds," she said.

"Perhaps if we work together . . ." Eloise suggested.

"God save me," was Colin's reply.

Eloise ignored him, saying to Penelope, "We could split the money."

Penelope opened her mouth to reply, but Lady Danbury's cane suddenly came into view, waving wildly through the air. Colin had to take a quick step to the side just to avoid getting his ear clipped off.

"Miss Featherington!" Lady D boomed. "You haven't told me who *you* suspect."

"No, Penelope," Colin said, a rather smirky smile on his face, "you haven't."

Penelope's first instinct was to mumble something under her breath and hope that Lady Danbury's age had left her hard enough of hearing that she would assume that any lack of understanding was the fault of her own ears and not Penelope's lips. But even without glancing to her side, she could feel Colin's presence, sense his quirky, cocky grin egging her on, and she found herself standing a little straighter, with her chin perched just a little higher than usual.

He made her more confident, more daring. He made her more . . . herself. Or at least the herself she wished she could be.

"Actually," Penelope said, looking Lady Danbury *almost* in the eye, "I think it's you."

A collective gasp echoed around them.

And for the first time in her life, Penelope Featherington found herself at the very center of attention.

Lady Danbury stared at her, her pale blue eyes shrewd and assessing. And then the most amazing thing happened. Her lips began to twitch at the corners. Then they widened until Penelope realized she was not just smiling, but positively grinning.

"I like you, Penelope Featherington," Lady Danbury said, tapping her right on the toe with her cane. "I wager half the ballroom is of the same notion, but no one else has the mettle to tell me so."

"I really don't, either," Penelope admitted, grunting slightly as Colin elbowed her in the ribs.

"Obviously," Lady Danbury said with a strange light in her eyes, "you do."

Penelope didn't know what to say to this. She looked at Colin, who was smiling at her encouragingly, then she looked back to Lady Danbury, who looked almost . . . maternal.

Which had to be the strangest thing of all. Penelope rather doubted that Lady Danbury had given maternal looks to her own children.

"Isn't it nice," the older lady said, leaning in so that only Penelope could hear her words, "to discover that we're not exactly what we thought we were?"

And then she walked away, leaving Penelope wondering if maybe she wasn't quite what she'd thought she was.

Maybe—just maybe—she was something a little bit more.

The next day was a Monday, which meant that Penelope took tea with the Bridgerton ladies at Number Five. She didn't know when, precisely, she'd fallen into that habit, but it had been so for close to a decade, and if she didn't show up on a Monday afternoon, she rather thought Lady Bridgerton would send someone over to fetch her.

Penelope rather enjoyed the Bridgerton custom of tea and biscuits in the afternoon. It wasn't a widespread ritual; indeed, Penelope knew of no one else who made a daily habit of it. But Lady Bridgerton insisted that she simply could not last from luncheon to supper, especially not when they were observing town hours and eating so late at night. And thus, every afternoon at four, she and any number of her children (and often a friend or two) met in the informal upstairs drawing room for a snack.

There was drizzle in the air, even though it was a fairly warm day, so Penelope took her black parasol with her for the short walk over to Number Five. It was a route she'd followed hundreds of times before, a few houses down to the corner of Mount and Davies Street, then along the edge of Berkeley Square to Bruton Street. But she was in an odd mood that day, a little bit lighthearted and maybe even a little bit childish, so she decided to cut across the northern corner of the Berkeley Square green for no other reason than she liked the squishy sound her boots made on the wet grass.

It was Lady Danbury's fault. It had to be. She'd been positively giddy since their encounter the night before.

"Not. What. I. Thought. I. Was," she sang to herself as she walked, adding a word every time the soles of her boots sank into the ground. "Something more. Something more."

She reached a particularly wet patch and moved like a skater on the grass, singing (softly, of course; she hadn't changed so much from the night before that she actually wanted someone to hear her singing in public), "Something moooore," as she slid forward.

Which was, of course (since it was fairly well established—in her own mind, at least—that she had the worst timing in the history of civilization), right when she heard a male voice call out her name.

She skidded to a halt and gave fervent thanks that she caught her balance at the very last moment instead of landing on her bottom on the wet and messy grass.

It was, of course, *him*.

"Colin!" she said in a slightly embarrassed voice, holding still as she waited for him to reach her side. "What a surprise."

He looked like he was trying not to smile. "Were you dancing?"

"Dancing?" she echoed.

"It looked like you were dancing."

"Oh. No." She swallowed guiltily, because even though she wasn't technically lying, it felt as if she were. "Of course not."

His eyes crinkled slightly at the corners. "Pity, then. I would have felt compelled to partner you, and I've never danced in Berkeley Square."

If he'd said the same to her just two days earlier, she would have laughed at his joke and let him be the witty and charming one. But she must have heard Lady Danbury's voice at the back of her head again, because she suddenly decided she didn't want to be the same old Penelope Featherington.

She decided to join in the fun.

She smiled a smile she didn't think she'd even known how to smile. It was wicked and she was mysterious, and she knew it wasn't all in her head because Colin's eyes widened markedly as she murmured, "That's a shame. It's rather enjoyable."

"Penelope Featherington," he drawled, "I thought you said you weren't dancing."

She shrugged. "I lied."

"If that's the case," he said, "then surely this must be my dance."

Penelope's insides suddenly felt very queer. This was why she shouldn't let whispers from Lady Danbury go to her head. She might manage daring and charm for a fleeting moment, but she had no idea how to follow through.

Unlike Colin, obviously, who was grinning devilishly as he held his arms out in perfect waltz position.

"Colin," she gasped, "we're in Berkeley Square!"

"I know. I just finished telling you I've never danced here, don't you recall?"

"But—"

Colin crossed his arms. "Tsk. Tsk. You can't issue a dare like that and then try to weasel out of it. Besides, dancing in Berkeley Square seems like the sort of thing a person ought to do at least once in his life, wouldn't you agree?"

"Anyone might see," she whispered urgently.

He shrugged, trying to hide the fact that he was rather entertained by her reaction. "I don't care. Do you?"

Her cheeks grew pink, then red, and it seemed to take her a great deal of effort to form the words, "People will think you are courting me."

He watched her closely, not understanding why she was disturbed. Who cared if people thought they were courting? The rumor would soon be proven false, and they'd have a good laugh at society's expense. It was on the tip of his tongue to say, *Hang society*, but he held silent. There was something lurking deep in the brown depths of her eyes, some emotion he couldn't even begin to identify.

An emotion he suspected he'd never even felt.

And he realized that the last thing he wanted to do was hurt Penelope Featherington. She was his sister's best friend, and moreover, she was, plain and simple, a very nice girl.

He frowned. He supposed he shouldn't be calling her a girl anymore. At eight-and-twenty she was no more a girl than he was still a boy at three-and-thirty.

Finally, with great care and what he hoped was a good dose of sensitivity, he asked, "Is there a reason why we should worry if people think we are courting?"

She closed her eyes, and for a moment Colin actually thought she might be in pain. When she opened them, her gaze was almost bittersweet. "It would be very funny, actually," she said. "At first."

He said nothing, just waited for her to continue.

"But eventually it would become apparent that we are not actually courting, and it would . . ." She stopped, swallowed, and Colin realized that she was not as composed on the inside as she hoped to appear.

"It would be assumed," she continued, "that you were the one to break things off, because—well, it just would be."

He didn't argue with her. He knew that her words were true.

She let out a sad-sounding exhale. "I don't want to subject myself to that. Even Lady Whistledown would probably write about it. How could she not? It would be far too juicy a piece of gossip for her to resist."

"I'm sorry, Penelope," Colin said. He wasn't sure what he was apologizing for, but it still seemed like the right thing to say.

She acknowledged him with a tiny nod. "I know I shouldn't care what other people say, but I do."

He found himself turning slightly away as he considered her

words. Or maybe he was considering the tone of her voice. Or maybe both.

He'd always thought of himself as somewhat above society. Not really outside of it, precisely, since he certainly moved within it and usually enjoyed himself quite a bit. But he'd always assumed that his happiness did not depend upon the opinions of others.

But maybe he wasn't thinking about this the right. way. It was easy to assume that you didn't care about the opinions of others when those opinions were consistently favorable. Would he be so quick to dismiss the rest of society if they treated him the way they treated Penelope?

She'd never been ostracized, never been made the subject of scandal. She just hadn't been . . . popular.

Oh, people were polite, and the Bridgertons had all befriended her, but most of Colin's memories of Penelope involved her standing at the perimeter of a ballroom, trying to look anywhere but at the dancing couples, clearly pretending that she really didn't want to dance. That was usually when he went over and asked her himself. She always looked grateful for the request, but also a little bit embarrassed, because they both knew he was doing it at least a little bit because he felt sorry for her.

Colin tried to put himself in her shoes. It wasn't easy. He'd always been popular; his friends had looked up to him at school and the women had flocked to his side when he'd entered society. And as much as he could say he didn't care what people thought, when it came right down to it . . .

He rather liked being liked.

Suddenly he didn't know what to say. Which was strange, because he *always* knew what to say. In fact, he was somewhat famous for always knowing what to say. It was, he reflected, probably one of the reasons he was so well liked.

But he sensed that Penelope's feelings depended on his next

words, and at some point in the last ten minutes, her feelings had become very important to him.

"You're right," he finally said, deciding that it was always a good idea to tell someone she was correct. "It was very insensitive of me. Perhaps we should start anew?"

She blinked. "I beg your pardon?"

He waved his hand about, as if the motion could explain everything. "Make a fresh start."

She looked quite adorably confused, which confused *him*, since he'd never thought Penelope the least bit adorable.

"But we've known each other for twelve years," she said.

"Has it really been that long?" He searched his brain, but for the life of him, he couldn't recall the event of their first meeting. "Never mind that. I meant just for this afternoon, you ninny."

She smiled, clearly in spite of herself, and he knew that calling her a ninny had been the exact right thing to do, although in all truth he had no idea why.

"Here we go," he said slowly, drawing his words out with a long flourish of his arm. "You are walking across Berkeley Square, and you spy me in the distance. I call out your name, and you reply by saying . . ."

Penelope caught her lower lip between her teeth, trying, for some unknown reason, to contain her smile. What magical star had Colin been born under, that he *always* knew what to say? He was the pied piper, leaving nothing but happy hearts and smiling faces in his wake. Penelope would have bet money—far more than the thousand pounds Lady Danbury had offered up—that she was not the only woman in London desperately in love with the third Bridgerton.

He dipped his head to the side and then righted it in a prompting sort of motion.

"I would reply . . ." Penelope said slowly. "I would reply . . ."

Colin waited two seconds, then said, "Really, any words will do."

Penelope had planned to fix a bright grin on her face, but she discovered that the smile on her lips was quite genuine. "Colin!" she said, trying to sound as if she'd just been surprised by his arrival. "What are you doing about?"

"Excellent reply," he said.

She shook her finger at him. "You're breaking out of character."

"Yes, yes, of course. Apologies." He paused, blinked twice, then said, "Here we are. How about this: Much the same as you, I imagine. Heading to Number Five for tea."

Penelope found herself falling into the rhythm of the conversation. "You sound as if you're just going for a visit. Don't you live there?"

He grimaced. "Hopefully just for the next week. A fortnight at most. I'm trying to find a new place to live. I had to give up the lease on my old set of rooms when I left for Cyprus, and I haven't found a suitable replacement yet. I had a bit of business down on Piccadilly and thought I'd walk back."

"In the rain?"

He shrugged. "It wasn't raining when I left earlier this morning. And even now it's just drizzle."

Just drizzle, Penelope thought. Drizzle that clung to his obscenely long eyelashes, framing eyes of such perfect green that more than one young lady had been moved to write (extremely bad) poetry about them. Even Penelope, levelheaded as she liked to think herself, had spent many a night in bed, staring at the ceiling and seeing nothing but those eyes.

Just drizzle, indeed.

"Penelope?"

She snapped to attention. "Right. Yes. I'm going to your mother's for tea as well. I do so every Monday. And often on other days, too," she admitted. "When there's, er, nothing interesting occurring at my house."

"No need to sound so guilty about it. My mother's a lovely woman. If she wants you over for tea, you should go."

Penelope had a bad habit of trying to hear between the lines of people's conversations, and she had a suspicion that Colin was really saying that he didn't blame her if she wanted to escape her own mother from time to time.

Which somehow, unaccountably, made her feel a little sad.

He rocked on his heels for a moment, then said, "Well, I shouldn't keep you out here in the rain."

She smiled, since they'd been standing outside for at least fifteen minutes. Still, if he wanted to continue with the ruse, she would do so as well. "I'm the one with the parasol," she pointed out.

His lips curved slightly. "So you are. But still, I wouldn't be much of a gentleman if I didn't steer you toward a more hospitable environment. Speaking of which . . ." He frowned, looking around.

"Speaking of what?"

"Of being a gentleman. I believe we're supposed to see to the welfare of ladies."

"And?"

He crossed his arms. "Shouldn't you have a maid with you?"

"I live just around the corner," she said, a little bit deflated that he didn't remember that. She and her sister were best friends with two of his sisters, after all. He'd even walked her home once or twice. "On Mount Street," she added, when his frown did not dissipate.

He squinted slightly, looking in the direction of Mount Street, although she had no idea what he hoped to accomplish by doing so.

"Oh, for heaven's sake, Colin. It's just near the corner of Davies Street. It can't be more than a five-minute walk to your mother's. Four, if I'm feeling exceptionally sprightly."

"I was just looking to see if there were any darkened or recessed spots." He turned back to face her. "Where a criminal might lurk."

"In *Mayfair*?"

"In Mayfair," he said grimly. "I really think you ought to have a maid accompany you when you journey to and fro. I should hate for something to happen to you."

She was oddly touched by his concern, even though she knew he would have extended equal thoughtfulness to just about every female of his acquaintance. That was simply the sort of man he was.

"I can assure you that I observe all of the usual proprieties when I am traveling longer distances," she said. "But truly, this is so close. Just a few blocks, really. Even my mother doesn't mind."

Colin's jaw suddenly looked quite stiff.

"Not to mention," Penelope added, "that I am eight-and-twenty."

"What has that to do with anything? I am three-and-thirty, if you care to know."

She knew that, of course, since she knew almost everything about him. "Colin," she said, a slightly annoyed whine creeping into her voice.

"Penelope," he replied, in exactly the same tone.

She let out a long exhale before saying, "I am quite firmly on the shelf, Colin. I needn't worry about all of the rules that plagued me when I was seventeen."

"I hardly think—"

One of Penelope's hands planted itself on her hip. "Ask your sister if you don't believe me."

He suddenly looked more serious than she had ever seen him. "I make it a point not to ask my sister on matters that relate to common sense."

"Colin!" Penelope exclaimed. "That's a terrible thing to say."

"I didn't say I don't love her. I didn't even say I don't like her. I adore Eloise, as you well know. However—"

"Anything that begins with *however* has got to be bad," Penelope muttered.

"Eloise," he said with uncharacteristic high-handedness, "should be married by now."

Now, *that* was really too much, especially in that tone of voice.

"Some might say," Penelope returned with a self-righteous little tilt of her chin, "that you should be married by now, too."

"Oh, pl—"

"You are, as you so proudly informed me, three-and-thirty."

His expression was slightly amused, but with that pale tinge of irritation which told her he would not remain amused for long. "Penelope, don't even—"

"Ancient!" she chirped.

He swore under his breath, which surprised her, since she didn't think she'd ever heard him do so in the presence of a lady. She probably should have taken it as a warning, but she was too riled up. She supposed the old saying was true—courage spawned more courage.

Or maybe it was more that recklessness emboldened more recklessness, because she just looked at him archly and said, "Weren't both of your older brothers married by the age of thirty?"

To her surprise, Colin merely smiled and crossed his arms as he leaned one shoulder against the tree they were standing beneath. "My brothers and I are very different men."

It was, Penelope realized, a very telling statement, because so many members of the *ton*, including the fabled Lady Whistledown, made so much of the fact that the Bridgerton brothers looked so alike. Some had even gone so far as to call them interchangeable. Penelope hadn't thought any of them were bothered by this—in fact, she'd assumed they'd all felt flattered by the comparison, since they seemed to like each other so well. But maybe she was wrong.

Or maybe she'd never looked closely enough.

Which was rather strange, because she felt as if she'd spent half her life watching Colin Bridgerton.

One thing she did know, however, and should have remembered, was that if Colin had any sort of a temper, he had never chosen to let her see it. Surely she'd flattered herself when she thought that her little quip about his brothers marrying before they turned thirty might set him off.

No, his method of attack was a lazy smile, a well-timed joke. If Colin ever lost his temper . . .

Penelope shook her head slightly, unable even to fathom it. Colin would never lose his temper. At least not in front of her. He'd have to be really, truly—no, *profoundly*—upset to lose his temper. And that kind of fury could only be sparked by someone you really, truly, *profoundly* cared about.

Colin liked her well enough—maybe even better than he liked most people—but he didn't *care*. Not that way.

"Perhaps we should just agree to disagree," she finally said.

"On what?"

"Er . . ." She couldn't remember. "Er, on what a spinster may or may not do?"

He seemed amused by her hesitation. "That would probably require that I defer to my younger sister's judgment in some capacity, which would be, as I'm sure you can imagine, very difficult for me."

"But you don't mind deferring to *my* judgment?"

His smile was lazy and wicked. "Not if you promise not to tell another living soul."

He didn't mean it, of course. And she knew he knew she knew he didn't mean it. But that was his way. Humor and a smile could smooth any path. And blast him, it worked, because she heard herself sighing and felt herself smiling, and before she knew it she was saying, "Enough! Let us be on our way to your mother's."

Colin grinned. "Do you think she'll have biscuits?"

Penelope rolled her eyes. "I *know* she'll have biscuits."

"Good," he said, taking off at a lope and half dragging her with him. "I do love my family, but I really just go for the food."

Chapter 4

It is difficult to imagine that there is any news from the Bridgerton ball other than Lady Danbury's determination to discern the identity of This Author, but the following items should be duly noted:

Mr. Geoffrey Albansdale was seen dancing with Miss Felicity Featherington.

Miss Felicity Featherington was also seen dancing with Mr. Lucas Hotchkiss.

Mr. Lucas Hotchkiss was also seen dancing with Miss Hyacinth Bridgerton.

Miss Hyacinth Bridgerton was also seen dancing with Viscount Burwick.

Viscount Burwick was also seen dancing with Miss Jane Hotchkiss.

Miss Jane Hotchkiss was also seen dancing with Mr. Colin Bridgerton.

Mr. Colin Bridgerton was also seen dancing with Miss Penelope Featherington.

And to round out this incestuous little ring-around-the-rosy, Miss Penelope Featherington was seen speaking with Mr. Geoffrey Albansdale. (It would have been too perfect if she'd actually danced with him, don't you agree, Dear Reader?)

LADY WHISTLEDOWN'S SOCIETY PAPERS,
12 April 1824

When Penelope and Colin entered the drawing room, Eloise and Hyacinth were already sipping tea, along with both of the Ladies Bridgerton. Violet, the dowager, was seated in front of a tea service, and Kate, her daughter-in-law and the wife of Anthony, the current viscount, was attempting, without much success, to control her two-year-old daughter Charlotte.

"Look who I bumped into in Berkeley Square," Colin said.

"Penelope," Lady Bridgerton said with a warm smile, "do sit down. The tea is still nice and hot, and Cook made her famous butter biscuits."

Colin made a beeline for the food, barely pausing to acknowledge his sisters.

Penelope followed Lady Bridgerton's wave to a nearby chair and took a seat.

"Biscuits are good," Hyacinth said, thrusting a plate in her direction.

"Hyacinth," Lady Bridgerton said in a vaguely disapproving voice, "do try to speak in complete sentences."

Hyacinth looked at her mother with a surprised expression. "Biscuits. Are. Good." She cocked her head to the side. "Noun. Verb. Adjective."

"Hyacinth."

Penelope could see that Lady Bridgerton was trying to look stern as she scolded her daughter, but she wasn't quite succeeding.

"Noun. Verb. Adjective," Colin said, wiping a crumb from his grinning face. "Sentence. Is. Correct."

"If you're barely literate," Kate retorted, reaching for a biscuit.

"These *are* good," she said to Penelope, a sheepish smile crossing her face. "This one's my fourth."

"I love you, Colin," Hyacinth said, ignoring Kate completely.

"Of course you do," he murmured.

"I myself," Eloise said archly, "prefer to place articles before my nouns in my own writings."

Hyacinth snorted. "Your *writings*?" she echoed.

"I write many letters," Eloise said with a sniff. "And I keep a journal, which I assure you is a very beneficial habit."

"It does keep one disciplined," Penelope put in, taking her cup and saucer from Lady Bridgerton's outstretched hands.

"Do you keep a journal?" Kate asked, not really looking at her, since she had just jumped up from her chair to grasp her daughter before the two-year-old climbed on a side table.

"I'm afraid not," Penelope said with a shake of her head. "It requires far too much discipline for me."

"I don't think it is always necessary to put an article before a noun," Hyacinth persisted, completely unable, as always, to let her side of the argument go.

Unfortunately for the rest of the assemblage, Eloise was equally tenacious. "You may leave off the article if you are referring to your noun in a general sense," she said, pursing her lips in a rather supercilious manner, "but in this case, as you were referring to *specific* biscuits . . ."

Penelope wasn't positive, but she thought she heard Lady Bridgerton groan.

". . . then specifically," Eloise said with an arch of her brows, "you are incorrect."

Hyacinth turned to Penelope. "I am positive she did not use *specifically* correctly in that last sentence."

Penelope reached for another butter biscuit. "I refuse to enter the conversation."

"Coward," Colin murmured.

"No, just hungry." Penelope turned to Kate. "These *are* good."

Kate nodded her agreement. "I have heard rumors," she said to Penelope, "that your sister may become betrothed."

Penelope blinked in surprise. She hadn't thought that Felicity's connection to Mr. Albansdale was public knowledge. "Er, where have you heard rumors?"

"Eloise, of course," Kate said matter-of-factly. "She always knows everything."

"And what I don't know," Eloise said with an easy grin, "Hyacinth usually does. It's very convenient."

"Are you certain that neither one of you is Lady Whistledown?" Colin joked.

"Colin!" Lady Bridgerton exclaimed. "How could you even think such a thing?"

He shrugged. "They're certainly both smart enough to carry off such a feat."

Eloise and Hyacinth beamed.

Even Lady Bridgerton couldn't quite dismiss the compliment. "Yes, well," she hemmed, "Hyacinth is much too young, and Eloise . . ." She looked over at Eloise, who was watching her with a most amused expression. "Well, Eloise is not Lady Whistledown. I'm sure of it."

Eloise looked at Colin. "I'm not Lady Whistledown."

"That's too bad," he replied. "You'd be filthy rich by now, I imagine."

"You know," Penelope said thoughtfully, "that might be a good way to discern her identity."

Five pairs of eyes turned in her direction.

"She has to be someone who has more money than she ought to have," Penelope explained.

"A good point," Hyacinth said, "except that I haven't a clue how much money people ought to have."

"Neither do I, of course," Penelope replied. "But most of the time one has a *general* idea." At Hyacinth's blank stare, she added, "For example, if I suddenly went out and bought myself a diamond parure, that would be very suspect."

Kate nudged Penelope with her elbow. "Bought any diamond parures lately, eh? I could use a thousand pounds."

Penelope let her eyes roll up for a second before replying, because as the current Viscountess Bridgerton, Kate most certainly did not need a thousand pounds. "I can assure you," she said, "I don't own a single diamond. Not even a ring."

Kate let out an "euf" of mock disgruntlement. "Well, you're no help, then."

"It's not so much the money," Hyacinth announced. "It's the glory."

Lady Bridgerton coughed on her tea. "I'm sorry, Hyacinth," she said, "but *what* did you just say?"

"Think of the accolades one would receive for having finally caught Lady Whistledown," Hyacinth said. "It would be glorious."

"Are you saying," Colin asked, a deceptively bland expression on his face, "that you don't care about the money?"

"I would never say *that*," Hyacinth said with a cheeky grin.

It occurred to Penelope that of all the Bridgertons, Hyacinth and Colin were the most alike. It was probably a good thing Colin was so often out of the country. If he and Hyacinth ever joined forces in earnest, they could probably take over the world.

"Hyacinth," Lady Bridgerton said firmly, "you are *not* to make the search for Lady Whistledown your life's work."

"But—"

"I'm not saying you cannot ponder the problem and ask a few questions," Lady Bridgerton hastened to add, holding up one hand to ward off further interruptions. "Good gracious, I would hope that after nearly forty years of motherhood I would know better than to try to stop you when you have your mind quite so set on something, nonsense as it may be."

Penelope brought her teacup to her mouth to cover her smile.

"It's just that you have been known to be rather"—Lady Bridgerton delicately cleared her throat—"single-minded at times . . ."

"Mother!"

Lady Bridgerton continued as if Hyacinth had never spoken. ". . . and I do not want you to forget that your primary focus at this time must be to look for a husband."

Hyacinth uttered the word "Mother" again, but this time it was more of a groan than a protest.

Penelope stole a glance at Eloise, who had her eyes fixed on the ceiling and was clearly trying not to break out in a grin. Eloise had endured years of relentless matchmaking at her mother's hands and did not mind in the least that she seemed to have given up and moved on to Hyacinth.

In truth, Penelope was surprised that Lady Bridgerton seemed to have finally accepted Eloise's unmarried state. She had never hidden the fact that her greatest aim in life was to see all eight of her children happily married. And she'd succeeded with four. First Daphne had married Simon and become the Duchess of Hastings. The following year Anthony had married Kate. There had been a bit of a lull after that, but both Benedict and Francesca had married within a year of each other, Benedict to Sophie, and Francesca to the Scottish Earl of Kilmartin.

Francesca, unfortunately, had been widowed only two years after her marriage. She now divided her time between her late husband's family in Scotland and her own in London. When in town, however, she insisted upon living at Kilmartin House instead of at Bridgerton House or Number Five. Penelope didn't blame her. If she were a widow, she'd want to enjoy all of her independence, too.

Hyacinth generally bore her mother's matchmaking with good humor since, as she had told Penelope, it wasn't as if she didn't want to get married eventually. Might as well let her mother do all the work and then she could choose a husband when the right one presented himself.

And it was with this good humor that she stood, kissed her mother on the cheek, and dutifully promised that her main focus in life was to look for a husband—all the while directing a cheeky, sneaky smile at her brother and sister. She was barely back in her seat when she said to the crowd at large, "So, do you think she'll be caught?"

"Are we still discussing that Whistledown woman?" Lady Bridgerton groaned.

"Have you not heard Eloise's theory, then?" Penelope asked.

All eyes turned to Penelope, then to Eloise.

"Er, what *is* my theory?" Eloise asked.

"It was just, oh, I don't know, maybe a week ago," Penelope said. "We were talking about Lady Whistledown, and I said that I didn't see how she could possibly go on forever, that eventually she would have to make a mistake. Then Eloise said she wasn't so sure, that it had been over ten years and if she were going to make a mistake, wouldn't she have already done so? Then I said, no, she was only human. Eventually she would have to slip up, because no one could go on forever, and—"

"Oh, I remember now!" Eloise cut in. "We were at your house, in your room. I had the most brilliant idea! I said to Penelope that I would wager that Lady Whistledown has already made a mistake, and it's just *we* were too stupid to have noticed it."

"Not very complimentary for us, I must say," Colin murmured.

"Well, I did intend *we* to mean all of society, not just us Bridgertons," Eloise demurred.

"So maybe," Hyacinth mused, "all I need to do to catch Lady Whistledown is peruse back issues of her column."

Lady Bridgerton's eyes filled with a mild panic. "Hyacinth Bridgerton, I don't like the look on your face."

Hyacinth smiled and shrugged. "I could have a great deal of fun with one thousand pounds."

"God help us all," was her mother's reply.

"Penelope," Colin said quite suddenly, "you never did finish telling us about Felicity. Is it true that she is to be engaged?"

Penelope gulped down the tea she'd been in the process of sipping. Colin had a way of looking at a person, his green eyes so focused and intent that you felt as if you must be the only two people in the universe. Unfortunately for Penelope, it also seemed to have a way of reducing her to a stammering imbecile. If they were in the midst of conversation, she could generally hold her own, but when he surprised her like that, turning his attention onto her just when she'd convinced herself she blended in perfectly with the wallpaper, she was completely and utterly lost.

"Er, yes, it is quite possible," she said. "Mr. Albansdale has been hinting at his intentions. But if he does decide to propose, I imagine he will travel to East Anglia to ask my uncle for her hand."

"Your uncle?" Kate asked.

"My uncle Geoffrey. He lives near Norwich. He's our closest male relative, although truth be told, we don't see him very often. But Mr. Albansdale is rather traditional. I don't think he would feel comfortable asking my mother."

"I hope he asks Felicity as well," Eloise said. "I've often thought it foolish that a man asks a woman's father for her hand before he asks her. The father doesn't have to live with him."

"This attitude," Colin said with an amused smile that was only partly hidden by his teacup, "may explain why you are as yet unmarried."

Lady Bridgerton gave her son a stern glare and said his name disapprovingly.

"Oh, no, Mother," Eloise said, "I don't mind. I'm perfectly comfortable as an old maid." She gave Colin a rather superior look. "I'd much rather be a spinster than be married to a bore. As," she added with a flourish, "would Penelope!"

Startled by Eloise's hand waving rather suddenly in her direction, Penelope straightened her spine and said, "Er, yes. Of course."

But Penelope had a feeling she wasn't quite as firm in her convictions as her friend. Unlike Eloise, she hadn't refused six offers of marriage. She hadn't refused any; she hadn't received even a one.

She'd told herself that she wouldn't have accepted in any case, since her heart belonged to Colin. But was that really the truth, or was she just trying to make herself feel better for having been such a resounding failure on the marriage mart?

If someone asked her to marry him tomorrow—someone perfectly kind and acceptable, whom she might never love but would in all probability like very well—would she say yes?

Probably.

And this made her melancholy, because admitting this to herself meant she'd really, truly given up hope on Colin. It meant she wasn't as true to her principles as she'd hoped she was. It meant she was willing to settle on a less-than-perfect husband in order to have a home and family of her own.

It wasn't anything that hundreds of women didn't do every year, but it was something that she'd never thought she'd do herself.

"You look very serious all of a sudden," Colin said to her.

Penelope jerked out of her musings. "Me? Oh. No, no. I just lost myself in my thoughts, that's all."

Colin acknowledged her statement with a brief nod before reaching for another biscuit. "Have we anything more substantial?" he asked, wrinkling his nose.

"If I'd known you were coming," his mother said in a dry voice, "I would have doubled the food."

He stood and walked to the bellpull. "I'll ring for more." After giving it a yank, he turned back and asked, "Did you hear about Penelope's Lady Whistledown theory?"

"No, I haven't," Lady Bridgerton replied.

"It's very clever, actually," Colin said, stopping to ask a maid for sandwiches before finishing with, "She thinks it's Lady Danbury."

"Ooooh." Hyacinth was visibly impressed. "That's very cunning, Penelope."

Penelope nodded her head to the side in thanks.

"And just the sort of thing Lady Danbury would do," Hyacinth added.

"The column or the challenge?" Kate asked, catching hold of the sash on Charlotte's frock before the little girl could scramble out of reach.

"Both," Hyacinth said.

"And," Eloise put in, "Penelope told her so. Right to her face."

Hyacinth's mouth dropped open, and it was obvious to Penelope that she'd just gone up—way up—in Hyacinth's estimation.

"I should have liked to have seen that!" Lady Bridgerton said with a wide, proud smile. "Frankly, I'm surprised that didn't show up in this morning's *Whistledown*."

"I hardly think Lady Whistledown would comment upon individual people's theories as to her identity," Penelope said.

"Why not?" Hyacinth asked. "It would be an excellent way for her to set out a few red herrings. For example"—she held her hand out toward her sister in a most dramatic pose—"say I thought it was Eloise."

"It is not Eloise!" Lady Bridgerton protested.

"It's not me," Eloise said with a grin.

"But say I *thought* it was," Hyacinth said in an extremely beleaguered voice. "And that I said so publicly."

"Which you would never do," her mother said sternly.

"Which I would never do," Hyacinth parroted. "But just to be academic, let us pretend that I did. And say that Eloise really was Lady Whistledown. Which she's not," she hastened to add before her mother could interrupt again.

Lady Bridgerton held up her hands in silent defeat.

"What better way to fool the masses," Hyacinth continued, "than to make fun of me in her column?"

"Of course, if Lady Whistledown really *were* Eloise . . ." Penelope mused.

"She's not!" Lady Bridgerton burst out.

Penelope couldn't help but laugh. "But if she were . . ."

"You know," Eloise said, "now I *really* wish I were."

"What a joke you'd be having on us all," Penelope continued. "Of course, then on Wednesday you couldn't run a column making fun of Hyacinth for thinking you are Lady Whistledown, because then we'd all know it had to be you."

"Unless it was *you*." Kate laughed, looking at Penelope. "*That* would be a devious trick."

"Let me see if I have it straight," Eloise said with a laugh. "Penelope is Lady Whistledown, and she is going to run a column on Wednesday making fun of Hyacinth's theory that *I'm* Lady Whistledown just to trick you into thinking that I really *am* Lady Whistledown, because Hyacinth suggested that that would be a cunning ruse."

"I am utterly lost," Colin said to no one in particular.

"Unless *Colin* were really Lady Whistledown . . ." Hyacinth said with a devilish gleam in her eye.

"Stop!" Lady Bridgerton said. "I beg you."

By then everyone was laughing too hard for Hyacinth to continue, anyway.

"The possibilities are endless," Hyacinth said, wiping a tear from her eye.

"Perhaps we should all simply look to the left," Colin suggested as he sat back down. "Who knows, that person may very well be our infamous Lady Whistledown."

Everyone looked left, with the exception of Eloise, who looked right . . . right to Colin. "Were you trying to tell me something," she asked with an amused smile, "when you sat down to my right?"

"Not at all," he murmured, reaching for the biscuit plate and then stopping when he remembered it was empty.

But he didn't quite meet Eloise's eyes when he said so.

If anyone other than Penelope had noticed his evasiveness, they were unable to question him on it, because that was when the sandwiches arrived, and he was useless for conversation after that.

Chapter 5

It has come to This Author's attention that Lady Blackwood turned her ankle earlier this week whilst chasing down a delivery boy for This Humble Newssheet.

One thousand pounds is certainly a great deal of money, but Lady Blackwood is hardly in need of funds, and moreover, the situation is growing absurd. Surely Londoners have better things to do with their time than chase down poor, hapless delivery boys in a fruitless attempt to uncover the identity of This Author.

Or maybe not.

This Author has chronicled the activities of the ton *for over a decade now and has found no evidence that they do indeed have anything better to do with their time.*

LADY WHISTLEDOWN'S SOCIETY PAPERS,
14 April 1824

Two days later Penelope found herself once again cutting across Berkeley Square, on her way to Number Five to see Eloise. This time, however, it was late morning, and it was sunny, and she did not bump into Colin along the way.

Penelope wasn't sure if that was a bad thing or not.

She and Eloise had made plans the week before to go shopping, but they'd decided to meet at Number Five so that they could head out together and forgo the accompaniment of their maids. It was a perfect sort of day, far more like June than April, and Penelope was looking forward to the short walk up to Oxford Street.

But when she arrived at Eloise's house, she was met with a puzzled expression on the butler's face.

"Miss Featherington," he said, blinking several times in rapid succession before locating a few more words. "I don't believe Miss Eloise is here at present."

Penelope's lips parted in surprise. "Where did she go? We made our plans over a week ago."

Wickham shook his head. "I do not know. But she departed with her mother and Miss Hyacinth two hours earlier."

"I see." Penelope frowned, trying to decide what to do. "May I wait, then? Perhaps she was merely delayed. It's not like Eloise to forget an appointment."

He nodded graciously and showed her upstairs to the informal drawing room, promising to bring a plate of refreshments and handing her the latest edition of *Whistledown* to read while she bided her time.

Penelope had already read it, of course; it was delivered quite early in the morning, and she made a habit of perusing the column at breakfast. With so little to occupy her mind, she wandered over to the window and peered out over the Mayfair streetscape. But there wasn't much new to see; it was the same buildings she'd seen a thousand times before, even the same people walking along the street.

Maybe it was because she was pondering the sameness of her life that she noticed the one object new to her vista: a bound book lying open on the table. Even from several feet away she could see that it was filled not with the printed word, but rather with neat handwritten lines.

She inched toward it and glanced down without actually touching the pages. It appeared to be a journal of sorts, and in the middle of the right-hand side there was a heading that was set apart from the rest of the text by a bit of space above and below:

22 February 1824
Troodos Mountains, Cyprus

One of her hands flew to her mouth. Colin had written this! He'd said just the other day that he'd visited Cyprus instead of Greece. She had no idea that he kept a journal.

She lifted a foot to take a step back, but her body didn't budge. She shouldn't read this, she told herself. This was Colin's private journal. She really ought to move away.

"Away," she muttered, looking down at her recalcitrant feet. "Away."

Her feet didn't move.

But maybe she wasn't quite so in the wrong. After all, was she really invading his privacy if she read only what she could see without turning a page? He *had* left it lying open on the table, for all the world to see.

But then again, Colin had every reason to think that no one would stumble across his journal if he dashed out for a few moments. Presumably, he was aware that his mother and sisters had departed for the morning. Most guests were shown to the formal drawing room on the ground floor; as far as Penelope knew, she and Felicity were the only non-Bridgertons who were taken straight up to the informal drawing room. And since Colin wasn't expecting her (or, more likely, hadn't thought of her one way or another), he wouldn't have thought there was any danger in leaving his journal behind while he ran an errand.

On the other hand, he *had* left it lying open.

Open, for heaven's sake! If there were any valuable secrets in that journal, surely Colin would have taken greater care to secret it when he left the room. He wasn't stupid, after all.

Penelope leaned forward.

Oh, bother. She couldn't read the writing from that distance. The heading had been legible since it was surrounded by so much white space, but the rest was a bit too close together to make out from far away.

Somehow she'd thought she wouldn't feel so guilty if she didn't have to step any closer to the book to read it. Never mind, of course, that she'd already crossed the room to get to where she was at that moment.

She tapped her finger against the side of her jaw, right near her ear. That was a good point. She had crossed the room some time ago, which surely meant that she'd already committed the biggest sin she was likely to that day. One little step was nothing compared to the length of the room.

She inched forward, decided that only counted as half a step, then inched forward again and looked down, beginning her reading right in the middle of a sentence.

> *in England. Here the sand ripples between tan and white, and the consistency is so fine that it slides over a bare foot like a whisper of silk. The water is a blue unimaginable in England, aquamarine with the glint of the sun, deep cobalt when the clouds take the sky. And it is warm—surprisingly, astoundingly warm, like a bath that was heated perhaps a half an hour earlier. The waves are gentle, and they lap up on the shore with a soft rush of foam, tickling the skin and turning the perfect sand into a squishy delight that slips and slides along the toes until another wave arrives to clean up the mess.*
>
> *It is easy to see why this is said to be the birthplace of Aphrodite. With every step I almost expect to see her as in Botticelli's painting,*

rising from the ocean, perfectly balanced on a giant shell, her long titian hair streaming around her.

If ever a perfect woman was born, surely this would be the place. I am in paradise. And yet . . .

And yet with every warm breeze and cloudless sky I am reminded that this is not my home, that I was born to live my life elsewhere. This does not quell the desire—no, the compulsion!— to travel, to see, to meet. But it does feed a strange longing to touch a dew-dampened lawn, or feel a cool mist on one's face, or even to remember the joy of a perfect day after a week of rain.

The people here can't know that joy. Their days are always perfect. Can one appreciate perfection when it is a constant in one's life?

> *22 February 1824*
> *Troodos Mountains, Cyprus*

It is remarkable that I am cold. It is, of course, February, and as an Englishman I'm quite used to a February chill (as well as that of any month with an R in its name), but I am not in England. I am in Cyprus, in the heart of the Mediterranean, and just two days ago I was in Paphos, on the southwest coast of the island, where the sun is strong and the ocean salty and warm. Here, one can see the peak of Mount Olympus, still capped with snow so white one is temporarily blinded when the sun glints off of it.

The climb to this altitude was treacherous, with danger lurking around more than one corner. The road is rudimentary, and along the way we met

Penelope let out a soft grunt of protest when she realized that the page ended in the middle of a sentence. Who had he met? What had happened? *What danger?*

She stared down at the journal, absolutely *dying* to flip the page and see what happened next. But when she'd started reading, she had managed to justify it by telling herself she wasn't really invading Colin's privacy; he'd left the book open, after all. She was only looking at what he had left exposed.

Turning the page, however, was something else altogether.

She reached out, then yanked her hand back. This wasn't right. She couldn't read his journal. Well, not beyond what she'd already read.

On the other hand, it was clear that these were words worth reading. It was a crime for Colin to keep them for himself. Words should be celebrated, shared. They should be—

"Oh, for God's sake," she muttered to herself. She reached for the edge of the page.

"What are you doing?"

Penelope whirled around. "Colin!"

"Indeed," he snapped.

Penelope lurched back. She'd never heard him use such a tone. She hadn't even thought him capable of it.

He strode across the room, grabbed the journal, and snapped it shut. "What are you doing here?" he demanded.

"Waiting for Eloise," she managed to get out, her mouth suddenly quite dry.

"In the upstairs drawing room?"

"Wickham always takes me here. Your mother told him to treat me like family. I . . . uh . . . he . . . uh . . ." She realized that she was wringing her hands together and willed herself to stop. "It's the same with my sister Felicity. Because she and Hyacinth are such good friends. I—I'm sorry. I thought you knew."

He threw the leather-bound book carelessly onto a nearby chair and crossed his arms. "And do you make a habit of reading the personal letters of others?"

"No, of course not. But it was open and—" She gulped, recognizing how awful the excuse sounded the second the words left her lips. "It's a public room," she mumbled, somehow feeling like she had to finish her defense. "Maybe you should have taken it with you."

"Where I went," he ground out, still visibly furious with her, "one doesn't ordinarily take a book."

"It's not very big," she said, wondering why why *why* she was still talking when she was so clearly in the wrong.

"For the love of God," he exploded. "Do you *want* me to say the word *chamberpot* in your presence?"

Penelope felt her cheeks blush deep red. "I'd better go," she said. "Please tell Eloise—"

"*I'll* go," Colin practically snarled. "I'm moving out this afternoon, anyway. Might as well leave now, since you've so obviously taken over the house."

Penelope had never thought that words could cause physical pain, but right then she would have sworn that she'd taken a knife to the heart. She hadn't realized until that very moment just how much it meant to her that Lady Bridgerton had opened her home to her.

Or how much it would hurt to know that Colin resented her presence there.

"Why do you have to make it so difficult to apologize?" she burst out, dogging his heels as he crossed the room to gather the rest of his things.

"And why, pray tell, should I make it easy?" he returned. He didn't face her as he said it; he didn't even break his stride.

"Because it would be the nice thing to do," she ground out.

That got his attention. He whirled around, his eyes flashing so furiously that Penelope stumbled back a step. Colin was the nice one, the easygoing one. He didn't lose his temper.

Until now.

"Because it would be the nice thing to do?" he thundered. "Is that what you were thinking when you read my journal? That it would be a nice thing to read someone's private papers?"

"No, Colin, I—"

"There is nothing you can say—" he said, jabbing her in the shoulder with his index finger.

"Colin! You—"

He turned around to gather his belongings, rudely giving her his back while he spoke. "Not a thing that could justify your behavior."

"No, of course not, but—"

"OW!"

Penelope felt the blood drain from her face. Colin's yell was one of real pain. His name escaped her lips in a panicked whisper and she rushed to his side. "What's—Oh, my heavens!"

Blood was gushing from a wound on the palm of his hand.

Never terribly articulate in a crisis, Penelope managed to say, "Oh! Oh! The carpet!" before leaping forward with a piece of writing paper that had been lying on a nearby table and sliding it under his hand to catch the blood before it ruined the priceless carpet below.

"Ever the attentive nurse," Colin said in a shaky voice.

"Well, you're not going to die," she explained, "and the carpet—"

"It's all right," he assured her. "I was trying to make a joke."

Penelope looked up at his face. Tight white lines were etched in the skin around his mouth, and he looked very pale. "I think you'd better sit down," she said.

He nodded grimly and sagged into a chair.

Penelope's stomach did a rather seasickish sway. She'd never been terribly good with blood. "Maybe I'd better sit down, too," she mumbled, sinking onto the low table opposite him.

"Are you going to be all right?" he asked.

She nodded, swallowing against a tiny wave of nausea. "We need to find something to wrap this," she said, grimacing as she looked down at the ridiculous setup below. The paper wasn't absorbent, and the blood was rolling precariously along its surface, with Penelope desperately trying to keep it from dripping over the side.

"I have a handkerchief in my pocket," he said.

She carefully set the paper down and retrieved the handkerchief from his breast pocket, trying not to notice the warm beat of his heart as her fingers fumbled for the creamy white scrap of cloth. "Does it hurt?" she asked as she wrapped it around his hand. "No, don't answer that. Of course it hurts."

He managed a very wobbly smile. "It hurts."

She peered down at the gash, forcing herself to look at it closely even though the blood made her stomach turn. "I don't think you'll need stitches."

"Do you know much about wounds?"

She shook her head. "Nothing. But it doesn't look too bad. Except for . . . ah, all the blood."

"Feels worse than it looks," he joked.

Her eyes flew to his face in horror.

"Another joke," he reassured her. "Well, not really. It *does* feel worse than it looks, but I assure you it's bearable."

"I'm sorry," she said, increasing pressure on the wound to staunch the flow of blood. "This is all my fault."

"That I sliced open my hand?"

"If you hadn't been so angry . . ."

He just shook his head, closing his eyes briefly against the pain. "Don't be silly, Penelope. If I hadn't gotten angry with you, I would have gotten angry with someone else some other time."

"And you'd of course have a letter opener by your side when that happened," she murmured, looking up at him through her lashes as she bent over his hand.

When his eyes met hers, they were filled with humor and maybe just a touch of admiration.

And something else she'd never thought to see—vulnerability, hesitancy, and even insecurity. He didn't know how good his writing was, she realized with amazement. He had no idea, and he was actually embarrassed that she'd seen it.

"Colin," Penelope said, instinctively pressing harder on his wound as she leaned in, "I must tell you. You—"

She broke off when she heard the sharp, even clatter of footsteps coming down the hall. "That will be Wickham," she said, glancing toward the door. "He insisted upon bringing me a small meal. Can you keep the pressure on this for now?"

Colin nodded. "I don't want him to know I've hurt myself. He'll only tell Mother, and then I'll never hear the end of it."

"Well, here, then." She stood and tossed him his journal. "Pretend you're reading this."

Colin barely had time to open it and lay it across his injured hand before the butler entered with a large tray.

"Wickham!" Penelope said, jumping to her feet and turning to face him as if she hadn't already known he was coming. "As usual you've brought far more than I could possibly eat. Luckily, Mr. Bridgerton has been keeping me company. I'm certain that with his help, I'll be able to do justice to your meal."

Wickham nodded and removed the covers from the serving dishes. It was a cold repast—pieces of meat, cheese, and fruit, accompanied by a tall pitcher of lemonade.

Penelope smiled brightly. "I hope you didn't think I could eat all of this myself."

"Lady Bridgerton and her daughters are expected soon. I thought they might be hungry as well."

"Won't be any left after I'm through with it," Colin said with a jovial smile.

Wickham bowed slightly in his direction. "If I'd known you were here, Mr. Bridgerton, I would have trebled the portions. Would you like me to fix you a plate?"

"No, no," Colin said, waving his uninjured hand. "I'll get up just as soon as I . . . ah . . . finish reading this chapter."

The butler said, "Let me know if you require further assistance," and exited the room.

"Aaaaaahhh," Colin groaned, the moment he heard Wickham's steps disappear down the hall. "Damn—I mean, dash it—it hurts."

Penelope plucked a napkin off the tray. "Here, let's replace that handkerchief." She peeled it away from his skin, keeping her eyes on the cloth rather than the wound. For some reason that didn't seem to bother her stomach quite as much. "I'm afraid your handkerchief is ruined."

Colin just closed his eyes and shook his head. Penelope was smart enough to interpret the action to mean, *I don't care.* And she was sensible enough not to say anything further on the subject. Nothing worse than a female who chattered forever about nothing.

He'd always liked Penelope, but how was it he'd never realized how intelligent she was up till now? Oh, he supposed if someone had asked him, he would have said she was bright, but he'd certainly never taken the time to think about it.

It was becoming clear to him, however, that she was very intelligent, indeed. And he thought he remembered his sister once telling him that she was an avid reader.

And probably a discriminating one as well.

"I think the bleeding is slowing down," she was saying as she wrapped the fresh napkin around his hand. "In fact, I'm sure it is, if only because I don't feel quite so sick every time I look at the wound."

He wished that she hadn't read his journal, but now that she *had* . . .

"Ah, Penelope," he began, startled by the hesitancy in his own voice.

She looked up. "I'm sorry. Am I pressing too hard?"

For a moment Colin did nothing but blink. How was it possible he'd never noticed how big her eyes were? He'd known they were brown, of course, and . . . No, come to think of it, if he were to be honest with himself, he would have to admit that if asked earlier this morning, he'd not have been able to identify the color of her eyes.

But somehow he knew that he'd never forget again.

She eased up on the pressure. "Is this all right?"

He nodded. "Thank you. I would do it myself, but it's my right hand, and—"

"Say no more. It's the very least I can do, after . . . after . . ." Her eyes slid slightly to the side, and he knew she was about to apologize another time.

"Penelope," he began again.

"No, wait!" she cried out, her dark eyes flashing with . . . could it be passion? Certainly not the brand of passion with which he was most familiar. But there were other sorts, weren't there? Passion for learning. Passion for . . . literature?

"I must tell you this," she said urgently. "I know it was unforgivably intrusive of me to look at your journal. I was just . . . bored . . . and waiting . . . and I had nothing to do, and then I saw the book and I was curious."

He opened his mouth to interrupt her, to tell her that what was done was done, but the words were rushing from her mouth, and he found himself oddly compelled to listen.

"I should have stepped away the moment I realized what it was," she continued, "but as soon as I read one sentence I had to read another! Colin, it was wonderful! It was just like I was there. I could feel the water—I knew exactly the temperature. It was so clever of you to describe it the way you did. Everyone knows exactly what a bath feels like a half an hour after it has been filled."

For a moment Colin could do nothing but stare at her. He'd never seen Penelope quite so animated, and it was strange and . . . good, really, that all that excitement was over his journal.

"You—you liked it?" he finally asked.

"Liked it? Colin, I loved it! I—"

"Ow!"

In her excitement, she'd started squeezing his hand a bit too hard.

"Oh, sorry," she said perfunctorily. "Colin, I really must know. What was the danger? I couldn't bear to be left hanging like that."

"It was nothing," he said modestly. "The page you read really wasn't a very exciting passage."

"No, it was mostly description," she agreed, "but the description was very compelling and evocative. I could see everything. But it wasn't—oh, dear, how do I explain this?"

Colin discovered that he was very impatient for her to figure out what she was trying to say.

"Sometimes," she finally continued, "when one reads a passage of description, it's rather . . . oh, I don't know . . . detached. Clinical, even. You brought the island to life. Other people might call the water warm, but you related it to something we all know and understand. It made me feel as if I were there, dipping my toe in right alongside you."

Colin smiled, ridiculously pleased by her praise.

"Oh! And I don't want to forget—there was another brilliant thing I wanted to mention."

Now he knew he must be grinning like an idiot. Brilliant brilliant brilliant. What a *good* word.

Penelope leaned in slightly as she said, "You also showed the reader how *you* relate to the scene and how it affects you. It becomes more than mere description because we see how you react to it."

Colin knew he was fishing for compliments, but he didn't much care as he asked, "What do you mean?"

"Well, if you look at—May I see the journal to refresh my memory?"

"Of course," he murmured, handing it to her. "Wait, let me find the correct page again."

Once he had done so, she scanned his lines until she found the section she was looking for. "Here we are. Look at this part about how you are reminded that England is your home."

"It's funny how travel can do that to a person."

"Do what to a person?" she asked, her eyes wide with interest.

"Make one appreciate home," he said softly.

Her eyes met his, and they were serious, inquisitive. "And yet you still like to go away."

He nodded. "I can't help it. It's like a disease."

She laughed, and it sounded unexpectedly musical. "Don't be ridiculous," she said. "A disease is harmful. It's clear that your travels feed your soul." She looked down to his hand, carefully peeling the napkin back to inspect his wound. "It's almost better," she said.

"Almost," he agreed. In truth, he suspected the bleeding had stopped altogether, but he was reluctant to let the conversation end. And he knew that the moment she was done caring for him, she would go.

He didn't think she wanted to go, but he somehow knew that she would. She'd think it was the proper thing to do, and she'd probably also think it was what he wanted.

Nothing, he was surprised to realize, could be further from the truth.

And nothing could have scared him more.

Chapter 6

Everyone has secrets.
Especially me.
LADY WHISTLEDOWN'S SOCIETY PAPERS,
14 April 1824

"I wish I'd known you kept a journal," Penelope said, reapplying pressure to his palm.

"Why?"

"I'm not sure," she said with a shrug. "It's always interesting to find out that there is more to someone than meets the eye, don't you think?"

Colin didn't say anything for several moments, and then, quite suddenly, he blurted out, "You really liked it?"

She looked amused. He was horrified. Here he was, considered one of the most popular and sophisticated men of the *ton*, and he'd been reduced to a bashful schoolboy, hanging on Penelope Featherington's every word, just for a single scrap of praise.

Penelope Featherington, for God's sake.

Not that there was anything wrong with Penelope, of course, he hastened to remind himself. Just that she was . . .well . . . Penelope.

"Of course I liked it," she said with a soft smile. "I just finished telling you so."

"What was the first thing that struck you about it?" he asked, deciding that he might as well act like a complete fool, since he was already more than halfway there.

She smiled wickedly. "Actually, the first thing that struck me was that your penmanship was quite a bit neater than I would have guessed."

He frowned. "What does that mean?"

"I have difficulty seeing you bent over a desk, practicing your flicks," she replied, her lips tightening at the corners to suppress a smile.

If ever there were a time for righteous indignation, this was clearly it. "I'll have you know I spent many an hour in the nursery schoolroom, bent over a desk, as you so delicately put it."

"I'm sure," she murmured.

"Hmmmph."

She looked down, clearly trying not to smile.

"I'm quite good with my flicks," he added. It was just a game now, but somehow it was rather fun to play the part of the petulant schoolboy.

"Obviously," she replied. "I especially liked them on the H's. Very well done. Quite . . . flicky of you."

"Indeed."

She matched his straight face perfectly. "Indeed."

His gaze slid from hers, and for a moment he felt quite unaccountably shy. "I'm glad you liked the journal," he said.

"It was lovely," she said in a soft, faraway kind of voice. "Very lovely, and . . ." She looked away, blushing. "You're going to think I'm silly."

"Never," he promised.

"Well, I think one of the reasons I enjoyed it so much is that I could somehow feel that *you'd* enjoyed writing it."

Colin was silent for a long moment. It hadn't ever occurred to him that he enjoyed his writing; it was just something he *did*.

He did it because he couldn't imagine not doing it. How could he travel to foreign lands and not keep a record of what he saw, what he experienced, and perhaps most importantly, what he felt?

But when he thought back, he realized that he felt a strange rush of satisfaction whenever he wrote a phrase that was exactly right, a sentence that was particularly true. He distinctly remembered the moment he'd written the passage Penelope had read. He'd been sitting on the beach at dusk, the sun still warm on his skin, the sand somehow rough and smooth at the same time under his bare feet. It had been a heavenly moment—full of that warm, lazy feeling one can truly only experience in the dead of summer (or on the perfect beaches of the Mediterranean), and he'd been trying to think of the exact right way to describe the water.

He'd sat there for ages—surely a full half an hour—his pen poised above the paper of his journal, waiting for inspiration. And then suddenly he'd realized the temperature was precisely that of slightly old bathwater, and his face had broken into a wide, delighted smile.

Yes, he enjoyed writing. Funny how he'd never realized it before.

"It's good to have something in your life," Penelope said quietly. "Something satisfying—that will fill the hours with a sense of purpose." She crossed her hands in her lap and looked down, seemingly engrossed by her knuckles. "I've never understood the supposed joys of a lazy life."

Colin wanted to touch his fingers to her chin, to see her eyes when he asked her—*And what do you do to fill your hours with a sense of purpose?* But he didn't. It would be far too forward, and it would mean admitting to himself just how interested he was in her answer.

So he asked the question, and he kept his own hands still.

"Nothing, really," she replied, still examining her fingernails.

Then, after a pause, she looked up quite suddenly, her chin rising so quickly it almost made him dizzy. "I like to read," she said. "I read quite a bit, actually. And I do a bit of embroidery now and then, but I'm not very good at it. I wish there were more, but, well . . ."

"What?" Colin prodded.

Penelope shook her head. "It's nothing. You should be grateful for your travels. I'm quite envious of you."

There was a long silence, not awkward, but strange nonetheless, and finally Colin said brusquely, "It's not enough."

The tone of his voice seemed so out of place in the conversation that Penelope could do nothing but stare. "What do you mean?" she finally asked.

He shrugged carelessly. "A man can't travel forever; to do so would take all the fun out of it."

She laughed, then looked at him and realized he was serious. "I'm sorry," she said. "I didn't mean to be rude."

"You weren't rude," he said, taking a swig of his lemonade. It sloshed on the table when he set the glass down; clearly, he was unused to using his left hand. "Two of the best parts of travel," he explained, wiping his mouth with one of the clean napkins, "are the leaving and the coming home, and besides, I'd miss my family too much were I to go off indefinitely."

Penelope had no reply—at least nothing that wouldn't sound like platitudes, so she just waited for him to continue.

For a moment he didn't say anything, then he scoffed and shut his journal with a resounding thud. "These don't count. They're just for me."

"They don't have to be," she said softly.

If he heard her, he made no indication. "It's all very well and good to keep a journal while you're traveling," he continued, "but once I'm home I still have nothing to do."

"I find that difficult to believe."

He didn't say anything, just reached for a piece of cheese off the tray. She watched him while he ate, and then, after he'd washed it down with more lemonade, his entire demeanor changed. He seemed more alert, more on edge as he asked, "Have you read *Whistledown* lately?"

Penelope blinked at the sudden change of subject. "Yes, of course, why? Doesn't everyone read it?"

He waved off her question. "Have you noticed how she describes me?"

"Er, it's almost always favorable, isn't it?"

His hand began to wave again—rather dismissively, in her opinion. "Yes, yes, that's not the point," he said in a distracted voice.

"You might think it more the point," Penelope replied testily, "if you'd ever been likened to an overripe citrus fruit."

He winced, and he opened and closed his mouth twice before finally saying, "If it makes you feel better, I didn't remember that she'd called you that until just now." He stopped, thought for a moment, then added, "In fact, I still don't remember it."

"It's all right," she said, putting on her best I'm-a-good-sport face. "I assure you, I'm quite beyond it. And I've always had a fondness for oranges and lemons."

He started to say something again, then stopped, then looked at her rather directly and said, "I hope what I'm about to say isn't abominably insensitive or insulting, given that when all is said and done, I've very little to complain about."

The implication being, Penelope realized, that perhaps *she* did.

"But I'm telling you," he continued, his eyes clear and earnest, "because I think maybe you'll understand."

It was a compliment. A strange, uncommon one, but a compliment nonetheless. Penelope wanted nothing more than to lay her hand across his, but of course she could not, so she just nodded and said, "You can tell me anything, Colin."

"My brothers—" he began. "They're—" He stopped, staring rather blankly toward the window before finally turning back to her and saying, "They're very accomplished. Anthony is the viscount, and God knows I wouldn't want that responsibility, but he has a purpose. Our entire heritage is in his hands."

"More than that, I should think," Penelope said softly.

He looked at her, question in his eyes.

"I think your brother feels responsible for your entire family," she said. "I imagine it's a heavy burden."

Colin tried to keep his face impassive, but he'd never been an accomplished stoic, and he must have shown his dismay on his face, because Penelope practically rose from her seat as she rushed to add, "Not that I think he minds it! It's part of who he is."

"Exactly!" Colin exclaimed, as if he'd just discovered something that was actually important. As opposed to this . . . this . . . this inane discussion about his life. He had nothing to complain about. He *knew* he had nothing to complain about, and yet . . .

"Did you know Benedict paints?" he found himself asking.

"Of course," she replied. "Everyone knows he paints. He has a painting in the National Gallery. And I believe they are planning to hang another soon. Another landscape."

"Really?"

She nodded. "Eloise told me."

He slumped again. "Then it must be true. I can't believe no one mentioned it to me."

"You *have* been away," she reminded him.

"What I'm trying to say," he continued, "is that they both have a purpose to their lives. I have nothing."

"That can't be true," she said.

"I should think I would be in a position to know."

Penelope sat back, startled by the sharp tone of his voice.

"I know what people think of me," he began, and although Penelope had told herself that she was going to remain silent, to allow him to speak his mind fully, she couldn't help but interrupt.

"Everyone likes you," she rushed to say. "They adore you."

"I know," he groaned, looking anguished and sheepish at the same time. "But . . ." He raked a hand through his hair. "God, how to say this without sounding a complete ass?"

Penelope's eyes widened.

"I'm sick of being thought an empty-headed charmer," he finally blurted out.

"Don't be silly," she said, faster than immediately, if that were possible.

"Penelope—"

"No one thinks you're stupid," she said.

"How would—"

"Because I've been stuck here in London for more years than anyone should have to," she said sharply. "I may not be the most popular woman in town, but after ten years, I've heard more than my fair share of gossip and lies and foolish opinions, and I have never—not once—heard someone refer to you as stupid."

He stared at her for a moment, a bit startled by her passionate defense. "I didn't mean *stupid*, precisely," he said in a soft, and he hoped humble, voice. "More . . . without substance. Even Lady Whistledown refers to me as a charmer."

"What's wrong with that?"

"Nothing," he replied testily, "if she didn't do it every other day."

"She only *publishes* every other day."

"My point exactly," he shot back. "If she thought there was anything to me other than my so-called legendary charm, don't you think she would have said so by now?"

Penelope was quiet for a long moment, then she said, "Does it really matter what Lady Whistledown thinks?"

He slumped forward, smacking his hands against his knees,

then yelping with pain when he (belatedly) remembered his injury. "You're missing the point," he said, wincing as he reapplied pressure to his palm. "I couldn't care less about Lady Whistledown. But whether we like it or not, she represents the rest of society."

"I would imagine that there are quite a few people who would take exception to that statement."

He raised one brow. "Including yourself?"

"Actually, I think Lady Whistledown is rather astute," she said, folding her hands primly in her lap.

"The woman called you an overripe melon!"

Two splotches of red burned in her cheeks. "An overripe citrus fruit," she ground out. "I assure you there is a very big difference."

Colin decided then and there that the female mind was a strange and incomprehensible organ—one which no man should even attempt to understand. There wasn't a woman alive who could go from point A to B without stopping at C, D, X, and 12 along the way.

"Penelope," he finally said, staring at her in disbelief, "the woman insulted you. How can you defend her?"

"She said nothing more than the truth," she replied, crossing her arms over her chest. "She's been rather kind, actually, since my mother started allowing me to pick out my own clothing."

Colin groaned. "Surely we were talking about something else at some point. Tell me we didn't *intend* to discuss your wardrobe."

Penelope's eyes narrowed. "I believe we were discussing your dissatisfaction with life as the most popular man in London."

Her voice rose on the last four words, and Colin realized he'd been scolded. Soundly.

Which he found extraordinarily irritating. "I don't know why I thought you'd understand," he bit off, hating the childish tinge in his voice but completely unable to edit it out.

"I'm sorry," she said, "but it's a little difficult for me to sit here and listen to you complain that your life is nothing."

"I didn't say that."

"You most certainly did!"

"I said I *have* nothing," he corrected, trying not to wince as he realized how stupid that sounded.

"You have more than anyone I know," she said, jabbing him in the shoulder. "But if you don't realize that, then maybe you are correct—your life is nothing."

"It's too hard to explain," he said in a petulant mutter.

"If you want a new direction for your life," she said, "then for heaven's sake, just pick something out and do it. The world is your oyster, Colin. You're young, wealthy, and you're a *man*." Penelope's voice turned bitter, resentful. "You can do anything you want."

He scowled, which didn't surprise her. When people were convinced they had problems, the last thing they wanted to hear was a simple, straightforward solution.

"It's not that simple," he said.

"It's exactly that simple." She stared at him for the longest moment, wondering, perhaps for the first time in her life, just who he was.

She'd thought she knew everything about him, but she hadn't known that he kept a journal.

She hadn't known that he possessed a temper.

She hadn't known that he felt dissatisfied with his life.

And she certainly hadn't known that he was petulant and spoiled enough to feel that dissatisfaction, when heaven knew he didn't deserve to. What right did he have to feel unhappy with his life? How dare he complain, especially to her?

She stood, smoothing out her skirts in an awkward, defensive gesture. "Next time you want to complain about the trials and tribulations of universal adoration, try being an on-the-shelf spinster for a day. See how that feels and then let me know what you want to complain about."

And then, while Colin was still sprawled on the sofa, gaping at her as if she were some bizarre creature with three heads, twelve fingers, and a tail, she swept out of the room.

It was, she thought as she descended the outer steps to Bruton Street, quite the most splendid exit of her existence.

It was really too bad, then, that the man she'd been leaving was the only one in whose company she'd ever wanted to remain.

Colin felt like hell all day.

His hand hurt like the devil, despite the brandy he'd sloshed both on his skin and into his mouth. The estate agent who'd handled the lease for the snug little terrace house he'd found in Bloomsbury had informed him that the previous tenant was having difficulties and Colin wouldn't be able to move in today as planned—would next week be acceptable?

And to top it off, he suspected that he might have done irreparable harm to his friendship with Penelope.

Which made him feel worst of all, since (A) he rather valued his friendship with Penelope and (B) he hadn't realized how much he valued his friendship with Penelope, which (C) made him feel slightly panicked.

Penelope was a constant in his life. His sister's friend—the one who was always at the fringes of the party; nearby, but not truly a part of things.

But the world seemed to be shifting. He'd only been back in England for a fortnight, but already Penelope had changed. Or maybe he'd changed. Or maybe she hadn't changed but the way he saw her had changed.

She mattered. He didn't know how else to put it.

And after ten years of her just being . . . *there*, it was rather bizarre for her to matter quite so much.

He didn't like that they'd parted ways that afternoon on such awkward terms. He couldn't remember feeling awkward with Penelope, ever—no, that wasn't true. There was that time . . . dear God, how many years ago was it? Six? Seven? His mother had been pestering him about getting married, which was nothing new, except this time she'd suggested Penelope as a potential bride, which *was* new, and Colin just hadn't been in the mood to deal with his mother's matchmaking in his usual manner, which was to tease her back.

And then she just hadn't stopped. She'd talked about Penelope all day and night, it seemed, until Colin finally fled the country. Nothing drastic—just a short jaunt to Wales. But really, what had his mother been thinking?

When he'd returned, his mother had wanted to speak with him, of course—except this time it had been because his sister Daphne was with child again and she had wanted to make a family announcement. But how was he to have known that? So he had not been looking forward to the visit, since he was sure it would involve a great deal of completely unveiled hints about marriage. Then he had run into his brothers, and they'd started tormenting him about the very same subject, as only brothers can do, and the next thing he knew, he announced, in a very loud voice, that he was not going to marry Penelope Featherington!

Except somehow Penelope had been standing right there in the doorway, her hand to her mouth, her eyes wide with pain and embarrassment and probably a dozen other unpleasant emotions that he'd been too ashamed to delve into.

It had been one of the most awful moments of his life. One, in fact, that he made an effort not to remember. He didn't think Penelope had ever fancied him—at least not any more than other ladies fancied him—but he'd embarrassed her. To single her out for such an announcement . . .

It had been unforgivable.

He'd apologized, of course, and she'd accepted, but he'd never quite forgiven himself.

And now he'd gone and insulted her again. Not in as direct a manner, of course, but he should have thought a bit longer and harder before complaining about his life.

Hell, it had sounded stupid, even to him. What did he have to complain about?

Nothing.

And yet there was still this nagging emptiness. A longing, really, for something he couldn't define. He was jealous of his brothers, for God's sake, for having found their passions, their legacies.

The only mark Colin had left on the world was in the pages of *Lady Whistledown's Society Papers.*

What a joke.

But all things were relative, weren't they? And compared to Penelope, he had little to complain about.

Which probably meant that he should have kept his thoughts to himself. He didn't like to think of her as an on-the-shelf spinster, but he supposed that was exactly what she was. And it wasn't a position of much reverence in British society.

In fact, it was a situation about which many people would complain. Bitterly.

Penelope had never once presented herself as anything less than a stoic—perhaps not content with her lot, but at least accepting of it.

And who knows? Maybe Penelope had hopes and dreams of a life beyond the one she shared with her mother and sister in their small home on Mount Street. Maybe she had plans and goals of her own but kept them to herself under a veil of dignity and good humor.

Maybe there was more to her than there seemed.

Maybe, he thought with a sigh, she deserved an apology. He wasn't precisely certain what he needed to apologize for; he wasn't certain there *was* a precise thing that needed it.

But the situation needed *some*thing.

Aw, hell. Now he was going to have to attend the Smythe-Smith musicale this evening. It was a painful, discordant, annual event; just when one was sure that all the Smythe-Smith daughters had grown up, some new cousin rose to take her place, each more tone deaf than the last.

But that was where Penelope was going to be that evening, and that meant that was where Colin would have to be as well.

Chapter 7

Colin Bridgerton had quite the bevy of young ladies at his side at the Smythe-Smith musicale Wednesday night, all fawning over his injured hand.

This Author does not know how the injury was sustained—indeed, Mr. Bridgerton has been rather annoyingly tight-lipped about it. Speaking of annoyances, the man in question seemed rather irritated by all of the attention. Indeed, This Author overheard him tell his brother Anthony that he wished he'd left the (unrepeatable word) bandage at home.

LADY WHISTLEDOWN'S SOCIETY PAPERS,
16 April 1824

Why why why did she do this to herself?

Year after year the invitation arrived by messenger, and year after year Penelope swore she would never, as God was her witness, ever attend another Smythe-Smith musicale.

And yet year after year she found herself seated in the Smythe-Smith music room, desperately trying not to cringe (at least not visibly) as the latest generation of Smythe-Smith girls butchered poor Mr. Mozart in musical effigy.

It was painful. Horribly, awfully, hideously painful. Truly, there was no other way to describe it.

Even more perplexing was that Penelope always seemed to end up in the front row, or close to it, which was beyond excruciating. And not just on the ears. Every few years, there would be one Smythe-Smith girl who seemed aware that she was taking part in what could only be termed a crime against auditory law. While the other girls attacked their violins and pianofortes with oblivious vigor, this odd one out played with a pained expression on her face—an expression Penelope knew well.

It was the face one put on when one wanted to be anywhere but where one was. You could try to hide it, but it always came out in the corners of the mouth, which were held tight and taut. And the eyes, of course, which floated either above or below everyone else's line of vision.

Heaven knew Penelope's face had been cursed with that same expression many a time.

Maybe that was why she never quite managed to stay home on a Smythe-Smith night. Someone had to smile encouragingly and pretend to enjoy the music.

Besides, it wasn't as if she were forced to come and listen more than once per year, anyway.

Still, one couldn't help but think that there must be a fortune to be made in discreet earplugs.

The quartet of girls were warming up—a jumble of discordant notes and scales that only promised to worsen once they began to play in earnest. Penelope had taken a seat in the center of the second row, much to her sister Felicity's dismay.

"There are two perfectly good seats in the back corner," Felicity hissed in her ear.

"It's too late now," Penelope returned, settling down on the lightly cushioned chair.

"God help me," Felicity groaned.

Penelope picked up her program and began leafing through it. "If we don't sit here, someone else will," she said.

"Precisely my desire!"

Penelope leaned in so that only her sister could hear her murmured words. "We can be counted on to smile and be polite. Imagine if someone like Cressida Twombley sat here and snickered all the way through."

Felicity looked around. "I don't think Cressida Twombley would be caught dead here."

Penelope chose to ignore the statement. "The last thing they need is someone seated right in front who likes to make unkind remarks. Those poor girls would be mortified."

"They're going to be mortified anyway," Felicity grumbled.

"No, they won't," Penelope said. "At least not that one, that one, or that one," she said, pointing to the two on violins and the one at the piano. But that one"—she motioned discreetly to the girl sitting with a cello between her knees—"is already miserable. The least we can do is not to make it worse by allowing someone catty and cruel to sit here."

"She's only going to be eviscerated later this week by Lady Whistledown," Felicity muttered.

Penelope opened her mouth to say more, but at that exact moment she realized that the person who had just occupied the seat on her other side was Eloise.

"Eloise," Penelope said with obvious delight. "I thought you were planning to stay home."

Eloise grimaced, her skin taking on a decidedly green pallor. "I can't explain it, but I can't seem to stay away. It's rather like a carriage accident. You just can't *not* look."

"Or listen," Felicity said, "as the case may be."

Penelope smiled. She couldn't help it.

"Did I hear you talking about Lady Whistledown when I arrived?" Eloise asked.

"I told Penelope," Felicity said, leaning rather inelegantly across her sister to speak to Eloise, "that they're going to be destroyed by Lady W later this week."

"I don't know," Eloise said thoughtfully. "She doesn't pick on the Smythe-Smith girls every year. I'm not sure why."

"I know why," cackled a voice from behind.

Eloise, Penelope, and Felicity all twisted in their seats, then lurched backward as Lady Danbury's cane came perilously close to their faces.

"Lady Danbury," Penelope gulped, unable to resist the urge to touch her nose—if only to reassure herself that it was still there.

"I have that Lady Whistledown figured out," Lady Danbury said.

"You do?" Felicity asked.

"She's soft at heart," the old lady continued. "You see that one"— she poked her cane in the direction of the cellist, nearly piercing Eloise's ear in the process—"right over there?"

"Yes," Eloise said, rubbing her ear, "although I don't think I'm going to be able to hear her."

"Probably a blessing," Lady Danbury said before turning back to the subject at hand. "You can thank me later."

"You were saying something about the cellist?" Penelope said swiftly, before Eloise said something entirely inappropriate.

"Of course I was. Look at her," Lady Danbury said. "She's miserable. And well she should be. She's clearly the only one who has a clue as to how dreadful they are. The other three don't have the musical sense of a gnat."

Penelope gave her younger sister a rather smug glance.

"You mark my words," Lady Danbury said. "Lady Whistledown won't have a thing to say about this musicale. She won't want to hurt that one's feelings. The rest of them—"

Felicity, Penelope, and Eloise all ducked as the cane came swinging by.

"Bah. She couldn't care less for the rest of them."

"It's an interesting theory," Penelope said.

Lady Danbury sat back contentedly in her chair. "Yes, it is. Isn't it?"

Penelope nodded. "I think you're right."

"Hmmph. I usually am."

Still twisted in her seat, Penelope turned first to Felicity, then to Eloise, and said, "It's the same reason why I keep coming to these infernal musicales year after year."

"To see Lady Danbury?" Eloise asked, blinking with confusion.

"No. Because of girls like her." Penelope pointed at the cellist. "Because I know exactly how she feels."

"Don't be silly, Penelope," Felicity said. "You've never played piano in public, and even if you did, you're quite accomplished."

Penelope turned to her sister. "It's not about the music, Felicity."

Then the oddest thing happened to Lady Danbury. Her face changed. Completely, utterly, astoundingly changed. Her eyes grew misty, wistful. And her lips, which were usually slightly pinched and sarcastic at the corners, softened. "I was that girl, too, Miss Featherington," she said, so quietly that both Eloise and Felicity were forced to lean forward, Eloise with an, "I beg your pardon," and Felicity with a considerably less polite, "What?"

But Lady Danbury only had eyes for Penelope. "It's why I attend, year after year," the older lady said. "Just like you."

And for a moment Penelope felt the oddest sense of connection to the older woman. Which was mad, because they had nothing in common aside from gender—not age, not status, nothing. And yet it was almost as if the countess had somehow chosen her—for what purpose Penelope could never guess. But she seemed determined to light a fire under Penelope's well-ordered and often boring life.

And Penelope couldn't help but think that it was somehow working.

Isn't it nice to discover that we're not exactly what we thought we were?

Lady Danbury's words from the other night still echoed in Penelope's head. Almost like a litany.

Almost like a dare.

"Do you know what I think, Miss Featherington?" Lady Danbury asked, her tone deceptively mild.

"I couldn't possibly begin to guess," Penelope said with great honesty—and respect—in her voice.

"I think *you* could be Lady Whistledown."

Felicity and Eloise gasped.

Penelope's lips parted with surprise. No one had ever even thought to accuse her of such before. It was unbelievable . . . unthinkable . . . and . . .

Rather flattering, actually.

Penelope felt her mouth sliding into a sly smile, and she leaned forward, as if getting ready to impart news of great import.

Lady Danbury leaned forward.

Felicity and Eloise leaned forward.

"Do you know what *I* think, Lady Danbury?" Penelope asked, in a compellingly soft voice.

"Well," Lady D said, a wicked gleam in her eye, "I would tell you that I am breathless with anticipation, but you've already told me once before that you think that *I* am Lady Whistledown."

"Are you?"

Lady Danbury smiled archly. "Maybe I am."

Felicity and Eloise gasped again, louder this time.

Penelope's stomach lurched.

"Are you admitting it?" Eloise whispered.

"Of course I'm not admitting it," Lady Danbury barked, straightening her spine and thumping her cane against the floor with enough force to momentarily stop the four amateur musicians in their warm-up. "Even if it were true—and I'm not saying whether or not it is—would I be fool enough to admit it?"

"Then why did you say—"

"Because, you ninnyhead, I'm trying to make a point."

She then proceeded to fall silent until Penelope was forced to ask, "Which is?"

Lady Danbury gave them all an extremely exasperated look. "That *anyone* could be Lady Whistledown," she exclaimed, thumping her cane on the floor with renewed vigor. "Anyone at all."

"Well, except *me*," Felicity put in. "I'm quite certain it's not me."

Lady Danbury didn't even honor Felicity with a glance. "Let me tell you something," she said.

"As if we could stop you," Penelope said, so sweetly that it came out like a compliment. And truth be told, it *was* a compliment. She admired Lady Danbury a great deal. She admired anyone who knew how to speak her mind in public.

Lady Danbury chuckled. "There's more to you than meets the eye, Penelope Featherington."

"It's true," Felicity said with a grin. "She can be rather cruel, for example. Nobody would believe it, but when we were young—"

Penelope elbowed her in the ribs.

"See?" Felicity said.

"What I was going to say," Lady Danbury continued, "was that the *ton* is going about my challenge all wrong."

"How do you suggest we go about it, then?" Eloise asked.

Lady Danbury waved her hand dismissively in Eloise's face. "I have to explain what people are doing wrong first," she said. "They keep looking toward the obvious people. People like your mother," she said, turning to Penelope and Felicity.

"Mother?" they both echoed.

"Oh, please," Lady Danbury scoffed. "A bigger busybody this town has never seen. She's exactly the sort of person everyone suspects."

Penelope had no idea what to say to that. Her mother *was* a notorious gossip, but it was difficult to imagine her as Lady Whistledown.

"Which is why," Lady Danbury continued, a shrewd look in her eye, "it can't be her."

"Well, *that*," Penelope said with a touch of sarcasm, "and the fact that Felicity and I could tell you for certain that it's not her."

"Pish. If your mother were Lady Whistledown, she'd have figured out a way to keep it from you."

"My mother?" Felicity said doubtfully. "I don't think so."

"What I am trying to *say*," Lady Danbury ground out, "prior to all of these infernal *interruptions*—"

Penelope thought she heard Eloise snort.

"—was that if Lady Whistledown were someone *obvious*, she'd have been found out by now, don't you think?"

Silence, until it became clear some response was required, then all three of them nodded with appropriate thoughtfulness and vigor.

"She must be someone that nobody suspects," Lady Danbury said. "She has to be."

Penelope found herself nodding again. Lady Danbury did make sense, in a strange sort of way.

"Which is why," the older lady continued triumphantly, "I am not a likely candidate!"

Penelope blinked, not quite following the logic. "I beg your pardon?"

"Oh, *please*." Lady Danbury gave Penelope quite the most disdainful glance. "Do you think you're the first person to suspect me?"

Penelope just shook her head. "I still think it's you."

That earned her a measure of respect. Lady Danbury nodded approvingly as she said, "You're cheekier than you look."

Felicity leaned forward and said in a rather conspiratorial voice, "It's true."

Penelope swatted her sister's hand. "Felicity!"

"I think the musicale is starting," Eloise said.

"Heaven help us all," Lady Danbury announced. "I don't know why I—Mr. Bridgerton!"

Penelope had turned to face the small stage area, but she whipped back around to see Colin making his way along the row to the empty seat beside Lady Danbury, apologizing good-naturedly as he bumped into people's knees.

His apologies, of course, were accompanied by one of his lethal smiles, and no fewer than three ladies positively melted in their seats as a result.

Penelope frowned. It was disgusting.

"Penelope," Felicity whispered. "Did you just growl?"

"Colin," Eloise said. "I didn't know you were coming."

He shrugged, his face alight with a lopsided grin. "Changed my mind at the last moment. I've always been a great lover of music, after all."

"Which would explain your presence here," Eloise said in an exceptionally dry voice.

Colin acknowledged her statement with nothing more than an arch of his brow before turning to Penelope and saying, "Good evening, Miss Featherington." He nodded at Felicity with another, "Miss Featherington."

It took Penelope a moment to find her voice. They had parted most awkwardly that afternoon, and now here he was with a friendly smile. "Good evening, Mr. Bridgerton," she finally managed.

"Does anyone know what is on the program tonight?" he asked, looking terribly interested.

Penelope had to admire that. Colin had a way of looking at you as if nothing in the world could be more interesting than your next sentence. It was a talent, that. Especially now, when they all knew that he couldn't possibly care one way or another what the Smythe-Smith girls chose to play that evening.

"I believe it's Mozart," Felicity said. "They almost always choose Mozart."

"Lovely," Colin replied, leaning back in his chair as if he'd just finished an excellent meal. "I'm a great fan of Mr. Mozart."

"In that case," Lady Danbury cackled, elbowing him in the ribs, "you might want to make your escape while the possibility still exists."

"Don't be silly," he said. "I'm sure the girls will do their best."

"Oh, there's no question of them doing their best," Eloise said ominously.

"Shhh," Penelope said. "I think they're ready to begin."

Not, she admitted to herself, that she was especially eager to listen to the Smythe-Smith version of *Eine Kleine Nachtmusik*. But she felt profoundly ill-at-ease with Colin. She wasn't sure what to say to him—except that whatever it was she *should* say definitely shouldn't be said in front of Eloise, Felicity, and most of all Lady Danbury.

A butler came around and snuffed out a few candles to signal that the girls were ready to begin. Penelope braced herself, swallowed in such a way as to clog her inner ear canals (it didn't work), and then the torture began.

And went on . . . and on . . . and on.

Penelope wasn't certain what was more agonizing—the music or the knowledge that Colin was sitting right behind her. The back of her neck prickled with awareness, and she found herself fidgeting like mad, her fingers tapping relentlessly on the dark blue velvet of her skirts.

When the Smythe-Smith quartet was finally done, three of the girls were beaming at the polite applause, and the fourth—the cellist—looked as if she wanted to crawl under a rock.

Penelope sighed. At least she, in all of her unsuccessful seasons, hadn't ever been forced to parade her deficiencies before all the *ton* like these girls had. She'd always been allowed to melt into the shadows, to hover quietly at the perimeter of the room, watching the other girls take their turns on the dance floor. Oh, her mother dragged her here and there, trying to place her in the path of some eligible gentleman or another, but that was nothing—nothing!—like what the Smythe-Smith girls were forced to endure.

Although, in all honesty, three out of the four seemed blissfully unaware of their musical ineptitude. Penelope just smiled and clapped. She certainly wasn't going to burst their collective bubble.

And if Lady Danbury's theory was correct, Lady Whistledown wasn't going to write a word about the musicale.

The applause petered out rather quickly, and soon everyone was milling about, making polite conversation with their neighbors and eyeing the sparsely laid refreshment table at the back of the room.

"Lemonade," Penelope murmured to herself. Perfect. She was dreadfully hot—really, what had she been thinking, wearing velvet on such a warm night?—and a cool beverage would be just the thing to make her feel better. Not to mention that Colin was trapped in conversation with Lady Danbury, so it was the ideal time to make her escape.

But as soon as Penelope had her glass in hand, she heard Colin's achingly familiar voice behind her, murmuring her name.

She turned around, and before she had any idea what she was doing, she said, "I'm sorry."

"You are?"

"Yes," she assured him. "At least I think I am."

His eyes crinkled slightly at the corners. "The conversation grows more intriguing by the second."

"Colin—"

He held out his arm. "Take a turn with me around the room, will you?"

"I don't think—"

He moved his arm closer to her—just by an inch or so, but the message was clear. "Please," he said.

She nodded and set her lemonade down. "Very well."

They walked in silence for almost a minute, then Colin said, "I would like to apologize to you."

"I was the one who stormed out of the room," Penelope pointed out.

He tilted his head slightly, and she could see an indulgent smile playing across his lips. "I'd hardly call it 'storming,' " he said.

Penelope frowned. She probably shouldn't have left in such a huff, but now that she had, she was oddly proud of it. It wasn't every day that a woman such as herself got to make such a dramatic exit.

"Well, I shouldn't have been so rude," she muttered, by now not really meaning it.

He arched a brow, then obviously decided not to pursue the matter. "I would like to apologize," he said, "for being such a whiny little brat."

Penelope actually tripped over her feet.

He helped her regain her balance, then said, "I am aware that I have many, many things in my life for which I should be grateful. For which I *am* grateful," he corrected, his mouth not quite smiling but certainly sheepish. "It was unforgivably rude to complain to you."

"No," she said, "I have spent all evening thinking about what you said, and while I . . ." She swallowed, then licked her lips, which had gone quite dry. She'd spent all day trying to think of the right words, and she'd thought that she'd found them, but now that he was here, at her side, she couldn't think of a deuced thing.

"Do you need another glass of lemonade?" Colin asked politely.

She shook her head. "You have every right to your feelings," she blurted out. "They may not be what I would feel, were I in your shoes, but you have every right to them. But—"

She broke off, and Colin found himself rather desperate to know what she'd planned to say. "But what, Penelope?" he urged.

"It's nothing."

"It's not nothing to me." His hand was on her arm, and so he squeezed slightly, to let her know that he meant what he said.

For the longest time, he didn't think she was actually going to respond, and then, just when he thought his face would crack from the smile he held so carefully on his lips—they were in public, after all, and it wouldn't do to invite comment and speculation by appearing urgent and disturbed—she sighed.

It was a lovely sound, strangely comforting, soft, and wise. And it made him want to look at her more closely, to see into her mind, to hear the rhythms of her soul.

"Colin," Penelope said quietly, "if you feel frustrated by your current situation, you should do something to change it. It's really that simple."

"That's what I do," he said with a careless shrug of his outside shoulder. "My mother accuses me of picking up and leaving the country completely on a whim, but the truth is—"

"You do it when you're feeling frustrated," she finished for him.

He nodded. She understood him. He wasn't sure how it had happened, or even that it made any sense, but Penelope Featherington understood him.

"I think you should publish your journals," she said.

"I couldn't."

"Why not?"

He stopped in his tracks, letting go of her arm. He didn't really have an answer, other than the odd pounding in his heart. "Who would want to read them?" he finally asked.

"I would," she said frankly. "Eloise, Felicity . . ." she added, ticking off names on her fingers. "Your mother, Lady Whistledown, I'm sure," she added with a mischievous smile. "She does write about you rather a lot."

Her good humor was infectious, and Colin couldn't quite suppress his smile. "Penelope, it doesn't count if the only people who buy the book are the people I know."

"Why not?" Her lips twitched. "You know a lot of people. Why, if you only count Bridgertons—"

He grabbed her hand. He didn't know why, but he grabbed her hand. "Penelope, stop."

She just laughed. "I think Eloise told me that you have piles and piles of cousins as well, and—"

"Enough," he warned. But he was grinning as he said it.

Penelope stared down at her hand in his, then said, "Lots of people will want to read about your travels. Maybe at first it will only be because you're a well-known figure in London, but it won't take long before everyone realizes what a good writer you are. And then they'll be clamoring for more."

"I don't want to be a success because of the Bridgerton name," he said.

She dropped his hand and planted hers on her hips. "Are you even *listening* to me? I just told you that—"

"What are you two talking about?"

Eloise. Looking very, very curious.

"Nothing," they both muttered at the same time.

Eloise snorted. "Don't insult me. It's not nothing. Penelope looked as if she might start breathing fire at any moment."

"Your brother is just being obtuse," Penelope said.

"Well, that is nothing new," Eloise said.

"Wait a moment!" Colin exclaimed.

"But what," Eloise probed, ignoring him entirely, "is he being obtuse about?"

"It's a private matter," Colin ground out.

"Which makes it all the more interesting," Eloise said. She looked to Penelope expectantly.

"I'm sorry," Penelope said. "I really can't say."

"I can't believe it!" Eloise cried out. "You're not going to tell me."

"No," Penelope replied, feeling rather oddly satisfied with herself, "I'm not."

"I can't believe it," Eloise said again, turning to her brother. "I can't believe it."

His lips quirked into the barest of smiles. "Believe it."

"You're keeping secrets from me."

He raised his brows. "Did you think I told you everything?"

"Of course not." She scowled. "But I thought Penelope did."

"But this isn't my secret to tell," Penelope said. "It's Colin's."

"I think the planet has shifted on its axis," Eloise grumbled. "Or perhaps England has crashed into France. All I know is this is not the same world I inhabited just this morning."

Penelope couldn't help it. She giggled.

"And you're laughing at me!" Eloise added.

"No, I'm not," Penelope said, laughing. "Really, I'm not."

"Do you know what you need?" Colin asked.

"Me?" Eloise queried.

He nodded. "A husband."

"You're as bad as Mother!"

"I could be a lot worse if I really put my mind to it."

"Of that I have no doubt," Eloise shot back.

"Stop, stop!" Penelope said, truly laughing in earnest now.

They both looked at her expectantly, as if to say, *Now what?*

"I'm so glad I came tonight," Penelope said, the words tumbling unbidden from her lips. "I can't remember a nicer evening. Truly, I can't."

Several hours later, as Colin was lying in bed, staring up at the ceiling in the bedroom of his new flat in Bloomsbury, it occurred to him that he felt the exact same way.

Chapter 8

Colin Bridgerton and Penelope Featherington were seen in conversation at the Smythe-Smith musicale, although no one seems to know what exactly they were discussing. This Author would venture to guess that their conversation centered upon This Author's identity, since that was what everyone else seemed to be talking about before, after, and (rather rudely, in This Author's esteemed opinion) during the performance.

In other news, Honoria Smythe-Smith's violin was damaged when Lady Danbury accidentally knocked it off a table while waving her cane.

Lady Danbury insisted upon replacing the instrument, but then declared that as it is not her habit to buy anything but the best, Honoria will have a Ruggieri violin, imported from Cremona, Italy.

It is This Author's understanding that, when one factors in manufacture and shipping time, along with a lengthy waiting list, it takes six months for a Ruggieri violin to reach our shores.

LADY WHISTLEDOWN'S SOCIETY PAPERS,
16 April 1824

There are moments in a woman's life when her heart flips in her chest, when the world suddenly seems uncommonly pink and perfect, when a symphony can be heard in the tinkle of a doorbell.

Penelope Featherington had just such a moment two days after the Smythe-Smith musicale.

All it took was a knock on her bedroom door, followed by her butler's voice, informing her:

"Mr. Colin Bridgerton is here to see you."

Penelope tumbled right off the bed.

Briarly, who had butlered for the Featherington family long enough so that he did not even so much as bat an eyelash at Penelope's clumsiness, murmured, "Shall I tell him you are not in?"

"No!" Penelope nearly shrieked, stumbling to her feet. "I mean, no," she added in a more reasonable voice. "But I will require ten minutes to prepare myself." She glanced in the mirror and winced at her disheveled appearance. "Fifteen."

"As you wish, Miss Penelope."

"Oh, and make certain to prepare a tray of food. Mr. Bridgerton is sure to be hungry. He's always hungry."

The butler nodded again.

Penelope stood stock-still as Briarly disappeared out the door, then, completely unable to contain herself, danced from foot to foot, emitting a strange squealing sort of noise—one that she was convinced—or at least hoped—had never before crossed her lips.

Then again, she couldn't remember the last time a gentleman had called upon her, much less the one with whom she'd been desperately in love for almost half of her life.

"Settle down," she said, spreading her fingers and pressing her flattened palms out in much the same motion she might make if she were trying to placate a small, unruly crowd. "You must remain calm. Calm," she repeated, as if that would actually do the trick. "Calm."

But inside, her heart was dancing.

She took a few deep breaths, walked over to her dressing table, and picked up her hairbrush. It would only take a few minutes to repin her hair; surely Colin wasn't going to flee if she kept him waiting for a short while. He'd expect her to take a bit of time to ready herself, wouldn't he?

But still, she found herself fixing her hair in record time, and by the time she stepped through the sitting room door, a mere five minutes had passed since the butler's announcement.

"That was quick," Colin said with a quirky grin. He'd been standing by the window, peering out at Mount Street.

"Oh, was it?" Penelope said, hoping that the heat she felt on her skin wasn't translating into a blush. A woman was supposed to keep a gentleman waiting, although not too long. Still, it made no sense to hold to such silly behavior with Colin, of all people. He would never be interested in her in a romantic fashion, and besides, they were friends.

Friends. It seemed like such an odd concept, and yet that was exactly what they were. They'd always been friendly acquaintances, but since his return from Cyprus, they'd become friends in truth.

It was magical.

Even if he never loved her—and she rather thought he never would—this was better than what they'd had before.

"To what do I owe the pleasure?" she asked, taking a seat on her mother's slightly faded yellow damask sofa.

Colin sat across from her in a rather uncomfortable straight-backed chair. He leaned forward, resting his hands on his knees, and Penelope knew instantly that something was wrong. It simply wasn't the pose a gentleman adopted for a regular social call. He looked too distraught, too intense.

"It's rather serious," he said, his face grim.

Penelope nearly rose to her feet. "Has something happened? Is someone ill?"

"No, no, nothing like that." He paused, let out a long breath, then raked his hand through his already mussed-up hair. "It's about Eloise."

"What is it?"

"I don't know how to say this. I—Do you have anything to eat?"

Penelope was ready to wring his neck. "For heaven's sake, Colin!"

"Sorry," he muttered. "I haven't eaten all day."

"A first, I'm sure," Penelope said impatiently. "I already told Briarly to fix a tray. Now, will you just tell me what is wrong, or do you plan to wait until I expire of impatience?"

"I think she's Lady Whistledown," he blurted out.

Penelope's mouth fell open. She wasn't sure what she'd expected him to say, but it wasn't this.

"Penelope, did you hear me?"

"Eloise?" she asked, even though she knew exactly who he was talking about.

He nodded.

"She can't be."

He stood and began to pace, too full of nervous energy to sit still. "Why not?"

"Because . . . because . . ." Because *why*? "Because there is no way she could have done that for ten years without my knowing."

His expression went from disturbed to disdainful in an instant. "I hardly think you're privy to everything that Eloise does."

"Of course not," Penelope replied, giving him a rather irritated look, "but I can tell you with absolute certainty that there is no way Eloise could keep a secret of that magnitude from me for over ten years. She's simply not capable of it."

"Penelope, she's the nosiest person I know."

"Well, that much is true," Penelope agreed. "Except for my mother, I suppose. But that's hardly enough to convict her."

Colin stopped his pacing and planted his hands on his hips. "She is always writing things down."

"Why would you think that?"

He held up his hand, rubbing his thumb briskly against his fingertips. "Inkstains. Constantly."

"Lots of people use pen and ink." Penelope motioned broadly at Colin. "You write in journals. I am certain you've had your share of ink on your fingers."

"Yes, but I don't *disappear* when I write in my journals."

Penelope felt her pulse quicken. "What do you mean?" she asked, her voice growing breathless.

"I mean that she locks herself in her room for hours on end, and it's after those periods that her fingers are covered with ink."

Penelope didn't say anything for an agonizingly long moment. Colin's "evidence" was damning, indeed, especially when combined with Eloise's well-known and well-documented penchant for nosiness.

But she wasn't Lady Whistledown. She couldn't be. Penelope would bet her life on it.

Finally Penelope just crossed her arms and, in a tone of voice that probably would have been more at home on an exceedingly stubborn six-year-old, said, "It's not her. It's not."

Colin sat back down, looking defeated. "I wish I could share your certainty."

"Colin, you need to—"

"Where the hell is the food?" he grumbled.

She should have been shocked, but somehow his lack of manners amused her. "I'm sure Briarly will be here shortly."

He sprawled into a chair. "I'm hungry."

"Yes," Penelope said, lips twitching, "I surmised as much."

He sighed, weary and worried. "If she's Lady Whistledown, it'll be a disaster. A pure, unmitigated disaster."

"It wouldn't be that bad," Penelope said carefully. "Not that I think she's Lady Whistledown, because I don't! But truly, if she were, would it be so very dreadful? I rather like Lady Whistledown myself."

"Yes, Penelope," Colin said rather sharply, "it would be so very dreadful. She'd be ruined."

"I don't think she'd be *ruined*. . . ."

"Of course she'd be ruined. Do you have any idea how many people that woman has insulted over the years?"

"I didn't realize you hated Lady Whistledown so much," Penelope said.

"I don't hate her," Colin said impatiently. "It doesn't matter if I hate her. Everyone else hates her."

"I don't think that's true. They all buy her paper."

"Of course they buy her paper! Everyone buys her bloody paper."

"Colin!"

"Sorry," he muttered, but it didn't really sound like he meant it.

Penelope nodded her acceptance of his apology.

"Whoever that Lady Whistledown is," Colin said, shaking his finger at her with such vehemence that she actually lurched backward, "when she is unmasked, she will not be able to show her face in London."

Penelope delicately cleared her throat. "I didn't realize you cared so much about the opinions of society."

"I don't," he retorted. "Well, not much, at least. Anyone who tells you they don't care at all is a liar and a hypocrite."

Penelope rather thought he was correct, but she was surprised he'd admitted it. It seemed men always liked to pretend that they were wholly self-contained, completely unaffected by the whims and opinions of society.

Colin leaned forward, his green eyes burning with intensity. "This isn't about me, Penelope, it's about Eloise. And if she is cast out of society, she will be crushed." He sat back, but his entire body radiated tension. "Not to mention what it would do to my mother."

Penelope let out a long breath. "I really think you're getting upset over nothing," she said.

"I hope you're right," he replied, closing his eyes. He wasn't sure when he'd started to suspect that his sister might be Lady Whistledown. Probably after Lady Danbury had issued her now famous challenge. Unlike most of London, Colin had never been terribly interested in Lady Whistledown's true identity. The column was entertaining, and he certainly read it along with everyone else, but to his mind, Lady Whistledown was simply . . . Lady Whistledown, and that was all she needed to be.

But Lady Danbury's dare had started him thinking, and like the rest of the Bridgertons, once he got hold of an idea, he was fundamentally incapable of letting it go. Somehow it had occurred to him that Eloise had the perfect temperament and skills to write such a column, and then, before he could convince himself that he was crazy, he'd seen the ink spots on her fingers. Since then he'd gone nearly mad, unable to think about anything but the possibility that Eloise had a secret life.

He didn't know which irritated him more—that Eloise might be Lady Whistledown, or that she had managed to hide it from him for over a decade.

How galling, to be hoodwinked by one's sister. He liked to think himself smarter than that.

But he needed to focus on the present. Because if his suspicions were correct, how on earth were they going to deal with the scandal when she was discovered?

And she *would* be discovered. With all of London lusting after the thousand-pound prize, Lady Whistledown didn't stand a chance.

"Colin! Colin!"

He opened his eyes, wondering how long Penelope had been calling his name.

"I really think you should stop worrying about Eloise," she said. "There are hundreds and hundreds of people in London. Lady Whistledown could be any one of them. Heavens, with your eye for detail"—she waggled her fingers to remind him of Eloise's ink-stained fingertips—"*you* could be Lady Whistledown."

He shot her a rather condescending look. "Except for the small detail of my having been out of the country half the time."

Penelope chose to ignore his sarcasm. "You're certainly a good enough writer to carry it off."

Colin had intended to say something droll and slightly gruff, dismissing her rather weak arguments, but the truth was he was so secretly delighted about her "good writer" compliment that all he could do was sit there with a loopy smile on his face.

"Are you all right?" Penelope asked.

"Perfectly fine," he replied, snapping to attention and trying to adopt a more sober mien. "Why would you ask?"

"Because you suddenly looked quite ill. Dizzy, actually."

"I'm fine," he repeated, probably a little louder than was necessary. "I'm just thinking about the scandal."

She let out a beleaguered sigh, which irritated him, because he didn't see that she had any reason to feel so impatient with him. "What scandal?" she asked.

"The scandal that is going to erupt when she is discovered," he ground out.

"She's not Lady Whistledown!" she insisted.

Colin suddenly sat up straight, his eyes alight with a new idea. "Do you know," he said in a rather intense sort of voice, "but I don't think it matters if she is Lady Whistledown or not."

Penelope stared at him blankly for a full three seconds before looking about the room, muttering, "Where's the food? I must be light-headed. Haven't you spent the last ten minutes positively going *mad* over the possibility that she is?"

As if on cue, Briarly entered the room with a heavily laden tray. Penelope and Colin watched in silence as the butler laid out the meal. "Would you like me to fix your plates?" he inquired.

"No, that's quite all right," Penelope said quickly. "We can manage for ourselves."

Briarly nodded and, as soon as he'd laid the flatware and filled the two glasses with lemonade, left the room.

"Listen to me," Colin said, jumping to his feet and moving the door so that it almost rested against the doorframe (but remained technically open, should anyone quibble about proprieties).

"Don't you want something to eat?" Penelope inquired, holding aloft a plate that she'd filled with various small snacks.

He snatched a piece of cheese, ate it in two rather indelicate bites, then continued, "Even if Eloise isn't Lady Whistledown— and mind you, I still think she is—it doesn't matter. Because if *I* suspect that she's Lady Whistledown, then surely someone else will as well."

"Your point being?"

Colin realized that his arms were reaching forward, and he stopped himself before he reached out to shake her shoulders. "It doesn't matter! Don't you see? If someone points his finger at her, she'll be ruined."

"But not," Penelope said, appearing to require a great deal of effort to unclench her teeth, "if she's not Lady Whistledown!"

"How could she prove it?" Colin returned, jumping to his feet. "Once a rumor is started, the damage is done. It develops a life of its own."

"Colin, you ceased to make sense five minutes ago."

"No, hear me out." He whirled to face her, and he was seized by a feeling of such intensity that he couldn't have ripped his eyes from hers if the house were falling down around them. "Suppose I told everyone that I had seduced you."

Penelope grew very, very still.

"You would be ruined forever," he continued, crouching down near the edge of the sofa so that they were more on the same level. "It wouldn't matter that we had never even kissed. *That*, my dear Penelope, is the power of the word."

She looked oddly frozen. And at the same time flushed. "I . . . I don't know what to say," she stammered.

And then the most bizarre thing happened. He realized that he didn't know what to say, either. Because he'd forgotten about rumors and the power of the word and all of that rot, and the only thing he could think of was the part about the kissing, and—

And—

And—

Good God in heaven, he wanted to kiss Penelope Featherington.

Penelope Featherington!

He might as well have said he wanted to kiss his sister.

Except—he stole a glance at her; she looked uncommonly fetching, and he wondered how he hadn't noticed that earlier that afternoon—she wasn't his sister.

She definitely wasn't his sister.

"Colin?" His name was a mere whisper on her lips, her eyes were quite adorably blinking and befuddled, and how was it he'd never noticed what an intriguing shade of brown they were? Almost gold near the pupil. He'd never seen anything like it, and yet it wasn't as if he hadn't seen her a hundred times before.

He stood—suddenly, drunkenly. Best if they weren't quite on the same latitude. Harder to see her eyes from up here.

She stood, too.

Damn it.

"Colin?" she asked, her voice barely audible. "Could I ask you a favor?"

Call it male intuition, call it insanity, but a very insistent voice inside of him was screaming that whatever she wanted *had* to be a very bad idea.

He was, however, an idiot.

He had to be, because he felt his lips part and then he heard a voice that sounded an awful lot like his own say, "Of course."

Her lips puckered, and for a moment he thought she was trying to kiss him, but then he realized that she was just bringing them together to form a word.

"Would—"

Just a word. Nothing but a word beginning with *W*. *W* always looked like a kiss.

"Would you kiss me?"

Chapter 9

Every week there seems to be one invitation that is coveted above all others, and this week's prize must surely go to the Countess of Macclesfield, who is hosting a grand ball on Monday night. Lady Macclesfield is not a frequent hostess here in London, but she is very popular, as is her husband, and it is expected that a great many bachelors plan to attend, including Mr. Colin Bridgerton (assuming he does not collapse from exhaustion after four days with the ten Bridgerton grandchildren), Viscount Burwick, and Mr. Michael Anstruther-Wetherby.

This Author anticipates that a great many young and unmarried ladies will choose to attend as well, following the publication of this column.

LADY WHISTLEDOWN'S SOCIETY PAPERS,
16 April 1824

His life as he knew it was over.

"What?" he asked, aware that he was blinking rapidly.

Her face turned a deeper shade of crimson than he'd thought humanly possible, and she turned away. "Never mind," she mumbled. "Forget I said anything."

Colin thought that a *very* good idea.

But then, just when he'd thought that his world might resume its normal course (or at least that he'd be able to pretend it had), she whirled back around, her eyes alight with a passionate fire that astonished him.

"No, I'm not going to forget it," she cried out. "I've spent my life forgetting things, not saying them, never telling anyone what I really want."

Colin tried to say something, but it was clear to him that his throat had begun to close. Any minute now he'd be dead. He was sure of it.

"It won't mean a thing," she said. "I promise you, it won't mean anything, and I'd never expect anything from you because of it, but I could die tomorrow, and—"

"*What?*"

Her eyes looked huge, and meltingly dark, and pleading, and . . .

He could feel his resolve melting away.

"I'm eight-and-twenty," she said, her voice soft and sad. "I'm an old maid, and I've never been kissed."

"Gah . . . gah . . . gah . . ." He knew he knew how to speak; he was fairly certain he'd been perfectly articulate just minutes earlier. But now he didn't seem able to form a word.

And Penelope kept talking, her cheeks delightfully pink, and her lips moving so quickly that he couldn't help but wonder what they'd feel like on his skin. On his neck, on his shoulder, on his . . . other places.

"I'm going to be an old maid at nine-and-twenty," she said, "and I'll be an old maid at thirty. I could die tomorrow, and—"

"You're not going to die tomorrow!" he somehow managed to get out.

"But I could! I could, and it would kill me, because—"

"You'd already be dead," he said, thinking his voice sounded rather strange and disembodied.

"I don't want to die without ever having been kissed," she finally finished.

Colin could think of a hundred reasons why kissing Penelope Featherington was a very bad idea, the number one being that he actually *wanted* to kiss her.

He opened his mouth, hoping that a sound would emerge and that it might actually be intelligible speech, but there was nothing, just the sound of breath on his lips.

And then Penelope did the one thing that could break his resolve in an instant. She looked up at him, deeply into his eyes, and uttered one, simple word.

"Please."

He was lost. There was something heartbreaking in the way she was gazing at him, as if she might die if he didn't kiss her. Not from heartbreak, not from embarrassment—it was almost as if she needed him for nourishment, to feed her soul, to fill her heart.

And Colin couldn't remember anyone else ever needing him with such fervor.

It humbled him.

It made him want her with an intensity that nearly buckled his knees. He looked at her, and somehow he didn't see the woman he'd seen so many times before. She was different. She glowed. She was a siren, a goddess, and he wondered how on earth no one had ever noticed this before.

"Colin?" she whispered.

He took a step forward—barely a half a foot, but it was close enough so that when he touched her chin and tipped her face up, her lips were mere inches from his.

Their breath mingled, and the air grew hot and heavy. Penelope was trembling—he could feel that under his fingers—but he wasn't so sure that he wasn't trembling, too.

He assumed he'd say something flip and droll, like the devil-may-care fellow he was reputed to be. *Anything for you*, perhaps, or maybe, *Every woman deserves at least one kiss.* But as he closed the bare distance between them, he realized that there were no words that could capture the intensity of the moment.

No words for the passion. No words for the need.

No words for the sheer epiphany of the moment.

And so, on an otherwise unremarkable Friday afternoon, in the heart of Mayfair, in a quiet drawing room on Mount Street, Colin Bridgerton kissed Penelope Featherington.

And it was glorious.

His lips touched hers softly at first, not because he was trying to be gentle, although if he'd had the presence of mind to think about such things, it probably would have occurred to him that this was her first kiss, and it ought to be reverent and beautiful and all the things a girl dreams about as she's lying in bed at night.

But in all truth, none of that was on Colin's mind. In fact, he was thinking of quite little. His kiss was soft and gentle because he was still so surprised that he was kissing her. He'd known her for years, had never even thought about touching his lips to hers. And now he couldn't have let her go if the fires of hell were licking his toes. He could barely believe what he was doing—or that he wanted to do it so damned much.

It wasn't the sort of a kiss one initiates because one is overcome with passion or emotion or anger or desire. It was a slower thing, a learning experience—for Colin just as much as for Penelope.

And he was learning that everything he thought he'd known about kissing was rubbish.

Everything else had been mere lips and tongue and softly murmured but meaningless words.

This was a kiss.

There was something in the friction, the way he could hear and feel her breath at the same time. Something in the way she held perfectly still, and yet he could feel her heart pounding through her skin.

There was something in the fact that he knew it was *her*.

Colin moved his lips slightly to the left, until he was nipping the corner of her mouth, softly tickling the very spot where her lips joined. His tongue dipped and traced, learning the contours of her mouth, tasting the sweet-salty essence of her.

This was more than a kiss.

His hands, which had been lightly splayed against her back, grew rigid, more tense as they pressed into the fabric of her dress. He could feel the heat of her under his fingertips, seeping up through the muslin, swirling in the delicate muscles of her back.

He drew her to him, pulling her closer, closer, until their bodies were pressed together. He could feel her, the entire length of her, and it set him on fire. He was growing hard, and he wanted her—dear God, how he wanted her.

His mouth grew more insistent, and his tongue darted forward, nudging her until her lips parted. He swallowed her soft moan of acquiescence, then pushed forward to taste her. She was sweet and a little tart from the lemonade, and she was clearly as intoxicating as fine brandy, because Colin was starting to doubt his ability to remain on his feet.

He moved his hands along the length of her—slowly, so as not to frighten her. She was soft, curvy, and lush, just as he'd always thought a woman should be. Her hips flared, and her bottom was perfect, and her breasts . . . good God, her breasts felt good pressing against his chest. His palms itched to cup them, but he forced his hands to remain where they were (rather enjoyably on her derrière, so it really wasn't that much of a sacrifice.) Beside the fact that he really shouldn't be groping a gently bred lady's breasts in the middle of her drawing room, he had a rather painful suspicion that if he touched her in that way, he would lose himself completely.

"Penelope, Penelope," he murmured, wondering why her name tasted so good on his lips. He was ravenous for her, heady and drugged by passion, and he wanted desperately for her to feel the same way. She felt perfect in his arms, but thus far, she had made no reaction. Oh, she had swayed in his arms and opened her mouth to welcome his sweet invasion, but other than that, she had done nothing.

And yet, from the pant of her breath and the beat of her heart, he knew that she was aroused.

He pulled back, just a few inches so that he could touch her chin and tilt her face up toward his. Her eyelids fluttered open, revealing eyes that were dazed with passion, perfectly matching her lips, which were lightly parted, completely soft, and thoroughly swollen from his kisses.

She was beautiful. Utterly, completely, soul-stirringly beautiful. He didn't know how he hadn't noticed it all these years.

Was the world populated with blind men, or merely stupid ones?

"You can kiss me, too," he whispered, leaning his forehead lightly against hers.

She did nothing but blink.

"A kiss," he murmured, lowering his lips to hers again, although just for a fleeting moment, "is for two people."

Her hand stirred at his back. "What do I do?" she whispered.

"Whatever you want to do."

Slowly, tentatively, she lifted one of her hands to his face. Her fingers trailed lightly over his cheek, skimming along the line of his jaw until they fell away.

"Thank you," she whispered.

Thank you?

He went still.

It was *exactly* the wrong thing to say. He didn't want to be thanked for his kiss.

It made him feel guilty.

And shallow.

As if it had been something done out of pity. And the worst part was he knew that if all this had come to pass only a few months earlier, it *would* have been out of pity.

What the hell did that say about him?

"Don't thank me," he said gruffly, shoving himself backward until they were no longer touching.

"But—"

"I said *don't*," he repeated harshly, turning away as if he couldn't bear the sight of her, when the truth was that he couldn't quite bear himself.

And the damnedest thing was—he wasn't sure why. This desperate, gnawing feeling—was it guilt? Because he shouldn't have kissed her? Because he shouldn't have liked it?

"Colin," she said, "don't be angry with yourself."

"I'm not," he snapped.

"I asked you to kiss me. I practically forced you—"

Now, there was a surefire way to make a man feel manly. "You didn't force me," he bit off.

"No, but—"

"For the love of God, Penelope, *enough*!"

She drew back, her eyes wide. "I'm sorry," she whispered.

He looked down at her hands. They were shaking. He closed his eyes in agony. Why why *why* was he being such an ass?

"Penelope . . ." he began.

"No, it's all right," she said, her words rushed. "You don't have to say anything."

"No, I should."

"I really wish you wouldn't."

And now she looked so quietly dignified. Which made him feel even worse. She was standing there, her hands clasped demurely in front of her, her eyes downward—not quite on the floor, but not on his face.

She thought he'd kissed her out of pity.

And he was a knave because a small part of him wanted her to think that. Because if she thought it, then maybe he could convince himself that it was true, that it was just pity, that it couldn't possibly be more.

"I should go," he said, the words quiet, and yet still too loud in the silent room.

She didn't try to stop him.

He motioned to the door. "I should go," he said again, even as his feet refused to move.

She nodded.

"I didn't—" he started to say, and then, horrified by the words that had nearly come out of his mouth, he actually did head toward the door.

But Penelope called out—of *course* she called out—"You didn't what?"

And he didn't know what to say, because what he'd started to say was, *I didn't kiss you out of pity.* If he wanted her to know that, if he wanted to convince himself of that, then that could only mean that he craved her good opinion, which could only mean—

"I have to go," he blurted out, desperate now, as if leaving the room might be the only way to keep his thoughts from traveling down such a dangerous road. He crossed the remaining distance to the door, waiting for her to say something, to call out his name.

But she didn't.

And he left.

And he'd never hated himself more.

Colin was in an exceedingly bad mood before the footman showed up at his front door with a summons from his mother. Afterward, he was beyond repair.

Bloody hell. She was going to start in on him again about getting married. Her summonses were *always* about getting married. And he really wasn't in the mood for it right now.

But she was his mother. And he loved her. And that meant he

couldn't very well ignore her. So with considerable grumbling and a fair bit of cursing while he was at it, he yanked on his boots and coat, and headed out the door.

He was living in Bloomsbury, not the most fashionable section of town for a member of the aristocracy, although Bedford Square, where he had taken out a lease on a small but elegant terrace house, was certainly an upscale and respectable address.

Colin rather liked living in Bloomsbury, where his neighbors were doctors and lawyers and scholars and people who actually *did* things other than attend party after party. He wasn't ready to trade in his heritage for a life in trade—it was rather good to be a Bridgerton, after all—but there was something stimulating about watching professional men going about their daily business, the lawyers heading east to the Inns of the Court, the doctors northwest to Portland Place.

It would have been easy enough to drive his curricle across town; it had only been brought back to the mews an hour ago upon his return from the Featheringtons'. But Colin was feeling a bit in need of some fresh air, not to mention perverse enough to take the slowest means possible to Number Five.

If his mother intended to deliver another lecture on the virtues of marriage, followed by a lengthy dissertation on the attributes of each and every eligible miss in London, she could bloody well wait for him.

Colin closed his eyes and groaned. His mood must be worse than even he had thought if he was cursing in relation to his mother, whom he (and all the Bridgertons, really) held in the highest esteem and affection.

It was Penelope's fault.

No, it was Eloise's fault, he thought, grinding his teeth. Better to blame a sibling.

No—he slumped back into his desk chair, groaning—it was his

fault. If he was in a bad mood, if he was ready to yank someone's head off with his bare hands, it was his fault and his fault alone.

He shouldn't have kissed Penelope. It didn't matter that he'd *wanted* to kiss her, even though he hadn't even *realized* that he wanted to until right before she'd mentioned it. He still shouldn't have kissed her.

Although, when he really thought about it, he wasn't quite sure *why* he shouldn't have kissed her.

He stood, then trudged to the window and let his forehead rest against the pane. Bedford Square was quiet, with only a few men walking along the pavement. Laborers, they looked to be, probably working on the new museum being built just to the east. (It was why Colin had taken a house on the west side of the square; the construction could get very noisy.)

His gaze traveled north, to the statue of Charles James Fox. Now, there was a man with a purpose. Led the Whigs for years. He hadn't always been very well liked, if some of the older members of the *ton* were to be believed, but Colin was coming to think that perhaps being well liked was overrated. Heaven knew that no one was better liked than he was, and look at him now, frustrated and malcontent, grumpy and ready to lash out at anyone who crossed his path.

He sighed, planting one hand on the window frame and pushing himself back to an upright position. He'd better get going, especially if he was planning to walk all the way to Mayfair. Although, in truth, it really wasn't that far. Probably not more than thirty minutes if he kept his pace brisk (and he always did), less if the pavements weren't littered with slow people. It was longer than most members of the *ton* cared to be outside in London unless they were shopping or fashionably strolling in the park, but Colin felt the need to clear his head. And if the air in London wasn't particularly fresh, well, it would still have to do.

His luck that day being what it was, however, by the time he reached the intersection of Oxford and Regent Streets, the first splats of raindrops began to dance against his face. By the time he was turning off Hanover Square onto St. George Street, it was pouring in earnest. And he was just close enough to Bruton Street that it would have been really ridiculous to have tried to hail a hackney to take him the rest of the way.

So he walked on.

After the first minute or so of annoyance, however, the rain began to feel oddly good. It was warm enough out that it didn't chill him to the bone, and the fat, wet sting of it almost felt like a penance.

And he felt like maybe that was what he deserved.

The door to his mother's house opened before Colin's foot had even found the top step; Wickham must have been waiting for him.

"Might I suggest a towel?" the butler intoned, handing him a large white cloth.

Colin took it, wondering how on earth Wickham had had time to get a towel. He couldn't have known that Colin would be fool enough to walk in the rain.

Not for the first time it occurred to Colin that butlers must be possessed of strange, mystical powers. Perhaps it was a job requirement.

Colin used the towel to dry his hair, causing great consternation to Wickham, who was terribly proper and surely expected Colin to retire to a private room for at least a half an hour to mend his appearance.

"Where's my mother?" Colin asked.

Wickham's lips tightened, and he looked pointedly down at Colin's feet, which were now creating small puddles. "She is in her office," he replied, "but she is speaking with your sister."

"Which sister?" Colin asked, keeping a sunny smile on his face, just to annoy Wickham, who had surely been trying to annoy him by omitting his sister's name.

As if you could simply say "your sister" to a Bridgerton and expect him to know who you were talking about.

"Francesca."

"Ah, yes. She's returning to Scotland soon, isn't she?"

"Tomorrow."

Colin handed the towel back to Wickham, who regarded it as he might a large insect. "I won't bother her, then. Just let her know I'm here when she's done with Francesca."

Wickham nodded. "Would you care to change your clothes, Mr. Bridgerton? I believe we have some of your brother Gregory's garments upstairs in his bedchamber."

Colin found himself smiling. Gregory was finishing up his final term at Cambridge. He was eleven years younger than Colin, and it was difficult to believe they could actually share clothing, but he supposed it was time to accept that his little brother had finally grown up.

"That's an excellent idea," Colin said. He gave his sodden sleeve a rueful glance. "I'll leave these here to be cleaned and fetch them later."

Wickham nodded again, murmured, "As you wish," and disappeared down the hall to parts unknown.

Colin took the steps two at a time up to the family quarters. As he sloshed down the hall, he heard the sound of a door opening. Turning around, he saw that it was Eloise.

Not the person he wanted to see. She immediately brought back all the memories of his afternoon with Penelope. Their conversation. The kiss.

Especially the kiss.

And even worse, the guilt he'd felt afterward.

The guilt he still felt.

"Colin," Eloise said brightly, "I didn't realize you—what did you do, *walk?*"

He shrugged. "I like the rain."

She eyed him curiously, her head cocking to the side as it always did when she was puzzling through something. "You're in a rather odd mood today."

"I'm soaking wet, Eloise."

"No need to snap at me about it," she said with a sniff. "I didn't force you to walk across town in the rain."

"It wasn't raining when I left," he felt rather compelled to say. There was something about a sibling that brought out the eight-year-old in a body.

"I'm sure the sky was gray," she returned.

Clearly, she had a bit of the eight-year-old in her as well.

"May we continue this discussion when I'm dry?" he asked, his voice deliberately impatient.

"Of course," she said expansively, all accommodation. "I'll wait for you right here."

Colin took his time while he changed into Gregory's clothes, taking more care with his cravat than he had in years. Finally, when he was convinced that Eloise must be grinding her teeth, he reentered the hall.

"I heard you went to see Penelope today," she said without preamble.

Wrong thing to say.

"Where did you hear that?" he asked carefully. He knew that his sister and Penelope were close, but surely Penelope wouldn't have told Eloise about *that*.

"Felicity told Hyacinth."

"And Hyacinth told you."

"Of course."

"Something," Colin muttered, "has got to be done about all the gossip in this town."

"I hardly think this counts as gossip, Colin," Eloise said. "It's not as if you're *interested* in Penelope."

If she had been talking about any other woman, Colin would have expected her to give him a sidelong glance, followed by a coy, *Are you?*

But this was Penelope, and even though Eloise was her very best friend, and thus her finest champion, even she couldn't imagine that a man of Colin's reputation and popularity would be interested in a woman of Penelope's reputation and (lack of) popularity.

Colin's mood shifted from bad to foul.

"Anyway," Eloise continued, completely oblivious to the thunderstorm that was brewing in her normally sunny and jovial brother, "Felicity told Hyacinth that Briarly told her that you'd visited. I was just wondering what it was about."

"It's none of your business," Colin said briskly, hoping she'd leave it at that, but not really believing she would. He took a step toward the stairwell, though, always optimistic.

"It's about my birthday, isn't it?" Eloise guessed, dashing in front of him with such suddenness that his toe crashed into her slipper. She winced, but Colin didn't feel particularly sympathetic.

"No, it's not about your birthday," he snapped. "Your birthday isn't even until—"

He stopped. Ah, hell.

"Until next week," he grumbled.

She smiled slyly. Then, as if her brain had just realized it had taken a wrong turn, her lips parted with dismay as she mentally backed up and headed in another direction. "So," she continued, moving slightly so that she better blocked his path, "if you didn't go over there to discuss my birthday—and there's nothing you could say now that would convince me you did—why *did* you go see Penelope?"

"Is nothing private in this world?"

"Not in *this* family."

Colin decided that his best bet was to adopt his usual sunny persona, even though he didn't feel the least bit charitable toward her at the moment, and so he slapped on the smoothest and easiest of his smiles, quirked his head to the side, and asked, "Do I hear Mother calling my name?"

"I didn't hear a thing," Eloise said pertly, "and what is wrong with you? You look very odd."

"I'm fine."

"You're not fine. You look as if you've been to the dentist."

His voice descended into a mutter. "It's always nice to receive compliments from family."

"If you can't trust your family to be honest with you," she volleyed, "who *can* you trust?"

He leaned fluidly back against the wall, crossing his arms. "I prefer flattery to honesty."

"No, you don't."

Dear God, he wanted to smack her. He hadn't done that since he was twelve. And he'd been horsewhipped for it. The only time he could recall his father laying a hand on him.

"What I want," Colin returned, arching one brow, "is an immediate cessation of this conversation."

"What you want," Eloise needled, "is for me to stop asking you why you went to see Penelope Featherington, but I think we both know *that* isn't likely to occur."

And that was when he knew it. Knew it deep in his bones, from his head to his toes, his heart to his mind that his sister was Lady Whistledown. All of the pieces fit. There was no one more stubborn and bullheaded, no one who could—or would—take the time to get to the bottom of every last piece of gossip and innuendo.

When Eloise wanted something, she didn't stop until she had it firmly in her grasp. It wasn't about money, or greed, or material goods. With her it was about knowledge. She liked knowing things, and she'd needle and needle and needle until you'd told her exactly what she wanted to hear.

It was a miracle no one had found her out sooner.

Out of nowhere he said, "I need to talk to you." He grabbed her arm and hauled her into the nearest room, which happened to be her own.

"Colin!" she shrieked, trying unsuccessfully to shake him off. "What are you doing?"

He slammed the door shut, let go of her, and crossed his arms, his stance wide, his expression menacing.

"Colin?" she repeated, her voice dubious.

"I know what you've been up to."

"What I've been—"

And then, damn her, she started laughing.

"Eloise!" he boomed. "I'm talking to you!"

"Clearly," she just barely managed to get out.

He held his ground, glaring at her.

She was looking away, nearly doubled over with laughter. Finally, she said, "What are you—"

But then she looked at him again and even though she'd tried to keep her mouth shut, she exploded again.

If she'd been drinking something, Colin thought without a trace of humor, it would have come out her nose. "What the hell is the matter with you?" he snapped.

That finally got her attention. He didn't know whether it was his tone of voice or maybe his use of profanity, but she sobered in an instant.

"My word," she said softly, "you're serious."

"Do I look like I'm joking?"

"No," Eloise said. "Although you did at first. I'm sorry, Colin, but it's just not like you to be glowering and yelling and all that. You looked rather like Anthony."

"You—"

"Actually," she said, giving him a look that was not nearly as wary as it should have been, "you looked more like yourself, trying to imitate Anthony."

He was going to kill her. Right here in her room, in his mother's house, he was going to commit sororicide.

"Colin?" she asked hesitantly, as if she'd just finally noticed that he had long since passed angry on his way to furious.

"Sit. Down." He jerked his head toward a chair. "Now."

"Are you all right?"

"SIT DOWN!" he roared.

And she did. With alacrity.

"I can't remember the last time you raised your voice," she whispered.

"I can't remember the last time I had cause to."

"What's wrong?"

He decided he might as well just come out and say it.

"Colin?"

"I know you're Lady Whistledown."

"Whaaaaat?"

"There's no use denying it. I've seen—"

Eloise jumped to her feet. "Except that it's not true!"

Suddenly he no longer felt quite so angry. Instead he felt tired, old. "Eloise, I've seen the proof."

"What proof?" she asked, her voice rising with disbelief. "How can there be proof of something that isn't true?"

He grabbed one of her hands. "Look at your fingers."

She did so. "What about them?"

"Inkstains."

Her mouth fell open. "From *that* you've deduced that I'm Lady Whistledown?"

"Why are they there, then?"

"You've never used a quill?"

"Eloise . . ." There was a great deal of warning in his voice.

"I don't have to tell you why I have inkstains on my fingers."

He said her name again.

"I don't," she protested. "I owe you no—oh, very well, fine." She crossed her arms mutinously. "I write letters."

He shot her an extremely disbelieving look.

"I do!" she protested. "Every day. Sometimes two in a day when Francesca is away. I'm quite a loyal correspondent. You should know. I've written enough letters with *your* name on the envelope, although I doubt half of them ever reached you."

"Letters?" he asked, his voice full of doubt . . . and derision. "For God's sake, Eloise, do you really think that will wash? Who the devil are you writing so many letters to?"

She blushed. Really, truly, deeply blushed. "It's none of your business."

He would have been intrigued by her reaction if he still weren't so sure that she was lying about being Lady Whistledown. "For God's sake, Eloise," he bit off, "who is going to believe that you're writing letters every day? I certainly don't."

She glared at him, her dark gray eyes flashing with fury. "I don't care what you think," she said in a very low voice. "No, that's not true. I am *furious* that you don't believe me."

"You're not giving me much to believe in," he said wearily.

She stood, walked over to him, and poked him in the chest. Hard. "You are my brother," she spat out. "You should believe me unquestioningly. Love me unconditionally. That's what it means to be family."

"Eloise," he said, her name coming out really as nothing more than a sigh.

"Don't try to make excuses now."

"I wasn't."

"That's even worse!" She stalked to the door. "You should be on your hands and knees, begging me for forgiveness."

He hadn't thought he had it in him to smile, but somehow that did it for him. "Now, that doesn't really seem in keeping with my character, does it?"

She opened her mouth to say something, but the sound that came out was not precisely English. All she managed was something along the lines of, "Oooooooooh," in an extremely irate voice, and then she stormed out, slamming the door behind her.

Colin slouched into a chair, wondering when she'd realize that she'd left him in her own bedchamber.

The irony was, he reflected, possibly the only bright spot in an otherwise miserable day.

Chapter 10

Dear Reader—

It is with a surprisingly sentimental heart that I write these words. After eleven years of chronicling the lives and times of the beau monde, This Author is putting down her pen.

Although Lady Danbury's challenge was surely the catalyst for the retirement, in truth the blame cannot be placed (entirely) upon that countess's shoulders. The column has grown wearisome of late, less fulfilling to write, and perhaps less entertaining to read. This Author needs a change. It is not so difficult to fathom. Eleven years is a long time.

And in truth, the recent renewal of interest in This Author's identity has grown disturbing. Friends are turning against friends, brothers against sisters, all in the futile attempt to solve an unsolvable secret. Furthermore, the sleuthing of the ton has grown downright dangerous. Last week it was Lady Blackwood's twisted ankle, this week's injury apparently belongs to Hyacinth Bridgerton, who was slightly hurt at Saturday's soirée held at the London home of Lord and Lady Riverdale. (It has not escaped This Author's notice that Lord Riverdale is Lady Danbury's nephew.) Miss Hyacinth must *have suspected someone in attendance, because she sustained her injuries while falling into the library after the door was opened while she had her ear pressed up to the wood.*

Listening at doors, chasing down delivery boys—and these are only the tidbits that have reached This Author's ears! What has London Society come to? This Author assures you, Dear Reader, that she never once listened at a door in all eleven years of her career. All gossip in this column was come by fairly, with no tools or tricks other than keen eyes and ears.

I bid you au revoir, London! It has been a pleasure to serve you.

LADY WHISTLEDOWN'S SOCIETY PAPERS,
19 April 1824

It was, not surprisingly, the talk of the Macclesfield ball.

"Lady Whistledown has retired!"

"Can you believe it?"

"What will I read with my breakfast?"

"How will I know what happened if I miss a party?"

"We'll never find out who she is now!"

"Lady Whistledown has retired!"

One woman fainted, nearly cracking her head against the side of a table as she slumped gracelessly to the floor. Apparently, she had not read that morning's column and thus heard the news for the first time right there at the Macclesfield ball. She was revived by smelling salts but then quickly swooned again.

"She's a faker," Hyacinth Bridgerton muttered to Felicity Featherington as they stood in a small group with the Dowager Lady Bridgerton and Penelope. Penelope was officially attending as Felicity's chaperone due to their mother's decision to remain home with an upset stomach.

"The first faint was real," Hyacinth explained. "Anyone could tell that by the clumsy way she fell. But this . . ." Her hand flicked toward the lady on the floor with a gesture of disgust. "No one swoons like a ballet dancer. Not even ballet dancers."

Penelope had overheard the entire conversation, as Hyacinth was directly to her left, and so she murmured, "Have you ever swooned?" all the while keeping her eyes on the unfortunate woman, who was now coming awake with a delicate fluttering of eyelashes as the smelling salts were once again wafted under her nose.

"Absolutely not!" Hyacinth replied, with no small measure of pride. "Swoons are for the tenderhearted and foolish," she added. "And if Lady Whistledown were still writing, mark my words, she would say the exact same thing in her next column."

"Alas, there are no words to mark anymore," Felicity answered with a sad sigh.

Lady Bridgerton agreed. "It's the end of an era," she said. "I feel quite bereft without her."

"Well, it's not as if we've had to go more than eighteen hours without her yet," Penelope felt compelled to point out. "We did receive a column this morning. What is there yet to feel bereft about?"

"It's the principle of it," Lady Bridgerton said with a sigh. "If this were an ordinary Monday, I would know that I'd receive a new report on Wednesday. But now . . ."

Felicity actually sniffled. "Now we're lost," she said.

Penelope turned to her sister in disbelief. "Surely you're being a little melodramatic."

Felicity's overblown shrug was worthy of the stage. "Am I? *Am I?*"

Hyacinth gave her a sympathetic pat on the back. "I don't think you are, Felicity. I feel precisely the same way."

"It's only a gossip column," Penelope said, looking around for any sign of sanity in her companions. Surely they realized that the world was not drawing to a close just because Lady Whistledown had decided to end her career.

"You're right, of course," said Lady Bridgerton, jutting her chin out and pursing her lips in a manner that was probably supposed to convey an air of practicality. "Thank you for being the voice of reason for our little party." But then she seemed to deflate slightly, and she said, "But I must admit, I'd grown rather used to having her around. Whoever she is."

Penelope decided it was well past time to change the topic. "Where is Eloise this evening?"

"Ill, I'm afraid. A headache," Lady Bridgerton said, small frowns of worry creasing her otherwise unlined face. "She hasn't been feeling the thing for almost a week now. I'm starting to grow concerned about her."

Penelope had been staring rather aimlessly at a sconce on the wall, but her attention was immediately brought back to Lady Bridgerton. "It's nothing serious, I hope?"

"It's nothing serious," Hyacinth answered, before her mother could even open her mouth. "Eloise never gets sick."

"Which is precisely why I'm worried," Lady Bridgerton said. "She hasn't been eating very well."

"That's not true," Hyacinth said. "Just this afternoon Wickham brought up a very heavy tray. Scones and eggs and I think I smelled gammon steak." She gave an arch look to no one in particular. "And when Eloise left the tray out in the hall it was completely empty."

Hyacinth Bridgerton, Penelope decided, had a surprisingly good eye for detail.

"She's been in a bad mood," Hyacinth continued, "since she quarreled with Colin."

"She quarreled with Colin?" Penelope asked, an awful feeling beginning to roil her stomach. "When?"

"Sometime last week," Hyacinth said.

WHEN? Penelope wanted to scream, but surely it would look odd if she demanded an exact day. Was it Friday? Was it?

Penelope would always remember that her first, and most probably only, kiss had occurred on a Friday.

She was strange that way. She always remembered the days of the week.

She'd met Colin on a Monday.

She'd kissed him on a Friday.

Twelve years later.

She sighed. It seemed fairly pathetic.

"Is something wrong, Penelope?" Lady Bridgerton asked.

Penelope looked at Eloise's mother. Her blue eyes were kind and filled with concern, and there was something about the way she tilted her head to the side that made Penelope want to cry.

She was getting far too emotional these days. Crying over the tilt of a head.

"I'm fine," she said, hoping that her smile looked true. "I'm just worried about Eloise."

Hyacinth snorted.

Penelope decided she needed to make her escape. All these Bridgertons—well, two of them, anyway—were making her think of Colin.

Which wasn't anything she hadn't been doing nearly every minute of the day for the past three days. But at least that had been in private where she could sigh and moan and grumble to her heart's content.

But this must have been her lucky night, because just then she heard Lady Danbury barking her name.

(What was her world coming to, that she considered herself lucky to be trapped in a corner with London's most acerbic tongue?)

But Lady Danbury would provide the perfect excuse to leave her current little quartet of ladies, and besides, she was coming to realize that in a very odd way, she rather liked Lady Danbury.

"Miss Featherington! Miss Featherington!"

Felicity instantly took a step away. "I think she means you," she whispered urgently.

"Of course she means me," Penelope said, with just a touch of hauteur. "I consider Lady Danbury a cherished friend."

Felicity's eyes bugged out. "You do?"

"Miss Featherington!" Lady Danbury said, thumping her cane an inch away from Penelope's foot as soon as she reached her side. "Not you," she said to Felicity, even though Felicity had done nothing more than smile politely as the countess had approached. "You," she said to Penelope.

"Er, good evening, Lady Danbury," Penelope said, which she considered an admirable number of words under the circumstances.

"I have been looking for you all evening," Lady D announced.

Penelope found that a trifle surprising. "You have?"

"Yes. I want to talk with you about that Whistledown woman's last column."

"Me?"

"Yes, you," Lady Danbury grumbled. "I'd be happy to talk with someone else if you could find me a body with more than half a brain."

Penelope choked on the beginnings of laughter as she motioned to her companions. "Er, I assure you that Lady Bridgerton—"

Lady Bridgerton was furiously shaking her head.

"She's too busy trying to get that oversized brood of hers married off," Lady Danbury announced. "Can't be expected to know how to conduct a decent conversation these days."

Penelope stole a frantic glance over at Lady Bridgerton to see if she was upset by the insult—after all, she had been trying to marry off her oversized brood for a decade now. But Lady Bridgerton didn't look the least bit upset. In fact, she appeared to be stifling laughter.

Stifling laughter and inching away, taking Hyacinth and Felicity with her.

Sneaky little traitors.

Ah, well, Penelope shouldn't complain. She'd wanted an escape from the Bridgertons, hadn't she? But she didn't particularly enjoy having Felicity and Hyacinth think they'd somehow pulled one over on her.

"They're gone now," Lady Danbury cackled, "and a good thing it is, too. Those two gels haven't an intelligent thing to say between them."

"Oh, now, that isn't true," Penelope felt compelled to protest. "Felicity and Hyacinth are both very bright."

"I never said they weren't smart," Lady D replied acidly, "just that they haven't an intelligent thing to say. But don't worry," she added, giving Penelope a reassuring—reassuring? whoever heard of Lady Danbury being reassuring?—pat on the arm. "It's not their fault that their conversation is useless. They'll grow out of it. People are like fine wines. If they start off good, they only get better with age."

Penelope had actually been glancing slightly to the right of Lady Danbury's face, peering over her shoulder at a man who she thought might be Colin (but wasn't), but this brought her attention right back to where the countess wanted it.

"Fine wines?" Penelope echoed.

"Hmmph. And here I thought you weren't listening."

"No, of course I was listening." Penelope felt her lips tugging into something that wasn't quite a smile. "I was just . . . distracted."

"Looking for that Bridgerton boy, no doubt."

Penelope gasped.

"Oh, don't look so shocked. It's written all over your face. I'm just surprised he hasn't noticed."

"I imagine he has," Penelope mumbled.

"Has he? Hmmph." Lady Danbury frowned, the corners of her mouth spilling into long vertical wrinkles on either side of her chin. "Doesn't speak well of him that he hasn't done anything about it."

Penelope's heart ached. There was something oddly sweet about the old lady's faith in her, as if men like Colin fell in love with women like Penelope on a regular basis. Penelope had had to beg him to kiss her, for heaven's sake. And look how that had ended up. He'd left the house in a fit of temper and they hadn't spoken for three days.

"Well, don't worry over him," Lady Danbury said quite suddenly. "We'll find you someone else."

Penelope delicately cleared her throat. "Lady Danbury, have you made me your *project*?"

The old lady beamed, her smile a bright and glowing streak in her wrinkled face. "Of course! I'm surprised it has taken you so long to figure it out."

"But why?" Penelope asked, truly unable to fathom it.

Lady Danbury sighed. The sound wasn't sad—more wistful, really. "Would you mind if we sat down for a spell? These old bones aren't what they used to be."

"Of course," Penelope said quickly, feeling terrible that she'd never once considered Lady Danbury's age as they stood there in the stuffy ballroom. But the countess was so vibrant; it was difficult to imagine her ailing or weak.

"Here we are," Penelope said, taking her arm and leading her to a nearby chair. Once Lady Danbury was settled, Penelope took a seat beside her. "Are you more comfortable now? Would you like something to drink?"

Lady Danbury nodded gratefully, and Penelope signaled to a footman to bring them two glasses of lemonade, since she didn't want to leave the countess while she was looking so pale.

"I'm not as young as I used to be," Lady Danbury told her once the footman had hied off to the refreshment table.

"None of us are," Penelope replied. It could have been a flip comment, but it was spoken with wry warmth, and somehow Penelope thought that Lady Danbury would appreciate the sentiment.

She was right. Lady D chuckled and sent Penelope an appreciative glance before saying, "The older I get, the more I realize that most of the people in this world are fools."

"You're only just figuring that out now?" Penelope asked, not to mock, but rather because, given Lady Danbury's usual demeanor, it was difficult to believe that she hadn't reached that conclusion years ago.

Lady Danbury laughed heartily. "No, sometimes I think I knew that before I was born. What I'm realizing now is that it's time I did something about it."

"What do you mean?"

"I couldn't care less what happens to the fools of this world, but the people like you"—lacking a handkerchief, she dabbed at her eyes with her fingers—"well, I'd like to see you settled."

For several seconds, Penelope did nothing but stare at her. "Lady Danbury," she said carefully, "I very much appreciate the gesture . . . and the sentiment . . . but you must know that I am not your responsibility."

"Of course I know that," Lady Danbury scoffed. "Have no fear, I feel no responsibility to you. If I did, this wouldn't be half so much fun."

Penelope knew she sounded the veriest ninny, but all she could think to say was, "I don't understand."

Lady Danbury held silent while the footmen returned with their lemonade, then began speaking once she had taken several small sips. "I like you, Miss Featherington. I don't like a lot of people. It's as simple as that. And I want to see you happy."

"But I am happy," Penelope said, more out of reflex than anything else.

Lady Danbury raised one arrogant brow—an expression that she did to perfection. "Are you?" she murmured.

Was she? What did it mean, that she had to stop and think about the answer? She wasn't *un*happy, of that she was sure. She had wonderful friends, a true confidante in her younger sister Felicity, and if her mother and older sisters weren't women she'd have chosen as close friends—well, she still loved them. And she knew they loved her.

Hers wasn't such a bad lot. Her life lacked drama and excitement, but she was content.

But contentment wasn't the same thing as happiness, and she felt a sharp, stabbing pain in her chest as she realized that she could not answer Lady Danbury's softly worded question in the affirmative.

"I've raised my family," Lady Danbury said. "Four children, and they all married well. I even found a bride for my nephew, who, truth be told"—she leaned in and whispered the last three words, giving Penelope the impression that she was about to divulge a state secret—"I like better than my own children."

Penelope couldn't help but smile. Lady Danbury looked so furtive, so naughty. It was rather cute, actually.

"It may surprise you," Lady Danbury continued, "but by nature I'm a bit of a meddler."

Penelope kept her expression scrupulously even.

"I find myself at loose ends," Lady Danbury said, holding up her hands as if in surrender. "I'd like to see one last person happily settled before I go."

"Don't talk that way, Lady Danbury," Penelope said, impulsively reaching out and taking her hand. She gave it a little squeeze. "You'll outlive us all, I am certain."

"Pfffft, don't be silly." Lady Danbury's tone was dismissive, but she made no move to remove her hand from Penelope's grasp. "I'm not being depressive," she added. "I'm just realistic. I've passed seventy years of age, and I'm not going to tell you how many years ago that was. I haven't much time left in this world, and that doesn't bother me one bit."

Penelope hoped she would be able to face her own mortality with the same equanimity.

"But I like you, Miss Featherington. You remind me of myself. You're not afraid to speak your mind."

Penelope could only look at her in shock. She'd spent the last ten years of her life never quite saying what she wanted to say. With people she knew well she was open and honest and even sometimes a little funny, but among strangers her tongue was quite firmly tied.

She remembered a masquerade ball she'd once attended. She'd attended many masquerade balls, actually, but this one had been unique because she'd actually found a costume—nothing special, just a gown styled as if from the 1600s—in which she'd truly felt her identity was hidden. It had probably been the mask. It was overly large and covered almost all of her face.

She had felt transformed. Suddenly free of the burden of being Penelope Featherington, she felt a new personality coming to the fore. It wasn't as if she had been putting on false airs; rather, it was more like her true self—the one she didn't know how to show to anyone she didn't know well—had finally broken loose.

She'd laughed; she'd joked. She'd even flirted.

And she'd sworn that the following night, when the costumes were all put away and she was once again attired in her finest evening dress, she'd remember how to be herself.

But it hadn't happened. She'd arrived at the ball and she'd nodded and smiled politely and once again found herself standing near the perimeter of the room, quite literally a wallflower.

It seemed that being Penelope Featherington meant something. Her lot had been cast years ago, during that first awful season when her mother had insisted she make her debut even though Penelope had begged otherwise. The pudgy girl. The awkward girl. The one always dressed in colors that didn't suit her. It didn't matter that she'd slimmed and grown graceful and finally thrown out all of her yellow dresses. In this world—the world of London society and the *ton*—she would always be the same old Penelope Featherington.

It was her own fault just as much as anyone else's. A vicious circle, really. Every time Penelope stepped into a ballroom, and she saw all those people who had known her for so long, she felt herself folding up inside, turning into the shy, awkward girl of years gone past, rather than the self-assured woman she liked to think she'd become—at least in her heart.

"Miss Featherington?" came Lady Danbury's soft—and surprisingly gentle—voice. "Is something wrong?"

Penelope knew she took longer than she should have to reply, but somehow she needed a few seconds to find her voice. "I don't think I know how to speak my mind," she finally said, turning to look at Lady Danbury only as she uttered the final words of the sentence. "I never know what to say to people."

"You know what to say to *me*."

"You're different."

Lady Danbury threw her head back and laughed. "If ever there was an understatement . . . Oh, Penelope—I hope you don't mind if I call you by your given name—if you can speak your mind to me, you can speak it to anyone. Half the grown men in this room run cowering into corners the minute they see me coming."

"They just don't know you," Penelope said, patting her on the hand.

"And they don't know *you*, either," Lady Danbury quite pointedly replied.

"No," Penelope said, a touch of resignation in her voice, "they don't."

"I'd say that it was their loss, but that would be rather cavalier of me," Lady Danbury said. "Not to them, but to you, because as often as I call them all fools—and I do call them fools often, as I'm sure you know—some of them are actually rather decent people, and it's a crime they haven't gotten to know you. I—Hmmm . . . I wonder what is going on."

Penelope found herself unaccountably sitting up a little straighter.

She asked Lady Danbury, "What do you mean?" but it was clear that something was afoot. People were whispering and motioning to the small dais where the musicians were seated.

"You there!" Lady Danbury said, poking her cane into the hip of a nearby gentleman. "What is going on?"

"Cressida Twombley wants to make some sort of announcement," he said, then quickly stepped away, presumably to avoid any further conversation with Lady Danbury or her cane.

"I hate Cressida Twombley," Penelope muttered.

Lady Danbury choked on a bit of laughter. "And you say you don't know how to speak your mind. Don't keep me in suspense. Why do you detest her so?"

Penelope shrugged. "She's always behaved quite badly toward me."

Lady Danbury nodded knowingly. "All bullies have a favorite victim."

"It's not so bad now," Penelope said. "But back when we were both out—when she was still Cressida Cowper—she never could resist the chance to torment me. And people . . . well . . ." She shook her head. "Never mind."

"No, please," Lady Danbury said, "do go on."

Penelope sighed. "It's nothing, really. Just that I've noticed that people don't often rush to another's defense. Cressida was popular— at least with a certain set—and she was rather frightening to the other girls our age. No one dared go against her. Well, almost no one."

That got Lady Danbury's attention, and she smiled. "Who was your champion, Penelope?"

"Champions, actually," Penelope replied. "The Bridgertons always came to my aid. Anthony Bridgerton once gave her the cut direct and took me in to dinner, and"—her voice rose with remembered excitement—"he really shouldn't have done so. It was a formal dinner party, and he was supposed to escort in some marchioness, I think." She sighed, treasuring the memory. "It was lovely."

"He's a good man, that Anthony Bridgerton."

Penelope nodded. "His wife told me that that was the day she fell in love with him. When she saw him being my hero."

Lady Danbury smiled. "And has the younger Mr. Bridgerton ever rushed to your aid?"

"Colin, you mean?" Penelope didn't even wait for Lady Danbury's nod before adding, "Of course, although never with quite so much drama. But I must say, as nice as it is that the Bridgertons are so supportive. . . ."

"What is it, Penelope?" Lady Danbury asked.

Penelope sighed again. It seemed a night for sighs. "I just wish they didn't have to defend me so often. You'd think I could defend myself. Or at least comport myself in such a manner so that no defending was necessary."

Lady Danbury patted her hand. "I think you get on a great deal better than you think you do. And as for that Cressida Twombley . . ." Lady Danbury's face soured with distaste. "Well, she got her just desserts, if you ask me. Although," she added sharply, "people don't ask me as often as they should."

Penelope could not quite suppress a little snort of laughter.

"Look where she is now," Lady Danbury said sharply. "Widowed and without even a fortune to show for it. She married that old lecher Horace Twombley and it turned out he'd managed to fool everyone into thinking he had money. Now she has nothing but fading good looks."

Honesty compelled Penelope to say, "She is still quite attractive."

"Hmmph. If you like flashy women." Lady Danbury's eyes narrowed. "There is something far too obvious about that woman."

Penelope looked toward the dais, where Cressida was waiting, standing there with a surprising amount of patience while the ballroom quieted down. "I wonder what she is going to say."

"Nothing that could possibly interest me," Lady Danbury retorted. "I—Oh." She stopped, and her lips curved into the oddest of expressions, a little bit frown, a little bit smile.

"What is it?" Penelope asked. She craned her neck to try to see Lady Danbury's line of vision, but a rather portly gentleman was blocking her way.

"Your Mr. Bridgerton is approaching," Lady Danbury said, the smile edging out the frown. "And he looks quite determined."

Penelope immediately twisted her head around.

"For the love of God, girl, don't look!" Lady Danbury exclaimed, jamming her elbow into Penelope's upper arm. "He'll know you're interested."

"I don't think there's much of a chance he hasn't figured that out already," Penelope mumbled.

And then there he was, standing splendidly in front of her, looking like some handsome god, deigning to grace earth with his presence. "Lady Danbury," he said, executing a smooth and graceful bow. "Miss Featherington."

"Mr. Bridgerton," Lady Danbury said, "how nice to see you."

Colin looked to Penelope.

"Mr. Bridgerton," she murmured, not knowing what else to say. What *did* one say to a man one had recently kissed? Penelope certainly had no experience in that area. Not to mention the added complication of his storming out of the house once they were through.

"I'd hoped . . ." Colin began, then stopped and frowned, looking up toward the dais. "What is everyone looking at?"

"Cressida Twombley has some sort of announcement," Lady Danbury said.

Colin's face slid into a vaguely annoyed frown. "Can't imagine what she has to say that I'd want to listen to," he muttered.

Penelope couldn't help but grin. Cressida Twombley was considered a leader in society, or at least she had been when she'd been

young and unmarried, but the Bridgertons had never liked her, and
somehow that had always made Penelope feel a little better.

Just then a trumpet blared, and the room fell silent as everyone
turned their attention to the Earl of Macclesfield, who was standing
on the dais next to Cressida, looking vaguely uncomfortable with all
the attention.

Penelope smiled. She'd been told the earl had once been a terrible
rake, but now he was a rather scholarly sort, devoted to his family.
He was still handsome enough to be a rake, though. Almost as handsome as Colin.

But only almost. Penelope knew she was biased, but it was difficult to imagine any creature quite as magnetically good-looking as
Colin when he was smiling.

"Good evening," the earl said loudly.

"Good evening to you!" came a drunken shout from the back of
the room.

The earl gave a good-natured nod, a tolerant half-smile playing along his lips. "My, er, esteemed guest here"—he motioned
to Cressida—"would like to make an announcement. So if you
would all give your attention to the lady beside me, I give you Lady
Twombley."

A low ripple of whispers spread across the room as Cressida
stepped forward, nodding regally at the crowd. She waited for the
room to fall into stark silence, and then she said, "Ladies and gentleman, thank you so much for taking time out of your festivities to
lend me your attention."

"Hurry up with it!" someone shouted, probably the same person
who had yelled good evening to the earl.

Cressida ignored the interruption. "I have come to the conclusion
that I can no longer continue the deception that has ruled my life for
the last eleven years."

The ballroom was rocked with the low buzz of whispers. Everyone knew what she was going to say, and yet no one could believe it was actually true.

"Therefore," Cressida continued, her voice growing in volume, "I have decided to reveal my secret.

"Ladies and gentleman, *I am Lady Whistledown.*"

Chapter 11

Colin couldn't remember the last time he'd entered a ballroom with quite so much apprehension.

The last few days had not been among his best. He'd been in a bad mood, which had only been worsened by the fact that he was rather renowned for his good humor, which meant that everyone had felt compelled to comment on his foul disposition.

There was nothing worse for a bad mood than being subjected to constant queries of, "Why are you in such a bad mood?"

His family had stopped asking after he'd actually snarled—snarled!—at Hyacinth when she'd asked him to accompany her to the theater the following week.

Colin hadn't even been aware that he knew how to snarl.

He was going to have to apologize to Hyacinth, which was going to be a chore, since Hyacinth never accepted apologies gracefully—at least not those that came from fellow Bridgertons.

But Hyacinth was the least of his problems. Colin groaned. His sister wasn't the only person who deserved his apology.

And that was why his heart was beating with this strange, nervous, and completely unprecedented rapidity as he entered the Macclesfield ballroom. Penelope would be here. He knew she'd be here because she always attended the major balls, even if she was now most often doing so as her sister's chaperone.

There was something quite humbling in feeling nervous about seeing Penelope. Penelope was . . . Penelope. It was almost as if she'd always been there, smiling politely at the perimeter of a ballroom. And he'd taken her for granted, in a way. Some things didn't change, and Penelope was one of them.

Except she *had* changed.

Colin didn't know when it had happened, or even if anyone other than himself had noticed it, but Penelope Featherington was not the same woman he used to know.

Or maybe she was, and *he* had changed.

Which made him feel even worse, because if that was the case, then Penelope had been interesting and lovely and kissable years ago, and he hadn't the maturity to notice.

No, better to think that Penelope had changed. Colin had never been a great fan of self-flagellation.

Whatever the case, he needed to make his apology, and he needed to do it soon. He had to apologize for the kiss, because she was a lady and he was (most of the time, at least) a gentleman. And he had to apologize for behaving like a raving idiot afterward, because it was simply the right thing to do.

God only knew what Penelope thought he thought of her now.

It wasn't difficult to find her once he entered the ballroom. He didn't bother to look among the dancing couples (which angered him—why didn't the other men think to ask her to dance?). Rather, he focused his attention along the walls, and sure enough, there she was, seated on a long bench next to—oh, *God*—Lady Danbury.

Well, there was nothing else to do but walk right up. The way Penelope and the old busybody were clutching each other's hands, he couldn't expect Lady Danbury to disappear anytime soon.

When he reached the pair of ladies, he turned first to Lady Danbury and swept into an elegant bow. "Lady Danbury," he said, before turning his attention to Penelope. "Miss Featherington."

"Mr. Bridgerton," Lady Danbury said, with a surprising lack of sharpness in her voice, "how nice to see you."

He nodded, then looked to Penelope, wondering what she was thinking, and whether he'd be able to see it in her eyes.

But whatever she was thinking—or feeling—it was hidden under a rather thick layer of nervousness. Or maybe the nervousness was all she was feeling. He couldn't really blame her. The way he'd stormed out of her drawing room without an explanation . . . she had to feel confused. And it was his experience that confusion invariably led to apprehension.

"Mr. Bridgerton," she finally murmured, her entire bearing scrupulously polite.

He cleared his throat. How to extract her from Lady Danbury's clutches? He'd really rather not humble himself in front of the nosy old countess.

"I'd hoped . . ." he began, intending to say that he'd hoped to have a private word with Penelope. Lady Danbury would be ferociously curious, but there was really no other course of action, and it would probably do her good to be left in the dark for once.

But just as his lips were forming his query, he realized that something strange was afoot in the Macclesfield ballroom. People were whispering and pointing toward the small orchestra, whose members had recently laid their instruments down. Furthermore, neither Penelope nor Lady Danbury were paying him the least attention.

"What is everyone looking at?" Colin asked.

Lady Danbury didn't even bother looking back at him as she replied, "Cressida Twombley has some sort of announcement."

How annoying. He'd never liked Cressida. She'd been mean and petty when she was Cressida Cowper, and she was meaner and pettier as Cressida Twombley. But she was beautiful, and she was intelligent, in a rather cruel sort of way, and so she was still considered a leader in certain society circles.

"Can't imagine what she has to say that I'd want to listen to," Colin muttered.

He spied Penelope trying to stifle a smile and flashed her an I-caught-you sort of look. But it was the sort of I-caught-you look that also said And-I-agree-completely.

"Good evening!" came the loud voice of the Earl of Macclesfield.

"Good evening to you!" replied some drunken fool in the back. Colin twisted to see who it was, but the crowd had grown too thick.

The earl spoke some more, then Cressida opened her mouth, at which point Colin ceased paying attention. Whatever Cressida had to say, it wasn't going to help him solve his main problem: figuring out exactly how he was going to apologize to Penelope. He'd tried rehearsing the words in his mind, but they never sounded quite right, and so he was hoping his famously glib tongue would lead him in the right direction when the time came. Surely she'd understand—

"Whistledown!"

Colin only caught the last word of Cressida's monologue, but there was no way he could have missed the massive collective indrawn breath that swept the ballroom.

Followed by the flurry of harsh, urgent whispers one generally only hears after someone is caught in a very embarrassing, very public compromising position.

"What?" he blurted out, turning to Penelope, who'd gone white as a sheet. "What did she say?"

But Penelope was speechless.

He looked to Lady Danbury, but the old lady had her hand over her mouth and looked as if she might possibly swoon.

Which was somewhat alarming, as Colin would have bet large sums of money that Lady Danbury had never once swooned in all of her seventy-odd years.

"What?" he demanded again, hoping one of them would break free of her stupor.

"It can't be true," Lady Danbury finally whispered, her mouth slack even as she spoke the words. "I don't believe it."

"*What?*"

She pointed toward Cressida, her extended index finger quivering in the flickering candlelight. "That lady is not Lady Whistledown."

Colin's head snapped back and forth. To Cressida. To Lady Danbury. To Cressida. To Penelope. "*She's* Lady Whistledown?" he finally blurted out.

"So she says," Lady Danbury replied, doubt written all over her face.

Colin tended to agree with her. Cressida Twombley was the last person he'd have pegged as Lady Whistledown. She was smart; there was no denying that. But she wasn't clever, and she wasn't terribly witty unless she was poking fun at others. Lady Whistledown had a rather cutting sense of humor, but with the exception of her infamous comments on fashion, she never seemed to pick on the less popular members of society.

When all was said and done, Colin had to say that Lady Whistledown had rather good taste in people.

"I can't believe this," Lady Danbury said with a loud snort of disgust. "If I'd dreamed *this* would happen, I would never have made that beastly challenge."

"This is horrible," Penelope whispered.

Her voice was quavering, and it made Colin uneasy. "Are you all right?" he asked.

She shook her head. "No, I don't think I am. I feel rather ill, actually."

"Do you want to leave?"

Penelope shook her head again. "But I'll sit right here, if you don't mind."

"Of course," he said, keeping a concerned eye on her. She was still terribly pale.

"Oh, for the love of . . ." Lady Danbury blasphemed, which took

Colin by surprise, but then she actually swore, which he thought might very well have tilted the planet on its axis.

"Lady Danbury?" he asked, gaping.

"She's coming this way," she muttered, jerking her head to the right. "I should have known I'd not escape."

Colin looked to his left. Cressida was trying to make her way through the crowd, presumably to confront Lady Danbury and collect her prize. She was, naturally, being accosted at every turn by fellow partygoers. She seemed to be reveling in the attention—no big surprise there; Cressida had always reveled in attention—but she also seemed rather determined to reach Lady Danbury's side.

"There's no way to avoid her, I'm afraid," Colin said to Lady Danbury.

"I know," she grumbled. "I've been trying to avoid her for years, and I've never succeeded. I thought I was so clever." She looked to Colin, shaking her head with disgust. "I thought it would be such fun to rout out Lady Whistledown."

"Er, well, it was fun," Colin said, not really meaning it.

Lady Danbury jabbed him in the leg with her cane. "It's not the least bit fun, you foolish boy. Now look what I have to do!" She waved the cane toward Cressida, who was drawing ever closer. "I never dreamed I'd have to deal with the likes of *her.*"

"Lady Danbury," Cressida said, swishing to a stop in front of her. "How nice to see you."

Lady Danbury had never been known for her pleasantries, but even she outdid herself by skipping any pretense of a greeting before snapping, "I suppose you're here to try to collect your money."

Cressida cocked her head to the side in a very pretty, very practiced manner. "You did say you would give a thousand pounds to whomever unmasked Lady Whistledown." She shrugged, lifting her hands in the air and then twisting them gracefully until her palms were up in a gesture of false humility. "You never stipulated that I couldn't unmask myself."

Lady Danbury rose to her feet, narrowed her eyes, and said, "I don't believe it's you."

Colin liked to think that he was rather suave and unflappable, but even he gasped at that.

Cressida's blue eyes blazed with fury, but she quickly regained control of her emotions and said, "I would be shocked if you did not behave with a degree of skepticism, Lady Danbury. After all, it is not your way to be trusting and gentle."

Lady Danbury smiled. Well, perhaps not a smile, but her lips did move. "I shall take that as a compliment," she said, "and allow you to tell me that you meant it as such."

Colin watched the stalemate with interest—and with a growing sense of alarm—until Lady Danbury turned quite suddenly to Penelope, who had risen to her feet mere seconds after she had.

"What do you think, Miss Featherington?" Lady Danbury asked.

Penelope visibly started, her entire body jerking slightly as she stammered, "What . . . I . . . I beg your pardon?"

"What do you think?" Lady Danbury persisted. "Is Lady Twombley Lady Whistledown?"

"I—I'm sure I don't know."

"Oh, come, now, Miss Featherington." Lady Danbury planted her hands on her hips and looked at Penelope with an expression that bordered on exasperation. "Surely you have an opinion on the matter."

Colin felt himself stepping forward. Lady Danbury had no right to speak to Penelope in such a manner. And furthermore, he didn't like the expression on Penelope's face. She looked trapped, like a fox in a hunt, her eyes darting to him with a panic he'd never seen there before.

He'd seen Penelope uncomfortable, and he'd seen her pained, but he'd never seen her truly panicked. And then it occurred to him— she hated being the center of attention. She might poke fun at her status as a wallflower and a spinster, and she'd probably have liked a little more attention from society, but this kind of attention . . . with everyone staring at her and awaiting the merest word from her lips . . .

She was miserable.

"Miss Featherington," Colin said smoothly, moving to her side, "you look unwell. Would you like to leave?"

"Yes," she said, but then something strange happened.

She changed. He didn't know how else to describe it. She simply changed. Right there, in the Macclesfield ballroom, by his side, Penelope Featherington became someone else.

Her spine stiffened, and he could swear the heat from her body increased, and she said, "No. No, I have something to say."

Lady Danbury smiled.

Penelope looked straight at the old countess and said, "I don't think she's Lady Whistledown. I think she's lying."

Colin instinctively pulled Penelope a little closer to his side. Cressida looked as if she might go for her throat.

"I've always liked Lady Whistledown," Penelope said, her chin rising until her bearing was almost regal. She looked to Cressida, and their eyes caught as she added, "And it would break my heart if she turned out to be someone like Lady Twombley."

Colin took her hand and squeezed it. He couldn't help himself.

"Well said, Miss Featherington!" Lady Danbury exclaimed, clapping her hands together in delight. "That is exactly what I was thinking, but I couldn't find the words." She turned to Colin with a smile. "She's very clever, you know."

"I know," he replied, a strange, new pride brimming within him.

"Most people don't notice it," Lady Danbury said, twisting so that her words were directed to—and probably only heard by—Colin.

"I know," he murmured, "but I do." He had to smile at Lady Danbury's behavior, which he was certain was chosen in part to annoy the devil out of Cressida, who did *not* like to be ignored.

"I will not be insulted by that . . . by that *nothing*!" Cressida fumed. She turned to Penelope with a seething glare and hissed, "I demand an apology."

Penelope just nodded slowly and said, "That is your prerogative."

And then she said nothing more.

Colin had to physically wipe the smile from his face.

Cressida clearly wanted to say more (and perhaps commit an act of violence while she was at it), but she held back, presumably because it was obvious that Penelope was among friends. She had always been renowned for her poise, however, and thus Colin was not surprised when she composed herself, turned to Lady Danbury, and said, "What do you plan to do about the thousand pounds?"

Lady Danbury looked at her for the longest second Colin had ever endured, then she turned to *him*—dear God, the last thing he wanted to do was get involved in this disaster—and asked, "And what do you think, Mr. Bridgerton? Is our Lady Twombley telling the truth?"

Colin gave her a practiced smile. "You must be mad if you think I'm going to offer an opinion."

"You're a surprisingly wise man, Mr. Bridgerton," Lady Danbury said approvingly.

He nodded modestly, then ruined the effect by saying, "I pride myself on it." But what the hell—it wasn't every day a man was called wise by Lady Danbury.

Most of her adjectives, after all, were of the decidedly negative variety.

Cressida didn't even bother to bat her eyelashes at him; as Colin had already reflected, she wasn't stupid, just mean, and after a dozen years out in society, she had to know that he didn't much like her and certainly wasn't about to fall prey to her charms. Instead, she looked squarely at Lady Danbury and kept her voice evenly modulated as she asked, "What shall we do now, my lady?"

Lady Danbury's lips pursed together until she almost appeared mouthless, then she said, "I need proof."

Cressida blinked. "I beg your pardon?"

"Proof!" Lady Danbury's cane slammed against the floor with remarkable force. "Which letter of the word did you not understand? I'm not handing over a king's ransom without proof."

"One thousand pounds is hardly a king's ransom," Cressida said, her expression growing petulant.

Lady Danbury's eyes narrowed. "Then why are you so keen to get it?"

Cressida was silent for a moment, but there was a tightness in everything about her—her stance, her posture, the line of her jaw. Everyone knew that her husband had left her in bad financial straits, but this was the first time anyone had hinted as such to her face.

"Get me proof," Lady Danbury said, "and I'll give you the money."

"Are you saying," Cressida said (and even as he despised her, Colin was forced to admire her ability to keep her voice even), "that my word is not good enough?"

"That's precisely what I'm saying," Lady Danbury barked. "Good God, girl, you don't get to be my age without being allowed to insult anyone you please."

Colin thought he heard Penelope choking, but when he stole a glance at her, there she was at his side, avidly watching the exchange. Her brown eyes were huge and luminous in her face, and she'd regained most of the color she'd lost when Cressida had made her unexpected announcement. In fact, now Penelope looked positively intrigued by the goings-on.

"Fine," Cressida said, her voice low and deadly. "I will bring you proof in a fortnight's time."

"What sort of proof?" Colin asked, then mentally kicked himself. The last thing he wanted to do was embroil himself in this mess, but his curiosity had gotten the better of him.

Cressida turned to him, her face remarkably placid considering the insult she'd just been dealt by Lady Danbury—before countless witnesses. "You shall know it when I deliver it," she told him archly. And then she held out her arm, waiting for one of her minions to take it and lead her away.

Which was really quite amazing, because a young man (a besotted fool, from all appearances) materialized at her side as if she'd conjured him by the mere tilt of her arm. A moment later they were gone.

"Well," Lady Danbury said, after everyone had stood in reflective—or maybe stunned—silence for nearly a minute. "That was unpleasant."

"I've never liked her," Colin said, to no one in particular. A small crowd had gathered around them, so his words were heard by more than Penelope and Lady Danbury, but he didn't much care.

"Colin!"

He turned to see Hyacinth skidding through the crowd, dragging along Felicity Featherington as she barreled to his side.

"What did she say?" Hyacinth asked breathlessly. "We tried to get here sooner, but it's been such a crush."

"She said exactly what you would have expected her to say," he replied.

Hyacinth pulled a face. "Men are never good for gossip. I want exact words."

"It's very interesting," Penelope said suddenly.

Something about the thoughtful tone of her voice demanded attention, and in seconds the entire crowd had quieted.

"Speak up," Lady Danbury instructed. "We're all listening."

Colin expected such a demand to make Penelope uncomfortable, but whatever silent infusion of confidence she'd experienced a few minutes earlier was still with her, because she stood straight and proud as she said, "Why would someone reveal herself as Lady Whistledown?"

"For the money, of course," Hyacinth said.

Penelope shook her head. "Yes, but you'd think that Lady Whistledown would be quite wealthy by now. We've all been paying for her paper for years."

"By God, she's right!" Lady Danbury exclaimed.

"Perhaps Cressida merely sought attention," Colin suggested. It wasn't such an unbelievable hypothesis; Cressida had spent the bulk of her adult life trying to place herself at the center of attention.

"I'd thought of that," Penelope allowed, "but does she really want *this* sort of attention? Lady Whistledown has insulted quite a few people over the years."

"No one who means anything to me," Colin joked. Then, when it became obvious that his companions required an explanation, he added, "Haven't you all noticed that Lady Whistledown only insults the people who need insulting?"

Penelope cleared her throat delicately. "I have been referred to as an overripe citrus fruit."

He waved off her concern. "Except for the bits about fashion, of course."

Penelope must have decided not to pursue the matter any further, because all she did was give Colin a long, assessing stare before turning back to Lady Danbury and saying, "Lady Whistledown has no motive to reveal herself. Cressida obviously does."

Lady Danbury beamed, then all at once her face scrunched into a frown. "I suppose I'll have to give her the fortnight to come up with her 'proof.' Fair play and all that."

"I, for one, will be very interested to see what she comes up with," Hyacinth put in. She turned to Penelope and added, "I say, you're very clever, did you know that?"

Penelope blushed modestly, then she turned to her sister and said, "We must be going, Felicity."

"So soon?" Felicity asked, and to his horror, Colin realized that he'd mouthed the very same words.

"Mother wanted us home early," Penelope said.

Felicity looked truly perplexed. "She did?"

"She did," Penelope said emphatically. "And besides that, I am not feeling well."

Felicity nodded glumly. "I shall instruct a footman to see that our carriage is brought around."

"No, you stay," Penelope said, placing a hand on her sister's arm. "I will see to it."

"I will see to it," Colin announced. Really, what was the use of being a gentleman when ladies insisted upon doing things for themselves?

And then, before he even realized what he was doing, he'd facilitated Penelope's departure, and she left the scene without his ever having apologized to her.

He supposed he should have deemed the evening a failure for that reason alone, but in all truth, he couldn't quite bring himself to do so.

After all, he'd spent the better part of five minutes holding her hand.

Chapter 12

It wasn't until Colin woke up the following morning that he realized he still hadn't apologized to Penelope. Strictly speaking, it probably was no longer necessary that he do so; even though they'd barely spoken at the Macclesfield ball the night before, they seemed to have forged an unspoken truce. Still, Colin didn't think he'd feel comfortable in his own skin until he spoke the words, "I'm sorry."

It was the right thing to do.

He was a gentleman, after all.

And besides, he rather fancied seeing her that morning.

He'd gone to Number Five for breakfast with his family, but he wanted to head straight for home after seeing Penelope, so he hopped in his carriage for the trip to the Featherington home on Mount Street, even though the distance was short enough to make him feel utterly lazy for doing so.

He smiled contentedly and lay back against the squabs, watching the lovely springtime scene roll by his window. It was one of those perfect sorts of days when everything simply felt right. The sun was shining, he felt remarkably energized, he'd had an excellent morning meal . . .

Life really didn't get better than this.

And he was going over to see Penelope.

Colin chose not to analyze why he was so eager to see her; that was the sort of thing an unmarried man of three-and-thirty didn't generally care to think about. Instead he simply enjoyed the day—the sun, the air, even the three neat townhouses he passed on Mount Street before spying Penelope's front door. There was nothing remotely different or original about any of them, but it was such a perfect morning that they seemed unusually charming butted up next to each other, tall and thin, and stately with their gray Portland stone.

It was a wonderful day, warm and serene, sunny and tranquil . . .

Except that just as he started to rise from his seat, a short flurry of movement across the street caught his eye.

Penelope.

She was standing on the corner of Mount and Penter streets—the far corner, the one that would be not be visible to anyone looking out a window in the Featherington home. And she was climbing into a hired hack.

Interesting.

Colin frowned, mentally smacking himself on the forehead. It wasn't *interesting*. What the hell was he thinking? It wasn't interesting at all. It might have been interesting, had she been, say, a *man*. Or it might have been interesting if the conveyance into which she'd just entered had been one from the Featherington mews and not some scruffy hired hack.

But no, this was Penelope, who was certainly not a man, and she was entering a carriage by herself, presumably heading to some completely unsuitable location, because if she were doing anything proper and normal, she'd be in a Featherington conveyance. Or better yet, with one of her sisters or a maid, or anyone, just not, damn it, by herself.

This wasn't interesting, it was idiotic.

"Fool woman," he muttered, hopping down from his carriage with every intention of dashing toward the hack, wrenching the

door open, and dragging her out. But just as his right foot left the
confines of his carriage, he was struck by the same madness that led
him to wander the world.

Curiosity.

Several choice curses were grumbled under his breath, all of them
self-directed. He couldn't help it. It was so unlike Penelope to be
taking off by herself in a hired hack; he *had* to know where she was
going.

And so, instead of forcibly shaking some sense into her, he directed his driver to follow the hack, and they rolled north toward
the busy thoroughfare of Oxford Street, where, Colin reflected,
surely Penelope intended to do a bit of shopping. There could be any
number of reasons she wasn't using the Featherington carriage. Perhaps it was damaged, or one of their horses had taken ill, or Penelope
was buying someone a gift and wanted to keep it a secret.

No, that wasn't right. Penelope would never embark on a shopping expedition by herself. She would take a maid, or one of her
sisters, or even one of *his* sisters. To stroll along Oxford Street by
herself was to invite gossip. A woman alone was practically an ad-
vertisement for the next *Whistledown* column.

Or used to be, he supposed. It was hard to get used to a life without *Whistledown*. He hadn't realized how accustomed he'd been to
seeing it at his breakfast table whenever he was in town.

And speaking of Lady Whistledown, he was even more certain
than ever that she was none other than his sister Eloise. He'd gone
over to Number Five for breakfast with the express purpose of questioning her, only to be informed that she was still feeling poorly and
would not be joining the family that morning.

It had not escaped Colin's notice, however, that a rather hefty
tray of food had been sent up to Eloise's room. Whatever ailed his
sister, it had not affected her appetite.

He hadn't made any mention of his suspicions at the breakfast
table; truly, he saw no reason to upset his mother, who would surely

be horrified at the thought. It was difficult to believe, however, that Eloise—whose love of discussing scandal was eclipsed only by her thrill at discovering it—would miss the opportunity to gossip about Cressida Twombley's revelation of the night before.

Unless *Eloise* was Lady Whistledown, in which case she'd be up in her room, plotting her next step.

The pieces all fit. It would have been depressing if Colin hadn't felt so oddly thrilled at having found her out.

After they rolled along for a few minutes, he poked his head outside to make sure his driver had not lost sight of Penelope's carriage. There she was, right in front of him. Or at least he thought it was her. Most hired hacks looked the same, so he was going to have to trust and hope that he was following the right one. But as he looked out, he realized that they'd traveled much farther east than he would have anticipated. In fact, they were just now passing Soho Street, which meant they were nearly to Tottenham Court Road, which meant—

Dear God, was Penelope taking the carriage to his house? Bedford Square was practically right around the corner.

A delicious thrill shot up his spine, because he couldn't imagine what she was doing in this part of town if not to see him; who else would a woman like Penelope know in Bloomsbury? He couldn't imagine that her mother allowed her to associate with people who actually worked for a living, and Colin's neighbors, though certainly well enough born, were not of the aristocracy and rarely even of the gentry. And they all plodded off to work each day, doctoring and lawyering, or—

Colin frowned. Hard. They'd just rolled past Tottenham Court Road. What the devil was she doing this far east? He supposed her driver might not know his way around town very well and thought to take Bloomsbury Street up to Bedford Square, even though it was a bit out of the way, but—

He heard something very strange and realized it was the sound of his teeth grinding together. They'd just passed Bloomsbury Street and were presently veering right onto High Holborn.

Devil take it, they were nearly in the City. What in God's name was Penelope planning to do in the City? It was no place for a woman. Hell, he hardly ever went there himself. The world of the *ton* was farther west, in the hallowed buildings of St. James's and Mayfair. Not here in the City, with its narrow, twisting, medieval roads and rather dangerous proximity to the tenements of the East End.

Colin's jaw dropped progressively lower as they rolled on . . . and on . . . and on . . . until he realized they were turning down Shoe Lane. He craned his head out the window. He'd only been here once before, at the age of nine when his tutor had dragged him and Benedict off to show them where the Great Fire of London had started in 1666. Colin remembered feeling vaguely disappointed when he'd learned that the culprit was a mere baker who'd not dampened the ashes in his oven properly. A fire like that should have had arson or intrigue in its origin.

A fire like that was nothing compared to the feelings coming to a boil in his chest. Penelope had better have a *damned* good reason for coming out here by herself. She shouldn't be going *anywhere* unaccompanied, much less the City.

Then, just when Colin was convinced that Penelope was going to travel all the way to the Dover coast, the carriages crossed Fleet Street and ground to a halt. Colin held still, waiting to see what Penelope was up to even though every fiber of his being was screaming to leap out of the carriage and tackle her right there on the pavement.

Call it intuition, call it madness, but somehow he knew that if he accosted Penelope right away, he would never learn of her true purpose here near Fleet Street.

Once she was far enough away so that he could alight unnoticed, he jumped down from the carriage and followed her south toward some church that looked decidedly like a wedding cake.

"For God's sake," Colin muttered, completely unaware of blasphemy or puns, "now is not the time to find religion, Penelope."

She disappeared into the church, and his legs ate up the pavement after her, slowing only when he reached the front door. He didn't want to surprise her too quickly. Not before he found out what exactly she was doing there. His earlier words notwithstanding, he did not for one moment think that Penelope had suddenly developed a desire to extend her churchgoing habits to midweek visits.

He slipped quietly into the church, keeping his footsteps as soft as he could. Penelope was walking down the center aisle, her left hand tapping along each pew, almost as if she were . . .

Counting?

Colin frowned as she picked her pew, then scooted in until she was in the middle. She sat utterly still for a moment, then reached into her reticule and pulled out an envelope. Her head moved the teeniest bit to the left, then to the right, and Colin could easily picture her face, her dark eyes darting in either direction as she checked the room for other people. He was safe from her gaze at the back, so far in the shadows that he was practically pressed up against the wall. And besides, she seemed intent upon remaining still and quiet in her movements; she certainly hadn't moved her head far enough to see him behind her.

Bibles and prayer books were tucked in little pockets on the backs of the pews, and Colin watched as Penelope surreptitiously slid the envelope behind one. Then she stood and edged her way out toward the center aisle.

And that was when Colin made his move.

Stepping out of the shadows, he strode purposefully toward her, taking grim satisfaction in the horror on her face when she saw him.

"Col—Col—" she gasped.

"That would be Colin," he drawled, grasping her arm just above the elbow. His touch was light, but his grip was firm, and there was no way she could think that she might make an escape.

Smart girl that she was, she didn't even try.

But smart girl that she was, she did attempt a play at innocence.

"Colin!" she finally managed to get out. "What a . . . what a . . ."

"Surprise?"

She gulped. "Yes."

"I'm sure it is."

Her eyes darted to the door, to the nave, everywhere but to the pew where she'd hidden her envelope. "I've—I've never seen you here before."

"I've never been."

Penelope's mouth moved several times before her next words emerged. "It's quite appropriate, actually, that you'd be here, actually, because, actually . . . uh . . . do you know the story of St. Bride's?"

He raised one brow. "Is that where we are?"

Penelope was clearly trying for a smile, but the result was more of the openmouthed idiot sort of look. Normally this would have amused him, but he was still angry with her for taking off on her own, not giving a care to her safety and welfare.

But most of all, he was furious that she had a secret.

Not so much that she'd *kept* a secret. Secrets were meant to be kept, and he couldn't blame her for that. Irrational as it was, he absolutely could not tolerate the fact that she *had* a secret. She was Penelope. She was supposed to be an open book. He knew her. He'd always known her.

And now it seemed he'd never known her.

"Yes," she finally replied, her voice squeaking on the word. "It's one of Wren's churches, actually, you know, the ones he did after the Great Fire, they're all over the City, and actually it's my favorite. I do so love the steeple. Don't you think it looks like a wedding cake?"

She was babbling. It was never a good sign when someone babbled. It generally meant they were hiding something. It was already obvious that Penelope was making an attempt at concealment, but the uncharacteristic rapidity of her words told him that her secret was exceedingly large, indeed.

He stared at her for a very long time, drawn out over many seconds just to torture her, then finally asked, "Is that why you think it's appropriate that I'm here?"

Her face went blank.

"The wedding cake . . ." he prompted.

"Oh!" she squealed, her skin flushing a deep, guilty red. "No! Not at all! It's just that—What I meant to say was that this is the church for writers. And publishers. I think. About the publishers, that is."

She was flailing and she knew she was flailing. He could see it in her eyes, on her face, in the very way her hands twisted as she spoke. But she kept trying, kept attempting to keep up the pretense, and so he did nothing but give her a sardonic stare as she continued with, "But I'm sure about the writers." And then, with a flourish that might have been triumphant if she hadn't ruined it with a nervous swallow, "And you're a writer!"

"So you're saying this is my church?"

"Er . . ." Her eyes darted to her left. "Yes."

"Excellent."

She gulped. "It is?"

"Oh, yes," he said, with a smooth casualness to his words that was intended to terrify her.

Her eyes darted to her left again . . . toward the pew where she'd hidden her correspondence. She'd been so good until now, keeping her attention off of her incriminating evidence. He'd almost been proud of her for it.

"My church," he repeated. "What a lovely notion."

Her eyes grew round, scared. "I'm afraid I don't catch your meaning."

He tapped his finger to his jaw, then held out his hand in a thoughtful manner. "I believe I'm developing a taste for prayer."

"Prayer?" she echoed weakly. "You?"

"Oh, yes."

"I . . . well . . . I . . . I . . ."

"Yes?" he queried, beginning to enjoy this in a sick sort of way. He'd never been the angry, brooding type. Clearly, he hadn't known what he was missing. There was something rather pleasing in making her squirm. "Penelope?" he continued. "Did you have something to say?"

She swallowed. "No."

"Good." He smiled blandly. "Then I believe I require a few moments for myself."

"I'm sorry?"

He stepped to his right. "I'm in a church. I believe I want to pray."

She stepped to her left. "I beg your pardon?"

He cocked his head very slightly to the side in question. "I said that I want to pray. It wasn't a terribly complicated sentiment."

He could tell that she was straining hard not to rise to his bait. She was trying to smile, but her jaw was tense, and he'd wager that her teeth were going to grind themselves to powder within minutes.

"I didn't think you were a particularly religious person," she said.

"I'm not." He waited for her to react, then added, "I intend to pray for *you*."

She swallowed uncontrollably. "Me?" she squeaked.

"Because," he began, unable to prevent his voice from rising in volume, "by the time I'm done, prayer is the only thing that is going to save you!"

And with that he brushed her aside and strode to where she'd hidden the envelope.

"Colin!" she yelled, running frantically after him. "No!"

He yanked the envelope out from behind the prayer book but didn't yet look at it. "Do you want to tell me what this is?" he demanded. "Before I look myself, do you want to tell me?"

"No," she said, her voice breaking on the word.

His heart breaking at the expression in her eyes.

"Please," she begged him. "Please give it to me." And then, when he did nothing but stare at her with hard, angry eyes, she whispered, "It's mine. It's a secret."

"A secret worth your welfare?" he nearly roared. "Worth your life?"

"What are you talking about?"

"Do you have any idea how dangerous it is for a woman alone in the City? Alone anywhere?"

All she said was, "Colin, please." She reached for the envelope, still held out of her reach.

And suddenly he didn't know what he was doing. This wasn't him. This insane fury, this anger—it couldn't be his.

And yet it was.

But the troubling part was . . . it was Penelope who had made him thus. And what had she done? Traveled across London by herself? He was rather irritated at her for her lack of concern for her own safety, but that paled in comparison to the fury he felt at her keeping of secrets.

His anger was entirely unwarranted. He had no right to expect that Penelope share her secrets with him. They had no commitments to each other, nothing beyond a rather nice friendship and a single, albeit disturbingly moving, kiss. He certainly wouldn't have shared his journals with her if she hadn't stumbled upon them herself.

"Colin," she whispered. "Please . . . don't."

She'd seen his secret writings. Why shouldn't he see hers? Did she have a lover? Was all that nonsense about never having been kissed exactly that—nonsense?

Dear God, was this fire burning in his belly . . . *jealousy*?

"Colin," she said again, choking now. She placed her hand on his, trying to prevent him from opening the envelope. Not with strength, for she could never match him on that, just with her presence.

But there was no way . . . no way he could have stopped himself at that point. He would have died before surrendering that envelope to her unopened.

He tore it open.

Penelope let out a strangled cry and ran from the church.

Colin read the words.

And then he sank to the pew, bloodless, breathless.

"Oh, my God," he whispered. *"Oh, my God."*

By the time Penelope reached the outer steps to St. Bride's Church, she was hysterical. Or at least as hysterical as she'd ever been. Her breath was coming in short, sharp gasps, tears pricked her eyes, and her heart felt . . .

Well, her heart felt as if it wanted to throw up, if such a thing were possible.

How could he have done this? He'd followed her. *Followed her!* Why would Colin follow her? What would he have to gain? Why would he—

She suddenly looked around.

"Oh, damn!" she wailed, not caring if anyone heard her. The hack had left. She'd given specific instructions to the driver to wait for her, that she'd only be a minute, but he was nowhere in sight.

Another transgression she could lay at Colin's door. He'd delayed her inside the church, and now the hack had left, and she was stuck here on the steps of St. Bride's Church, in the middle of the City of London, so far from her home in Mayfair that she might as well have been in France. People were staring at her and any minute now she was sure to be accosted, because who had ever seen a gently bred lady alone in the City, much less one who was so clearly on the verge of a nervous attack?

Why why *why* had she been so foolish as to think that he was the perfect man? She'd spent half her life worshiping someone who wasn't even real. Because the Colin she knew—no, the Colin she'd *thought* she'd known—clearly didn't exist. And whoever this man was, she wasn't even sure she liked him. The man she'd loved so faithfully over the years never would have behaved like this. He wouldn't have followed her—Oh, very well, he would have, but only to assure himself of her safety. But he wouldn't have been so cruel, and he certainly wouldn't have opened her private correspondence.

She had read two pages of his journal, that was true, but they hadn't been in a sealed envelope!

She sank onto the steps and sat down, the stone cool even through the fabric of her dress. There was little she could do now besides sit here and wait for Colin. Only a fool would take off on foot by herself so far from home. She supposed she could hail a hack on Fleet Street, but what if they were all occupied, and besides, was there really any point in running from Colin? He knew where she lived, and unless she decided to run to the Orkney Islands, she wasn't likely to escape a confrontation.

She sighed. Colin would probably find her in the Orkneys, seasoned traveler that he was. And she didn't even want to *go* to the Orkneys.

She choked back a sob. Now she wasn't even making sense. Why was she fixated on the Orkney Islands?

And then there was Colin's voice behind her, clipped and so very cold. "Get up," was all he said.

She did, not because he'd ordered her to (or at least that was what she told herself), and not because she was afraid of him, but rather because she couldn't sit on the steps of St. Bride's forever, and even if she wanted nothing more than to hide herself from Colin for the next six months, at the moment he was her only safe means home.

He jerked his head toward the street. "Into the carriage."

She went, climbing up as she heard Colin give the driver her address and then instruct him to "take the long way."

Oh, God.

They'd been moving a good thirty seconds before he handed her the single sheet of paper that had been folded into the envelope she'd left in the church. "I believe this is yours," he said.

She gulped and looked down, not that she needed to. She already had the words memorized. She'd written and rewritten them so many times the previous night, she didn't think they'd ever escape her memory.

> *There is nothing I despise more than a gentleman who thinks it amusing to give a lady a condescending pat on the hand as he murmurs, "It is a woman's prerogative to change her mind." And indeed, because I feel one should always support one's words with one's actions, I endeavor to keep my opinions and decisions steadfast and true.*
>
> *Which is why, Gentle Reader, when I wrote my column of 19 April, I truly intended it to be my last. However, events entirely beyond my control (or indeed beyond my approval) force me to put my pen to paper one last time.*
>
> *Ladies and Gentleman, This Author is NOT Lady Cressida Twombley. She is nothing more than a scheming imposter, and it would break my heart to see my years of hard work attributed to one such as her.*
>
> LADY WHISTLEDOWN'S SOCIETY PAPERS,
> 21 April 1824

Penelope refolded the paper with great precision, using the time to try to compose herself and figure out what on earth she was supposed to say at a moment like that. Finally, she attempted a smile, didn't quite meet his eyes, and joked, "Did you guess?"

He didn't say anything, so she was forced to look up. She immediately wished she hadn't. Colin looked completely unlike himself. The easy smile that always tugged at his lips, the good humor forever lurking in his eyes—they were all gone, replaced by harsh lines and cold, pure ice.

The man she knew, the man she'd loved for so very long—she didn't know who he was anymore.

"I'll take that as a no," she said shakily.

"Do you know what I am trying to do right now?" he asked, his voice startling and loud against the rhythmic clip-clop of the horses' hooves.

She opened her mouth to say no, but one look at his face told her he didn't desire an answer, so she held her tongue.

"I am trying to decide what, precisely, I am most angry with you about," he said. "Because there are so many things—so very *many* things—that I am finding it extraordinarily difficult to focus upon just one."

It was on the tip of Penelope's tongue to suggest something—her deception was a likely place to start—but on second thought, now seemed an excellent time to hold her counsel.

"First of all," he said, the terribly even tone of his voice suggesting that he was trying *very* hard to keep his temper in check (and this was, in and of itself, rather disturbing, as she hadn't been aware that Colin even possessed a temper), "I cannot believe you were stupid enough to venture into the City by yourself, and in a hired hack, no less!"

"I could hardly go by myself in one of our own carriages," Penelope blurted out before she remembered that she'd meant to remain silent.

His head moved about an inch to the left. She didn't know what that meant, but she couldn't imagine it was good, especially since it almost seemed as if his neck were tightening as it twisted. "I beg your pardon?" he asked, his voice still that awful blend of satin and steel.

Well, now she *had* to answer, didn't she? "Er, it's nothing," she said, hoping the evasion would reduce his attention on the rest of her reply. "Just that I'm not allowed to go out by myself."

"I am aware of that," he bit off. "There's a damned good reason for it, too."

"So if I wanted to go out by myself," she continued, choosing to ignore the second part of his reply, "I couldn't very well use one of our carriages. None of our drivers would agree to take me here."

"Your drivers," he snapped, "are clearly men of impeccable wisdom and sense."

Penelope said nothing.

"Do you have any idea what could have happened to you?" he demanded, his sharp mask of control beginning to crack.

"Er, very little, actually," she said, gulping on the sentence. "I've come here before, and——"

"*What?*" His hand closed over her upper arm with painful force. "What did you just say?"

Repeating it seemed almost dangerous to her health, so Penelope just stared at him, hoping that maybe she could break through the wild anger in his eyes and find the man she knew and loved so dearly.

"It's only when I need to leave an urgent message for my publisher," she explained. "I send a coded message, then he knows to pick up my note here."

"And speaking of which," Colin said roughly, snatching the folded paper back from her hands, "what the *hell* is this?"

Penelope stared at him in confusion. "I would have thought it was obvious. I'm——"

"Yes, of course, you're bloody Lady Whistledown, and you've probably been laughing at me for weeks as I insisted it was Eloise." His face twisted as he spoke, nearly breaking her heart.

"No!" she cried out. "No, Colin, never. I would never laugh at you!"

But his face told her clearly that he did not believe her. There was humiliation in his emerald eyes, something she'd never seen there, something she'd never expected to see. He was a Bridgerton. He was popular, confident, self-possessed. Nothing could embarrass him. No one could humiliate him.

Except, apparently, her.

"I couldn't tell you," she whispered, desperately trying to make that awful look in his eyes go away. "Surely you knew I couldn't tell you."

He was silent for an agonizingly long moment, and then, as if she'd never spoken, never tried to explain herself, he lifted the incriminating sheet of paper into the air and shook it, completely disregarding her impassioned outcry. "This is stupidity," he said. "Have you lost your mind?"

"I don't know what you mean."

"You had a perfectly good escape, just waiting for you. Cressida Twombley was willing to take the blame for you."

And then suddenly his hands were on her shoulders, and he was holding her so tightly she could barely breathe.

"Why couldn't you just let it die, Penelope?" His voice was urgent, his eyes blazing. It was the most feeling she'd ever seen in him, and it broke her heart that it was directed toward her in anger. And in shame.

"I couldn't let her do it," she whispered. "I couldn't let her be me."

Chapter 13

"Why the hell not?"

Penelope could do nothing but stare for several seconds. "Because . . . because . . ." she flailed, wondering how she was supposed to explain this. Her heart was breaking, her most terrifying—and exhilarating—secret had been shattered, and he thought she had the presence of mind to *explain* herself?

"I realize she's quite possibly the biggest bitch . . ."

Penelope gasped.

". . . that England has produced in this generation at least, but for God's sake, Penelope"—he raked his hand through his hair, then fixed a hard stare on her face—"she was going to take the blame—"

"The credit," Penelope interrupted testily.

"The blame," he continued. "Do you have any idea what will happen to you if people find out who you really are?"

The corners of her lips tightened with impatience . . . and irritation at being so obviously condescended to. "I've had over a decade to ruminate the possibility."

His eyes narrowed. "Are you being sarcastic?"

"Not at all," she shot back. "Do you really think I haven't spent a good portion of the last ten years of my life contemplating what would happen if I were found out? I'd be a blind idiot if I hadn't."

He grabbed her by the shoulders, holding tight even as the carriage bumped over uneven cobbles. "You will be ruined, Penelope. Ruined! Do you understand what I am saying?"

"If I did not," she replied, "I assure you I would now, after your lengthy dissertations on the subject when you were accusing Eloise of being Lady Whistledown."

He scowled, obviously annoyed at having his errors thrown in his face. "People will stop talking to you," he continued. "They will cut you dead—"

"People never talked to me," she snapped. "Half the time they didn't even know I was there. How do you think I was able to keep up the ruse for so long in the first place? I was invisible, Colin. No one saw me, no one talked to me. I just stood and listened, *and no one noticed.*"

"That's not true." But his eyes slid from hers as he said it.

"Oh, it *is* true, and you know it. You only deny it," she said, jabbing him in the arm, "because you feel guilty."

"I do not!"

"Oh, *please*," she scoffed. "Everything you do, you do out of guilt."

"Pen—"

"That involves me, at least," she corrected. Her breath was rushing through her throat, and her skin was pricking with heat, and for once, her soul was on fire. "Do you think I don't know how your family pities me? Do you think it escapes my notice that anytime you or your brothers happen to be at the same party as me, you ask me to dance?"

"We're polite," he ground out, "and we *like* you."

"*And* you feel sorry for me. You like Felicity but I don't see you dancing with her every time your paths cross."

He let go of her quite suddenly and crossed his arms. "Well, I don't like her as well as I do you."

She blinked, knocked rather neatly off her verbal stride. Trust him to go and *compliment* her in the middle of an argument. Nothing could have disarmed her more.

"And," he continued with a rather arch and superior lifting of his chin, "you have not addressed my original point."

"Which was?"

"That Lady Whistledown will ruin you!"

"For God's sake," she muttered, "you talk as if she were a separate person."

"Well, excuse me if I still have difficulty reconciling the woman in front of me with the harridan writing the column."

"Colin!"

"Insulted?" he mocked.

"Yes! I've worked very hard on that column." She clenched her fists around the thin fabric of her mint-green morning dress, oblivious to the wrinkled spirals she was creating. She had to do something with her hands or she'd quite possibly explode with the nervous energy and anger coursing through her veins. Her only other option seemed to be crossing her arms, and she refused to give in to such an obvious show of petulance. Besides, he was crossing his arms, and one of them needed to act older than six.

"I wouldn't dream of denigrating what you've done," he said condescendingly.

"Of course you would," she interrupted.

"No, I wouldn't."

"Then what do you think you're doing?"

"Being an adult!" he answered, his voice growing loud and impatient. "One of us has to be."

"Don't you dare speak to me of adult behavior!" she exploded. "You, who run at the very hint of responsibility."

"And what the hell does that mean?" he bit off.

"I thought it was rather obvious."

He drew back. "I can't believe you're speaking to me like this."

"You can't believe I'm doing it," she taunted, "or that I possess the nerve to do so?"

He just stared at her, obviously surprised by her question.

"There's more to me than you think, Colin," she said. And then, in a quieter tone of voice, she added, "There's more to me than *I* used to think."

He said nothing for several moments, and then, as if he just couldn't drag himself away from the topic, he asked, practically between his teeth, "What did you mean when you said I run from responsibility?"

She pursed her lips, then relaxed as she let out what she hoped would be a calming exhale. "Why do you think you travel so much?"

"Because I like it," he replied, his tone clipped.

"And because you're bored out of your mind here in England."

"And that makes me a child because . . . ?"

"Because you're not willing to grow up and do something adult that would keep you in one place."

"Like what?"

Her hands came up in an I-should-think-it-was-obvious sort of gesture. "Like get married."

"Is that a proposal?" he mocked, one corner of his mouth rising into a rather insolent smile.

She could feel her cheeks flushing deep and hot, but she forced herself to continue. "You know it's not, and don't try to change the subject by being deliberately cruel." She waited for him to say something, perhaps an apology. His silence was an insult, and so she let out a snort and said, "For heaven's sake, Colin, you're three-and-thirty."

"And you're eight-and-twenty," he pointed out, and not in a particularly kind tone of voice.

It felt like a punch in the belly, but she was too riled up to retreat into her familiar shell. "Unlike you," she said with low precision, "I don't have the luxury of asking someone. And unlike *you*," she added, her intention now solely to induce the guilt she'd accused him of just minutes earlier, "I don't have a massive pool of prospective suitors, so I've never had the luxury of saying no."

His lips tightened. "And you think that your unveiling as Lady Whistledown is going to increase the number of your suitors?"

"Are you *trying* to be insulting?" she ground out.

"I'm trying to be realistic! Something which you seem to have completely lost sight of."

"I never said I was planning to unveil myself as Lady Whistledown."

He snatched the envelope with the final column in it back up off the cushioned bench. "Then what is this about?"

She grabbed it back, yanking the paper from the envelope. "I beg your pardon," she said, every syllable heavy with sarcasm. "I must have missed the sentence proclaiming my identity."

"You think this swan song of yours will do anything to dampen the frenzy of interest in Lady Whistledown's identity? Oh, excuse me"—he placed one insolent hand over his heart—"perhaps I should have said *your* identity. After all, I don't want to deny you your *credit*."

"Now you're just being ugly," she said, a little voice at the back of her brain wondering why she wasn't crying by now. This was Colin, and she'd loved him forever, and he was acting as if he hated her. Was there anything else in the world more worthy of tears?

Or maybe that wasn't it at all. Maybe all this sadness building up inside of her was for the death of a dream. Her dream of him. She'd built up the perfect image of him in her mind, and with every word he spat in her face, it was becoming more and more obvious that her dream was quite simply wrong.

"I'm making a point," he said, snatching the paper back from her hands. "Look at this. It might as well be an invitation for further investigation. You're mocking society, daring them to uncover you."

"That's not at all what I'm doing!"

"It may not be your intention, but it is certainly the end result."

He probably had something of a point there, but she was loath to give him credit for it. "It's a chance I'll have to take," she replied, crossing her arms and looking pointedly away from him. "I've gone eleven years without detection. I don't see why I'm in need of undue worry now."

His breath left him in a short punch of exasperation. "Do you have any concept of money? Any idea how many people would like Lady Danbury's thousand pounds?"

"I have more of a concept of money than you do," she replied, bristling at the insult. "And besides, Lady Danbury's reward doesn't make my secret any more vulnerable."

"It makes everyone else more determined, and that makes you more vulnerable. Not to mention," he added with a wry twist to his lips, "as my youngest sister pointed out, there is the glory."

"Hyacinth?" she asked.

He nodded grimly, setting the paper down on the bench beside him. "And if Hyacinth thinks the glory at having uncovered your identity is enviable, then you can be sure she's not the only one. It may very well be why Cressida is pursuing her stupid ruse."

"Cressida's doing it for the money," Penelope grumbled. "I'm sure of it."

"Fine. It doesn't matter why she's doing it. All that matters is that she is, and once you dispose of her with your idiocy"—he slammed his hand against the paper, causing Penelope to wince as a loud crinkle filled the air—"someone else will take her place."

"This is nothing I don't already know," she said, mostly because she couldn't bear to give him the last word.

"Then for the love of God, woman," he burst out, "let Cressida get away with her scheme. She's the answer to your prayers."

Her eyes snapped up to his. "You don't know my prayers."

Something in her tone hit Colin squarely in the chest. She hadn't changed his mind, hadn't even budged it, but he couldn't seem to find the right words to fill the moment. He looked at her, then he looked out the window, his mind absently focusing on the dome of St. Paul's Cathedral.

"We really are taking the long way home," he murmured.

She didn't say anything. He didn't blame her. It had been a stupid non sequitur, words to fill the silence and nothing else.

"If you let Cressida—" he began.

"Stop," she implored him. "Please, don't say any more. I can't let her do it."

"Have you really thought about what you'd gain?"

She looked at him sharply. "Do you think I've been able to think of anything else these past few days?"

He tried another tactic. "Does it truly matter that people know you were Lady Whistledown? *You* know that you were clever and fooled us all. Can't that be enough?"

"You're not listening to me!" Her mouth remained frozen open, in an odd incredulous oval, as if she couldn't quite believe that he didn't understand what she was saying. "I don't need for people to know it was me. I just need for them to know it wasn't *her.*"

"But clearly you don't mind if people think someone else is Lady Whistledown," he insisted. "After all, you've been accusing Lady Danbury for weeks."

"I had to accuse *some*one," she explained. "Lady Danbury asked me point-blank who I thought it was, and I couldn't very well say myself. Besides, it wouldn't be so very bad if people thought it was Lady Danbury. At least I like Lady Danbury."

"Penelope—"

"How would you feel if your journals were published with Nigel Berbrooke as the author?" she demanded.

"Nigel Berbrooke can barely string two sentences together," he said with a derisive snort. "I hardly think anyone would believe he could have written my journals." As an afterthought, he gave her a little nod as an apology, since Berbrooke was, after all, married to her sister.

"Try to imagine it," she ground out. "Or substitute whomever you think is similar to Cressida."

"Penelope," he sighed, "I'm not you. You can't compare the two. Besides, if I were to publish my journals, they would hardly ruin me in the eyes of society."

She deflated in her seat, sighing loudly, and he knew that his point had been well made. "Good," he announced, "then it is decided. We will tear this up——" He reached for the sheet of paper.

"No!" she cried out, practically leaping from her seat. "Don't!"

"But you just said——"

"I said nothing!" she shrilled. "All I did was sigh."

"Oh, for God's sake, Penelope," he said testily. "You clearly agreed with——"

She gaped at his audacity. "When did I give you leave to interpret my sighs?"

He looked at the incriminating paper, still held in his hands, and wondered what on earth he was meant to do with it at this moment.

"And *anyway*," she continued, her eyes flashing with an anger and fire that made her almost beautiful, "it isn't as if I don't have every last word memorized. You can destroy that paper, but you can't destroy me."

"I'd like to," he muttered.

"*What* did you say?"

"Whistledown," he ground out. "I'd like to destroy Whistledown. You, I'm happy to leave as is."

"But I *am* Whistledown."

"God help us all."

And then something within her simply snapped. All her rage, all her frustration, every last negative feeling she'd kept bottled up inside over the years broke forth, all directed at Colin, who, of all the *ton*, was probably the least deserving of it.

"Why are you so angry with me?" she burst out. "What have I done that is so repellent? Been cleverer than you? Kept a secret? Had a good laugh at the expense of society?"

"Penelope, you—"

"No," she said forcefully. "You be quiet. It's my turn to speak."

His jaw went slack as he stared at her, shock and disbelief crowding in his eyes.

"I am proud of what I've done," she managed to say, her voice shaking with emotion. "I don't care what you say. I don't care what anyone says. No one can take that from me."

"I'm not trying—"

"I don't need for people to know the truth," she said, jumping on top of his ill-timed protest. "But I will be *damned* if I allow Cressida Twombley, the very person who . . . who . . ." Her entire body was trembling now, as memory after memory swept over her, all of them bad.

Cressida, renowned for her grace and carriage, tripping and spilling punch on Penelope's gown that first year—the only one her mother had allowed her to buy that wasn't yellow or orange.

Cressida, sweetly begging young bachelors to ask Penelope to dance, her requests made with such volume and fervor that Penelope could only be mortified by them.

Cressida, saying before a crowd how worried she was about Penelope's appearance. "It's just not *healthful* to weigh more than ten stone at our age," she'd cooed.

Penelope never knew whether Cressida had been able to hide her smirk following her barb. She'd fled the room, blinded by tears, unable to ignore the way her hips jiggled as she ran away.

Cressida had always known exactly where to stick her sword, and she'd known how to twist her bayonet. It didn't matter that Eloise remained Penelope's champion or that Lady Bridgerton always tried to bolster her confidence. Penelope had cried herself to sleep more times than she could remember, always due to some well-placed barb from Cressida Cowper Twombley.

She'd let Cressida get away with so much in the past, all because she hadn't the courage to stand up for herself. But she couldn't let Cressida have *this*. Not her secret life, not the one little corner of her soul that was strong and proud and completely without fear.

Penelope might not know how to defend herself, but by God, Lady Whistledown did.

"Penelope?" Colin asked cautiously.

She looked at him blankly, taking several seconds to remember that it was 1824, not 1814, and she was here in a carriage with Colin Bridgerton, not cowering in the corner of a ballroom, trying to escape Cressida Cowper.

"Are you all right?" he asked.

She nodded. Or at least she tried to.

He opened his mouth to say something, then paused, his lips remaining parted for several seconds. Finally, he just placed his hand on hers, saying, "We'll talk about this later?"

This time she did manage a short nod. And truly, she just wanted the entire awful afternoon to be over, but there was one thing she couldn't quite let go of yet.

"Cressida wasn't ruined," she said quietly.

He turned to her, a slight veil of confusion descending over his eyes. "I beg your pardon?"

Her voice rose slightly in volume. "Cressida said she was Lady Whistledown, and she wasn't ruined."

"That's because no one believed her," Colin replied. "And besides," he added without thinking, "she's . . . different."

She turned to him slowly. Very slowly, with steadfast eyes. "Different how?"

Something akin to panic began to pound in Colin's chest. He'd known he wasn't saying the right words even as they'd spilled from his lips. How could one little sentence, one little word be so very wrong?

She's different.

They both knew what he'd meant. Cressida was popular, Cressida was beautiful, Cressida could carry it all off with aplomb.

Penelope, on the other hand . . .

She was Penelope. Penelope Featherington. And she hadn't the clout nor the connections to save her from ruin. The Bridgertons could stand behind her and offer support, but even they wouldn't be able prevent her downfall. Any other scandal might have been manageable, but Lady Whistledown had, at one time or another, insulted almost every person of consequence in the British Isles. Once people were over their surprise, that was when the unkind remarks would begin.

Penelope wouldn't be praised for being clever or witty or daring.

She'd be called mean, and petty, and jealous.

Colin knew the *ton* well. He knew how his peers acted. The aristocracy was capable of individual greatness, but collectively they tended to sink to the lowest common denominator.

Which was very low, indeed.

"I see," Penelope said into the silence.

"No," he said quickly, "you don't. I—"

"No, Colin," she said, sounding almost painfully wise, "I do. I suppose I'd just always hoped *you* were different."

His eyes caught hers, and somehow his hands were on her shoulders, gripping her with such intensity that she couldn't possibly look away. He didn't say anything, letting his eyes ask his questions.

"I thought you believed in me," she said, "that you saw beyond the ugly duckling."

Her face was so familiar to him; he'd seen it a thousand times before, and yet until these past few weeks, he couldn't have said he truly knew it. Would he have remembered that she had a small birthmark near her left earlobe? Had he ever noticed the warm glow to her skin? Or that her brown eyes had flecks of gold in them, right near the pupil?

How had he danced with her so many times and never noticed that her mouth was full and wide and made for kissing?

She licked her lips when she was nervous. He'd seen her do that just the other day. Surely she'd done that at some point in the dozen years of their acquaintance, and yet it was only now that the mere sight of her tongue made his body clench with need.

"You're not ugly," he told her, his voice low and urgent.

Her eyes widened.

And he whispered, "You're beautiful."

"No," she said, the word barely more than a breath. "Don't say things you don't mean."

His fingers dug into her shoulders. "You're beautiful," he repeated. "I don't know how . . . I don't know when . . ." He touched her lips, feeling her hot breath on his fingertips. "But you are," he whispered.

He leaned forward and kissed her, slowly, reverently, no longer quite so surprised that this was happening, that he wanted her so badly. The shock was gone, replaced by a simple, primitive need to claim her, to brand her, to mark her as his.

His?

He pulled back and looked at her for a moment, his eyes searching her face.

Why not?

"What is it?" she whispered.

"You *are* beautiful," he said, shaking his head in confusion. "I don't know why nobody else sees it."

Something warm and lovely began to spread in Penelope's chest. She couldn't quite explain it; it was almost as if someone had heated her blood. It started in her heart and then slowly swept through her arms, her belly, down to the tips of her toes.

It made her light-headed. It made her content.

It made her whole.

She wasn't beautiful. She knew she wasn't beautiful, she knew she'd never be more than passably attractive, and that was only on her good days. But he thought she was beautiful, and when he looked at her . . .

She *felt* beautiful. And she'd never felt that way before.

He kissed her again, his lips hungrier this time, nibbling, caressing, waking her body, rousing her soul. Her belly had begun to tingle, and her skin felt hot and needy where his hands touched her through the thin green fabric of her dress.

And never once did she think, *This is wrong.* This kiss was everything she'd been brought up to fear and avoid, but she knew—body, mind, and soul—that nothing in her life had ever been so right. She had been born for this man, and she'd spent so many years trying to accept the fact that he had been born for someone else.

To be proven wrong was the most exquisite pleasure imaginable.

She wanted him, she wanted this, she wanted the way he made her feel.

She wanted to be beautiful, even if it was only in one man's eyes.

They were, she thought dreamily as he laid her down on the plush cushion of the carriage bench, the only eyes that mattered.

She loved him. She had always loved him. Even now, when he was so angry with her that she barely recognized him, when he was so angry with her that she wasn't even sure she *liked* him, she loved him.

And she wanted to be his.

The first time he had kissed her, she had accepted his advances with a passive delight, but this time she was determined to be an active partner. She still couldn't quite believe that she was here, with him, and she certainly wasn't ready to let herself dream that he might ever be kissing her on a regular basis.

This might never happen again. She might never again feel the exquisite weight of him pressing against her, or the scandalous tickle of his tongue against hers.

She had one chance. One chance to make a memory that would have to last a lifetime. One chance to reach for bliss.

Tomorrow would be awful, knowing that he would find some other woman with whom to laugh and joke and even marry, but today . . .

Today was hers.

And by God, she was going to make this a kiss to remember.

She reached up and touched his hair. She was hesitant at first— just because she was determined to be an active, willing partner didn't mean she had a clue what she was doing. His lips were slowly easing all the reason and intelligence from her mind, but still, she couldn't quite help noticing that his hair felt exactly like Eloise's, which she had brushed countless times during their years of friendship. And heaven help her . . .

She giggled.

That got his attention, and he lifted his head, his lips touched by an amused smile. "I beg your pardon?" he queried.

She shook her head, trying to fight off her smile, knowing she was losing the battle.

"Oh, no, you must," he insisted. "I couldn't possibly continue without knowing the reason for the giggle."

She felt her cheeks burning, which struck her as ridiculously ill-timed. Here she was, completely misbehaving in the back of a carriage, and it was only *now* that she had the decency to blush?

"Tell me," he murmured, nibbling at her ear.

She shook her head.

His lips found the exact point where her pulse beat in her throat. "Tell me."

All she did—all she could do—was moan, arching her neck to give him greater access.

Her dress, which she hadn't even realized had been partially unbuttoned, slid down until her collarbone was exposed, and she watched with giddy fascination as his lips traced the line of it, until his entire face was nuzzled perilously close to her bosom.

"Will you tell me?" he whispered, grazing her skin with his teeth.

"Tell you what?" she gasped.

His lips were wicked, moving lower, then lower still. "Why you were laughing?"

For several seconds Penelope couldn't even remember what he was talking about.

His hand cupped her breast through her dress. "I'll torment you until you tell me," he threatened.

Penelope's answer was an arch of her back, settling her breast even more firmly in his grasp.

She liked his torment.

"I see," he murmured, simultaneously sliding her bodice down and moving his hand so that his palm grazed her nipple. "Then perhaps I'll"—his hand stilled, then lifted—"stop."

"No," she moaned.

"Then tell me."

She stared at her breast, mesmerized by the sight of it, bare and open to his gaze.

"Tell me," he whispered, blowing softly so that his breath brushed across her.

Something clenched inside Penelope, deep inside of her, in places that were never talked about.

"Colin, please," she begged.

He smiled, slow and lazy, satisfied and still somehow hungry. "Please what?" he asked.

"Touch me," she whispered.

His index finger slid along her shoulder. "Here?"

She shook her head frantically.

He trailed down the column of her neck. "Am I getting closer?" he murmured.

She nodded, her eyes never leaving her breast.

He found her nipple again, his fingers tracing slow, tantalizing spirals around it, then on it, and all the while she watched, her body growing tighter and tighter.

And all she could hear was her breath, hot and heavy from her lips.

Then—

"Colin!" His name flew from her mouth in a strangled gasp. Surely he couldn't—

His lips closed around her, and before she'd even felt more than the heat of him, she bucked off the bench in surprise, her hips pressing shamelessly against his, then settling back down as he ground against her, holding her immobile as he pleasured her.

"Oh, Colin, Colin," she gasped, her hands flying around to his back, pressing desperately into his muscles, wanting nothing other than to hold him and keep him and never let him go.

He yanked at his shirt, pulling it free from the waist of his breeches, and she followed his cue by slipping her hands under the fabric and running them along the hot skin of his back. She'd never touched a man this way; she'd never touched *anyone* like this, except maybe herself, and even then, it wasn't like she could easily reach her own back.

He groaned when she touched him, then tensed when her fingers skimmed along his skin. Her heart leaped. He liked this; he liked the way she was touching him. She hadn't the least clue what to do with herself, but he liked it just the same.

"You're perfect," he whispered against her skin, his lips blazing a trail back up to the underside of her chin. His mouth claimed hers again, this time with increased fervor, and his hands slid underneath to cup her derriere, squeezing and kneading and pressing her up against his arousal.

"My God, I want you," he gasped, grinding his hips down. "I want to strip you bare and sink into you and never let you go."

Penelope groaned with desire, unable to believe how much pleasure she could feel from mere words. He made her feel wicked, naughty, and oh-so-desirable.

And she never wanted it to end.

"Oh, Penelope," he was groaning, his lips and hands growing more frantic. "Oh, Penelope. Oh, Penelope, oh—" He lifted his head. Very abruptly.

"Oh, God."

"What is it?" she asked, trying to lift the back of her head from the cushion.

"We've stopped."

It took her a moment to recognize the import of this. If they'd stopped, that meant they'd most likely reached their destination, which was . . .

Her home.

"Oh, God!" She started yanking at the bodice of her gown with frantic motions. "Can't we just ask the driver to keep going?"

She'd already proven herself a complete wanton. There seemed little harm at this point in adding "shameless" to her list of behaviors.

He grabbed the bodice for her and hauled it into place. "What is the possibility your mother won't have noticed my carriage in front of your house yet?"

"Fairly good, actually," she said, "but Briarly will have done."

"Your butler will recognize my carriage?" he asked in disbelief.

She nodded. "You came the other day. He always remembers things like that."

His lips twisted in a grimly determined manner. "Very well, then," he said. "Make yourself presentable."

"I can race up to my room," Penelope said. "No one will see me."

"I doubt that," he said ominously, tucking in his shirt and smoothing his hair.

"No, I assure you—"

"And I assure you," he said, leaping on top of her words. "You will be seen." He licked his fingers, then ran them through his hair. "Do I look presentable?"

"Yes," she lied. In truth, he looked rather flushed, with swollen lips, and hair that didn't remotely adhere to a current style.

"Good." He hopped down from the carriage and held his hand out to her.

"You're coming in as well?" she asked.

He looked at her as if she'd suddenly gone daft. "Of course."

She didn't move, too perplexed by his actions to give her legs the orders to step down. There was certainly no reason he had to accompany her inside. Propriety didn't really demand it, and—

"For God's sake, Penelope," he said, grabbing her hand and yanking her down. "Are you going to marry me or not?"

Chapter 14

She hit the pavement.

Penelope was—in her opinion, at least—a bit more graceful than most people gave her credit for. She was a good dancer, could play the piano with her fingers arched perfectly, and could usually navigate a crowded room without bumping into an uncommon amount of people or furniture.

But when Colin made his rather matter-of-fact proposal, her foot—at the time halfway out of the carriage—found only air, her left hip found the curb, and her head found Colin's toes.

"Good God, Penelope," he exclaimed, crouching down. "Are you all right?"

"Just fine," she managed to get out, searching for the hole in the ground that must have just opened up, so that she could crawl into it and die.

"Are you certain?"

"It's nothing, really," she replied, holding her cheek, which she was certain now sported a perfect imprint of the top of Colin's boot. "Just a bit surprised, that is all."

"Why?"

"Why?" she echoed.

"Yes, why?"

She blinked. Once, twice, then again. "Er, well, it might have to do with your mentioning marriage."

He yanked her unceremoniously to her feet, nearly dislocating her shoulder in the process. "Well, what did you think I would say?"

She stared at him in disbelief. Was he mad? "Not *that*," she finally replied.

"I'm not a complete boor," he muttered.

She brushed dust and pebbles off her sleeves. "I never said you were, I just—"

"I can assure you," he continued, now looking mortally offended, "that I do not behave as I did with a woman of your background without rendering a marriage proposal."

Penelope's mouth fell open, leaving her feeling rather like an owl.

"Don't you have a reply?" he demanded.

"I'm still trying to figure out what you said," she admitted.

He planted his hands on his hips and stared at her with a decided lack of indulgence.

"You must admit," she said, her chin dipping until she was regarding him rather dubiously through her lashes, "it did sound rather like you've, er—how did you say it—rendered marriage proposals before."

He scowled at her. "Of course I haven't. Now take my arm before it starts to rain."

She looked up at the clear blue sky.

"At the rate you're going," he said impatiently, "we'll be here for days."

"I . . . well . . ." She cleared her throat. "Surely you can forgive me my lack of composure in the face of such tremendous surprise."

"Now who's speaking in circles?" he muttered.

"I beg your pardon."

His hand tightened on her arm. "Let's just get going."

"Colin!" she nearly shrieked, tripping over her feet as she stumbled up the stairs. "Are you sure—"

"No time like the present," he said, almost jauntily. He seemed quite pleased with himself, which puzzled her, because she would have bet her entire fortune—and as Lady Whistledown, she'd amassed quite a fortune—that he had not intended to ask her to marry him until the moment his carriage had ground to a halt in front her house.

Perhaps not even until the words had left his lips.

He turned to her. "Do I need to knock?"

"No, I—"

He knocked anyway, or rather banged, if one wanted to be particular about it.

"Briarly," Penelope said through an attempted smile as the butler opened the door to receive them.

"Miss Penelope," he murmured, one brow rising in surprise. He nodded at Colin. "Mr. Bridgerton."

"Is Mrs. Featherington at home?" Colin asked brusquely.

"Yes, but—"

"Excellent." Colin barged in, pulling Penelope along with him. "Where is she?"

"In the drawing room, but I should tell you—"

But Colin was already halfway down the hall, Penelope one step behind him. (Not that she could be anywhere else, seeing as how his hand was wrapped rather tightly around her upper arm.)

"Mr. Bridgerton!" the butler yelled out, sounding slightly panicked.

Penelope twisted, even as her feet continued to follow Colin. Briarly never panicked. About anything. If he didn't think she and Colin ought to enter the drawing room, he had to have a very good reason.

Maybe even—

Oh, *no.*

Penelope dug in her heels, skidding along the hardwood floor as Colin dragged her along by the arm. "Colin," she said, gulping on the first syllable. "Colin!"

"What?" he asked, not breaking his stride.

"I really think—Aaack!" Her skidding heels hit the edge of the runner carpet, sending her flying forward.

He caught her neatly and set her on her feet. "What is it?"

She glanced nervously at the door to the drawing room. It was slightly ajar, but maybe there was enough noise inside so that her mother hadn't yet heard them approaching.

"Penelope . . ." Colin prompted impatiently.

"Er . . ." There was still time to escape, wasn't there? She looked frantically about, not that she was likely to find a solution to her problems anywhere in the hall.

"Penelope," Colin said, now tapping his foot, "what the devil is the matter?"

She looked back to Briarly, who simply shrugged his shoulders. "This really might not be the best time to speak to my mother."

He raised one brow, looking rather like the butler had just seconds earlier. "You're not planning to refuse me, are you?"

"No, of course not," she said hastily, even though she hadn't truly accepted the fact that he even intended to offer for her.

"Then this is an excellent time," he stated, his tone inviting no further protest.

"But it's—"

"What?"

Tuesday, she thought miserably. And it was just past noon, which meant—

"Let's go," Colin said, striding forward, and before she could stop him, he pushed open the door.

Colin's first thought upon stepping into the drawing room was that the day, while certainly not proceeding in any manner he might have anticipated when he'd risen from bed that morning, was turning out to be a most excellent endeavor. Marriage to Penelope was an eminently sensible idea, and surprisingly appealing as well, if their recent encounter in the carriage was any indication.

His second thought was that he'd just entered his worst nightmare.

Because Penelope's mother was not alone in the drawing room. Every last Featherington, current and former, was there, along with assorted spouses and even a cat.

It was the most frightening assemblage of people Colin had ever witnessed. Penelope's family was . . . well . . . except for Felicity (whom he'd always held in some suspicion; how could one truly trust anyone who was such good friends with Hyacinth?), her family was . . . well . . .

He couldn't think of a good word for it. Certainly nothing complimentary (although he'd like to think he could have avoided an outright insult), and really, was there a word that effectively combined slightly dim, overly talkative, rather meddlesome, excruciatingly dull, and—and one couldn't forget this, not with Robert Huxley a recent addition to the clan—uncommonly loud.

So Colin just smiled. His great, big, friendly, slightly mischievous smile. It almost always worked, and today was no exception. The Featheringtons all smiled right back at him, and—thank God—said nothing.

At least not right away.

"Colin," Mrs. Featherington said with visible surprise. "How nice of you to bring Penelope home for our family meeting."

"Your family meeting?" he echoed. He looked to Penelope, who was standing next to him, looking rather ill.

"Every Tuesday," she said, smiling weakly. "Didn't I mention it?"

"No," he replied, even though it was obvious her question had been for the benefit of their audience. "No, you didn't mention it."

"Bridgerton!" bellowed Robert Huxley, who was married to Penelope's eldest sister Prudence.

"Huxley," Colin returned, taking a discreet step back. Best to protect his eardrums in case Penelope's brother-in-law decided to leave his post near the window.

Thankfully, Huxley stayed put, but Penelope's other brother-in-law, the well-meaning but vacant-minded Nigel Berbrooke, did cross the room, greeting Colin with a hearty slap on the back. "Wasn't expecting you," Berbrooke said jovially.

"No," Colin murmured, "I wouldn't think so."

"Just family, after all," Berbrooke said, "and you're not family. Not my family, at least."

"Not yet, anyway," Colin murmured, stealing a glance at Penelope. She was blushing.

Then he looked back at Mrs. Featherington, who looked as if she might faint from excitement. Colin groaned through his smile. He hadn't meant for her to hear his comment about possibly joining the family. For some reason he'd wanted to retain an element of surprise before he asked for Penelope's hand. If Portia Featherington knew his intentions ahead of time, she'd likely twist the whole thing around (in her mind, at least) so that she had somehow orchestrated the match herself.

And for some reason, Colin found that exceedingly distasteful.

"I hope I'm not intruding," he said to Mrs. Featherington.

"No, of course not," she said quickly. "We are delighted to have you here, at a *family* gathering." But she looked rather odd, not precisely undecided about his presence there, but certainly unsure of what her next move should be. She was chewing on her lower lip, and then she darted a furtive glance at Felicity, of all people.

Colin turned to Felicity. She was looking at Penelope, a small secret smile fixed to her face. Penelope was glaring at her mother, her mouth twisted into an irritated grimace.

Colin's gaze went from Featherington to Featherington to Featherington. Something was clearly simmering under the surface here and if he weren't trying to figure out (A) how to avoid being trapped into conversation with Penelope's relations while (B) somehow managing to issue a proposal of marriage at the same time—well, he'd be rather curious as to what was causing all the secret, underhanded glances being tossed back and forth between the Featherington women.

Mrs. Featherington cast one last glance at Felicity, did a little gesture that Colin could have sworn meant, *Sit up straight,* then fixed her attention on Colin. "Won't you sit down?" she asked, smiling widely and patting the seat next to her on the sofa.

"Of course," he murmured, because there was really no getting out of it now. He still had to ask for Penelope's hand in marriage, and even if he didn't particularly want to do it in front of every last Featherington (and their two inane spouses), he was stuck here, at least until a polite opportunity to make his escape presented itself.

He turned and offered his arm to the woman he intended to make his bride. "Penelope?"

"Er, yes, of course," she stammered, placing her hand at the crook of his elbow.

"Oh, yes," Mrs. Featherington said, as if she'd completely forgotten about her daughter's presence. "Terribly sorry, Penelope. Didn't see you. Won't you please go and ask Cook to increase our order? We'll surely need more food with Mr. Bridgerton here."

"Of course," Penelope said, the corners of her lips quivering.

"Can't she ring for it?" Colin asked loudly.

"What?" Mrs. Featherington said distractedly. "Well, I suppose she could, but it would take longer, and Penelope doesn't mind, do you?"

Penelope gave her head a little shake.

"I mind," Colin said.

Mrs. Featherington let out a little "Oh" of surprise, then said, "Very well. Penelope, er, why don't you sit right there?" She motioned to a chair that was not quite situated to be a part of the inner conversation circle.

Felicity, who was seated directly across from her mother, jumped up. "Penelope, please take my seat."

"No," Mrs. Featherington said firmly. "You have been feeling under the weather, Felicity. You need to sit."

Colin thought Felicity looked the picture of perfect health, but she sat back down.

"Penelope," Prudence said loudly, from over by the window. "I need to speak with you."

Penelope glanced helplessly from Colin to Prudence to Felicity to her mother.

Colin yanked her in closer. "I need to speak with her as well," he said smoothly.

"Right, well, I suppose there is room for both of you," Mrs. Featherington said, scooting over on the sofa.

Colin was caught between the good manners that had been drummed into his head since birth and the overwhelming urge to strangle the woman who would someday be his mother-in-law. He had no idea why she was treating Penelope like some sort of lesser-favored stepchild, but really, it had to stop.

"What brings you this way?" yelled Robert Huxley.

Colin touched his ears—he couldn't help himself—then said, "I was—"

"Oh, goodness," fluttered Mrs. Featherington, "we do not mean to interrogate our guest, do we?"

Colin hadn't really thought Huxley's question constituted an interrogation, but he didn't really want to insult Mrs. Featherington by saying so, so he merely nodded and said something completely meaningless like, "Yes, well, of course."

"Of course what?" asked Philippa.

Philippa was married to Nigel Berbrooke, and Colin had always thought it was a rather good match, indeed.

"I'm sorry?" he queried.

"You said, 'Of course,' " Philippa said. "Of course what?"

"I don't know," Colin said.

"Oh. Well, then, why did you—"

"Philippa," Mrs. Featherington said loudly, "perhaps you should fetch the food, since Penelope has forgotten to ring for it."

"Oh, I'm sorry," Penelope said quickly, starting to rise to her feet.

"Don't worry," Colin said through a smooth smile, grabbing hold of her hand and yanking her back down. "Your mother said Prudence could go."

"Philippa," Penelope said.

"What about Philippa?"

"She said Philippa could go, not Prudence."

He wondered what had happened to her brain, because somewhere between his carriage and this sofa, it had clearly disappeared. "Does it matter?" he asked.

"No, not really, but—"

"Felicity," Mrs. Featherington interrupted, "why don't you tell Mr. Bridgerton about your watercolors?"

For the life of him, Colin couldn't imagine a less interesting topic (except, maybe, for Philippa's watercolors), but he nonetheless turned to the youngest Featherington with a friendly smile and asked, "And how are your watercolors?"

But Felicity, bless her heart, gave him a rather friendly smile herself and said nothing but, "I imagine they're fine, thank you."

Mrs. Featherington looked as if she'd just swallowed a live eel, then exclaimed, "Felicity!"

"Yes?" Felicity said sweetly.

"You didn't tell him that you'd won an award." She turned to

Colin. "Felicity's watercolors are very unique." She turned back to Felicity. "Do tell Mr. Bridgerton about your award."

"Oh, I don't imagine he is interested in that."

"Of course he is," Mrs. Featherington ground out.

Normally, Colin would have chimed in with, *Of course I am*, since he was, after all, an exceedingly affable fellow, but doing so would have validated Mrs. Featherington's statement and, perhaps more critically, ruined Felicity's good fun.

And Felicity appeared to be having a *lot* of fun. "Philippa," she said, "weren't you going to go after the food?"

"Oh, right," Philippa replied. "Forgot all about it. I do that a lot. Come along, Nigel. You can keep me company."

"Right-o!" Nigel beamed. And then he and Philippa left the room, giggling all the way.

Colin reaffirmed his conviction that the Berbrooke-Featherington match had been a good one, indeed.

"I think I shall go out to the garden," Prudence suddenly announced, taking hold of her husband's arm. "Penelope, why don't you come with me?"

Penelope opened her mouth a few seconds before she figured out what to say, leaving her looking a little bit like a confused fish (but in Colin's opinion a rather fetching fish, if such a thing were possible). Finally, her chin took on a resolute mien, and she said, "I don't think so, Prudence."

"Penelope!" Mrs. Featherington exclaimed.

"I need you to show me something," Prudence ground out.

"I really think I'm needed here," Penelope replied. "I can join you later this afternoon, if you like."

"I need you *now*."

Penelope looked to her sister in surprise, clearly not expecting quite so much resistance. "I'm sorry, Prudence," she reiterated. "I believe I'm needed here."

"Nonsense," Mrs. Featherington said breezily. "Felicity and I can keep Mr. Bridgerton company."

Felicity jumped to her feet. "Oh, no!" she exclaimed, her eyes round and innocent. "I forgot something."

"What," Mrs. Featherington asked between her teeth, "could you possibly have forgotten?"

"Uhh . . . my watercolors." She turned to Colin with a sweet, mischievous smile. "You did want to see them, didn't you?"

"Of course," he murmured, deciding he very much liked Penelope's younger sister. "Seeing as how they are so unique."

"One might say they are uniquely ordinary," Felicity said with an overly earnest nod.

"Penelope," Mrs. Featherington said, obviously trying to hide her annoyance, "would you be so kind as to fetch Felicity's watercolors?"

"Penelope doesn't know where they are," Felicity said quickly.

"Why don't you tell her?"

"For God's sake," Colin finally exploded, "let Felicity go. I need a private moment with you, anyway."

Silence reigned. It was the first time Colin Bridgerton had ever lost his temper in public. Beside him, Colin heard Penelope let out a little gasp, but when he glanced at her, she was hiding a tiny smile behind her hand.

And that made him feel ridiculously good.

"A private moment?" Mrs. Featherington echoed, her hand fluttering to her chest. She glanced over at Prudence and Robert, who were still standing by the window. They immediately left the room, although not without a fair bit of grumbling on Prudence's part.

"Penelope," Mrs. Featherington said, "perhaps you should accompany Felicity."

"Penelope will remain," Colin ground out.

"Penelope?" Mrs. Featherington asked doubtfully.

"Yes," he said slowly, in case she still didn't understand his meaning, "Penelope."

"But—"

Colin gave her such a glare that she actually drew back and folded her hands in her lap.

"I'm gone!" Felicity chirped, sailing out of the room. But before she closed the door behind her, Colin saw her give a quick wink to Penelope.

And Penelope smiled, love for her younger sister shining clearly in her eyes.

Colin relaxed. He hadn't realized just how tense Penelope's misery was making him. And she was definitely miserable. Good God, he couldn't wait to remove her from the bosom of her ridiculous family.

Mrs. Featherington's lips spread into a feeble attempt at a smile. She looked from Colin to Penelope and back again, and then finally said, "You desired a word?"

"Yes," he replied, eager to get this done with. "I would be honored if you would grant me your daughter's hand in marriage."

For a moment Mrs. Featherington made no reaction. Then her eyes grew round, her mouth grew round, her body—well, her body was already round—and she clapped her hands together, unable to say anything other than, "Oh! Oh!"

And then, "Felicity! Felicity!"

Felicity?

Portia Featherington jumped to her feet, ran to the door and actually screamed like a fishwife. "Felicity! Felicity!"

"Oh, Mother," Penelope moaned, closing her eyes.

"Why are you summoning Felicity?" Colin asked, rising to his feet.

Mrs. Featherington turned to him quizzically. "Don't you want to marry Felicity?"

Colin actually thought he might be sick. "No, for God's sake, I don't want to marry Felicity," he snapped. "If I'd wanted to marry Felicity, I'd hardly have sent her upstairs for her bloody watercolors, would I?"

Mrs. Featherington swallowed uncomfortably. "Mr. Bridgerton," she said, wringing her hands together. "I don't understand."

He stared at her in horror, which then turned to disgust. "Penelope," he said, grabbing her hand and yanking her until she was pressed close to his side. "I want to marry Penelope."

"Penelope?" Mrs. Featherington echoed. "But——"

"But what?" he interrupted, his voice pure menace.

"But—but——"

"It's all right, Colin," Penelope said hastily. "I——"

"No, it is not all right," he exploded. "I've never given any indication I'm the least bit interested in Felicity."

Felicity appeared in the doorway, clapped her hand over her mouth, and quickly disappeared, wisely shutting the door behind her.

"Yes," Penelope said placatingly, shooting a quick look at her mother, "but Felicity is unmarried, and——"

"So are you," he pointed out.

"I know, but I'm old, and——"

"And Felicity is an *infant*," he spat. "Good God, marrying her would be like marrying Hyacinth."

"Er, except for the incest," Penelope said.

He gave her an extremely unamused look.

"Right," she said, mostly to fill the silence. "It's just a terrible misunderstanding, isn't it?"

No one said anything. Penelope looked at Colin pleadingly. "Isn't it?"

"It certainly is," he muttered.

She turned to her mother. "Mama?"

"Penelope?" she murmured, and Penelope knew that her mother wasn't asking her a question; rather, she was still expressing her disbelief that Colin would want to marry her.

And oh, but it hurt so much. You'd think she'd be used to it by now.

"I would like to marry Mr. Bridgerton," Penelope said, trying to summon up as much quiet dignity as she could manage. "He asked me, and I said yes."

"Well, of course you would say yes," her mother retorted. "You'd have to be an idiot to say no."

"Mrs. Featherington," Colin said tightly, "I suggest you begin treating my future wife with a bit more respect."

"Colin, it's not necessary," Penelope said, placing her hand on his arm, but the truth was—her heart was soaring. He might not love her, but he cared about her. No man could defend a woman with such fierce protectiveness without caring for her a little.

"It *is* necessary," he returned. "For God's sake, Penelope, I arrived with you. I made it abundantly clear that I required your presence in the room, and I practically shoved Felicity out the door to fetch her watercolors. Why on earth would anyone think I wanted Felicity?"

Mrs. Featherington opened and closed her mouth several times before finally saying, "I love Penelope, of course, but—"

"But do you know her?" Colin shot back. "She's lovely and intelligent and has a fine sense of humor. Who wouldn't want to marry a woman like that?"

Penelope would have melted to the floor if she weren't already holding on to his hand. "Thank you," she whispered, not caring if her mother heard her, not even really caring if Colin heard her. Somehow she needed to say the words for herself.

Not what she thought she was.

Lady Danbury's face swam before her eyes, her expression warm and just a little bit cunning.

Something more. Maybe Penelope was something more, and maybe Colin was the only other person to realize that as well.

It made her love him all the more.

Her mother cleared her throat, then stepped forward and gave

Penelope a hug. It was, at first, a hesitant embrace on both of their parts, but then Portia tightened her arms around her thirdborn daughter, and with a choked cry, Penelope found herself returning the hug in equal measure.

"I do love you, Penelope," Portia said, "and I am very pleased for you." She drew back and wiped a tear from her eye. "I shall be lonely without you, of course, since I'd assumed we would grow old together, but this is what's best for you, and that, I suppose, is what being a mother is all about."

Penelope let out a loud sniffle, then blindly reached for Colin's handkerchief, which he had already pulled from his pocket and was holding in front of her.

"You'll learn someday," Portia said, patting her on the arm. She turned to Colin and said, "We are delighted to welcome you to the family."

He nodded, not terribly warmly, but Penelope thought he made a rather nice effort considering how angry he'd been just moments earlier.

Penelope smiled and squeezed his hand, aware that she was about to embark upon the adventure of her life.

Chapter 15

"You know," Eloise said, three days after Colin and Penelope made their surprise announcement, "it's really a pity that Lady Whistledown has retired, because this would have been the coup of the decade."

"Certainly from Lady Whistledown's viewpoint," Penelope murmured, lifting her teacup to her lips and keeping her eyes trained on the wall clock in Lady Bridgerton's informal drawing room. Better not to look at Eloise directly. She had a way of noticing secrets in a person's eyes.

It was funny. Penelope had gone years without worrying that Eloise would discover the truth about Lady Whistledown. At least, not worrying overmuch. But now that Colin knew, it somehow felt as if her secret were floating about in the air, like particles of dust just waiting to form into a cloud of knowledge.

Maybe the Bridgertons were like dominoes. Once one found out, it was only a matter of time before they all fell.

"What do you mean?" Eloise asked, breaking into Penelope's nervous thoughts.

"If I recall correctly," Penelope said, very carefully, "she once wrote that she would have to retire if I ever married a Bridgerton."

Eloise's eyes bugged out. "She did?"

"Or something like that," Penelope said.

"You're joking," Eloise said, making a "pffft" sort of sound as she waved her hand dismissively. "She would never have been that cruel."

Penelope coughed, not really thinking that she could end the topic by faking a biscuit crumb in her throat, but trying nonetheless.

"No, really," Eloise persisted. "What did she say?"

"I don't recall, precisely."

"Try."

Penelope stalled by setting her cup down and reaching for another biscuit. They were alone for tea, which was odd. But Lady Bridgerton had dragged Colin off on some errand regarding the upcoming wedding—set for only a month hence!—and Hyacinth was off shopping with Felicity, who had, upon hearing Penelope's news, thrown her arms around her sister and shrieked her delight until Penelope's ears had gone numb.

As far as sisterly moments went, it had been something wonderful.

"Well," Penelope said, chewing on a bite of biscuit, "I believe she said that if I married a Bridgerton, it would be the end of the world as she knew it, and as she wouldn't be able to make heads or tails of such a world, she would have to retire immediately."

Eloise stared at her for a moment. "That's not a precise recollection?"

"One doesn't forget things like that," Penelope demurred.

"Hmmmph." Eloise's nose wrinkled with disdain. "Well, that was rather horrid of her, I must say. Now I doubly wish she were still writing, because she would have to eat an entire gaggle of crow."

"Do crows gather in gaggles?"

"I don't know," Eloise replied promptly, "but they should."

"You're a very good friend, Eloise," Penelope said quietly.

"Yes," Eloise said with an affected sigh, "I know. The very best."

Penelope smiled. Eloise's breezy reply made it clear that she wasn't in the mood for emotion or nostalgia. Which was fine. There was a time and a place for everything. Penelope had said what she wanted to say, and she knew that Eloise returned the sentiment, even if she preferred to joke and tease at that moment.

"I must confess, though," Eloise said, reaching for another biscuit, "you and Colin did surprise me."

"We surprised me as well," Penelope admitted wryly.

"Not that I'm not delighted," Eloise hastened to add. "There is no one I'd rather have as a sister. Well, aside from the ones I already have, of course. And if I'd ever dreamed the two of you were inclined in that direction, I'm sure I would have meddled horribly."

"I know," Penelope said, laughter forcing her lips up at the corners.

"Yes, well"—Eloise waved the comment away—"I'm not known for minding my own business."

"What's that on your fingers?" Penelope asked, leaning forward for a better look.

"What? That? Oh, nothing." But she settled her hands in her lap nonetheless.

"It's not nothing," Penelope said. "Let me see. It looks like ink."

"Well, of course it does. It *is* ink."

"Then why didn't you say so when I asked?"

"Because," Eloise said pertly, "it's none of your business."

Penelope drew back in shock at Eloise's sharp tone. "I'm terribly sorry," she said stiffly. "I had no idea it was such a sensitive subject."

"Oh, it's not," Eloise said quickly. "Don't be silly. It's just that I'm clumsy and I can't write without getting ink all over my fingers. I suppose I could wear gloves, but then *they'd* be stained, and I'd be forever replacing them, and I can assure you that I have no wish to spend my entire allowance—meager as it is—on gloves."

Penelope stared at her through her lengthy explanation, then asked, "What were you writing?"

"Nothing," Eloise said dismissively. "Just letters."

Penelope could tell from Eloise's brisk tone that she didn't particularly want to subject the topic to further exploration, but she was being so uncharacteristically evasive that Penelope couldn't resist asking, "To whom?"

"The letters?"

"Yes," Penelope replied, even though she thought that was rather obvious.

"Oh, no one."

"Well, unless they're a diary, they're not to *no one*," Penelope said, impatience adding a short tinge to her voice.

Eloise gave her a vaguely affronted look. "You're rather nosy today."

"Only because you're being so evasive."

"They're just to Francesca," Eloise said with a little snort.

"Well, then, why didn't you say so?"

Eloise crossed her arms. "Perhaps I didn't appreciate your questioning me."

Penelope's mouth fell open. She couldn't remember the last time she and Eloise had had anything even remotely approaching a row. "Eloise," she said, her shock showing in her voice, "what is wrong?"

"Nothing is wrong."

"I know that's not true."

Eloise said nothing, just pursed her lips and glanced toward the window, a clear attempt to end the conversation.

"Are you angry with me?" Penelope persisted.

"Why would I be angry with you?"

"I don't know, but it's clear that you are."

Eloise let out a little sigh. "I'm not angry."

"Well, you're *some*thing."

"I'm just . . . I'm just . . ." She shook her head. "I don't know what I am. Restless, I suppose. Out of sorts."

Penelope was silent as she digested that, then said quietly, "Is there anything I can do?"

"No." Eloise smiled wryly. "If there were, you can be sure I'd have already asked it of you."

Penelope felt something that was almost a laugh rising within her. How like Eloise to make such a comment.

"I suppose it's . . ." Eloise began, her chin lifting in thought. "No, never mind."

"No," Penelope said, reaching out and taking her friend's hand. "Tell me."

Eloise pulled her hand free and looked away. "You'll think I'm silly."

"Maybe," Penelope said with a smile, "but you'll still be my very closest friend."

"Oh, Penelope, but I'm not," Eloise said sadly. "I'm not worthy of it."

"Eloise, don't talk such madness. I'd have gone right-out insane trying to navigate London and society and the *ton* without you."

Eloise smiled. "We did have fun, didn't we?"

"Well, yes, when I was with you," Penelope admitted. "The rest of the time I was bloody miserable."

"Penelope! I don't believe I've ever heard you curse before."

Penelope gave her a sheepish smile. "It slipped out. And besides, I couldn't possibly think of a better adjective to describe life for a wallflower among the *ton*."

Eloise let out an unexpected chuckle. "Now, that's a book I would like to read: *A Wallflower Among the Ton*."

"Not unless you're given to tragedies."

"Oh, come, now, it couldn't be a tragedy. It would have to be a romance. You're getting your happy ending, after all."

Penelope smiled. As strange as it was, she *was* getting her happy ending. Colin had been a lovely and attentive fiancé, at least for the three days that he'd been playing that role. And it couldn't have been particularly easy; they'd been subject to more speculation and scrutiny than Penelope could have imagined.

She wasn't surprised, though; when she (as Lady Whistledown) had written that the world would end as she knew it if a Featherington married a Bridgerton, she rather thought she'd been echoing a prevalent sentiment.

To say that the *ton* had been shocked by Penelope's engagement would have been an understatement, indeed.

But much as Penelope liked to anticipate and reflect upon her upcoming marriage, she was still a bit disturbed about Eloise's strange mood. "Eloise," she said seriously, "I want you to tell me what has you so upset."

Eloise sighed. "I'd hoped you'd forgotten about it."

"I've learned tenacity from the master," Penelope commented.

That made Eloise smile, but only for a moment. "I feel so disloyal," she said.

"What have you done?"

"Oh, nothing." She patted her heart. "It's all inside. I—" She stopped, looked to the side, her eyes settling on the fringed corner of the carpet, but Penelope suspected that she didn't see much of anything. At least nothing beyond what was rumbling about in her mind.

"I'm so happy for you," Eloise said, the words tumbling forth in odd bursts, punctuated by awkward pauses. "And I honestly think I can really, truly say that I'm not jealous. But at the same time . . ."

Penelope waited for Eloise to collect her thoughts. Or maybe she was collecting her courage.

"At the same time," she said, so softly that Penelope could barely hear her, "I suppose I always thought you'd be a spinster right along with me. I've chosen this life. I know that I have. I could have married."

"I know," Penelope said quietly.

"But I never did, because it never seemed right, and I didn't want to settle for anything less than what my brothers and sister have. And now Colin, too," she said, motioning toward Penelope.

Penelope didn't mention that Colin had never said he loved her. It didn't seem like the right time, or, frankly, the sort of thing she cared to share. Besides, even if he didn't love her, she still thought he cared about her, and that was enough.

"I would never have wanted you *not* to marry," Eloise explained, "I just never thought you would." She closed her eyes, looking quite agonized. "That came out all wrong. I've insulted you terribly."

"No, you haven't," Penelope said, meaning it. "I never thought I would marry, either."

Eloise nodded sadly. "And somehow, it made it all . . . all right. I was almost twenty-eight and unmarried, and you were already twenty-eight and unmarried, and we'd always have each other. But now you have Colin."

"I still have you, too. At least I hope I do."

"Of course you do," Eloise said fervently. "But it won't be the same. You must cleave unto your husband. Or at least that's what they all say," she added with a slightly mischievous spark in her eyes. "Colin will come first, and that is how it should be. And frankly," she added, her smile growing a bit sly, "I'd have to kill you if he didn't. He *is* my favorite brother, after all. It really wouldn't do for him to have a disloyal wife."

Penelope laughed out loud at that.

"Do you hate me?" Eloise asked.

Penelope shook her head. "No," she said softly. "If anything I love you all the more, because I know how difficult it must have been to be honest with me about this."

"I'm so glad you said that," Eloise said with a loud, dramatic sigh. "I was terrified you'd say that the only solution would be for me to find myself a husband as well."

The thought had crossed Penelope's mind, but she shook her head and said, "Of course not."

"Good. Because my mother has been saying it constantly."

Penelope smiled wryly. "I'd be surprised if she hadn't."

"Good afternoon, ladies!"

The two women looked up to see Colin entering the room. Penelope's heart did a little flip upon seeing him, and she found herself oddly out of breath. Her heart had been doing little flips for years whenever he walked into a room, but it was somehow different now, more intense.

Perhaps because she *knew.*

Knew what it was like to be with him, to be wanted by him.

To know that he would be her husband.

Her heart flipped again.

Colin let out a loud groan. "You ate all the food?"

"There was only one small plate of biscuits," Eloise said in their defense.

"That's not what I was led to believe," Colin grumbled.

Penelope and Eloise shared a glance, then both burst out laughing.

"What?" Colin demanded, leaning down to press a quick, dutiful kiss on Penelope's cheek.

"You sounded so sinister," Eloise explained. "It's just food."

"It's never just food," Colin said, plopping down in a chair.

Penelope was still wondering when her cheek would stop tingling.

"So," he said, taking a half-eaten biscuit off of Eloise's plate, "what were you two talking about?"

"Lady Whistledown," Eloise said promptly.

Penelope choked on her tea.

"Were you?" Colin said softly, but Penelope detected a definite edge in his voice.

"Yes," Eloise said. "I was telling Penelope that it is really too bad she's retired, since your engagement would have been quite the most newsworthy piece of gossip we've had all year."

"Interesting how that works out," Colin murmured.

"Mmmm," Eloise agreed, "and she surely would have devoted an entire column just to your engagement ball tomorrow night."

Penelope did not lower her teacup from her mouth.

"Do you want some more?" Eloise asked her.

Penelope nodded and handed her the cup, although she very much missed having it in front of her face as a shield. She knew that Eloise had blurted out Lady Whistledown's name because she did not want Colin to know that she had mixed feelings about his marriage, but still, Penelope fervently wished that Eloise had said anything else in reply to Colin's question.

"Why don't you ring for more food?" Eloise asked Colin.

"Already did so," he answered. "Wickham intercepted me in the hall and asked if I was hungry." He popped the last bite of Eloise's biscuit into his mouth. "Wise man, that Wickham."

"Where did you go today, Colin?" Penelope asked, eager to get the topic firmly off of Lady Whistledown.

He gave his head a beleaguered shake. "Devil if I know. Mother dragged me from shop to shop."

"Aren't you thirty-three years old?" Eloise inquired sweetly.

He answered her with a scowl.

"Just thought you'd be beyond the age of having Mother drag you about, that's all," she murmured.

"Mother will be dragging all of us about when we're doddering old fools, and you know it," he replied. "Besides, she's so delighted to see me married, I really can't bring myself to spoil her fun."

Penelope sighed. This had to be why she loved the man. Anyone who treated his mother so well would surely be an excellent husband.

"And how are your wedding preparations coming along?" Colin asked Penelope.

She hadn't meant to pull a face, but she did, anyway. "I have never been so exhausted in all my life," she admitted.

He reached over and grabbed a large crumb off of her plate. "We should elope."

"Oh, could we *really*?" Penelope asked, the words flying from her lips in an unsummoned rush.

He blinked. "Actually, I was joking, mostly, although it does seem a prime idea."

"I shall arrange for a ladder," Eloise said, clapping her hands together, "so that you might climb to her room and steal her away."

"There's a tree," Penelope said. "Colin will have no difficulty with it."

"Good God," he said, "you're not serious, are you?"

"No," she sighed. "But I could be. If you were."

"I can't be. Do you know what it would do to my mother?" He rolled his eyes. "Not to mention yours."

Penelope groaned. "I know."

"She'd hunt me down and kill me," Colin said.

"Mine or yours?"

"Both. They'd join forces." He craned his neck toward the door. "*Where* is the food?"

"You just got here, Colin," Eloise said. "Give them time."

"And here I thought Wickham a sorcerer," he grumbled, "able to conjure food with the snap of his hand."

"Here you are, sir!" came Wickham's voice as he sailed into the room with a large tray.

"See?" Colin said, raising his brows first at Eloise and then at Penelope. "I told you so."

"Why," Penelope asked, "do I sense that I will be hearing those words from your lips far too many times in my future?"

"Most likely because you will," Colin replied. "You'll soon learn"—he shot her an extremely cheeky grin—"that I am almost always right."

"Oh, *please*," Eloise groaned.

"I may have to side with Eloise on this one," Penelope said.

"Against your husband?" He placed a hand on his heart (while the other one reached for a sandwich). "I'm wounded."

"You're not my husband yet."

Colin turned to Eloise. "The kitten has claws."

Eloise raised her brows. "You didn't realize that before you proposed?"

"Of course I did," he said, taking a bite of his sandwich. "I just didn't think she'd use them on me."

And then he looked at her with such a hot, masterful expression that Penelope's bones went straight to water.

"Well," Eloise announced, rising quite suddenly to her feet, "I think I shall allow you two soon-to-be-newlyweds a moment or two of privacy."

"How positively forward-thinking of you," Colin murmured.

Eloise looked to him with a peevish twist to her mouth. "Anything for you, dear brother. Or rather," she added, her expression growing arch, "anything for Penelope."

Colin stood and turned to his betrothed, "I seem to be slipping down the pecking order."

Penelope just smiled behind her teacup and said, "I am making it my policy never to get in the middle of a Bridgerton spat."

"Oh ho!" Eloise chortled. "You'll not be able to keep to that one, I'm afraid, Mrs. Soon-to-be-Bridgerton. Besides," she added with a wicked grin, "if you think this is a spat, I can't wait until you see us in full form."

"You mean I haven't?" Penelope asked.

Both Eloise and Colin shook their heads in a way that made her extremely fearful.

Oh, dear.

"Is there something I should know?" Penelope asked.

Colin grinned rather wolfishly. "It's too late now."

Penelope gave Eloise a helpless glance, but all she did was laugh as she left the room, closing the door firmly behind her.

"Now, *that* was nice of Eloise," Colin murmured.

"What?" Penelope asked innocently.

His eyes gleamed. "The door."

"The door? Oh!" she yelped. "The door."

Colin smiled, moving over to the sofa beside her. There was something rather delightful about Penelope on a rainy afternoon.

He'd hardly seen her since they'd become engaged—wedding plans had a way of doing that to a couple—and yet she'd not been out of his thoughts, even as he slept.

Funny how that happened. He'd spent years not really ever thinking about her unless she was standing in front of his face, and now she had permeated his every last thought.

His every last desire.

How had this happened?

When had it happened?

And did it really matter? Maybe the only important thing was that he wanted her and she was—or at least she would be—his. Once he put his ring on her finger, the hows, whys, and whens would become irrelevant, provided that this madness he felt never went away.

He touched his finger to her chin, tipping her face up to the light. Her eyes shone with anticipation, and her lips—dear God, how was it possible that the men of London had never noticed how perfect they were?

He smiled. This was a permanent madness. And he couldn't have been more pleased.

Colin had never been opposed to marriage. He'd simply been opposed to a dull marriage. He wasn't picky; he just wanted passion and friendship and intellectual conversation and a good laugh every now and then. A wife from whom he wouldn't want to stray.

Amazingly, he seemed to have found that in Penelope.

All he needed to do now was make sure her Big Secret remained just that. A secret.

Because he didn't think he could bear the pain he'd see in her eyes if she were cast out of society.

"Colin?" she whispered, her breath quivering across her lips, making him *really* want to kiss her.

He leaned in. "Hmmm?"

"You were so quiet."

"Just thinking."

"About what?"

He gave her an indulgent smile. "You really have been spending too much time with my sister."

"What does that mean?" she asked, her lips twitching in such a way that he knew she'd never feel any compunction at poking fun at him. She would keep him on his toes, this woman.

"You seem," he said, "to have developed a certain penchant for persistence."

"Tenacity?"

"That, too."

"But that's a good thing."

Their lips were still mere inches apart, but the urge to continue the teasing conversation was too strong. "When you're persistently avowing your obedience for your husband," he murmured, "that's a good thing."

"Oh, really?"

His chin dipped into the barest hint of a nod. "And when you're tenaciously holding on to my shoulders when I'm kissing you, that's a good thing as well."

Her dark eyes widened so delightfully that he had to add, "Don't you think?"

And then she surprised him.

"Like this?" she asked, placing her hands on his shoulders. Her tone was daring, her eyes pure flirtation.

Lord, he loved that she surprised him.

"That's a start," he said. "You might have to"—he moved one of his hands to cover hers, pressing her fingers into his skin—"hold me a little more tenaciously."

"I see," she murmured. "So what you're saying is that I should never let go?"

He thought about that for a moment. "Yes," he answered, realizing that there was a deeper meaning in her words, whether she'd intended it or not. "That's exactly what I'm saying."

And then words were simply not enough. He brought his lips to hers, remaining gentle for barely a second before his hunger overtook him. He kissed her with a passion he hadn't even known he possessed. It wasn't about desire—or at least it wasn't *just* about desire.

It was about need.

It was about a strange sensation, hot and fierce inside of him, urging him to lay claim to her, to somehow brand her as his.

He wanted her desperately, and he had absolutely no idea how he could possibly make it through an entire month before the wedding.

"Colin?" Penelope gasped, just as he was easing her down onto her back on the sofa.

He was kissing her jaw, and then her neck, and his lips were far too busy for anything other than a low, "Mmm?"

"We're—Oh!"

He smiled, even as he nipped her earlobe gently with his teeth. If she could finish a sentence, then he clearly wasn't befuddling her as much as he ought.

"You were saying?" he murmured, then kissed her deeply on the mouth, just to torture her.

He lifted his lips off hers just long enough for her to say, "I just—" and then he kissed her again, reeling with pleasure when she groaned with desire.

"I'm sorry," he said, scooting his hands under the hem of her dress and then using them to do all sorts of wicked things to her calves, "you were saying?"

"I was?" she asked, her eyes glazed.

He moved his hands higher, until they were tickling the back of her knee. "You were saying *some*thing," he said, pressing his hips against her because he honestly thought he would burst into flame at that very moment if he did not. "I think," he whispered, sliding his hand over the soft skin of her thigh, "that you were going to say that you wanted me to touch you *here*."

She gasped, then groaned, then somehow managed to say, "I don't think that was what I was going to say."

He grinned against her neck. "Are you sure?"

She nodded.

"So then you want me to stop?"

She shook her head. Frantically.

He could take her now, he realized. He could make love to her right there on his mother's sofa and not only would she let him, she would enjoy herself in every way a woman should.

It wouldn't be a conquest, it wouldn't even be seduction.

It would be more than that. Maybe even . . .

Love.

Colin froze.

"Colin?" she whispered, opening her eyes.

Love?

It wasn't possible.

"Colin?"

Or maybe it was.

"Is something wrong?"

It wasn't that he feared love, or didn't believe in it. He just hadn't . . . expected it.

He'd always thought love would hit a man like a thunderbolt, that one day you'd be loitering about at some party, bored to tears, and then you'd see a woman, and you'd know instantly that your life would be changed forever. That was what had happened to his brother Benedict, and heaven knew that he and his wife Sophie were blissfully happy rusticating away in the country.

But this thing with Penelope . . . it had crept up on him. The change had been slow, almost lethargic, and if it was love, well . . .

If it was love, wouldn't he *know*?

He watched her closely, curiously, thinking that maybe he'd find his answer in her eyes, or the sweep of her hair, or the way the bodice of her gown hung slightly crookedly. Maybe if he watched her long enough, he'd know.

"Colin?" she whispered, starting to sound slightly anxious.

He kissed her again, this time with a fierce determination. If this was love, wouldn't it become obvious when they kissed?

But if his mind and body were working separately, then the kiss was clearly in league with his body, because while his mind's confusion remained just as blurry as ever, his body's need was brought into sharper focus.

Hell, now he was in pain. And he really couldn't do anything about it here in his mother's drawing room, even if Penelope would have been a willing participant.

He pulled back, letting his hand slip down her leg toward the edge of her skirt. "We can't do this here."

"I know," she said, sounding so sad that his hand stilled on her knee, and he almost lost his resolve to do the right thing and mind the dictates of propriety.

He thought hard and fast. It was possible that he could make love to her and no one would walk in on them. Heaven knew that in his current state, it would be an embarrassingly fast endeavor, anyway.

"When is the wedding?" he growled.

"A month."

"What would it take to change that to a fortnight?"

She thought about that for a moment. "Bribery or blackmail. Maybe both. Our mothers will not be easily swayed."

He groaned, letting his hips sink against hers for one delicious moment before heaving himself off. He couldn't take her now. She was going to be his wife. There would be plenty of time for midday tumbles on illicit sofas, but he owed it to her to use a bed for the first time, at least.

"Colin?" she asked, straightening her dress and smoothing her hair, even though there was no way she was going to make the latter look anything even approaching presentable without a mirror, hair-brush, and maybe even a maid. "Is something wrong?"

"I want you," he whispered.

She looked up at him, startled.

"I just wanted you to know that," he said. "I didn't want you to think I stopped because you didn't please me."

"Oh." She looked as if she wanted to say something; she looked almost absurdly happy at his words. "Thank you for saying that."

He took her hand and squeezed.

"Do I look a mess?" she asked.

He nodded. "But you're *my* mess," he whispered.

And he was very glad for that.

Chapter 16

As Colin liked to walk, and in fact frequently did so to clear his mind, it was no surprise that he spent much of the next day traversing Bloomsbury . . . and Fitzrovia . . . and Marylebone . . . and in fact several other London neighborhoods, until he looked up and realized that he was standing in the heart of Mayfair, in Grosvenor Square, to be precise, outside of Hastings House, town home of the Dukes of Hastings, the latest of whom happened to be married to his sister Daphne.

It had been a while since they'd had a conversation, anything above the usual family chitchat, that was. Of all his siblings, Daphne was the closest in age to him, and they'd always shared a rather special bond, even though they didn't see each other as much as they used to, what with Colin's frequent travels and Daphne's busy family life.

Hastings House was one of those enormous mansions that one could find scattered throughout Mayfair and St. James's. Large and square and constructed of elegant Portland stone, it was thoroughly imposing in its ducal splendor.

Which made it all the more amusing, Colin thought with a wry grin, that his sister was the current duchess. He couldn't imagine anyone less haughty or imposing. In fact, Daphne had had difficulty finding a husband when she'd been out on the marriage mart, precisely because she *was* so friendly and easy to be with. Gentlemen had tended to think of her as their friend and not as a prospective bride.

But all that had changed when she'd met Simon Bassett, Duke of Hastings, and now she was a respectable society matron with four children, aged ten, nine, eight, and seven. It still sometimes seemed odd to Colin that his sister was a mother, of all things, while he still lived the free and unfettered life of a bachelor. With only one year between them, he and Daphne had always passed through the various stages of life together. Even when she'd married, things hadn't seemed so very different; she and Simon attended the same parties he did and had many of the same interests and pursuits.

But then she'd started reproducing, and while Colin was always delighted to welcome a new niece or nephew into his life, each arrival had brought home the fact that Daphne had moved on in a way he had not.

But, he thought, smiling as Penelope's face drifted through his mind, he supposed all that would soon change.

Children. It was a rather nice thought, actually.

He hadn't consciously meant to visit Daphne, but now that he was here, he figured he might as well stop by and say hello, so he marched up the steps and gave the big brass knocker a sturdy clanking. Jeffries, the butler, opened the door almost immediately.

"Mr. Bridgerton," he said. "Your sister was not expecting you."

"No, I decided to surprise her. Is she at home?"

"I shall see," the butler said with a nod, even though they both knew that Daphne would never refuse to see a member of her family.

Colin waited in the drawing room while Jeffries informed Daphne of his presence, wandering idly about, feeling too restless to sit or even stand in one place. After a few minutes, Daphne appeared in the doorway, looking slightly disheveled but happy as always.

And why shouldn't she be? Colin wondered. All she'd ever wanted in life was to be a wife and mother, and it seemed that reality had more than surpassed her dreams.

"Hello there, sister," he said with a sloppy smile as he crossed the room to give her a quick hug. "You've got . . ." He motioned to his shoulder.

She looked down at her own shoulder, then smiled sheepishly as she saw the large dark gray smudge on the pale pink fabric of her dress. "Charcoal," she explained ruefully. "I've been trying to teach Caroline to draw."

"You?" Colin asked doubtfully.

"I know, I know," she said. "She really couldn't have picked a worse tutor, but she only decided yesterday that she loves art, so I'm all she's got on such short notice."

"You should pack her off to see Benedict," Colin suggested. "I'm sure he'd be happy to give her a lesson or two."

"The thought had already crossed my mind, but I'm sure she'll have moved on to some other pursuit by the time I can make the arrangements." She motioned to a sofa. "Sit. You look rather like a caged cat over there, pacing as you are."

He sat, even though he felt uncommonly fidgety.

"And before you ask," Daphne said, "I already told Jeffries to see to food. Will sandwiches be enough?"

"Could you hear my stomach grumbling from across the room?"

"From across town, I'm afraid." She laughed. "Did you know that whenever it thunders, David says that it's your stomach?"

"Oh, good God," Colin muttered, but he was chuckling all the while. His nephew was a rather clever little fellow.

Daphne smiled broadly as she settled down against the sofa cushions, folding her hands elegantly in her lap. "What brings you by, Colin? Not that you need a reason, of course. It's always lovely to see you."

He shrugged. "Just passing by."

"Did you visit Anthony and Kate?" she asked. Bridgerton House, where their eldest brother lived with his family, was just across the square from Hastings House. "Benedict and Sophie are already there with the children, helping to prepare for your engagement ball tonight."

He shook his head. "No, you're my chosen victim, I'm afraid."

She smiled again, but this time it was a softer expression, tempered by a fair dose of curiosity. "Is something wrong?"

"No, of course not," he said quickly. "Why would you ask that?"

"I don't know." She cocked her head to the side. "You seem odd, that's all."

"Just tired."

She nodded knowingly. "Wedding plans, I'm sure."

"Yes," he said, jumping on the excuse, although for the life of him, he wasn't even sure what it was he was trying to hide from her.

"Well, remember that whatever you're going through," she said with a peevish twist to her lips, "it's a thousand times worse for Penelope. It's always worse for women. Trust me."

"For weddings or for everything?" he asked mildly.

"Everything," she said promptly. "I know you men think you're actually in charge, but—"

"I wouldn't dream of thinking we're actually in charge," Colin said, and not entirely sarcastically.

Her face pinched into a peevish expression. "Women have far more to do than men. *Especially* with weddings. With all the fittings I'm sure Penelope has had for her wedding gown, she probably feels like a pincushion."

"I suggested eloping," Colin said conversationally, "and I think she rather hoped I was serious."

Daphne chuckled. "I'm so glad you're marrying her, Colin."

He nodded, not planning to say anything, and then somehow, he was saying her name. "Daff—"

"Yes?"

He opened his mouth, and then—"Never mind."

"Oh, no, you don't," she said. "Now you really have my curiosity piqued."

He drummed his fingers against the sofa. "Do you suppose the food might arrive soon?"

"Are you even hungry or are you merely trying to change the subject?"

"I'm always hungry."

She was silent for several seconds. "Colin," she finally asked, her voice soft and carefully gentle, "what were you going to say?"

He jumped to his feet, too restless to remain still, and began to pace. He stopped, turned to her, looked at her concerned face. "It's nothing," he started to say, except it wasn't nothing, and—

"How does one know?" he blurted out, not even aware that he hadn't completed his question until she replied, "How does one know what?"

He stopped in front of the window. It looked like it might rain. He'd have to borrow a carriage from Daphne unless he wanted to get soaked on the long walk home. Yet, he didn't know why he was even thinking about precipitation, because what he really wanted to know was—

"How does one know *what*, Colin?" Daphne repeated.

He turned around and just let the words break free. "How do you know if it's love?"

For a moment she just stared at him, her large brown eyes wide with surprise, her lips parted and utterly still.

"Forget I asked," he muttered.

"No!" she exclaimed, jumping to her feet. "I'm *glad* you asked. Very glad. I'm just . . . surprised, I must say."

He closed his eyes, thoroughly disgusted with himself. "I can't believe I just asked you that."

"No, Colin, don't be silly. It's really rather . . . sweet that you asked. And I can't even begin to tell you how flattered I am that you would come to me when—"

"Daphne . . ." he said warningly. She had a way of wandering off the topic, and he really wasn't in the right frame of mind to follow her errant thoughts.

Impulsively, she reached out and hugged him; then, her hands still on his shoulders, she said, "I don't know."

"I beg your pardon?"

She gave her head a little shake. "I don't know how you know it's love. I think it's different for everyone."

"How did you know?"

She chewed on her lower lip for several seconds before replying, "I don't know."

"What?"

She shrugged helplessly. "I don't remember. It's been so long. I just . . . *knew.*"

"So what you're saying," he said, leaning against the windowsill and crossing his arms, "is that if one doesn't know one's in love, then one probably isn't."

"Yes," she said firmly. "No! No, that's not what I mean at all."

"Then what do you mean?"

"I don't know," she said weakly.

He stared at her. "And how long have you been married?" he muttered.

"Colin, don't tease. I'm trying to be helpful."

"And I appreciate the attempt, but truly, Daphne, you—"

"I know, I know," she interrupted. "I'm useless. But listen to me. Do you like Penelope?" Then she gasped in horror. "We are talking about Penelope, aren't we?"

"Of course we are," he snapped.

She let out a relieved sigh. "Good, because if we weren't, then I can assure you I would have had no advice whatsoever."

"I'll go," he said abruptly.

"No, don't," she pleaded, placing her hand on his arm. "Stay, Colin, please."

He looked at her, sighing, feeling defeated. "I feel like an ass."

"Colin," she said, guiding him to the sofa and pushing him down until he sat, "listen to me. Love grows and changes every day. And it isn't like some thunderbolt from the sky, instantly transforming you into a different man. I know Benedict says it was that way for him, and that's just lovely, but you know, Benedict is *not* normal."

Colin very much wanted to take that bait, but he just couldn't summon the energy.

"It wasn't like that for me," Daphne said, "and I don't think it was like that for Simon, although truthfully, I don't think I've ever asked."

"You should."

She paused while her mouth was forming a word, leaving her looking like a surprised bird. "Why?"

He shrugged. "So you can tell me."

"What, do you think it's different for men?"

"Everything else is."

She grimaced. "I'm beginning to develop a fair dose of pity for Penelope."

"Oh, absolutely you should," he agreed. "I'll make a dreadful husband, to be sure."

"You will not," she said, batting his arm. "Why on earth would you say that? You would never be unfaithful to her."

"No," he agreed. He was quiet for a moment, and when he finally spoke again, his voice was soft. "But I might not love her the way she deserves."

"But you *might*." She threw up her hands in a gesture of exasperation. "For heaven's sake, Colin, just the fact that you're sitting here asking your *sister* about love probably means you're more than halfway there."

"Do you think?"

"If I didn't *think* so," she said, "I wouldn't have *said* so." She sighed.

"Stop thinking so hard, Colin. You'll find marriage a lot easier if you simply allow it to be."

He eyed her suspiciously. "When did you grow so philosophical?"

"When you came by to see me and forced the issue," she said promptly. "You're marrying the right person. Stop worrying so much."

"I'm not worrying," he said automatically, but of course he *was* worrying, so he didn't even bother to defend himself when Daphne shot him an extremely sarcastic look. But it wasn't as if he were worrying whether Penelope was the right woman. He was certain of that.

And he wasn't worried about whether his marriage would be a good one. He was certain of that, as well.

No, he was worrying about stupid things. About whether or not he loved her, not because it would be the end of the world if he did (or the end of the world if he didn't), but because he found it extremely unsettling not to know exactly what it was he was feeling.

"Colin?"

He looked over at his sister, who was regarding him with a rather bemused expression. He stood, intending to leave before he embarrassed himself beyond repair, then leaned down and kissed her cheek. "Thank you," he said.

She narrowed her eyes. "I can't tell if you're serious or are teasing me for being an utter lack of help."

"You *were* an utter lack of help," he said, "but it's an honest thank-you, nonetheless."

"Points for effort?"

"Something like that."

"Are you going over to Bridgerton House now?" she asked.

"Why, so I may embarrass myself with Anthony next?"

"Or Benedict," she said. "He's there, too."

The thing about large families was, there was never a lack of opportunity to make a fool of oneself with a sibling. "No," he said with a small, wry smile, "I think I'll walk home."

"Walk?" she echoed, gaping.

He squinted toward the window. "Do you think it might rain?"

"Take my carriage, Colin," she insisted, "and please wait for the sandwiches. There is sure to be a mountain of them, and if you leave before they arrive, I know I'll eat half, and then I'll hate myself for the rest of the day."

He nodded and sat back down, and was glad he did. He'd always been partial to smoked salmon. In fact, he took a plate with him in the carriage, staring out the window the whole way home at the pouring rain.

When the Bridgertons threw a party, they did it right.

And when the Bridgertons threw an engagement ball . . . well, had Lady Whistledown still been writing, it would have taken at least three columns to chronicle the event.

Even this engagement ball, thrown together at the last minute (due to the fact that neither Lady Bridgerton nor Mrs. Featherington were willing to allow their children the possibility of changing their minds during a long engagement), easily qualified as *the* party of the season.

Although part of that, Penelope thought wryly, had little to do with the party itself and everything to do with the continued speculation over why on earth Colin Bridgerton would choose a nobody like Penelope Featherington to be his wife. It hadn't even been this bad when Anthony Bridgerton had married Kate Sheffield, who, like Penelope, had never been considered a diamond of the first water. But at least Kate hadn't been *old*. Penelope couldn't even begin to count the number of times she'd heard the word *spinster* whispered behind her back during the past few days.

But while the gossip was a bit tedious, it didn't really bother her, because she was still floating along on the cloud of her own bliss. A woman couldn't spend her entire adult life in love with one man and then not be almost stupid with happiness after he asked her to marry him.

Even if she couldn't quite figure out how it had all happened.

It *had* happened. That was all that mattered.

And Colin was everything anyone could dream of in a fiancé. He stuck to her side like glue the entire evening, and Penelope didn't even think he was doing it to protect her from gossip. In all truth, he seemed rather oblivious to the talk.

It was almost as if . . . Penelope smiled dreamily. It was almost as if Colin were remaining by her side because he wanted to be there.

"Did you see Cressida Twombley?" Eloise whispered in her ear while Colin was off dancing with his mother. "She's green with envy."

"That's just her dress," Penelope said with an impressively straight face.

Eloise laughed. "Oh, I wish Lady Whistledown were writing. She would *skewer* her."

"I think Lady Whistledown is supposed to *be* her," Penelope said carefully.

"Oh, pish and tosh. I don't believe for one moment that Cressida is Lady Whistledown, and I can't believe that you do, either."

"Probably not," Penelope allowed. She knew that her secret would be better protected if she claimed to believe Cressida's story, but anyone who knew her would have found that so out of character that it would have been quite suspicious indeed.

"Cressida just wanted the money," Eloise continued disdainfully. "Or maybe the notoriety. Probably both."

Penelope watched her nemesis, holding court on the other side of the room. Her regular crowd of cronies milled about, but they were joined by new people, as well, most likely curious about the

Whistledown gossip. "Well, she's succeeded with the notoriety, at least."

Eloise nodded her agreement. "I cannot even imagine why she was invited. There is certainly no love lost between the two of you, and none of us like her."

"Colin insisted upon it."

Eloise turned to her with gaping jaw. "Why?"

Penelope suspected that the main reason was Cressida's recent claim to be Lady Whistledown; most of the *ton* wasn't sure whether or not she was lying, but no one was willing to deny her an invitation to an event, just in case she really was telling the truth.

And Colin and Penelope shouldn't have had any reason to know for certain otherwise.

But Penelope couldn't reveal this to Eloise, so she told her the rest of the story, which was still the truth. "Your mother didn't want to cause any gossip by cutting her, and Colin also said . . ."

She blushed. It was really too sweet.

"What?" Eloise demanded.

Penelope couldn't speak without smiling. "He said he wanted Cressida to be forced to watch me in my triumph."

"Oh. My. Word." Eloise looked as if she might need to sit down. "My brother is in love."

Penelope's blush turned a furious red.

"*He is*," Eloise exclaimed. "He must be. Oh, you must tell me. Has he said so?"

There was something both wonderful and horrible in listening to Eloise gush. On the one hand, it was always lovely to share life's most perfect moments with one's best friend, and Eloise's joy and excitement were certainly contagious.

But on the other hand, they weren't necessarily warranted, because Colin didn't love her. Or at least he hadn't said so.

But he acted like he did! Penelope clung to that thought, trying to focus on that, rather than the fact that he'd never said the words.

Actions spoke louder than words, didn't they?

And his actions made her feel like a princess.

"Miss Featherington! Miss Featherington!"

Penelope looked to her left and beamed. That voice could belong to no one other than Lady Danbury.

"Miss Featherington," Lady D said, poking her cane through the crowd until she was standing right in front of Penelope and Eloise.

"Lady Danbury, how nice to see you."

"Heh heh heh." Lady Danbury's wrinkled face became almost young again from the force of her smile. "It's always nice to see me, regardless of what anyone else says. And *you*, you little devil. Look what you did."

"Isn't it the *best*?" Eloise asked.

Penelope looked to her closest friend. For all her mixed emotions, Eloise was truly, honestly, and forever would be thrilled for her. Suddenly it didn't matter that they were standing in the middle of a crowded ballroom, with everyone staring at her as if she were some sort of specimen on a biology plate. She turned and gave Eloise a fierce hug, whispering, "I do love you," in her ear.

"I know you do," Eloise whispered back.

Lady Danbury banged her cane—loudly—on the floor. "I'm still standing here, ladies!"

"Oh, sorry," Penelope said sheepishly.

"It's all right," Lady D said, with an uncharacteristic level of indulgence. "It's rather nice to see two girls who'd rather embrace than stab each other in the back, if you must know."

"Thank you for coming over to congratulate me," Penelope said.

"I wouldn't have missed this for the world," Lady Danbury said. "Heh heh heh. All these fools, trying to figure out what you did to get him to marry you, when all you really did was be yourself."

Penelope's lips parted, and tears pricked her eyes. "Why, Lady Danbury, that's just about the nicest—"

"No, no," Lady D interrupted loudly, "none of that. I haven't the time nor the inclination for sentiment."

But Penelope noticed that she'd pulled out her handkerchief and was discreetly dabbing her eyes.

"Ah, Lady Danbury," Colin said, returning to the group and sliding his arm possessively through Penelope's. "Good to see you."

"Mr. Bridgerton," she said in curt greeting. "Just came over to congratulate your bride."

"Ah, but I am surely the one who deserves the congratulations."

"Hmmmph. Truer words, and all that," Lady D said. "I think you might be right. She's more of a prize than anyone realizes."

"I realize," he said, his voice so low and deadly serious that Penelope thought she might faint from the thrill of it.

"And if you'll excuse us," Colin continued smoothly, "I must take my fiancée over to meet my brother—"

"I've met your brother," Penelope interrupted.

"Consider it tradition," he said. "We need to officially welcome you to the family."

"Oh." She felt rather warm inside at the thought of becoming a Bridgerton. "How lovely."

"As I was saying," Colin said, "Anthony would like to make a toast, and then I must lead Penelope in a waltz."

"Very romantic," Lady Danbury said approvingly.

"Yes, well, I am a romantic sort," Colin said airily.

Eloise let out a loud snort.

He turned to her with one arrogantly arched brow. "I am."

"For Penelope's sake," she retorted, "I certainly hope so."

"Are they always like this?" Lady Danbury asked Penelope.

"Most of the time."

Lady D nodded. "That's a good thing. My children rarely even speak to one another. Not out of any ill will, of course. They just have nothing in common. Sad, really."

Colin tightened his hand on Penelope's arm. "We really must be going."

"Of course," she murmured, but as she turned to walk toward Anthony, whom she could see across the room, standing near the small orchestra, she heard a loud and sudden commotion at the door.

"Attention! Attention!"

The blood drained from her face in under a second. "Oh, no," she heard herself whisper. This wasn't supposed to happen. Not tonight, anyway.

"Attention!"

Monday, her mind screamed. She'd told her printer Monday. At the Mottram ball.

"What is going on?" Lady Danbury demanded.

Ten young boys were racing into the room, nothing more than urchins, really, holding sheaves of paper, tossing them about like large rectangles of confetti.

"Lady Whistledown's final column!" they all yelled. "Read it now! Read the truth."

Chapter 17

Colin Bridgerton was famous for many things.

He was famous for his good looks, which was no surprise; all the Bridgerton men were famous for their good looks.

He was famous for his slightly crooked smile, which could melt a woman's heart across a crowded ballroom and had even once caused a young lady to faint dead away, or at least to swoon delicately, then hit her head on a table, which did produce the aforementioned dead faint.

He was famous for his mellow charm, his ability to set anyone at ease with a smooth grin and an amusing comment.

What he was *not* famous for, and in fact what many people would have sworn he did not even possess, was a temper.

And, in fact, due to his remarkable (and heretofore untapped) self-control, no one was going to get a glimpse of it that night, either, although his soon-to-be wife might wake up the next day with a *serious* bruise on her arm.

"Colin," she gasped, looking down at where he was gripping her.

But he couldn't let go. He knew he was hurting her, he knew it wasn't a terribly nice thing that he was hurting her, but he was so damned *furious* at that moment, and it was either squeeze her arm for all he was worth or lose his temper in front of five hundred of their nearest and dearest acquaintances.

All in all, he thought he was making the right choice.

He was going to kill her. As soon as he figured out some way to remove her from this godforsaken ballroom, he was absolutely going to kill her. They had agreed that Lady Whistledown was a thing of the past, that they were going to let matters lie. This was not supposed to happen. She was inviting disaster. Ruin.

"This is fabulous!" Eloise exclaimed, snatching a newssheet from the air. "Absolutely, positively smashing. I'll bet she came out of retirement to celebrate your engagement."

"Wouldn't that be nice?" Colin drawled.

Penelope said nothing, but she looked very, very pale.

"Oh, my heavens!"

Colin turned to his sister, whose mouth was hanging open as she read the column.

"Grab one of those for me, Bridgerton!" Lady Danbury ordered, swatting him in the leg with her cane. "Can't believe she's publishing on a Saturday. Must be a good one."

Colin leaned down and picked up two pieces of paper from the floor, handing one to Lady Danbury and looking down at the one in his hand, even though he was fairly certain he knew exactly what it would say.

He was right.

> *There is nothing I despise more than a gentleman who thinks it amusing to give a lady a condescending pat on the hand as he murmurs, "It is a woman's prerogative to change her mind." And indeed, because I feel one should always support one's words with one's actions, I endeavor to keep my opinions and decisions steadfast and true.*
>
> *Which is why, Gentle Reader, when I wrote my column of 19 April, I truly intended it to be my last. However, events entirely beyond my control (or indeed my approval) force me to put my pen to paper one last time.*

Ladies and Gentleman, This Author is NOT Lady Cressida Twombley. She is nothing more than a scheming imposter, and it would break my heart to see my years of hard work attributed to one such as her.

LADY WHISTLEDOWN'S SOCIETY PAPERS,
24 April 1824

"This is the best thing I have ever seen," Eloise said in a gleeful whisper. "Maybe I am a bad person at heart, because I have never before felt such happiness at another person's downfall."

"Balderdash!" Lady Danbury said. "I *know* I am not a bad person, and I find this delightful."

Colin said nothing. He didn't trust his voice. He didn't trust himself.

"Where is Cressida?" Eloise asked, craning her neck. "Does anyone see her? I'll bet she's already fled. She must be mortified. I would be mortified if I were her."

"You would never be her," Lady Danbury said. "You're much too decent a person."

Penelope said nothing.

"Still," Eloise continued jovially, "one almost feels sorry for her."

"But only almost," Lady D said.

"Oh, for certain. Barely almost, truth be told."

Colin just stood there, grinding his teeth into powder.

"And I get to keep my thousand pounds!" cackled Lady Danbury.

"Penelope!" Eloise exclaimed, jostling her with her elbow. "You haven't said a word. Isn't this marvelous?"

Penelope nodded and said, "I can't believe it."

Colin's grip on her arm tightened.

"Your brother's coming," she whispered.

He looked to his right. Anthony was striding toward him, Violet and Kate hot on his heels.

"Well, this rather upstages us," Anthony said as he drew up

alongside Colin. He nodded at the ladies present. "Eloise, Penelope, Lady Danbury."

"I don't think anyone is going to listen to Anthony's toast now," Violet said, glancing about the room. The buzz of activity was relentless. Errant newssheets still floated in the air, and all about them, people were slipping on the ones that had already landed on the floor. The hum of the whispers was constant and almost grating, and Colin felt like the top of his skull was going to blow off.

He had to get away. Now. Or at least as soon as possible.

His head was screaming and he felt too hot in his own skin. It was almost like passion, except this wasn't passion, it was fury, and it was outrage, and it was this awful, black feeling that he'd been betrayed by the one person who should have stood by him without question.

It was strange. He knew that Penelope was the one with the secret, the one with the most to lose. This was about her, not him; he knew that, intellectually, at least. But somehow that had ceased to matter. They were a team now, and she had acted without him.

She had no right to put herself in such a precarious position without consulting him first. He was her husband, or would be, and it was his God-given duty to protect her whether she desired it or not.

"Colin?" his mother was saying. "Are you well? You look a bit odd."

"Make the toast," he said, turning to Anthony. "Penelope isn't feeling well, and I need to take her home."

"You're not feeling well?" Eloise asked Penelope. "What's wrong? You didn't say anything."

To Penelope's credit, she managed a rather credible, "A bit of a headache, I'm afraid."

"Yes, yes, Anthony," Violet said, "do go ahead and make the toast now so that Colin and Penelope may have their dance. She really can't leave until you do."

Anthony nodded his agreement, then motioned for Colin and Penelope to follow him to the front of the ballroom. A trumpeter let out a loud squawk on his horn, signaling the partygoers to be quiet. They all obeyed, probably because they assumed the ensuing announcement would be about Lady Whistledown.

"Ladies and gentlemen," Anthony said loudly, accepting a flute of champagne from a footman. "I know that you are all intrigued by Lady Whistledown's recent intrusion into our party, but I must entreat you all to remember our purpose for gathering here tonight."

It should have been a perfect moment, Colin thought dispassionately. It was to have been Penelope's night of triumph, her night to shine, to show the world how beautiful and lovely and smart she really was.

It was his night to make his intentions well and truly public, to make sure that everyone knew that he had chosen her, and just as importantly, that she had chosen him.

And all he wanted to do was take her by the shoulders and shake her until he ran out of strength. She was jeopardizing everything. She was putting her very future at risk.

"As the head of the Bridgerton family," Anthony continued, "it gives me great joy whenever one of my siblings chooses a bride. Or groom," he added with a smile, nodding toward Daphne and Simon.

Colin looked down at Penelope. She was standing very straight and very still in her dress of ice-blue satin. She wasn't smiling, which must have looked odd to the hundreds of people staring at her. But maybe they would just think she was nervous. There were hundreds of people staring at her, after all. Anyone would be nervous.

Although if one was standing right next to her, as Colin was, one could see the panic in her eyes, the rapid rise and fall of her chest as her breathing grew faster and more erratic.

She was scared.

Good. She should be scared. Scared of what could happen to her if her secret came out. Scared of what *would* happen to her once they had a chance to talk.

"Therefore," Anthony concluded, "it gives me great pleasure to lift my glass in a toast to my brother Colin, and his soon-to-be bride, Penelope Featherington. To Colin and Penelope!"

Colin looked down at his hand and realized that someone had placed a glass of champagne in it. He lifted his glass, started to raise it to his lips, then thought the better of it and touched it to Penelope's mouth instead. The crowd cheered wildly, and he watched as she took a sip, and then another and another, forced to keep drinking until he removed the glass, which he did not do until she was finished.

Then he realized that his childish display of power had left him without a drink, which he badly needed, so he plucked Penelope's glass from her hand and downed it in a single gulp.

The crowd cheered even harder.

He leaned down and whispered in her ear, "We're going to dance now. We're going to dance until the rest of the party joins us and we're no longer the center of attention. And then you and I will slip outside. And then we will talk."

Her chin moved in a barely perceptible nod.

He took her hand and led her onto the dance floor, placing his other hand at her waist as the orchestra began the first strains of a waltz.

"Colin," she whispered, "I didn't mean for this to happen."

He affixed a smile on his face. This was supposed to be his first official dance with his intended, after all. "Not now," he ordered.

"But—"

"In ten minutes, I will have a great deal to say to you, but for right now, we are simply going to dance."

"I just wanted to say—"

His hand tightened around hers in a gesture of unmistakable warning. She pursed her lips and looked at his face for the briefest of moments, then looked away.

"I should be smiling," she whispered, still not looking at him.

"Then smile."

"*You* should be smiling."

"You're right," he said. "I should."

But he didn't.

Penelope felt like frowning. She felt like crying, in all honesty, but somehow she managed to nudge her lips up at the corners. The entire world was watching her—her entire world, at least—and she knew they were examining her every move, cataloguing each expression that crossed her face.

Years she'd spent, feeling like she was invisible and hating it. And now she'd have given anything for a few brief moments of anonymity again.

No, not anything. She wouldn't have given up Colin. If having him meant that she would spend the rest of her life under close scrutiny from the *ton*, it would be worth it. And if having to endure his anger and disdain at a time like this was to be a part of marriage as well, then that would be worth it, too.

She'd known that he would be furious with her for publishing one last column. Her hands had been shaking as she'd rewritten the words, and she'd been terrified the entire time she'd been at St. Bride's Church (as well as the ride to and from), sure that he was going to jump out at her at any moment, calling off the wedding because he couldn't bear to be married to Lady Whistledown.

But she'd done it anyway.

She knew he thought she was making a mistake, but she simply could not allow Cressida Twombley to take the credit for her life's work. But was it so much to ask that Colin at least make the attempt to see it all from her point of view? It would have been hard enough allowing anyone to pretend to be Lady Whistledown, but Cressida was unbearable. Penelope had worked too hard and endured too much at Cressida's hands.

Plus, she knew that Colin would never jilt her once their engagement became public. That was part of the reason she'd specifically instructed her publisher to have the papers delivered on *Monday* to the Mottram ball. Well, that and the fact that it seemed terribly wrong to do it at her own engagement ball, especially when Colin was so opposed to the idea.

Damn Mr. Lacey! He'd surely done this to maximize circulation and exposure. He knew enough about society from reading Whistle-down to know that a Bridgerton engagement ball would be the most coveted invitation of the season. Why this should matter, she didn't know, since increasing interest in *Whistledown* would not lead to more money in his pocket; *Whistledown* was well and truly through, and neither Penelope nor Mr. Lacey would receive another pound from its publication.

Unless . . .

Penelope frowned and sighed. Mr. Lacey must be hoping that she would change her mind.

Colin's hand tightened at her waist, and she looked back up. His eyes were on hers, startlingly green even in the candlelight. Or maybe it was just that she knew they were so green. She probably would have thought them emerald in the dark.

He nodded toward the other dancers on the floor, which was now crowded with revelers. "Time to make our escape," he said.

She returned his nod with one of her own. They had already told his family that she wasn't feeling well and wanted to go home, so no one would think overmuch of their departure. And if it wasn't quite *de rigeur* for them to be alone in his carriage, well, sometimes rules were stretched for affianced couples, especially on such romantic evenings.

A bubble of ridiculous, panicky laughter escaped her lips. The night was turning out to be the least romantic of her life.

Colin looked at her sharply, one arrogant brow raised in question.

"It's nothing," Penelope said.

He squeezed her hand, although not terribly affectionately. "I want to know," he said.

She shrugged fatalistically. She couldn't imagine what she could do or say to make the night any worse than it already was. "I was just thinking about how this evening was supposed to be romantic."

"It could have been," he said cruelly.

His hand slipped from its position at her waist, but he held on to her other hand, grasping her fingers lightly to weave her through the crowd until they stepped through the French doors out onto the terrace.

"Not here," Penelope whispered, glancing anxiously back toward the ballroom.

He didn't even dignify her comment with a reply, instead pulling her farther into the inky night, drifting around a corner until they were quite alone.

But they didn't stop there. With a quick glance to make sure that no one was about, Colin pushed open a small, unobtrusive side door.

"What's this?" Penelope asked.

His answer was a little shove at the small of her back, until she was fully inside the dark hallway.

"Up," he said, motioning to the steps.

Penelope didn't know whether to be scared or thrilled, but she climbed the stairs anyway, ever aware of Colin's hot presence, right at her back.

After they'd climbed several flights, Colin stepped ahead of her and pushed open a door, peeking out into the hall. It was empty, so he stepped out, pulling her along with him, dashing quietly through the hall (which Penelope now recognized as the family's private chambers) until they reached a room she had never before entered.

Colin's room. She'd always known where it was. Through all her years of coming here to visit with Eloise, she'd never once done more than trail her fingers along the heavy wood of the door. It had been years since he'd lived here at Number Five on a permanent basis, but his mother had insisted upon maintaining his room for him. One never knew when he might need it, she'd said, and she'd been proven right earlier that season when Colin had returned from Cyprus without a house under lease.

He pushed open the door and pulled her inside after him. But the room was dark, and she was stumbling, and when she stopped moving it was because his body was right there in front of hers.

He touched her arms to steady her, but then he didn't let go, just held her there in the dark. It wasn't an embrace, not really, but the length of her body was touching the length of his. She couldn't see anything, but she could feel him, and she could smell him, and she could hear his breathing, swirling through the night air, gently caressing her cheek.

It was agony.

It was ecstasy.

His hands slid slowly down her bare arms, torturing her every nerve, and then, abruptly, he stepped away.

Followed by—silence.

Penelope wasn't sure what she had expected. He would yell at her, he would berate her, he would order her to explain herself.

But he was doing none of those things. He was just standing there in the dark, forcing the issue, forcing her to say something.

"Could you . . . could you light a candle?" she finally asked.

"You don't like the dark?" he drawled.

"Not now. Not like this."

"I see," he murmured. "So you're saying you might like it like this?" His fingers were suddenly on her skin, trailing along the edge of her bodice.

And then they were gone.

"Don't," she said, her voice shaking.

"Don't touch you?" His voice grew mocking, and Penelope was glad that she couldn't see his face. "But you're mine, aren't you?"

"Not yet," she warned him.

"Oh, but you are. You saw to that. It was rather clever timing, actually, waiting until our engagement ball to make your final announcement. You knew I didn't want you to publish that last column. I forbade it! We agreed—"

"We never agreed!"

He ignored her outburst. "You waited until—"

"We never agreed," Penelope cried out again, needing to make it clear that she had not broken her word. Whatever else she had done, she had not lied to him. Well, aside from keeping *Whistledown* a secret for nearly a dozen years, but he certainly hadn't been alone in that deception. "And yes," she admitted, because it didn't seem right to start lying now, "I knew you wouldn't jilt me. But I hoped—"

Her voice broke, and she was unable to finish.

"You hoped what?" Colin asked after an interminable silence.

"I hoped that you would forgive me," she whispered. "Or at least that you would understand. I always thought you were the sort of man who . . ."

"What sort of man?" he asked, this time after the barest hint of a pause.

"It's my fault, really," she said, sounding tired and sad. "I've put you on a pedestal. You've been so nice all these years. I suppose I thought you were incapable of anything else."

"What the hell have I done that hasn't been nice?" he demanded. "I've protected you, I've offered for you, I've—"

"You haven't tried to see this from my point of view," she interrupted.

"Because you're acting like an idiot!" he nearly roared.

There was silence after that, the kind of silence that grates at ears, gnaws at souls.

"I can't imagine what else there is to say," Penelope finally said.

Colin looked away. He didn't know why he did so; it wasn't as if he could see her in the dark, anyway. But there was something about the tone of her voice that made him uneasy. She sounded vulnerable, tired. Wishful and heartbroken. She made him want to understand her, or at least to try, even though he *knew* she had made a terrible mistake. Every little catch in her voice put a damper on his fury. He was still angry, but somehow he'd lost the will to display it.

"You are going to be found out, you know," he said, his voice low and controlled. "You have humiliated Cressida; she will be beyond furious, and she's not going to rest until she unearths the real Lady Whistledown."

Penelope moved away; he could hear her skirts rustling. "Cressida isn't bright enough to figure me out, and besides, I'm not going to write any more columns, so there will be no opportunity for me to slip up and reveal something." There was a beat of silence, and then she added, "You have my promise on that."

"It's too late," he said.

"It's not too late," she protested. "No one knows! No one knows but you, and you're so ashamed of me, I can't bear it."

"Oh, for the love of God, Penelope," he snapped, "I'm not ashamed of you."

"Would you *please* light a candle?" she wailed.

Colin crossed the room and fumbled in a drawer for a candle and the means with which to light it. "I'm not ashamed of you," he reiterated, "but I do think you're acting foolishly."

"You may be correct," she said, "but I have to do what I think is right."

"You're not thinking," he said dismissively, turning and looking at her face as he sparked a flame. "Forget, if you will—although I cannot—what will happen to your reputation if people find out who you really are. Forget that people will cut you, that they will talk about you behind your back."

"Those people aren't worth worrying about," she said, her back ramrod straight.

"Perhaps not," he agreed, crossing his arms and staring at her. Hard. "But it will hurt. You will not like it, Penelope. And *I* won't like it."

She swallowed convulsively. Good. Maybe he was getting through to her.

"But forget all of that," he continued. "You have spent the last decade insulting people. Offending them."

"I have said lots of very nice things as well," she protested, her dark eyes glistening with unshed tears.

"Of course you have, but those aren't the people you are going to have to worry about. I'm talking about the angry ones, the insulted ones." He strode forward and grabbed her by her upper arms. "Penelope," he said urgently, "there will be people who want to *hurt* you."

His words had been meant for her, but they turned around and pierced his own heart.

He tried to picture a life without Penelope. It was impossible.

Just weeks ago she'd been . . . He stopped, thought. What *had* she been? A friend? An acquaintance? Someone he saw and never really noticed?

And now she was his fiancée, soon to be his bride. And maybe . . . maybe she was something more than that. Something deeper. Something even more precious.

"What I want to know," he asked, deliberately forcing the conversation back on topic so his mind wouldn't wander down such dangerous roads, "is why you're not jumping on the perfect alibi if the point is to remain anonymous."

"Because remaining anonymous isn't the point!" she fairly yelled.

"You want to be found out?" he asked, gaping at her in the candlelight.

"No, of course not," she replied. "But this is my work. This is my life's work. This is all I have to show for my life, and if I can't take the credit for it, I'll be *damned* if someone else will."

Colin opened his mouth to offer a retort, but to his surprise, he had nothing to say. *Life's work.* Penelope had a life's work.

He did not.

She might not be able to put her name on her work, but when she was alone in her room, she could look at her back issues, and point to them, and say to herself, *This is it. This is what my life has been about.*

"Colin?" she whispered, clearly startled by his silence.

She was amazing. He didn't know how he hadn't realized it before, when he'd already known that she was smart and lovely and witty and resourceful. But all those adjectives, and a whole host more he hadn't yet thought of, did not add up to the true measure of her.

She was amazing.

And he was . . . Dear God above, he was jealous of her.

"I'll go," she said softly, turning and walking toward the door.

For a moment he didn't react. His mind was still frozen, reeling with revelations. But when he saw her hand on the doorknob, he knew he could not let her go. Not this night, not ever.

"No," he said hoarsely, closing the distance between them in three long strides. "No," he said again, "I want you to stay."

She looked up at him, her eyes two pools of confusion. "But you said—"

He cupped her face tenderly with his hands. "Forget what I said."

And that was when he realized that Daphne had been right. His love hadn't been a thunderbolt from the sky. It had started with a smile, a word, a teasing glance. Every second he had spent in her presence it had grown, until he'd reached this moment, and he suddenly *knew.*

He loved her.

He was still furious with her for publishing that last column, and he was bloody ashamed of himself that he was actually jealous of her for having found a life's work and purpose, but even with all that, he loved her.

And if he let her walk out the door right now, he would never forgive himself.

Maybe this, then, was the definition of love. When you wanted someone, needed her, adored her still, even when you were utterly furious and quite ready to tie her to the bed just to keep her from going out and making more trouble.

This was the night. This was the moment. He was brimming with emotion, and he had to tell her. He had to *show* her.

"Stay," he whispered, and he pulled her to him, roughly, hungrily, without apology or explanation.

"Stay," he said again, leading her to his bed.

And when she didn't say anything, he said it for a third time.

"Stay."

She nodded.

He took her into his arms.

This was Penelope, and this was love.

Chapter 18

The moment Penelope nodded—the moment before she nodded, really—she knew that she had agreed to more than a kiss. She wasn't sure what had made Colin change his mind, why he had been so angry one minute and then so loving and tender the next.

She wasn't sure, but the truth was—she didn't care.

One thing she knew—he wasn't doing this, kissing her so sweetly, to punish her. Some men might use desire as a weapon, temptation as revenge, but Colin wasn't one of them.

It just wasn't in him.

He was, for all his rakish and mischievous ways, for all his jokes and teasing and sly humor, a good and noble man. And he would be a good and noble husband.

She knew this as well as she knew herself.

And if he was kissing her passionately, lowering her to his bed, covering her body with his own, then it was because he wanted her, cared enough to overcome his anger.

Cared for her.

Penelope kissed him back with every ounce of her emotion, every last corner of her soul. She had years and years of love for this man, and what she lacked in technique, she made up in fervor. She clutched at his hair, writhed beneath him, unmindful of her own appearance.

They weren't in a carriage or his mother's drawing room this time. There was no fear of discovery, no need to make sure that she looked presentable in ten minutes.

This was the night she could show him everything she felt for him. She would answer his desire with her own, and silently make her vows of love and fidelity and devotion.

When the night was through, he would know that she loved him. She might not say the words—she might not even whisper them—but he would know.

Or maybe he already knew. It was funny; it had been so easy to hide her secret life as Lady Whistledown, but so unbelievably hard to keep her heart from her eyes every time she looked at him.

"When did I start needing you so much?" he whispered, raising his head very slightly from hers until the tips of their noses touched and she could see his eyes, dark and colorless in the dim candlelight, but so very green in her mind, focusing on hers. His breath was hot, and his gaze was hot, and he was making her feel hot in areas of her body she never even allowed herself to think about.

His fingers moved to the back of her gown, moving expertly along the buttons until she felt the fabric loosening, first around her breasts, then around her ribs, then around her waist.

And then it wasn't even there at all.

"My God," he said, his voice a mere shadow louder than breath, "you're so beautiful."

And for the first time in her life, Penelope truly believed that it might be true.

There was something very wicked and titillating about being so intimately bared before another human being, but she didn't feel shame. Colin was looking at her so warmly, touching her so reverently, that she could feel nothing but an overwhelming sense of destiny.

His fingers skimmed along the sensitive skin at the outside edge of her breast, first teasing her with his fingernails, then stroking her more gently as his fingertips returned to their original position near her collarbone.

Something tightened within her. She didn't know if it was his touch or the way he was looking at her, but something was making her change.

She felt strange, odd.

Wonderful.

He was kneeling on the bed beside her, still fully clothed, gazing down at her with a sense of pride, of desire, of ownership. "I never dreamed you would look like this," he whispered, moving his hand until his palm was lightly grazing her nipple. "I never dreamed I would want you this way."

Penelope sucked in her breath as a spasm of sensation shot through her. But something in his words was unsettling, and he must have seen her reaction in her eyes, because he asked, "What is it? What is wrong?"

"Nothing," she started to say, then checked herself. Their marriage ought to be based on honesty, and she did neither of them a service by withholding her true feelings.

"What did you think I would look like?" she asked quietly.

He just stared at her, clearly confused by her question.

"You said you never dreamed I would look this way," she explained. "What did you think I would look like?"

"I don't know," he admitted. "Until the last few weeks, honestly I don't think I thought about it."

"And since then?" she persisted, not quite sure why she needed him to answer, just knowing that she did.

In one swift moment he straddled her, then leaned down until the fabric of his waistcoat scraped her belly and breasts, until his nose touched hers and his hot breath swarmed across her skin.

"Since then," he growled, "I've thought of this moment a thousand times, pictured a hundred different pairs of breasts, all lovely and desirable and full and begging for my attention, but nothing, and let me repeat this in case you didn't quite hear me the first time, *nothing* comes close to reality."

"Oh." It was really all she could think to say.

He shrugged off his jacket and waistcoat until he was clad only in his fine linen shirt and breeches, then did nothing but stare at her, a wicked, wicked smile lifting one corner of his lips as she squirmed beneath him, growing hot and hungry under his relentless gaze.

And then, just when she was certain that she couldn't take it for one more second, he reached out and covered her with both his hands, squeezing lightly as he tested the weight and shape of her. He moaned raggedly, then sucked in his breath as he adjusted his fingers so that her nipples popped up between them.

"I want to see you sitting up," he groaned, "so I can see them full and lovely and large. And then I want to crawl behind you and cup you." His lips found her ear and his voice dropped to a whisper. "And I want to do it in front of a mirror."

"Now?" she squeaked.

He seemed to consider that for a moment, then shook his head. "Later," he said, and then repeated it in a rather resolute tone. "Later."

Penelope opened her mouth to ask him something—she had no idea what—but before she could utter a word, he murmured, "First things first," and lowered his mouth to her breast, teasing her first with a soft rush of air, then closing his lips around her, chuckling softly as she yelped in surprise and bucked off the bed.

He continued this torture until she thought she might scream, then he moved to the other breast and repeated it all over again. But this time he'd freed up one of his hands, and it seemed to be everywhere—teasing, tempting, tickling. It was on her belly, then on her hip, then on her ankle, sliding up under her skirt.

"Colin," Penelope gasped, squirming beneath him as his fingers stroked the delicate skin behind her knee.

"Are you trying to get away or come closer?" he murmured, his lips never once leaving her breast.

"I don't know."

He lifted his head and smiled down at her wolfishly. "Good."

He climbed off of her and slowly removed the remainder of his clothing, first his fine linen shirt and then his boots and breeches. And all the while, he never once allowed his eyes to stray from hers. When he was done, he nudged her dress, already pooling about her waist, around her hips, his fingers pressing lightly against her soft bottom as he lifted her up to slide the fabric under her.

She was left before him in nothing but her sheer, whisper-soft stockings. He paused then, and smiled, too much of a man not to enjoy the view, then eased them from her legs, letting them flitter to the floor after he'd slid them over her toes.

She was shivering in the night air, and so he lay beside her, pressing his body to hers, infusing her with his warmth as he savored the silky softness of her skin.

He needed her. It was humbling how much he needed her.

He was hard, hot, and so desperately wracked with desire it was a wonder he could still see straight. And yet even as his body screamed for release, he was possessed of a strange calm, an unexpected sense of control. Somewhere along the way this had ceased to be about him. It was about her—no, it was about *them*, about this wondrous joining and miraculous love that he was only now beginning to appreciate.

He wanted her—God above, he wanted her—but he wanted her to tremble beneath him, to scream with desire, to thrash her head from side to side as he teased her toward completion.

He wanted her to love this, to love him, and to *know*, when they were lying in each other's arms, sweaty and spent, that she belonged to him.

Because he already knew that he belonged to her.

"Tell me if I do anything you don't like," he said, surprised by the way his voice was shaking over his words.

"You couldn't," she whispered, touching his cheek.

She didn't understand. It almost made him smile, probably *would* have made him smile if he weren't so concerned with making this, her first experience, a good one. But her whispered words—*you couldn't*—could mean only one thing—that she had no idea what it meant to make love with a man.

"Penelope," he said softly, covering her hand with his own, "I need to explain something to you. I could hurt you. I would never mean to, but I could, and—"

She shook her head. "You couldn't," she said again. "I know you. Sometimes I think I know you better than I know myself. And you would never do anything that would hurt me."

He gritted his teeth and tried not to groan. "Not on purpose," he said, the barest hint of exasperation tinging his voice, "but I could, and—"

"Let me be the judge," she said, taking his hand and bringing it to her mouth for a single, heartfelt kiss. "And as for the other . . ."

"What other?"

She smiled, and Colin had to blink, because he could swear she almost looked as if she were amused by him. "You told me to tell you if you did anything I didn't like," she said.

He watched her face closely, suddenly mesmerized by the way her lips were forming words.

"I promise you," she vowed, "I will like it all."

A strange bubble of joy began to rise within him. He didn't know what benevolent god had chosen to bestow her upon him, but he was thinking that he needed to be a bit more attentive next time he went to church.

"I will like it all," she said again, "because I'm with you."

He took her face in his hands, gazing down at her as if she were the most wondrous creature ever to walk the earth.

"I love you," she whispered. "I've loved you for years."

"I know," he said, surprising himself with his words. He had known, he supposed, but he'd thrust it from his mind because her love made him uncomfortable. It was hard to be loved by someone decent and good when you didn't return the emotion. He couldn't dismiss her, because he liked her and he'd not have been able to forgive himself if he'd trampled on her emotions. And he couldn't flirt with her, for much the same reasons.

And so he had told himself that what she felt wasn't really love. It had been easier to try to convince himself that she was merely infatuated with him, that she didn't understand what true love was (as if he did!), and that eventually she would find someone else and settle down into a happy and contented life.

Now that thought—that she might have married another—nearly left him paralyzed with fear.

They were side by side, and she was staring at him with her heart in her eyes, her entire face alive with happiness and contentment, as if she finally felt free now that she had spoken the words. And he realized that her expression held not one trace of expectation. She hadn't told him she loved him simply to hear his reply. She wasn't even waiting for his answer.

She had told him she loved him simply because she wanted to. Because that was what she felt.

"I love you, too," he whispered, pressing an intense kiss against her lips before moving away so that he could see her reaction.

Penelope gazed at him for a very long while before responding. Finally, with an odd, convulsive swallow, she said, "You don't have to say that just because I did."

"I know," he replied, smiling.

She just looked at him, her widening eyes the only movement on her face.

"And you know that, too," he said softly. "You said you know me better than you know yourself. And you know I would never say the words if I didn't mean them."

And as she lay there, naked in his bed, cradled in his embrace, Penelope realized that she *did* know. Colin didn't lie, not about anything important, and she couldn't imagine anything more important than the moment they were sharing.

He loved her. It wasn't anything she'd expected, nor anything she'd even allowed herself to hope for, and yet here it was, like a bright and shining miracle in her heart.

"Are you sure?" she whispered.

He nodded, his arms drawing her closer. "I realized it this evening. When I asked you to stay."

"How . . ." But she didn't finish the question. Because she wasn't even really sure what the question was. How did he know he loved her? How had it happened? How did it make him feel?

But somehow he must have known what she could not verbalize, because he answered, "I don't know. I don't know when, I don't know how, and to be honest, I don't care. But I know this much is true: I love you, and I hate myself for not seeing the real you all these years."

"Colin, don't," she pleaded. "No recriminations. No regrets. Not tonight."

But he just smiled, placing a single finger on her lips to silence her plea. "I don't think you changed," he said. "At least not very much. But then one day I realized I was seeing something different when I looked at you." He shrugged. "Maybe I changed. Maybe I grew up."

She placed her finger on his lips, quieting him in the same manner he'd done to her. "Maybe I grew up, too."

"I love you," he said, leaning forward to kiss her. And this time she couldn't reply, because his mouth remained on hers, hungry, demanding, and very, very seductive.

He seemed to know exactly what to do. Each flick of his tongue, each nibble of his teeth sent shivers to the very core of her being, and she gave herself over to the pure joy of the moment, to the white-hot flame of desire. His hands were everywhere, and she felt him everywhere, his fingers on her skin, his leg nudging its way between hers.

He was pulling her closer, rolling her on top of him as he slid onto his back. His hands were on her bottom, pulling her so tightly against him that the proof of his desire seared itself into her skin.

Penelope gasped at the astounding intimacy of it all, but her breath was caught by his lips, still kissing her with fierce tenderness.

And then she was on her back, and he was on top of her, and the weight of him was pressing her into the mattress, squeezing the air from her lungs. His mouth moved to her ear, then to her throat, and Penelope felt herself arching beneath him, as if she could somehow curve her body closer to his.

She didn't know what she was supposed to do, but she knew she had to move. Her mother had already conducted her "little talk," as she'd put it, and she'd told Penelope that she must lie still beneath her husband and allow him his pleasures.

But there was no way she could have remained motionless, no way she could have stopped her hips from pressing up against him, nor her legs from wrapping around his. And she didn't want to *allow* him his pleasures—she wanted to encourage them, to share them.

And she wanted them for herself as well. Whatever this was, building inside of her—this tension, this desire—it needed release, and Penelope couldn't imagine that that moment, that those feelings wouldn't be the most exquisite of her life.

"Tell me what to do," she said, urgency making her voice hoarse.

Colin spread her legs wide, running his hands along her sides until they reached her thighs and squeezed. "Let me do everything," he said, breathing hard.

She grabbed at his buttocks, pulling him closer. "No," she insisted. "Tell me."

He stopped moving for the barest of moments, looking at her in surprise. "Touch me," he said.

"Where?"

"Anywhere."

Her hands on his bottom relaxed slightly, and she smiled. "I *am* touching you."

"Move," he groaned. "Move them."

She let her fingers drift to his thighs, swirling gently as she felt the soft springiness of hair. "Like this?"

He nodded jerkily.

Her hands slid forward, until they were dangerously close to his member. "Like this?"

Abruptly, he covered one of her hands with his. "Not now," he said harshly.

She looked at him in confusion.

"You'll understand later," he grunted, spreading her legs even wider before sliding his hand between their bodies and touching her most intimate place.

"Colin!" she gasped.

He smiled devilishly. "Did you think I wouldn't touch you like this?" As if to illustrate his point, one of his fingers began to dance across her sensitive flesh, causing her to arch off the bed, her hips actually lifting them both before sagging back down as she shuddered with desire.

His lips found her ear. "There's much more," he whispered.

Penelope didn't dare ask what. This was already an awful lot more than her mother had mentioned.

He slid one finger inside her, causing her to gasp again (which caused him to laugh with delight), then began to stroke her slowly.

"Oh, my *God*," Penelope moaned.

"You're almost ready for me," he said, his breath coming faster now. "So wet, but so tight."

"Colin, what are you—"

He slid another finger inside, effectively ending any chance she had for intelligent speech.

She felt stretched wide, and yet she loved it. She must be very wicked, a wanton at heart, because all she wanted was to spread her legs wider and wider until she was completely open to him. As far as she was concerned, he could do anything to her, touch her in any way he pleased.

Just as long as he didn't stop.

"I can't wait much longer," he gasped.

"Don't wait."

"I need you."

She reached up and grasped his face, forcing him to look at her. "I need you, too."

And then his fingers were gone. Penelope felt oddly hollow and empty, but only for a second, because then there was something else at her entrance, something hard and hot, and very, very demanding.

"This may hurt," Colin said, gritting his teeth as if he expected pain himself.

"I don't care."

He had to make this good for her. He had to. "I'll be gentle," he said, although his desire was now so fierce he had no idea how he could possibly keep such a promise.

"I want you," she said. "I want you and I need something and I don't know what."

He pushed forward, just an inch or so, but it felt like she was swallowing him whole.

She went silent beneath him, her only sound her breath running raggedly across her lips.

Another inch, another step closer to heaven. "Oh, Penelope," he moaned, using his arms to hold himself above her so as not to crush her with his weight. "Please tell me this feels good. *Please.*"

Because if she said otherwise, it was going to kill him to pull out.

She nodded, but said, "I need a moment."

He swallowed, forcing his breath through his nose in short bursts. It was the only way he could concentrate on holding back. She probably needed to stretch around him, to allow her muscles to relax. She'd never taken a man before, and she was so exquisitely tight.

All the same, he couldn't wait until they'd had a chance to do this enough so that he didn't have to hold back.

When he felt her relax slightly beneath him, he pushed forward a bit more, until he reached the undeniable proof of her innocence. "Oh, God," he groaned. "This is going to hurt. I can't help it, but I promise you, it's only this one time, and it won't hurt much."

"How do you know?" she asked him.

He closed his eyes in agony. Trust Penelope to question him. "Trust me," he said, weaseling out of the question.

And then he thrust forward, embedding himself to the hilt, sinking into her warmth until he knew he was home.

"Oh!" she gasped, her face showing her shock.

"Are you all right?"

She nodded. "I think so."

He moved slightly. "Is this all right?"

She nodded again, but her face looked surprised, maybe a little dazed.

Colin's hips began to move of their own volition, unable to remain still when he was so obviously near to a climax. She was pure perfection around him, and when he realized that her gasps were of desire and not of pain, he finally let himself go and gave in to the overwhelming desire surging through his blood.

She was quickening beneath him, and he prayed that he could hold out until she climaxed. Her breath was fast and hot, and her fingers were pressing relentlessly into his shoulders, and her hips were squirming under him, whipping his need into a near-frenzy.

And then it came. A sound from her lips, sweeter than anything ever to touch his ears. She cried out his name as her entire body tensed in pleasure, and he thought—*Someday I will watch her. I will see her face when she reaches the height of pleasure.*

But not today. He was already coming, and his eyes were shut with the fierce ecstasy of it all. Her name was ripped from his lips as he thrust one last time, then slumped atop her, completely bereft of strength.

For a full minute there was silence, nothing but the rise and fall of their chests as they fought for breath, waited for the tremendous rush of their bodies to settle down into that tingly bliss one feels in the arms of one's beloved.

Or at least that was what Colin thought this must be. He had been with women before, but he had only just realized that he had never made love until he'd laid Penelope onto his bed and begun their intimate dance with a single kiss upon her lips.

This was like nothing he'd ever felt before.

This was love.

And he was going to hold on with both hands.

Chapter 19

It was not very difficult to get the wedding date pushed forward.

It occurred to Colin as he was returning to his home in Bloomsbury (after sneaking an extremely disheveled Penelope into her own house in Mayfair), that there might be a very good reason why they should be married sooner rather than later.

Of course, it was quite unlikely that she would become pregnant after only one encounter. And, he had to admit, even if she did become pregnant, the child would be an eight-month baby, which wasn't too terribly suspect in a world full of children born a mere six months or so following a wedding. Not to mention that first babies were usually late (Colin was uncle to enough nieces and nephews to know this to be true), which would make the baby an eight-and-a-half-month baby, which wasn't unusual at all.

So really, there was no urgent need to move up the wedding.

Except that he wanted to.

So he had a little "talk" with the mothers, in which he conveyed a great deal without actually saying anything explicit, and they hastily agreed to his plan to rush the wedding.

Especially since he *might* have *possibly* misled them to believe that his and Penelope's intimacies had occurred several weeks prior.

Ah, well, little white lies really weren't such a large transgression when they were told to serve the greater good.

And a hasty wedding, Colin reflected as he lay in bed each night, reliving his time with Penelope and fervently wishing she were there beside him, *definitely* served the greater good.

The mothers, who had become inseparable in recent days as they planned the wedding, initially protested the change, worrying about unsavory gossip (which in this case would have been entirely true), but Lady Whistledown came, somewhat indirectly, to their rescue.

The gossip surrounding Lady Whistledown and Cressida Twombley and whether the two were actually the same person raged like nothing London had heretofore seen or heard. In fact, the talk was so ubiquitous, so utterly impossible to escape, that no one paused to consider the fact that the date of the Bridgerton-Featherington wedding had been altered.

Which suited the Bridgertons and the Featheringtons just fine.

Except, perhaps, for Colin and Penelope, neither of whom were especially comfortable when talk turned to Lady Whistledown. Penelope was used to it by now, of course; nary a month had gone by in the past ten years when someone had not made idle speculation in her presence about the identity of Lady Whistledown. But Colin was still so upset and angry over her secret life that she'd grown uncomfortable herself. She'd tried to broach the subject with him a few times, but he'd become tight-lipped and told her (in a very un-Colin-like tone) that he didn't want to talk about it.

She could only deduce that he was ashamed of her. Or if not of her, precisely, then of her work as Lady Whistledown. Which was like a blow to her heart, because her writing was the one segment in her life that she could point to with a great sense of pride and accomplishment. She had *done* something. She had, even if she could not put her own name on her work, become a wild success. How many of her contemporaries, male or female, could claim the same?

She might be ready to leave Lady Whistledown behind and live her new life as Mrs. Colin Bridgerton, wife and mother, but that in no way meant that she was ashamed of what she had done.

If only Colin could take pride in her accomplishments as well.

Oh, she believed, with every fiber of her being, that he loved her. Colin would never lie about such a thing. He had enough clever words and teasing smiles to make a woman feel happy and content without actually uttering words of love he did not feel. But perhaps it was possible—indeed, after regarding Colin's behavior, she was now sure it was possible—that someone could love another person and still feel shame and displeasure with that person.

Penelope just hadn't expected it to hurt quite so much.

They were strolling through Mayfair one afternoon, just days before the wedding, when she attempted to broach the subject once again. Why, she didn't know, since she couldn't imagine that his attitude would have miraculously changed since the last time she'd mentioned it, but she couldn't seem to stop herself. Besides, she was hoping that their position out in public, where all the world could see them, would force Colin to keep a smile on his face and listen to what she had to say.

She gauged the distance to Number Five, where they were expected for tea. "I think," she said, estimating that she had five minutes of conversation before he could usher her inside and change the subject, "that we have unfinished business that must be discussed."

He raised a brow and looked at her with a curious but still very playful grin. She knew exactly what he was trying to do: use his charming and witty personality to steer the conversation where he wanted it. Any minute now, that grin would turn boyishly lopsided, and he would say something designed to change the topic without her realizing, something like—

"Rather serious for such a sunny day."

She pursed her lips. It wasn't precisely what she'd expected, but it certainly echoed the sentiment.

"Colin," she said, trying to remain patient, "I wish you wouldn't try to change the subject every time I bring up Lady Whistledown."

His voice grew even, controlled. "I don't believe I heard you mention her name, or I suppose I should say *your* name. And besides, all I did was compliment the fine weather."

Penelope wanted more than anything to plant her feet firmly on the pavement and yank him to a startling halt, but they were in public (her own fault, she supposed, for choosing such a place to initiate the conversation) and so she kept walking, her gait smooth and sedate, even as her fingers curled into tense little fists. "The other night, when my last column was published—you were furious with me," she continued.

He shrugged. "I'm over it."

"I don't think so."

He turned to her with a rather condescending expression. "And now you're telling me what I feel?"

Such a nasty shot could not go unreturned. "Isn't that what a wife is supposed to do?"

"You're not my wife yet."

Penelope counted to three—no, better make that ten—before replying. "I am sorry if what I did upset you, but I had no other choice."

"You had every choice in the world, but I am certainly not going to debate the issue right here on Bruton Street."

And they *were* on Bruton Street. Oh, *bother*, Penelope had completely misjudged how quickly they were walking. She only had another minute or so at the most before they ascended the front steps to Number Five.

"I can assure you," she said, "that you-know-who will never again emerge from retirement."

"I can hardly express my relief."

"I wish you wouldn't be so sarcastic."

He turned to face her with flashing eyes. His expression was so different from the mask of bland boredom that had been there just moments earlier that Penelope nearly backed up a step. "Be careful what you wish for, Penelope," he said. "The sarcasm is the only thing keeping my real feelings at bay, and believe me, you don't want *those* in full view."

"I think I do," she said, her voice quite small, because in truth she wasn't sure that she did.

"Not a day goes by when I'm not forced to stop and consider what on earth I am going to do to protect you should your secret get out. I love you, Penelope. God help me, but I do."

Penelope could have done without the plea for God's help, but the declaration of love was quite nice.

"In three days," he continued, "I will be your husband. I will take a solemn vow to protect you until death do us part. Do you understand what that means?"

"You'll save me from marauding minotaurs?" she tried to joke.

His expression told her he did not find that amusing.

"I wish you wouldn't be so angry," she muttered.

He turned to her with a disbelieving expression, as if he didn't think she had the right to mutter about anything. "If I'm angry, it's because I did not appreciate finding out about your last column at the same time as everyone else."

She nodded, catching her bottom lip between her teeth before saying, "I apologize for that. You certainly had the right to know ahead of time, but how could I have told you? You would have tried to stop me."

"Exactly."

They were now just a few houses away from Number Five. If Penelope wanted to ask him anything more, she would have to do it quickly. "Are you sure—" she began, then cut herself off, not certain if she wanted to finish the question.

"Am I sure of what?"

She gave her head a little shake. "It's nothing."

"It's obviously not nothing."

"I was just wondering . . ." She looked to the side, as if the sight of the London cityscape could somehow give her the necessary courage to continue. "I was just wondering . . ."

"Spit it out, Penelope."

It was unlike him to be so curt, and his tone prodded her into action. "I was wondering," she said, "if perhaps your unease with my, er . . ."

"Secret life?" he supplied in a drawl.

"If that is what you want to call it," she acceded. "It had occurred to me that perhaps your unease does not stem entirely from your desire to protect my reputation should I be found out."

"What, precisely," he asked in a clipped tone, "do you mean by that?"

She'd already voiced her question; there was nothing to do now but supply complete honesty. "I think you're ashamed of me."

He stared at her for three full seconds before answering, "I'm not ashamed of you. I told you once already I wasn't."

"What, then?"

Colin's steps faltered, and before he realized what his body was doing, he was standing still in front of Number Three, Bruton Street. His mother's home was only two houses away, and he was fairly certain they were expected for tea about five minutes ago, and . . .

And he couldn't quite get his feet to move.

"I'm not ashamed of you," he said again, mostly because he couldn't bring himself to tell her the truth—that he was jealous. Jealous of her achievements, jealous of her.

It was such a distasteful feeling, such an unpleasant emotion. It ate at him, creating a vague sense of shame every time someone mentioned Lady Whistledown, which, given the tenor of London's current gossip, was about ten times each day. And he wasn't quite certain what to do about it.

His sister Daphne had once commented that he always seemed to know what to say, how to set others at ease. He'd thought about that for several days after she'd said it, and he'd come to the conclusion that his ability to make others feel good about themselves must stem from his own sense of self.

He was a man who had always felt supremely comfortable in his own skin. He didn't know why he was so blessed—perhaps it was good parents, maybe simple luck. But now he felt awkward and uncomfortable and it was spilling into every corner of his life. He snapped at Penelope, he barely spoke at parties.

And it was all due to this detestable jealousy, and its attendant shame.

Or was it?

Would he be jealous of Penelope if he hadn't already sensed a lack in his own life?

It was an interesting psychological question. Or at least it would be if it were about anyone else but him.

"My mother will be expecting us," he said curtly, knowing that he was avoiding the issue, and hating himself for it, but quite unable to do anything else. "And your mother will be there as well, so we had better not be late."

"We're already late," she pointed out.

He took her arm and tugged her toward Number Five. "All the more reason not to dally."

"You're avoiding me," she said.

"How can I be avoiding you if you're right here on my arm?"

That made her scowl. "You're avoiding my question."

"We will discuss it later," he said, "when we are not standing in the middle of Bruton Street, with heaven knows whom staring at us through their windows."

And then, to demonstrate that he would brook no further protest, he placed his hand at her back and steered her none-too-gently up the steps to Number Five.

One week later, nothing had changed, except, Penelope reflected, her last name.

The wedding had been magical. It was a small affair, much to the dismay of London society. And the wedding night—well, that had been magical, too.

And, in fact, marriage was magical. Colin was a wonderful husband—teasing, gentle, attentive . . .

Except when the topic of Lady Whistledown arose.

Then he became . . . well, Penelope wasn't sure what he became, except that he was not himself. Gone was his easy grace, his glib tongue, everything wonderful that made him the man she'd loved for so very long.

In a way, it was almost funny. For so long, all of her dreams had revolved around marrying this man. And at some point those dreams had come to include her telling him about her secret life. How could they not? In Penelope's dreams, her marriage to Colin had been a perfect union, and that meant complete honesty.

In her dreams, she sat him down, shyly revealed her secret. He reacted first with disbelief, then with delight and pride. How remarkable she was, to have fooled all of London for so many years. How witty to have written such clever turns of phrase. He admired her for her resourcefulness, praised her for her success. In some of the dreams, he even suggested that he become her secret reporter.

It had seemed the sort of thing Colin would enjoy, just the sort of amusing, devious task that he would relish.

But that wasn't the way it had turned out.

He said he wasn't ashamed of her, and maybe he even thought that was true, but she couldn't quite bring herself to believe him. She'd seen his face when he swore that all he wanted was to protect her. But protectiveness was a fierce, burning feeling, and when Colin was talking about Lady Whistledown, his eyes were shuttered and flat.

She tried not to feel so disappointed. She tried to tell herself that she had no right to expect Colin to live up to her dreams, that her vision of him had been unfairly idealized, but . . .

But she still wanted him to be the man she'd dreamed of.

And she felt so guilty for every pang of disappointment. This was Colin! Colin, for heaven's sake. Colin, who was as close to perfect as any human being could ever hope to be. She had no right to find fault with him, and yet . . .

And yet she did.

She wanted him to be proud of her. She wanted it more than anything in the world, more even than she'd wanted *him* all those years when she'd watched him from afar.

But she cherished her marriage, and awkward moments aside, she cherished her husband. And so she stopped mentioning Lady Whistledown. She was tired of Colin's hooded expression. She didn't want to see the tight lines of displeasure around his mouth.

It wasn't as if she could avoid the topic forever; any trip out into society seemed to bring mention of her alter ego. But she didn't have to introduce the subject at home.

And so, as they sat at breakfast one morning, chatting amiably as they each perused that morning's newspaper, she searched for other topics.

"Do you think we shall take a honeymoon trip?" she asked, spreading a generous portion of raspberry jam on her muffin. She probably ought not to eat so much, but the jam was really quite tasty, and besides, she always ate a lot when she was anxious.

She frowned, first at the muffin and then at nothing in particular. She hadn't realized she was so anxious. She'd thought she'd been able to push the Lady Whistledown problem to the back of her mind.

"Perhaps later in the year," Colin replied, reaching for the jam once she was through with it. "Pass me the toast, would you?"

She did so, silently.

He glanced up, either at her or over at the plate of kippers—she couldn't be sure. "You look disappointed," he said.

She supposed she should be flattered that he'd looked up from his food. Or maybe he was looking at the kippers and she just got in the way. Probably the latter. It was difficult to compete with food for Colin's attention.

"Penelope?" he queried.

She blinked.

"You looked disappointed?" he reminded her.

"Oh. Yes, well, I am, I suppose." She gave him a faltering smile. "I've never been anywhere, and you've been everywhere, and I guess I thought you could take me someplace you especially liked. Greece, perhaps. Or maybe Italy. I've always wanted to see Italy."

"You would like it," he murmured distractedly, his attention more on his eggs than on her. "Venice especially, I think."

"Then why don't you take me?"

"I will," he said, spearing a pink piece of bacon and popping it into his mouth. "Just not now."

Penelope licked a bit of jam off her muffin and tried not to look too crestfallen.

"If you must know," Colin said with a sigh, "the reason I don't want to leave is . . ." He glanced at the open door, his lips pursing with annoyance. "Well, I can't say it here."

Penelope's eyes widened. "You mean . . ." She traced a large *W* on the tablecloth.

"Exactly."

She stared at him in surprise, a bit startled that he had brought up the subject, and even more so that he didn't seem terribly upset by it. "But why?" she finally asked.

"Should the secret come out," he said cryptically, just in case there were any servants about, which there usually were, "I should like to be in town to control the damage."

Penelope deflated in her chair. It was never pleasant to be referred to as damage. Which was what he had done. Well, indirectly, at least. She stared at her muffin, trying to decide if she was hungry. She wasn't, not really.

But she ate it, anyway.

Chapter 20

A few days later, Penelope returned from a shopping expedition with Eloise, Hyacinth, and Felicity to find her husband seated behind his desk in his study. He was reading something, uncharacteristically hunched as he pored over some unknown book or document.

"Colin?"

His head jerked up. He must not have heard her coming, which was surprising, since she hadn't made any effort to soften her steps. "Penelope," he said, rising to his feet as she entered the room, "how was your, er, whatever it was you did when you went out?"

"Shopping," she said with an amused smile. "I went shopping."

"Right. So you did." He rocked slightly from foot to foot. "Did you buy anything?"

"A bonnet," she replied, tempted to add *and three diamond rings*, just to see if he was listening.

"Good, good," he murmured, obviously eager to get back to whatever it was on his desk.

"What are you reading?" she asked.

"Nothing," he replied, almost reflexively, then he added, "Well, actually it's one of my journals."

His face took on a strange expression, a little sheepish, a little defiant, almost as if he were embarrassed that he'd been caught, and at the same time daring her to ask more.

"May I look at it?" she asked, keeping her voice soft and, she hoped, unthreatening. It was strange to think that Colin was insecure about anything. Mention of his journals, however, seemed to bring out a vulnerability that was surprising . . . and touching.

Penelope had spent so much of her life regarding Colin as an invincible tower of happiness and good cheer. He was self-confident, handsome, well liked, and intelligent. How easy it must be to be a Bridgerton, she'd thought on more than one occasion.

There had been so many times—more than she could count—that she'd come home from tea with Eloise and her family, curled up on her bed, and wished that she'd been born a Bridgerton. Life was easy for them. They were smart and attractive and rich and everyone seemed to like them.

And you couldn't even hate them for living such splendid existences because they were so *nice*.

Well, now she was a Bridgerton, by marriage if not by birth, and it was true—life *was* better as a Bridgerton, although that had less to do with any great change in herself than it did because she was madly in love with her husband, and by some fabulous miracle, he actually returned the emotion.

But life wasn't perfect, not even for the Bridgertons.

Even Colin—the golden boy, the man with the easy smile and devilish humor—had raw spots of his own. He was haunted by unfulfilled dreams and secret insecurities. How unfair she had been when she'd pondered his life, not to allow him his weaknesses.

"I don't need to see it in its entirety," she reassured him. "Maybe just a short passage or two. Of your own choosing. Perhaps something you especially like."

He looked down at the open book, staring blankly, as if the words were written in Chinese. "I wouldn't know what to pick out," he mumbled. "It's all the same, really."

"Of course it's not. I understand that more than anyone. I—" She suddenly looked about, realized the door was open, and quickly went to shut it. "I've written countless columns," she continued, "and I assure you, they are not all the same. Some I adored." She smiled nostalgically, remembering the rush of contentment and pride that washed over her whenever she'd written what she thought was an especially good installment. "It was lovely, do you know what I mean?"

He shook his head.

"That feeling you get," she tried to explain, "when you just *know* that the words you've chosen are exactly right. And you can only really appreciate it after you've sat there, slumped and dejected, staring at your blank sheet of paper, not having a clue what to say."

"I know *that*," he said.

Penelope tried not to smile. "I know you know the first feeling. You're a splendid writer, Colin. I've read your work."

He looked up, alarmed.

"Just the bit you know about," she assured him. "I would never read your journals without your invitation." She blushed, remembering that that was exactly how she'd read the passage about his trip to Cyprus. "Well, not now, anyway," she added. "But it was *good*, Colin. Almost magical, and somewhere inside of you, you have to know that."

He just stared at her, looking like he simply didn't know what to say. It was an expression she'd seen on countless faces, but never on *his* face, and it was so very odd and strange. She wanted to cry, she wanted to throw her arms around him. Most of all, she was gripped by an intense need to restore a smile to his face.

"I know you must have had those days I described," she insisted. "The ones when you know you've written something good." She looked at him hopefully. "You know what I mean, don't you?"

He made no response.

"You do," she said. "I know you do. You can't be a writer and not know it."

"I'm not a writer," he said.

"Of course you are." She motioned to the journal. "The proof is right there." She stepped forward. "Colin, please. Please may I read a little bit more?"

For the first time, he looked undecided, which Penelope took as a small victory. "You've already read almost everything *I've* ever written," she cajoled. "It's really only fair to—"

She stopped when she saw his face. She didn't know how to describe it, but he looked shuttered, cut off, utterly unreachable.

"Colin?" she whispered.

"I'd rather keep this to myself," he said curtly. "If you don't mind."

"No, of course I don't mind," she said, but they both knew she was lying.

Colin stood so still and silent that she had no choice but to excuse herself, leaving him alone in the room, staring helplessly at the door.

He'd hurt her.

It didn't matter that he hadn't meant to. She'd reached out to him, and he'd been unable to take her hand.

And the worst part was that he knew she didn't understand. She thought he was ashamed of her. He'd told her that he wasn't, but since he'd not been able to bring himself to tell her the truth—that he was jealous—he couldn't imagine that she'd believed him.

Hell, he wouldn't have believed him, either. He'd clearly looked like he was lying, because in a way, he was lying. Or at least withholding a truth that made him uncomfortable.

But the minute she'd reminded him that he'd read everything she'd written, something had turned ugly and black inside of him.

He'd read everything she'd written because she'd *published* everything she'd written. Whereas his scribblings sat dull and lifeless in his journals, tucked away where no one would see them.

Did it matter what a man wrote if no one ever read it? Did words have meaning if they were never heard?

He had never considered publishing his journals until Penelope had suggested it several weeks earlier; now the thought consumed him day and night (when he wasn't consumed with Penelope, of course). But he was gripped by a powerful fear. What if no one wanted to publish his work? What if someone did publish it, but only because his was a rich and powerful family? Colin wanted, more than anything, to be his own man, to be known for his accomplishments, not for his name or position, or even his smile or charm.

And then there was the scariest prospect of all: What if his writing was published but no one liked it?

How could he face that? How would he exist as a failure?

Or was it worse to remain as he was now: a coward?

Later that evening, after Penelope had finally pulled herself out of her chair and drunk a restorative cup of tea and puttered aimlessly about the bedchamber and finally settled against her pillows with a book that she couldn't quite make herself read, Colin appeared.

He didn't say anything at first, just stood there and smiled at her, except it wasn't one of his usual smiles—the sort that light from within and compel their recipient to smile right back.

This was a small smile, a sheepish smile.

A smile of apology.

Penelope let her book rest, spine up, on her belly.

"May I?" Colin inquired, motioning to the empty spot beside her.

Penelope scooted over to the right. "Of course," she murmured, moving her book to the night table next to her.

"I've marked a few passages," he said, holding forward his journal as he perched on the side of the bed. "If you'd like to read them, to"—he cleared his throat—"offer an opinion, that would be—" He coughed again. "That would be acceptable."

Penelope looked at the journal in his hand, elegantly bound in crimson leather, then she looked up at him. His face was serious, and his eyes were somber, and although he was absolutely still—no twitching or fidgeting—she could tell he was nervous.

Nervous. Colin. It seemed the strangest thing imaginable.

"I'd be honored," she said softly, gently tugging the book from his fingers. She noticed that a few pages were marked with ribbons, and with careful fingers, she opened to one of the selected spots.

14 March 1819
The Highlands are oddly brown.

"That was when I visited Francesca in Scotland," he interrupted.

Penelope gave him a slightly indulgent smile, meant as a gentle scolding for his interruption.

"Sorry," he mumbled.

> *One would think, at least one from England would think, that the hills and dales would be a rich emerald green. Scotland resides, after all, on the same isle, and by all accounts suffers from the same rain that plagues England.*
>
> *I am told that these strange beige hills are called tablelands, and they are bleak and brown and desolate.*
>
> *And yet they stir the soul.*

"That was when I was rather high up in elevation," he explained. "When you're lower, or near the lochs, it's quite different."

Penelope turned to him and gave him a look.

"Sorry," he mumbled.

"Maybe you'd be more comfortable if you didn't read over my shoulder?" she suggested.

He blinked in surprise.

"I would think you've already read all this before." At his blank stare, she added, "So you don't need to read it now." She waited for a reaction and got none. "So you don't need to hover over my shoulder," she finally finished.

"Oh." He inched away. "Sorry."

Penelope eyed him dubiously. "Off the bed, Colin."

Looking much chastened, Colin pushed himself off the bed and flopped into a chair in the far corner of the room, crossing his arms and tapping his foot in a mad dance of impatience.

Tap tap tap. Tappity tap tap tap.

"Colin!"

He looked up in honest surprise. "What?"

"Stop tapping your foot!"

He looked down as if his foot were a foreign object. "Was I tapping it?"

"Yes."

"Oh." He pulled his arms in more tightly against his chest. "Sorry."

Penelope refocused her attention on the journal.

Tap tap.

Penelope jerked head up. "Colin!"

He planted his feet down firmly on the carpet. "I couldn't help myself. Didn't even realize I was doing it." He uncrossed his arms, resting them on the upholstered side of the chair, but he didn't look relaxed; the fingers on both of his hands were tense and arched.

She stared at him for several moments, waiting to see if he was truly going to be able to hold still.

"I won't do it again," he assured her. "I promise."

She gave him one last assessing stare, then turned her attention back to the words in front of her.

As a people, the Scots despise the English, and many would say rightfully so. But individually, they are quite warm and friendly, eager to share a glass of whisky, a hot meal, or to offer a warm place to sleep. A group of Englishmen—or, in truth, any Englishman in any sort of uniform—will not find a warm welcome in a Scottish village. But should a lone Sassenach amble

down their High Street—*the local population will greet him
with open arms and broad smiles.*

*Such was the case when I happened upon Inveraray, upon the
banks of Loch Fyne. A neat, well-planned town that was designed by Robert Adam when the Duke of Argyll decided to
move the entire village to accommodate his new castle, it sits on
the edge of the water, its whitewashed buildings in neat rows that
meet at right angles (surely a strangely ordered existence for one
such as I, brought up amid the crooked intersections of London).*

*I was partaking of my evening meal at the George Hotel, en-
joying a fine whisky instead of the usual ale one might drink at
a similar establishment in England, when I realized that I had
no idea how to get to my next destination, nor any clue how
long it would take to get there. I approached the proprietor (one
Mr. Clark), explained my intention to visit Blair Castle, and
then could do nothing but blink in wonder and confusion as the
rest of the inn's occupants chimed in with advice.*

*"Blair Castle?" Mr. Clark boomed. (He was a booming sort
of man, not given to soft speech.) "Well, now, if ye're wanting
to go to Blair Castle, ye'll certainly be wanting to head west
toward Pitlochry and then north from there."*

*This was met by a chorus of approval—and an equally loud
echo of disapproval.*

*"Och, no!" yelled another (whose name I later learned was
MacBogel). "He'll be having to cross Loch Tay, and a greater
recipe for disaster has never been tasted. Better to head north
now, and then move west."*

*"Aye," chimed in a third, "but then he'll be having Ben Nevis
in his way. Are you saying a mountain is a lesser obstacle than
a puny loch?"*

*"Are you calling Loch Tay puny? I'll be telling you I was
born on the shores of Loch Tay, and no one will be calling it puny
in my presence." (I have no idea who said this, or indeed, almost*

everything forthwith, but it was all said with great feeling and conviction.)

"He doesn't need to go all the way to Ben Nevis. He can turn west at Glencoe."

"Oh, ho, ho, and a bottle of whisky. There isn't a decent road heading west from Glencoe. Are you trying to kill the poor lad?"

And so on and so forth. If the reader has noticed that I stopped writing who said what, it is because the din of voices was so overwhelming that it was impossible to tell anyone apart, and this continued for at least ten minutes until finally, old Angus Campbell, eighty years if he was a day, spoke, and out of respect, everyone quieted down.

"What he needs to do," Angus wheezed, "is travel south to Kintyre, turn back north and cross the Firth of Lorne to Mull so that he can scoot out to Iona, sail up to Skye, cross over to the mainland to Ullapool, back down to Inverness, pay his respects at Culloden, and from there, he can proceed south to Blair Castle, stopping in Grampian if he chooses so he can see how a proper bottle of whisky is made."

Absolute silence met this pronouncement. Finally, one brave man pointed out, "But that'll take months."

"And who's saying it won't?" old Campbell said, with the barest trace of belligerence. "The Sassenach is here to see Scotland. Are you telling me he can say he's done that if all he's done is taken a straight line from here to Perthshire?"

I found myself smiling, and made my decision on the spot. I would follow his exact route, and when I returned to London, I would know in my heart that I knew Scotland.

Colin watched Penelope as she read. Every now and then she would smile, and his heart would leap, and then suddenly he realized that her smile had become permanent, and her lips were puckering as if she were suppressing a laugh.

Colin realized he was smiling, too.

He'd been so surprised by her reaction the first time she'd read his writing; her response had been so passionate, and yet she'd been so analytical and precise when she spoke to him about it. It all made sense now, of course. She was a writer, too, probably a better one than he, and of all the things she understood in this world, she understood words.

It was hard to believe it had taken him this long to ask for her advice. Fear, he supposed, had stopped him. Fear and worry and all those stupid emotions he'd pretended were beneath him.

Who would have guessed that one woman's opinion would become so important to him? He'd worked on his journals for years, carefully recording his travels, trying to capture more than what he saw and did, trying to capture what he *felt*. And he'd never once showed them to anyone.

Until now.

There had been no one he'd wanted to show them to. No, that wasn't true. Deep down, he'd wanted to show them to a number of people, but the time had never seemed right, or he thought they would lie and say something was good when it wasn't, just to spare his feelings.

But Penelope was different. She was a writer. She was a damned good one, too. And if she said his journal entries were good, he could almost believe that it was true.

She pursed her lips slightly as she turned a page, then frowned as her fingers couldn't find purchase. After licking her middle finger, she caught hold of the errant page and began to read again.

And smiled again.

Colin let out a breath he didn't realize he'd been holding.

Finally, she laid the book down in her lap, leaving it open to the section she'd been reading. Looking up, she said, "I assume you wanted me to stop at the end of the entry?"

It wasn't quite what he'd expected her to say, and that befuddled him. "Er, if you want to," he stammered. "If you want to read more, that would be fine, I guess."

It was as if the sun had suddenly taken up residence in her smile. "Of *course* I want to read more," she gushed. "I can't wait to see what happened when you went to Kintyre and Mull and"—frowning, she checked the open book—"and Skye and Ullapool and Culloden and Grampian"—she glanced back down at the book again—"oh, yes, and Blair Castle, of course, if you ever made it. I assume you were planning to visit friends."

He nodded. "Murray," he said, referring to a school chum whose brother was the Duke of Atholl. "But I should tell you, I didn't end up following the exact route prescribed by old Angus Campbell. For one thing, I didn't even find roads connecting half the places he mentioned."

"Maybe," she said, her eyes growing dreamy, "that is where we ought to go for our honeymoon trip."

"Scotland?" he asked, thoroughly surprised. "Don't you want to travel someplace warm and exotic?"

"To one who has never traveled more than one hundred miles from London," she said pertly, "Scotland *is* exotic."

"I can assure you," he said with a smile as he walked across the room and perched on the edge of the bed, "that Italy is *more* exotic. And more romantic."

She blushed, which delighted him. "Oh," she said, looking vaguely embarrassed. (He wondered how long he'd be able to embarrass her with talk of romance and love and all the splendid activities that went with them.)

"We'll go to Scotland another time," he assured her. "I usually find myself heading north every few years or so to visit Francesca, anyway."

"I was surprised that you asked for my opinion," Penelope said after a short silence.

"Who else would I ask?"

"I don't know," she replied, suddenly very interested in the way her fingers were plucking at the bedcovers. "Your brothers, I suppose."

He laid his hand on hers. "What do *they* know about writing?"

Her chin lifted and her eyes, clear, warm, and brown, met his. "I know you value their opinions."

"That is true," he acceded, "but I value yours more."

He watched her face closely, as emotions played across her features. "But you don't like my writing," she said, her voice hesitant and hopeful at the same time.

He moved his hand to the curve of her cheek, holding it there gently, making sure that she was looking at him as he spoke. "Nothing could be further from the truth," he said, a burning intensity firing his words. "I think you are a marvelous writer. You cut right into the essence of a person with a simplicity and wit that is matchless. For years, you have made people laugh. You've made them wince. You've made them *think*, Penelope. You have made people think. I don't know what could be a higher achievement.

"Not to mention," he continued, almost as if he couldn't quite stop now that he'd gotten started, "that you write about *society*, of all things. You write about society, and you make it fun and interesting and witty, when we all know that more often than not it's beyond dull."

For the longest time, Penelope couldn't say anything. She had been proud of her work for years, and had secretly smiled whenever she had heard someone reciting from one of her columns or laughing at one of her quips. But she'd had no one with whom to share her triumphs.

Being anonymous had been a lonely prospect.

But now she had Colin. And even though the world would never know that Lady Whistledown was actually plain, overlooked, spinster-until-the-last-possible-moment Penelope Featherington, *Colin* knew.

And Penelope was coming to realize that even if that wasn't all that mattered, it was what mattered most.

But she still didn't understand his actions.

"Why, then," she asked him, her words slow and carefully measured, "do you grow so distant and cold every time I bring it up?"

When he spoke, his words were close to a mumble. "It's difficult to explain."

"I'm a good listener," she said softly.

His hand, which had been cradling her face so lovingly, dropped to his lap. And he said the one thing she never would have expected.

"I'm jealous." He shrugged helplessly. "I'm so sorry."

"I don't know what you mean," she said, not intending to whisper, but lacking the voice to do anything else.

"Look at yourself, Penelope." He took both of her hands in his and twisted so that they were facing one another. "You're a huge success."

"An anonymous success," she reminded him.

"But *you* know, and *I* know, and besides, that's not what I'm talking about." He let go of one of her hands, raking his fingers through his hair as he searched for words. "You have done something. You have a body of work."

"But you have—"

"What do I have, Penelope?" he interrupted, his voice growing agitated as he rose to his feet and began to pace. "What do I have?"

"Well, you have me," she said, but her words lacked force. She knew that wasn't what he meant.

He looked at her wearily. "I'm not talking about that, Penelope—"

"I know."

"—I need something I can point to," he said, right on top of her soft sentence. "I need a purpose. Anthony has one, and Benedict has one, but I'm at odds and ends."

"Colin, you're not. You're—"

"I'm tired of being thought of as nothing but an—" He stopped short.

"What, Colin?" she asked, a bit startled by the disgusted expression that suddenly crossed his face.

"Christ above," he swore, his voice low, the S hissing from his lips.

Her eyes widened. Colin was not one for frequent profanity.

"I can't believe it," he muttered, his head moving jerkily to the left, almost as if he was flinching.

"What?" she pleaded.

"I complained to you," he said incredulously. "I complained to you about Lady Whistledown."

She grimaced. "A lot of people have done that, Colin. I'm used to it."

"I can't believe it. I complained to you about how Lady Whistledown called me charming."

"She called me an overripe citrus fruit," Penelope said, attempting levity.

He stopped his pacing for just long enough to shoot her an annoyed look. "Were you laughing at me the whole time I was moaning about how the only way I would be remembered by future generations was in *Whistledown* columns?"

"No!" she exclaimed. "I would hope you know me better than that."

He shook his head in a disbelieving manner. "I can't believe I sat there, complaining to you that I had no accomplishments, when you had all of *Whistledown*."

She got off the bed and stood. It was impossible just to sit there while he was pacing like a caged tiger. "Colin, you couldn't have known."

"Still." He let out a disgusted exhale. "The irony would be beautiful, if it weren't directed at me."

Penelope parted her lips to speak, but she didn't know how to say everything that was in her heart. Colin had so many achievements, she couldn't even begin to count them all. They weren't something you could pick up, like an edition of *Lady Whistledown's Society Papers*, but they were just as special.

Perhaps even more so.

Penelope remembered all the moments he had made people smile, all the times he had walked past all of the popular girls at balls and asked a wallflower to dance. She thought of the strong, almost magical bond he shared with his siblings. If those weren't achievements, she didn't know what was.

But she knew that those weren't the sorts of milestones he was talking about. She knew what he needed: a purpose, a calling.

Something to show the world that he was more than they thought he was.

"Publish your travel memoirs," she said.

"I'm not—"

"Publish them," she said again. "Take a chance and see if you soar."

His eyes met hers for a moment, then they slid back down to his journal, still clutched in her hands. "They need editing," he mumbled.

Penelope laughed, because she knew she had won. And he had won, too. He didn't know it yet, but he had.

"Everyone needs editing," she said, her smile broadening with each word. "Well, except me, I guess," she teased. "Or maybe I did need it," she added with a shrug. "We'll never know, because I had no one to edit me."

He looked up quite suddenly. "How did you do it?"

"How did I do what?"

His lips pursed impatiently. "You know what I mean. How did you do the column? There was more to it than the writing. You had to print and distribute. Someone had to have known who you were."

She let out a long breath. She'd held these secrets so long it felt strange to share them, even with her husband. "It's a long story," she told him. "Perhaps we should sit."

He led her back to the bed, and they both made themselves comfortable, propped up against the pillows, their legs stretched out before them.

"I was very young when it started," Penelope began. "Only seventeen. And it happened quite by accident."

He smiled. "How does something like that happen by accident?"

"I wrote it as a joke. I was so miserable that first season." She looked up at him earnestly. "I don't know if you recall, but I weighed over a stone more back then, and it's not as if I'm fashionably slender now."

"I think you're perfect," he said loyally.

Which was, Penelope thought, part of the reason she thought he was perfect as well.

"Anyway," she continued, "I wasn't terribly happy, and so I wrote a rather scathing report of the party I'd been to the night before. And then I did another, and another. I didn't sign them Lady Whistledown; I just wrote them for fun and hid them in my desk. Except one day, I forgot to hide them."

He leaned forward, utterly rapt. "What happened?"

"My family were all out, and I knew they'd be gone for some time, because that was when Mama still thought she could turn Prudence into a diamond of the first water, and their shopping trips took all day."

Colin rolled his hand through the air, signaling that she should get to the point.

"Anyway," Penelope continued, "I decided to work in the drawing room because my room was damp and musty because someone— well, I suppose it was me—left the window open during a rainstorm. But then I had to . . . well, you know."

"No," Colin said abruptly. "I don't know."

"Attend to my business," Penelope whispered, blushing.

"Oh. Right," he said dismissively, clearly not interested in that part of the story, either. "Go on."

"When I got back, my father's solicitor was there. And he was reading what I wrote. I was horrified!"

"What happened?"

"I couldn't even speak for the first minute. But then I realized he was laughing, and it wasn't because he thought I was foolish, it was because he thought I was good."

"Well, you *are* good."

"I know that now," she said with a wry smile, "but you have to remember, I was seventeen. And I'd said some pretty horrid things in there."

"About horrid people, I'm sure," he said.

"Well, yes, but still . . ." She closed her eyes as all the memories swam through her head. "They were popular people. Influential people. People who didn't like me very much. It didn't really matter that they were horrid if what I said got out. In fact, it would have been worse because they were horrid. I would have been ruined, and I would have ruined my entire family along with me."

"What happened then? I assume it was his idea to publish."

Penelope nodded. "Yes. He made all the arrangements with the printer, who in turn found the boys to deliver. And it was his idea to give it away for free for the first two weeks. He said we needed to addict the *ton*."

"I was out of the country when the column began," Colin said, "but I remember my mother and sisters telling me all about it."

"People grumbled when the newsboys demanded payment after two weeks for free," Penelope said. "But they all paid."

"A bright idea on the part of your solicitor," Colin murmured.

"Yes, he was quite savvy."

He picked up on her use of the past tense. "Was?"

She nodded sadly. "He passed on a few years ago. But he knew he was ill and so before he died he asked me if I wanted to continue. I suppose I could have stopped then, but I had nothing else in my life, and certainly no marriage prospects." She looked up quickly. "I don't mean to—That is to say—"

His lips curved into a self-deprecating smile. "You may scold me all you wish for not having proposed years ago."

Penelope returned his smile with one of her own. Was it any wonder she loved this man?

"But," he said rather firmly, "only if you finish the story."

"Right," she said, forcing her mind back to the matter at hand. "After Mr—" She looked up hesitantly. "I'm not certain I should say his name."

Colin knew she was torn between her love and trust for him, and her loyalty to a man who had, in all probability, been a father to her once her own had departed this earth. "It's all right," he said softly. "He's gone. His name doesn't matter."

She let out a soft breath. "Thank you," she said, chewing on her lower lip. "It's not that I don't trust you. I—"

"I know," he said reassuringly, squeezing her fingers with his. "If you want to tell me later, that's fine. And if you don't, that will be fine as well."

She nodded, her lips tight at the corners, in that strained expression people get when they are trying hard not to cry. "After he died, I worked directly with the publisher. We set up a system for delivery of the columns, and the payments continued the way they had always been made—into a discreet account in my name."

Colin sucked in his breath as he thought about how much money she must have made over the years. But how could she have spent it without incurring suspicion? "Did you make any withdrawals?" he asked.

She nodded. "After I'd been working about four years, my great-aunt passed away and left her estate to my mother. My father's solicitor wrote the will. She didn't have very much, so we took my money and pretended it was hers." Penelope's face brightened slightly as she shook her head in bewilderment. "My mother was surprised. She'd never dreamed Aunt Georgette had been so wealthy. She smiled for months. I've never seen anything like it."

"It was very kind of you," Colin said.

Penelope shrugged. "It was the only way I could actually use my money."

"But you gave it to your mother," he pointed out.

"She's my mother," she said, as if that ought to explain everything. "She supported me. It all trickled down."

He wanted to say more, but he didn't. Portia Featherington was Penelope's mother, and if Penelope wanted to love her, he wasn't going to stop her.

"Since then," Penelope said, "I haven't touched it. Well, not for myself. I've given some money to charities." Her face took on a wry expression. "Anonymously."

He didn't say anything for a moment, just took the time to think about everything she had done in the last decade, all on her own, all in secret. "If you want the money now," he finally said, "you should use it. No one will question your suddenly having more funds. You're a Bridgerton, after all." He shrugged modestly. "It's well known that Anthony settled ample livings upon all of his brothers."

"I wouldn't even know what to do with it all."

"Buy something new," he suggested. Didn't all women like to shop?

She looked at him with an odd, almost inscrutable expression. "I'm not sure you understand how much money I have," she said hedgingly. "I don't think I could spend it all."

"Put it aside for our children, then," he said. "I've been fortunate that my father and brother saw fit to provide for me, but not all younger sons are so lucky."

"And daughters," Penelope reminded him. "Our daughters should have money of their own. *Separate* from their dowries."

Colin had to smile. Such arrangements were rare, but trust Penelope to insist upon it. "Whatever you wish," he said fondly.

She smiled and sighed, settling back against the pillows. Her fingers idly danced across the skin on the back of his hand, but her eyes were far away, and he doubted she was even aware of her movements.

"I have a confession to make," she said, her voice quiet and even just a touch shy.

He looked at her doubtfully. "Bigger than *Whistledown*?"

"Different."

"What is it?"

She dragged her eyes off of the random spot on the wall she seemed to be focused upon and gave him her full attention. "I've been feeling a bit"—she chewed on her lip as she paused, searching for the right words—"impatient with you lately. No, that's not right," she said. "Disappointed, really."

An odd feeling began to prickle in his chest. "Disappointed how?" he asked carefully.

Her shoulders gave a little shrug. "You seemed so upset with me. About Whistledown."

"I already told you that was because—"

"No, please," she said, placing a gently restraining hand on his chest. "Please let me finish. I told you I thought it was because you were ashamed of me, and I tried to ignore it, but it hurt so much, really. I thought I knew who you were, and I couldn't believe that person would think himself so far above me that he would feel such shame at my achievements."

He stared at her silently, waiting for her to continue.

"But the funny thing is . . ." She turned to him with a wise smile. "The funny thing is that it wasn't because you were ashamed at all. It was all because you wanted something like that for your own.

Something like *Whistledown*. It seems silly now, but I was so worried because you weren't the perfect man of my dreams."

"No one is perfect," he said quietly.

"I know." She leaned over and planted an impulsive kiss on his cheek. "You're the imperfect man of my heart, and that's even better. I'd always thought you infallible, that your life was charmed, that you had no worries or fears or unfulfilled dreams. But that wasn't really fair of me."

"I was never ashamed of you, Penelope," he whispered. "Never."

They sat in companionable silence for a few moments, and then Penelope said, "Do you remember when I asked you if we might take a belated honeymoon trip?"

He nodded.

"Why don't we use some of my Whistledown money for that?"

"*I* will pay for the honeymoon trip."

"Fine," she said with a lofty expression. "You may take it out of your quarterly allowance."

He stared at her in shock, then hooted with laughter. "You're going to give me pin money?" he asked, unable to control the grin that spread across his face.

"Pen money," she corrected. "So you can work on your journals."

"Pen money," he mused. "I like that."

She smiled and placed her hand on his. "I like you."

He squeezed her fingers. "I like you, too."

Penelope sighed as she settled her head on his shoulder. "Is life supposed to be this wonderful?"

"I think so," he murmured. "I really do."

Chapter 21

One week later, Penelope was sitting at the desk in her drawing room, reading Colin's journals and making notes on a separate piece of paper whenever she had a question or comment. He had asked her to help him edit his writing, a task she found thrilling.

She was, of course, overjoyed that he had entrusted this critical job to her. It meant he trusted her judgment, thought she was smart and clever, felt that she could take what he had written and make it even better.

But there was more to her happiness than that. She'd needed a project, something to do. In the first days after giving up *Whistledown*, she'd reveled in her newfound free time. It was like having a holiday for the first time in years. She'd read like mad—all those novels and books she'd purchased but never gotten around to reading. And she'd taken long walks, ridden her horse in the park, sat in the small courtyard behind her house on Mount Street, enjoying the fine spring weather and tipping her face up toward the sun for a minute or so at a time—long enough to bask in the warmth, but not so long as to turn her cheeks brown.

Then, of course, the wedding and its myriad details had consumed all of her time. So she really hadn't had much opportunity to realize what might be missing in her life.

When she had been doing the column, the actual writing of it hadn't taken too terribly long, but she always had to be on the alert, watching and listening. And when she wasn't writing the column she was thinking about writing the column or desperately trying to remember some clever turn of phrase until she could get home and jot it down.

It had been mentally engaging, and she hadn't realized how much she'd missed having her mind challenged until now, when she'd finally been given the opportunity again.

She was jotting down a question about Colin's description of a Tuscan villa on page 143 in volume two of his journals when the butler knocked discreetly on the open door to alert her to his presence.

Penelope smiled sheepishly. She tended to absorb herself entirely in her work, and Dunwoody had learned through trial and error that if he wanted to get her attention, he had to make some noise.

"A visitor to see you, Mrs. Bridgerton," he said.

Penelope looked up with a smile. It was probably one of her sisters, or maybe one of the Bridgerton siblings. "Really? Who is it?"

He stepped forward and handed her a card. Penelope looked down and gasped, first in shock, and then in misery. Engraved in classic, stately black on a creamy white background were two simple words: Lady Twombley.

Cressida Twombley? Why on earth would she come calling?

Penelope began to feel uneasy. Cressida would never call unless it was for some unpleasant purpose. Cressida never did anything unless it was for an unpleasant purpose.

"Would you like me to turn her away?" Dunwoody asked.

"No," Penelope said with a sigh. She wasn't a coward, and Cressida Twombley wasn't going to turn her into one. "I'll see her. Just give me a moment to put my papers away. But . . ."

Dunwoody stopped in his tracks and cocked his head slightly to the side, waiting for her to go on.

"Oh, never mind," Penelope muttered.

"Are you certain, Mrs. Bridgerton?"

"Yes. No." She groaned. She was dithering and it was one more transgression to add to Cressida's already long list of them—she was turning Penelope into a stammering fool. "What I mean is—if she's still here after ten minutes, would you devise some sort of emergency that requires my presence? My *immediate* presence?"

"I believe that can be arranged."

"Excellent, Dunwoody," Penelope said with a weak smile. It was, perhaps, the easy way out, but she didn't trust herself to be able to find the perfect point in the conversation to insist that Cressida leave, and the last thing she wanted was to be trapped in the drawing room with her all afternoon.

The butler nodded and left, and Penelope shuffled her papers into a neat stack, closing Colin's journal and setting it on top so that the breeze from the open window couldn't blow the papers off the desk. She stood and walked over to the sofa, sitting down in the center, hoping that she looked relaxed and composed.

As if a visit from Cressida Twombley could ever be called relaxing.

A moment later, Cressida arrived, stepping through the open doorway as Dunwoody intoned her name. As always, she looked beautiful, every golden hair on her head in its perfect place. Her skin was flawless, her eyes sparkled, her clothing was of the latest style, and her reticule matched her attire to perfection.

"Cressida," Penelope said, "how surprising to see you." *Surprising* being the most polite adjective she could come up with under the circumstances.

Cressida's lips curved into a mysterious, almost feline smile. "I'm sure it is," she murmured.

"Won't you sit down?" Penelope asked, mostly because she had to. She'd spent a lifetime being polite; it was difficult to stop now. She motioned to a nearby chair, the most uncomfortable one in the room.

Cressida sat on the edge of the chair, and if she found it less than pleasing, Penelope could not tell from her mien. Her posture was elegant, her smile never faltered, and she looked as cool and composed as anyone had a right to be.

"I'm sure you're wondering why I'm here," Cressida said.

There seemed little reason to deny it, so Penelope nodded.

And then, abruptly, Cressida asked, "How are you finding married life?"

Penelope blinked. "I beg your pardon?"

"It must be an amazing change of pace," Cressida said.

"Yes," Penelope said carefully, "but a welcome one."

"Mmmm, yes. You must have a dreadful amount of free time now. I'm sure you don't know what to do with yourself."

A prickling feeling began to spread along Penelope's skin. "I don't understand your meaning," she said.

"Don't you?"

When it became apparent that Cressida required an answer, Penelope replied, somewhat testily, "No, I don't."

Cressida was silent for a moment, but her cat-with-cream expression spoke volumes. She glanced about the room until her eyes fell on the writing desk where Penelope had so recently been sitting. "What are those papers?" she inquired.

Penelope's eyes flew to the papers on the desk, stacked neatly under Colin's journal. There was no way that Cressida could have known that they were anything special. Penelope had already been seated on the sofa when Cressida had entered the room. "I fail to see how my personal papers could be of your concern," she said.

"Oh, do not take offense," Cressida said with a little tinkle of laughter that Penelope found rather frightening. "I was merely making polite conversation. Inquiring about your interests."

"I see," Penelope said, trying to fill the ensuing silence.

"I'm very observant," Cressida said.

Penelope raised her brows in question.

"In fact, my keen powers of observation are quite well known among the very best circles of society."

"I must not be a link in those impressive circles, then," Penelope murmured.

Cressida, however, was far too involved in her own speech to acknowledge Penelope's. "It's why," she said in a thoughtful tone of voice, "I thought I might be able to convince the *ton* that I was really Lady Whistledown."

Penelope's heart thundered in her chest. "Then you admit that you're not?" she asked carefully.

"Oh, I think you know I'm not."

Penelope's throat began to close. Somehow—she'd never know how—she managed to keep her composure and say, "I beg your pardon?"

Cressida smiled, but she managed to take that happy expression and turn it into something sly and cruel. "When I came up with this ruse, I thought: *I can't lose.* Either I convince everyone I'm Lady Whistledown or they won't believe me and I look very cunning when I say that I was just pretending to be Lady Whistledown in order to ferret out the true culprit."

Penelope held very silent, very still.

"But it didn't quite play out the way I had planned. Lady Whistledown turned out to be far more devious and mean-spirited than I would have guessed." Cressida's eyes narrowed, then narrowed some more until her face, normally so lovely, took on a sinister air. "Her last little column turned me into a laughingstock."

Penelope said nothing, barely daring to breathe.

"And then . . ." Cressida continued, her voice dropping into lower registers. "And then you—*you!*—had the effrontery to insult me in front of the entire *ton.*"

Penelope breathed a tiny sigh of relief. Maybe Cressida didn't know her secret. Maybe this was all about Penelope's public insult, when she'd accused Cressida of lying, and she'd said—dear God, what had she said? Something terribly cruel, she was sure, but certainly well deserved.

"I might have been able to tolerate the insult if it had come from someone else," Cressida continued. "But from someone such as you—well, that could not go unanswered."

"You should think twice before insulting me in my own home," Penelope said in a low voice. And then she added, even though she hated to hide behind her husband's name, "I am a Bridgerton now. I carry the weight of their protection."

Penelope's warning made no dent in the satisfied mask that molded Cressida's beautiful face. "I think you had better listen to what I have to say before you make threats."

Penelope knew she had to listen. It was better to know what Cressida knew than to close her eyes and pretend all was well. "Go on," she said, her voice deliberately curt.

"You made a critical mistake," Cressida said, pointing her index finger at Penelope and wagging it back and forth in short ticktocky motions. "It didn't occur to you that I *never* forget an insult, did it?"

"What are you trying to say, Cressida?" Penelope had wanted her words to seem strong and forceful, but they came out as a whisper.

Cressida stood and walked slowly away from Penelope, her hips swaying slightly as she moved, the motion almost like a swagger. "Let me see if I can remember your exact words," she said, tapping one finger against her cheek. "Oh, no, no, don't remind me. I'm sure it will come to me. Oh, yes, I recall now." She turned around to face Penelope. "I believe you said you'd always liked Lady Whistledown. And then—and to give you credit, it was an evocative, memorable turn of phrase—you said that it would break your heart if she turned out to be someone like Lady Twombley." Cressida smiled. "Which would be me."

Penelope's mouth went dry. Her fingers shook. And her skin turned to ice.

Because while she hadn't remembered exactly what she'd said in her insult to Cressida, she did remember what she'd written in that last, final, column, the one which had been mistakenly distributed at her engagement ball. The one which—

The one which Cressida was now slapping down onto the table in front of her.

Ladies and Gentleman, This Author is NOT Lady Cressida Twombley. She is nothing more than a scheming imposter, and it would break my heart to see my years of hard work attributed to one such as her.

Penelope stared down at the words even though she knew each one by heart. "What do you mean?" she asked, even though she knew her attempt to pretend that she didn't know exactly what Cressida meant was futile.

"You're smarter than that, Penelope Featherington," Cressida said. "You know I know."

Penelope kept staring at the single, incriminating sheet of paper, unable to tear her eyes from those fateful words—

It would break my heart.

Break my heart.

Break my heart.

Break my—

"Nothing to say?" Cressida asked, and even though Penelope could not see her face, she felt her hard, supercilious smile.

"No one will believe you," Penelope whispered.

"I can barely believe it myself," Cressida said with a harsh laugh. "You, of all people. But apparently you had hidden depths and were a bit more clever than you let on. Clever enough," she added with noticeable emphasis, "to know that once I light the spark of this particular piece of gossip, the news will spread like wildfire."

Penelope's mind whirled in dizzying, unpleasant circles. Oh, God, what was she going to tell Colin? How would she tell him? She knew she had to, but where would she find the words?

"No one will believe it at first," Cressida continued. "You were right about that. But then they'll start to think, and slowly but surely, the pieces of the puzzle will fall into place. Someone will remember that they said something to you that ended up in a column. Or that you were at a particular house party. Or that they'd seen Eloise Bridgerton snooping about, and doesn't everyone know that the two of you tell each other everything?"

"What do you want?" Penelope asked, her voice low and haunted as she finally lifted her head to face her enemy.

"Ah, now, there's the question I've been waiting for." Cressida clasped her hands together behind her back and began to pace. "I've been giving the matter a great deal of thought. In fact, I put off coming here to see you for almost a full week until I could decide upon the matter."

Penelope swallowed, uncomfortable with the notion that Cressida had known her deepest secret for nearly a week, and she'd been blithely living her life, unaware that the sky was about to come crashing down.

"I knew from the outset, of course," Cressida said, "that I wanted money. But the question was—how much? Your husband is a Bridgerton, of course, and so he has ample funds, but then again, he's a younger son, and not as plump in the pocket as the viscount."

"How much, Cressida?" Penelope ground out. She knew that Cressida was drawing this out just to torture her, and she held little hope that she would actually name a figure before she was good and ready.

"Then I realized," Cressida continued, ignoring Penelope's question (and proving her point), "that you must be quite wealthy, too. Unless you're an utter fool—and considering your success at hiding your little secret for so long, I've revised my initial opinion of you, so I don't think you are—you'd have to have made a fortune after writing the column for all those years. And from all outward appearances"—she gave a scornful glance to Penelope's afternoon dress—"you haven't been spending it. So I can only deduce that it is all sitting in a discreet little bank account somewhere, just waiting for a withdrawal."

"How much, Cressida?"

"Ten thousand pounds."

Penelope gasped. "You're mad!"

"No." Cressida smiled. "Just very, very clever."

"I don't have ten thousand pounds."

"I think you're lying."

"I can assure you I'm not!" And she wasn't. The last time Penelope had checked her account balance, she'd had £8246, although she supposed that with interest, it had grown by a few pounds since then. It was an enormous sum of money, to be sure, enough to keep any reasonable person happy for several lifetimes, but it wasn't ten thousand, and it wasn't anything she wished to hand over to Cressida Twombley.

Cressida smiled serenely. "I'm sure you'll figure out what to do. Between your savings and your husband's money, ten thousand pounds is a paltry sum."

"Ten thousand pounds is *never* a paltry sum."

"How long will you need to gather your funds?" Cressida asked, completely ignoring Penelope's outburst. "A day? Two days?"

"Two days?" Penelope echoed, gaping. "I couldn't do it in two weeks!"

"Aha, so then you *do* have the money."

"I don't!"

"One week," Cressida said, her voice turning sharp. "I want the money in one week."

"I won't give it to you," Penelope whispered, more for her own benefit than Cressida's.

"You will," Cressida replied confidently. "If you don't, I'll ruin you."

"Mrs. Bridgerton?"

Penelope looked up to see Dunwoody standing in the doorway.

"There is an urgent matter which requires your attention," he said. "Immediately."

"Just as well," Cressida said, walking toward the door. "I'm done here." She walked through the doorway, then turned around once she reached the hall, so that Penelope was forced to look at her, perfectly framed in the portal. "I'll hear from you soon?" she inquired, her voice mild and innocent, as if she were talking about nothing more weighty than an invitation to a party, or perhaps the agenda for a charity meeting.

Penelope gave her a little nod, just to be rid of her.

But it didn't matter. The front door may have thunked shut, and Cressida might be gone, but Penelope's troubles weren't going anywhere.

Chapter 22

Three hours later, Penelope was still in the drawing room, still sitting on the sofa, still staring into space, still trying to figure out how she was going to solve her problems.

Correction: problem, singular.

She had only one problem, but for the size of it, she might as well have had a thousand.

She wasn't an aggressive person, and she couldn't remember the last time she had a violent thought, but at that moment, she could have gladly wrung Cressida Twombley's neck.

She watched the door with a morose sense of fatalism, waiting for her husband to come home, knowing that each ticking second brought her closer to her moment of truth, when she would have to confess everything to him.

He wouldn't say, *I told you so*. He would never say such a thing.

But he would be thinking it.

It never occurred to her, not even for a minute, that she might keep this from him. Cressida's threats weren't the sort of thing one hid from one's husband, and besides, she was going to need his help.

She wasn't certain what she needed to do, but whatever it was, she didn't know how to do it alone.

But there was one thing she knew for sure—she didn't want to pay Cressida. There was no way Cressida would be satisfied with ten thousand pounds, not when she thought she could get more. If Penelope capitulated now, she'd be handing money over to Cressida for the rest of her life.

Which meant that in one week's time, Cressida Twombley would tell all the world that Penelope Featherington Bridgerton was the infamous Lady Whistledown.

Penelope reckoned she had two choices. She could lie, and call Cressida a fool, and hope that everyone believed her; or she could try to find some way to twist Cressida's revelation to her advantage.

But for the life of her, she didn't know how.

"Penelope?"

Colin's voice. She wanted to fling herself into his arms, and at the same time, she could barely bring herself to turn around.

"Penelope?" He sounded concerned now, his footsteps increasing in speed as he crossed the room. "Dunwoody said that Cressida was here."

He sat next to her and touched her cheek. She turned and saw his face, the corners of his eyes crinkled with worry, his lips, slightly parted as they murmured her name.

And that was when she finally allowed herself to cry.

Funny how she could hold herself together, keep it all inside until she saw him. But now that he was here, all she could do was bury her face in the warmth of his chest, snuggle closer as his arms wrapped around her.

As if somehow he could make all her problems go away by his presence alone.

"Penelope?" he asked, his voice soft and worried. "What happened? What's wrong?"

Penelope just shook her head, the motion having to suffice until she could think of the words, summon the courage, stop the tears.

"What did she do to you?"

"Oh, Colin," she said, somehow summoning the energy to pull herself far enough back so that she could see his face. "She knows."

His skin went white. "How?"

Penelope sniffled, wiping her nose with the back of her hand. "It's my fault," she whispered.

He handed her a handkerchief without ever taking his eyes off of her face. "It's not your fault," he said sharply.

Her lips slid into a sad smile. She knew that his harsh tone was meant for Cressida, but she deserved it as well. "No," she said, her voice laced with resignation, "it is. It happened exactly as you said it would. I wasn't paying attention to what I wrote. I slipped up."

"What did you do?" he asked.

She told him everything, starting with Cressida's entrance and ending with her demands for money. She confessed that her poor choice of words was going to be her ruin, but wasn't it ironic, because it really did feel like her heart was breaking.

But the whole time she spoke, she felt him slipping away. He was listening to her, but he wasn't there with her. His eyes took on a strange, faraway look, and yet they were narrowed, intense.

He was plotting something. She was sure of it.

It terrified her.

And thrilled her.

Whatever he was planning, whatever he was thinking, it was all for her. She hated that it had been her stupidity that had forced him into this dilemma, but she couldn't stem the tingle of excitement that swept across her skin as she watched him.

"Colin?" she asked hesitantly. She'd been done speaking for a full minute, and still he hadn't said anything.

"I'll take care of everything," he said. "I don't want you to worry about a thing."

"I assure you that that is impossible," she said with shaking voice.

"I take my wedding vows quite seriously," he replied, his tone almost frighteningly even. "I believe I promised to honor and keep you."

"Let me help you," she said impulsively. "Together we can solve this."

One corner of his mouth lifted into a hint of a smile. "Have you a solution?"

She shook her head. "No. I've been thinking all day, and I don't know . . . although . . ."

"Although what?" he asked, his brows rising.

Her lips parted, then pursed, then parted again as she said, "What if I enlisted the aid of Lady Danbury?"

"You're planning to ask her to pay off Cressida?"

"No," she said, even though the tone of his voice told her that his had not been a serious question. "I'm going to ask her to be me."

"I beg your pardon?"

"Everyone thinks she's Lady Whistledown, anyway," Penelope explained. "At least, quite a lot of people do. If she were to make an announcement—"

"Cressida would refute it instantly," Colin interrupted.

"Who would believe Cressida over Lady Danbury?" Penelope turned to him with wide, earnest eyes. "I wouldn't dare cross Lady Danbury in any matter. If she were to say she was Lady Whistledown, I'd probably believe her myself."

"What makes you think you can convince Lady Danbury to lie for you?"

"Well," Penelope replied, chewing on her lower lip, "she likes me."

"She likes you?" Colin echoed.

"She does, rather. I think she might like to help me, especially since she detests Cressida almost as much as I do."

"You think her fondness for you will lead her to lie to the entire *ton*?" he asked doubtfully.

She sagged in her seat. "It's worth asking."

He stood, his movements abrupt, and walked to the window. "Promise me you won't go to her."

"But—"

"Promise me."

"I promise," she said, "but—"

"No buts," he said. "If we need to, we'll contact Lady Danbury, but not until I have a chance to think of something else." He raked his hand through his hair. "There must be something else."

"We have a week," she said softly, but she didn't find her words reassuring, and it was difficult to imagine that Colin did, either.

He turned around, his about-face so precise he might have been in the military. "I'll be back," he said, heading for the door.

"But where are you going?" Penelope cried out, jumping to her feet.

"I have to think," he said, pausing with his hand on the doorknob.

"You can't think here with me?" she whispered.

His face softened, and he crossed back to her side. He murmured her name, tenderly taking her face in his hands. "I love you," he said, his voice low and fervent. "I love you with everything I am, everything I've been, and everything I hope to be."

"Colin . . ."

"I love you with my past, and I love you for my future." He bent forward and kissed her, once, softly, on the lips. "I love you for the children we'll have and for the years we'll have together. I love you for every one of my smiles, and even more, for every one of your smiles."

Penelope sagged against the back of a nearby chair.

"I love you," he repeated. "You know that, don't you?"

She nodded, closing her eyes as her cheeks rubbed against his hands.

"I have things to do," he said, "and I won't be able to concentrate if I'm thinking about you, worrying if you're crying, wondering if you're hurt."

"I'm fine," she whispered. "I'm fine now that I've told you."

"I will make this right," he vowed. "I just need you to trust me."

She opened her eyes. "With my life."

He smiled, and suddenly she knew that his words were true. Everything would be all right. Maybe not today and maybe not tomorrow, but soon. Tragedy couldn't coexist in a world with one of Colin's smiles.

"I don't think it will come to that," he said fondly, giving her cheek one affectionate stroke before returning his arms to his sides. He walked back to the door, turning the moment his hand touched the knob. "Don't forget about my sister's party tonight."

Penelope let out a short groan. "Do we have to? The last thing I want to do is go out in public."

"We have to," Colin said. "Daphne doesn't host balls very often, and she'd be crushed if we did not attend."

"I know," Penelope said with a sigh. "I know. I knew it even as I complained. I'm sorry."

He smiled wryly. "It's all right. You're entitled to a bit of a bad mood today."

"Yes," she said, trying to return the smile. "I am, aren't I?"

"I'll be back later," he promised.

"Where are you—" she started to ask, then caught herself. He obviously didn't want questions just then, even from her.

But to her surprise, he answered, "To see my brother."

"Anthony?"

"Yes."

She nodded encouragingly, murmuring, "Go. I will be fine." The Bridgertons had always found strength in other Bridgertons. If Colin felt he needed his brother's counsel, then he should go without delay.

"Don't forget to prepare for Daphne's ball," he reminded her.

She gave him a halfhearted salute and watched as he left the room.

Then she moved to the window to watch him walk by, but he never appeared. He must have headed straight out the back to the mews. She sighed, allowing her bottom to rest against the windowsill for support. She hadn't realized just how much she'd wanted to catch one last glimpse of him.

She wished she knew what he was planning.

She wished she could be sure he even had a plan.

But at the same time, she felt oddly at ease. Colin would make this right. He'd said he would, and he never lied.

She knew that her idea to enlist the aid of Lady Danbury wasn't a perfect solution, but unless Colin came up with a better idea, what else could they do?

For now, she would try to push it all from her mind. She was so weary, and so very tired, and right now what she needed was to close her eyes and think of nothing but the green of her husband's eyes, the shining light of his smile.

Tomorrow.

Tomorrow she would help Colin solve their problems.

Today she would rest. She would take a nap and pray for sleep and try to figure out how she would face all of society this evening, knowing that Cressida would be there, watching and waiting for her to make a false move.

One would think that after nearly a dozen years of pretending she was nothing more than the wallflowerish Penelope Featherington, she'd be used to playing roles and hiding her true self.

But that was when her secret had been safe. Everything was different now.

Penelope curled up on the sofa and closed her eyes.

Everything was different now, but that didn't mean that it had to be worse, did it?

Everything would be fine. It would. It had to.

Didn't it?

Colin was starting to regret his decision to take a carriage over to his brother's house.

He'd wanted to walk—the vigorous use of his legs and feet and muscles seemed the only socially acceptable outlet for his fury. But he'd recognized that time was of the essence, and even with traffic, a carriage could convey him to Mayfair faster than could his own two feet.

But now the walls seemed too close and the air too thick, *and goddamn it*, was that an overturned milkwagon blocking the street?

Colin poked his head out the door, hanging out of the carriage even as they were still rolling to a halt. "God above," he muttered, taking in the scene. Broken glass littered the street, milk was flowing everywhere, and he couldn't tell who was screeching louder—the horses, which were still tangled in the reins, or the ladies on the pavement, whose dresses had been completely splattered with milk.

Colin jumped down from his carriage, intending to help clear the scene, but it quickly became apparent that Oxford Street would be a snarl for at least an hour, with or without his help. He checked to make sure that the milkwagon horses were being properly cared for, informed his driver that he would be continuing on foot, and took off walking.

He stared defiantly in the faces of each person he passed, perversely enjoying the way they averted their gaze when faced with his obvious hostility. He almost wished one of them would make a comment, just so he could have someone to lash out at. It didn't matter that the only person he really wanted to throttle was Cressida Twombley; by this point anyone would have made a fine target.

His anger was making him unbalanced, unreasonable. Unlike himself.

He still wasn't certain what had happened to him when Penelope had told him of Cressida's threats. This was more than anger, greater than fury. This was physical; it coursed through his veins, pulsed beneath his skin.

He wanted to hit someone.

He wanted to kick things, put his fist through a wall.

He'd been furious when Penelope had published her last column. In fact, he'd thought he couldn't possibly experience a greater anger.

He was wrong.

Or perhaps it was just that this was a different sort of anger. Someone was trying to hurt the one person he loved above all others.

How could he tolerate that? How could he allow it to happen?

The answer was simple. He couldn't.

He had to stop this. He had to *do* something.

After so many years of ambling through life, laughing at the antics of others, it was time to take action himself.

He looked up, somewhat surprised that he was already at Bridgerton House. Funny how it no longer seemed like home. He'd grown up here, but now it was so obviously his brother's house.

Home was in Bloomsbury. Home was with Penelope.

Home was anywhere with Penelope.

"Colin?"

He turned around. Anthony was on the pavement, obviously returning from an errand or appointment.

Anthony nodded toward the door. "Were you planning to knock?"

Colin looked blankly at his brother, just then realizing that he'd been standing perfectly still on the steps for God only knew how long.

"Colin?" Anthony asked again, his brow furrowing with concern.

"I need your help," Colin said. It was all he needed to say.

Penelope was already dressed for the ball when her maid brought in a note from Colin.

"Dunwoody got it from the messenger," the maid explained before bobbing a quick curtsy and leaving Penelope to read the note in privacy.

Penelope slid her gloved finger under the envelope flap and nudged it open, pulling out the single sheet of paper on which she saw the fine, neat handwriting that had become so familiar to her since she'd started editing Colin's journals.

*I will make my own way over to the ball this evening. Please
proceed to Number Five. Mother, Eloise, and Hyacinth are
waiting to accompany you to Hastings House.*

All my love,
Colin

For someone who wrote so well in his journals, he wasn't much of
a correspondent, Penelope thought with a wry smile.

She stood, smoothing out the fine silk of her skirts. She'd chosen
a dress of her favorite color—sage green—in hopes that it might
lend her courage. Her mother had always said that when a woman
looked good, she felt good, and she rather thought her mother was
right. Heaven knows, she'd spent a good eight years of her life
feeling rather *bad* in the dresses her mother had insisted looked
good.

Her hair had been dressed in a loosely upswept fashion that flattered her face, and her maid had even combed something through
the strands (Penelope was afraid to ask what) that seemed to bring
out the red highlights.

Red hair wasn't very fashionable, of course, but Colin had once
said he liked the way the candlelight made her hair more colorful,
so Penelope had decided that this was one case upon which she and
fashion would have to disagree.

By the time she made her way downstairs, her carriage was waiting for her, and the driver had already been instructed to take her
to Number Five.

Colin had clearly taken care of everything. Penelope wasn't sure
why this surprised her; he wasn't the sort of man who forgot details.
But he was preoccupied today. It seemed odd that he would have
taken the time to send instructions to the staff about her delivery
to his mother's house when she could have conveyed the order just
as well herself.

He had to be planning something. But what? Was he going to intercept Cressida Twombley and have her shipped off to a penal colony?

No, too melodramatic.

Maybe he'd found a secret about her, and was planning to cross-blackmail her. Silence for silence.

Penelope nodded approvingly as her carriage rolled along Oxford Street. That had to be the answer. It was just like Colin to come up with something so diabolically fitting and clever. But what could he possibly have unearthed about Cressida in so short a time? In all her years as Lady Whistledown, she'd never heard even a whisper of anything truly scandalous attached to Cressida's name.

Cressida was mean, and Cressida was petty, but she'd never stepped outside the rules of society. The only truly daring thing she'd ever done was claim to be Lady Whistledown.

The carriage turned south into Mayfair, and a few minutes later, they came to a stop in front of Number Five. Eloise must have been watching at the window, because she virtually flew down the steps and would have crashed into the carriage had the driver not stepped down at that precise moment and blocked her path.

Eloise jumped from foot to foot as she waited for the driver to open the carriage door; in fact, she looked so impatient that Penelope was surprised she didn't brush past him and wrench the door open herself. Finally, ignoring the driver's offer of help, she climbed into the carriage, nearly tripping on her skirts and tumbling to the floor in the process. As soon as she'd righted herself, she looked both ways, her face pursed into an extremely furtive expression, and yanked the door shut, nearly taking off the driver's nose in the process.

"What," Eloise demanded, "is going on?"

Penelope just stared at her. "I could ask the same of you."

"You could? Why?"

"Because you nearly knocked over the carriage in your haste to climb inside!"

"Oh," Eloise sniffed dismissively. "You have only yourself to blame for that."

"Me?"

"Yes, you! I want to know what's going on. And I need to know tonight."

Penelope was quite certain that Colin would not have told his sister about Cressida's blackmail demands, not unless his plan was to have Eloise harangue Cressida to death. "I don't know what you mean," she said.

"You *have* to know what I mean!" Eloise insisted, glancing back up toward the house. The front door was opening. "Oh, bother. Mother and Hyacinth are coming already. *Tell* me!"

"Tell you *what*?"

"Why Colin sent us that abominably cryptic note instructing us to stick to you like *glue* all evening."

"He did?"

"Yes, and may I point out that he underlined the word *glue*?"

"And here I thought the emphasis was yours," Penelope said dryly.

Eloise scowled. "Penelope, this is not the time to poke fun at me."

"When *is* the time?"

"Penelope!"

"Sorry, I couldn't resist."

"Do you know what the note was about?"

Penelope shook her head. Which wasn't a complete lie, she told herself. She really didn't know what Colin had planned for this evening.

Just then the door opened, and Hyacinth bounded in. "Penelope!" she said with great enthusiasm. "*What* is going on?"

"She doesn't know," Eloise said.

Hyacinth shot her sister an annoyed look. "It figures you'd sneak out here early."

Violet poked her head in. "Are they quarreling?" she asked Penelope.

"Just a little," Penelope replied.

Violet sat next to Hyacinth across from Penelope and Eloise. "Very well, it's not as if I could stop them, anyway. But do tell, what did Colin mean when he instructed us to stick to you like glue?"

"I'm sure I don't know."

Violet's eyes narrowed, as if assessing Penelope's honesty. "He was quite emphatic. He underlined the word *glue*, you know."

"I know," Penelope replied, just as Eloise said, "I told her."

"He underlined it twice," Hyacinth added. "If his ink had been any darker, I'm sure I would have had to go out and slaughter a horse myself."

"Hyacinth!" Violet exclaimed.

Hyacinth just shrugged. "It's all very intriguing."

"Actually," Penelope said, eager to change the subject, or at least to twist it slightly, "what I'm wondering is, what will Colin wear?"

That got everyone's attention.

"He left home in his afternoon clothes," Penelope explained, "and didn't come back. I can't imagine your sister would accept anything less than full evening kit for her ball."

"He'll have borrowed something from Anthony," Eloise said dismissively. "They're precisely the same size. Same as Gregory, actually. Only Benedict is different."

"Two inches taller," Hyacinth said.

Penelope nodded, feigning interest as she glanced out the window. They'd just slowed down, the driver presumably trying to navigate through the crush of carriages that were choking Grosvenor Square.

"How many people are expected tonight?" Penelope asked.

"I believe five hundred were invited," Violet replied. "Daphne doesn't host parties very often, but what she lacks in frequency she makes up for in size."

"I'll say," Hyacinth muttered. "I hate crowds. I'm not going to be able to get a decent breath tonight."

"I'm lucky you were my last," Violet told her with weary affection. "I'd not have had the energy for any more after you, I'm sure."

"Pity I wasn't first, then," Hyacinth said with a cheeky smile. "Think of all the attention I could have had. Not to mention the fortune."

"You're already quite the heiress as it is," Violet said.

"And you always manage to find your way to the center of attention," Eloise teased.

Hyacinth just grinned.

"Did you know," Violet said, turning to Penelope, "that all of my children are going to be in attendance tonight? I can't remember the last time we were all together."

"What about your birthday party?" Eloise asked.

Violet shook her head. "Gregory wasn't able to get away from university."

"We're not expected to line up according to height and sing a festive tune, are we?" Hyacinth asked, only half joking. "I can see us now: The Singing Bridgertons. We'd make a fortune on the stage."

"You're in a punchy mood tonight," Penelope said to her.

Hyacinth shrugged. "Just getting myself ready for my upcoming transformation into glue. It seems to require a certain mental preparedness."

"A gluey frame of mind?" Penelope inquired mildly.

"Precisely."

"We must get her married off soon," Eloise said to her mother.

"You first," Hyacinth shot back.

"I'm working on it," Eloise said cryptically.

"*What?*" The word's volume was rather amplified by the fact that it exploded from three mouths at once.

"That's all I'm going to say," Eloise said, and in such a tone of voice that they all knew she meant it.

"I will get to the bottom of *this*," Hyacinth assured her mother and Penelope.

"I'm sure you will," Violet replied.

Penelope turned to Eloise and said, "You don't stand a chance."

Eloise just lifted her chin in the air and looked out the window. "We're here," she announced.

The four ladies waited until the driver had opened the door, and then one by one they alighted.

"My goodness," Violet said approvingly, "Daphne has truly outdone herself."

It was difficult not to stop and look. All of Hastings House was ablaze with light. Every window had been adorned with candles, and outdoor sconces held torches, as did a fleet of footmen who were greeting the carriages.

"It's too bad Lady Whistledown isn't here," Hyacinth said, her voice for once losing its cheeky edge. "She would have loved this."

"Maybe she *is* here," Eloise said. "In fact, she probably is."

"Did Daphne invite Cressida Twombley?" Violet asked.

"I'm sure she did," Eloise said. "*Not* that I think she's Lady Whistledown."

"I don't think anyone thinks that any longer," Violet replied as she lifted her foot onto the first step. "Come along, girls, our night awaits."

Hyacinth stepped forward to accompany her mother, while Eloise fell into line beside Penelope.

"There's magic in the air," Eloise said, looking around as if she'd never seen a London ball before. "Do you feel it?"

Penelope just looked at her, afraid that if she opened her mouth, she'd blurt out all of her secrets. Eloise was right. There was something strange and electric about the night, a crackling sort of energy—the kind one felt just before a thunderstorm.

"It almost feels like a turning point," Eloise mused, "as if one's life could change completely, all in one night."

"What are you saying, Eloise?" Penelope asked, alarmed by the look in her friend's eyes.

"Nothing," Eloise said with a shrug. But a mysterious smile remained upon her lips as she hooked her arm through Penelope's and murmured, "Let's be off. The night awaits."

Chapter 23

Penelope had been to Hastings House a number of times, both for formal parties and more casual visits, but never had she seen the stately old building look more lovely—or more magical—than it did that evening.

She and the Bridgerton ladies were among the first to arrive; Lady Bridgerton had always said that it was rude for family members even to consider fashionably late entrances. It was nice to be so early, though; Penelope was actually able to see the decorations without having to push through crushing crowds.

Daphne had decided not to use a theme for her ball, unlike the Egyptian ball last week and the Grecian one the week before. Rather, she had decorated the house with the same simple elegance with which she lived her everyday life. Hundreds of candles adorned the walls and tables, flickering in the night, reflecting off the enormous chandeliers that hung from the ceilings. The windows were swathed in a shimmery, silvery fabric, the sort of thing one might imagine a fairy to wear. Even the servants had changed their livery. Penelope knew that the Hastings servants usually wore blue and gold, but tonight their blue was adorned with silver.

It could almost make a woman feel like a princess in a fairy tale.

"I wonder how much this cost," Hyacinth said, eyes wide.

"Hyacinth!" Violet scolded, batting her daughter on the arm. "You know that it's impolite to ask about such things."

"I didn't ask," Hyacinth pointed out, "I wondered. And besides, it's only Daphne."

"Your sister is the Duchess of Hastings," Violet said, "and as such she has certain responsibilities to her station. You would do well to remember that fact."

"But wouldn't you agree," Hyacinth said, linking her arm around her mother's and giving her hand a little squeeze, "that it's more important simply to remember that she's my sister?"

"She has you there," Eloise said with a smile.

Violet sighed. "Hyacinth, I declare that you will be the death of me."

"No, I won't," Hyacinth replied. "Gregory will."

Penelope found herself stifling a laugh.

"I don't see Colin here yet," Eloise said, craning her neck.

"No?" Penelope scanned the room. "That's surprising."

"Did he tell you that he would be here before you arrived?"

"No," Penelope replied, "but for some reason I rather thought he would."

Violet patted her arm. "I'm sure he'll be here soon, Penelope. And then we'll all know what this big secret is that has him insisting we remain by your side. Not," she added hastily, her eyes widening with alarm, "that we view it as any sort of *chore*. You know we adore your company."

Penelope gave her a reassuring smile. "I know. The feeling is mutual."

There were only a few people ahead of them in the receiving line, so it wasn't very long before they were able to greet Daphne and her husband Simon.

"*What*," Daphne asked without preamble, just as soon as she was sure her other guests were out of earshot, "is going on with Colin?"

Since the question appeared to be directed mostly at her, Penelope felt compelled to say, "I don't know."

"Did he send you a note as well?" Eloise asked.

Daphne nodded. "Yes, we're to keep an eye on her, he said."

"It could be worse," Hyacinth said. "We're to stick to her like glue." She leaned forward. "He underlined *glue*."

"And here I thought I wasn't a chore," Penelope quipped.

"Oh, you're not," Hyacinth said breezily, "but there's something rather enjoyable about the word *glue*. Slides off the tongue rather pleasingly, don't you think? Glue. Gloooooooo."

"Is it me," Eloise asked, "or has she gone mad in the head?"

Hyacinth ignored her with a shrug. "Not to mention the drama of it. I feel as if I'm a part of some grand espionage plot."

"Espionage," Violet groaned. "Heaven help us all."

Daphne leaned forward with great drama. "Well, he told *us*—"

"It's not a competition, wife," Simon put in.

She shot him an annoyed look before turning back to her mother and sisters and saying, "He told us to make sure she stays away from Lady Danbury."

"Lady Danbury!" they all exclaimed.

Except for Penelope, who had a very good idea why Colin might want her to stay away from the elderly countess. He must have come up with something better than her plan to convince Lady Danbury to lie and tell everyone that *she* was Lady Whistledown.

It had to be the double-blackmail theory. What else could it be? He must have uncovered some horrible secret about Cressida.

Penelope was almost giddy with delight.

"I thought you were rather good friends with Lady Danbury," Violet said to her.

"I am," Penelope replied, trying to act perplexed.

"This is very curious," Hyacinth said, tapping her index finger against her cheek. "Very curious indeed."

"Eloise," Daphne suddenly put in, "you're very quiet tonight."

"Except for when she called me mad," Hyacinth pointed out.

"Hmmm?" Eloise had been staring off into space—or perhaps at something behind Daphne and Simon—and hadn't been paying attention. "Oh, well, nothing to say, I suppose."

"*You?*" Daphne asked doubtfully.

"Precisely what I was thinking," Hyacinth said.

Penelope agreed with Hyacinth, but she decided to keep that to herself. It wasn't like Eloise not to weigh in with an opinion, especially not on a night like this, which was growing more and more shrouded with mystery as each second passed.

"You all were saying everything so well," Eloise said. "What could I have possibly added to the conversation?"

Which struck Penelope as very odd. The sly sarcasm was in character, but Eloise *always* thought she had something to add to a conversation.

Eloise just shrugged.

"We should be moving along," Violet said. "We're beginning to hold up your other guests."

"I shall see you later," Daphne promised. "And—Oh!"

Everyone leaned in.

"You will probably want to know," she whispered, "that Lady Danbury is not here yet."

"Simplifies my job," Simon said, looking a bit weary of all the intrigue.

"Not mine," Hyacinth said. "I still have to stick to her—"

"—like glue," they all—including Penelope—finished for her.

"Well, I do," Hyacinth said.

"Speaking of glue," Eloise said as they stepped away from Daphne and Simon, "Penelope, do you think you can make do with only two batches for a bit? I should like to step out for a moment."

"I will go with you," Hyacinth announced.

"You can't both go," Violet said. "I'm certain Colin didn't want Penelope left with only *me*."

"May I go when she's back, then?" Hyacinth grimaced. "It's not something I can avoid."

Violet turned to Eloise expectantly.

"What?" Eloise demanded.

"I was waiting for you to say the same thing."

"I'm far too dignified," Eloise sniffed.

"Oh, please," Hyacinth muttered.

Violet groaned. "Are you certain you wish us to remain by your side?" she asked Penelope.

"I didn't think I had a choice," Penelope replied, amused by the interchange.

"Go," Violet said to Eloise. "Just hurry back."

Eloise gave her mother a nod, and then, much to everyone's surprise, she reached forward and gave Penelope a quick hug.

"What was that for?" Penelope asked with an affectionate smile.

"No reason," Eloise replied, her returning grin rather like one of Colin's. "I just think this is going to be a special night for you."

"You do?" Penelope asked carefully, unsure of what Eloise might have figured out.

"Well, it's obvious *some*thing is afoot," Eloise said. "It's not like Colin to act with such secrecy. And I wanted to offer my support."

"You'll be back in just a few minutes," Penelope said. "Whatever is going to happen—if indeed anything is going to happen—you're not likely to miss it."

Eloise shrugged. "It was an impulse. An impulse born from a dozen years of friendship."

"Eloise Bridgerton, are you growing sentimental on me?"

"At this late date?" Eloise said with a look of mock outrage. "I think not."

"Eloise," Hyacinth interrupted, "will you *leave*? I can't wait all night."

And with a quick wave, Eloise was off.

For the next hour, they just milled about, mingling with the other guests, and moving—Penelope, Violet, and Hyacinth—as one giant being.

"Three heads and six legs have we," Penelope remarked as she walked toward the window, the two Bridgerton women bustling right alongside her.

"I beg your pardon?" Violet asked.

"Did you really want to look out the window," Hyacinth muttered, "or were you just testing us? And *where* is Eloise?"

"Mostly just testing you," Penelope admitted. "And I'm sure Eloise was detained by some other guest. You know as well as I that there are many people here from whom it is rather difficult to extract oneself from conversation."

"Hmmph," was Hyacinth's reply. "Someone needs to recheck her definition of *glue.*"

"Hyacinth," Penelope said, "if you need to excuse yourself for a few minutes, please do go ahead. I shall be just fine." She turned to Violet. "You as well. If you need to leave, I promise I shall remain right here in the corner until you return."

Violet looked at her in horror. "And break our word to Colin?"

"Er, did you actually give him your word?" Penelope asked.

"No, but it was implied in his request, I'm sure. Oh, look!" she suddenly exclaimed. "There he is!"

Penelope tried to signal discreetly at her husband, but all her attempts at circumspection were drowned out by Hyacinth's vigorous wave and holler of, "Colin!"

Violet groaned.

"I know, I know," Hyacinth said unrepentantly, "I must be more ladylike."

"If you know it," Violet said, sounding every inch the mother she was, "then why don't you *do* it?"

"What would be the fun in that?"

"Good evening, ladies," Colin said, kissing his mother's hand before smoothly taking his place beside Penelope and sliding his arm around her waist.

"Well?" Hyacinth demanded.

Colin merely quirked a brow.

"Are you going to *tell* us?" she persisted.

"All in good time, dear sister."

"You're a wretched, wretched man," Hyacinth grumbled.

"I say," Colin murmured, looking about, "what happened to Eloise?"

"That's a very good question," Hyacinth muttered, just as Penelope said, "I'm sure she'll be back soon."

He nodded, not looking terribly interested. "Mother," he said, turning toward Violet, "how have you been?"

"You've been sending cryptic notes all over town," Violet demanded, "and you want to know how I've *been*?"

He smiled. "Yes."

Violet actually started wagging her finger at him, something she'd forbidden her own children from ever doing in public. "Oh, no, you don't, Colin Bridgerton. You are not going to get out of explaining yourself. I am your mother. Your mother!"

"I am aware of the relation," he murmured.

"You are not going to waltz in here and distract me with a clever phrase and a beguiling smile."

"You think my smile is beguiling?"

"Colin!"

"But," he acceded, "you did make an excellent point."

Violet blinked. "I did?"

"Yes. About the waltz." He cocked his head slightly to the side. "I believe I hear one beginning."

"I don't hear anything," Hyacinth said.

"Don't you? Pity." He grabbed Penelope's hand. "Come along, wife. I do believe this is our dance."

"But no one is dancing," Hyacinth ground out.

He flashed her a satisfied smile. "They will be."

And then, before anyone had a chance to comment, he'd yanked on Penelope's hand, and they were weaving through the crowds.

"Didn't you want to waltz?" Penelope asked breathlessly, right after they'd passed the small orchestra, the members of whom appeared to be taking an extended break.

"No, just to escape," he explained, slipping through a side door and pulling her along with him.

A few moments later they had ascended a narrow staircase and were secreted in some small parlor, their only light the flickering torches that blazed outside the window.

"Where are we?" Penelope asked, looking around.

Colin shrugged. "I don't know. It seemed as good a place as any."

"Are you going to tell me what is going on?"

"No, first I'm going to kiss you."

And before she had a chance to respond to that (not that she would have protested!) his lips found hers in a kiss that was hungry and urgent and tender all in one.

"Colin!" she gasped, in that split second when he took a breath.

"Not now," he murmured, kissing her again.

"But—" this was muffled, lost against his lips.

It was the sort of kiss that enveloped her, from her head to her toes, from the way his teeth nibbled her lips, to his hands, squeezing her bottom and sliding across her back. It was the sort of kiss that could easily have turned her knees to water and led her to swoon on the sofa and allow him to do anything to her, the more wicked the better, even though they were mere yards away from over five hundred members of the *ton*, except—

"Colin!" she exclaimed, somehow breaking her mouth free of his.

"Shush."

"Colin, you have to stop!"

He looked like a lost puppy. "Must I?"

"Yes, you must."

"I suppose you're going to say it's because of all the people just next door."

"No, although that's a very good reason to consider restraint."

"To consider and then reject, perhaps?" he asked hopefully.

"No! Colin—" She pulled herself from his arms and moved several feet away, lest his nearness tempt her into forgetting herself. "Colin, you need to tell me what is going on."

"Well," he said slowly, "I *was* kissing you. . . ."

"That's not what I meant, and you know it."

"Very well." He walked away, his footsteps echoing loudly in her ears. When he turned back around, his expression had turned deadly serious. "I have decided what to do about Cressida."

"You have? What? Tell me."

His face took on a slightly pained expression. "Actually, I think it might be best if I didn't tell you until the plan is under way."

She stared at him in disbelief. "You're not serious."

"Well . . ." He was looking longingly at the door, clearly hoping for an escape.

"Tell me," she insisted.

"Very well." He sighed, then sighed again.

"Colin!"

"I'm going to make an announcement," he said, as if that would explain everything.

At first she said nothing, thinking that maybe it would all become clear if she just waited a moment and thought about it. But that didn't work, and so she asked, her words slow and careful, "What sort of announcement?"

His face turned resolute. "I'm going to tell the truth."

She gasped. "About me?"

He nodded.

"But you can't!"

"Penelope, I think it's best."

Panic began to rise within her, and her lungs felt impossibly tight. "No, Colin, you can't! You can't do that! It's not your secret to reveal!"

"Do you want to pay Cressida for the rest of your life?"

"No, of course not, but I can ask Lady Danbury—"

"You're not going to ask Lady Danbury to lie on your behalf," he snapped. "That's beneath you and you know it."

Penelope gasped at his sharp tone. But deep down, she knew he was right.

"If you were so willing to allow someone else to usurp your identity," he said, "then you should have just allowed Cressida to do it."

"I couldn't," she whispered. "Not her."

"Fine. Then it's time we both stood up and faced the music."

"Colin," she whispered, "I'll be ruined."

He shrugged. "We'll move to the country."

She shook her head, desperately trying to find the right words.

He took her hands in his. "Does it really matter so much?" he said softly. "Penelope, I love you. As long as we're together, we'll be happy."

"It's not that," she said, trying to tug her hand from his so that she could wipe the tears from her eyes.

But he wouldn't let go. "What, then?" he asked.

"Colin, you'll be ruined, too," she whispered.

"I don't mind."

She stared at him in disbelief. He sounded so flip, so casual about something that would change his entire life, alter it in ways he couldn't possibly imagine.

"Penelope," he said, his voice so reasonable she could barely stand it, "it's the only solution. Either we tell the world, or Cressida does."

"We could pay her," she whispered.

"Is that what you really want to do?" he asked. "Give her all the money you've worked so hard to earn? You might as well have just let her tell the world she was Lady Whistledown."

"I can't let you do this," she said. "I don't think you understand what it means to be outside of society."

"And you do?" he countered.

"Better than you!"

"Penelope—"

"You're trying to act as if it doesn't matter, but I know you don't feel that way. You were so angry with me when I published that last column, all because you thought I shouldn't have risked the secret getting out."

"As it turns out," he remarked, "I was right."

"See?" she said urgently. "Do you see? You're still upset with me over that!"

Colin let out a long breath. The conversation was not moving in the direction he'd hoped. He certainly hadn't intended for her to throw his earlier insistence that she not tell anyone about her secret life back in his face. "If you hadn't published that last column," he said, "we wouldn't be in this position, that is true, but the point is now moot, don't you think?"

"Colin," she whispered. "If you tell the world I'm Lady Whistledown, and they react the way we think they will, you'll never see your journals published."

His heart stood still.

Because that was when he finally understood her.

She had told him before that she loved him, and she had shown her love as well, in all the ways he'd taught her. But never before had it been so clear, so frank, *so* raw.

All this time she'd been begging him not to make the announcement—it had all been for him.

He swallowed against the lump that was forming in his throat, fought for words, fought even for breath.

She reached out and touched his hand, her eyes pleading, her cheeks still wet with tears. "I could never forgive myself," she said. "I don't want to destroy your dreams."

"They were never my dreams until I met you," he whispered.

"You don't want to publish your journals?" she asked, blinking in confusion. "You were just doing it for me?"

"No," he said, because she deserved nothing less than complete honesty. "I do want it. It *is* my dream. But it's a dream you gave me."

"That doesn't mean I can take it away."

"You're not."

"Yes, I—"

"*No*," he said forcefully, "you're not. And getting my work published . . . well, it doesn't hold a candle to my real dream, which is spending the rest of my life with you."

"You'll always have that," she said softly.

"I know." He smiled, and then it turned rather cocky. "So what do we have to lose?"

"Possibly more than we could ever guess."

"And possibly less," he reminded her. "Don't forget that I'm a Bridgerton. And you are now, too. We wield a bit of power in this town."

Her eyes widened. "What do you mean?"

He shrugged modestly. "Anthony is prepared to give you his full support."

"You told Anthony?" she gasped.

"I had to tell Anthony. He's the head of the family. And there are very few people on this earth who would dare to cross him."

"Oh." Penelope chewed on her lower lip, considering all this. And then, because she had to know: "What did he say?"

"He was surprised."

"I expected as much."

"And rather pleased."

Her face lit up. "Really?"

"And amused. He said he had to admire someone who could keep a secret like that for so many years. He said he couldn't wait to tell Kate."

She nodded. "I suppose you'll have to make an announcement now. The secret is out."

"Anthony will hold his counsel if I ask him to," Colin said. "That has nothing to do with why I want to tell the world the truth."

She looked at him expectantly, warily.

"The truth is," Colin said, tugging on her hand and pulling her close, "I'm rather proud of you."

She felt herself smiling, and it was so strange, because just a few moments earlier, she couldn't imagine ever smiling again.

He leaned down until his nose touched hers. "I want everyone to know how proud I am of you. By the time I'm through, there won't be a single person in London who doesn't recognize how clever you are."

"They may still hate me," she said.

"They may," he agreed, "but that will be their problem, not ours."

"Oh, Colin," she sighed. "I do love you. It's an excellent thing, really."

He grinned. "I know."

"No, I really do. I thought I loved you before, and I'm sure I did, but it's nothing like what I feel now."

"Good," he said, a rather possessive gleam appearing in his eyes, "that's the way I like it. Now come with me."

"Where?"

"Here," he said, pushing open a door.

To Penelope's amazement, she found herself on a small balcony, overlooking the entire ballroom. "Oh. Dear. God," she gulped, trying to yank him back into the darkened room behind them. No one had seen them yet; they could still make their escape.

"Tsk tsk," he scolded. "Bravery, my sweet."

"Couldn't you post something in the paper?" she whispered urgently. "Or just tell someone and allow the rumor to spread?"

"There's nothing like a grand gesture to get the point across."

She swallowed convulsively. As gestures went, this was going to be grand. "I'm not very good at being the center of attention," she said, trying to remember how to breathe in a normal rhythm.

He squeezed her hand. "Don't worry. I am." He looked out over the crowd until his eyes found those of their host, his brother-in-law, the Duke of Hastings. At Colin's nod, the duke began to move toward the orchestra.

"Simon knows?" Penelope gasped.

"I told him when I arrived," Colin murmured absently. "How do you think I knew how to find the room with the balcony?"

And then the most remarkable thing happened. A veritable fleet of footmen appeared as if from nowhere and began handing tall flutes of champagne to every guest.

"Here's ours," Colin said approvingly, picking up two glasses that were waiting in the corner. "Just as I asked."

Penelope took hers silently, still unable to comprehend all that was unfolding around her.

"It's probably a little flat by now," Colin said in a conspiratorial sort of whisper that she knew was meant to set her at ease. "But it's the best I could do under the circumstances."

As Penelope clutched Colin's hand in terror, she watched helplessly as Simon quieted the orchestra and directed the throng of partygoers to turn their attention to his brother and sister on the balcony.

His brother and sister, she thought in wonder. The Bridgertons really did inspire a bond. She never thought she'd see the day when a duke referred to her as his sister.

"Ladies and gentlemen," Colin announced, his strong, confident voice booming throughout the hall, "I would like to propose a toast to the most remarkable woman in the world."

A low murmur spread across the room, and Penelope stood frozen, watching everyone watching her.

"I am a newlywed," Colin continued, beguiling the partygoers with his lopsided smile, "and therefore you are all required to indulge me in my lovesick ways."

Friendly laughter rippled through the crowd.

"I know that many of you were surprised when I asked Penelope Featherington to be my wife. I was surprised myself."

A few unkind titters wafted through the air, but Penelope held herself perfectly still, completely proud. Colin would say the right thing. She knew he would. Colin always said the right thing.

"I wasn't surprised that I had fallen in love with her," he said pointedly, giving the crowd a look that dared them to comment, "but rather that it had taken so long.

"I've known her for so many years, you see," he continued, his voice softening, "and somehow I'd never taken the time to look inside, to see the beautiful, brilliant, witty woman she'd become."

Penelope could feel the tears trickling down her face, but she couldn't move. She could barely breathe. She had expected him to reveal her secret, and instead he was giving her this incredible gift, this spectacular declaration of love.

"Therefore," Colin said, "with all of you here as my witnesses, I would like to say—Penelope—" He turned to her, taking her free hand in his, and said:

"I love you. I adore you. I worship the ground you walk upon."

He turned back out to the crowd, lifted his glass, and said, "To my wife!"

"To your wife!" they all boomed, caught up in the magic of the moment.

Colin drank, and Penelope drank, even though she couldn't help but wonder when he was going to tell them all the real reason for this announcement.

"Put down your glass, dear," he murmured, plucking it from her fingers and setting it aside.

"But—"

"You interrupt far too much," he scolded, and then he swept her into a passionate kiss, right there on the balcony in front of the entire *ton.*

"Colin!" she gasped, once he gave her a chance to breathe.

He grinned wolfishly as their audience roared its approval.

"Oh, and one last thing!" he called to the crowd.

They were now stamping their feet, hanging on his every word.

"I'm leaving the party early. Right now, as a matter of fact." He shot a wicked, sideways grin at Penelope. "I'm sure you'll understand."

The men in the crowd hooted and hollered as Penelope turned beet red.

"But before I do, I have one last thing to say. One last little thing, in case you still don't believe me when I tell you that my wife is the wittiest, cleverest, most enchanting woman in all of London."

"Nooooo!" came a voice from the back, and Penelope knew it was Cressida.

But even Cressida was no match for the crowd, none of whom would let her pass, or even listen to her cries of distress.

"You might say that my wife has two maiden names," he said thoughtfully. "Of course you all knew her as Penelope Featherington, as did I. But what you didn't know, and what even I was not clever enough to figure out until she told me herself . . ."

He paused, waiting for silence to fall over the room.

". . . is that she is also the brilliant, the witty, the breathtakingly magnificent—Oh, you all know who I am talking about," he said, his arm sweeping out toward the crowd.

"I give you my wife!" he said, his love and pride flowing across the room. "Lady Whistledown!"

For a moment there was nothing but silence. It was almost as if no one even dared to breathe.

And then it came. Clap. Clap. Clap. Slow and methodical, but with such force and determination that everyone had to turn and look to see who had dared to break the shocked silence.

It was Lady Danbury.

She had shoved her cane into someone else's arms and was holding her arms high, clapping loud and proud, beaming with pride and delight.

And then someone else began to clap. Penelope jerked her head to the side to see who . . .

Anthony Bridgerton.

And then Simon Basset, the Duke of Hastings.

And then the Bridgerton women, and then the Featherington women, and then another and another and more and more until the entire room was cheering.

Penelope couldn't believe it.

Tomorrow they might remember to be angry with her, to feel irritated at having been fooled for so many years, but tonight . . .

Tonight all they could do was admire and cheer.

For a woman who had had to carry out all of her accomplishments in secret, it was everything she'd ever dreamed of.

Well, almost everything.

Everything she'd truly ever dreamed of was standing next to her, his arm around her waist. And when she looked up at him, at his beloved face, he was smiling down at her with such love and pride that her breath caught in her throat.

"Congratulations, Lady Whistledown," he murmured.

"I prefer Mrs. Bridgerton," she replied.

He grinned. "Excellent choice."

"Can we leave?" she whispered.

"Right now?"

She nodded.

"Oh, *yes*," he said enthusiastically.

And no one saw them for several days.

Epilogue

Bedford Square, Bloomsbury
London, 1825

"It's here! It's here!"

Penelope looked up from the papers spread over her desk. Colin was standing in the doorway of her small office, jumping from foot to foot like a schoolboy.

"Your book!" she exclaimed, jumping to her feet as quickly as her rather ungainly body would allow. "Oh, Colin, let me see. Let me see. I can't wait!"

He couldn't contain his grin as he handed her his book.

"Ohhhh," she said reverently, holding the slim, leather-bound volume in her hands. "Oh, my." She held the book up to her face and inhaled deeply. "Don't you just love the smell of new books?"

"Look at this, look at this," he said impatiently, pointing to his name on the front cover.

Penelope beamed. "Look at that. And so elegant, too." She ran her finger over the words as she read, "*An Englishman in Italy*, by Colin Bridgerton."

He looked ready to burst with pride. "It looks good, doesn't it?"

"It looks better than good, it looks perfect! When will *An Englishman in Cyprus* be available?"

"The publisher says every six months. They want to release *An Englishman in Scotland* after that."

"Oh, Colin, I'm so proud of you."

He drew her into his arms, letting his chin rest on top of her head. "I couldn't have done it without you."

"Yes, you could," she replied loyally.

"Just be quiet and accept the praise."

"Very well," she said, grinning even though he couldn't see her face, "you couldn't. Clearly, you could never have been published without such a talented editor."

"You won't hear any disagreement from me," he said softly, kissing the top of her head before he let her go. "Sit down," he added. "You shouldn't be on your feet for so long."

"I'm fine," she assured him, but she sat down, anyway. Colin had been overly protective since the first moment she'd told him she was pregnant; now that she was only a month from her due date, he was insufferable.

"What are these papers?" he asked, glancing down at her scribblings.

"This? Oh, it's nothing." She started to gather them into piles. "Just a little project I was working on."

"Really?" He sat down across from her. "What is it?"

"It's . . . well . . . actually . . ."

"What is it, Penelope?" he asked, looking exceedingly amused by her stammers.

"I've been at loose ends since I finished editing your journals," she explained, "and I found I rather missed writing."

He was smiling as he leaned forward. "What are you working on?"

She blushed; she wasn't sure why. "A novel."

"A novel? Why, that's brilliant, Penelope!"

"You think so?"

"Of course I think so. What is it called?"

"Well, I've only written a few dozen pages," she said, "and there's much work to be done, but I think, if I don't decide to change it overmuch, that I will call it *The Wallflower*."

His eyes grew warm, almost misty. "Really?"

"It's a little bit autobiographical," she admitted.

"Just a little bit?" he returned.

"Just a little."

"But it has a happy ending?"

"Oh, yes," she said fervently. "It *has* to."

"It has to?"

She reached her hand across the table and rested it atop his. "Happy endings are all I can do," she whispered. "I wouldn't know how to write anything else."

Dear Reader,

Have you ever wondered what happened to your favorite characters after you closed the final page? Wanted just a little bit more of a favorite novel? I have, and if the questions from my readers are any indication, I'm not the only one. So after countless requests from Bridgerton fans, I decided to try something a little different, and I wrote a "2nd Epilogue" for each of the novels. These are the stories that come after the stories.

At first, the Bridgerton 2nd Epilogues were available exclusively online; later they were published (along with a novella about Violet Bridgerton) in a collection called The Bridgertons: Happily Ever After. *Now, for the first time, each 2nd Epilogue is being included with the novel it follows. I hope you enjoy Penelope and Colin as they continue their journey.*

Warmly,
Julia Quinn

Romancing Mister Bridgerton:
The 2nd Epilogue

"You didn't tell her?"

Penelope Bridgerton would have said more, and in fact would have liked to say more, but words were difficult, what with her mouth hanging slack. Her husband had just returned from a mad dash across the south of England with his three brothers, in pursuit of his sister Eloise, who had, by all accounts, run off to elope with—

Oh, dear God.

"Is she married?" Penelope asked frantically.

Colin tossed his hat on a chair with a clever little twist of his wrist, one corner of his mouth lifting in a satisfied smile as it spun through the air on a perfect horizontal axis. "Not yet," he replied.

So she hadn't eloped. But she *had* run away. And she'd done it in secret. Eloise, who was Penelope's closest friend. Eloise, who told Penelope everything. Eloise, who apparently *didn't* tell Penelope everything, had run off to the home of a man none of them knew, leaving a note assuring her family that all would be well and not to worry.

Not to worry????

Good heavens, one would think Eloise Bridgerton knew her family better than that. They had been frantic, every last one of them. Penelope had stayed with her new mother-in-law while the men were searching for Eloise. Violet Bridgerton had put up a good front, but her skin was positively ashen, and Penelope could not help but notice the way her hands shook with every movement.

And now Colin was back, acting as if nothing was amiss, answering none of her questions to her satisfaction, and beyond all that—

"How could you not have told her?" she said again, dogging his heels.

He sprawled into a chair and shrugged. "There really wasn't an appropriate time."

"You were gone five days!"

"Yes, well, not all of them were with Eloise. A day's travel on either end, after all."

"But—but—"

Colin summoned just enough energy to glance about the room. "Don't suppose you ordered tea?"

"Yes, of course," Penelope said reflexively, since it had not taken more than a week of marriage to learn that when it came to her new husband, it was best to always have food at the ready. "But Colin—"

"I did hurry back, you know."

"I can see that," she said, taking in his dampened, windblown hair. "Did you ride?"

He nodded.

"From Gloucestershire?"

"Wiltshire, actually. We retired to Benedict's."

"But—"

He smiled disarmingly. "I missed you."

And Penelope was not so accustomed to his affection that she did not blush. "I missed you, too, but—"

"Come sit with me."

Where? Penelope almost demanded. Because the only flat surface was his lap.

His smile, which had been charm personified, grew more heated. "I'm missing you right now," he murmured.

Much to her extreme embarrassment, her gaze moved instantly to the front of his breeches. Colin let out a bark of laughter, and Penelope crossed her arms. "*Don't*, Colin," she warned.

"Don't what?" he asked, all innocence.

"Even if we weren't in the sitting room, and even if the draperies weren't open—"

"An easily remedied nuisance," he commented with a glance to the windows.

"And *even*," she ground out, her voice growing in depth, if not quite in volume, "were we not expecting a maid to enter at any moment, the poor thing staggering under the weight of your tea tray, the fact of the matter is—"

Colin let out a sigh.

"—you *have not answered my question*!"

He blinked. "I've quite forgotten what it was."

A full ten seconds elapsed before she spoke. And then: "I'm going to kill you."

"Of that, I'm certain," he said offhandedly. "Truly, the only question is when."

"Colin!"

"Might be sooner rather than later," he murmured. "But in truth, I thought I'd go in an apoplexy, brought on by bad behavior."

She stared at him.

"*Your* bad behavior," he clarified.

"I didn't have bad behavior before I met you," she retorted.

"Oh, ho, ho," he chortled. "Now *that* is rich."

And Penelope was forced to shut her mouth. Because, blast it all, he was right. And that was what all of this was about, as it happened. Her husband, after entering the hall, shrugging off his coat, and kissing her rather soundly on the lips (in front of the butler!), had blithely informed her, "Oh, and by the by, I never did tell her you were Whistledown."

And if there was anything that might count as bad behavior, it had to be over ten years as the author of the now infamous *Lady Whistledown's Society Papers*. Penelope had, in her pseudonymous guise, managed to insult just about everyone in society, even herself. (Surely, the *ton* would have grown suspicious if she had never poked fun at herself, and besides, she really did look like an overripe citrus fruit in the dreadful yellows and oranges her mother had always forced her to wear.)

Penelope had "retired" just before her marriage, but a blackmail attempt had convinced Colin that the best course of action was to reveal her secret in a grand gesture, and so he had announced her identity at his sister Daphne's ball. It had all been very romantic and very, well, *grand*, but by the end of the night it had become apparent that Eloise had disappeared.

Eloise had been Penelope's closest friend for years, but even she had not known Penelope's big secret. And now she still didn't. She'd left the party before Colin had announced it, and he apparently had not seen fit to say anything once he'd found her.

"Frankly," Colin said, his voice holding an uncharacteristic strain of irritability, "it's less than she deserved, after what she put us through."

"Well, yes," Penelope murmured, feeling rather disloyal even as she said it. But the entire Bridgerton clan had been mad with worry. Eloise had left a note, it was true, but it had somehow got mixed into her mother's correspondence, and an entire day had passed before the family was reassured that Eloise had not been abducted. And even then, no one's mind was set at ease; Eloise may have left of her own accord, but it had taken another day of tearing her bedchamber to bits before they found a letter from Sir Phillip Crane that indicated where she might have run off to.

Considering all that, Colin did have something of a point.

"We have to go back in a few days for the wedding," he said. "We'll tell her then."

"Oh, but we can't!"

He paused. Then he smiled. "And why is that?" he asked, his eyes resting on her with great appreciation.

"It will be her wedding day," Penelope explained, aware that he'd been hoping for a far more diabolical reason. "She must be the center of all attention. I cannot tell her something such as *this*."

"A bit more altruistic than I'd like," he mused, "but the end result is the same, so you have my approval—"

"I don't need your approval," Penelope cut in.

"But nonetheless, you have it," he said smoothly. "We shall keep Eloise in the dark." He tapped his fingertips together and sighed with audible pleasure. "It will be a most excellent wedding."

The maid arrived just then, carrying a heavily laden tea tray. Penelope tried not to notice that she let out a little grunt when she was finally able to set it down.

"You may close the door behind you," Colin said, once the maid had straightened.

Penelope's eyes darted to the door, then to her husband, who had risen and was shutting the draperies.

"Colin!" she yelped, because his arms had stolen around her, and his lips were on her neck, and she could feel herself going quite liquid in his embrace. "I thought you wanted food," she gasped.

"I do," he murmured, tugging on the bodice of her dress. "But I want you more."

And as Penelope sank to the cushions that had somehow found their way to the plush carpet below, she felt very loved indeed.

Several days later, Penelope was seated in a carriage, gazing out the window and scolding herself.

Colin was asleep.

She was a widgeon for feeling so nervous about seeing Eloise again. Eloise, for heaven's sake. They had been as close as sisters for over a decade. Closer. Except, maybe . . . not quite as close as either had thought. They had kept secrets, both of them. Penelope wanted to wring Eloise's neck for not telling her about her suitor, but really, she hadn't a leg to stand on. When Eloise found out that Penelope was Lady Whistledown . . .

Penelope shuddered. Colin might be looking forward to the moment—he was positively devilish in his glee—but she felt rather ill, quite frankly. She hadn't eaten all day, and she was *not* the sort to skip breakfast.

She wrung her hands, craned her neck to get a better view out the window—she thought they might have turned onto the drive for Romney Hall, but she wasn't precisely certain—then looked back to Colin.

He was still asleep.

She kicked him. Gently, of course, because she did not think herself overly violent, but really, it wasn't fair that he had slept like a baby from the moment the carriage had started rolling. He had settled into his seat, inquired after her comfort, and then, before she'd even managed the *you* in "Very well, thank you," his eyes were closed.

Thirty seconds later he was snoring.

It really wasn't fair. He always fell asleep before she did at night as well.

She kicked him again, harder this time.

He mumbled something in his sleep, shifted positions ever so slightly, and slumped into the corner.

Penelope scooted over. Closer, closer . . .

Then she organized her elbow in a sharp point and jabbed him in the ribs.

"Wha . . . ? " Colin shot straight awake, blinking and coughing. "What? What? What?"

"I think we're here," Penelope said.

He looked out the window, then back at her. "And you needed to inform me of this by taking a weapon to my body?"

"It was my elbow."

He glanced down at her arm. "You, my dear, are in possession of exceedingly bony elbows."

Penelope was quite sure her elbows—or any part of her, for that matter—were not the least bit bony, but there seemed little to gain by contradicting him, so she said, again, "I think we're here."

Colin leaned toward the glass with a couple of sleepy blinks. "I think you're right."

"It's lovely," Penelope said, taking in the exquisitely maintained grounds. "Why did you tell me it was run-down?"

"It is," Colin replied, handing her her shawl. "Here," he said with a gruff smile, as if he weren't yet used to caring for another person's welfare in quite the way he did hers. "It will be chilly yet."

It was still fairly early in the morning; the inn at which they had slept was only an hour's ride away. Most of the family had stayed with Benedict and Sophie, but their home was not large enough to accommodate all of the Bridgertons. Besides, Colin had explained, they were newlyweds. They needed their privacy.

Penelope hugged the soft wool to her body and leaned against him to get a better look out the window. And, to be honest, just because she liked to lean against him. "I think it looks lovely," she said. "I have never seen such roses."

"It's nicer on the outside than in," Colin explained as the carriage drew to a halt. "But I expect Eloise will change that."

He opened the door himself and hopped out, then offered his arm to assist her down. "Come along, Lady Whistledown—"

"Mrs. Bridgerton," she corrected.

"Whatever you wish to call yourself," he said with a grand smile, "you're still mine. And this is your swan song."

As Colin stepped across the threshold of what was to be his sister's new home, he was struck by an unexpected sense of relief. For all his irritation with her, he loved his sister. They had not been particularly intimate while growing up; he had been much closer in age to Daphne, and Eloise had often seemed nothing so much as a pesky afterthought. But the previous year had brought them closer, and if it hadn't been for Eloise, he might never have discovered Penelope.

And without Penelope, he'd be . . .

It was funny. He couldn't imagine what he'd be without her.

He looked down at his new wife. She was glancing around the entry hall, trying not to be too obvious about it. Her face was impassive, but he knew she was taking everything in. And tomorrow, when they were musing about the events of the day, she would have remembered every last detail.

Mind like an elephant, she had. He loved it.

"Mr. Bridgerton," the butler said, greeting them with a little nod of his head. "Welcome back to Romney Hall."

"A pleasure, Gunning," Colin murmured. "So sorry about the last time."

Penelope looked to him in askance.

"We entered rather . . . suddenly," Colin explained.

The butler must have seen Penelope's expression of alarm, because he quickly added, "I stepped out of the way."

"Oh," she started to say, "I'm so—"

"Sir Phillip did not," Gunning cut in.

"Oh." Penelope coughed awkwardly. "Is he going to be all right?"

"Bit of swelling around the throat," Colin said, unconcerned. "I expect he's improved by now." He caught her glancing down at his hands and let out a chuckle. "Oh, it wasn't me," he said, taking her arm to lead her down the hall. "I just watched."

She grimaced. "I think that might be worse."

"Quite possibly," he said with great cheer. "But it all turned out well in the end. I quite like the fellow now, and I rather—Ah, Mother, there you are."

And sure enough, Violet Bridgerton was bustling down the hall. "You're late," she said, even though Colin was fairly certain they were not. He bent down to kiss her proffered cheek, then stepped to the side as his mother came forward to take both of Penelope's hands in hers. "My dear, we need you in back. You are the matron of honor, after all."

Colin had a sudden vision of the scene—a gaggle of chatty females, all talking over one another about minutiae he couldn't begin to care about, much less understand. They told each other everything, and—

He turned sharply. "Don't," he warned, "say a word."

"I beg your pardon." Penelope let out a little huff of righteous indignation. "I'm the one who said we couldn't tell her on her wedding day."

"I was talking to my mother," he said.

Violet shook her head. "Eloise is going to kill us."

"She nearly killed us already, running off like an idiot," Colin said, with uncharacteristic shortness of temper. "I've already instructed the others to keep their mouths shut."

"Even Hyacinth?" Penelope asked doubtfully.

"Especially Hyacinth."

"Did you bribe her?" Violet asked. "Because it won't work unless you bribe her."

"Good Lord," Colin muttered. "One would think I'd joined this family yesterday. Of course I bribed her." He turned to Penelope. "No offense to recent additions."

"Oh, none taken," she said. "What did you give her?"

He thought about his bargaining session with his youngest sister and nearly shuddered. "Twenty pounds."

"Twenty pounds!" Violet exclaimed. "Are you mad?"

"I suppose you could have done better," he retorted. "And I've only given her half. I wouldn't trust that girl as far as I could throw her. But if she keeps her mouth shut, I'll be another ten pounds poorer."

"I wonder how far you *could* throw her," Penelope mused.

Colin turned to his mother. "I tried for ten, but she wouldn't budge." And then to Penelope: "Not nearly far enough."

Violet sighed. "I ought to scold you for that."

"But you won't." Colin flashed her a grin.

"Heaven help me," was her only reply.

"Heaven help whatever chap is mad enough to marry her," he remarked.

"I think there is more to Hyacinth than the two of you allow," Penelope put in. "You ought not to underestimate her."

"Good Lord," Colin replied, "we don't do *that*."

"You're so sweet," Violet said, leaning forward to give Penelope an impromptu hug.

"It's only through sheer force of luck she hasn't taken over the world," Colin muttered.

"Ignore him," Violet said to Penelope. "And you," she added, turning to Colin, "must head immediately to the church. The rest of the men have already gone down. It's only a five-minute walk."

"You're planning to walk?" he asked doubtfully.

"Of course not," his mother replied dismissively. "And we certainly cannot spare a carriage for you."

"I wouldn't dream of asking for one," Colin replied, deciding that a solitary stroll through the fresh morning air was decidedly preferable to a closed carriage with his female relations.

He leaned down to kiss his wife's cheek. Right near her ear. "Remember," he whispered, "no telling."

"I can keep a secret," she replied.

"It's far easier to keep a secret from a thousand people than it is from just one," he said. "Far less guilt involved."

Her cheeks flushed, and he kissed her again near her ear. "I know you so well," he murmured.

He could practically hear her teeth gnashing as he left.

———

"Penelope!"

Eloise started to jump from her seat to greet her, but Hyacinth, who was supervising the dressing of her hair, jammed her hand on her shoulder with a low, almost menacing, "*Down.*"

And Eloise, who normally would have slain Hyacinth with a glare, meekly resumed her seat.

Penelope looked to Daphne, who appeared to be supervising Hyacinth.

"It has been a long morning," Daphne said.

Penelope walked forward, pushed gently past Hyacinth, and carefully embraced Eloise so as not to muss her coiffure. "You look beautiful," she said.

"Thank you," Eloise replied, but her lips were trembling, and her eyes were wet and threatening to spill over at any moment.

More than anything, Penelope wanted to take her aside and tell her that everything was going to be all right, and she didn't *have* to marry Sir Phillip if she didn't want to, but when all was said and done, Penelope *didn't* know that everything was going to be all right, and she rather suspected that Eloise did have to marry her Sir Phillip.

She'd heard bits and pieces. Eloise had been in residence at Romney Hall for over a week without a chaperone. Her reputation would be in tatters if it got out, which it surely would. Penelope knew better than anyone the power and tenacity of gossip. Plus, Penelope had heard that Eloise and Anthony had had A Talk.

The matter of the wedding, it seemed, was final.

"I'm so glad you're here," Eloise said.

"Goodness, you know I would never miss your wedding."

"I know." Eloise's lips trembled, and then her face took on that expression one makes when one is trying to appear brave and actually thinks one might be succeeding. "I know," she said again, a little more evenly. "Of course you wouldn't. But that does not lessen my pleasure in seeing you."

It was an oddly stiff sentence for Eloise, and for a moment Penelope forgot her own secrets, her own fears and worries. Eloise was her dearest friend. Colin was her love, her passion, and her soul, but it was Eloise, more than anyone, who had shaped Penelope's adult life. Penelope could not imagine what the last decade would have been like without Eloise's smile, her laughter, and her indefatigable good cheer.

Even more than her own family, Eloise had loved her.

"Eloise," Penelope said, crouching down beside her so that she might put her arm around her shoulders. She cleared her throat, mostly because she was about to ask a question for which the answer probably did not matter. "Eloise," she said again, her voice dropping to a near whisper. "Do you want this?"

"Of course," Eloise replied.

But Penelope wasn't sure she believed her. "Do you lo—" She caught herself. And she did that little thing with her mouth that tried to be a smile. And she asked, "Do you like him? Your Sir Phillip?"

Eloise nodded. "He's . . . complicated."

Which made Penelope sit down. "You're joking."

"At a time like this?"

"Aren't you the one who always said that men were simple creatures?"

Eloise looked at her with an oddly helpless expression. "I thought they were."

Penelope leaned in, aware that Hyacinth's auditory skills were positively canine. "Does he like you?"

"He thinks I talk too much."

"You do talk too much," Penelope replied.

Eloise shot her a look. "You could at least smile."

"It's the truth. But I find it endearing."

"I think he does as well." Eloise grimaced. "Some of the time."

"Eloise!" called Violet from the doorway. "We really must be on our way."

"We wouldn't want the groom to think you've run off," Hyacinth quipped.

Eloise stood and straightened her shoulders. "I've done quite enough running off recently, wouldn't you say?" She turned to Penelope with a wise, wistful smile. "It's time I began running to and stopped running from."

Penelope looked at her curiously. "What did you say?"

But Eloise only shook her head. "It's just something I heard recently."

It was a curious statement, but this wasn't the time to delve further, so Penelope moved to follow the rest of the family. After she'd taken a few steps, however, she was halted by the sound of Eloise's voice.

"Penelope!"

Penelope turned. Eloise was still in the doorway, a good ten feet behind her. She had an odd look on her face, one that Penelope could not quite interpret. Penelope waited, but Eloise did not speak.

"Eloise?" Penelope said quietly, because it looked as if Eloise *wished* to say something, just wasn't sure how. Or possibly what.

And then—

"*I'm sorry.*" Eloise blurted it out, the words rushing across her lips with a speed that was remarkable, even for her.

"You're sorry," Penelope echoed, mostly out of surprise. She hadn't really considered what Eloise might say in that moment, but an apology would not have topped the list. "For what?"

"For keeping secrets. That wasn't well-done of me."

Penelope swallowed. *Good Lord.*

"Forgive me?" Eloise's voice was soft, but her eyes were urgent, and Penelope felt like the worst sort of fraud.

"Of course," she stammered. "It is nothing." And it *was* nothing, at least when compared to her own secrets.

"I should have told you about my correspondence with Sir Phillip. I don't know why I didn't at the outset," Eloise continued. "But then, later, when you and Colin were falling in love . . . I think it was . . . I think it was just because it was *mine*."

Penelope nodded. She knew a great deal about wanting something of one's own.

Eloise let out a nervous laugh. "And now look at me."

Penelope did. "You look beautiful." It was the truth. Eloise was not a serene bride, but she was a glowing one, and Penelope felt her worries lift and lighten and finally disappear. All would be well. Penelope did not know if Eloise would experience the same bliss in her marriage as she'd found, but she would at least be happy and content.

And who was she to say that the new married couple wouldn't fall madly in love? Stranger things had happened.

She linked her arm through Eloise's and steered her out into the hall, where Violet had raised her voice to heretofore unimagined volumes.

"I think your mother wants us to make haste," Penelope whispered.

"Eloeeeeeeeeeeeeese!" Violet positively bellowed. "NOW!"

Eloise's brows rose as she gave Penelope a sideways glance. "Whatever makes you think so?"

But they didn't hurry. Arm in arm they glided down the hall, as if it were the church aisle.

"Who would have thought we'd both marry within months of each other?" Penelope mused. "Weren't we meant to be old crones together?"

"We can still be old crones," Eloise replied gaily. "We shall simply be married old crones."

"It will be grand."

"Magnificent!"

"Stupendous!"

"We shall be leaders of crone fashion!"

"Arbiters of cronish taste."

"What," Hyacinth demanded, hands on hips, "are the two of you talking about?"

Eloise lifted her chin and looked down her nose at her. "You're far too young to understand."

And she and Penelope practically collapsed in a fit of giggles.

"They've gone mad, Mother," Hyacinth announced.

Violet gazed lovingly at her daughter and daughter-in-law, both of whom had reached the unfashionable age of twenty-eight before becoming brides. "Leave them alone, Hyacinth," she said, steering her toward the waiting carriage. "They'll be along shortly." And then she added, almost as an afterthought: "You're too young to understand."

After the ceremony, after the reception, and after Colin was able to assure himself once and for all that Sir Phillip Crane would indeed make an acceptable husband to his sister, he managed to find a quiet corner into which he could yank his wife and speak with her privately.

"Does she suspect?" he asked, grinning.

"You're terrible," Penelope replied. "It's her *wedding*."

Which was not one of the two customary answers to a yes-or-no question. Colin resisted the urge to let out an impatient breath, and instead offered a rather smooth and urbane "By this you mean . . . ?"

Penelope stared at him for a full ten seconds, and then she muttered, "I don't know what Eloise was talking about. Men are *abysmally* simple creatures."

"Well . . . *yes*," Colin agreed, since it had long been obvious to him that the female mind was an utter and complete mystery. "But what has that got to do with anything?"

Penelope glanced over both shoulders before dropping her voice to a harsh whisper. "Why would she even be thinking about Whistledown at a time like this?"

She had a point there, loath as Colin was to admit it. In his mind, this had all played out with Eloise somehow being aware that she was the only person who didn't know the secret of Lady Whistledown's identity.

Which was ridiculous to be sure, but still, a satisfying daydream.

"Hmmmm," he said.

Penelope looked at him suspiciously. "What are you thinking?"

"Are you certain we cannot tell her on her wedding day?"

"Colin . . ."

"Because if we *don't*, she's sure to find out from *some*one, and it doesn't seem fair that we not be present to see her face."

"Colin, *no.*"

"After all you've been through, wouldn't you say you deserve to see her reaction?"

"No," Penelope said slowly. "No. No, I wouldn't."

"Oh, you sell yourself too cheaply, my darling," he said, smiling benevolently at her. "And besides that, think of Eloise."

"I fail to see what else it is I have been doing all morning."

He shook his head. "She would be devastated. Hearing the awful truth from a complete stranger."

"It's not awful," Penelope shot back, "and how do you know it would be a stranger?"

"We've sworn my entire family to secrecy. Who else does she know out in this godforsaken county?"

"I rather like Gloucestershire," Penelope said, her teeth now charmingly clenched. "I find it delightful."

"Yes," he said equably, taking in her furrowed brow, pinched mouth, and narrowed eyes. "You look delighted."

"Weren't you the one who insisted we keep her in the dark for as long as humanly possible?"

"*Humanly possible* being the phrase of note," Colin replied. "*This* human"—he gestured rather unnecessarily to himself—"finding it quite impossible to maintain his silence."

"I can't believe you've changed your mind."

He shrugged. "Isn't it a man's prerogative?"

At that her lips parted, and Colin found himself wishing he'd found a corner as private as it was quiet, because she was practically begging to be kissed, whether she knew it or not.

But he was a patient man, and they did still have that comfortable room reserved at the inn, and there was still much mischief to be made right here at the wedding. "Oh, Penelope," he said huskily, leaning in more than was proper, even with one's wife, "don't you want to have some fun?"

She flushed scarlet. "Not *here*."

He laughed aloud at that.

"I wasn't talking about that," she muttered.

"Neither was I, as a matter of fact," he returned, completely unable to keep the humor off his face, "but I *am* pleased that it comes to mind so readily." He pretended to glance about the room. "When do you think it would be polite to leave?"

"Definitely not yet."

He pretended to ponder. "Mmmm, yes, you're probably correct at that. Pity. But"—at that he pretended to brighten—"it does leave us time to make mischief."

Again, she was speechless. He liked that. "Shall we?" he murmured.

"I don't know what I'm going to do with you."

"We need to work on this," he said, giving his head a shake. "I'm not sure you fully understand the mechanics of a yes-or-no question."

"I think you should sit down," she said, her eyes now taking on that glint of cautious exhaustion usually reserved for small children.

Or adult fools.

"And then," she continued, "I think you should remain in your seat."

"Indefinitely?"

"*Yes.*"

Just to torture her, he sat. And then—

"*Nooooo*, I think I'd rather make mischief."

Back to his feet he was, and striding off to find Eloise before Penelope could even attempt to lunge for him.

"Colin, *don't!*" she called out, her voice echoing off the walls of the reception room. She managed to yell—of course—at the precise moment when every other wedding guest paused to take a breath.

A roomful of Bridgertons. What were the odds?

Penelope jammed a smile on her face as she watched two dozen heads swivel in her direction. "Nothing about it," she said, her voice coming out strangled and chirpy. "So sorry to disturb."

And apparently Colin's family was well used to his embarking on something requiring the rejoinder "Colin, don't!" because they all resumed their conversations with barely another glance in her direction.

Except Hyacinth.

"Oh, blast," Penelope muttered under her breath, and she raced forward.

But Hyacinth was quick. "What's going on?" she asked, falling into stride beside Penelope with remarkable agility.

"Nothing," Penelope replied, because the last thing she wanted was Hyacinth adding to the disaster.

"He's going to tell her, isn't he?" Hyacinth persisted, let out an "*Euf??*" and an "Excuse me," when she pushed past one of her brothers.

"No," Penelope said firmly, darting around Daphne's children, "he's not."

"He *is.*"

Penelope actually stopped for a moment and turned. "Do any of you ever listen to anyone?"

"Not me," Hyacinth said cheerfully.

Penelope shook her head and moved forward, Hyacinth hot on

her heels. When she reached Colin, he was standing next to the newlyweds and had his arms linked through Eloise's and was smiling down at her as if he had never once considered:

a. Teaching her to swim by tossing her in a lake.
b. Cutting off three inches of her hair while she slept.

or

c. Tying her to a tree so that she did not follow him to a local public inn.

Which of course he had, all three of them, and two he'd actually done. (Even Colin wouldn't have dared something so permanent as a shearing.)

"Eloise," Penelope said, somewhat breathless from trying to shake off Hyacinth.

"Penelope." But Eloise's voice sounded curious. Which did not surprise Penelope; Eloise was no fool, and she was well aware that her brother's normal modes of behavior did not include beatific smiles in her direction.

"Eloise," Hyacinth said, for no reason Penelope could deduce.

"Hyacinth."

Penelope turned to her husband. "Colin."

He looked amused. "Penelope. Hyacinth."

Hyacinth grinned. "Colin." And then: "Sir Phillip."

"Ladies." Sir Phillip, it seemed, favored brevity.

"Stop!" Eloise burst out. "What is going on?"

"A recitation of our Christian names, apparently," Hyacinth said.

"Penelope has something to say to you," Colin said.

"I don't."

"She does."

"I *do*," Penelope said, thinking quickly. She rushed forward, taking Eloise's hands in her own. "Congratulations. I'm so happy for you."

"That's what you needed to say?" Eloise asked.

"Yes."

"*No.*"

And from Hyacinth: "I am enjoying myself immensely."

"Er, it's very kind of you to say so," Sir Phillip said, looking a bit perplexed at her sudden need to compliment the host. Penelope closed her eyes for a brief moment and let out a weary sigh; she was going to need to take the poor man aside and instruct him on the finer points of marrying into the Bridgerton family.

And because she did know her new relations so well, and she knew that there was no way she was going to avoid revealing her secret, she turned to Eloise and said, "Might I have a moment alone?"

"With me?"

It was enough to make Penelope wish to strangle someone. Anyone. "Yes," she said patiently, "with you."

"And me," Colin put in.

"And me," Hyacinth added.

"*Not* you," Penelope said, not bothering to look at her.

"But still me," Colin added, looping his free arm through Penelope's.

"Can this wait?" Sir Phillip asked politely. "This is her wedding day, and I expect that she does not wish to miss it."

"I know," Penelope said wearily. "I'm so sorry."

"It's all right," Eloise said, breaking free of Colin's grasp and turning to her new husband. She murmured a few words to him that Penelope could not hear, then said, "There is a small salon just through that door. Shall we?"

She led the way, which suited Penelope because it gave her time to say to Colin, "You will say nothing."

He surprised her by nodding, and then, maintaining his silence, he held open the door for her as she entered the room behind Eloise.

"This won't take long," Penelope said apologetically. "At least, I hope it won't."

Eloise said nothing, just looked at her with an expression that was, Penelope had just enough presence of mind to notice, uncharacteristically serene.

Marriage must agree with her, Penelope thought, because the Eloise *she* knew would have been chomping at the bit at such a moment. A big secret, a mystery to be revealed—Eloise loved that sort of thing.

But she was just standing there, calmly waiting, a light smile touching her features. Penelope looked to Colin in confusion, but he was apparently taking her instructions to heart, and his mouth was clamped firmly shut.

"Eloise," Penelope began.

Eloise smiled. A bit. Just at the corners, as if she wanted to smile more. "Yes?"

Penelope cleared her throat. "Eloise," she said again, "there is something I must tell you."

"Really?"

Penelope's eyes narrowed. Surely the moment did not call for sarcasm. She took a breath, tamping down the urge to fire off an equally dry rejoinder, and said, "I did not wish to tell you on your wedding day"—at this she *speared* her husband with a glare—"but it seems I have no choice."

Eloise blinked a few times, but other than that, her placid demeanor did not change.

"I can think of no other way to say it," Penelope plodded on, feeling positively sick, "but while you were gone . . . That is to say, the night you left, as a matter of fact . . ."

Eloise leaned forward. The movement was slight, but Penelope caught it, and for a moment she thought—Well, she didn't think anything clearly, certainly nothing that she could have expressed in a proper sentence. But she did get a feeling of unease—a different sort of unease than the one she was already feeling. It was a suspicious sort of unease, and—

"I am Whistledown," she blurted out, because if she waited any longer she thought her brain might explode.

And Eloise said, "I know."

Penelope sat down on the nearest solid object, which happened to be a table. "You know."

Eloise shrugged. "I know."

"How?"

"Hyacinth told me."

"*What?*" This from Colin, looking fit to be tied. Or perhaps more accurately, fit to tie Hyacinth.

"I'm sure she's at the door," Eloise murmured, with a nod. "In case you want to—"

But Colin was one step ahead of her, wrenching open the door to the small salon. Sure enough, Hyacinth tumbled in.

"Hyacinth!" Penelope said disapprovingly.

"Oh, please," Hyacinth retorted, smoothing her skirts. "You didn't think I wouldn't eavesdrop, did you? You know me better than that."

"I'm going to wring your neck," Colin ground out. "We had an agreement."

Hyacinth shrugged. "I don't really need twenty pounds, as it happens."

"I already *gave* you ten."

"I know," Hyacinth said with a cheerful smile.

"Hyacinth!" Eloise exclaimed.

"Which isn't to say," Hyacinth continued modestly, "that I don't *want* the other ten."

"She told me last night," Eloise explained, her eyes narrowing dangerously, "but only after informing me that she knew who Lady

Whistledown was, and in fact the whole of society knew, but that the knowledge would cost me twenty-*five* pounds."

"Did it not occur to you," Penelope asked, "that if the whole of society knew, that you could simply have asked someone else?"

"The whole of society wasn't in my bedchamber at two in the morning," Eloise snapped.

"I am thinking of buying a hat," Hyacinth mused. "Or maybe a pony."

Eloise shot her a nasty look, then turned to Penelope. "Are you really Whistledown?"

"I am," Penelope admitted. "Or rather—" She looked over at Colin, not exactly certain why she was doing so except that she loved him so much, and he knew her so well, and when he saw her helpless little wobbly smile, he would smile in return, no matter how irate he was with Hyacinth.

And he did. Somehow, amidst everything, he knew what she needed. He always did.

Penelope turned back to Eloise. "I *was*," she amended. "No longer. I've retired."

But of course Eloise already knew that. Lady W's letter of retirement had circulated long before Eloise had left town.

"For good," Penelope added. "People have asked, but I shan't be induced to pick up my quill again." She paused, thinking of the scribblings she'd embarked upon at home. "At least not as Whistledown." She looked at Eloise, who had sat down next to her on the table. Her face was somewhat blank, and she hadn't said anything in *ages*—well, ages for Eloise, at least.

Penelope tried to smile. "I am thinking of writing a novel, actually."

Still nothing from Eloise, although she was blinking quite rapidly, and her brow was scrunched up as if she were thinking quite hard.

And so Penelope took one of her hands and said the one thing she was really feeling. "I'm sorry, Eloise."

Eloise had been staring rather blankly at an end table, but at that, she turned, her eyes finding Penelope's. "You're sorry?" she echoed, and she sounded dubious, as if sorry couldn't possibly be the correct emotion, or at least, not *enough* of it.

Penelope's heart sank. "I'm so sorry," she said again. "I should have told you. I should have—"

"Are you *mad*?" Eloise asked, finally seeming to snap to attention. "Of *course* you should not have told me. I could never have kept this a secret."

Penelope thought it rather remarkable of her to admit it.

"I am so *proud* of you," Eloise continued. "Forget the writing for a moment—I cannot even fathom the logistics of it all, and someday— when it is not my wedding day—I shall insist upon hearing every last detail."

"You were surprised, then?" Penelope murmured.

Eloise gave her a rather dry look. "To put it mildly."

"I had to get her a chair," Hyacinth supplied.

"I was already sitting down," Eloise ground out.

Hyacinth waved her hand in the air. "Nevertheless."

"Ignore her," Eloise said, focusing firmly on Penelope. "Truly, I cannot begin to tell you how impressed I am—now that I've got over the shock, that is."

"Really?" It hadn't occurred to Penelope until that very moment just how much she'd wished for Eloise's approval.

"Keeping us all in the dark for so long," Eloise said, shaking her head with slow admiration. "From me. From *her*." She jabbed a finger in Hyacinth's direction. "It's really very well-done of you." At that she leaned forward and enveloped Penelope in a warm hug.

"You're not angry with me?"

Eloise moved back and opened her mouth, and Penelope could see that she'd been about to say, "No," probably to be followed by "Of course not."

But the words remained in Eloise's mouth, and she just sat

there, looking slightly thoughtful and surprised until she finally said . . . "No."

Penelope felt her brows lift. "Are you certain?" Because Eloise didn't sound certain. She didn't much sound like Eloise, to be honest.

"It would be different if I were still in London," Eloise said quietly, "with nothing else to do. But this—" She glanced around the room, gesturing rather vaguely toward the window. "*Here*. It's just not the same. It's a different life," she said quietly. "I'm a different person. A little bit, at least."

"Lady Crane," Penelope reminded her.

Eloise smiled. "Good of you to remind me of that, Mrs. Bridgerton."

Penelope almost laughed. "Can you believe it?"

"Of you, or me?" Eloise asked.

"Both."

Colin, who had been keeping a respectful distance—one hand firmly clamped around Hyacinth's arm to keep *her* at a respectful distance—stepped forward. "We should probably return," he said quietly. He held out his hand, and helped first Penelope, then Eloise, to her feet. "You," he said, leaning forward to kiss his sister on the cheek, "should *certainly* return."

Eloise smiled wistfully, the blushing bride once again, and nodded. With one last squeeze of Penelope's hands, she brushed past Hyacinth (rolling her eyes as she did so) and made her way back to her wedding party.

Penelope watched her go, linking her arm in Colin's and leaned gently into him. They both stood there in contented silence, idly watching the now empty doorway, listening to the sounds of the party wafting through the air.

"Do you think it would be polite if we left?" he murmured.

"Probably not."

"Do you think Eloise would mind?"

Penelope shook her head.

Colin's arms tightened around her, and she felt his lips gently brush her ear. "Let's go," he said.

She did not argue.

On the twenty-fifth of May, in the year 1824, precisely one day after the wedding of Eloise Bridgerton to Sir Phillip Crane, three missives were delivered to the room of Mr. and Mrs. Colin Bridgerton, guests at the Rose and Bramble Inn, near Tetbury, Gloucestershire. They arrived together; all were from Romney Hall.

"Which shall we open first?" Penelope asked, spreading them before her on the bed.

Colin yanked off the shirt he'd donned to answer the knock. "I defer to your good judgment as always."

"As always?"

He crawled back into bed beside her. She was remarkably adorable when she was being sarcastic. He couldn't think of another soul who could carry that off. "As whenever it suits me," he amended.

"Your mother, then," Penelope said, plucking one of the letters off the sheet. She broke open the seal and carefully unfolded the paper.

Colin watched as she read. Her eyes widened, then her brows rose, then her lips pinched slightly at the corners, as if she were smiling despite herself. "What does she have to say?" he asked.

"She forgives us."

"I don't suppose it would make any sense for me to ask for what."

Penelope gave him a stern look. "For leaving the wedding early."

"You told me Eloise wouldn't mind."

"And I'm sure she did not. But this is your *mother.*"

"Write back and assure her that should she ever remarry, I will stay to the bitter end."

"I will do no such thing," Penelope replied, rolling her eyes. "I don't think she expects a reply, in any case."

"Really?" Now he was curious, because his mother always expected replies. "What did we do to earn her forgiveness, then?"

"Er, she mentioned something about the timely delivery of grand-children."

Colin grinned. "Are you blushing?"

"No."

"You *are*."

She elbowed him in the ribs. "I'm not. Here, read it yourself if you are so inclined. I shall read Hyacinth's."

"I don't suppose she returned my ten pounds," Colin grumbled.

Penelope unfolded the paper and shook it out. Nothing fluttered down.

"That minx is lucky she's my sister," he muttered.

"What a bad sport you are," Penelope chided. "She bested you, and rather brilliantly, too."

"Oh, please," he scoffed. "I did not see *you* praising her cunning yesterday afternoon."

She waved off his protests. "Yes, well, some things are more easily seen in hindsight."

"What does she have to say?" Colin asked, leaning over her shoulder. Knowing Hyacinth, it was probably some scheme to extort more money from his pockets.

"It's rather sweet, actually," Penelope said. "Nothing nefarious at all."

"Did you read both sides?" Colin asked dubiously.

"She only wrote on one side."

"Uncharacteristically uneconomical of her," he added, with suspicion.

"Oh, heavens, Colin, it is just an account of the wedding after we left. And I must say, she has a superior eye for humor and detail. She would have made a fine Whistledown."

"God help us all."

The last letter was from Eloise, and unlike the other two, it was addressed to Penelope alone. Colin was curious, of course—who wouldn't be? But he moved away to allow Penelope her privacy. Her friendship with his sister was something he held in both awe and respect. He was close to his brothers—extremely so. But he had never seen a bond of friendship quite so deep as that between Penelope and Eloise.

"Oh!" Penelope let out, as she turned a page. Eloise's missive was a good deal longer than the previous two, and she'd managed to fill two sheets, front and back. "That minx."

"What did she do?" Colin asked.

"Oh, it was nothing," Penelope replied, even though her expression was rather peeved. "You weren't there, but the morning of the wedding she kept apologizing for keeping secrets, and it never even occurred to me that she was trying to get me to admit to keeping secrets of my own. Made me feel wretched, she did."

Her voice trailed off as she read through another page. Colin leaned back against the fluffy pillows, his eyes resting on his wife's face. He liked watching her eyes move from left to right, following the words. He liked watching her lips move as she smiled or frowned. It was rather amazing, actually, how contented he felt, simply watching his wife read.

Until she gasped, that was, and turned utterly white.

He shoved himself up on his elbows. "What is it?"

Penelope shook her head and groaned. "Oh, she is devious."

Privacy be damned. He grabbed the letter. "What did she say?"

"Down there," Penelope said, pointing miserably at the bottom. "At the end."

Colin brushed her finger away and began to read. "Good Lord, she's wordy," he muttered. "I can't make heads or tails of it."

"Revenge," Penelope said. "She says my secret was bigger than hers."

"It was."

"She says she's owed a boon."

Colin pondered that. "She probably is."

"To even the score."

He patted her hand. "I'm afraid that's how we Bridgertons think. You've never played a sporting game with us, have you?"

Penelope moaned. "She said she is going to consult *Hyacinth*."

Colin felt the blood leave his face.

"I know," Penelope said, shaking her head. "We'll never be safe again."

Colin slid his arm around her and pulled her close. "Didn't we say we wanted to visit Italy?"

"Or India."

He smiled and kissed her on the nose. "Or we could just stay here."

"At the Rose and Bramble?"

"We're supposed to depart tomorrow morning. It's the last place Hyacinth would look."

Penelope glanced up at him, her eyes growing warm and perhaps just a little bit mischievous. "I have no pressing engagements in London for at least a fortnight."

He rolled atop her, tugging her down until she was flat on her back. "My mother did say she would not forgive us unless we produced a grandchild."

"She did not put it in quite so uncompromising terms."

He kissed her, right on the sensitive spot behind her earlobe that always made her squirm. "Pretend she did."

"Well, in that case—oh!"

His lips slid down her belly. "Oh?" he murmured.

"We had best get to—oh!"

He looked up. "You were saying?"

"To work," she just barely managed to get out.

He smiled against her skin. "Your servant, Mrs. Bridgerton. Always."

About the Author

#1 *New York Times* bestselling author JULIA QUINN began writing one month after graduating from college and, aside from a brief stint in medical school, she has been tapping away at her keyboard ever since. Her novels have been translated into thirty-seven languages and are beloved the world over. A graduate of Harvard and Radcliffe Colleges, she lives with her family in the Pacific Northwest.